Praise for the *Aeneid*

"A new edition of the *Aeneid*, Virgil's imperial masterpiece, has arrived just as the whole world is witnessing the stress fractures in our own imperial enterprise. And I'm here to report that it is magnificent. When you are faced with something incredibly complex yet beautifully simple, you must bow your head before inexplicable greatness. That's the case with Robert Fagles's translation. . . . This work, this miraculous beast of a text, is so enjoyable that you will hardly know you are reading an ancient masterpiece. . . . Fortune has certainly favored Fagles for his bravery and sped this bold, unwearied translator to his tripartite kudos."
—Thomas Cahill, *Los Angeles Times Book Review*

"Fagles's new version of Virgil's epic delicately melds the stately rhythms of the original to a contemporary cadence. Having previously produced well-received translations of the *Iliad* and the *Odyssey*, he illuminates the poem's Homeric echoes while remaining faithful to Virgil's distinctive voice." —*The New Yorker*

"Robert Fagles's wonderful new version of Virgil's *Aeneid* (Penguin) caps his career as a translator, Fagles may be a Hellenist, but his Virgil is the best thing he has done, and Simon Callow's recording for the audio book is superb."
—Denis Feeney, *London Review of Books*

"Fagles, who has rendered the best contemporary translations of Homer, now interprets the cooler, more stately and in many ways less accessible Virgil. The result: a triumph, and the *Aeneid* for our age, if not necessarily for the ages."
—*The Atlantic Monthly*

"Robert Fagles once more carries through an epic task, rendering Virgil's *Aeneid* with a rigorous sense of its beauty and of the often brutal power that coexists with strokes of humanity and love. To this work and its centuried greatness, Fagles brings his fresh impetus, unexampled experience, mastery, devotion."
—Shirley Hazzard

"A bonus of this new volume, as of Fagles's *Iliad* and *Odyssey*, is the long introduction by Bernard Knox, humane, graceful, and authoritative. . . . Robert Fagles . . . finds a good blend of the objective and the personal: he wants to serve Virgil, not to draw attention to himself, but his translation is unmistakably, though unobtrusively, of its time and of its maker. It is likely to be the *Aeneid* for our new century."
—Richard Jenkyns, *The Times Literary Supplement* (London)

"Fagles boldly chooses to render Virgil's historical present in the present tense more consistently than most other modern translations. . . . In this lively and accurate translation, students, new readers, and readers returning to this cornerstone of Western civilization will not have to choose, as poor Aeneas did, between duty and pleasure." —A.E. Stallings, *The American Scholar*

"Fagles, better than any other translator, captures the weird, scintillating coexistence of Virgil's defense of the Roman vision and his sympathy for those who must submit to it. . . . Fagles is able to draw on the best model of modern English as a language suited to the epic form. Virgil's verse, thus carefully transformed, remains both epigrammatic and fluid." —Rafil Kroll-Zaidi, *Harper's*

"A generation may, without too much presumption, expect its healthy share of illustrious novelists, poets, playwrights, and journalists. Great translators, however, do not always abound. Thankfully, we have Robert Fagles. . . . Though he modestly insists that he is only one of many to translate all three of the great epics of antiquity, his fans can't help but feel otherwise. The Greeks referred to Homer as 'the poet.' Since Fagles has already attracted a readership in the hundreds of thousands, our generation may well recognize him as 'the translator.'"
—Max Carter, *Vanity Fair*

"Fitzgerald was the best modern translator to this point. There is no way to deny that. [But with Fagles's *Aeneid*] . . . a very good version has been replaced by a better one." —Garry Wills, *Poetry*

"Fagles is incredibly successful at producing something that reads like English poetry and at the same time gives you an idea of what Virgil is like."
—Denis Feeney, Chair, Department of Classics, Princeton University

"One of the greatest difficulties is producing a translation that is a worthy poem in its own light but is not a different poem from the original. . . . What Fagles does is he gives us as good a poem as possible while still staying as faithful to the original as possible." —Alexander Nehamas, Professor of Philosophy and Comparative Literature, Princeton University

"The main point to convey about his *Aeneid* is that it accomplishes three things: it reflects the meaning of the Latin very closely; it does this in very comfortable and accessible English; and it makes the poem sing. Doing any one of these things consistently is unbelievably difficult. That it does all three at once is astonishing. It is truly a great translation, which will make the poem readable for many people for the first time." —Robert Kaster, Professor of Classics, Princeton University

"One of the virtues of Robert Fagles's impressive translation is its slashing energy, which stays true to the Virgilian aesthetics while keeping the reader's eye fixed on the ethical tensions of the tale." —*Book Forum*

"Robert Fagles's new translation of the *Aeneid* is a fluid, lyrical rendering of the epic. One of the world's leading classicists, whose versions of the *Iliad* and the *Odyssey* have sold more than a million copies, Fagles brings a contemporary vigor to Virgil's lines. . . . Fagles's lively, accessible translation includes a glossary and notes, which serve to put this seminal saga in context." —*Bookpage*

"Robert Fagles, the poem's newest translator, comes to the fray well armed. . . . Viking has accoutered him handsomely. . . . Fagles renders the pilgrimage in cadences that are encompassing without feeling cluttered. . . . The *Aeneid* hauntingly captures the psyche of a weathered soldier who has had enough. . . . Robert Fagles emerges as a new and noble standard bearer."
—Brad Leithauser, *The New York Times Book Review* (front page)

PENGUIN  CLASSICS

THE AENEID

PUBLIUS VERGILIUS MARO (70–19 B.C.), known as Virgil, was born near Mantua in the last days of the Roman Republic. In his comparatively short life he became the supreme poet of his age, whose *Aeneid* gave the Romans a great national epic equal to the Greeks', celebrating their city's origins and the creation of their empire. In addition to this, he was also the author of the *Eclogues* and the *Georgics*.

ROBERT FAGLES was the Arthur W. Marks '19 Professor of Comparative Literature, Emeritus, at Princeton University. In 2006, he received a National Humanities Medal and was the recipient of the 1997 PEN/ Ralph Manheim Medal for Translation and a 1996 Academy Award in Literature from the American Academy of Arts and Letters. Fagles was elected to the Academy, the American Academy of Arts and Sciences, and the American Philosophical Society. He won the Harold Morton Landon Translation Award from The Academy of American Poets twice, once for the *Iliad* in 1991 and then again in 2007 for his *Aeneid*, and was twice honored by the New Jersey Council of the Humanities (the second time for lifetime achievement). His translations of Sophocles' *Three Theban Plays*, Aeschylus' *Oresteia* (nominated for a National Book Award), Homer's *Iliad* (which also won an award from The Translation Center of Columbia University), and Homer's *Odyssey* are all published in Penguin Classics. He died in 2008.

BERNARD KNOX is Director Emeritus of Harvard's Center for Hellenic Studies in Washington, D.C. He taught at Yale University for many years. Among his numerous honors are awards from the National Institute of Arts and Letters and the National Endowment for the Humanities. A Guggenheim Fellow, he has published widely, and in 1978 he won the George Jean Nathan Award for Dramatic Criticism. His works include *The Heroic Temper: Studies in Sophoclean Tragedy*; *Oedipus at Thebes: Sophocles' Tragic Hero and His Time*; and *Essays Ancient and Modern* (awarded the 1989 PEN/Spielvogel-Diamonstein Award). Mr. Knox also collaborated with Robert Fagles on the *Odyssey*, the *Iliad*, and *Three Theban Plays*.

VIRGIL

The Aeneid

TRANSLATED BY
Robert Fagles

INTRODUCTION BY
BERNARD KNOX

PENGUIN BOOKS

PENGUIN BOOKS

Published by the Penguin Group
Penguin Group (USA) Inc., 375 Hudson Street, New York, New York 10014, U.S.A.
Penguin Group (Canada), 90 Eglinton Avenue East, Suite 700, Toronto,
Ontario, Canada M4P 2Y3 (a division of Pearson Penguin Canada Inc.)
Penguin Books Ltd, 80 Strand, London WC2R 0RL, England
Penguin Ireland, 25 St Stephen's Green, Dublin 2, Ireland (a division of Penguin Books Ltd)
Penguin Group (Australia), 250 Camberwell Road, Camberwell,
Victoria 3124, Australia (a division of Pearson Australia Group Pty Ltd)
Penguin Books India Pvt Ltd, 11 Community Centre, Panchsheel Park, New Delhi – 110 017, India
Penguin Group (NZ), 67 Apollo Drive, Rosedale, North Shore 0632,
New Zealand (a division of Pearson New Zealand Ltd)
Penguin Books (South Africa) (Pty) Ltd, 24 Sturdee Avenue,
Rosebank, Johannesburg 2196, South Africa

Penguin Books Ltd, Registered Offices:
80 Strand, London WC2R 0RL, England

First published in the United States of America by Viking Penguin,
a member of Penguin Group (USA) Inc. 2006
Published in Penguin Books 2008
This edition published 2010

9   10

Translation and notes copyright © Robert Fagles, 2006
Introduction copyright © Bernard Knox, 2006
All rights reserved

An extract from Book Two (under the title "The Death of Priam") and two extracts
from Book Six ("Dido in the Underworld" and "Aeneas and His Father's Ghost")
originally appeared in *The Kenyon Review*, Fall 2006.

Grateful acknowledgments is made for permission to reprint
excerpts from the following copyrighted works:
"Secondary Epic" from *Collected Poems* by W. H. Auden. Copyright © 1960 by W. H. Auden.
Used by permission of Random House, Inc.
The Georgics by Virgil, translated with an introduction and notes by L. P. Wilkinson
(Penguin Classics, 1982). Copyright © L. P. Wilkinson, 1982.
Used by permission of Penguin Books Ltd.

Illustrations by David Cain. Copyright © David Cain, 2006.

ISBN 978-0-670-03803-9 (hc.)
ISBN 978-0-14-310629-6 (pbk.)
CIP data available

Printed in the United States of America
Set in Meridien   •   Designed by Francesca Belanger

For Lynne

tendimus in Latium

CONTENTS

INTRODUCTION

ROME

When Publius Vergilius Maro—Virgil in common usage—was born in 70 B.C., the Roman Republic was in its last days. In 71 it had just finished suppressing the three-year-long revolt of the slaves in Italy, who, organized by Spartacus, a gladiator, had defeated four Roman armies but were finally crushed by Marcus Crassus. Crassus celebrated his victory by crucifying six thousand captured slaves along the Appian Way, the road that ran south from Rome to the Bay of Naples and from there on to Brundisium (Brindisi). In 67 B.C. Gnaeus Pompeius (Pompey) was given an extraordinary, wide command to clear the Mediterranean, which the Romans claimed was "our sea"—*mare nostrum*—of the pirates who made commerce and travel dangerous. (The young Julius Caesar was captured by pirates and held for ransom around 70 B.C.; he paid it but came back at once with an armed force and crucified them all.) In 65 B.C. Catiline conspired against the Republic but was suppressed in 63 through the action of the consul, Cicero. From 58 to 51 B.C. Julius Caesar added what are now Switzerland, France, and Belgium to the Roman Empire, creating in the course of these campaigns a superb army loyal to him rather than to the Republic, while in 53 B.C. Crassus invaded Parthia, a part of modern-day Iraq, but was killed at Carrhae, where many of his soldiers were taken prisoner and the legions' standards displayed as trophies of the Parthian victory. From 49 to 45 B.C. there was civil war as Caesar crossed the Rubicon River into Italy with his victorious army, which defeated Pompey's forces in Greece at Pharsalus in 48 B.C. Pompey escaped by sea and took refuge on the shore of Egypt, the only country on the Mediterranean not yet part of the Roman Empire, but he was killed by the Alexandrians and his head taken to Alexandria to be given to Caesar when he arrived. Caesar went on to defeat another republican army in Africa at Thapsus, and in the next year vanquished the last republican army at Munda in Spain. Back in Rome he appointed himself dictator, a position that had always been held for a short term in an emergency, for ten years.

But on the Ides of March, 44 B.C., Caesar was assassinated in the Senate House by conspirators led by Brutus and Cassius. However, Marcus Antonius (Mark Antony), Caesar's right-hand man in Gaul as in Rome, and young Octavian, great-nephew and adopted son of Caesar, soon drove the republicans to Greece and defeated the republican army at Philippi. Brutus and Cassius subsequently committed suicide. Antony took over the pacification of the eastern half of the Empire, making Alexandria, where he became the lover of the Hellenistic queen Cleopatra, his base, while Octavian, making Rome his headquarters, dealt with problems in Spain and the west.

Tension between Antony and Octavian grew steadily over time, in spite of attempts at reconciliation, and in 31 B.C. Antony and Cleopatra's fleet was defeated by Octavian and his admiral, Agrippa, off the Greek promontory of Actium. Antony and Cleopatra committed suicide in Alexandria rather than walk to execution in Rome in Octavian's triumph, and Egypt became a Roman province. Virgil died in 19 B.C. Octavian, who assumed the title of Augustus in 27 B.C., ruled what was now the Roman Empire until his death in A.D. 14, when he was succeeded peacefully by Tiberius.

In his comparatively short life Virgil became the supreme Roman poet; his work overshadowed that of his successors, and his epic poem, the *Aeneid*, gave Homeric luster to the story of Rome's origins and its achievement— the creation of an empire that gave peace and the rule of law to all the territory surrounding the Mediterranean, to what are now Switzerland, France, and Belgium, and later to England. Yet when Virgil was born in the village of Andes, near Mantua (Mantova), he, like all the other Italians living north of the Po River, was not a Roman citizen.

Full Roman citizenship had been gradually conceded over the centuries to individuals and communities, but in the years 91 to 87 B.C. those communities still excluded fought a successful civil war against Rome, which ended with the grant of full Roman citizenship to all Italians living south of the Po River. The territory north of the river continued to be a *provincia*, ruled by a proconsul from Rome, with an army. Full Roman citizenship was finally granted to the inhabitants of the area by Julius Caesar in 49 B.C., when Virgil was already a young man.

Virgil was an Italian long before he became a Roman, and in the second book of the *Georgics* he follows a passage celebrating the riches of the East with a hymn of praise for the even greater riches of Italy:

But neither Media's land most rich in forests,
The gorgeous Ganges or the gold-flecked Hermus

Could rival Italy . . . the land is full
Of teeming fruits and Bacchus' Massic liquor.
Olives are everywhere and prosperous cattle . . .
And then the cities,
So many noble cities raised by our labors,
So many towns we've piled on precipices,
And rivers gliding under ancient walls . . .
Hail, mighty mother of fruits, Saturnian land
And mighty mother of men . . .
The same has bred a vigorous race of men,
Marsians, the Sabine stock, Ligurians
Inured to hardship, Volscians javelin-armed.

(2.136–69, trans. L. P. Wilkinson, et seq.)

And in the *Aeneid,* Virgil's poem about the origins of Rome, though his hero, Aeneas, and the Trojan invaders of Italy are to build the city from which Rome will eventually be founded, there is a constant and vibrant undertone of sympathy for and identification with the Italians, which becomes a major theme in the story of the Volscian warrior princess Camilla.

Biographical information about Virgil is scant and much of it unreliable, but we learn from Suetonius' "Life" of the poet, written probably in the early years of the second century A.D., that Virgil "was tall . . . with a dark complexion and a rustic appearance" and that "he spoke very slowly and almost like an uneducated man." Yet when he read his own poems, his delivery of them "was sweet and wonderfully effective" (pp. 467–73, trans. J. C. Rolfe, et seq.). And we learn from the same author that when he read to Augustus and his sister Octavia the second, fourth, and sixth books of the *Aeneid,* when he reached in the sixth book the lines about her son Marcellus, who had died young, she fainted, and it was difficult to revive her. We know too that Virgil and his father somehow escaped the fate of so many of the landowners in the area that Virgil refers to as Mantua—"but Mantua / Stands far too close for comfort to poor Cremona" (*Eclogues* 9.28, trans. C. Day Lewis, et seq.)—confiscation of the land to reward the veterans of the armies of Octavian and Mark Antony after the defeat of Brutus and Cassius at Philippi in 42 B.C. We know this mainly by inference from Virgil's first poems, the *Eclogues,* published around 39 to 38 B.C.

THE *ECLOGUES*

Like most Roman poems, the *Eclogues* (a word that means something like "Selections") have a Greek model. In this case it is the poems of Theocritus, a resident of the Greek city of Syracuse in Sicily who, writing in the Doric dialect of the western Greeks, invented a genre of poetry that used the Homeric hexameter for very un-Homeric themes: the singing contests, love affairs, and rivalries of shepherds and herdsmen who relieved the boredom of their lonely rural life by competing in song accompanied by pipes and pursuing their love affairs and rivalries far from the city and the farmlands, in the hills with their sheep, goats, and cattle. Their names, and the names of their lady loves—Lycidas, Daphnis, Amaryllis—have become famous through the long tradition of pastoral poetry that began with Theocritus, flourished in Virgil, and had a splendid rebirth in the Italian Renaissance and in Elizabethan England; Spenser's *Shepheardes Calender* was published in 1579, and Milton's *Lycidas* (written in 1637) is a masterpiece of the genre. It reached what might well be considered its end in the parodic performance of Marie Antoinette, queen of France, and her court ladies playing the role, at the Petit Trianon palace, of simple milkmaids.

Not all of Theocritus' poems feature shepherds; one of them, for example, is a delightful dramatic sketch of two light-headed, gossipy housewives on their way to the festival of Adonis in Alexandria, and another is a hymn of praise to Ptolemy II, the ruler of Alexandria and Egypt. Similarly, one of Virgil's ten *Eclogues,* the fourth, has nothing to do with shepherds; it prophesies the birth of a son who will bring back the Golden Age on earth. Many Christians, from Lactantius on, later took this to be a prophecy of the birth of Christ, but it seems clear that Virgil was referring to the expectation that Octavian's sister, married to Mark Antony and pregnant by him, would bear a son, and that this would heal the growing breach between the two leaders. But the child turned out to be a daughter, and in any case, Cleopatra's hold on Antony was permanent.

But Virgil differs from his model in one significant particular: he makes two of the *Eclogues* that are dialogues of shepherds, the first and ninth, reflect the sorrows and passions of the real world of 41 B.C.—the confiscation of land in the area north of the river Po, to reward the veterans of the armies of Octavian and Antony. The first *Eclogue* features Tityrus, who, as a result of a visit to Rome, has been granted, by a "young man"* whom he will always worship as a god, a favorable response to his plea: "'Pasture your cattle, breed from your bulls, as you did of old'" (1.45). But the speaker, Meliboeus, must go on his sad way,

> "To Scythia, bone-dry Africa, the chalky spate of the Oxus,
> Even to Britain—that place cut off at the very world's end . . .
> To think of some godless soldier owning my well-farmed fallow,
> A foreigner reaping these crops!"   (1.64–71)

And in the ninth *Eclogue*, Moeris laments his eviction from his land, the day

> ". . . that I should have lived to see an outsider
> Take over my little farm—a thing I had never feared—
> And tell me, 'You're dispossessed, you old tenants,
>   you've got to go.'"   (9.2–4)

It seems clear from all this that somehow Virgil, or rather Virgil's father, escaped the fate of Meliboeus and Moeris. Either his farm was exempt from confiscation or he was given another in exchange. The "young man" can only have been Octavian, and somehow Asinius Pollio, who is mentioned in *Eclogue* 4, and who was a patron of poets and the arts, sensing the young Virgil's talent, brought him to Octavian's notice and secured his future education in the capital of the province, Mediolanum (Milan), at Rome, and later at Naples and at nearby Herculaneum, where his name appears on a burned papyrus as a student of Epicurean philosophy. At some point he was brought to the attention of Maecenas, who was Octavian's friend and another benefactor of poets. We have from Virgil's friend and fellow poet Horace an account of their meeting on the way to Brundisium with Maecenas on his mission to Greece to negotiate with Antony in 37 B.C. In his fifth *Satire* of the first book, written in hexameter verse, Horace describes the journey from Rome with Maecenas; at Sinuessa they meet with another group, of which Virgil is part. *O qui complexus et gaudia,* "Oh what embraces and joy!" And later at Capua they stay for the night at an inn. *Lusum it Maecenas,* writes Horace, "Maecenas goes off to exercise," *dormitum ego Vergiliusque,* "and Virgil and I to bed" (1.5.43, 48, trans. Knox).

Virgil's *Eclogues* were an immediate success and soon gained all the

---

*Bernard Knox's slight variation on the original translation.

trappings of general approval—some of the dialogues of shepherds were performed in theaters, quotations and parodies abounded. But what made them a landmark in the history of Latin poetry were the music and elegance of the hexameter verse, the exquisite control of the rhythmic patterns.

The Latin hexameter, modeled on Homer's, had been used by Latin poets ever since Quintus Ennius (239–169 B.C.) had adapted it to celebrate in his *Annales* the history of Rome from the founding by Aeneas down to his own day. Virgil knew and often used phrases of this poet; he also knew the great hexameter poem of his older contemporary, Lucretius, whose *De Rerum Natura* (*On the Nature of Things*) celebrated the Epicurean philosophy of which Virgil was a devotee: Virgil's lines often show the influence of Lucretius' poem. But only Virgil's own poetic genius can explain the lightness, the dexterity, the rhythmic music of the *Eclogues*, and this is even truer of his next, and most perfect, poem, the *Georgics*.

THE *GEORGICS*

This poem, of more than two thousand lines in four books, was first read to Octavian soon after the suicides of Antony and Cleopatra in 30 B.C., which made him sole ruler of the Roman world, at Atella near Naples by Maecenas and Virgil in 29 B.C. It is, like the *Eclogues*, modeled on a Greek poem, Hesiod's *Works and Days*, but whereas Hesiod writes of farming from firsthand experience, Virgil has to draw on a prose work written on the subject, the *De Re Rustica* of Varro, which had been published in 37–36 B.C. Of Virgil's four books the first is on field crops, the second on trees, the third on herds, and the fourth on bees. The only source of sweetness available to the ancient Western world was honey—hence the importance of bee-keeping. Virgil's poem, with its devotion to the land, the crops, and the herds, fits admirably into the old Roman ideal: the Roman farmer is equally adapted to work on the land and to do the work of a soldier in the legion in time of war. The model was the legendary figure Cincinnatus, who in 458 B.C. was called from his farm and given dictatorial power; he rescued the state by defeating the Aequi and, after holding supreme power for sixteen days, resigned it and returned to his plow. But the *Georgics* is no more a real manual for the soldier turned farmer than the Augustan ideal of the Roman soldier-farmer was realistic; as a manual for farmers the *Georgics* has huge omissions and as a practical handbook would be as useless as Augustus's program of re-creating the Roman farmer-soldier was impractical. Most of Italy was cultivated by slave labor on land owned by absentee landlords who lived in Rome. The *Georgics* is a work of art—as Dryden declared, "the best Poem by the best Poet"—on which Virgil worked for seven years; he compared his work on it to that of a mother bear licking her cubs into shape.

In the opening lines of the poem, addressed to Maecenas, he announces the subject of the four books:

> What makes the corncrops glad, under which star
> To turn the soil, Maecenas, and wed your vines
> To elms, the care of cattle, keeping of flocks,
> All the experience thrifty bees demand—
> Such are the themes of my song.   (1.1–5, trans. Wilkinson)

With an invocation of the country gods, Virgil proceeds to describe the farmer's life of hard work as in his model, Hesiod. Later he writes about the weather signs that the farmer must recognize as prophecies of what is to come, sometimes evil, as he ends the book with memories of the recent civil wars, of Roman blood shed on the fields of Greece, and with a finale that is a prayer and a dark vision of the future:

> Gods of our fathers, Heroes of our land . . .
> Do not prevent at least this youthful prince
> From saving a world in ruins . . .
> For right and wrong change places; everywhere
> So many wars, so many shapes of crime
> Confront us; no due honor attends the plow.
> The fields, bereft of tillers, are all unkempt . . .
> . . . throughout the world
> Impious War is raging.   (1.498–511)

Book 2 is concerned with trees and vines, principally with the olive and the wine grape. There is much good advice here for the farmer, but the book is notable not only for the hymn of praise for Italy already quoted, but also for its praise of the happy life of the farmer as compared to that of the city dweller:

> How lucky, if they know their happiness,
> Are farmers, more than lucky, they for whom,

> Far from the clash of arms, the earth herself,
> Most fair in dealing, freely lavishes
> An easy livelihood . . .
> . . . Peace they have and a life of innocence
> Rich in variety; they have for leisure
> Their ample acres, caverns, living lakes,
> . . . cattle low, and sleep is soft
> Under a tree . . .   (2.458–70)

Book 3 is concerned with the breeding and raising of farm animals: horses and cattle in the first part and sheep and goats in the later section. After an exordium in which Virgil promises to celebrate the victories of Octavian, a promise fulfilled in the *Aeneid*, he proceeds to his subject. His discussion of farm animals contains the famous lines that apply equally to the human animal:

> Life's earliest years for wretched mortal creatures
> Are best, and fly most quickly: soon come on
> Diseases, suffering and gloomy age,
> Till Death's unpitying harshness carries them off.   (3.66–68)

Virgil ends this book, as he did Book 1, on a sad note: an account of a plague that struck cattle in the northern region of the Alps, in which he draws much from Lucretius' portrayal of the plague that struck humans in the Athens of Pericles, described in exact detail by Thucydides.

In his introduction to Book 4, about bee-keeping, Virgil assures Maecenas that he will describe

> . . . a world in miniature,
> Gallant commanders and the institutions
> Of a whole nation, its character, pursuits,
> Communities and warfare.   (4.3–5)

And this theme, of the hive as a community, in harmony or dissension, is a constant in the book.

A great deal of misinformation about bees is conveyed to the reader. Bees were not properly observed in the hive until the invention of the glass observation hive, and until the seventeenth century it was believed that the leader of the hive was the king, not the queen. But what has made Book 4 famous is the end—the long tale of Aristaeus and his bees and of Orpheus and Eurydice.

Virgil first describes the process of *bougonia* (the Greek word means something like "birth from a steer"), for re-creating the hive of bees in case the original bees die. A two-year-old steer is brought to a specially constructed hut that has windows facing in all four directions. The animal is then beaten to death and the remains left in place through the spring. Suddenly, in the rotting flesh a whole cluster of bees is born. This is not true, but it was widely believed in the ancient world (except by Aristotle) and appears also in the riddle Samson asked the Philistines to answer: "out of the strong came forth sweetness" (Judges 14:14).

Virgil's account of the origin of this method is told through the story of the farmer Aristaeus, whose hive of bees has died. He goes to his mother, the nymph Cyrene, and she tells him to find out what has gone wrong from Proteus, the Old Man of the Sea, who "knows / All that has been, is now, and lies in store" (4.392–93). Aristaeus must seize Proteus as he comes out of the water with his seals and hold him tightly as he changes shape, "for suddenly / He'll be a bristly boar or a savage tiger / or a scaly serpent or a lioness" (4.407–8). But he must be held fast until he gives up and resumes his own shape, and then he will answer questions. (This scene is adapted from Menelaus' similar interrogation of Proteus in the *Odyssey* 4.428–641.)* Aristaeus follows directions faithfully, and finally Proteus, back in his own shape, tells Aristaeus what is wrong. "Piteous Orpheus / It is that seeks to invoke this penalty / Against you" (4.454–55). It is revenge for the death of his wife, the nymph Eurydice, who, fleeing Aristaeus' advances, ran along the banks of a river where she was killed by a serpent. After mourning for her, Orpheus decided to seek her in the land of the dead.

> And entering the gloomy grove of terror
> Approached the shades and their tremendous king . . .
> [Orpheus'] music shook them . . .   (4 468–71)

And Virgil goes on to describe the dark kingdom and its denizens in lines that foreshadow his more detailed description of the Underworld later, in Book 6 of the *Aeneid*. Orpheus' music wins him his Eurydice.

---

*Here and throughout, unless otherwise indicated, line numbers of the *Iliad*, the *Odyssey*, and the *Aeneid* refer to the Fagles translations, where the line numbers of the Greek and Latin texts will be found at the top of every page.

She is allowed to follow him back to the land of the living, but on condition that he does not look back at her until they reach the light of the upper world. But Orpheus,

> . . . on the very brink of light, alas,
> Forgetful, yielding in his will, looked back
> At his own Eurydice. . . .   (4.490–91)

And as she reproached him bitterly, she

>   . . . suddenly
> Out of his sight, like smoke into thin air,
> Vanished away . . .
>   For seven whole months on end, they say, he wept . . .
> Alone in the wild . . .
> And sang his tale of woe . . .   (4.499–510)

And finally, wandering in Thrace in the north, he was torn to pieces by Bacchantes in their Dionysiac frenzy, his limbs were scattered far and wide, and his head was thrown into the Hebrus River. And there,

> His head, now severed from his marble neck,
> "Eurydice!" the voice and frozen tongue
> Still called aloud, "Ah, poor Eurydice!"   (4.523–26)

So Proteus departed and Aristaeus, instructed by his mother Cyrene, made sacrifices to the shade of Orpheus and to the nymphs, the sisters of Eurydice, and then left for his *bougonia* for the regeneration of his bees. And the story of Orpheus and Eurydice, in Virgil's musical verse, has inspired poetry and song ever since.

In the final lines of the *Georgics*, published probably in 29 B.C., two years after the battle of Actium, which made Octavian master of the Roman world, Virgil tells us that he finished the poem at Naples (to which he gives its Greek name, Parthenope), while Octavian, soon to be given the title Augustus, was making a triumphant progress through the East.

> This song of the husbandry of crops and beasts
> And fruit-trees I was singing while great Caesar
> Was thundering beside the deep Euphrates
> In war, victoriously for grateful peoples

Appointing laws and setting his course for Heaven.
I, Virgil, at that time lay in the lap
Of sweet Parthenope, enjoying there
The studies of inglorious ease, who once
Dallied in pastoral verse and with youth's boldness
Sang of you, Tityrus, lazing under a beech-tree.   (4.559–66)

That last line is a quotation, slightly adapted, of the opening line of his
first book, the *Eclogues*.

THE *AENEID*

Near the opening of the third book of the *Georgics* Virgil speaks of what
will be his next work:

Yet soon I will gird myself to celebrate
The fiery fights of Caesar, make his name
Live in the future . . .   (3.46–47)

This promise would be kept by the writing of his last and most grandly
ambitious poem, the *Aeneid*, which he never finished to his full satisfac-
tion. After reading Books 2, 4, and 6 to Augustus and Octavia and com-
pleting his work on Book 12, he decided to visit Greece in 19 B.C. and
spend three years on correction and revision. But he met Augustus in
Athens on Augustus' return from the East and was persuaded to return to
Italy with him. However, passing from Athens to Corinth, at Megara Vir-
gil contracted a fever, which grew worse during the voyage to Brundis-
ium, where he died on September 21. He was buried near Naples, and on
his tomb were inscribed verses that he is said to have composed himself:

Mantua me genuit, Calabri rapuere, tenet nunc
Parthenope. Cecini pascua, rura, duces.

Mantova gave me life, the Calabrians took it away, Naples
holds me now; I sang of pastures, farms, and commanders.

(trans. Knox)

There is a report that he had ordered his literary executors, Varius
and Tucca, to destroy the unfinished manuscript; if so, these orders were

immediately canceled by Augustus. Imperfections remain: some incomplete hexameters, which Virgil would certainly have tidied up, and several minor contradictions, which he would certainly have dealt with. One passage (2.702–28), which is not in the oldest manuscripts, was removed, according to the much later commentator Servius, by Varius and Tucca. (In the most recent editions of Virgil's text, for example that of Fairclough, revised in 1999–2000 by George P. Goold, the passage is marked as spurious. Other recent commentators, however, notably R. G. Austin and R. D. Williams, consider it genuine.) The passage pictures Helen as seeking sanctuary at the shrine of Vesta, fearing the vengeance of the Trojans for the ruin she has brought on them, and Aeneas' angry decision to kill her. This passage contradicts a long and intricate story of Helen triumphantly welcoming the Greeks and organizing the mutilation and death of Deiphobus, the Trojan whom she had married after the death of Paris (6.573–623). But however it may complicate the narrative, and however Virgil might have revised it later, one may still be impressed by its strong Virgilian style and the effectiveness with which it suits its context, setting the scene for Venus, who redirects Aeneas' energies to the rescue of his family. So we have bracketed the passage and kept it in the translation.

The *Aeneid,* of course, is based on and often uses characters and incidents from the Homeric epics. In the *Iliad* Aeneas is an important warrior fighting on the Trojan side. He is the son of the love-goddess Aphrodite (Venus in the Roman pantheon) and Anchises, and he is often rescued from death at the hands of Greek warriors by divine intervention: from Diomedes by Aphrodite (*Iliad* 5.495–517), and from Achilles by Poseidon (Neptune) at *Iliad* 20.314–386. On this occasion Poseidon comments on Aeneas' piety toward the gods: "He always gave us gifts to warm our hearts, / gifts for the gods who rule the vaulting skies" (20.345–46). He also says something else about Aeneas:

> "He is destined to survive.
> Yes, so the generation of Dardanus shall not perish . . .
> Dardanus, dearest to Zeus of all the sons
> That mortal women brought to birth for Father."   (20.349–53)

Dardanus was the founder of the race of Trojan kings, ancestor not only of Priam and Hector but also of Anchises and Aeneas. And Poseidon goes on to say: "and now Aeneas will rule the men of Troy in power— / his sons' sons and the sons born in future years" (20.355–56).

Poseidon's mention of Aeneas' insistence on gifts of sacrifice to the gods anticipates the adjective that Virgil often attaches to him—*pius*, and its abstract noun *pietas*. He is called in the early lines of the poem (1.10) "a man outstanding in his piety," *insignem pietate virum*, and in 1.457 he introduces himself to his mother, Venus (whom he has not yet recognized), with the words "I am pious Aeneas," *sum pius Aeneas* (trans. Knox). The adjective and the abstract noun occur often in the poem and are attributed to its hero. Virgil's mastery of the hexameter line rules out the Homeric reason for the repetition of such modifiers—metrical necessity; in Virgil the frequent reappearance of these words in connection with the hero has a meaning and an emphasis, though not those of Yeats's sailor who told him Aeneas sounded more like a priest than a hero.

The word *pius* does indeed refer, like its English derivative, to devotion and duty to the Divine; this is the reason cited by Poseidon in the *Iliad* for saving Aeneas from death at the hand of Achilles. And in the *Aeneid* he is always mindful of the gods, constant in prayer and thanks and dutiful in sacrifice. But the words *pius* and *pietas* have in Latin a wider meaning. Perhaps the best English equivalent is something like "dutiful," "mindful of one's duty"—not only to the gods but also to one's family and to one's country.

Aeneas' devotion to his family was famous. Book 2 describes how, after realizing that fighting was no longer of use, that Troy was doomed, he carries his father, Anchises, on his shoulders out of the burning city, holding his son Ascanius by the hand, with his wife, Creusa, following behind. But she is lost on the way, and he arrives at the rendezvous outside the city with only his father and son. In desperation he rushes back into the burning city to find her, but finds only her ghost, which tells him what his future and his duty are now:

> "'A long exile is your fate . . .
> the vast plains of the sea are yours to plow
> until you reach Hesperian land, where Lydian Tiber
> flows with its smooth march through rich and loamy fields,
> a land of hardy people. There great joy and a kingdom
> are yours to claim, and a queen to make your wife . . .
> And now farewell. Hold dear the son we share,
> we love together.'"   (2.967–80)

He tries to embrace her only to find

> "... her phantom
> sifting through my fingers,
> light as wind, quick as a dream in flight."   (2.984–86)

But *pietas* describes another loyalty and duty, besides that to the gods and to the family. It is for the Roman, to Rome, and in Aeneas' case, to his mission to found it in Hesperia, the western country, Italy. And it is noticeable that this adjective is not applied to him when, in love with Dido, in Book 4, he actually takes part in helping to build her city, Carthage, "founding the city fortifications, / building homes in Carthage" (4.324–25). Jupiter in heaven, enraged that Aeneas has forgotten his mission, sends his messenger, Mercury, down to him with the single-word command *Naviget!* "Let him set sail!" (4.296). Only when Aeneas realizes he must leave Dido, and suffers from her rage as he makes his reply to her accusations, only when he leaves for the shore and gives his fleet the order to set sail, is he called *pius* again (4.494–95). He has given up her love, and left her to die, as he fulfills his duty to his son—for as Mercury reminds him, "you owe him Italy's realm, the land of Rome!" (4.343)—and his own duty to found the western Troy that is to be.

But *pietas* is not a virtue confined to Aeneas; it is also an ideal for all Romans. Unlike the Greeks whom they added to their empire, and admired for their artistic and literary skills, but who never acted as a united nation, not even when invaded by the forces of the Persian Empire in 480 B.C., the Romans had a profound sense of national unity, and the talents and virtues necessary for a race of conquerors and organizers, of empire-builders and rulers. One of the virtues besides *pietas* that they admired was *gravitas,* a profound seriousness in matters political and religious, in which they distrusted attempts to change; they deferred on these and other matters to *auctoritas,* the power and respect won by men of experience, of successful leadership in war and peace. They admired discipline, the mark of their legionary soldiers who conquered and held for centuries an empire that included almost the whole of western Europe and much of the Middle East.

Many of these Roman characteristics appear early in Virgil's poem in the simile that describes how Neptune restored order to the chaos created by Juno, who had loosed all of the Aeolian winds against the Trojan fleet:

> Just as, all too often,
> some huge crowd is seized by a vast uprising,

the rabble runs amok, all slaves to passion,
rocks, firebrands flying. Rage finds them arms
but then, if they chance to see a man among them,
one whose devotion and public service lend him weight [*pietate
    gravem*],
they stand there, stock-still with their ears alert as
he rules their furor with his words and calms their passion.

(1.174–81)

Here *pietas, gravitas,* and the *auctoritas* conferred by his public service (*meritis*) are enough to calm the mob and restore order.

The continuation of the *Iliad,* the *Iliou Persis* (*The Sack of Troy*), exists now only in fragmentary quotations, but it records Aeneas' exit from the burning city and his stay with his family and followers on Mount Ida, near Troy, before departing on his travels to the West. These are mentioned by the Greek writer Hellanicus of Lesbos as early as the fifth century B.C., and the final object of his travels was established as Italy perhaps as early as the fifth century but certainly by the third. As the Romans in that century began to find themselves opposed by Macedonian and Greek powers in the East, the legend of Rome's Trojan ancestry became increasingly popular; it was eagerly embraced when in 280 B.C. Pyrrhus of Epirus invaded Italy, claiming descent from Achilles and labeling Rome a second Troy. He defeated several Roman armies, with increasing losses—hence the phrase *Pyrrhic victory*—but finally left Italy in 275 B.C. and was killed soon afterward. In Rome the legend of Aeneas' arrival in Italy and the founding by his son Ascanius of Alba Longa, where many centuries later, Romulus, founder of Rome, would be born, was celebrated in the *Annales* of Ennius, written in hexameter verse, which carried on the history of Rome from its founding until Ennius' own time—the second century B.C.

The first six books of the *Aeneid* contain many references to and imitations of incidents and passages found in the Homeric *Odyssey.* Aeneas' stay at Carthage with Dido corresponds to Odysseus' stay (much longer and against his will) with the nymph Calypso, and his account of his wanderings from Troy, told to Dido in Book 3, to Odysseus' long account of his wanderings told to the Phaeacians in Books 9 through 12 of the *Odyssey.* Aeneas encounters and rescues one of Odysseus' sailors who has been left behind on the island of the Cyclops, where Aeneas too encounters Polyphemus and his Cyclopean relatives. The funeral games for Anchises in Book 5 of the *Aeneid* are modeled on those for Patroclus in Book 23 of the *Iliad*, except that a ship-race in the *Aeneid* replaces a horse race in the *Iliad*. And of course Aeneas visits the land of the dead in Book 6 of the *Aeneid* to see his father, just as Odysseus goes there to meet his mother in Book 11 of the *Odyssey*. Yet these correspondences are of quite different episodes: the stay with Calypso is long and uneventful, that with Dido is short and tragic; the encounters in the lower world are very different in length as in nature. And many correspondences in the later books, such as the shield made for Achilles by Hephaestus and that made for Aeneas by Vulcan are superficial resemblances between entirely different objects. As for the fact that the last six books of the *Aeneid* resemble the *Iliad* more than the *Odyssey*, because they deal with war not voyaging, this is not their only resemblance. In both epics an older man has entrusted to the hero a companion to fight with him and sustain his cause. In the *Iliad* Achilles' father gives him an older companion, Patroclus, and in the *Aeneid* Evander gives his young son Pallas to fight at Aeneas' side. In both cases this man is killed by the enemy chieftain, and in both cases that killing is avenged by the hero's killing of the enemy champion, of Hector in the *Iliad*, and in the last lines of the *Aeneid*, of Turnus.

The *Aeneid* is to be Rome's *Iliad* and *Odyssey*, and it derives also from Homer its picture of two different worlds, each with its own passions and actions. One is the world of heaven above, in Homer the world of Zeus, the supreme god, his wife and sister, Hera, the love-goddess Aphrodite, the smith-god Hephaestus, the sea-god Poseidon and the others; and below, on earth, the world of Achilles, Patroclus, Diomedes and of Hector, his wife Andromache, and his father Priam. In the *Aeneid* the heavens are the home of Jupiter (or Jove) the supreme god, his wife and sister Juno, the love-goddess Venus, the smith-god Vulcan, the sea-god Neptune, and the minor gods. They preside over the world of the heroes— Aeneas, Turnus, Evander, Pallas, and Camilla down below. As in Homer, the passions and actions of the gods affect the actions and passions of the heroes on earth.

Jupiter knows what the Fates have decreed, what will happen in the end—that Aeneas will reach Italy and found Lavinium, the beginning of the process that over the centuries will lead to the founding of Rome. But Juno is bitterly opposed to this vision of the future; she hated Troy while it stood, and all Trojans since with a vicious aversion, and she is determined that Aeneas will not reach Italy. This hatred of Trojans has many causes: the fact that their ancestor was Dardanus, the son of Zeus and Electra, daughter of Atlas—"the Trojan stock she loathed" (1.35); the fact that Ganymede, a beautiful boy whose father was Laomedon, a Trojan prince, had been carried up to Olympus by Zeus, who assumed the shape of an eagle, to be his cupbearer—"the honors showered on Ganymede" (1.35)—and lastly the so-called Judgment of Paris, delivered while Troy still stood secure at peace behind its walls. Three goddesses, Juno, Athena, and Venus, disputed which was the most beautiful and finally decided on a beauty contest to be judged by Paris, a son of Priam, king of Troy. As he surveyed their charms, each one offered him a bribe to win his vote. The virgin goddess Athena offered him success in war, Juno success in every walk of life, but Venus offered the love and the hand of the most beautiful woman in the world, Helen, wife of Menelaus, king of Sparta in Greece. He judges Venus the most beautiful, goes to Sparta, runs off to Troy with Helen, and the ten-year war begins. Juno never forgot this insult; it is mentioned at the beginning of Virgil's poem, "the judgment of Paris, the unjust slight to her beauty" (1.34). And this is one of the reasons why she

> drove over endless oceans
> Trojans left by the Greeks . . .
> Juno kept them far from Latium, forced by the Fates
> to wander round the seas of the world, year in, year out.
> Such a long hard labor it was to found the Roman people.   (1.37–41)

NARRATIVE

After this line the narrative begins. It is the opening of an epic poem, divided into twelve books containing roughly ten thousand lines. The story plunges, in Horace's famous phrase, *in medias res,* into the middle of events. Aeneas' fleet is just off Sicily when Juno arrives, bribes the divine keeper of the winds, Aeolus, to let them loose in a storm that scatters Aeneas' fleet and lands him, with only seven of his ships, on the African shore. But Neptune suddenly realizes that a vast storm has raged without his permission; he rebukes Aeolus and calms the weather, and the rest of Aeneas' fleet re-forms in quiet waters.

On the African shore Aeneas tries to cheer his despondent crews in words that summarize their hard lot and their final reward promised by Fate:

"A joy it will be one day, perhaps, to remember even this.
Through so many hard straits, so many twists and turns
our course holds firm for Latium. There Fate holds out
a homeland, calm, at peace. There the gods decree
the kingdom of Troy will rise again. Bear up.
Save your strength for better times to come."   (1.239–44)

Meanwhile there are fresh developments in heaven above. Venus reminds
Jupiter of his promises about Aeneas' future and complains of Juno's in-
terference. Why is Aeneas kept away from the Rome he was promised?
Jupiter's reply is long and favorable: "the fate of your children stands un-
changed," he reassures her, and "unrolling the scroll of Fate" (1.308–13)
he tells her that

                              "Aeneas will wage
a long, costly war in Italy . . .
and build high city walls for the people there . . .
But his son Ascanius, now that he gains the name
of Iulus . . .
[will] raise up Alba Longa's mighty ramparts."   (1.314–25)

There, after three hundred years, the priestess Ilia will bear to the Roman
war-god Mars twin sons; one of them, Romulus, will build Rome's
walls and call his people Romans. Jupiter goes on: "On them I set no lim-
its, space or time: / I have granted them power, empire without end"
(1.333–34). And he concludes with a vision of the future, the Roman
conquest of Greece, the coming of a Trojan Caesar, Julius, "a name passed
down from Iulus, his great forebear" (1.344). This is Augustus, under
whom "the violent centuries, battles set aside, / [will] grow gentle, kind"
(1.348–49).

Below, on earth, Aeneas, who now sets out with one companion,
Achates, to explore the territory, has landed in the area where Dido, an
exile from Tyre, is building her new city, Carthage. His mother, Venus, dis-
guised as a girl huntress, tells him the story of Dido, and he eventually
comes to the city that is being built, to find the rest of his surviving
crews being welcomed by the queen. She realizes who he is and invites
him to a banquet, at which, in Books 2 and 3, he tells her the story of
the fall of Troy, his escape with his father and young son, and the long
voyage west with his Trojans toward their destined home. Meanwhile,
not without the intervention of Venus, Dido has fallen madly in love

with Aeneas, and on the next day, in Book 4, at a hunt Juno sends down a storm that drives the pair to take refuge in a cave, where their love is consummated. Dido regards this as a marriage, and Aeneas seems to agree, since he takes part in the building of her new city. But Jupiter soon sends his messenger, Mercury, to remind Aeneas of his duty, and in spite of Dido's appeals and denunciations, he sets sail with his fleet. Dido curses him and all his race and calls for an avenger to arise from her bones as she commits suicide. In Book 5, Aeneas in Sicily organizes the funeral games for Anchises. Juno attempts, unsuccessfully, to burn his ships. In a dream he sees his dead father, Anchises, who tells him he must go to the land of the dead, guided by the Sibyl, to meet him in Elysium, "the luminous fields where the true / and faithful gather" (5.814–15). His guide to the Underworld will be the Sibyl whom he will find in Italy. And in Book 6, after his journey with the Sibyl through the darker regions of the world below, he meets Anchises and is shown a pageant of the great Romans, who in future days will establish the Roman Empire and the peace of the world.

In Book 7 Aeneas finally reaches the Tiber River, and the second part of the *Aeneid* starts: the wandering is over and the wars begin. Virgil invokes the Muse Erato to tell "who were the kings, the tides and times, how stood / the old Latin state" (7.40–41). He asks the goddess

> "inspire your singer, come!
> I will tell of horrendous wars
> . . . all Hesperia called to arms . . .
> I launch a greater labor."   (7.45–50)

Erato is the Muse of lyric poetry and love; she seems an unusual Muse to call on for inspiration in a tale of "horrendous wars." Calliope, the Muse of epic poetry, might seem more appropriate, but these wars are waged because of a marriage contested between the two champions, Aeneas and Turnus. Since there is no Muse specifically associated with war, Erato is the natural choice.

In Book 7 Aeneas establishes a fortified camp on the shore by the river Tiber,

> And Aeneas himself lines up
> his walls with a shallow trench, he starts to work the site
> and rings his first settlement on the coast with mounds,
> redoubts and ramparts built like an armed camp.   (7.180–83)

The words used—*fossa, pinnis, aggere, castrorum*—identify it with the camps (*castra*) that in the future Roman legionary soldiers will build at the end of the day's march—*castra,* which will be built all over Europe and have often left their mark on the names of the cities that occupy those sites— Lancaster, Manchester, Worcester. From this camp Aeneas sends an embassy to King Latinus, asking for a grant of land and the hand of his daughter Lavinia in marriage. The king has been warned of such an approach by visions and seers, and is agreeable. But Juno intervenes again—this is where she makes her famous proclamation: "if I cannot sway the heavens, I'll wake the powers of hell!" *Flectere si nequeo superos, Acheronta movebo* (7.365). (Many centuries later these words would appear on the title page of Sigmund Freud's book *The Interpretation of Dreams,* a clear announcement that he is drawing some sort of analogy between the psychic and the infernal, and the dark energies of both.) Juno sends the Fury Allecto to rouse against the marriage first Lavinia's mother Amata, and then the Rutulian leader Turnus, who presumes that Lavinia will become his bride. Both are filled with furious rage against the new proposal, and Turnus (and Juno) stir Italy against its terms. War against the intruders is declared, and Book 7 ends with a long catalog of the Italian forces and leaders, prominent among them Mezentius, the Etruscan king whose own people (who eventually fight on the Trojan side) had driven him out because of his cruelty; and Turnus, the leader of the fight against Aeneas, and the virgin cavalry leader Camilla, the Volscian.

As Book 8 opens, the god of the river Tiber appears to Aeneas in a dream, explains to him that Evander, whose kingdom lies upriver, is an enemy of the Latins and will help Aeneas. The river-god himself will help him on his way in his ships. Aeneas chooses a pair of galleys and sets off for Evander's town, which is on the site, with its hills, where Rome will one day rise. They are hailed by Pallas, Evander's son, and welcomed by the king. He has been celebrating their liberation by Hercules from the fire-breathing monster Cacus, which lived in a cave on what later, in Roman times, was named the Aventine hill. And Evander tells the long story of Hercules' ultimate destruction of Cacus. He then shows Aeneas all around his kingdom, the places that will in later times be famous, the future sites of the Capitol—"they saw herds of cattle . . . / in the Roman Forum and Carinae's elegant district" (8.423–24). That night, as they sleep, Venus persuades her husband, the smith-god Vulcan, to make arms and a shield for Aeneas. Meanwhile Evander tells Aeneas of certain allies for him—the Etruscans, who have expelled their cruel king, Mezentius, and burn to fight the Rutulian forces of Turnus but have been told by a seer to await a captain from overseas. Aeneas and Pallas ride for Etruria with their cavalry, meet the Etruscan forces and, as the "weary troops take rest" (8.716), Venus gives her son his new arms and shield. And on the shield "There is the story of Italy, / Rome in all her triumphs" (8.738–39). Across its surface is pictured the whole history of Rome, from the she-wolf that suckled Romulus and Remus to the battle of Actium, which made Augustus master of the world. Aeneas

> knows nothing of these events but takes delight
> in their likeness, lifting onto his shoulders now
> the fame and fates of all his children's children.   (8.856–58)

Back at the seashore Turnus, spurred on by Juno, leads his troops against the Trojan camp, but unable to breach the walls, attacks with fire the ships of Aeneas, moored by the camp. But these ships were built outside Troy from trees in a wood sacred to Jupiter's mother, Cybebe (Cybele), and she now calls on her son to save them. He changes them into sea-nymphs, and Turnus calls off the attack on the camp until the next day. One of the Trojans, Nisus, proposes to steal at night through the sleeping enemy contingents to go and warn Aeneas of the danger to his base, and his young lover, Euryalus, insists, in spite of Nisus' protests, on accompanying him. They carry out a wild slaughter among the sleeping Italians but as they move off, toward the river perhaps, they are intercepted and killed by a fresh enemy contingent just arriving. The next day Turnus renews the attack on the camp and even manages to get in alone through a gate that has been opened by overconfident Trojans. He creates great slaughter among the Trojans as he fights his way to the water and swims to safety.

At the beginning of Book 10, which follows, Jupiter calls together an assembly of the gods at which both Venus and Juno make their long complaints, but Jupiter declares neutrality. He will leave the outcome to the champions themselves:

> "How each man weaves
> his web will bring him to glory or to grief . . .
> The Fates will find the way."   (10.135–38)

The attack on the camp resumes, while far upriver, Aeneas joins the Etruscan leaders, who combine their fleet with his to sail down to the relief of the Trojan camp. At this point (10.202ff.) Virgil names and describes

the Etruscan leaders, another of those catalogs in which he lovingly re-
cites the various parts of Italy from which they come . . . Pisa, Caere, Li-
guria, Mantua—part of that hymn of praise of Italy that is a main feature
of the *Aeneid*. As Aeneas sails down the river, the nymph Cymodocea, who
had been one of the nymphs that had been changed into a ship outside
the camp, warns him that the camp is under attack by Turnus, and as
Aeneas comes in sight of it he raises the shield his mother had made for
him, and the signal is greeted with joy and relief by the Trojans in the
camp. There follows a vivid account of an opposed landing and an equally
fierce battle afterward "on Italy's very doorstep" (10.420), in which, as
young Pallas' troops begin to fall back, he rallies them and kills one en-
emy chieftain after another, until Turnus comes to the rescue and routs
the Arcadians, killing Pallas and taking from him as a trophy Pallas' en-
graved sword-belt, which will turn out to be his own death warrant.

Aeneas hears the news and comes on, slaughtering enemy champions
right and left as he looks for Turnus. But Juno obtains from Jupiter a
respite, no more, for Turnus, and full of grief she spirits him out of the
fighting to his home. Book 10 ends with an account of the many success-
ful duels of Mezentius, the Etruscan king fighting on the Latin side. He
kills one Trojan champion after another until he meets Aeneas, who
wounds him and then kills his son Lausus, as he comes to his father's aid.
Aeneas, thinking no doubt of Pallas, is sorry for him, but goes on to kill
his father, Mezentius. In Book 11 Aeneas, his camp no longer besieged,
proceeds to the burial of the dead. He mourns over the body of Pallas
and sends it off with his arms, his warhorse, and a huge escort, to his
father. He gives envoys from the Latin city permission to bury their
dead, and Drances, an enemy of Turnus, announces his intention to seek
peace. Evander mourns over the body of Pallas and sends word to Aeneas
that his "right arm / . . . owes . . . the life of Turnus / to son and father
both" (11.210–12).

Now, as the Latins bury their dead, the discontent with the war,
fanned by Drances, grows and is increased by bad news that arrives from
the city that Diomedes the Greek champion was building in Italy, and
whom the Latin envoys had counted on for support against the enemy he
had fought at Troy. But Diomedes' answer is negative: he advises them to
make peace with Aeneas, whose bravery he praises. Latinus offers to give
the Trojans the territory they ask for, and Drances proposes that the king
give his daughter Lavinia to Aeneas in marriage. Turnus makes a long and
furious reply, urging continuation of the war, and offering, if it comes to

that, to fight Aeneas man to man as Drances has proposed. But the council is interrupted by the news that Aeneas with all his troops is advancing on the city. The citizens man the walls, and Turnus orders his captains to their stations and rides off himself to meet, at the head of her cavalry, Camilla the Volscian. He arranges for her to engage the Trojan cavalry, while he hopes to ambush Aeneas and his troops, who are attacking the city from a different direction. The rest of Book 11 is mainly concerned with the feats and fate of Camilla, who, after killing many adversaries, is brought down by the Etruscan Arruns, who has stalked her all over the battlefield. Her death is avenged by that of Arruns at the hand of the nymph Opis, sent down by the goddess Diana, who loves Camilla, her devotee. And now, in the last book, Turnus sends the challenge to Aeneas, to fight him man to man. As all the preparations are made, the dueling ground paced off, Juno intervenes. She tells Turnus' sister, Juturna, a river-nymph, "Pluck your brother from death, if there's a way, / or drum up war and abort that treaty they conceived" (12.187–88).

And she does. Disguised as Camers, a famous Italian warrior, she begins to stir discontent among the Rutulians, and soon fighting breaks out. Aeneas, as he vainly tries to stop it, is hit by an arrow and retreats from the lines. Turnus attacks, the war resumes. Aeneas and his friends try to pull the broken arrowhead out of the wound; their efforts and those of the old healer Iapyx are unsuccessful until Venus intervenes and supplies Iapyx, without his knowledge, with herbs that restore Aeneas to health. Venus also inspires Aeneas to put Latinus' city to the torch, and the Trojan attack is successful enough to cause the queen, Amata, to hang herself as the walls are breached. The news is brought to Turnus, and abandoning his chariot, which, he now realizes, is driven by his sister Juturna the nymph, who is trying to save him, he comes to meet Aeneas and settle the issue man to man.

As they fight, Venus and Juturna both intervene to help their relatives, and finally Jupiter forbids any further interference by Juno or her helper. And reluctantly Juno yields. But she makes a request:

"never command the Latins, here on native soil,
to change their age-old name,
to become Trojans, called the kin of Teucer,
alter their language, change their style of dress.
Let Latium endure. Let Alban kings hold sway for all time.
Let Roman stock grow strong with Italian strength.

Troy has fallen—and fallen let her stay—
with the very name of Troy!"   (12.954–61)

And Jupiter grants her wish:

"Latium's sons will retain their fathers' words and ways.
Their name till now is the name that shall endure.
Mingling in stock alone, the Trojans will subside.
And I will add the rites and the forms of worship,
make them Latins all, who speak the Latin tongue."   (12.967–71)

Juno accepts, with joy. But Jupiter must now deal with Juturna. He sends
down one of the Furies, who assumes the form of an owl that flutters in
Turnus' face, screeches, drums Turnus' shield with its wings. Juturna rec-
ognizes the signal and, lamenting, leaves Turnus to face Aeneas. In the
end, Turnus, helpless, lies at Aeneas' feet and begs for his life. Turnus'
pleas begin to sway him, when suddenly he sees "the fateful sword-belt of
Pallas, / swept over Turnus' shoulder . . . like a trophy" and "plants /
his iron sword hilt-deep in his enemy's heart" (12.1098–1110).

HISTORY

All this intervention of gods in human affairs to advance their own in-
terests and satisfy their own passions is Homeric, but what is not Homeric
is the constant reference to history, in particular to Roman history, which
is a recurring feature of the *Aeneid*. The Homeric epics have no historical
background to speak of—as C. S. Lewis puts it, "There is no pretence, in-
deed no possibility of pretending, that the world, or even Greece, would
have been much altered if Odysseus had never got home at all" (*Preface*,
p. 26). But the *Aeneid* is always conscious of history, Roman history, many
centuries of it. Very often this reference is explicit, as in the long list and
description of great Romans not yet born, whose spirits are shown to Ae-
neas by his father in Elysium in Book 6. But often the allusion is not ex-
plicit, and though it was obvious to Virgil's Roman readers, it may not be
so without explanation today.

For example, in Book 2, Aeneas' account to Dido of the sack of Troy
by the Greeks, the final disposition of the corpse of Priam, king of Troy,
slaughtered in his palace by Pyrrhus, son of Achilles, is described by Virgil
in these words:

"Such was the fate of Priam . . .
the monarch who once had ruled in all his glory
the many lands of Asia, Asia's many tribes.
A powerful trunk is lying on the shore.
The head wrenched from the shoulders.
A corpse without a name."   (2.686–92)

Any Roman who read these lines in the years after Virgil's poem was published or heard them recited would at once remember a real and recent ruler over "the many lands of Asia," whose headless corpse lay on the shore. It was the corpse of Gnaeus Pompeius (Pompey), who had been ruler of all the lands of Asia; from 67 to 62 B.C. he had been given a wide and extended command to settle the Middle East, had defeated the army of Mithridates, king of Pontus, and reorganized the whole area, adding new provinces to the Empire. But many years later, after his defeat by Caesar at Pharsalus in 48 B.C., his body lay headless on the Egyptian shore.

But this is far from being the only such reference to Roman history. Dido's last words, in which she curses Aeneas and predicts eternal war between her people and his, reminded Roman readers of the three wars the Romans had to fight against the Carthaginians: the Punic Wars, they called them, a word formed from their name—*Poeni*—for the settlers from Tyre, who had founded the great commercial and naval power of Carthage.

As she prepares to kill herself after Aeneas leaves her, Dido curses him, foretelling a sad end for him and commanding her people to wage endless war on Aeneas' descendants:

"And you, my Tyrians,
harry with hatred all his line, his race to come . . .
No love between our peoples, ever—no pacts of peace! . . .
Shore clash with shore, sea against sea and sword
against sword—this is my curse—war between all
our peoples, all their children, endless war!"   (4.775–84)

The Phoenicians, inhabitants of two cities, Tyre and Sidon on the Palestinian coast, were the great sailors, traders, and explorers of the ancient world. They provided, for example, the fleet that backed the Persian king Xerxes' invasion of Greece in 480 B.C. They also, from their colony at Carthage, founded, probably in the second half of the eighth century B.C., colonies in western Sicily, which regularly fought against the Greek colonies in the east of that island. And they colonized southern Spain, from which they exported those metals that were so rare in the eastern Mediterranean area. Their relations with Rome were friendly at first but soon, as Rome began to intervene in Sicily, degenerated, and in 264 B.C. the First Punic War began, to end in 241 with a hard-won Roman victory and the annexation of Sicily as Rome's first province.

But the Second Punic War (218–201 B.C.) was an entirely different matter; it saw the fulfillment of another part of Dido's curse:

> "Come rising up from my bones, you avenger still unknown,
> to stalk those Trojan settlers, hunt with fire and iron,
> now or in time to come, whenever the power is yours."   (4.779–81)

This was the Carthaginian Hannibal, whose feats are also predicted by Jupiter in Book 10:

> "one day when savage Carthage will loose enormous ruin
> down on the Roman strongholds, breach and unleash
> the Alps against her walls."   (10.15–17)

Hannibal moved from his base in Spain north to what is now the French coast and then, war elephants and all, crossed the Alps and came down on Italy. He defeated the Roman troops in one battle after another, at the Trebia River, at Lake Trasimenus, and in 216 at Cannae he annihilated a superior Roman force with tactics that were carefully studied by the German general staff in 1914. But though he remained in Italy until 202, he was unable to break the loyalty of the Latin cities to Rome's federation and was gradually confined to a small area in the South of Italy. Meanwhile the Roman general Scipio took southern Spain from the Carthaginians as Hasdrubal made his way over the Alps with a relief force to join Hannibal. Hasdrubal's army was defeated in northern Italy in 207; Scipio crossed to Africa in 204, and Hannibal was recalled to defend Carthage. He was defeated by Scipio in 202 B.C. at Zama, and Carthage made peace with Rome on very harsh terms.

But Carthage, with its superb harbor and trading contacts, soon began to revive, and the Roman senator Cato became famous for ending every speech he made in the Senate, no matter what the subject under discussion happened to be, with the words: "And furthermore, my opinion is that Carthage should be destroyed—*delendam esse Carthaginem.*" Finally, in 149 B.C., the Romans took his advice; the Third Punic War came to an end in 146 B.C. with the total defeat of Carthage and the destruction of the city.

But of course it was eventually rebuilt, to become the heart of Rome's North African province, and in Virgil's lifetime the emperor Augustus established a Roman colony on the site, and it flourished as a commercial and cultural center well into the Christian centuries. St. Augustine as a young man went to the university there in the fourth century A.D., and it was in Carthage that he fell in love with Virgil, yet he later ascribed that love to sins of youth. He says of his school days there in his *Confessions*: "The singsong One and one makes two, two and two makes four was detestable to me, but sweet were the visions of absurdity—the wooden horse cargoed with men, Troy in flames, and Creusa herself ghosting by" (1.IV.22, trans. Garry Wills).

ANCHISES' PAGEANT

But the most copious rehearsal of Roman history occurs in Book 6, when in Elysium Anchises shows Aeneas the spirits of the great Romans to come, a pageant of Roman history from the earliest, legendary times right up to Virgil's own day. Following the instructions given him by Anchises in a dream in Sicily, Aeneas sails to Cumae in Italy, to meet the Sibyl who will be his guide for his visit to the land of the dead. He begs her to take him to his father and receives the famous reply:

> "the descent to the Underworld is easy.
> Night and day the gates of shadowy Death stand open wide,
> but to retrace your steps, to climb back to the upper air—
> there the struggle, there the labor lies."   (6.149–52)

She tells him he must have the golden bough as a gift for the goddess Proserpina. He goes to get it and soon they are on their way "through gloom and the empty halls of Death's ghostly realm" (6.308) to the river Acheron and its ferryman Charon. By the river there is a huge host of souls stretching out their arms in longing toward the farther bank, but Charon will take only those who have been properly buried; the others must wait on the bank for a hundred years. Here they see the shade of Palinurus, Aeneas' pilot on the way to Italy, who was put to sleep by the god Somnus and fell overboard. He now lies unburied on the shore, but the Sibyl tells him he will be buried soon by the local people. As Aeneas and the Sibyl approach Charon, he refuses to take living passengers, but the Sibyl shows him the bough and he takes them aboard. On the other side they pass the hell-hound Cerberus as the Sibyl gives him the proverbial "sop," "slumbrous with honey and drugged seed" (6.483).

Now they see the ghosts of those who died in infancy, of those condemned to death on a false charge, of suicides, and lastly, in the Fields of Mourning, of those who died of love. And here Aeneas sees the ghost of Dido. He approaches her, full of remorse, and makes his excuse: "I left your shores, my Queen, against my will" (6.535), but—in what T. S. Eliot calls "perhaps the most telling snub in all poetry" (*What Is a Classic?* p. 62)—she tears herself away, "his enemy forever" (6.548). Next they meet the "throngs of the great war heroes" who "live apart"—the Trojans who come "crowding around him" and the Greeks who "turn tail and run" (6.556–69). It is here that he meets the ghost of Deiphobus and hears the dreadful story of Helen's treachery and his ghastly death. Soon they reach the place where the road divides; on the left lies a fortress surrounded by Tartarus' River of Fire and guarded by Tisiphone, a Fury. It is the place, the Sibyl tells him, where the great sinners for whom there is only eternal punishment are confined. Besides the great sinners of the remote, mythical past—Salmoneus, Ixion, Tityos—are the human sinners, the parricides, the tyrants, the traitors . . . "No," she says,

> "not if I had a hundred tongues and a hundred mouths
> . . . I could never capture
> all the crimes or run through all the torments." (6.724–26)

And now they hurry away, and after Aeneas dedicates the golden bough to Proserpina, they come at last to the Elysian Fields, "the land of joy . . . / . . . where the blessed make their homes" (6.741–42). Aeneas sees them exercising or feasting as he goes to meet the ghost of his father, Anchises. There are the founders of the line of Trojan kings—Ilus, Assaracus and Dardanus—and Aeneas sees also

> troops of men
> who had suffered wounds, fighting to save their country,
> and those who had been pure priests while still alive,
> and the faithful poets whose songs were fit for Phoebus;

those who enriched our lives with the newfound arts they forged
and those we remember well for the good they did mankind.

(6.764–69)

In this paradise Aeneas finally meets the ghost of his father, who explains
to him the workings of this spiritual world and in particular the nature of
the spirits who throng the banks of the river Lethe, the river of forgetful-
ness. They are the souls of those, who after many years of punishment for
their sins in life, are destined to return to the world after drinking the wa-
ter of the Lethe and forgetting their previous existence. The spirits he sees
are those of the great Romans to come and Anchises will "reveal them all"
(6.878).

The background of this doctrine, of purgatorial suffering followed by
rebirth, seems to be a purely Virgilian invention. It is, as one critic, R. G.
Austin, puts it, "a poetic synthesis, blending the Stoic doctrine of the *an-
ima mundi* [the spirit or mind of the universe] with Platonic and Orphic-
Pythagorean teaching of rebirth." He also adds: "The manner is constantly
and pointedly Lucretian; the matter would have excited Lucretius' dis-
dain" (*Sextus*, 1977, note 724–51). What this religio-philosophical mélange
enables Virgil to do is to display the future descendants of Aeneas who
will one day rule the world. Virgil's whole picture of the lower world,
with its separation of the great sinners, for whom there is no forgiveness,
from those who, through many years of punishment, win some kind of
redemption, and those who are immediately admitted to heaven, re-
appears in many ways in Dante's *Divina Commedia*.

The first spirit waiting to be reborn is Silvius, the first king of Alba
Longa. He will be of half Italian blood, the child of Aeneas in his old age
by Lavinia. The "tipless spear of honor" (6.879) that Silvius holds is the
Roman award given to a young warrior for his first success in battle. There
follow the names of "brave young men" who will build the towns near
Rome, "famous names in the future, nameless places now"—Nomentum,
Gabii, Fidena, Collatia, and many others (6.893–96). Next comes Romu-
lus, son of the Roman war-god Mars (like him, he wears a helmet with
twin plumes), who is to found Rome, which will one day rule the world.
But now Anchises goes across the centuries to "Caesar and all the line of
Iulus," and Caesar Augustus who "will bring back the Age of Gold" and
"expand his empire past the Garamants and the Indians" (6.911–17). An-
chises now moves back from the glories of Augustan Rome to the history
of Roman kings after Romulus: Numa the lawgiver, next Tullus, a king

"who rouse[s] a stagnant people / . . . back to war again" (6.937–38), and Ancus who was "too swayed by the breeze of public favor" (6.940). Next the expulsion of the last Roman king, Tarquin, by Brutus, who reclaims those symbols of power, the fasces—bundles of rods wrapped around an axe—and as the first consul of the new Republic sets a dreadful example by executing his own two sons for treason against the new Roman state. Next are the spirits of famous republican heroes; the Decii, father and son, who each in turn won a battle for Rome with a victorious but suicidal charge; the Drusi, another great patrician family, which gave Rome many victorious generals (and incidentally, was the family of Augustus' wife). Torquatus was another stern Roman father who executed his son for disobedience. Camillus brought home the standards taken by the Gauls when they occupied Rome in 387 B.C. Other sources say that he took back from the Gauls not the standards but the gold they had taken. Virgil obviously preferred his version because it would remind readers that in 20 B.C. Augustus had recovered from the Parthians (by negotiation, not by war) the legionary standards lost by Crassus in his ill-fated expedition of 53 B.C.

Anchises makes another historical jump—to 49 B.C., when Julius Caesar was about to cross the Rubicon and start civil war against Pompey. Anchises points out that they are

> "equals now at peace . . .
> but if they should reach the light of life, what war
> they'll rouse between them! . . . Caesar,
> the bride's father, marching down from his Alpine ramparts
> . . . Pompey her husband set to oppose him."   (6.952–56)

Caesar's daughter had been married to Pompey in a vain attempt to reconcile them; Virgil's words recall the contemporary lines of Catullus: *socer generque, perdidistis omnia*—"Son and father-in-law, you have ruined everything" (29.24, trans. Knox). Anchises begs them not to start civil war and particularly appeals to Caesar: "born of my blood, throw down your weapons now!" (6.961).

But after this dramatic outcry Anchises returns to his catalog of Roman conquerors, this time of some of those who will avenge Troy by subduing Greece: Lucius Mummius, who sacked Corinth in 146 B.C., and Aemilius Paullus, who defeated Perseus, king of Macedon, who claimed descent from Achilles, at Pydna in 168 B.C. He briefly mentions Cato, known as the Censor, who strongly disapproved of the new Greek cultural influences on the Romans and insisted on the destruction of Carthage. Cossus was the second Roman commander to win the *spolia opima*, the "rich spoils," an award given to the general who killed the opposing general in single combat. The Gracchi were a family that produced many famous Romans, among them the two tribunes who attempted the reform of the Roman landholding system in favor of the small farmers and were both killed and their movement suppressed. The elder Scipio defeated Hannibal at Zama, and the younger defeated the Carthaginians in the battle that was followed by the total destruction of Carthage. More great republican heroes are invoked as Anchises sweeps on—Fabricius, who conquered Pyrrhus and was known for his austere integrity, Serranus (the Sower), who was called to the consulship from work on his farm, and the great family of the Fabii, of whom Anchises mentions only one, Fabius Maximus, the consul who after the terrible Roman defeat at Cannae denied battle to Hannibal in order to defeat him, harassing him but always refusing major engagement. He was known as Cunctator, the Delayer—"the one man / whose delaying tactics save our Roman state" (6.974–75), a phrase in which Virgil quotes the words of his forerunner Ennius, adding honor and antiquity to Fabius Maximus' exploit.

Anchises suddenly changes tone: he gives us no more great Romans for the moment but rather the moral of all these tales—the Roman character and the Roman mission in the world. But first he tells us what the Romans are not, listing the achievements of "others," by which he means the Greeks:

> "Others, I have no doubt,
> will forge the bronze to breathe with suppler lines,
> draw from the block of marble features quick with life,
> plead their cases better, chart with their rods the stars
> that climb the sky and foretell the times they rise."   (6.976–80)

But the Roman arts are different:

> "But you, Roman, remember, rule with all your power
> the peoples of the earth—these will be your arts:
> to put your stamp on the works and ways of peace,
> to spare the defeated, break the proud in war."   (6.981–84)

And then Anchises introduces another Roman hero, Marcellus, who won the *spolia opima* at Clastidium in 222 B.C. by killing the chief commanding the Insubrian Gauls. And Aeneas, who sees a handsome but sad young man walking by Marcellus' side, asks who he is, to receive the answer that he is also named Marcellus but is destined, after a short but brilliant career, to die young. He is the son of Octavia, Augustus' sister, and when he died suddenly, perhaps at age twenty, in 23 B.C. he had been considered a likely successor to Augustus. "Oh, child of heartbreak! If only you could burst / the stern decrees of Fate!" (6.1017–18).

There is no more to be seen, and Anchises, after warning Aeneas of hard wars to come in Italy, ushers his son and the Sibyl out of the land of the dead by the ivory gates along which the dead "send false dreams up toward the sky" (6.1033). And Aeneas heads for his ships and his waiting men.

The Gate of Ivory is adapted from the *Odyssey* (19.634–38), where Penelope speaks of the two gates for our dreams:

"one is made of ivory, the other made of horn.
Those that pass through the ivory cleanly carved
are will-o'-the-wisps, their message bears no fruit.
The dreams that pass through the gates of polished horn
are fraught with truth, for the dreamer who can see them."

There has been much discussion of the passage in Virgil. Aeneas and the Sibyl are not dreams to start with; and why must they go out of the land of the dead through the gate of false dreams? The obvious answer is that since the other party, the shades of noble Romans to come, must go through the Gate of Horn, which "offers easy passage to all true shades" (6.1031), Aeneas and the Sibyl must go out through the Gate of Ivory. But the real question is: why did Virgil use the Odyssean gates of dreams for the two exits from the land of the dead, one for the living, one for the Roman spirits, back to temporary oblivion? The answer is suggested by Goold in his revision of Fairclough's *Virgil* (1999, note 6.57), where he writes: "By making Aeneas leave by the gate of delusive dreams Virgil represents his vision of Rome's destiny as a dream which he is not to remember on his return to the real world; the poet will have us know that from the beginning of Book 7 his hero has not been endowed with superhuman knowledge to confront the problems which face him."

This interpretation is strengthened by the passage in Virgil's poem that deals with the other display given to Aeneas of Roman history and Roman heroes and villains to come: the pictures on the shield that Vulcan at the request of Venus makes for him in Book 8. After the long recital of the pageant of Roman history right up to Virgil's own day, that Aeneas sees on the shield, we are told:

> He fills with wonder—
> he knows nothing of these events but takes delight
> in their likeness.   (8.855–57)

Once again, as in Book 6, he has seen the future, but will not remember it.

THE SHIELD OF AENEAS

The vision Aeneas sees, the pictures on the shield, is another image of Rome's future. The incident is clearly modeled on the shield of Achilles in the *Iliad* (Book 18.558–709). Both shields were made by the smith-god at a mother's request, but they could not be more different. Aeneas' shield is decorated with the deeds and names of those who through the ages have brought Rome to its position of world mastery, but the shield made for Achilles has no names but those drawn from myth, no history; it is a picture of the world and human life. On it the smith-god Hephaestus makes the earth, sky, and sea, the sun, moon, and constellations and two cities "filled / with mortal men" (18.572–73). One is at peace and celebrates a wedding, "choir on choir the wedding song rose high" (18.576). And elsewhere, in the marketplace a quarrel breaks out and is to be settled by a judge. The other city is attacked and the horrors of wounding and killing on the battlefield parallel the wedding songs in the city at peace.

The god made also a broad plowland, a king's estate where harvesters are working, a thriving vineyard, a herd of longhorn cattle, and a dancing circle on which young boys and girls "danced and danced" (18.694). And round it all "he forged the Ocean River's mighty power girdling / round the outmost rim of the welded indestructible shield" (18.708–9). It is a whole world and it has no history.

On the shield of Aeneas, however, the smith-god forged

> . . . the story of Italy,
> Rome in all her triumphs . . .
> all in order the generations born of Ascanius' stock
> and all the wars they waged.   (8.738–42)

Vulcan forged the mother wolf, with Romulus and Remus, "twin boys at her dugs . . . suckling" (8.744), and newly built Rome and the Circus games there at which the Romans carried off the Sabine women to marry them—the so-called Rape of the Sabines—and the reconciliation with the Sabine tribe afterward. There was Mettus, king of Alba Longa, who broke his word to Tullus, third king of Rome, who tore him apart as punishment. Then Lars Porsenna, the Etruscan commanding the Romans to take back their banished king, Tarquin, and attacking the city from across the Tiber. But Cocles (better known to English-speaking readers by his other name, Horatius) tears the bridge down and swims to safety, as does the maiden Cloelia, who has been taken as a hostage. Next Manlius, who when the Gauls invaded Rome by night in 390 B.C. was awakened by the cackling of the sacred geese and saved the Capitol. And Vulcan forged the Salii, the dancing priests of Mars and the "chaste matrons . . . [who] led the sacred marches through the city" (8.779–80). And "far apart . . . he forged the homes of hell" with the great criminal Catiline "dangling from a beetling crag" and "the virtuous souls, with Cato giving laws" (8.783–85). This is not Cato the Censor but his great-grandson, the Cato who, defeated by Julius Caesar at Utica in Africa, committed suicide rather than live under Caesar's dictatorship, after reading Plato's *Phaedo*.

But the rest of the shield is devoted to the decisive victory of Augustus at Actium, the naval defeat of Antony and Cleopatra, their suicides, and the great triumph of Augustus, master of the Roman world, at Rome. The Roman fleet, led by Augustus on one flank and Agrippa on the other, faces and defeats Antony,

> leading on
> the riches of the Orient, troops of every stripe—
> . . . all the might of the East   (8.803–6)

and Cleopatra, "that outrage, that Egyptian wife!" (8.808), who eventually leads the flight of the Eastern fleet—"pale / with imminent death" (8.831–32), commits suicide, accompanied by Antony's, in Alexandria. And lastly the vision of Augustus' great triumph in Rome. Augustus

> reviews the gifts brought on by the nations of the earth . . .
> as the vanquished people move in a long slow file,
> their dress, their arms as motley as their tongues.   (8.844–47)

The battle of Actium is shown to the Roman reader as the victory of Italy and the West over the barbarous tribes of the East.

In the *Aeneid* Virgil combines mythological epic with themes from Roman history. But there is one field of Roman history where Virgil's material is mythological rather than historical, and that is his account of the Etruscans. In Book 8 (575ff.) he describes them as "Lydian people . . . / brilliant in war" (8.565–66), who inhabit the city of Agylla (now called Cervetri). They have recently expelled their king, Mezentius, for his oppression and atrocities, and he has found refuge with Turnus, "his old friend" (8.580). The Etruscans are eager to fight against him and his allies, but they have been told by "an aged prophet" that they must "choose leaders from overseas" (8.585–92). They are the perfect ally for Aeneas; after his meeting with their leader, Tarchon, they sail down the river with Aeneas' ships to relieve the beleaguered camp and fight with him to the end.

This has little to do with history. About the only detail that may be authentic is the adjective *Lydian,* since Lydia in Asia Minor was thought to be the original home of the Etruscans, a belief mentioned by Herodotus. Their language, recorded in a script based on the Greek alphabet, still defies attempts to decipher it; the buildings of their many cities, from the Arno to the Tiber and farther south, have vanished. But we know them from the large tombs, built below ground in the rock, where the bones of their upper classes rested, with frescoes painted on the walls, and from their treasures, bronze metalwork and imported painted Greek vases from the great periods of the black- and red-figure vases, which now, as a result of excavations both legal and illegal, adorn the museums of Europe and America.

Excavation has also confirmed that Rome too was for some time under Etruscan occupation or domination, a fact acknowledged by the legends of early Rome and the items of Etruscan origin in Roman religion and especially divination. Among the early kings of Rome, the fifth and the last were called Tarquin, an Etruscan name, the second of whom was expelled and whose reimposition was attempted by Lars Porsenna (an Etruscan name if ever there was one) of Clusium (Chiusi), an important Etruscan city. The attempt was foiled by Horatius' stand while the bridge over the Tiber was destroyed.

Nonetheless, Virgil (who knew less about the Etruscans than we do) gives us in Book 10 (202–60) a list of the Etruscan chieftains who came "speeding to rescue Troy" (10.259). They all come from cities that we know were Etruscan—Clusium, Cosae, Populonia, the source of the copper from which they made the bronze for weapons and statues, the island of Ilva (Elba), their source of iron, and Pisa, Caere, Pyrgi, and Graviscae. And Virgil includes his own hometown, Mantua. But the catalog of the Etruscans was another opportunity to do what he does so well—to recall in his lines the glories of the Italian countryside, its towns and its history, to celebrate Elba, "the Blacksmiths' inexhaustible island rife with iron ore" (10.210) or Mantua's own river, "the Mincius, / son of Father Benacus gowned in gray-green reeds" (10.248–49).

VIRGIL'S AFTERLIFE

Even before it became generally available as a written text, Virgil's *Aeneid* was famous. A younger poet, Propertius, wrote in elegiac verse an announcement:

> Give way, you Roman writers, give way, Greeks.
>   Something greater than the *Iliad* is being born.
>
> (2.34.65–66, trans. Knox)

As copies appeared and multiplied, the *Aeneid* became the textbook for the Roman school and the medieval school after that. The Roman satyric poet Juvenal, writing in the second century A.D., describes, in *Satire* 6 (434–35), among the many intolerable wives he catalogs, the one "who as soon as she's taken her place at dinner is praising Virgil and forgiving [Dido] on her deathbed" (trans. Susanna M. Braund, et seq.). In *Satire* 7 (226–27) he speaks of schoolboys thumbing a Horace that "gets totally discolored and the soot sticks to your blackened Virgil." And the poor schoolteacher is liable to be asked questions that eventually a reader of the *Aeneid* might be able to answer: who was "Anchises' nurse and . . . the name and birthplace of the stepmother of Anchemolus and how long Acestes lived and how many jars of Sicilian wine he gave to the Trojans" (234–36). And Juvenal is not alone in his knowledge and citation of Virgil. As J. M. Mackail put it in his edition of the *Aeneid*, published in 1930 (two thousand years after Virgil's birth; it is dedicated, *Principi Poetarum Natalii MM*): "The whole of post-Virgilian Latin literature, in prose as well as in poetry, is saturated with Virgilian quotations, adaptations, and allusions, as much as English literature for the last three hundred years has been with Shakespeare, and even more" (Introduction, p. lxx).

But in addition to its literary supremacy, the *Aeneid* acquired a semi-religious stature. It became an oracle known as the *Sortes Virgilianae*, the Virgilian lottery: you took a passage at random and it foretold your future. Often it was consulted in temples, as it was regarded as an oracle; Hadrian and other men who became Roman emperors first learned of their future eminence from this source. And when the English monarch Charles I, barred from London by revolutionary parliamentarians, made Oxford his headquarters during the civil war, he consulted the Virgilian lottery in the Bodleian Library and put his finger by chance on Dido's curse on Aeneas:

> ". . . let him be plagued in war by a nation proud in arms, . . .
> let him grovel for help and watch his people die
> a shameful death! And then, once he has bowed down
> to an unjust peace, may he never enjoy his realm
> . . . let him die
> before his day. . . . "   (4.767–73)

When the Roman world became Christian, Virgil remained as its classic poet, not only because of the fourth *Eclogue*, which many Christians regarded as a prophecy of the birth of Christ, but also because of a recognition of a fellow spirit—*anima naturaliter Christiana*, a naturally Christian spirit he was called by Tertullian, the great Christian figure of second century Carthage. And Virgil's significance in the European Christian tradition is emphasized by the important part he takes, both in the many borrowings from his work and also in the prominent role he plays himself in the *Divina Commedia* of Dante (1265–1321).

Not only are there striking resemblances between Dante's account of *Inferno, Purgatorio,* and *Paradiso* and Book 6 of the *Aeneid,* not only does he choose Virgil as his guide through the first two countries of the next world, he thanks him also for the gift of *bello stilo,* which Virgil had given to the Latin language, and which Dante has re-created for the Italian. And recalls of Virgil's language occur at once as he recognizes the figure before him; he addresses him in a reminiscence of his own *Aeneid,* "*Or se'tu quel Virgilio . . . / che . . .* ?" (*Inferno* 1.79–80), "Are you that Virgil who . . . ?" It is a recall of Dido's question as she realizes who her visitor must be: "*Tune ille Aeneas quem . . .* ?" (1.617). And the reminiscences are not just verbal; subject matter and character are borrowed too. The same Charon ferries spirits across the same river and refuses again to take a living passenger at first. Minos judges the dead; Cerberus must have his "sop." And there are even wider resemblances—the special place in both poems for suicides, and for those who died for love. And on a broader scale between Elysium and *Paradiso*, between *Purgatorio* and Virgil's "souls" who are "drilled in punishments, they must pay for their old offenses" (6.854–55), with the difference that in Dante the souls who have finished purgation drink the water of Lethe and go to Paradise, where in Virgil, except for those who go to Elysium, they go, after drinking the water of Lethe, back to life in a fresh incarnation to become the Romans.

And there is one reference to Virgil in Dante that echoes down the centuries to the twentieth. It is the passage in Canto I of *Inferno* (106–8, trans. Robert and Jean Hollander):

Di quella umile Italia fia salute
per cui morì la vergine Cammilla,
Eurialo e Turno e Niso di ferute.

"He shall be the salvation of low-lying Italy
for which maiden Camilla, Euryalus,
Turnus, and Nisus died of their wounds."

Why Italy is lowly and who her savior is are matters still disputed by scholars, but the phrase *"umile Italia"* is obviously a memory of *Aeneid* 3.522–23: *"umilemque videmus / Italiam"*—"and low-lying we see / Italy" (trans. Knox). It is Aeneas' first sight of Italy, as indeed it looks still to the traveler coming from Greece—a low line on the horizon. And the heroes who have laid down their lives for this Italy fought on both sides. This tercet of Dante's, among the most copious of his references to Virgil's text, was destined to echo down the ages until its appearance in a remarkable twentieth-century context in the Italy of Mussolini, who was trying to restore the warlike image of Roman Italy and make the Mediterranean once more *mare nostrum,* "our sea."

In this endeavor he made opponents and enemies whom he silenced and punished in various ways. One of his critics and opponents, Carlo Levi, was sent into a sort of exile in a small poverty-stricken town in Calabria, a town so poor that its inhabitants claimed that Christ, on his way through Italy, had stopped at Eboli, and never reached them. In Levi's somber and beautiful account of his life there, published under the title *Christ Stopped at Eboli* (trs. 1947), he tells how the local Fascist official came to see him, and asked him why on earth he, an educated, talented

man, did not support Mussolini's regime, which aimed at restoring Italy
to its old eminence as master of the Mediterranean. His reply was to say
that his idea of Italy was different; it was

"*Di quella umile Italia . . .*
per cui morì la vergine Cammilla,
Eurialo e Turno e Niso di ferute."

Carlo Levi's reply brought Virgil through Dante into the realities of the
modern world, and to compare small things to great, I too brought Vir-
gil back to life in Italy some years later. I consulted the Virgilian lottery
in April 1945. The year before, while a captain in the U.S. Army, I had
worked with French partisans behind the lines against German troops in
Brittany, and after a leave I was finally sent to Italy to work with partisans
there. No doubt the OSS moguls in Washington figured that since I had
studied Latin at Cambridge I would have no trouble picking up Italian.
The partisans this time were on our side of the lines; things had got too
difficult for them in the Po Valley and they had come through the moun-
tains. The U.S. Army, very short of what the soldiers called "warm bod-
ies," since so many of its best units had been called in for the invasion of
southern France, armed them and put them under the command of
American officers to hold sections of the mountain line where no German
breakthrough was expected. I had about twelve hundred of them, in var-
ious units ranging from Communist to officers of the crack corps of the
Italian army, the Alpini; but they had two things in common—great
courage and still greater hatred of Germans. For several months we held
the sector, which contained the famous Passo dell' Abettone, then im-
passable for wheeled vehicles since the German engineers had blown its
sides down. We made frequent long patrols into enemy territory, some-
times bringing back prisoners for interrogation, sometimes passing civil-
ian agents through the lines. In April we were given a small role in the
final move north that brought about the German surrender of Italy. The
main push was to the left and right of us, where tanks and wheeled vehi-
cles could move—on the coast road to our left and on our right through
the Futa Pass to Bologna. We were to attack German positions on the
heights opposite us, take the town of Fanano, and then go on to Modena
in the valley.

We killed or captured the German troops holding the heights without
too many losses, liberated Fanano, and started north on the road to Mo-
dena. As we marched along I could not help thinking that the legions of

Octavian and Mark Antony had marched and countermarched in these regions in 43 B.C. Like them, we had no wheeled transport; like them, we had no communications (our walkie-talkies had a very short range); like them, we hoisted our weapons onto our shoulders when we forded the Reno River with the water up to our waists.

Every now and then we met a German machine-gun crew holed up in a building that delayed our passage. Usually we too occupied a building to house our machine guns and keep the enemy under fire while we sent out a flanking party to dislodge them. On one of these occasions we occupied a villa off the road that had evidently been hit by one of our bombers; it had not much roof left and the inside was a shambles, but it would do. At one point in the sporadic exchanges of fire I handed over the gun to a sergeant and retreated into the debris of the room to smoke a cigarette. As I looked at the tangled wreckage on the floor I noticed what looked like a book, and investigation with my foot revealed part of its spine, on which I saw, in gold capitals, the letters "MARONIS." It was a text of Virgil, published by the Roman Academy "IUSSU BENEDICTI MUS-SOLINI," "By Order of Benito Mussolini." There were not many Italians who would call him "blessed" now; in fact, a few weeks later his blood-stained corpse, together with that of his mistress, Clara Petacci, and that of his right-hand man, Starace, would be hanging upside-down outside a gas station in Milan.

And then I remembered the *Sortes Virgilianae*. I closed my eyes, opened the book at random and put my finger on the page. What I got was not so much a prophecy about my own future as a prophecy for Italy; it was from lines at the end of the first *Georgic*:

> . . . a world in ruins . . .
> For right and wrong change places; everywhere
> So many wars, so many shapes of crime
> Confront us; no due honor attends the plow.
> The fields, bereft of tillers, are all unkempt . . .
> . . . throughout the world
> Impious War is raging.   (1.500–11)

"A world in ruins." It was an exact description of the Italy we were fighting in—its railroads and its ancient buildings shattered by Allied aircraft, its elegant bridges blown into the water by the retreating Germans, and its fields sown not with seed by the farmers but with mines by the German engineers.

The fighting stopped; it was time to move on. I tried to get the Virgil into my pack, but it was too big, and I threw it back to the cluttered floor. But I remember thinking: "If I get out of this alive, I'll go back to the classics, and Virgil especially." And I did. My first scholarly article, written when I was an assistant professor at Yale, was about the imagery of Book 2 of the *Aeneid*, entitled "The Serpent and the Flame."

Lake Benacus
Timavus River
Mincius R.
Padua
Mantua
Po River
ILLYRIA
LIGURIA
ITALY
UMBRIA
(HESPERIA)
ETRURIA
Populonia
ILVA (ELBA)
Cosae
Tiber R.
Cures
Adriatic Sea
CORSICA
Caere
Pallanteum (Rome)
TROJAN CAMP
Alba Longa
Lavinium
LATIUM
C. GARGANUS
Argyripa (Arpi)
Caieta
Cumae
CAMPANIA
APULIA
Lake Avernus
Baiae
C. MISENUM
SIRENS?
SARDINIA
CAPREAE (CAPRI)
Tarentum
TEMPLE OF MINERVA
Gulf of Tarentum
Tyrrhenian Sea
C. PALINURUS
AEOLIAN IS.
SILA
Ionian Sea
MT. ERYX
CHARYBDIS?
SCYLLA?
Drepanum
Eryx
Acesta
C. PELORUS
Cyclops Harbor?
MT. ETNA
SICILY
Carthage
Syracuse
LIBYA
C. PACHYNUS
Mediterranean Sea

the VOYAGES of
AENEAS

⊙ Port of call

0   100   200
Scale in Miles

Black
Sea

MACEDONIA

THRACE

⊙ Aenus?

SAMOTHRACE
MT. ATHOS
LEMNOS

C. RHOETEUM
Simois R.
Troy (Ilium)
MT. IDA
Xanthus
(Scamander) River
Antandros

PHRYGIA

TENEDOS

Acroceraunia

THESSALY
MT. OLYMPUS

Aegean
Sea

LESBOS

Buthrotum
Dodona
EPIRUS
PHAEACIA
(CORFU)
GREECE

LYDIA

SCYROS

LEUCAS
LEUCATA
ITHACA?
SAME

Actium
AETOLIA
MT. NERITON

EUBOEA

Athens

SAMOS

ZACYNTHOS

PELOPONNESE
ARCADIA
Alpheus R.

Mycenae
Argos

CYCLADES

DELOS
PAROS

MYCONOS

NAXOS

STROFIIADES

Sparta

C. MALEA
CYTHERA

Pergamum?

Cnossus

CRETE
MT. IDA

MT. DICTE

VIRGIL:
THE AENEID

BOOK ONE

Safe Haven
After Storm

Wars and a man I sing—an exile driven on by Fate,
he was the first to flee the coast of Troy,
destined to reach Lavinian shores and Italian soil,
yet many blows he took on land and sea from the gods above—
thanks to cruel Juno's relentless rage—and many losses
he bore in battle too, before he could found a city,
bring his gods to Latium, source of the Latin race,
the Alban lords and the high walls of Rome.

                                   Tell me,
Muse, how it all began. Why was Juno outraged?
What could wound the Queen of the Gods with all her power?   10
Why did she force a man, so famous for his devotion,
to brave such rounds of hardship, bear such trials?
Can such rage inflame the immortals' hearts?

    There was an ancient city held by Tyrian settlers,

Carthage, facing Italy and the Tiber River's mouth
but far away—a rich city trained and fierce in war.
Juno loved it, they say, beyond all other lands
in the world, even beloved Samos, second best.
Here she kept her armor, here her chariot too,
and Carthage would rule the nations of the earth   20
if only the Fates were willing. This was Juno's goal
from the start, and so she nursed her city's strength.
But she heard a race of men, sprung of Trojan blood,
would one day topple down her Tyrian stronghold,
breed an arrogant people ruling far and wide,
proud in battle, destined to plunder Libya.
So the Fates were spinning out the future . . .
This was Juno's fear
and the goddess never forgot the old campaign
that she had waged at Troy for her beloved Argos.   30
No, not even now would the causes of her rage,
her bitter sorrows drop from the goddess' mind.
They festered deep within her, galled her still:
the Judgment of Paris, the unjust slight to her beauty,
the Trojan stock she loathed, the honors showered on Ganymede
ravished to the skies. Her fury inflamed by all this,
the daughter of Saturn drove over endless oceans
Trojans left by the Greeks and brute Achilles.
Juno kept them far from Latium, forced by the Fates
to wander round the seas of the world, year in, year out.   40
Such a long hard labor it was to found the Roman people.

    Now, with the ridge of Sicily barely out of sight,
they spread sail for the open sea, their spirits buoyant,
their bronze beaks churning the waves to foam as Juno,
nursing deep in her heart the everlasting wound,
said to herself: "Defeated, am I? Give up the fight?
Powerless now to keep that Trojan king from Italy?
Ah but of course—the Fates bar my way.
And yet Minerva could burn the fleet to ash
and drown my Argive crews in the sea, and all for one,   50
one mad crime of a single man, Ajax, son of Oileus!

She hurled Jove's all-consuming bolt from the clouds,
she shattered a fleet and whipped the swells with gales.
And then as he gasped his last in flames from his riven chest
she swept him up in a cyclone, impaled the man on a crag.
But I who walk in majesty, I the Queen of the Gods,
the sister and wife of Jove—I must wage a war,
year after year, on just one race of men!
Who will revere the power of Juno after this—
lay gifts on my altar, lift his hands in prayer?"   60

    With such anger seething inside her fiery heart
the goddess reached Aeolia, breeding-ground of storms,
their home swarming with raging gusts from the South.
Here in a vast cave King Aeolus rules the winds,
brawling to break free, howling in full gale force
as he chains them down in their dungeon, shackled fast.
They bluster in protest, roaring round their prison bars
with a mountain above them all, booming with their rage.
But high in his stronghold Aeolus wields his scepter,
soothing their passions, tempering their fury.   70
Should he fail, surely they'd blow the world away,
hurling the land and sea and deep sky through space.
Fearing this, the almighty Father banished the winds
to that black cavern, piled above them a mountain mass
and imposed on all a king empowered, by binding pact,
to rein them back on command or let them gallop free.

    Now Juno made this plea to the Lord of Winds:
"Aeolus, the Father of Gods and King of Men gave you
the power to calm the waves or rouse them with your gales.
A race I loathe is crossing the Tuscan sea, transporting   80
Troy to Italy, bearing their conquered household gods—
thrash your winds to fury, sink their warships, overwhelm them
or break them apart, scatter their crews, drown them all!
I happen to have some sea-nymphs, fourteen beauties,
Deiopea the finest of all by far . . .
I'll join you in lasting marriage, call her yours
and for all her years to come she will live with you

and make you the proud father of handsome children.
Such service earns such gifts."
                                    Aeolus warmed
to Juno's offer: "Yours is the task, my queen,   90
to explore your heart's desires. Mine is the duty
to follow your commands. Yes, thanks to you
I rule this humble little kingdom of mine.
You won me the scepter, Jupiter's favors too,
and a couch to lounge on, set at the gods' feasts—
you made me Lord of the Stormwind, King of Cloudbursts."

    With such thanks, swinging his spear around he strikes home
at the mountain's hollow flank and out charge the winds
through the breach he'd made, like armies on attack
in a blasting whirlwind tearing through the earth.   100
Down they crash on the sea, the Eastwind, Southwind,
all as one with the Southwest's squalls in hot pursuit,
heaving up from the ocean depths huge killer-breakers
rolling toward the beaches. The crews are shouting,
cables screeching—suddenly cloudbanks blotting out
the sky, the light of day from the Trojans' sight
as pitch-black night comes brooding down on the sea
with thunder crashing pole to pole, bolt on bolt
blazing across the heavens—death, everywhere
men facing instant death.   110
At once Aeneas, limbs limp in the chill of fear,
groans and lifting both his palms toward the stars
cries out: "Three, four times blest, my comrades
lucky to die beneath the soaring walls of Troy—
before their parents' eyes! If only I'd gone down
under your right hand—Diomedes, strongest Greek afield—
and poured out my life on the battlegrounds of Troy!
Where raging Hector lies, pierced by Achilles' spear,
where mighty Sarpedon lies, where the Simois River
swallows down and churns beneath its tides so many   120
shields and helmets and corpses of the brave!"
                                    Flinging cries
as a screaming gust of the Northwind pounds against his sail,
raising waves sky-high. The oars shatter, prow twists round,

taking the breakers broadside on and over Aeneas' decks
a mountain of water towers, massive, steep.
Some men hang on billowing crests, some as the sea
gapes, glimpse through the waves the bottom waiting,
a surge aswirl with sand.
                              Three ships the Southwind grips
and spins against those boulders lurking in mid-ocean—
rocks the Italians call the Altars, one great spine   130
breaking the surface—three the Eastwind sweeps
from open sea on the Syrtes' reefs, a grim sight,
girding them round with walls of sand.
                                One ship
that carried the Lycian units led by staunch Orontes—
before Aeneas' eyes a toppling summit of water
strikes the stern and hurls the helmsman overboard,
pitching him headfirst, twirling his ship three times,
right on the spot till the ravenous whirlpool gulps her down.
Here and there you can sight some sailors bobbing in heavy seas,
strewn in the welter now the weapons, men, stray spars   140
and treasures saved from Troy.
                              Now Ilioneus' sturdy ship,
now brave Achates', now the galley that carried Abas,
another, aged Aletes, yes, the storm routs them all,
down to the last craft the joints split, beams spring
and the lethal flood pours in.
                              All the while Neptune
sensed the furor above him, the roaring seas first and
the storm breaking next—his standing waters boiling up
from the sea-bed, churning back. And the mighty god,
stirred to his depths, lifts his head from the crests
and serene in power, gazing out over all his realm,   150
he sees Aeneas' squadrons scattered across the ocean,
Trojans overwhelmed by the surf and the wild crashing skies.
Nor did he miss his sister Juno's cunning wrath at work.
He summons the East- and Westwind, takes them to task:
"What insolence! Trusting so to your lofty birth?
You winds, you dare make heaven and earth a chaos,
raising such a riot of waves without my blessings.

You—what I won't do! But first I had better set
to rest the flood you ruffled so. Next time, trust me,
you will pay for your crimes with more than just a scolding.   160
Away with you, quick! And give your king this message:
Power over the sea and ruthless trident is mine,
not his—it's mine by lot, by destiny. His place,
Eastwind, is the rough rocks where you are all at home.
Let him bluster there and play the king in his court,
let Aeolus rule his bolted dungeon of the winds!"

Quicker than his command he calms the heaving seas,
putting the clouds to rout and bringing back the sun.
Struggling shoulder-to-shoulder, Triton and Cymothoë
hoist and heave the ships from the jagged rocks   170
as the god himself whisks them up with his trident,
clearing a channel through the deadly reefs, his chariot
skimming over the cresting waves on spinning wheels
to set the seas to rest. Just as, all too often,
some huge crowd is seized by a vast uprising,
the rabble runs amok, all slaves to passion,
rocks, firebrands flying. Rage finds them arms
but then, if they chance to see a man among them,
one whose devotion and public service lend him weight,
they stand there, stock-still with their ears alert as   180
he rules their furor with his words and calms their passion.
So the crash of the breakers all fell silent once their Father,
gazing over his realm under clear skies, flicks his horses,
giving them free rein, and his eager chariot flies.

Now bone-weary, Aeneas' shipmates make a run
for the nearest landfall, wheeling prows around
they turn for Libya's coast. There is a haven shaped
by an island shielding the mouth of a long deep bay, its flanks
breaking the force of combers pounding in from the sea
while drawing them off into calm receding channels.   190
Both sides of the harbor, rock cliffs tower, crowned
by twin crags that menace the sky, overshadowing
reaches of sheltered water, quiet and secure.

Over them as a backdrop looms a quivering wood,
above them rears a grove, bristling dark with shade,
and fronting the cliff, a cave under hanging rocks
with fresh water inside, seats cut in the native stone,
the home of nymphs. Never a need of cables here to moor
a weathered ship, no anchor with biting flukes to bind her fast.

Aeneas puts in here with a bare seven warships   200
saved from his whole fleet. How keen their longing
for dry land underfoot as the Trojans disembark,
taking hold of the earth, their last best hope,
and fling their brine-wracked bodies on the sand.
Achates is first to strike a spark from flint,
then works to keep it alive in dry leaves,
cups it around with kindling, feeds it chips
and briskly fans the tinder into flame.
Then, spent as they were from all their toil,
they set out food, the bounty of Ceres, drenched   210
in sea-salt, Ceres' utensils too, her mills and troughs,
and bend to parch with fire the grain they had salvaged,
grind it fine on stones.
                              While they see to their meal
Aeneas scales a crag, straining to scan the sea-reach
far and wide . . . is there any trace of Antheus now,
tossed by the gales, or his warships banked with oars?
Or Capys perhaps, or Caicus' stern adorned with shields?
Not a ship in sight. But he does spot three stags
roaming the shore, an entire herd behind them
grazing down the glens in a long ranked line.   220
He halts, grasps his bow and his flying arrows,
the weapons his trusty aide Achates keeps at hand.
First the leaders, antlers branching over their high heads,
he brings them down, then turns on the herd, his shafts
stampeding the rest like rabble into the leafy groves.
Shaft on shaft, no stopping him till he stretches
seven hefty carcasses on the ground—a triumph,
one for each of his ships—and makes for the cove,
divides the kill with his whole crew and then shares out

the wine that good Acestes, princely man, had brimmed   230
in their casks the day they left Sicilian shores.

    The commander's words relieve their stricken hearts:
"My comrades, hardly strangers to pain before now,
we all have weathered worse. Some god will grant us
an end to this as well. You've threaded the rocks
resounding with Scylla's howling rabid dogs,
and taken the brunt of the Cyclops' boulders, too.
Call up your courage again. Dismiss your grief and fear.
A joy it will be one day, perhaps, to remember even this.
Through so many hard straits, so many twists and turns   240
our course holds firm for Latium. There Fate holds out
a homeland, calm, at peace. There the gods decree
the kingdom of Troy will rise again. Bear up.
Save your strength for better times to come."
                                Brave words.
Sick with mounting cares he assumes a look of hope
and keeps his anguish buried in his heart.
The men gird up for the game, the coming feast,
they skin the hide from the ribs, lay bare the meat.
Some cut it into quivering strips, impale it on skewers,
some set cauldrons along the beach and fire them to the boil.   250
Then they renew their strength with food, stretched out
on the beachgrass, fill themselves with seasoned wine
and venison rich and crisp. Their hunger sated,
the tables cleared away, they talk on for hours,
asking after their missing shipmates—wavering now
between hope and fear: what to believe about the rest?
Were the men still alive or just in the last throes,
forever lost to their comrades' far-flung calls?
Aeneas most of all, devoted to his shipmates,
deep within himself he moans for the losses . . .   260
now for Orontes, hardy soldier, now for Amycus,
now for the brutal fate that Lycus may have met,
then Gyas and brave Cloanthus, hearts of oak.

    Their mourning was over now as Jove from high heaven,

gazing down on the sea, the whitecaps winged with sails,
the lands outspread, the coasts, the nations of the earth,
paused at the zenith of the sky and set his sights
on Libya, that proud kingdom. All at once,
as he took to heart the struggles he beheld,
Venus approached in rare sorrow, tears abrim   270
in her sparkling eyes, and begged: "Oh you who rule
the lives of men and gods with your everlasting laws
and your lightning bolt of terror, what crime could my Aeneas
commit against you, what dire harm could the Trojans do
that after bearing so many losses, this wide world
is shut to them now? And all because of Italy.
Surely from them the Romans would arise one day
as the years roll on, and leaders would as well,
descended from Teucer's blood brought back to life,
to rule all lands and seas with boundless power—   280
you promised! Father, what motive changed your mind?
With that, at least, I consoled myself for Troy's demise,
that heartrending ruin—weighing fate against fate.
But now after all my Trojans suffered, still
the same disastrous fortune drives them on and on.
What end, great king, do you set to their ordeals?

     "Antenor could slip out from under the Greek siege,
then make his passage through the Illyrian gulfs and,
safe through the inlands where the Liburnians rule,
he struggled past the Timavus River's source.   290
There, through its nine mouths as the mountain caves
roar back, the river bursts out into full flood,
a thundering surf that overpowers the fields.
Reaching Italy, he erected a city for his people,
a Trojan home called Padua—gave them a Trojan name,
hung up their Trojan arms and there, after long wars,
he lingers on in serene and settled peace.
                                        "But we,
your own children, the ones you swore would hold
the battlements of heaven—now our ships are lost,
appalling! We are abandoned, thanks to the rage   300

of a single foe, cut off from Italy's shores.
Is this our reward for reverence,
this the way you give us back our throne?"

    The Father of Men and Gods, smiling down on her
with the glance that clears the sky and calms the tempest,
lightly kissing his daughter on the lips, replied:
"Relieve yourself of fear, my lady of Cythera,
the fate of your children stands unchanged, I swear.
You will see your promised city, see Lavinium's walls
and bear your great-hearted Aeneas up to the stars on high.   310
Nothing has changed my mind. No, your son, believe me—
since anguish is gnawing at you, I will tell you more,
unrolling the scroll of Fate
to reveal its darkest secrets. Aeneas will wage
a long, costly war in Italy, crush defiant tribes
and build high city walls for his people there
and found the rule of law. Only three summers
will see him govern Latium, three winters pass
in barracks after the Latins have been broken.
But his son Ascanius, now that he gains the name   320
of Iulus—Ilus he was, while Ilium ruled on high—
will fill out with his own reign thirty sovereign years,
a giant cycle of months revolving round and round,
transferring his rule from its old Lavinian home
to raise up Alba Longa's mighty ramparts.
There, in turn, for a full three hundred years
the dynasty of Hector will hold sway till Ilia,
a royal priestess great with the brood of Mars,
will bear the god twin sons. Then one, Romulus,
reveling in the tawny pelt of a wolf that nursed him,   330
will inherit the line and build the walls of Mars
and after his own name, call his people Romans.
On them I set no limits, space or time:
I have granted them power, empire without end.
Even furious Juno, now plaguing the land and sea and sky
with terror: she will mend her ways and hold dear with me
these Romans, lords of the earth, the race arrayed in togas.

This is my pleasure, my decree. Indeed, an age will come,
as the long years slip by, when Assaracus' royal house
will quell Achilles' homeland, brilliant Mycenae too,   340
and enslave their people, rule defeated Argos.
From that noble blood will arise a Trojan Caesar,
his empire bound by the Ocean, his glory by the stars:
Julius, a name passed down from Iulus, his great forebear.
And you, in years to come, will welcome him to the skies,
you rest assured—laden with plunder of the East,
and he with Aeneas will be invoked in prayer.
Then will the violent centuries, battles set aside,
grow gentle, kind. Vesta and silver-haired Good Faith
and Romulus flanked by brother Remus will make the laws.   350
The terrible Gates of War with their welded iron bars
will stand bolted shut, and locked inside, the Frenzy
of civil strife will crouch down on his savage weapons,
hands pinioned behind his back with a hundred brazen shackles,
monstrously roaring out from his bloody jaws."
                                                            So
he decrees and speeds the son of Maia down the sky
to make the lands and the new stronghold, Carthage,
open in welcome to the Trojans, not let Dido,
unaware of fate, expel them from her borders.
Down through the vast clear air flies Mercury,   360
rowing his wings like oars and in a moment
stands on Libya's shores, obeys commands
and the will of god is done.
The Carthaginians calm their fiery temper
and Queen Dido, above all, takes to heart
a spirit of peace and warm good will to meet
the men of Troy.
                        But Aeneas, duty-bound,
his mind restless with worries all that night,
reached a firm resolve as the fresh day broke.
Out he goes to explore the strange terrain . . .   370
what coast had the stormwinds brought him to?
Who lives here? All he sees is wild, untilled—
what men, or what creatures? Then report the news

to all his comrades. So, concealing his ships
in the sheltered woody narrows overarched by rocks
and screened around by trees and trembling shade,
Aeneas moves out, with only Achates at his side,
two steel-tipped javelins balanced in his grip.
Suddenly, in the heart of the woods, his mother
crossed his path. She looked like a young girl,   380
a Spartan girl decked out in dress and gear
or Thracian Harpalyce tiring out her mares,
outracing the Hebrus River's rapid tides.
Hung from a shoulder, a bow that fit her grip,
a huntress for all the world, she'd let her curls
go streaming free in the wind, her knees were bare,
her flowing skirts hitched up with a tight knot.

    She speaks out first: "You there, young soldiers,
did you by any chance see one of my sisters?
Which way did she go? Roaming the woods,   390
a quiver slung from her belt,
wearing a spotted lynx-skin, or in full cry,
hot on the track of some great frothing boar?"

    So Venus asked and the son of Venus answered:
"Not one of your sisters have I seen or heard . . .
but how should I greet a young girl like you?
Your face, your features—hardly a mortal's looks
and the tone of your voice is hardly human either.
Oh a goddess, without a doubt! What, are you
Apollo's sister? Or one of the breed of Nymphs?   400
Be kind, whoever you are, relieve our troubled hearts.
Under what skies and onto what coasts of the world
have we been driven? Tell us, please. Castaways,
we know nothing, not the people, not the place—
lost, hurled here by the gales and heavy seas.
Many a victim will fall before your altars,
we'll slaughter them for you!"
                                    But Venus replied:
"Now there's an honor I really don't deserve.
It's just the style for Tyrian girls to sport

a quiver and high-laced hunting boots in crimson.   410
What you see is a Punic kingdom, people of Tyre
and Agenor's town, but the border's held by Libyans
hard to break in war. Phoenician Dido is in command,
she sailed from Tyre, in flight from her own brother.
Oh it's a long tale of crime, long, twisting, dark,
but I'll try to trace the high points in their order . . .

  "Dido was married to Sychaeus, the richest man in Tyre,
and she, poor girl, was consumed with love for him.
Her father gave her away, wed for the first time,
a virgin still, and these her first solemn rites.   420
But her brother held power in Tyre—Pygmalion,
a monster, the vilest man alive.
A murderous feud broke out between both men.
Pygmalion, catching Sychaeus off guard at the altar,
slaughtered him in blood. That unholy man, so blind
in his lust for gold he ran him through with a sword,
then hid the crime for months, deaf to his sister's love,
her heartbreak. Still he mocked her with wicked lies,
with empty hopes. But she had a dream one night.
The true ghost of her husband, not yet buried,   430
came and lifting his face—ashen, awesome in death—
showed her the cruel altar, the wounds that pierced his chest
and exposed the secret horror that lurked within the house.
He urged her on: 'Take flight from our homeland, quick!'
And then he revealed an unknown ancient treasure,
an untold weight of silver and gold, a comrade
to speed her on her way.
                          "Driven by all this,
Dido plans her escape, collects her followers
fired by savage hate of the tyrant or bitter fear.
They seize some galleys set to sail, load them with gold—   440
the wealth Pygmalion craved—and they bear it overseas
and a woman leads them all. Reaching this haven here,
where now you will see the steep ramparts rising,
the new city of Carthage—the Tyrians purchased land as
large as a bull's-hide could enclose but cut in strips for size

and called it Byrsa, the Hide, for the spread they'd bought.
But you, who are you? What shores do you come from?
Where are you headed now?"
                                        He answered her questions,
drawing a labored sigh from deep within his chest:
"Goddess, if I'd retrace our story to its start,   450
if you had time to hear the saga of our ordeals,
before I finished the Evening Star would close
the gates of Olympus, put the day to sleep . . .
From old Troy we come—Troy it's called, perhaps
you've heard the name—sailing over the world's seas
until, by chance, some whim of the winds, some tempest
drove us onto Libyan shores. I ~~am Aeneas~~, duty-bound.
I carry aboard my ships the gods of house and home
we seized from enemy hands. My fame goes past the skies.
I seek my homeland—Italy—born as I am from highest Jove.   460
I launched out on the Phrygian sea with twenty ships,
my goddess mother marking the way, and followed hard
on the course the Fates had charted. A mere seven,
battered by wind and wave, survived the worst.
I myself am a stranger, utterly at a loss,
trekking over this wild Libyan wasteland,
forced from Europe, Asia too, an exile—"

        Venus could bear no more of his laments
and broke in on his tale of endless hardship:
"Whoever you are, I scarcely think the Powers hate you: 470
you enjoy the breath of life, you've reached a Tyrian city.
So off you go now. Take this path to the queen's gates.
I have good news. Your friends are restored to you,
your fleet's reclaimed. The winds swerved from the North
and drove them safe to port. True, unless my parents
taught me to read the flight of birds for nothing.
Look at those dozen swans triumphant in formation!
The eagle of Jove had just swooped down on them all
from heaven's heights and scattered them into open sky,
but now you can see them flying trim in their long ranks,   480
landing or looking down where their friends have landed—

home, cavorting on ruffling wings and wheeling round
the sky in convoy, trumpeting in their glory.
So homeward bound, your ships and hardy shipmates
anchor in port now or approach the harbor's mouth,
full sail ahead. Now off you go, move on,
wherever the path leads you, steer your steps."

                      At that,
as she turned away her neck shone with a rosy glow,
her mane of hair gave off an ambrosial fragrance,
her skirt flowed loose, rippling down to her feet   490
and her stride alone revealed her as a goddess.
He knew her at once—his mother—
and called after her now as she sped away:
"Why, you too, cruel as the rest? So often
you ridicule your son with your disguises!
Why can't we clasp hands, embrace each other,
exchange some words, speak out, and tell the truth?"

   Reproving her so, he makes his way toward town
but Venus screens the travelers off with a dense mist,
pouring round them a cloak of clouds with all her power,   500
so no one could see them, no one reach and hold them,
cause them to linger now or ask why they had come.
But she herself, lifting into the air, wings her way
toward Paphos, racing with joy to reach her home again
where her temples stand and a hundred altars steam
with Arabian incense, redolent with the scent
of fresh-cut wreaths.
                 Meanwhile the two men
are hurrying on their way as the path leads,
now climbing a steep hill arching over the city,
looking down on the facing walls and high towers.   510
Aeneas marvels at its mass—once a cluster of huts—
he marvels at gates and bustling hum and cobbled streets.
The Tyrians press on with the work, some aligning the walls,
struggling to raise the citadel, trundling stones up slopes;
some picking the building sites and plowing out their boundaries,
others drafting laws, electing judges, a senate held in awe.

Here they're dredging a harbor, there they lay foundations
deep for a theater, quarrying out of rock great columns
to form a fitting scene for stages still to come.
As hard at their tasks as bees in early summer,   520
that work the blooming meadows under the sun,
they escort a new brood out, young adults now,
or press the oozing honey into the combs, the nectar
brimming the bulging cells, or gather up the plunder
workers haul back in, or close ranks like an army,
driving the drones, that lazy crew, from home.
The hive seethes with life, exhaling the scent
of honey sweet with thyme.
                              "How lucky they are,"
Aeneas cries, gazing up at the city's heights,
"their walls are rising now!" And on he goes,   530
cloaked in cloud—remarkable—right in their midst
he blends in with the crowds, and no one sees him.

   Now deep in the heart of Carthage stood a grove,
lavish with shade, where the Tyrians, making landfall,
still shaken by wind and breakers, first unearthed that sign:
Queen Juno had led their way to the fiery stallion's head
that signaled power in war and ease in life for ages.
Here Dido of Tyre was building Juno a mighty temple,
rich with gifts and the goddess' aura of power.
Bronze the threshold crowning a flight of stairs,   540
the doorposts sheathed in bronze, and the bronze doors
groaned deep on their hinges.
                              Here in this grove
a strange sight met his eyes and calmed his fears
for the first time. Here, for the first time,
Aeneas dared to hope he had found some haven,
for all his hard straits, to trust in better days.
For awaiting the queen, beneath the great temple now,
exploring its features one by one, amazed at it all,
the city's splendor, the work of rival workers' hands
and the vast scale of their labors—all at once he sees,   550
spread out from first to last, the battles fought at Troy,

the fame of the Trojan War now known throughout the world,
Atreus' sons and Priam—Achilles, savage to both at once.
Aeneas came to a halt and wept, and "Oh, Achates,"
he cried, "is there anywhere, any place on earth
not filled with our ordeals? There's Priam, look!
Even here, merit will have its true reward . . .
even here, the world is a world of tears
and the burdens of mortality touch the heart.
Dismiss your fears. Trust me, this fame of ours   560
will offer us some haven."
                                    So Aeneas says,
feeding his spirit on empty, lifeless pictures,
groaning low, the tears rivering down his face
as he sees once more the fighters circling Troy.
Here Greeks in flight, routed by Troy's young ranks,
there Trojans routed by plumed Achilles in his chariot.
Just in range are the snow-white canvas tents of Rhesus—
he knows them at once, and sobs—Rhesus' men betrayed
in their first slumber, droves of them slaughtered
by Diomedes splattered with their blood, lashing   570
back to the Greek camp their high-strung teams
before they could ever savor the grass of Troy
or drink at Xanthus' banks.
                                    Next Aeneas sees
Troilus in flight, his weapons flung aside,
unlucky boy, no match for Achilles' onslaught—
horses haul him on, tangled behind an empty war-car,
flat on his back, clinging still to the reins, his neck
and hair dragging along the ground, the butt of his javelin
scrawling zigzags in the dust.
                                    And here the Trojan women
are moving toward the temple of Pallas, their deadly foe,   580
their hair unbound as they bear the robe, their offering,
suppliants grieving, palms beating their breasts
but Pallas turns away, staring at the ground.
                                    And Hector—
three times Achilles has hauled him round the walls of Troy
and now he's selling his lifeless body off for gold.

Aeneas gives a groan, heaving up from his depths,
he sees the plundered armor, the car, the corpse
of his great friend, and Priam reaching out
with helpless hands . . .
                              He even sees himself
swept up in the melee, clashing with Greek captains,   590
sees the troops of the Dawn and swarthy Memnon's arms.
And Penthesilea leading her Amazons bearing half-moon shields—
she blazes with battle fury out in front of her army,
cinching a golden breastband under her bared breast,
a girl, a warrior queen who dares to battle men.

                              And now
as Trojan Aeneas, gazing in awe at all the scenes of Troy,
stood there, spellbound, eyes fixed on the war alone,
the queen aglow with beauty approached the temple,
Dido, with massed escorts marching in her wake.
Like Diana urging her dancing troupes along   600
the Eurotas' banks or up Mount Cynthus' ridge
as a thousand mountain-nymphs crowd in behind her,
left and right—with quiver slung from her shoulder,
taller than any other goddess as she goes striding on
and silent Latona thrills with joy too deep for words.
Like Dido now, striding triumphant among her people,
spurring on the work of their kingdom still to come.
And then by Juno's doors beneath the vaulted dome,
flanked by an honor guard beside her lofty seat,
the queen assumed her throne. Here as she handed down   610
decrees and laws to her people, sharing labors fairly,
some by lot, some with her sense of justice, Aeneas
suddenly sees his men approaching through the crowds,
Antheus, Sergestus, gallant Cloanthus, other Trojans
the black gales had battered over the seas
and swept to far-flung coasts.
                              Aeneas, Achates,
both were amazed, both struck with joy and fear.
They yearn to grasp their companions' hands in haste
but both men are unnerved by the mystery of it all.
So, cloaked in folds of mist, they hide their feelings,   620

waiting, hoping to see what luck their friends have found.
Where have they left their ships, what coast? Why have they come?
These picked men, still marching in from the whole armada,
pressing toward the temple amid the rising din
to plead for some good will.
            Once they had entered,
allowed to appeal before the queen—the eldest,
Prince Ilioneus, calm, composed, spoke out:
"Your majesty, empowered by Jove to found
your new city here and curb rebellious tribes
with your sense of justice—we poor Trojans,   630
castaways, tossed by storms over all the seas,
we beg you: keep the cursed fire off our ships!
Pity us, god-fearing men! Look on us kindly,
see the state we are in. We have not come
to put your Libyan gods and homes to the sword,
loot them and haul our plunder toward the beach.
No, such pride, such violence has no place
in the hearts of beaten men.
           "There is a country—
the Greeks called it Hesperia, Land of the West,
an ancient land, mighty in war and rich in soil.   640
Oenotrians settled it; now we hear their descendants
call their kingdom Italy, after their leader, Italus.
Italy-bound we were when, surging with sudden breakers
stormy Orion drove us against blind shoals and from the South
came vicious gales to scatter us, whelmed by the sea,
across the murderous surf and rocky barrier reefs.
We few escaped and floated toward your coast.
What kind of men are these? What land is this,
that you can tolerate such barbaric ways?
We are denied the sailor's right to shore—   650
attacked, forbidden even a footing on your beach.
If you have no use for humankind and mortal armor,
at least respect the gods. They know right from wrong.
They don't forget.
          "We once had a king, Aeneas . . .
none more just, none more devoted to duty, none

more brave in arms. If Fate has saved that man,
if he still draws strength from the air we breathe,
if he's not laid low, not yet with the heartless shades,
fear not, nor will you once regret the first step
you take to compete with him in kindness.   660
We have cities too, in the land of Sicily,
arms and a king, Acestes, born of Trojan blood.
Permit us to haul our storm-racked ships ashore,
trim new oars, hew timbers out of your woods, so that,
if we are fated to sail for Italy—king and crews restored—
to Italy, to Latium we will sail with buoyant hearts.
But if we have lost our haven there, if Libyan waters
hold you now, my captain, best of the men of Troy,
and all our hopes for Iulus have been dashed,
at least we can cross back over Sicilian seas,   670
the straits we came from, homes ready and waiting,
and seek out great Acestes for our king."

    So Ilioneus closed. And with one accord
the Trojans murmured Yes.
                              Her eyes lowered,
Dido replies with a few choice words of welcome:
"Cast fear to the winds, Trojans, free your minds.
Our kingdom is new. Our hard straits have forced me
to set defenses, station guards along our far frontiers.
Who has not heard of Aeneas' people, his city, Troy,
her men, her heroes, the flames of that horrendous war?   680
We are not so dull of mind, we Carthaginians here.
When he yokes his team, the Sun shines down on us as well.
Whatever you choose, great Hesperia—Saturn's fields—
or the shores of Eryx with Acestes as your king,
I will provide safe passage, escorts and support
to speed you on your way. Or would you rather
settle here in my realm on equal terms with me?
This city I build—it's yours. Haul ships to shore.
Trojans, Tyrians: they will be all the same to me.
If only the storm that drove you drove your king   690
and Aeneas were here now! Indeed, I'll send out

trusty men to scour the coast of Libya far and wide.
Perhaps he's shipwrecked, lost in woods or towns."

    Spirits lifting at Dido's welcome, brave Achates
and captain Aeneas had long chafed to break free
of the mist, and now Achates spurs Aeneas on:
"Son of Venus, what feelings are rising in you now?
You see the coast is clear, our ships and friends restored.
Just one is lost. We saw him drown at sea ourselves.
All else is just as your mother promised."   700

    He'd barely ended when all at once the mist
around them parted, melting into the open air,
and there Aeneas stood, clear in the light of day,
his head, his shoulders, the man was like a god.
His own mother had breathed her beauty on her son,
a gloss on his flowing hair, and the ruddy glow of youth,
and radiant joy shone in his eyes. His beauty fine
as a craftsman's hand can add to ivory, or aglow
as silver or Parian marble ringed in glinting gold.

    Suddenly, surprising all, he tells the queen: 710
"Here I am before you, the man you are looking for.
Aeneas the Trojan, plucked from Libya's heavy seas.
You alone have pitied the long ordeals of Troy—unspeakable—
and here you would share your city and your home with us,
this remnant left by the Greeks. We who have drunk deep
of each and every disaster land and sea can offer.
Stripped of everything, now it's past our power
to reward you gift for gift, Dido, theirs as well,
whoever may survive of the Dardan people still,
strewn over the wide world now. But may the gods,   720
if there are Powers who still respect the good and true,
if justice still exists on the face of the earth,
may they and their own sense of right and wrong
bring you your just rewards.
What age has been so blest to give you birth?
What noble parents produced so fine a daughter?

So long as rivers run to the sea, so long as shadows
travel the mountain slopes and the stars range the skies,
your honor, your name, your praise will live forever,
whatever lands may call me to their shores."
                              With that,   730
he extends his right hand toward his friend Ilioneus,
greeting Serestus with his left, and then the others,
gallant Gyas, gallant Cloanthus.
                         Tyrian Dido marveled,
first at the sight of him, next at all he'd suffered,
then she said aloud: "Born of a goddess, even so
what destiny hunts you down through such ordeals?
What violence lands you on this frightful coast?
Are you that Aeneas whom loving Venus bore
to Dardan Anchises on the Simois' banks at Troy?
Well I remember . . . Teucer came to Sidon once,   740
banished from native ground, searching for new realms,
and my father Belus helped him. Belus had sacked Cyprus,
plundered that rich island, ruled with a victor's hand.
From that day on I have known of Troy's disaster,
known your name, and all the kings of Greece.
Teucer, your enemy, often sang Troy's praises,
claiming his own descent from Teucer's ancient stock.
So come, young soldiers, welcome to our house.
My destiny, harrying me with trials hard as yours,
led me as well, at last, to anchor in this land.   750
Schooled in suffering, now I learn to comfort
those who suffer too."
                    With that greeting
she leads Aeneas into the royal halls, announcing
offerings in the gods' high temples as she goes.
Not forgetting to send his shipmates on the beaches
twenty bulls and a hundred huge, bristling razorbacks
and a hundred fatted lambs together with their mothers:
gifts to make this day a day of joy.
                       Within the palace
all is decked with adornments, lavish, regal splendor.
In the central hall they are setting out a banquet,   760

draping the gorgeous purple, intricately worked,
heaping the board with grand displays of silver
and gold engraved with her fathers' valiant deeds,
a long, unending series of captains and commands,
traced through a line of heroes since her country's birth.

Aeneas—a father's love would give the man no rest—
quickly sends Achates down to the ships to take
the news to Ascanius, bring him back to Carthage.
All his paternal care is focused on his son.
He tells Achates to fetch some gifts as well,   770
plucked from the ruins of Troy: a gown stiff
with figures stitched in gold, and a woven veil
with yellow sprays of acanthus round the border.
Helen's glory, gifts she carried out of Mycenae,
fleeing Argos for Troy to seal her wicked marriage—
the marvelous handiwork of Helen's mother, Leda.
Aeneas adds the scepter Ilione used to bear,
the eldest daughter of Priam; a necklace too,
strung with pearls, and a crown of double bands,
one studded with gems, the other, gold. Achates,   780
following orders, hurries toward the ships.

But now Venus is mulling over some new schemes,
new intrigues. Altered in face and figure, Cupid
would go in place of the captivating Ascanius,
using his gifts to fire the queen to madness,
weaving a lover's ardor through her bones.
No doubt Venus fears that treacherous house
and the Tyrians' forked tongues,
and brutal Juno inflames her anguish too
and her cares keep coming back as night draws on.   790
So Venus makes an appeal to Love, her winged son:
"You, my son, are my strength, my greatest power—
you alone, my son, can scoff at the lightning bolts
the high and mighty Father hurled against Typhoeus.
Help me, I beg you. I need all your immortal force.
Your brother Aeneas is tossed round every coast on earth,

thanks to Juno's ruthless hatred, as you well know,
and time and again you've grieved to see my grief.
But now Phoenician Dido has him in her clutches,
holding him back with smooth, seductive words,   800
and I fear the outcome of Juno's welcome here . . .
She won't sit tight while Fate is turning on its hinge.
So I plan to forestall her with ruses of my own
and besiege the queen with flames,
and no goddess will change her mood—she's mine,
my ally-in-arms in my great love for Aeneas.

    "Now how can you go about this? Hear my plan.
His dear father has just sent for the young prince—
he means the world to me—and he's bound for Carthage now,
bearing presents saved from the sea, the flames of Troy.   810
I'll lull him into a deep sleep and hide him far away
on Cythera's heights or high Idalium, my shrines,
so he cannot learn of my trap or spring it open
while it's being set. And you with your cunning,
forge his appearance—just one night, no more—put on
the familiar features of the boy, boy that you are,
so when the wine flows free at the royal board
and Dido, lost in joy, cradles you in her lap,
caressing, kissing you gently, you can breathe
your secret fire into her, poison the queen   820
and she will never know."
                                   Cupid leaps at once
to his loving mother's orders. Shedding his wings
he masquerades as Iulus, prancing with his stride.
But now Venus distills a deep, soothing sleep
into Iulus' limbs, and warming him in her breast
the goddess spirits him off to her high Idalian grove
where beds of marjoram breathe and embrace him with aromatic
flowers and rustling shade.
                            Now Cupid is on the move,
under her orders, bringing the Tyrians royal gifts,
his spirits high as Achates leads him on.   830
Arriving, he finds the queen already poised

on a golden throne beneath the sumptuous hangings,
commanding the very center of her palace. Now Aeneas,
the good captain, enters, then the Trojan soldiers,
taking their seats on couches draped in purple.
Servants pour them water to rinse their hands,
quickly serving them bread from baskets, spreading
their laps with linens, napkins clipped and smooth.
In the kitchens are fifty serving-maids assigned
to lay out foods in a long line, course by course,   840
and honor the household gods by building fires high.
A hundred other maids and a hundred men, all matched in age,
are spreading the feast on trestles, setting out the cups.
And Tyrians join them, bustling through the doors,
filling the hall with joy, to take invited seats
on brocaded couches. They admire Aeneas' gifts,
admire Iulus now—the glowing face of the god
and the god's dissembling words—and Helen's gown
and the veil adorned with a yellow acanthus border.

    But above all, tragic Dido, doomed to a plague   850
about to strike, cannot feast her eyes enough,
thrilled both by the boy and gifts he brings
and the more she looks the more the fire grows.
But once he's embraced Aeneas, clung to his neck
to sate the deep love of his father, deluded father,
Cupid makes for the queen. Her gaze, her whole heart
is riveted on him now, and at times she even warms him
snugly in her breast, for how can she know, poor Dido,
what a mighty god is sinking into her, to her grief?
But he, recalling the wishes of his mother Venus,   860
blots out the memory of Sychaeus bit by bit,
trying to seize with a fresh, living love
a heart at rest for long—long numb to passion.
                                                 Then,
with the first lull in the feast, the tables cleared away,
they set out massive bowls and crown the wine with wreaths.
A vast din swells in the palace, voices reverberating
through the echoing halls. They light the lamps,

hung from the coffered ceilings sheathed in gilt,
and blazing torches burn the night away.
The queen calls for a heavy golden bowl,   870
studded with jewels and brimmed with unmixed wine,
the bowl that Belus and all of Belus' sons had brimmed,
and the hall falls hushed as Dido lifts a prayer:
"Jupiter, you, they say, are the god who grants
the laws of host and guest. May this day be one
of joy for Tyrians here and exiles come from Troy,
a day our sons will long remember. Bacchus,
giver of bliss, and Juno, generous Juno,
bless us now. And come, my people, celebrate
with all good will this feast that makes us one!"   880

    With that prayer, she poured a libation to the gods,
tipping wine on the board, and tipping it, she was first
to take the bowl, brushing it lightly with her lips,
then gave it to Bitias—laughing, goading him on
and he took the plunge, draining the foaming bowl,
drenching himself in its brimming, overflowing gold,
and the other princes drank in turn. Then Iopas,
long-haired bard, strikes up his golden lyre
resounding through the halls. Giant Atlas
had been his teacher once, and now he sings   890
the wandering moon and laboring sun eclipsed,
the roots of the human race and the wild beasts,
the source of storms and the lightning bolts on high,
Arcturus, the rainy Hyades and the Great and Little Bears,
and why the winter suns so rush to bathe themselves in the sea
and what slows down the nights to a long lingering crawl . . .
And time and again the Tyrians burst into applause
and the Trojans took their lead. So Dido, doomed,
was lengthening out the night by trading tales
as she drank long draughts of love—asking Aeneas   900
question on question, now about Priam, now Hector,
what armor Memnon, son of the Morning, wore at Troy,
how swift were the horses of Diomedes? How strong was Achilles?

"Wait, come, my guest," she urges, "tell us your own story,
start to finish—the ambush laid by the Greeks, the pain
your people suffered, the wanderings you have faced.
For now is the seventh summer that has borne you
wandering all the lands and seas on earth."

BOOK TWO

The Final Hours of Troy

Silence. All fell hushed, their eyes fixed on Aeneas now
as the founder of his people, high on a seat of honor,
set out on his story: "Sorrow, unspeakable sorrow,
my queen, you ask me to bring to life once more,
how the Greeks uprooted Troy in all her power,
our kingdom mourned forever. What horrors I saw,
a tragedy where I played a leading role myself.
Who could tell such things—not even a Myrmidon,
a Dolopian, or comrade of iron-hearted Ulysses—
and still refrain from tears? And now, too,   10
the dank night is sweeping down from the sky
and the setting stars incline our heads to sleep.
But if you long so deeply to know what we went through,
to hear, in brief, the last great agony of Troy,
much as I shudder at the memory of it all—
I shrank back in grief—I'll try to tell it now . . .

"Ground down by the war and driven back by Fate,
the Greek captains had watched the years slip by
until, helped by Minerva's superhuman skill,
they built that mammoth horse, immense as a mountain,   20
lining its ribs with ship timbers hewn from pine.
An offering to secure safe passage home, or so
they pretend, and the story spreads through Troy.
But they pick by lot the best, most able-bodied men
and stealthily lock them into the horse's dark flanks
till the vast hold of the monster's womb is packed
with soldiers bristling weapons.
                    "Just in sight of Troy
an island rises, Tenedos, famed in the old songs,
powerful, rich, while Priam's realm stood fast.
Now it's only a bay, a treacherous cove for ships.   30
Well there they sail, hiding out on its lonely coast
while we thought—gone! Sped home on the winds to Greece.
So all Troy breathes free, relieved of her endless sorrow.
We fling open the gates and stream out, elated to see
the Greeks' abandoned camp, the deserted beachhead.
Here the Dolopians formed ranks—
                    "Here savage Achilles
pitched his tents—
                    "Over there the armada moored
and here the familiar killing-fields of battle.
Some gaze wonderstruck at the gift for Pallas,
the virgin never wed—transfixed by the horse,   40
its looming mass, our doom. Thymoetes leads the way.
'Drag it inside the walls,' he urges, 'plant it high
on the city heights!' Inspired by treachery now
or the fate of Troy was moving toward this end.
But Capys with other saner heads who take his side,
suspecting a trap in any gift the Greeks might offer,
tells us: 'Fling it into the sea or torch the thing to ash
or bore into the depths of its womb where men can hide!'
The common people are split into warring factions.

"But now, out in the lead with a troop of comrades,   50

down Laocoön runs from the heights in full fury,
calling out from a distance: 'Poor doomed fools,
have you gone mad, you Trojans?
You really believe the enemy's sailed away?
Or any gift of the Greeks is free of guile?
Is that how well you know Ulysses? Trust me,
either the Greeks are hiding, shut inside those beams,
or the horse is a battle-engine geared to breach our walls,
spy on our homes, come down on our city, overwhelm us—
or some other deception's lurking deep inside it.   60
Trojans, never trust that horse. Whatever it is,
I fear the Greeks, especially bearing gifts.'

    "In that spirit, with all his might he hurled
a huge spear straight into the monster's flanks,
the mortised timberwork of its swollen belly.
Quivering, there it stuck, and the stricken womb
came booming back from its depths with echoing groans.
If Fate and our own wits had not gone against us,
surely Laocoön would have driven us on, now,
to rip the Greek lair open with iron spears   70
and Troy would still be standing—
proud fortress of Priam, you would tower still!

    "Suddenly, in the thick of it all, a young soldier,
hands shackled behind his back, with much shouting
Trojan shepherds were haling him toward the king.
They'd come on the man by chance, a total stranger.
He'd given himself up, with one goal in mind:
to open Troy to the Greeks and lay her waste.
He trusted to courage, nerved for either end,
to weave his lies or face his certain death.   80
Young Trojan recruits, keen to have a look,
came scurrying up from all sides, crowding round,
outdoing each other to make a mockery of the captive.
Now, hear the treachery of the Greeks and learn
from a single crime the nature of the beast . . .
Haggard, helpless, there in our midst he stood,

all eyes riveted on him now, and turning a wary glance
at the lines of Trojan troops he groaned and spoke:
'Where can I find some refuge, where on land, on sea?
What's left for me now? A man of so much misery!   90
Nothing among the Greeks, no place at all. And worse,
I see my Trojan enemies crying for my blood.'
                              "His groans
convince us, cutting all our show of violence short.
We press him: 'Tell us where you were born, your family.
What news do you bring? Tell us what you trust to,
such a willing captive.'
                    "'All of it, my king,
I'll tell you, come what may, the whole true story.
Greek I am, I don't deny it. No, that first.
Fortune may have made me a man of misery
but, wicked as she is,   100
she can't make Sinon a lying fraud as well.
                              "'Now,
perhaps you've caught some rumor of Palamedes,
Belus' son, and his shining fame that rings in song.
The Greeks charged him with treason, a trumped-up charge,
an innocent man, and just because he opposed the war
they put him to death, but once he's robbed of the light,
they mourn him sorely. Now I was his blood kin,
a youngster when my father, a poor man, sent me
off to the war at Troy as Palamedes' comrade.
Long as he kept his royal status, holding forth   110
in the councils of the kings, I had some standing too,
some pride of place. But once he left the land of the living,
thanks to the jealous, forked tongue of our Ulysses—
you're no stranger to *his* story—I was shattered,
I dragged out my life in the shadows, grieving,
seething alone, in silence . . .
outraged by my innocent friend's demise until
I burst out like a madman, swore if I ever returned
in triumph to our native Argos, ever got the chance
I'd take revenge, and my oath provoked a storm of hatred. 120

That was my first step on the slippery road to ruin.
From then on, Ulysses kept tormenting me, pressing
charge on charge; from then on, he bruited about
his two-edged rumors among the rank and file.
Driven by guilt, he looked for ways to kill me,
he never rested until, making Calchas his henchman—
but why now? Why go over that unforgiving ground again?
Why waste words? If you think all Greeks are one,
if hearing the name *Greek* is enough for you,
it's high time you made me pay the price.   130
How that would please the man of Ithaca,
how the sons of Atreus would repay you!'

                                            "Now, of course,
we burn to question him, urge him to explain—
blind to how false the cunning Greeks could be.
All atremble, he carries on with his tale,
lying from the cockles of his heart:

                                      "'Time and again
the Greeks had yearned to abandon Troy—bone-tired
from a long hard war—to put it far behind and
beat a clean retreat. Would to god they had.
But time and again, as they were setting sail,   140
the heavy seas would keep them confined to port
and the Southwind filled their hearts with dread
and worst of all, once this horse, this mass of timber
with locking planks, stood stationed here at last,
the thunderheads rumbled up and down the sky.
So, at our wit's end, we send Eurypylus off
to question Apollo's oracle now, and back
he comes from the god's shrine with these bleak words:
"With blood you appeased the winds, with a virgin's sacrifice
when you, you Greeks, first sought the shores of Troy.   150
With blood you must seek fair winds to sail you home,
must sacrifice one more Greek life in return."

      "'As the word spread, the ranks were struck dumb
and icy fear sent shivers down their spines.
Whom did the god demand? Who'd meet his doom?

Just that moment the Ithacan haled the prophet,
Calchas, into our midst—he'd twist it out of him,
what was the gods' will? The army rose in uproar.
Even then our soldiers sensed that I was the one,
the target of that Ulysses' vicious schemes—   160
they saw it coming, still they held their tongues.
For ten days the seer, silent, closed off in his tent,
refused to say a word or betray a man to death.
But at last, goaded on by Ulysses' mounting threats
but in fact conniving in their plot, he breaks his silence
and dooms me to the altar. And the army gave consent.
The death that each man dreaded turned to the fate
of one poor soul: a burden they could bear.

    "'The day of infamy soon came . . .
the sacred rites were all performed for the victim,   170
the salted meal strewn, the bands tied round my head.
But I broke free of death, I tell you, burst my shackles,
yes, and hid all night in the reeds of a marshy lake,
waiting for them to sail—if only they would sail!
Well, no hope now of seeing the land where I was born
or my sweet children, the father I longed for all these years.
Maybe they'll wring from *them* the price for my escape,
avenge my guilt with my loved ones' blood, poor things.
I beg you, king, by the Powers who know the truth,
by any trust still uncorrupt in the world of men,   180
pity a man whose torment knows no bounds.
Pity me in my pain.
I know in my soul I don't deserve to suffer.'

    "He wept and won his life—our pity, too.
Priam takes command, has him freed from the ropes
and chains that bind him fast, and hails him warmly:
'Whoever you are, from now on, now you've lost the Greeks,
put them out of your mind and you'll be one of us.
But answer my questions. Tell me the whole truth.
Why did they raise up this giant, monstrous horse?   190
Who conceived it? What's it for? its purpose?

A gift to the gods? A great engine of battle?'

"He broke off. Sinon, adept at deceit,
with all his Greek cunning lifted his hands,
just freed from their fetters, up to the stars
and prayed: 'Bear witness, you eternal fires of the sky
and you inviolate will of the gods! Bear witness,
altar and those infernal knives that I escaped
and the sacred bands I wore myself: the victim.
It's right to break my sworn oath to the Greeks,   200
it's right to detest those men and bring to light
all they're hiding now. No laws of my native land
can bind me here. Just keep your promise, Troy,
and if I can save you, you must save me too—
if I reveal the truth and pay you back in full.

"'All the hopes of the Greeks, their firm faith
in a war they'd launched themselves
had always hinged on Pallas Athena's help.
But from the moment that godless Diomedes,
flanked by Ulysses, the mastermind of crime,   210
attacked and tore the fateful image of Pallas
out of her own hallowed shrine, and cut down
the sentries ringing your city heights and seized
that holy image and even dared touch the sacred bands
on the virgin goddess' head with hands reeking blood—
from that hour on, the high hopes of the Greeks
had trickled away like a slow, ebbing tide . . .
They were broken, beaten men,
the will of the goddess dead set against them.
Omens of this she gave in no uncertain terms.   220
They'd hardly stood her image up in the Greek camp
when flickering fire shot from its glaring eyes
and salt sweat ran glistening down its limbs
and three times the goddess herself—a marvel—
blazed forth from the ground, shield clashing, spear brandished.
The prophet spurs them at once to risk escape by sea:
"You cannot root out Troy with your Greek spears unless

you seek new omens in Greece and bring the god back here"—
the image they'd borne across the sea in their curved ships.
So now they've sailed away on the wind for home shores,   230
just to rearm, recruit their gods as allies yet again,
then measure back their course on the high seas and
back they'll come to attack you all off guard.

    "'So Calchas read the omens. At his command
they raised this horse, this effigy, all to atone
for the violated image of Pallas, her wounded pride,
her power—and expiate the outrage they had done.
But he made them do the work on a grand scale,
a tremendous mass of interlocking timbers towering
toward the sky, so the horse could not be trundled   240
through your gates or hauled inside your walls
or guard your people if they revered it well
in the old, ancient way. For if your hands
should violate this great offering to Minerva,
a total disaster—if only god would turn it
against the seer himself!—will wheel down
on Priam's empire, Troy, and all your futures.
But if your hands will rear it up, into your city,
then all Asia in arms can invade Greece, can launch
an all-out war right up to the walls of Pelops.   250
That's the doom that awaits our sons' sons.'

    "Trapped by his craft, that cunning liar Sinon,
we believed his story. His tears, his treachery seized
the men whom neither Tydeus' son nor Achilles could defeat,
nor ten long years of war, nor all the thousand ships.

    "But a new portent strikes our doomed people
now—a greater omen, far more terrible, fatal,
shakes our senses, blind to what was coming.
Laocoön, the priest of Neptune picked by lot,
was sacrificing a massive bull at the holy altar   260
when—I cringe to recall it now—look there!
Over the calm deep straits off Tenedos swim

twin, giant serpents, rearing in coils, breasting
the sea-swell side by side, plunging toward the shore,
their heads, their blood-red crests surging over the waves,
their bodies thrashing, backs rolling in coil on mammoth coil
and the wake behind them churns in a roar of foaming spray,
and now, their eyes glittering, shot with blood and fire,
flickering tongues licking their hissing maws, yes, now
they're about to land. We blanch at the sight, we scatter.   270
Like troops on attack they're heading straight for Laocoön—
first each serpent seizes one of his small young sons,
constricting, twisting around him, sinks its fangs
in the tortured limbs, and gorges. Next Laocoön
rushing quick to the rescue, clutching his sword—
they trap him, bind him in huge muscular whorls,
their scaly backs lashing around his midriff twice
and twice around his throat—their heads, their flaring necks
mounting over their victim writhing still, his hands
frantic to wrench apart their knotted trunks,   280
his priestly bands splattered in filth, black venom
and all the while his horrible screaming fills the skies,
bellowing like some wounded bull struggling to shrug
loose from his neck an axe that's struck awry,
to lumber clear of the altar . . .
Only the twin snakes escape, sliding off and away
to the heights of Troy where the ruthless goddess
holds her shrine, and there at her feet they hide,
vanishing under Minerva's great round shield.
                                        "At once,
I tell you, a stranger fear runs through the harrowed crowd.   290
Laocoön deserved to pay for his outrage, so they say,
he desecrated the sacred timbers of the horse,
he hurled his wicked lance at the beast's back.
'Haul Minerva's effigy up to her house,' we shout,
'Offer up our prayers to the power of the goddess!'
We breach our own ramparts, fling our defenses open,
all pitch into the work. Smooth running rollers
we wheel beneath its hoofs, and heavy hempen ropes
we bind around its neck, and teeming with men-at-arms

the huge deadly engine climbs our city walls . . .   300
And round it boys and unwed girls sing hymns,
thrilled to lay a hand on the dangling ropes
as on and on it comes, gliding into the city,
looming high over the city's heart.

                              "Oh my country!
Troy, home of the gods! You great walls of the Dardans
long renowned in war!

                     "Four times it lurched to a halt
at the very brink of the gates—four times the armor
clashed out from its womb. But we, we forged ahead,
oblivious, blind, insane, we stationed the monster
fraught with doom on the hallowed heights of Troy.   310
Even now Cassandra revealed the future, opening
lips the gods had ruled no Trojan would believe.
And we, poor fools—on this, our last day—we deck
the shrines of the gods with green holiday garlands
all throughout the city . . .

                       "But all the while
the skies keep wheeling on and night comes sweeping in
from the Ocean Stream, in its mammoth shadow swallowing up
the earth, and the pole star, and the treachery of the Greeks.
Dead quiet. The Trojans slept on, strewn throughout
their fortress, weary bodies embraced by slumber.   320
But the Greek armada was under way now, crossing
over from Tenedos, ships in battle formation
under the moon's quiet light, their silent ally,
homing in on the berths they know by heart—
when the king's flagship sends up a signal flare,
the cue for Sinon, saved by the Fates' unjust decree,
and stealthily loosing the pine bolts of the horse,
he unleashes the Greeks shut up inside its womb.
The horse stands open wide, fighters in high spirits
pouring out of its timbered cavern into the fresh air: 330
the chiefs, Thessandrus, Sthenelus, ruthless Ulysses
rappeling down a rope they dropped from its side,
and Acamas, Thoas, Neoptolemus, son of Achilles,
captain Machaon, Menelaus, Epeus himself,

the man who built that masterpiece of fraud.
They steal on a city buried deep in sleep and wine,
they butcher the guards, fling wide the gates and hug
their cohorts poised to combine forces. Plot complete.

"This was the hour when rest, that gift of the gods
most heaven-sent, first comes to beleaguered mortals,   340
creeping over us now . . . when there, look,
I dreamed I saw Prince Hector before my eyes,
my comrade haggard with sorrow, streaming tears,
just as he once was, when dragged behind the chariot,
black with blood and grime, thongs piercing his swollen feet—
what a harrowing sight! What a far cry from the old Hector
home from battle, decked in Achilles' arms—his trophies—
or fresh from pitching Trojan fire at the Greek ships.
His beard matted now, his hair clotted with blood,
bearing the wounds, so many wounds he suffered   350
fighting round his native city's walls . . .
I dreamed I addressed him first, in tears myself
I forced my voice from the depths of all my grief:
'Oh light of the Trojans—last, best hope of Troy!
What's held you back so long? How long we've waited,
Hector, for you to come, and now from what far shores?
How glad we are to see you, we battle-weary men,
after so many deaths, your people dead and gone,
after your citizens, your city felt such pain.
But what outrage has mutilated your face   360
so clear and cloudless once? Why these wounds?'

"Wasting no words, no time on empty questions,
heaving a deep groan from his heart he calls out:
'Escape, son of the goddess, tear yourself from the flames!
The enemy holds our walls. Troy is toppling from her heights.
You have paid your debt to our king and native land.
If one strong arm could have saved Troy, my arm
would have saved the city. Now, into your hands
she entrusts her holy things, her household gods.
Take them with you as comrades in your fortunes.   370

Seek a city for them, once you have roved the seas,
erect great walls at last to house the gods of Troy!'

"Urging so, with his own hands he carries Vesta forth
from her inner shrine, her image clad in ribbons,
filled with her power, her everlasting fire.
                                        "But now,
chaos—the city begins to reel with cries of grief,
louder, stronger, even though father's palace
stood well back, screened off by trees, but still
the clash of arms rings clearer, horror on the attack.
I shake off sleep and scrambling up to the pitched roof   380
I stand there, ears alert, and I hear a roar like fire
assaulting a wheatfield, whipped by a Southwind's fury,
or mountain torrent in full spate, flattening crops,
leveling all the happy, thriving labor of oxen,
dragging whole trees headlong down in its wake—
and a shepherd perched on a sheer rock outcrop
hears the roar, lost in amazement, struck dumb.
No doubting the good faith of the Greeks now,
their treachery plain as day.
                                "Already, there,
the grand house of Deiphobus stormed by fire,   390
crashing in ruins—
                    "Already his neighbor Ucalegon
up in flames—
              "The Sigean straits shimmering back the blaze,
the shouting of fighters soars, the clashing blare of trumpets.
Out of my wits, I seize my arms—what reason for arms?
Just my spirit burning to muster troops for battle,
rush with comrades up to the city's heights,
fury and rage driving me breakneck on
as it races through my mind
what a noble thing it is to die in arms!
                                        "But now, look,
just slipped out from under the Greek barrage of spears,   400
Panthus, Othrys' son, a priest of Apollo's shrine
on the citadel—hands full of the holy things,

the images of our conquered gods—he's dragging along
his little grandson, making a wild dash for our doors.
'Panthus, where's our stronghold? our last stand?'—
words still on my lips as he groans in answer:
'The last *day* has come for the Trojan people,
no escaping this moment. Troy's no more.
Ilium, gone—our awesome Trojan glory.
Brutal Jupiter hands it all over to Greece,   410
Greeks are lording over our city up in flames.
The horse stands towering high in the heart of Troy,
disgorging its armed men, with Sinon in his glory,
gloating over us—Sinon fans the fires.
The immense double gates are flung wide open,
Greeks in their thousands mass there, all who ever
sailed from proud Mycenae. Others have choked
the cramped streets, weapons brandished now
in a battle line of naked, glinting steel
tense for the kill. Only the first guards   420
at the gates put up some show of resistance,
fighting blindly on.'

    "Spurred by Panthus' words and the gods' will,
into the blaze I dive, into the fray, wherever
the din of combat breaks and war cries fill the sky,
wherever the battle-fury drives me on and now
I'm joined by Rhipeus, Epytus mighty in armor,
rearing up in the moonlight—
Hypanis comes to my side, and Dymas too,
flanked by the young Coroebus, Mygdon's son.   430
Late in the day he'd chanced to come to Troy
incensed with a mad, burning love for Cassandra:
son-in-law to our king, *he* would rescue Troy. Poor man,
if only he'd marked his bride's inspired ravings!

    "Seeing their close-packed ranks, hot for battle,
I spur them on their way: 'Men, brave hearts,
though bravery cannot save us—if you're bent on
following me and risking all to face the worst,

look around you, see how our chances stand.
The gods who shored our empire up have left us,   440
all have deserted their altars and their shrines.
You race to defend a city already lost in flames.
But let us die, go plunging into the thick of battle.
One hope saves the defeated: they know they can't be saved!'
That fired their hearts with the fury of despair.

                                                    "Now
like a wolfpack out for blood on a foggy night,
driven blindly on by relentless, rabid hunger,
leaving cubs behind, waiting, jaws parched—
so through spears, through enemy ranks we plow
to certain death, striking into the city's heart,   450
the shielding wings of the darkness beating round us.
Who has words to capture that night's disaster,
tell that slaughter? What tears could match
our torments now? An ancient city is falling,
a power that ruled for ages, now in ruins.
Everywhere lie the motionless bodies of the dead,
strewn in her streets, her homes and the gods' shrines
we held in awe. And not only Trojans pay the price in blood—
at times the courage races back in their conquered hearts
and they cut their enemies down in all their triumph.   460
Everywhere, wrenching grief, everywhere, terror
and a thousand shapes of death.
                              "And the first Greek
to cross our path? Androgeos leading a horde of troops
and taking *us* for allies on the march, the fool,
he even gives us a warm salute and calls out:
'Hurry up, men. Why holding back, why now,
why drag your heels? Troy's up in flames,
the rest are looting, sacking the city heights.
But you, have you just come from the tall ships?'
Suddenly, getting no password he can trust,   470
he sensed he'd stumbled into enemy ranks!
Stunned, he recoiled, swallowing back his words
like a man who threads his way through prickly brambles,
pressing his full weight on the ground, and blindly treads

on a lurking snake and back he shrinks in instant fear
as it rears in anger, puffs its blue-black neck.
Just so Androgeos, seeing us, cringes with fear,
recoiling, struggling to flee but we attack,
flinging a ring of steel around his cohorts—
panic takes the Greeks unsure of their ground   480
and we cut them all to pieces.
Fortune fills our sails in that first clash
and Coroebus, flushed, fired with such success,
exults: 'Comrades, wherever Fortune points the way,
wherever the first road to safety leads, let's soldier on.
Exchange shields with the Greeks and wear their emblems.
Call it cunning or courage: who would ask in war?
Our enemies will arm us to the hilt.'
                            "With that he dons
Androgeos' crested helmet, his handsome blazoned shield
and straps a Greek sword to his hip, and comrades,   490
spirits rising, take his lead. Rhipeus, Dymas too
and our corps of young recruits—each fighter
arms himself in the loot that he just seized
and on we forge, blending in with the enemy,
battling time and again under strange gods,
fighting hand-to-hand in the blind dark
and many Greeks we send to the King of Death.
Some scatter back to their ships, making a run
for shore and safety. Others disgrace themselves,
so panicked they clamber back inside the monstrous horse,   500
burying into the womb they know so well.
                            "But, oh
how wrong to rely on gods dead set against you!
Watch: the virgin daughter of Priam, Cassandra,
torn from the sacred depths of Minerva's shrine,
dragged by the hair, raising her burning eyes
to the heavens, just her eyes, so helpless,
shackles kept her from raising her gentle hands.
Coroebus could not bear the sight of it—mad with rage
he flung himself at the Greek lines and met his death.

Closing ranks we charge after him, into the thick of battle   510
and face our first disaster. Down from the temple roof
come showers of lances hurled by our own comrades there,
duped by the look of our Greek arms, our Greek crests
that launched this grisly slaughter. And worse still,
the Greeks roaring with anger—we had saved Cassandra—
attack us from all sides! Ajax, fiercest of all and
Atreus' two sons and the whole Dolopian army,
wild as a rampaging whirlwind, gusts clashing,
the West- and the South- and Eastwind riding high
on the rushing horses of the Dawn, and the woods howl   520
and Nereus, thrashing his savage trident, churns up
the sea exploding in foam from its rocky depths.
And those Greeks we had put to rout, our ruse
in the murky night stampeding them headlong on
throughout the city—back they come, the first
to see that our shields and spears are naked lies,
to mark the words on our lips that jar with theirs.
In a flash, superior numbers overwhelm us.
Coroebus is first to go,
cut down by Peneleus' right hand he sprawls   530
at Minerva's shrine, the goddess, power of armies.
Rhipeus falls too, the most righteous man in Troy,
the most devoted to justice, true, but the gods
had other plans.
              "Hypanis, Dymas die as well,
run through by their own men—
                    "And you, Panthus,
not all your piety, all the sacred bands you wore
as Apollo's priest could save you as you fell.
Ashes of Ilium, last flames that engulfed my world—
I swear by you that in your last hour I never shrank
from the Greek spears, from any startling hazard of war—   540
if Fate had struck me down, my sword-arm earned it all.
Now we are swept away, Iphitus, Pelias with me,
one weighed down with age and the other slowed
by a wound Ulysses gave him—heading straight

for Priam's palace, driven there by the outcries.

"And there, I tell you, a pitched battle flares!
You'd think no other battles could match its fury,
nowhere else in the city were people dying so.
Invincible Mars rears up to meet us face-to-face
with waves of Greeks assaulting the roofs, we see them   550
choking the gateway, under a tortoise-shell of shields,
and the scaling ladders cling to the steep ramparts—
just at the gates the raiders scramble up the rungs,
shields on their left arms thrust out for defense,
their right hands clutching the gables.
Over against them, Trojans ripping the tiles
and turrets from all their roofs—the end is near,
they can see it now, at the brink of death, desperate
for weapons, some defense, and these, these missiles they send
reeling down on the Greeks' heads—the gilded beams,   560
the inlaid glory of all our ancient fathers.
Comrades below, posted in close-packed ranks,
block the entries, swordpoints drawn and poised.
My courage renewed, I rush to relieve the palace,
brace the defenders, bring the defeated strength.

"There was a secret door, a hidden passage
linking the wings of Priam's house—remote,
far to the rear. Long as our realm still stood,
Andromache, poor woman, would often go this way,
unattended, to Hector's parents, taking the boy   570
Astyanax by the hand to see grandfather Priam.
I slipped through the door, up to the jutting roof
where the doomed Trojans were hurling futile spears.
There was a tower soaring high at the peak toward the sky,
our favorite vantage point for surveying all of Troy
and the Greek fleet and camp. We attacked that tower
with iron crowbars, just where the upper-story planks
showed loosening joints—we rocked it, wrenched it free
of its deep moorings and all at once we heaved it toppling
down with a crash, trailing its wake of ruin to grind   580

the massed Greeks assaulting left and right. But on
came Greek reserves, no letup, the hail of rocks,
the missiles of every kind would never cease.

    "There at the very edge of the front gates
springs Pyrrhus, son of Achilles, prancing in arms,
aflash in his shimmering brazen sheath like a snake
buried the whole winter long under frozen turf,
swollen to bursting, fed full on poisonous weeds
and now it springs into light, sloughing its old skin
to glisten sleek in its newfound youth, its back slithering,   590
coiling, its proud chest rearing high to the sun,
its triple tongue flickering through its fangs.
Backing him now comes Periphas, giant fighter,
Automedon too, Achilles' henchman, charioteer
who bore the great man's armor—backing Pyrrhus,
the young fighters from Scyros raid the palace,
hurling firebrands at the roofs. Out in the lead,
Pyrrhus seizes a double-axe and batters the rocky sill
and ripping the bronze posts out of their sockets,
hacking the rugged oaken planks of the doors,   600
makes a breach, a gaping maw, and there, exposed,
the heart of the house, the sweep of the colonnades,
the palace depths of the old kings and Priam lie exposed
and they see the armed sentries bracing at the portals.

    "But all in the house is turmoil, misery, groans,
the echoing chambers ring with cries of women,
wails of mourning hit the golden stars.
Mothers scatter in panic down the palace halls
and embrace the pillars, cling to them, kiss them hard.
But on he comes, Pyrrhus with all his father's force,   610
no bolts, not even the guards can hold him back—
under the ram's repeated blows the doors cave in,
the doorposts, prised from their sockets, crash flat.
Force makes a breach and the Greeks come storming through,
butcher the sentries, flood the entire place with men-at-arms.
No river so wild, so frothing in spate, bursting its banks

to overpower the dikes, anything in its way, its cresting
tides stampeding in fury down on the fields to sweep
the flocks and stalls across the open plain.
I saw him myself, Pyrrhus crazed with carnage   620
and Atreus' two sons just at the threshold—

                                        "I saw
Hecuba with her hundred daughters and daughters-in-law,
saw Priam fouling with blood the altar fires
he himself had blessed.

                        "Those fifty bridal-chambers
filled with the hope of children's children still to come,
the pillars proud with trophies, gilded with Eastern gold,
they all come tumbling down—
and the Greeks hold what the raging fire spares.

    "Perhaps you wonder how Priam met his end.
When he saw his city stormed and seized, his gates   630
wrenched apart, the enemy camped in his palace depths,
the old man dons his armor long unused, he clamps it
round his shoulders shaking with age and, all for nothing,
straps his useless sword to his hip, then makes
for the thick of battle, out to meet his death.
At the heart of the house an ample altar stood,
naked under the skies,
an ancient laurel bending over the shrine,
embracing our household gods within its shade.
Here, flocking the altar, Hecuba and her daughters   640
huddled, blown headlong down like doves by a black storm—
clutching, all for nothing, the figures of their gods.
Seeing Priam decked in the arms he'd worn as a young man,
'Are you insane?' she cries, 'poor husband, what impels you
to strap that sword on now? Where are you rushing?
Too late for such defense, such help. Not even
my own Hector, if *he* came to the rescue now . . .
Come to me, Priam. This altar will shield us all
or else you'll die with us.'

                        "With those words,
drawing him toward her there, she made a place   650

for the old man beside the holy shrine.
          "Suddenly,
look, a son of Priam, Polites, just escaped
from slaughter at Pyrrhus' hands, comes racing in
through spears, through enemy fighters, fleeing down
the long arcades and deserted hallways—badly wounded,
Pyrrhus hot on his heels, a weapon poised for the kill,
about to seize him, about to run him through and pressing
home as Polites reaches his parents and collapses,
vomiting out his lifeblood before their eyes.
At that, Priam, trapped in the grip of death,   660
not holding back, not checking his words, his rage:
'You!' he cries, 'you and your vicious crimes!
If any power on high recoils at such an outrage,
let the gods repay you for all your reckless work,
grant you the thanks, the rich reward you've earned.
You've made me see my son's death with my own eyes,
defiled a father's sight with a son's lifeblood.
You say you're Achilles' son? You lie! Achilles
never treated his enemy Priam so. No, he honored
a suppliant's rights, he blushed to betray my trust,   670
he restored my Hector's bloodless corpse for burial,
sent me safely home to the land I rule!'
          "With that
and with all his might the old man flings his spear—
but too impotent now to pierce, it merely grazes
Pyrrhus' brazen shield that blocks its way
and clings there, dangling limp from the boss,
all for nothing. Pyrrhus shouts back: 'Well then,
down you go, a messenger to my father, Peleus' son!
Tell him about my vicious work, how Neoptolemus
degrades his father's name—don't you forget.   680
Now—die!'
      "That said, he drags the old man
straight to the altar, quaking, slithering on through
slicks of his son's blood, and twisting Priam's hair
in his left hand, his right hand sweeping forth his sword—
a flash of steel—he buries it hilt-deep in the king's flank.

"Such was the fate of Priam, his death, his lot on earth,
with Troy blazing before his eyes, her ramparts down,
the monarch who once had ruled in all his glory
the many lands of Asia, Asia's many tribes.
A powerful trunk is lying on the shore.   690
The head wrenched from the shoulders.
A corpse without a name.

                                      "Then, for the first time
the full horror came home to me at last. I froze.
The thought of my own dear father filled my mind
when I saw the old king gasping out his life
with that raw wound—both men were the same age—
and the thought of my Creusa, alone, abandoned,
our house plundered, our little Iulus' fate.
I look back—what forces still stood by me?
None. Totally spent in war, they'd all deserted,   700
down from the roofs they'd flung themselves to earth
or hurled their broken bodies in the flames.

                                      ["So,*
at just that moment I was the one man left
and then I saw her, clinging to Vesta's threshold,
hiding in silence, tucked away—Helen of Argos.
Glare of the fires lit my view as I looked down,
scanning the city left and right, and there she was . . .
terrified of the Trojans' hate, now Troy was overpowered,
terrified of the Greeks' revenge, her deserted husband's rage—
that universal Fury, a curse to Troy and her native land   710
and here she lurked, skulking, a thing of loathing
cowering at the altar: Helen. Out it flared,
the fire inside my soul, my rage ablaze to avenge
our fallen country—pay Helen back, crime for crime.

    "'So, this woman,' it struck me now, 'safe and sound
she'll look once more on Sparta, her native Greece?
She'll ride like a queen in triumph with her trophies?
Feast her eyes on her husband, parents, children too?

    *See Introduction, pp. 11–12.

Her retinue fawning round her, Phrygian ladies, slaves?
That—with Priam put to the sword? And Troy up in flames?   720
And time and again our Dardan shores have sweated blood?
Not for all the world. No fame, no memory to be won
for punishing a woman: such victory reaps no praise
but to stamp this abomination out as she deserves,
to punish her now, they'll sing my praise for *that*.
What joy, to glut my heart with the fires of vengeance,
bring some peace to the ashes of my people!'

   "Whirling words—I was swept away by fury now]
when all of a sudden there my loving mother stood
before my eyes, but I had never seen her so clearly,   730
her pure radiance shining down upon me through the night,
the goddess in all her glory, just as the gods behold
her build, her awesome beauty. Grasping my hand
she held me back, adding this from her rose-red lips:
'My son, what grief could incite such blazing anger?
Why such fury? And the love you bore me once,
where has it all gone? Why don't you look first
where you left your father, Anchises, spent with age?
Do your wife, Creusa, and son Ascanius still survive?
The Greek battalions are swarming round them all,   740
and if my love had never rushed to the rescue,
flames would have swept them off by now or
enemy sword-blades would have drained their blood.
Think: it's not that beauty, Helen, you should hate,
not even Paris, the man that you should blame, no,
it's the gods, the ruthless gods who are tearing down
the wealth of Troy, her toppling crown of towers.
Look around. I'll sweep it all away, the mist
so murky, dark, and swirling around you now,
it clouds your vision, dulls your mortal sight.   750
You are my son. Never fear my orders.
Never refuse to bow to my commands.
                              "'There,
yes, where you see the massive ramparts shattered,
blocks wrenched from blocks, the billowing smoke and ash—

it's Neptune himself, prising loose with his giant trident
the foundation-stones of Troy, he's making the walls quake,
ripping up the entire city by her roots.

                "'There's Juno,
cruelest in fury, first to commandeer the Scaean Gates,
sword at her hip and mustering comrades, shock troops
streaming out of the ships.

                "'Already up on the heights—   760
turn around and look—there's Pallas holding the fortress,
flaming out of the clouds, her savage Gorgon glaring.
Even Father himself, he's filling the Greek hearts
with courage, stamina—Jove in person spurring the gods
to fight the Trojan armies!

                "'Run for your life, my son.
Put an end to your labors. I will never leave you,
I will set you safe at your father's door.'

"Parting words. She vanished into the dense night.
And now they all come looming up before me,
terrible shapes, the deadly foes of Troy,   770
the gods gigantic in power.

                "Then at last
I saw it all, all Ilium settling into her embers,
Neptune's Troy, toppling over now from her roots
like a proud, veteran ash on its mountain summit,
chopped by stroke after stroke of the iron axe as
woodsmen fight to bring it down, and over and
over it threatens to fall, its boughs shudder,
its leafy crown quakes and back and forth it sways
till overwhelmed by its wounds, with a long last groan
it goes—torn up from its heights it crashes down   780
in ruins from its ridge . . .
Venus leading, down from the roof I climb
and win my way through fires and massing foes.
The spears recede, the flames roll back before me.

"At last, gaining the door of father's ancient house,
my first concern was to find the man, my first wish

to spirit him off, into the high mountain range,
but father, seeing Ilium razed from the earth,
refused to drag his life out now and suffer exile.
'You,' he argued, 'you in your prime, untouched by age,   790
your blood still coursing strong, you hearts of oak,
you are the ones to hurry your escape. Myself,
if the gods on high had wished me to live on,
they would have saved my palace for me here.
Enough—more than enough—that I have seen
one sack of my city, once survived its capture.
Here I lie, here laid out for death. Come say
your parting salutes and leave my body so.
I will find my own death, sword in hand:
my enemies keen for spoils will be so kind.   800
Death without burial? A small price to pay.
For years now, I've lingered out my life,
despised by the gods, a dead weight to men,
ever since the Father of Gods and King of Mortals
stormed at me with his bolt and scorched me with its fire.'

"So he said, planted there. Nothing could shake him now.
But we dissolved in tears, my wife, Creusa, Ascanius,
the whole household, begging my father not to pull
our lives down with him, adding his own weight
to the fate that dragged us down.   810
He still refuses, holds to his resolve,
clings to the spot. And again I rush to arms,
desperate to die myself. Where could I turn?
What were our chances now, at this point?
'What!' I cried. 'Did you, my own father,
dream that I could run away and desert you here?
How could such an outrage slip from a father's lips?
If it please the gods that nothing of our great city
shall survive—if you are bent on adding your own death
to the deaths of Troy and of all your loved ones too,   820
the doors of the deaths you crave are spread wide open.
Pyrrhus will soon be here, bathed in Priam's blood,
Pyrrhus who butchers sons in their fathers' faces,

slaughters fathers at the altar. Was it for this,
my loving mother, you swept me clear of the weapons,
free of the flames? Just to see the enemy camped
in the very heart of our house, to see my son, Ascanius,
see my father, my wife, Creusa, with them, sacrificed,
massacred in each other's blood?
                            'Arms, my comrades,
bring me arms! The last light calls the defeated.   830
Send me back to the Greeks, let me go back
to fight new battles. Not all of us here
will die today without revenge.'
                            "Now buckling on
my sword again and working my left arm through
the shieldstrap, grasping it tightly, just as I
was rushing out, right at the doors my wife, Creusa,
look, flung herself at my feet and hugged my knees
and raised our little Iulus up to his father.
'If you are going off to die,' she begged,
'then take us with you too,   840
to face the worst together. But if your battles
teach you to hope in arms, the arms you buckle on,
your first duty should be to guard our house.
Desert us, leave us now—to whom? Whom?
Little Iulus, your father and your wife,
so I once was called.'
                            "So Creusa cries,
her wails of anguish echoing through the house
when out of the blue an omen strikes—a marvel!
Now as we held our son between our hands
and both our grieving faces, a tongue of fire,   850
watch, flares up from the crown of Iulus' head,
a subtle flame licking his downy hair, feeding
around the boy's brow, and though it never harmed him,
panicked, we rush to shake the flame from his curls
and smother the holy fire, damp it down with water.
But Father Anchises lifts his eyes to the stars in joy
and stretching his hands toward the sky, sings out:
'Almighty Jove! If any prayer can persuade you now,

look down on us—that's all I ask—if our devotion
has earned it, grant us another omen, Father,   860
seal this first clear sign.'
                              "No sooner said
than an instant peal of thunder crashes on the left
and down from the sky a shooting star comes gliding,
trailing a flaming torch to irradiate the night
as it comes sweeping down. We watch it sailing
over the topmost palace roofs to bury itself,
still burning bright, in the forests of Mount Ida,
blazing its path with light, leaving a broad furrow,
a fiery wake, and miles around the smoking sulfur fumes.
Won over at last, my father rises to his full height   870
and prays to the gods and reveres that holy star:
'No more delay, not now! You gods of my fathers,
now I follow wherever you lead me, I am with you.
Safeguard our house, safeguard my grandson Iulus!
This sign is yours: Troy rests in your power.
I give way, my son. No more refusals.
I will go with you, your comrade.'
                                    "So he yielded
but now the roar of flames grows louder all through Troy
and the seething floods of fire are rolling closer.
'So come, dear father, climb up onto my shoulders!   880
I will carry you on my back. This labor of love
will never wear me down. Whatever falls to us now,
we both will share one peril, one path to safety.
Little Iulus, walk beside me, and you, my wife,
follow me at a distance, in my footsteps.
Servants, listen closely . . .
Just past the city walls a grave-mound lies
where an old shrine of forsaken Ceres stands
with an ancient cypress growing close beside it—
our fathers' reverence kept it green for years.   890
Coming by many routes, it's there we meet,
our rendezvous. And you, my father, carry
our hearth-gods now, our fathers' sacred vessels.
I, just back from the war and fresh from slaughter,

I must not handle the holy things—it's wrong—
not till I cleanse myself in running springs.'
                              "With that,
over my broad shoulders and round my neck I spread
a tawny lion's skin for a cloak, and bowing down,
I lift my burden up. Little Iulus, clutching
my right hand, keeps pace with tripping steps.   900
My wife trails on behind. And so we make our way
along the pitch-dark paths, and I who had never flinched
at the hurtling spears or swarming Greek assaults—
now every stir of wind, every whisper of sound
alarms me, anxious both for the child beside me
and burden on my back. And then, nearing the gates,
thinking we've all got safely through, I suddenly
seem to catch the steady tramp of marching feet
and father, peering out through the darkness, cries:
'Run for it now, my boy, you must. They're closing in,   910
I can see their glinting shields, their flashing bronze!'

    "Then in my panic something strange, some enemy power
robbed me of my senses. Lost, I was leaving behind
familiar paths, at a run down blind dead ends
when—
        "Oh dear god, my wife, Creusa—
torn from me by a brutal fate! What then,
did she stop in her tracks or lose her way?
Or exhausted, sink down to rest? Who knows?
I never set my eyes on her again.
I never looked back, she never crossed my mind—   920
Creusa, lost—not till we reached that barrow
sacred to ancient Ceres where, with all our people
rallied at last, she alone was missing. Lost
to her friends, her son, her husband—gone forever.
Raving, I blamed them all, the gods, the human race—
what crueler blow did I feel the night that Troy went down?
Ascanius, father Anchises, and all the gods of Troy,
entrusting them to my friends, I hide them well away
in a valley's shelter, don my burnished gear

and back I go to Troy . . .   930
my mind steeled to relive the whole disaster,
retrace my route through the whole city now
and put my life in danger one more time.
                                          "First then,
back to the looming walls, the shadowy rear gates
by which I'd left the city, back I go in my tracks,
retracing, straining to find my footsteps in the dark,
with terror at every turn, the very silence makes me cringe.
Then back to my house I go—if only, only she's gone there—
but the Greeks have flooded in, seized the entire place.
All over now. Devouring fire whipped by the winds   940
goes churning into the rooftops, flames surging
over them, scorching blasts raging up the sky.
On I go and again I see the palace of Priam
set on the heights, but there in colonnades
deserted now, in the sanctuary of Juno, there
stand the elite watchmen, Phoenix, ruthless Ulysses
guarding all their loot. All the treasures of Troy
hauled from the burning shrines—the sacramental tables,
bowls of solid gold and the holy robes they'd seized
from every quarter—Greeks, piling high the plunder.   950
Children and trembling mothers rounded up
in a long, endless line.
                          "Why, I even dared fling
my voice through the dark, my shouts filled the streets
as time and again, overcome with grief I called out
'Creusa!' Nothing, no reply, and again 'Creusa!'
But then as I madly rushed from house to house,
no end in sight, abruptly, right before my eyes
I saw her stricken ghost, my own Creusa's shade.
But larger than life, the life I'd known so well.
I froze. My hackles bristled, voice choked in my throat,   960
and my wife spoke out to ease me of my anguish:
'My dear husband, why so eager to give yourself
to such mad flights of grief? It's not without
the will of the gods these things have come to pass.
But the gods forbid you to take Creusa with you,

bound from Troy together. The king of lofty Olympus
won't allow it. A long exile is your fate . . .
the vast plains of the sea are yours to plow
until you reach Hesperian land, where Lydian Tiber
flows with its smooth march through rich and loamy fields,   970
a land of hardy people. There great joy and a kingdom
are yours to claim, and a queen to make your wife.
Dispel your tears for Creusa whom you loved.
I will never behold the high and mighty pride
of their palaces, the Myrmidons, the Dolopians,
or go as a slave to some Greek matron, no, not I,
daughter of Dardanus that I am, the wife of Venus' son.
The Great Mother of Gods detains me on these shores.
And now farewell. Hold dear the son we share,
we love together.'
                          "These were her parting words   980
and for all my tears—I longed to say so much—
dissolving into the empty air she left me now.
Three times I tried to fling my arms around her neck,
three times I embraced—nothing . . . her phantom
sifting through my fingers,
light as wind, quick as a dream in flight.
                                              "Gone—
and at last the night was over. Back I went to my people
and I was amazed to see what throngs of new companions
had poured in to swell our numbers, mothers, men,
our forces gathered for exile, grieving masses.   990
They had come together from every quarter,
belongings, spirits ready for me to lead them
over the sea to whatever lands I'd choose.
And now the morning star was mounting above
the high crests of Ida, leading on the day.
The Greeks had taken the city, blocked off every gate.
No hope of rescue now. So I gave way at last and
lifting my father, headed toward the mountains."

BOOK THREE

Landfalls, Ports of Call

" Now that it pleased the gods to crush the power of Asia
and Priam's innocent people, now proud Troy had fallen—
Neptune's city a total ruin smoking on the ground—
signs from the high gods drive us on, exiles now,
searching earth for a home in some neglected land.
We labor to build a fleet—hard by Antandros,
under the heights of Phrygian Ida—knowing nothing.
Where would destiny take us? Where are we to settle?
We muster men for crews. Summer has just begun
when father commands us: 'Hoist our sails to Fate!'   10
And I launch out in tears and desert our native land,
the old safe haven, the plains where Troy once stood.
So I take to the open sea, an exile outward bound
with son and comrades, gods of hearth and home
and the great gods themselves.

                    "Just in the offing

lies the land of Mars, the boundless farmlands tilled
by the Thracian fieldhands, ruled in the old days
by merciless Lycurgus. His realm was a friend
of Troy for years, our household gods in league
so long as our fortunes lasted. Well, here I sail   20
and begin to build our first walls on the curving shore,
though Fate will block our way—and I give the town
the name of Aenus modeled on my own.
                                                    "Now,
making offerings to my mother, Dione's daughter,
and to the gods who bless new ventures, I was poised,
there on the beach, to slaughter a pure white bull
to Jove above all who rules the Powers on high.
Nearby I chanced on a rise of ground topped off
by thickets bristling dogwood and myrtle spears.
I tried to tear some green shoots from the brush   30
to make a canopy for the altar with leafy boughs,
when a dreadful, ghastly sight, too strange for words,
strikes my eyes.
                        "Soon as I tear the first stalk
from its roots and rip it up from the earth . . .
dark blood oozes out and fouls the soil with filth.
Icy shudders rack my limbs—my blood chills with fear.
But again I try, I tear at another stubborn stalk—
I'll probe this mystery to its hidden roots,
and again the dark blood runs from the torn bark.
Deeply shaken, I pray to the country nymphs   40
and Father Mars who strides the fields of Thrace:
'Make this sight a blessing, lift the omen's weight!'
But now as I pitch at a third stalk, doubling my effort,
knees bracing against the sand, struggling to pry it loose—
shall I tell you or hold my tongue?—I hear it, clearly,
a wrenching groan rising up from the deep mound,
a cry heaving into the air: 'Why, Aeneas,
why mangle this wretched flesh? Spare the body
buried here—spare your own pure hands, don't stain them!
I am no stranger to you. I was born in Troy,   50
and the blood you see is oozing from no tree.

Oh escape from this savage land, I beg you,
flee these grasping shores! I am Polydorus.
Here they impaled me, an iron planting of lances
covered my body—now they sprout in stabbing spears!'

    "Then I was awestruck, stunned by doubt and dread.
My hackles bristled, voice choked in my throat.
                                    "This Polydorus:
the doomed Priam had once dispatched him in secret,
bearing a great weight of gold, to be maintained
by the King of Thrace when Priam lost his faith   60
in Trojan arms and saw his city gripped by siege.
That Thracian, once the power of Troy was shattered,
our Trojan fortunes gone—he joins forces with Agamemnon,
siding with his victorious arms, and breaks all human laws.
He hacks Polydorus down and commandeers the gold.
To what extremes won't you compel our hearts,
you accursed lust for gold?
When dread has left my bones, I bring this omen
sent by the gods before our chosen Trojan captains,
my father first of all: I had to have their judgment.   70
With one mind they insist we leave this wicked land
where the bonds of hospitality are so stained—
sail out on the Southwind now!
                            "And so
we give Polydorus a fresh new burial,
piling masses of earth on his first mound,
raising to all the shades below an altar dark
with the wreaths of grief and dead-black cypress
ringed by Trojan women, hair unbound in mourning.
We offer up full bowls, foaming with warm milk,
and our cups of hallowed blood. And so we lay   80
his soul in the grave as our voices raise his name,
the resounding last farewell.
                            "Then in the first light
when we can trust the waves—a breeze has calmed the surf
and a gentle rustling Southwind makes the rigging sing,
inviting us to sea—my crewmen crowd the beaches,

launch the ships, and out from port we sail,
leaving the land and cities sinking in our wake.
Mid-sea there lies the sacred island of Delos,
loved by the Nereids' mother, Aegean Neptune too.
Apollo the Archer, finding his birthplace drifting   90
shore to shore, like a proper son had chained it fast
to Myconos' steep coast and Gyaros, made it stable,
a home for men that scorns the winds' assaults.
Here I sail, and here a haven, still, serene,
receives our weary bodies safe and sound . . .
Landing, we just begin to admire Apollo's city
when King Anius, king of men and priest of the god,
his brow wreathed with the bands and holy laurel leaves,
comes to meet us, spotting a long-lost friend, Anchises.
Clasping our host's hands, we file toward his palace.
                                        "There,   100
awed by the shrine of god, built strong of ancient stone,
I begged Apollo: 'Grant us our own home, god of Thymbra!
Grant us weary men some walls of our own, some sons,
a city that will last. Safeguard this second Troy,
this remnant left by the Greeks and cruel Achilles.
Whom do we follow? Where do we go? Command us,
where do we settle now? Grant us a sign, Father,
flow into our hearts!'
                        "I had barely spoken
when all at once, everything seemed to tremble,
the gates of the god, Apollo's laurel-tree,   110
the entire mountain around us seemed to quake,
the tripod moaned, the sacred shrine swung open.
We flung ourselves on the ground, and a voice sounded out:
'Sons of Dardanus, hardy souls, your fathers' land
that gave you birth will take you back again,
restored to her fertile breast.
Search for your ancient mother. There your house,
the line of Aeneas, will rule all parts of the world—
your sons' sons and all their descendants down the years.'
And Phoebus' words were met by a ringing burst of joy   120
mixed with confusion, all our voices rising, asking:

'Where is this city? Where is the land that Apollo
calls us wanderers to, the land of our return?'

　"Then my father, mulling over our old traditions,
answers: 'Lords of Troy, learn where your best hopes rest.
An island rises in mid-sea—Crete, great Jove's own land
where the first Mount Ida rears, the cradle of our people.
The Cretans live in a hundred spacious cities, rich domains.
From there—if I recall what I heard—our first father,
Teucer sailed to Troy, Cape Rhoeteum, picked the point   130
and founded his kingdom on those shores. But Troy
and her soaring ramparts were not standing yet,
the people lived in valleys, deep in lowlands.
From Crete came our Great Mother of Mount Cybelus,
her Corybantes' clashing cymbals, her grove on Ida,
the sacred binding silence kept for her mystic rites
and the team of lions yoked to our Lady's chariot.
So come, follow the gods' commands that lead us on.
Placate the winds, set sail for Cnossus' country.
It's no long journey. If only Jove is with us now,   140
the third dawn will find us beached on the shores of Crete.'

　"With that, he slaughtered fitting beasts on the altars:
a bull to Neptune, a bull to you, our noble Apollo,
a black ram to the winter storms, and a white ram
to the Zephyrs fair and warm.
　　　　　　　　"Rumor flies that Idomeneus,
famous Cretan prince, has fled his father's kingdom,
an exile, and the shores of Crete are now deserted,
clear of enemies, homes derelict, standing ready
for us to settle. Out of Ortygia's port we sail,
winging the sea to race on past the Naxos ridge   150
where the Maenads revel, past the lush green
islands of Donusa and Olearos, Paros, gleaming
white as its marble—through the Cyclades strewn
across the sea and through the straits we speed,
their waters churned to foam by the crowded shorelines,
shipmates racing each other, spurring each other on:

'On to Crete,' they're shouting, 'back to our fatherland!'
And a rising sternwind surges, drives our vessels on
and at last we're gliding into the old Curetes' harbor.
Inspired, I start to build the city walls we crave.   160
I call it Pergamum, yes, and my people all rejoice
at the old Trojan name. I urge them to cherish
their hearths and homes, erect a citadel strong
to shield them well.
                        "Our ships were no sooner hauled
onto dry land, our young crewmen busy with weddings,
plowing the fresh soil while I was drafting laws
and assigning homes, when suddenly, no warning,
out of some foul polluted quarter of the skies
a plague struck now, a heartrending scourge
attacking our bodies, rotting trees and crops,   170
one whole year of death . . .
Men surrendered their own sweet lives
or dragged their decrepit bodies on and on.
And the Dog Star scorched the green fields barren,
the grasses shriveled, blighted crops refused us food.

    "'Double back on the sea-lanes, back to Delos now,
Apollo's oracle!'—so my father Anchises urges—
'Pray for the god's good will and ask him there:
where will they end, our backbreaking labors?
Where can we turn for help from all our toil?   180
What new course do we set?'
                        "Night had fallen
and sleep embraced all living things on earth.
But the sacred images of our Trojan household gods,
those I'd saved from the fires that swept through Troy . . .
Now as I lay asleep they seemed to stand before me,
clear before my eyes, so vivid, washed in the light
of the full moon flooding in through deepset windows.
Then the Powers spoke out to ease me of my anguish:
'All that Apollo will predict if you return to Delos,
he tells you here, of his own free will he sends us   190
here before your doors. You and your force-at-arms,

we followed you all when Troy was burnt to rubble.
We are the gods, with you at the helm, who crossed
the billowing sea in ships. And one day we shall lift
your children to the stars and exalt your city's power.
For a destiny so great, great walls you must erect
and never shrink from the long labor of exile, no,
you must leave this home. These are not the shores
Apollo of Delos urged. He never commanded you
to settle here on Crete.
                         "'There is a country—   200
the Greeks called it Hesperia, Land of the West,
an ancient land, mighty in war and rich in soil.
Oenotrians settled it; now we hear their descendants
call their kingdom Italy, after their leader, Italus.
There lies our true home. There Dardanus was born,
there Iasius. Fathers, founders of our people.
Rise up now! Rejoice, relay our message, certain
beyond all doubt, to your father full of years.
Seek out the town of Corythus, sail for Italy!
Jove denies you the fields of Dicte: Crete.'   210

"Thunderstruck by the vision, the gods' voice—
this was no empty dream, I saw them clear before me,
their features, face-to-face, their hair crowned with wreaths.
At the sight an icy sweat goes rippling down my body,
I tear myself from bed, I raise my hands and voice
in prayer to the skies and tip a pure, unmixed
libation on the hearth. Gladly, the rite performed,
I unfold the whole event to Anchises, point by point.
He recalls at once the two lines of our race, two parents:
his own error, his late mistake about ancient places.   220
'My son,' he says, 'so pressed by the fate of Troy—
Cassandra alone made such a prophecy to me . . .
Now I recall how she'd reveal our destination,
Hesperia: time and again repeating it by name,
repeating the name of Italy. But who believed
a Trojan expedition could reach Italian shores?
Who was moved by Cassandra's visions then?

Yield to Apollo now and take the better course—
the god shows the way!'
                           "So Anchises urges
and all are overjoyed to follow his command.   230
Leaving a few behind, we launch out from Crete,
deserting another home, and set our sails again,
scudding on buoyant hulls through wastes of ocean.

                                             "As soon
as our ships had reached the high seas, no land in sight,
no longer—water at all points, at all points the sky—
looming over our heads a pitch-dark thunderhead
brings on night and storm, ruffling the swells black.
At once the winds whip up the sea, huge waves heaving,
strewing, flinging us down the sheer abyss, the cloudbanks
swallowing up the daylight, rain-soaked night wipes out the sky   240
and flash on flash of lightning bursts from the torn clouds—
we're whirled off course, yawing blind in the big waves.
Even Palinurus, he swears he can't tell night from day,
scanning the heavens he finds nothing but walls of sea,
the pilot's bearings lost. For three whole days we rush,
the waves driving us wildly on, the sun blotted out,
for as many nights we're robbed of stars to steer by.
Then at last, at the fourth dawn—landfall, rearing
up into view, some mountains clear in the offing,
a rising curl of smoke. Down come the sails,   250
the crewmen leap to the oars, no time to lose,
they bend to it, churn the spray and sweep
the clear blue sea.
                      "So I was saved from the deep,
the shores of the Strophades first to take me in.
Strophades—Greek name for the Turning Islands—
lie in the Great Ionian Sea.
Here grim Celaeno and sister Harpies settled
after Phineus' doors were locked against them all
and they fled in fear from the tables where they'd gorged.
The Harpies . . . no monsters on earth more cruel,   260
no scourge more savage, no wrath of the gods has
ever raised its head from the Styx's waters.

The faces of girls, but birds! A loathsome ooze
discharges from their bellies, talons for hands,
their jaws deathly white with a hunger never sated.

  "Gaining that landfall, making port, what do we see
but sleek lusty herds of cattle grazing the plains,
flocks of goats unguarded, cropping grassland?
We charge them with drawn swords, calling out
to the gods, to Jove himself, to share our kill.   270
Then on the halfmoon bay we build up mounds of turf
and fall to the rich feast. But all of a sudden, watch,
with a ghastly swoop from the hills the Harpies swarm us—
ruffling, clattering wingbeats—ripping our food to bits,
polluting it all with their foul, corrupting claws,
their obscene shrieks bursting from the stench.
Again, in a deep recess under rocky cliffs,
[screened around by trees and trembling shade,]
we deck our tables out, relight the altar-fire
but again, from some new height, some hidden nest   280
the rout comes screaming at their quarry, flapping round us,
slashing with claw-feet, hook-beaks fouling our meal.
'To arms!' I command the men,
'wage all-out war against this brutal crew!'
All hands snap to orders, hiding swords away
in the tall grasses, covering shields as well.
So when they make their roaring swoop along the bay,
Misenus, poised on a lookout, sounds the alarm,
a brazen trumpet blast, and the men attack,
geared for a strange new form of combat, fighting   290
to hack these vile seabirds down with bloody swords.
But their feathers take no stab-wounds, backs no scars
and swift on their wings they soar toward the heavens,
leaving behind half-eaten prey and trails of filth.

  "All but one. Perched on a beetling crag, Celaeno,
prophet of doom—her shrieks erupted from her breast:
'So, war as well now? Gearing for battle, are you?
You, the sons of Laomedon, as if to atone

for the butchery of our cattle, our young bulls?
You'd force the innocent Harpies from their fathers' kingdom?   300
Take what I say to heart and stamp it in your minds:
this prophecy the almighty Father made to Phoebus
and Phoebus made to me, the greatest of the Furies,
and I reveal to you. Italy is the land you seek?
You call on the winds to sweep you there by sea?
To Italy you will go. Permitted to enter port
but never granted a city girded round by ramparts,
not before some terrible hunger and your attack on us—
outrageous slaughter—drive you to gnaw your platters
with your teeth!'
                              "So Celaeno shrieked   310
and taking flight, dashed back to the forest.
The blood of my comrades froze with instant dread.
Their morale sank, they lost all heart for war,
pressing me now to pray, to beg for peace, whether
our foes are goddesses, yes, or filthy, lethal birds.
Then father Anchises, stretching his hands toward the sea,
cries out to the Great Powers, pledging them their due rites:
'Gods, ward off these threats. Gods, beat back disaster!
Be gracious, guard your faithful.'"

    "We cast off cables and let the sheets run free,   320
unfurling sail as a Southwind bellies out the canvas.
We launch out on the foaming waves as wind and helmsman
call our course. Now over the high seas we raise up
woody Zacynthos, Dulichium, Same, Neritos' crags,
past Ithaca's rocky coast we race, Laertes' realm,
cursing the land that spawned the vicious Ulysses.
And soon Leucata's cloudy summit comes into view and
Apollo's shrine on its rugged headland, dread of sailors.
Exhausted, we land at Actium, trek to the little town.
Anchors run from prows, the sterns line the shore.
                                        "So,   330
exceeding our hopes, we win our way to solid ground at last.
We cleanse ourselves with the rites we owe to Jove
and make the altars blaze with votive gifts,

then crowd the Actian shore with Trojan games.
My shipmates strip and glistening sleek with oil,
wrestle the old Trojan way, our spirits high—
we'd skimmed past such a flurry of Argive cities,
holding true to our flight through waters held by foes.
Then as the sun rolls round the giant arc of the year,
icy winter arrives and a Northwind roughens up the seas.   340
Fronting the temple doors, I bolt the brazen shield
great Abas bore, and I engrave the offering
with a verse:

       AENEAS DEVOTES THESE ARMS
      SEIZED FROM GRECIAN VICTORS.

              "Then I command
the crews to embark from harbor, man the thwarts.
And shipmates race each other, thrashing the waves,
plunging along Phaeacia's mist-enshrouded heights
to lose them far astern, skirting Epirus' coasts,
sailing into Chaonia's port and we finally reach
the hilltop town, Buthrotum.

              "Here an incredible story   350
meets our ears: that Helenus, Priam's son, holds sway
over these Greek towns, that he had won the throne
and wife of Pyrrhus, son of Achilles—Andromache
was wed once more to a man of Trojan stock.
Astonishing! My heart burned with longing,
irresistible longing to see my old friend
and learn about this remarkable twist of fate . . .
Setting out from the harbor, leaving ships and shore
I chanced to see Andromache pouring out libations
to the dead—the ritual foods, the gifts of grief—   360
in a grove before the city, banked by a stream
the exiles made believe was Simois River. Just now
tipping wine to her husband's ashes, she implored
Hector's shade to visit his tomb, an empty mound
of grassy earth, crowned with the double altars
she had blessed, a place to shed her tears.
As she saw me coming, flanked by Trojan troops,
she lost control, afraid of a wonder so extreme.

Watching, rigid, suddenly warmth leaves her bones,
she faints, and after a long pause barely finds   370
the breath to whisper: 'That face, it's really you?
You're real, a messenger come my way? Son of the goddess—
still alive? Or if the light of life has left you,
where's my Hector now?'
                                        "Breaking off,
Andromache wept, her wailing filled the grove,
inconsolable. I could scarcely interject a word,
dismayed, I stuttered a few breathless phrases:
'Alive, yes. Still dragging out my life . . .
through the worst the world can offer. Have no doubt,
what you see is real. Oh what fate has overpowered you,   380
robbed of such a husband? Or does fortune shine again
on you, Hector's Andromache, just as you deserve?
Are you still married to Pyrrhus?'
                                        "Eyes lowered,
her voice subdued, she murmured: 'She was the one,
the happiest one of all, Priam's virgin daughter
doomed to die at our enemy's tomb—Achilles—
under the looming walls of Troy. No captive slave
allotted to serve the lust of a conquering hero's bed!
But I, our home in flames, was shipped over strange seas,
I bowed to the high and mighty pride of Achilles' son,   390
produced him a child—in slavery. Then, keen to marry
a Spartan bride, Hermione, granddaughter of Leda,
he turned me over to Helenus, slave to slave.
But Orestes burned with love for his stolen bride,
spurred by the Furies for his crimes, he seized Pyrrhus,
quite off guard, and butchered him at his father's altar.
At Pyrrhus' death, part of his kingdom passed to Helenus,
who named the plains Chaonian—all this realm, Chaonia,
after the Trojan Chaon, and built a Trojan fortress,
the Ilian stronghold rising on this ridge.
                                        "'But you,   400
what following winds, what Fates have sailed you here?
What god urged you, all unknowing, to our shores?
And what of your son, Ascanius? Still alive,

still breathing the breath of life? Your son,
whom in the old days at Troy . . .
does he still love his mother lost and gone?
Do his father Aeneas and uncle Hector fire his heart
with the old courage, his heroic forebears' spirit?'

   "A torrent of questions—weeping futile tears,
she sobs her long lament as Priam's warrior son,   410
Helenus, comes from the walls with full cortege.
Recognizing his kin, he gladly leads us home,
each word of welcome breaking through his tears.
And I as I walk, I recognize a little Troy,
a miniature, mimicking our great Trojan towers,
and a dried-up brook they call the river Xanthus,
and I put my arms around a cutdown Scaean Gate.
And all my Trojans join me,
drinking deep of a Trojan city's welcome.
The king ushered us into generous colonnades,   420
in the heart of the court we offered Bacchus wine
and feasted from golden plates, all cups held high.

   "Now time wears on, day in, day out, and the breezes
lure our sails, a Southwind rippling in our canvas.
So I approach the prophet-king with questions:
'Son of Troy and seer of the gods, you know the will
of Phoebus Apollo, know his Clarian tripods and his laurel,
know the stars, the cries of birds, the omens quick on the wing.
Please, tell me—all the signs foretold me a happy voyage,
yes, and the will of all the gods impels me now   430
to sail for Italy, seek that far-off land.
The Harpy Celaeno alone foretold a monstrous sign,
chanting out the unspeakable—withering wrath to come
and the ghastly pangs of famine. What dangers, tell me,
to steer away from first? What course to set
to master these ordeals?'
                              "At that, Helenus
first performs a sacrifice, slaughters many bulls.
He prays the gods for peace, he looses the sacred ribbons

round his hallowed head and taking me by the hand
he leads me to your shrine, Apollo, stirred with awe   440
by your vibrant power, and at once this prophecy
comes singing from the priest's inspired lips:
'Son of the goddess, surely proof is clear,
the highest sanctions shine upon your voyage.
So the King of the Gods has sorted out your fate,
so rolls your life, as the world rolls through its changes.
Now, few out of many truths I will reveal to you,
so you can cross the welcoming seas more safely,
moor secure in a Latian harbor. The Fates
have forbidden Helenus to know the rest.   450
Saturnian Juno says I may not speak a word . . .

    "'First, that Italian land you think so near—
all unknowing, planning to ease into its harbors—
lies far off. A long wandering path will part you
miles from that shore by a lengthy stretch of coast.
So, first you must bend your oar in Sicilian seas
and cross in your ships the salt Italian waves,
the lakes of the Underworld and Aeaea, Circe's isle,
before you can build your city safe on solid ground.
I will give you a sign. Guard it in your heart.   460
When at an anxious time by a secret river's run,
under the oaks along the bank you find a great sow
stretched on her side with thirty pigs just farrowed,
a snow-white mother with snow-white young at her dugs:
that will be the place to found your city, there
your repose from labor lies. No reason to fear
that prophecy, the horror of eating your own platters.
The Fates will find the way. Apollo comes to your call.

    "'But set sail from our land, steer clear of Italy's coast,
the closest coast to our own, washed by our own seas—   470
every seaboard town is manned by hostile Greeks.
Here the Narycian Locri built their walls
and troops of Cretan Idomeneus from Lyctos
commandeered the Sallentine level fields.

Here little Petelia built by Philoctetes,
the Meliboean chief, lies safe behind its walls.
Once you have passed them all, moored your ships
on the far shore and set up altars on the beach
to perform your vows, then cloak yourselves in purple,
veil your heads, so while the hallowed fires are burning   480
in honor of the gods, no enemy presence can break in
and disrupt the omens. Your comrades, you yourself
must hold fast to this sacred rite, this custom.
Your sons' sons must keep it pure forever.
                                    "'Now then,
launching out as the wind bears you toward Sicilian shores
and Pelorus' crowded headlands open up a passage,
steer for the lands to port, the seas to port,
in a long southern sweep around the coast,
but stay clear of the heavy surf to starboard.
These lands, they say, were once an immense unbroken mass   490
but long ago—such is the power of time to work great change
as the ages pass—some vast convulsion sprang them apart,
a surge of the sea burst in between them, cleaving
Sicily clear of Hesperia's flanks, dividing lands
and towns into two coasts, rushing between them
down a narrow tiderip.
                        "'But now Scylla to starboard
blocks your way, with never-sated Charybdis off to port—
three times a day, into the plunging whirlpool of her abyss
she gulps down floods of sea, then heaves them back in the air,
pelting the stars with spray. Scylla lurks in her blind cave,   500
thrusting out her mouths and hauling ships on her rocks.
She's human at first glance, down to the waist a girl
with lovely breasts, but a monster of the deep below,
her body a writhing horror, her belly spawns wolves
flailing with dolphins' tails. Better to waste time,
skirting Sicily then in a long arc rounding Cape Pachynus,
than once set eyes on gruesome Scylla deep in her cave,
her rocks booming with all her sea-green hounds.
                                    "'What's more,
if a prophet has second sight, if Helenus earns your trust

and Apollo fills his soul with truth, one prophecy, one   510
above all, son of the goddess, I will make to you,
over and over repeat this warning word. Revere
great Juno's power first in all your prayers,
to Juno chant your vows with a full heart and win
the mighty goddess over with gifts to match your vows.
Only then can you leave Sicilian shores at last,
dispatched to Italy's coast, a conquering hero.
Once ashore, when you reach the city of Cumae
and Avernus' haunted lakes and murmuring forests,
there you will see the prophetess in her frenzy,   520
chanting deep in her rocky cavern, charting the Fates,
committing her vision to words, to signs on leaves.
Whatever verses the seer writes down on leaves
she puts in order, sealed in her cave, left behind.
There they stay, motionless, never slip from sequence.
But the leaves are light—if the door turns on its hinge,
the slightest breath of air will scatter them all about
and she never cares to retrieve them, flitting through her cave,
or restore them to order, join them as verses with a vision.
So visitors may depart, deprived of her advice,   530
and hate the Sibyl's haunts.
                            "'But never fear delay,
though crewmen press you hard and the course you set
calls out to your sails to take the waves, and you could
fill those sails with good fair winds. Still you must
approach her oracle, beg the seer with prayers
to chant her prophecies, all of her own accord,
unlock her lips and sing with her own voice.
She will reveal to you the Italian tribes,
the wars that you must fight, and the many ways
to shun or shoulder each ordeal that you must meet.   540
Revere her power and she will grant safe passage.
That far I may go with my words of warning.
Now sail on. By your own brave work exalt
our Trojan greatness to the skies.'
                            "Friendly words,
and when he had closed, the prophet ordered presents,

hoards of gold and ivory inlays, brought to our ships,
crowding our holds with a massive weight of silver,
Dodona cauldrons, a breastplate linked with mail
and triple-meshed in gold, a magnificent helmet
peaked with a plumed crest—Neoptolemus' arms—   550
and then the gifts of honor for my father.
He adds horses too, pilots to guide our way,
fills out our crews, rearms our fighting comrades.

     "Meanwhile Anchises gave the command to spread sail,
no time to waste, we'd lose the good fair winds,
and Apollo's seer addressed him with deep respect:
'Anchises, worthy to wed the proudest, Venus herself,
how the gods do love you. Twice they plucked you safe
from the ruins of Troy. Italy waits you now, look,
sail on and make it yours!   560
But first you must hurry past the coastline here,
the part of Italy that the god unfolds for you
lies far at sea. "Set sail now," the god commands,
"blest in the dedication of your son." Enough.
Why waste time with talk when the wind is rising?'

     "Andromache grieves no less at our final parting.
She brings out robes shot through with gilded thread
and a Phrygian cloak for Ascanius. Not to be outdone
in kindness, weighing him down with woven gifts
she says: 'Please take these as well, the work   570
of my hands, reminders of me to you, dear boy,
and tokens of my love . . .
the love of Hector's Andromache that never dies.
Take them. The last gifts from your own people.
You are the only image of my Astyanax that's left.
His eyes, his hands, his features, so like yours—
he would be growing up now, just your age.'
                                        "Turning
to leave, my tears brimmed and I said a last farewell:
'Live on in your blessings, your destiny's been won!
But ours calls us on from one ordeal to the next.   580

You've earned your rest at last. No seas to plow,
no questing after Italian fields forever
receding on the horizon. Now you see before you
Xanthus and Troy in replica, built with your own hands,
under better stars, I trust, and less exposed to the Greeks.
If I ever reach the Tiber, the fields on Tiber's banks,
and see my people secure behind their promised walls,
then of our neighboring kin and kindred cities, both
in Epirus and Hesperia—both have the same founder,
Dardanus, the same fate too—someday we will make   590
our peoples one, one Troy in heart and soul.
Let this mission challenge all our children.'

　　"North we sail and skirt Ceraunia's cliffs
to the narrow straits, the shortest route to Italy,
while the sun sinks and darkness shrouds the hills.
Landing, drawing lots for tomorrow's stint at the oars,
we stretch out in the lap of welcome land at water's edge
and scattered along the dry beach refresh ourselves
as sleep comes streaming through our weary bodies.
Night, drawn by the Hours, approaches mid-career   600
when Palinurus, on the alert, leaps up from bed
to test the winds, his ears keen for the first stir,
scanning the constellations wheeling down the quiet sky,
Arcturus, the rainy Hyades and the Great and Little Bears,
his eyes roving to find Orion geared in gold. And then,
when he sees the entire sky serene, all clear,
he gives the trumpet signal from his stern
and we strike camp at once,
set out on our way and spread our canvas wings.

　　"The dawn was a red glow now, putting stars to flight   610
as we glimpse the low-lying hills, dim in the distance . . .
Italy. 'Italy!'—Achates was first to shout the name—
'Italy!' comrades cried out too with buoyant hearts.
Father Anchises crowned a great bowl with wreaths,
brimmed it with unmixed wine,
and standing tall in the stern, he prayed the gods:

'You Powers that rule the land and sea and storms,
grant us wind for an easy passage, blow us safe to port!'
As the wind we pray for quickens, a harbor opens wide and
closer till we can see Minerva's temple on the heights.   620
Shipmates furl the sails and swing the prows toward land.
The harbor curves like a bow, bent by Eastern combers,
rocky breakwaters foam with the salt surf spray,
the haven's just behind them. Towering cliffs
fling out their arms like steep twin walls
and the temple rests securely back from shore.

"Here I saw it—our first omen: four horses,
snow-white, cropping the grasslands far and wide.
'War!' Father Anchises calls out, 'Land of welcome,
that's what you bring us, true, horses are armed for war,   630
these pairs of horses threaten war. But then again,
the same beasts are trained to harness as teams
and bow to the yoke, at one with bit and bridle.
There's hope for peace as well.'
                              "At once we pray
to the force of Pallas, goddess of clashing armies,
the first to receive our band of happy men.
We stand at the altar, heads under Trojan veils,
and following Helenus' orders first and foremost,
duly burn our offerings, just as bidden,
to Juno, Queen of Argos.
                              "No time for delay.   640
Our rites complete, at once we swing our sails
to the wind on yardarm spars and put astern
this home of Greeks, the fields we dare not trust.
First we sight the Gulf of Tarentum, Hercules' town,
if the tale is true, then looming over the waves ahead,
Lacinian Juno's temple, Caulon's fort on the rugged coast
of Scylaceum, wrecker of ships, then far across the seas,
rising up from the swells, we can see Mount Etna, Sicily,
hear the tremendous groaning of waters, pounding rocks,
the resounding roar of breakers crashing on the shore—   650
reefs spring up, swirling sand in the sea-surge.

Father Anchises cries out: 'Surely that's Charybdis,
those the cliffs that Helenus warned of, craggy deathtraps.
Row for your lives, my shipmates—backs in the oars, now stroke!'

   "They snapped to commands, pulled hard, Palinurus first
to swerve his shuddering prow to port for open sea
and the whole fleet swung to port with oars and sails.
Up to the sky an immense billow hoists us, then at once,
as the wave sank down, down we plunge to the pit of hell.
Three times the cliffs roared out from between the hollow caves,   660
three times we saw the spume exploding to spray the stars.
At last the sun and the wind went down, abandoned us,
broken men, our bearings lost . . . floating adrift
toward the Cyclops' coast.
                                    "There is a harbor
clear of the wind, and spacious, calm, a haven,
but Etna rumbles, hard by, showering deadly scree
and now it heaves into the sky a thundering dark cloud,
a whirlwind pitch-black with smoke and red-hot coals
and it hurls up huge balls of fire that lap the stars—
and now it vomits rocks ripped from the mountain's bowels   670
erupting lava into the air, enormous molten boulders,
groaning magma roiling up from its bedrock depths.
They say Enceladus' body, half-devoured by lightning,
lies crushed under Etna's mass, the mighty volcano piled
over him, breathing flames from its furnaces blasting open,
and every time the giant rolls on his bone-weary side
all Sicily moans, quakes, shrouds the sky with smoke.
Covered by woods that night we brave out horrors,
unable to see what made such a monstrous uproar.
The stars were extinguished, the high skies black,   680
the luminous heavens blotted out by a thick cloud cover,
the dead of night had wrapped the moon in mist.
                                    "At last
the day was breaking, the morning star on the rise,
Aurora had just burned off the night's dank fog,
when suddenly out of the woods the weird shape
of a man, a stranger, all but starved to death,

in wretched condition, emerges, staggers toward us,
hands outstretched to us on the beaches, begging mercy.
We turned, looked back at him . . . his filth appalling,
his beard all tangled, his rags hooked up with thorns.   690
Still, head to foot a Greek, a man once sent to Troy
equipped with his country's arms. Soon as he saw
our Dardan dress from afar, our Trojan swords,
he froze in his tracks a moment, gripped by fear,
then breakneck made for the shore with tears and prayers:
'I beg you, Trojans, beg by the stars, the gods above,
the clear bright air we breathe—sail me off and away!
Anywhere, any land you please, that's all I want.
I am, I confess, a man from the Greek fleets,
I admit I fought to seize your household gods.   700
For that, if my crime against you is so wicked,
rip me to bits and fling the bits in the sea,
plunge me into the depths! If die I must,
death at the hands of *men* will be a joy!'

                                        "With that,
he clutched my knees and kneeling, groveling, clung fast.
We press him hard—who is he? Who are his parents?
What rough fortune has driven him to despair?
Father Anchises, barely pausing, gives the man his hand
and the friendly gesture lifts the stranger's spirits.
Setting his fears aside, he starts out on his story: 710
'I come from Ithaca, my country . . .
unlucky Ulysses' comrade. Call me Achaemenides.
My father Adamastus was poor, and so I sailed to Troy—
Oh if only our poverty lasted longer! But here
my comrades left me, forgot me—this monstrous cave
of the Cyclops—fleeing in terror from its brutal mouth.
This gruesome house. Gory with its hideous feasts.
Pitch-dark inside. Immense. The giant himself,
his head scrapes the stars! God save our earth
from such a scourge! No looking him in the face,   720
no trying to reach him with a word. He gorges himself
on the innards and black blood of all his wretched victims.
With my own eyes I've seen him snatch a pair of our men

in one massive hand and, sprawling amidst his lair,
crush their bodies on the rocks till the cave's maw
swam with splashing blood. I've seen him gnawing limbs,
oozing dark filth, and the warm flesh twitching still
between his grinding jaws.
                              "'But what a price he paid!
Ulysses would not tolerate such an outrage,
always true to himself when it's life-or-death.   730
Soon as the monster gorged himself to bursting,
buried deep in wine, his neck slumping to one side,
spreading his huge hulk across his cave, dead asleep
but retching chunks of flesh and wine awash with filth—
we prayed to the great gods, drew lots, rushed in a ring
around him there and drilled out with a stabbing spike
his one enormous eye, lodged deep in his grisly brow,
big as a Greek shield or Apollo's torch, the sun.
So at last we avenged our comrades' shades—elated.

     "'But you, poor men, run now, run for your lives,   740
cut your hawsers, sail away! Just as horrible,
huge as Polyphemus here in his rocky cavern,
penning his woolly sheep, milking their udders dry,
there are a hundred more accursed Cyclops, everywhere,
crowding the deep inlets, lumbering over the ridged hills.
Three times now the horns of the moon have filled with light
since I've dragged out my lonely days through the woods,
where only the wild things have their dens and lairs,
and watched from a lookout crag for the giant Cyclops,
quaking to hear their rumbling tread, their shouts.   750
I live on the meager fare the branches offer,
berries and cornel nuts as hard as rocks, and feed
on roots I tear from the earth. As I scanned the horizon,
yours were the first ships that I'd seen come ashore.
I throw myself on your mercy, whoever you may be.
Enough for me to escape that barbarous crew!
Better for *you* to take this wretched life—
by any death you please.'
                         "He'd barely finished

when there, up on a ridge we saw him, Polyphemus!
The shepherd among his flock, hauling his massive hulk,   760
groping toward the shore he knew by heart. The monster,
immense, gargantuan, hideous—blind, his lone eye gone —
clutching a pine-tree trunk to keep his footing firm.
His woolly sheep at his side, his sole pleasure,
his only solace in pain . . .
Soon as the giant gained deep water and offshore swells,
he washed the blood still trickling down from his dug-out socket,
gnashing his teeth, groaning, and wades out in the surf
but the breakers still can't douse his soaring thighs.
In panic we rush to escape, get clear of his reach,   770
take aboard the fugitive—he had earned his way—
and we cut our lines, dead quiet, put our backs
in a racing stroke that makes the waters churn.

     "He hears us, wheels to follow our splashing oars
but he has no chance to seize us in his clutches,
he's no match for Ionian tides in his pursuit,
so he gives a tremendous howl that shakes the sea
and all its waves, all Italy inland shudders in fear
and Etna's echoing caverns bellow from their depths.
Down from the woods and high hills they lumber in alarm,   780
the tribe of Cyclops, down to the harbor, crowding the shore,
the brotherhood of Etna! We see them standing there, powerless,
each with his one glaring eye, their heads towering up,
an horrendous muster looming into the vaulting sky
like mountain oaks or cypress heavy with cones
in Jupiter's soaring woods or Diana's sacred grove.

     "Breakneck on, impelled by the sharp edge of fear,
we shake our sheets out, spread our sails to the wind,
wherever it may blow. But we run counter to Helenus'
warnings not to steer between Scylla and Charybdis—   790
only a razor-edge between the devil and deep blue sea—
so it's come about, we must swing back, when look,
a Northwind speeds to our rescue, sweeping South
from the narrow cape of Pelorus, driving us past

the Pantagias' mouth, that haven of native rock,
past the bay of Megara, Thapsus lying low,
sea-marks pointed out by Achaemenides now,
retracing the shores he once had coasted past
as luckless Ulysses' shipmate.
                              "There is an island
fronting the bay of Syracuse—over against Plemyrium's   800
headland rocked by breakers—called Ortygia once
by men in the old days. They tell how Alpheus,
the Elean river, forcing his passage undersea
by secret channels, now, Arethusa, mixes streams
at your fountain's mouth with your Sicilian waters.
We act on command, we worship the Powers of the place,
then sail on past the Helorus' rich, marshy fields,
then brush by the jutting reefs of craggy Cape Pachynus,
then distant Camerina heaves into view, a town the Fates
will never allow to move, then Gela's fields and Gela   810
named for its rushing torrent. Next in the offing
Acragas rears, steep city, once a famous breeder
of fiery steeds, and shows its mighty ramparts.
Next we run with the winds and leave Selinus,
city of palms, astern, then pick our way
by the shoals and hidden spurs of Lilybaeum.
Then, at last, the port of Drepanum takes me in,
a shore that brought no joy.
                            "Here, after all the blows
of sea and storm I lost my father, my mainstay
in every danger and defeat. Spent as I was,   820
you left me here, Anchises, best of fathers,
plucked from so many perils, all for nothing.
Not even Helenus, filled with dreadful warnings,
foresaw such grief for me—not even foul Celaeno.
This was my last ordeal, my long journey's end.
From here I sailed. God drove me to your shores."
                                            So Aeneas,
with all eyes fixed on him alone, the founder of his people
recalled his wanderings now, the fates the gods had sent.
He fell hushed at last, his tale complete, at rest.

BOOK FOUR

The Tragic Queen
of Carthage

But the queen—too long she has suffered the pain of love,
hour by hour nursing the wound with her lifeblood,
consumed by the fire buried in her heart.
The man's courage, the sheer pride of his line,
they all come pressing home to her, over and over.
His looks, his words, they pierce her heart and cling—
no peace, no rest for her body, love will give her none.

A new day's dawn was moving over the earth, Aurora's torch
cleansing the sky, burning away the dank shade of night
as the restless queen, beside herself, confides now   10
to the sister of her soul: "Dear Anna, the dreams
that haunt my quaking heart! Who is this stranger
just arrived to lodge in our house—our guest?
How noble his face, his courage, and what a soldier!
I'm sure—I know it's true—the man is born of the gods.

Fear exposes the lowborn man at once. But, oh, how tossed
he's been by the blows of fate. What a tale he's told,
what a bitter bowl of war he's drunk to the dregs.
If my heart had not been fixed, dead set against
embracing another man in the bonds of marriage—   20
ever since my first love deceived me, cheated me
by his death—if I were not as sick as I am
of the bridal bed and torch, this, perhaps,
is my one lapse that might have brought me down.
I confess it, Anna, yes. Ever since my Sychaeus,
my poor husband met his fate, and my own brother
shed his blood and stained our household gods,
this is the only man who's roused me deeply,
swayed my wavering heart . . .
The signs of the old flame, I know them well.   30
I pray that the earth gape deep enough to take me down
or the almighty Father blast me with one bolt to the shades,
the pale, glimmering shades in hell, the pit of night,
before I dishonor you, my conscience, break your laws.
He's carried my love away, the man who wed me first—
may he hold it tight, safeguard it in his grave."

    She broke off, her voice choking with tears
that brimmed and wet her breast.
                              But Anna answered:
"Dear one, dearer than light to me, your sister,
would you waste away, grieving your youth away, alone,   40
never to know the joy of children, all the gifts of love?
Do you really believe that's what the dust desires,
the ghosts in their ashen tombs? Have it your way.
But granted that no one tempted you in the past,
not in your great grief,
no Libyan suitor, and none before in Tyre,
you scorned Iarbas and other lords of Africa,
sons bred by this fertile earth in all their triumph:
why resist it now, this love that stirs your heart?
Don't you recall whose lands you settled here,   50
the men who press around you? On one side

the Gaetulian cities, fighters matchless in battle,
unbridled Numidians—Syrtes, the treacherous Sandbanks.
On the other side an endless desert, parched earth
where the wild Barcan marauders range at will.
Why mention the war that's boiling up in Tyre,
your brother's deadly threats? I think, in fact,
the favor of all the gods and Juno's backing drove
these Trojan ships on the winds that sailed them here.
Think what a city you will see, my sister, what a kingdom   60
rising high if you marry such a man! With a Trojan army
marching at our side, think how the glory of Carthage
will tower to the clouds! Just ask the gods for pardon,
win them with offerings. Treat your guests like kings.
Weave together some pretext for delay, while winter
spends its rage and drenching Orion whips the sea—
the ships still battered, weather still too wild."

    These were the words that fanned her sister's fire,
turned her doubts to hopes and dissolved her sense of shame.
And first they visit the altars, make the rounds,   70
praying the gods for blessings, shrine by shrine.
They slaughter the pick of yearling sheep, the old way,
to Ceres, Giver of Laws, to Apollo, Bacchus who sets us free
and Juno above all, who guards the bonds of marriage.
Dido aglow with beauty holds the bowl in her right hand,
pouring wine between the horns of a pure white cow
or gravely paces before the gods' fragrant altars,
under their statues' eyes refreshing her first gifts,
dawn to dusk. And when the victims' chests are splayed,
Dido, her lips parted, pores over their entrails,   80
throbbing still, for signs . . .
But, oh, how little they know, the omniscient seers.
What good are prayers and shrines to a person mad with love?
The flame keeps gnawing into her tender marrow hour by hour
and deep in her heart the silent wound lives on.
Dido burns with love—the tragic queen.
She wanders in frenzy through her city streets
like a wounded doe caught all off guard by a hunter

stalking the woods of Crete, who strikes her from afar
and leaves his winging steel in her flesh, and he's unaware   90
but she veers in flight through Dicte's woody glades,
fixed in her side the shaft that takes her life.
                                                            And now
Dido leads her guest through the heart of Carthage,
displaying Phoenician power, the city readied for him.
She'd speak her heart but her voice chokes, mid-word.
Now at dusk she calls for the feast to start again,
madly begging to hear again the agony of Troy,
to hang on his lips again, savoring his story.
Then, with the guests gone, and the dimming moon
quenching its light in turn, and the setting stars   100
inclining heads to sleep—alone in the echoing hall,
distraught, she flings herself on the couch that he left empty.
Lost as he is, she's lost as well, she hears him, sees him
or she holds Ascanius back and dandles him on her lap,
bewitched by the boy's resemblance to his father,
trying to cheat the love she dare not tell.
The towers of Carthage, half built, rise no more,
and the young men quit their combat drills in arms.
The harbors, the battlements planned to block attack,
all work's suspended now, the huge, threatening walls   110
with the soaring cranes that sway across the sky.

     Now, no sooner had Jove's dear wife perceived
that Dido was in the grip of such a scourge—
no thought of pride could stem her passion now—
than Juno approaches Venus and sets a cunning trap:
"What a glittering prize, a triumph you carry home!
You and your boy there, you grand and glorious Powers.
Just look, one woman crushed by the craft of two gods!
I am not blind, you know. For years you've looked askance
at the homes of rising Carthage, feared our ramparts.   120
But where will it end? What good is all our strife?
Come, why don't we labor now to live in peace?
Eternal peace, sealed with the bonds of marriage.

You have it all, whatever your heart desires—
Dido's ablaze with love,
drawing the frenzy deep into her bones. So,
let us rule this people in common: joint command.
And let her marry her Phrygian lover, be his slave
and give her Tyrians over to your control,
her dowry in your hands!"

                Perceiving at once   130
that this was all pretense, a ruse to shift
the kingdom of Italy onto Libyan shores,
Venus countered Juno: "Now who'd be so insane
as to shun your offer and strive with you in war?
If only Fortune crowns your proposal with success!
But swayed by the Fates, I have my doubts. Would Jove
want one city to hold the Tyrians and the Trojan exiles?
Would he sanction the mingling of their peoples,
bless their binding pacts? You are his wife,
with every right to probe him with your prayers.   140
You lead the way. I'll follow."

                "The work is mine,"
imperious Juno carried on, "but how to begin
this pressing matter now and see it through?
I'll explain in a word or so. Listen closely.
Tomorrow Aeneas and lovesick Dido plan to hunt
the woods together, soon as the day's first light
climbs high and the Titan's rays lay bare the earth.
But while the beaters scramble to ring the glens with nets,
I'll shower down a cloudburst, hail, black driving rain—
I'll shatter the vaulting sky with claps of thunder.   150
The huntsmen will scatter, swallowed up in the dark,
and Dido and Troy's commander will make their way
to the same cave for shelter. And I'll be there,
if I can count on your own good will in this—
I'll bind them in lasting marriage, make them one.
Their wedding it will be!"

              So Juno appealed
and Venus did not oppose her, nodding in assent

and smiling at all the guile she saw through . . .

   Meanwhile Dawn rose up and left her Ocean bed
and soon as her rays have lit the sky, an elite band   160
of young huntsmen streams out through the gates,
bearing the nets, wide-meshed or tight for traps
and their hunting spears with broad iron heads,
troops of Massylian horsemen galloping hard,
packs of powerful hounds, keen on the scent.
Yet the queen delays, lingering in her chamber
with Carthaginian chiefs expectant at her doors.
And there her proud, mettlesome charger prances
in gold and royal purple, pawing with thunder-hoofs,
champing a foam-flecked bit. At last she comes,   170
with a great retinue crowding round the queen
who wears a Tyrian cloak with rich embroidered fringe.
Her quiver is gold, her hair drawn up in a golden torque
and a golden buckle clasps her purple robe in folds.
Nor do her Trojan comrades tarry. Out they march,
young Iulus flushed with joy.
Aeneas in command, the handsomest of them all,
advancing as her companion joins his troop with hers.
So vivid. Think of Apollo leaving his Lycian haunts
and Xanthus in winter spate, he's out to visit Delos,   180
his mother's isle, and strike up the dance again
while round the altars swirls a growing throng
of Cretans, Dryopians, Agathyrsians with tattoos,
and a drumming roar goes up as the god himself
strides the Cynthian ridge, his streaming hair
braided with pliant laurel leaves entwined
in twists of gold, and arrows clash on his shoulders.
So no less swiftly Aeneas strides forward now
and his face shines with a glory like the god's.

   Once the huntsmen have reached the trackless lairs   190
aloft in the foothills, suddenly, look, some wild goats
flushed from a ridge come scampering down the slopes

and lower down a herd of stags goes bounding across
the open country, ranks massed in a cloud of dust,
fleeing the high ground. But young Ascanius,
deep in the valley, rides his eager mount
and relishing every stride, outstrips them all,
now goats, now stags, but his heart is racing, praying—
if only they'd send among this feeble, easy game
some frothing wild boar or a lion stalking down   200
from the heights and tawny in the sun.
                                        Too late.
The skies have begun to rumble, peals of thunder first
and the storm breaking next, a cloudburst pelting hail
and the troops of hunters scatter up and down the plain,
Tyrian comrades, bands of Dardans, Venus' grandson Iulus
panicking, running for cover, quick, and down the mountain
gulleys erupt in torrents. Dido and Troy's commander
make their way to the same cave for shelter now.
Primordial Earth and Juno, Queen of Marriage,
give the signal and lightning torches flare   210
and the high sky bears witness to the wedding,
nymphs on the mountaintops wail out the wedding hymn.
This was the first day of her death, the first of grief,
the cause of it all. From now on, Dido cares no more
for appearances, nor for her reputation, either.
She no longer thinks to keep the affair a secret,
no, she calls it a marriage,
using the word to cloak her sense of guilt.

    Straightway Rumor flies through Libya's great cities,
Rumor, swiftest of all the evils in the world.   220
She thrives on speed, stronger for every stride,
slight with fear at first, soon soaring into the air
she treads the ground and hides her head in the clouds.
She is the last, they say, our Mother Earth produced.
Bursting in rage against the gods, she bore a sister
for Coeus and Enceladus: Rumor, quicksilver afoot
and swift on the wing, a monster, horrific, huge

and under every feather on her body—what a marvel—
an eye that never sleeps and as many tongues as eyes
and as many raucous mouths and ears pricked up for news.   230
By night she flies aloft, between the earth and sky,
whirring across the dark, never closing her lids
in soothing sleep. By day she keeps her watch,
crouched on a peaked roof or palace turret,
terrorizing the great cities, clinging as fast
to her twisted lies as she clings to words of truth.
Now Rumor is in her glory, filling Africa's ears
with tale on tale of intrigue, bruiting her song
of facts and falsehoods mingled . . .
"Here this Aeneas, born of Trojan blood,   240
has arrived in Carthage, and lovely Dido deigns
to join the man in wedlock. Even now they warm
the winter, long as it lasts, with obscene desire,
oblivious to their kingdoms, abject thralls of lust."

     Such talk the sordid goddess spreads on the lips of men,
then swerves in her course and heading straight for King Iarbas,
stokes his heart with hearsay, piling fuel on his fire.

     Iarbas—son of an African nymph whom Jove had raped—
raised the god a hundred splendid temples across
the king's wide realm, a hundred altars too,   250
consecrating the sacred fires
that never died, eternal sentinels of the gods.
The earth was rich with blood of slaughtered herds
and the temple doorways wreathed with riots of flowers.
This Iarbas, driven wild, set ablaze by the bitter rumor,
approached an altar, they say, as the gods hovered round,
and lifting a suppliant's hands, he poured out prayers to Jove:
"Almighty Jove! Now as the Moors adore you, feasting away
on their gaudy couches, tipping wine in your honor—
do you see this? Or are we all fools, Father,   260
to dread the bolts you hurl? All aimless then,
your fires high in the clouds that terrify us so?
All empty noise, your peals of grumbling thunder?

That woman, that vagrant! Here in my own land
she founded her paltry city for a pittance.
We tossed her some beach to plow—on my terms—
and then she spurns our offer of marriage, she
embraces Aeneas as lord and master in her realm.
And now this second Paris . . .
leading his troupe of eunuchs, his hair oozing oil,   270
a Phrygian bonnet tucked up under his chin, he revels
in all that he has filched, while we keep bearing gifts
to your temples—yes, yours—coddling your reputation,
all your hollow show!"

                 So King Iarbas appealed,
his hand clutching the altar, and Jove Almighty heard
and turned his gaze on the royal walls of Carthage
and the lovers oblivious now to their good name.
He summons Mercury, gives him marching orders:
"Quick, my son, away! Call up the Zephyrs,
glide on wings of the wind. Find the Dardan captain   280
who now malingers long in Tyrian Carthage, look,
and pays no heed to the cities Fate decrees are his.
Take my commands through the racing winds and tell him
this is not the man his mother, the lovely goddess, promised,
not for *this* did she save him twice from Greek attacks.
Never. He would be the one to master an Italy
rife with leaders, shrill with the cries of war,
to sire a people sprung from Teucer's noble blood
and bring the entire world beneath the rule of law.
If such a glorious destiny cannot fire his spirit,   290
if he will not shoulder the task for his own fame,
does the father of Ascanius grudge his son
the walls of Rome? What is he plotting now?
What hope can make him loiter among his foes,
lose sight of Italian offspring still to come
and all the Lavinian fields? Let him set sail!
This is the sum of it. This must be our message."

     Jove had spoken. Mercury made ready at once
to obey the great commands of his almighty father.

First he fastens under his feet the golden sandals,   300
winged to sweep him over the waves and earth alike
with the rush of gusting winds. Then he seizes the wand
that calls the pallid spirits up from the Underworld
and ushers others down to the grim dark depths,
the wand that lends us sleep or sends it away,
that unseals our eyes in death. Equipped with this,
he spurs the winds and swims through billowing clouds
till in mid-flight he spies the summit and rugged flanks
of Atlas, whose long-enduring peak supports the skies.
Atlas: his pine-covered crown is forever girded   310
round with black clouds, battered by wind and rain;
driving blizzards cloak his shoulders with snow,
torrents course down from the old Titan's chin
and shaggy beard that bristles stiff with ice.
Here the god of Cyllene landed first,
banking down to a stop on balanced wings.
From there, headlong down with his full weight
he plunged to the sea as a seahawk skims the waves,
rounding the beaches, rounding cliffs to hunt for fish inshore.
So Mercury of Cyllene flew between the earth and sky   320
to gain the sandy coast of Libya, cutting the winds
that sweep down from his mother's father, Atlas.

                            Soon
as his winged feet touched down on the first huts in sight,
he spots Aeneas founding the city fortifications,
building homes in Carthage. And his sword-hilt
is studded with tawny jasper stars, a cloak
of glowing Tyrian purple drapes his shoulders,
a gift that the wealthy queen had made herself,
weaving into the weft a glinting mesh of gold.
Mercury lashes out at once: "You, so now you lay   330
foundation stones for the soaring walls of Carthage!
Building her gorgeous city, doting on your wife.
Blind to your own realm, oblivious to your fate!
The King of the Gods, whose power sways earth and sky—
he is the one who sends me down from brilliant Olympus,
bearing commands for you through the racing winds.

What are you plotting now?
Wasting time in Libya—what hope misleads you so?
If such a glorious destiny cannot fire your spirit,
[if you will not shoulder the task for your own fame,]   340
at least remember Ascanius rising into his prime,
the hopes you lodge in Iulus, your only heir—
you owe him Italy's realm, the land of Rome!"
This order still on his lips, the god vanished
from sight into empty air.
                                    Then Aeneas
was truly overwhelmed by the vision, stunned,
his hackles bristle with fear, his voice chokes in his throat.
He yearns to be gone, to desert this land he loves,
thunderstruck by the warnings, Jupiter's command . . .
But what can he do? What can he dare say now   350
to the queen in all her fury and win her over?
Where to begin, what opening? Thoughts racing,
here, there, probing his options, turning
to this plan, that plan—torn in two until,
at his wits' end, this answer seems the best.
He summons Mnestheus, Sergestus, staunch Serestus,
gives them orders: "Fit out the fleet, but not a word.
Muster the crews on shore, all tackle set to sail,
but the cause for our new course, you keep it secret."
Yet he himself, since Dido who means the world to him   360
knows nothing, never dreaming such a powerful love
could be uprooted—he will try to approach her,
find the moment to break the news gently,
a way to soften the blow that he must leave.
All shipmates snap to commands,
glad to do his orders.
                            True, but the queen—
who can delude a lover?—soon caught wind
of a plot afoot, the first to sense the Trojans
are on the move . . . She fears everything now,
even with all secure. Rumor, vicious as ever,   370
brings her word, already distraught, that Trojans
are rigging out their galleys, gearing to set sail.

She rages in helpless frenzy, blazing through
the entire city, raving like some Maenad
driven wild when the women shake the sacred emblems,
when the cyclic orgy, shouts of "Bacchus!" fire her on
and Cithaeron echoes round with maddened midnight cries.

    At last she assails Aeneas, before he's said a word:
"So, you traitor, you really believed you'd keep
this a secret, this great outrage? Steal away   380
in silence from my shores? Can nothing hold you back?
Not our love? Not the pledge once sealed with our right hands?
Not even the thought of Dido doomed to a cruel death?
Why labor to rig your fleet when the winter's raw,
to risk the deep when the Northwind's closing in?
You cruel, heartless— Even if you were not
pursuing alien fields and unknown homes,
even if ancient Troy were standing, still,
who'd sail for Troy across such heaving seas?
You're running away—from me? Oh, I pray you   390
by these tears, by the faith in your right hand—
what else have I left myself in all my pain?—
by our wedding vows, the marriage we began,
if I deserve some decency from you now,
if anything mine has ever won your heart,
pity a great house about to fall, I pray you,
if prayers have any place—reject this scheme of yours!
Thanks to you, the African tribes, Numidian warlords
hate me, even my own Tyrians rise against me.
Thanks to you, my sense of honor is gone,   400
my one and only pathway to the stars,
the renown I once held dear. In whose hands,
my guest, do you leave me here to meet my death?
'Guest'—that's all that remains of 'husband' now.
But why do I linger on? Until my brother Pygmalion
batters down my walls? Or Iarbas drags me off, his slave?
If only you'd left a baby in my arms—our child—
before you deserted me! Some little Aeneas
playing about our halls, whose features at least

would bring you back to me in spite of all,   410
I would not feel so totally devastated,
so destroyed."
                    The queen stopped but he,
warned by Jupiter now, his gaze held steady,
fought to master the torment in his heart. At last
he ventured a few words: "I . . . you have done me
so many kindnesses, and you could count them all.
I shall never deny what you deserve, my queen,
never regret my memories of Dido, not while I
can recall myself and draw the breath of life.
I'll state my case in a few words. I never dreamed   420
I'd keep my flight a secret. Don't imagine that.
Nor did I once extend a bridegroom's torch
or enter into a marriage pact with you.
If the Fates had left me free to live my life,
to arrange my own affairs of my own free will,
Troy is the city, first of all, that I'd safeguard,
Troy and all that's left of my people whom I cherish.
The grand palace of Priam would stand once more,
with my own hands I would fortify a second Troy
to house my Trojans in defeat. But not now.   430
Grynean Apollo's oracle says that I must seize
on Italy's noble land, his Lycian lots say 'Italy!'
There lies my love, there lies my homeland now.
If you, a Phoenician, fix your eyes on Carthage,
a Libyan stronghold, tell me, why do you grudge
the Trojans their new homes on Italian soil?
What is the crime if *we* seek far-off kingdoms too?

        "My father, Anchises, whenever the darkness shrouds
the earth in its dank shadows, whenever the stars
go flaming up the sky, my father's anxious ghost   440
warns me in dreams and fills my heart with fear.
My son Ascanius . . . I feel the wrong I do
to one so dear, robbing him of his kingdom,
lands in the West, his fields decreed by Fate.
And now the messenger of the gods—I swear it,

by your life and mine—dispatched by Jove himself
has brought me firm commands through the racing winds.
With my own eyes I saw him, clear, in broad daylight,
moving through your gates. With my own ears I drank
his message in. Come, stop inflaming us both   450
with your appeals. I set sail for Italy—
all against my will."
                        Even from the start
of his declaration, she has glared at him askance,
her eyes roving over him, head to foot, with a look
of stony silence . . . till abruptly she cries out
in a blaze of fury: "No goddess was your mother!
No Dardanus sired your line, you traitor, liar, no,
Mount Caucasus fathered you on its flinty, rugged flanks
and the tigers of Hyrcania gave you their dugs to suck!
Why hide it? Why hold back? To suffer greater blows?   460
Did *he* groan when *I* wept? Even look at me? Never!
Surrender a tear? Pity the one who loves him?
What can I say first? So much to say. Now—
neither mighty Juno nor Saturn's son, the Father,
gazes down on this with just, impartial eyes.
There's no faith left on earth!
He was washed up on my shores, helpless, and I,
I took him in, like a maniac let him share my kingdom,
salvaged his lost fleet, plucked his crews from death.
Oh I am swept by the Furies, gales of fire! Now   470
it's Apollo the Prophet, Apollo's Lycian oracles:
they're his masters now, and now, to top it off,
the messenger of the gods, dispatched by Jove himself,
comes rushing down the winds with his grim-set commands.
Really! What work for the gods who live on high,
what a concern to ruffle their repose!
I won't hold you, I won't even refute you—go!—
strike out for Italy on the winds, your realm across the sea.
I hope, I pray, if the just gods still have any power,
wrecked on the rocks mid-sea you'll drink your bowl   480
of pain to the dregs, crying out the name of Dido

over and over, and worlds away I'll hound you then
with pitch-black flames, and when icy death has severed
my body from its breath, then my ghost will stalk you
through the world! You'll pay, you shameless, ruthless—
and I will hear of it, yes, the report will reach me
even among the deepest shades of Death!"
                                        She breaks off
in the midst of outbursts, desperate, flinging herself
from the light of day, sweeping out of his sight,
leaving him numb with doubt, with much to fear   490
and much he means to say.
Catching her as she faints away, her women
bear her back to her marble bridal chamber
and lay her body down upon her bed.
                                  But Aeneas
is driven by duty now. Strongly as he longs
to ease and allay her sorrow, speak to her,
turn away her anguish with reassurance, still,
moaning deeply, heart shattered by his great love,
in spite of all he obeys the gods' commands
and back he goes to his ships.   500
Then the Trojans throw themselves in the labor,
launching their tall vessels down along the beach
and the hull rubbed sleek with pitch floats high again.
So keen to be gone, the men drag down from the forest
untrimmed timbers and boughs still green for oars.
You can see them streaming out of the whole city,
men like ants that, wary of winter's onset, pillage
some huge pile of wheat to store away in their grange
and their army's long black line goes marching through the field,
trundling their spoils down some cramped, grassy track. 510
Some put shoulders to giant grains and thrust them on,
some dress the ranks, strictly marshal stragglers,
and the whole trail seethes with labor.

    What did you feel then, Dido, seeing this?
How deep were the groans you uttered, gazing now

from the city heights to watch the broad beaches
seething with action, the bay a chaos of outcries
right before your eyes?
                            Love, you tyrant!
To what extremes won't you compel our hearts?
Again she resorts to tears, driven to move the man,   520
or try, with prayers—a suppliant kneeling, humbling
her pride to passion. So if die she must,
she'll leave no way untried.
                                "Anna, you see
the hurly-burly all across the beach, the crews
swarming from every quarter? The wind cries for canvas,
the buoyant oarsmen crown their sterns with wreaths.
This terrible sorrow: since I saw it coming, Anna,
I can endure it now. But even so, my sister,
carry out for me one great favor in my pain.
To you alone he used to listen, the traitor,   530
to you confide his secret feelings. You alone
know how and when to approach him, soothe his moods.
Go, my sister! Plead with my imperious enemy.
Remind him I was never at Aulis, never swore a pact
with the Greeks to rout the Trojan people from the earth!
I sent no fleet to Troy, I never uprooted the ashes
of his father, Anchises, never stirred his shade.
Why does he shut his pitiless ears to my appeals?
Where's he rushing now? If only he would offer
one last gift to the wretched queen who loves him: 540
to wait for fair winds, smooth sailing for his flight!
I no longer beg for the long-lost marriage he betrayed,
nor would I ask him now to desert his kingdom, no,
his lovely passion, Latium. All I ask is time,
blank time: some rest from frenzy, breathing room
till my fate can teach my beaten spirit how to grieve.
I beg him—pity your sister, Anna—one last favor,
and if he grants it now, I'll pay him back,
with interest, when I die."
                            So Dido pleads and
so her desolate sister takes him the tale of tears   550

again and again. But no tears move Aeneas now.
He is deaf to all appeals. He won't relent.
The Fates bar the way
and heaven blocks his gentle, human ears.
As firm as a sturdy oak grown tough with age
when the Northwinds blasting off the Alps compete,
fighting left and right, to wrench it from the earth,
and the winds scream, the trunk shudders, its leafy crest
showers across the ground but it clings firm to its rock,
its roots stretching as deep into the dark world below   560
as its crown goes towering toward the gales of heaven—
so firm the hero stands: buffeted left and right
by storms of appeals, he takes the full force
of love and suffering deep in his great heart.
His will stands unmoved. The falling tears are futile.

                                        Then,
terrified by her fate, tragic Dido prays for death,
sickened to see the vaulting sky above her.
And to steel her new resolve to leave the light,
she sees, laying gifts on the altars steaming incense—
shudder to hear it now—the holy water going black   570
and the wine she pours congeals in bloody filth.
She told no one what she saw, not even her sister.
Worse, there was a marble temple in her palace,
a shrine built for her long-lost love, Sychaeus.
Holding it dear she tended it—marvelous devotion—
draping the snow-white fleece and festal boughs.
Now from its depths she seemed to catch his voice,
the words of her dead husband calling out her name
while night enclosed the earth in its dark shroud,
and over and over a lonely owl perched on the rooftops   580
drew out its low, throaty call to a long wailing dirge.
And worse yet, the grim predictions of ancient seers
keep terrifying her now with frightful warnings.
Aeneas the hunter, savage in all her nightmares,
drives her mad with panic. She always feels alone,
abandoned, always wandering down some endless road,
not a friend in sight, seeking her own Phoenicians

in some godforsaken land. As frantic as Pentheus
seeing battalions of Furies, twin suns ablaze
and double cities of Thebes before his eyes.   590
Or Agamemnon's Orestes hounded off the stage,
fleeing his mother armed with torches, black snakes,
while blocking the doorway coil her Furies of Revenge.

    So, driven by madness, beaten down by anguish,
Dido was fixed on dying, working out in her mind
the means, the moment. She approaches her grieving
sister, Anna—masking her plan with a brave face
aglow with hope, and says: "I've found a way,
dear heart—rejoice with your sister—either
to bring him back in love for me or free me   600
of love for him. Close to the bounds of Ocean,
west with the setting sun, lies Ethiopian land,
the end of the earth, where colossal Atlas turns
on his shoulder the heavens studded with flaming stars.
From there, I have heard, a Massylian priestess comes
who tended the temple held by Hesperian daughters.
She'd safeguard the boughs in the sacred grove
and ply the dragon with morsels dripping loops
of oozing honey and poppies drowsy with slumber.
With her spells she vows to release the hearts   610
of those she likes, to inflict raw pain on others—
to stop the rivers in midstream, reverse the stars
in their courses, raise the souls of the dead at night
and make earth shudder and rumble underfoot—you'll see—
and send the ash trees marching down the mountains.
I swear by the gods, dear Anna, by your sweet life,
I arm myself with magic arts against my will.
                                                    "Now go,
build me a pyre in secret, deep inside our courtyard
under the open sky. Pile it high with his arms—
he left them hanging within our bridal chamber—   620
the traitor, so devoted then! and all his clothes
and crowning it all, the bridal bed that brought my doom.
I must obliterate every trace of the man, the curse,

and the priestess shows the way!"
                              She says no more
and now as the queen falls silent, pallor sweeps her face.
Still, Anna cannot imagine these outlandish rites
would mask her sister's death. She can't conceive
of such a fiery passion. She fears nothing graver
than Dido's grief at the death of her Sychaeus.
So she does as she is told.
                              But now the queen,   630
as soon as the pyre was built beneath the open sky,
towering up with pitch-pine and cut logs of oak—
deep in the heart of her house—she drapes the court
with flowers, crowning the place with wreaths of death,
and to top it off she lays his arms and the sword he left
and an effigy of Aeneas, all on the bed they'd shared,
for well she knows the future. Altars ring the pyre.
Hair loose in the wind, the priestess thunders out
the names of her three hundred gods, Erebus, Chaos
and triple Hecate, Diana the three-faced virgin.   640
She'd sprinkled water, simulating the springs of hell,
and gathered potent herbs, reaped with bronze sickles
under the moonlight, dripping their milky black poison,
and fetched a love-charm ripped from a foal's brow,
just born, before the mother could gnaw it off.
And Dido herself, standing before the altar,
holding the sacred grain in reverent hands—
with one foot free of its sandal, robes unbound—
sworn now to die, she calls on the gods to witness,
calls on the stars who know her approaching fate.   650
And then to any Power above, mindful, evenhanded,
who watches over lovers bound by unequal passion,
Dido says her prayers.
                              The dead of night,
and weary living creatures throughout the world
are enjoying peaceful sleep. The woods and savage seas
are calm, at rest, and the circling stars are gliding on
in their midnight courses, all the fields lie hushed
and the flocks and gay and gorgeous birds that haunt

the deep clear pools and the thorny country thickets
all lie quiet now, under the silent night, asleep.   660
But not the tragic queen . . .
torn in spirit, Dido will not dissolve
into sleep—her eyes, her mind won't yield tonight.
Her torments multiply, over and over her passion
surges back into heaving waves of rage—
she keeps on brooding, obsessions roil her heart:
"And now, what shall I do? Make a mockery of myself,
go back to my old suitors, tempt them to try again?
Beg the Numidians, grovel, plead for a husband—
though time and again I scorned to wed their like?   670
What then? Trail the Trojan ships, bend to the Trojans'
every last demand? So pleased, are they, with all the help,
the relief I lent them once? And memory of my service past
stands firm in grateful minds! And even if I were willing,
would the Trojans allow me to board their proud ships—
a woman they hate? Poor lost fool, can't you sense it,
grasp it yet—the treachery of Laomedon's breed?
What now? Do I take flight alone, consorting
with crews of Trojan oarsmen in their triumph?
Or follow them out with all my troops of Tyrians   680
thronging the decks? Yes, hard as it was to uproot
them once from Tyre! How can I force them back to sea
once more, command them to spread their sails to the winds?
No, no, die!
            You deserve it—
                           end your pain with the sword!
You, my sister, you were the first, won over by my tears,
to pile these sorrows on my shoulders, mad as I was,
to throw me into my enemy's arms. If only I'd been free
to live my life, untested in marriage, free of guilt
as some wild beast untouched by pangs like these!
I broke the faith I swore to the ashes of Sychaeus."   690

   Such terrible grief kept breaking from her heart
as Aeneas slept in peace on his ship's high stern,

bent on departing now, all tackle set to sail.
And now in his dreams it came again—the god,
his phantom, the same features shining clear.
Like Mercury head to foot, the voice, the glow,
the golden hair, the bloom of youth on his limbs
and his voice rang out with warnings once again:
"Son of the goddess, how can you sleep so soundly
in such a crisis? Can't you see the dangers closing   700
around you now? Madman! Can't you hear the Westwind
ruffling to speed you on? That woman spawns her plots,
mulling over some desperate outrage in her heart,
lashing her surging rage, she's bent on death.
Why not flee headlong?
Flee headlong while you can! You'll soon see
the waves a chaos of ships, lethal torches flaring,
the whole coast ablaze, if now a new dawn breaks
and finds you still malingering on these shores.
Up with you now. Enough delay. Woman's a thing   710
that's always changing, shifting like the wind."
With that he vanished into the black night.

        Then, terrified by the sudden phantom,
Aeneas, wrenching himself from sleep, leaps up
and rouses his crews and spurs them headlong on:
"Quick! Up and at it, shipmates, man the thwarts!
Spread canvas fast! A god's come down from the sky
once more—I've just seen him—urging us on
to sever our mooring cables, sail at once!
We follow you, blessed god, whoever you are—   720
glad at heart we obey your commands once more.
Now help us, stand beside us with all your kindness,
bring us favoring stars in the sky to blaze our way!"

        Tearing sword from sheath like a lightning flash,
he hacks the mooring lines with a naked blade.
Gripped by the same desire, all hands pitch in,
they hoist and haul. The shore's deserted now,

the water's hidden under the fleet—they bend to it,
churn the spray and sweep the clear blue sea.

                                        By now
early Dawn had risen up from the saffron bed   730
of Tithonus, scattering fresh light on the world.
But the queen from her high tower, catching sight
of the morning's white glare, the armada heading out
to sea with sails trimmed to the wind, and certain
the shore and port were empty, stripped of oarsmen—
three, four times over she beat her lovely breast,
she ripped at her golden hair and "Oh, by God,"
she cries, "will the stranger just sail off
and make a mockery of our realm? Will no one
rush to arms, come streaming out of the whole city,   740
hunt him down, race to the docks and launch the ships?
Go, quick—bring fire!
                          Hand out weapons!
                                        Bend to the oars!
What am I saying? Where am I? What insanity's this
that shifts my fixed resolve? Dido, oh poor fool,
is it only *now* your wicked work strikes home?
It should have then, when you offered him your scepter.
Look at his hand clasp, look at his good faith now—
that man who, they say, carries his fathers' gods,
who stooped to shoulder his father bent with age!
Couldn't I have seized him then, ripped him to pieces,   750
scattered them in the sea? Or slashed his men with steel,
butchered Ascanius, served him up as his father's feast?
True, the luck of battle might have been at risk—
well, risk away! Whom did I have to fear?
I was about to die. I should have torched their camp
and flooded their decks with fire. The son, the father,
the whole Trojan line—I should have wiped them out,
then hurled myself on the pyre to crown it all!

     "You, Sun, whose fires scan all works of the earth,
and you, Juno, the witness, midwife to my agonies—   760

Hecate greeted by nightly shrieks at city crossroads—
and you, you avenging Furies and gods of dying Dido!
Hear me, turn your power my way, attend my sorrows—
I deserve your mercy—hear my prayers! If that curse
of the earth must reach his haven, labor on to landfall—
if Jove and the Fates command and the boundary stone is fixed,
still, let him be plagued in war by a nation proud in arms,
torn from his borders, wrenched from Iulus' embrace,
let him grovel for help and watch his people die
a shameful death! And then, once he has bowed down   770
to an unjust peace, may he never enjoy his realm
and the light he yearns for, never, let him die
before his day, unburied on some desolate beach!

    "That is my prayer, my final cry—I pour it out
with my own lifeblood. And you, my Tyrians,
harry with hatred all his line, his race to come:
make that offering to my ashes, send it down below.
No love between our peoples, ever, no pacts of peace!
Come rising up from my bones, you avenger still unknown,
to stalk those Trojan settlers, hunt with fire and iron,   780
now or in time to come, whenever the power is yours.
Shore clash with shore, sea against sea and sword
against sword—this is my curse—war between all
our peoples, all their children, endless war!"

    With that, her mind went veering back and forth—
what was the quickest way to break off from the light,
the life she loathed? And so with a few words
she turned to Barce, Sychaeus' old nurse—her own
was now black ashes deep in her homeland lost forever:
"Dear old nurse, send Anna my sister to me here.   790
Tell her to hurry, sprinkle herself with river water,
bring the victims marked for the sacrifice I must make.
So let her come. And wrap your brow with the holy bands.
These rites to Jove of the Styx that I have set in motion,
I yearn to consummate them, end the pain of love,

give that cursed Trojan's pyre to the flames."
The nurse bustled off with an old crone's zeal.

                                        But Dido,
trembling, desperate now with the monstrous thing afoot—
her bloodshot eyes rolling, quivering cheeks blotched
and pale with imminent death—goes bursting through   800
the doors to the inner courtyard, clambers in frenzy
up the soaring pyre and unsheathes a sword, a Trojan sword
she once sought as a gift, but not for such an end.
And next, catching sight of the Trojan's clothes
and the bed they knew by heart, delaying a moment
for tears, for memory's sake, the queen lay down
and spoke her final words: "Oh, dear relics,
dear as long as Fate and the gods allowed,
receive my spirit and set me free of pain.
I have lived a life. I've journeyed through   810
the course that Fortune charted for me. And now
I pass to the world below, my ghost in all its glory.
I have founded a noble city, seen my ramparts rise.
I have avenged my husband, punished my blood-brother,
our mortal foe. Happy, all too happy I would have been
if only the Trojan keels had never grazed our coast."
She presses her face in the bed and cries out:
"I shall die unavenged, but die I will! So—
so—I rejoice to make my way among the shades.
And may that heartless Dardan, far at sea,   820
drink down deep the sight of our fires here
and bear with him this omen of our death!"

    All at once, in the midst of her last words,
her women see her doubled over the sword, the blood
foaming over the blade, her hands splattered red.
A scream goes stabbing up to the high roofs,
Rumor raves like a Maenad through the shocked city—
sobs, and grief, and the wails of women ringing out
through homes, and the heavens echo back the keening din—
for all the world as if enemies stormed the walls   830

and all of Carthage or old Tyre were toppling down
and flames in their fury, wave on mounting wave
were billowing over the roofs of men and gods.

    Anna heard and, stunned, breathless with terror,
raced through the crowd, her nails clawing her face,
fists beating her breast, crying out to her sister now
at the edge of death: "Was it all for *this*, my sister?
You deceived me all along? Is this what your pyre
meant for me—this, your fires—this, your altars?
You deserted me—what shall I grieve for first?   840
Your friend, your sister, you scorn me now in death?
You should have called me on to the same fate.
The same agony, same sword, the one same hour
had borne us off together. Just to think I built
your pyre with my own hands, implored our fathers' gods
with my own voice, only to be cut off from you—
how very cruel—when you lay down to die . . .
You have destroyed your life, my sister, mine too,
your people, the lords of Sidon and your new city here.
Please, help me to bathe her wounds in water now,   850
and if any last, lingering breath still hovers,
let me catch it on my lips."
                     With those words
she had climbed the pyre's topmost steps and now,
clasping her dying sister to her breast, fondling her
she sobbed, stanching the dark blood with her own gown.
Dido, trying to raise her heavy eyes once more, failed—
deep in her heart the wound kept rasping, hissing on.
Three times she tried to struggle up on an elbow,
three times she fell back, writhing on her bed.
Her gaze wavering into the high skies, she looked   860
for a ray of light and when she glimpsed it, moaned.

    Then Juno in all her power, filled with pity
for Dido's agonizing death, her labor long and hard,
sped Iris down from Olympus to release her spirit

wrestling now in a deathlock with her limbs.
Since she was dying a death not fated or deserved,
no, tormented, before her day, in a blaze of passion—
Proserpina had yet to pluck a golden lock from her head
and commit her life to the Styx and the dark world below.
So Iris, glistening dew, comes skimming down from the sky   870
on gilded wings, trailing showers of iridescence shimmering
into the sun, and hovering over Dido's head, declares:
"So commanded, I take this lock as a sacred gift
to the God of Death, and I release you from your body."

    With that, she cut the lock with her hand and all at once
the warmth slipped away, the life dissolved in the winds.

Funeral Games
for Anchises

All the while Aeneas, steeled for a mid-sea passage,
held the fleet on course, well on their way now,
plowing the waves blown dark by a Northwind
as he glanced back at the walls of Carthage
set aglow by the fires of tragic Dido's pyre.
What could light such a conflagration? A mystery—
but the Trojans know the pains of a great love
defiled, and the lengths a woman driven mad can go,
and it leads their hearts down ways of grim foreboding.

Once they had reached the high seas, no land in sight,   10
no longer—water at all points, at all points the sky—
looming over their heads a pitch-dark thunderhead
brought on night and storm, ruffling the swells black.
Even the pilot Palinurus, high astern at his station,
cries out: "Why such cloudbanks wrapped around the sky?

Father Neptune, what are you whipping up for us now?"
And with that he issues orders:
                              "Trim your sails!
Bend to your sturdy oars!"—
                              and setting canvas
aslant to work the wind, he calls out to his captain:
"Great-hearted Aeneas, no, not even if Jove himself   20
would pledge me with all his power, could I dream
of reaching Italy under skies like these.
The wind's shifted, surging athwart our beam,
roaring out of the black West, building into clouds!
There's no fighting it, no making way against it,
we're too weak. Since Fortune's got the upper hand,
let's follow her where she calls and change course.
No long way off, I think, there are friendly shores,
the coast of your brother Eryx, Sicily's havens,
if I remember rightly and take our bearings   30
back by the stars I marked when we set out."

    "That's what the wind demands," says good Aeneas.
"For long I've watched you trying to fight against it,
all for nothing. Shorten sail, change course. What land
could please me more, and where would I rather beach
our battered ships than Sicily? Home that harbors
my Dardan friend Acestes, earth that holds
my father Anchises' bones."
                              At that, they head for port
and a following Westwind bellies out their sails.
The fleet goes skimming over the whitecaps now,   40
the men rejoicing to wheel their prows around
to a coast they know, at last.
                              But far away,
high on a mountain lookout, quite amazed to see
the fleet of his old friends coming in, Acestes
rushes down to meet them there—a wild figure
bristling spears and a Libyan she-bear's hide.
Born of a Trojan mother to the river-god Crinisus,
Acestes, never forgetting his age-old lineage,

gladly welcomes his Trojan friends' return.
He warms them in with treasures of the field,   50
he cheers the exhausted men with generous care.
                                        And next,
once day broke in the East and put the stars to flight,
Aeneas summons his crews from down along the beach
and greets them all from a mounded rise of ground:
"Gallant sons of Dardanus, born of the gods' high blood,
the wheeling year has passed, rounding out its months,
since we committed to earth my godlike father's bones,
his relics, and sanctified the altars with our tears.
The day has returned, if I am not mistaken, the day
always harsh to my heart, I'll always hold in honor.   60
So you gods have willed. Were I passing the hours,
an exile lost in the swirling sands of Carthage
or caught in Greek seas, imprisoned in Mycenae,
I would still perform my anniversary vows,
carry out our processions grand and grave
and heap the altars high with fitting gifts.
But now, beyond our dreams, here we stand
by the very bones and ashes of my father—not,
I know, without the plan and power of the gods—
borne by the seas we've reached this friendly haven.   70
So come, all of us celebrate our happy, buoyant rites!
Pray for fair winds! And may it please my father,
once my city is built with temples in his name,
that I offer him these rites year in, year out.

    "Acestes born in Troy will give you cattle,
two head for every ship. Invite to the feast
our household gods, the gods of our own home
and those our host Acestes worships, too.
Then, if the ninth dawn brings a brilliant day
to the race of men and her rays lay bare the earth,   80
I shall hold games for all our Trojans. First a race
for our swift ships, then for our fastest man afoot,
and then our best and boldest can step up to win
the javelin-hurl or wing the wind-swift arrow

or dare to fight with bloody rawhide gauntlets.
Come all! See who takes the victory prize, the palm.
A reverent silence, all, and crown your brows with wreaths."

With that, he binds his own brows with his mother's myrtle.
So does Helymus, so does Acestes ripe in years, the boy
Ascanius too, and the other young men take his lead.   90
Leaving the council now with thousands in his wake,
amid his immense cortege, Aeneas gains the tomb
and here he pours libations, each in proper order.
Two bowls of unmixed wine he tips on the ground
and two of fresh milk, two more of hallowed blood,
then scatters crimson flowers with this prayer:
"Hail, my blessed father, hail again! I salute
your ashes, your spirit and your shade—my father
I rescued once, but all for nothing. Not with you
would it be my fate to search for Italy's shores   100
and destined fields and, whatever it may be,
the Italian river Tiber."
                            At his last words
a serpent slithered up from the shrine's depths,
drawing its seven huge coils, seven rolling coils
calmly enfolding the tomb, gliding through the altars:
his back blazed with a maze of sea-blue flecks, his scales
with a sheen of gold, shimmering as a rainbow showers
iridescent sunlight arcing down the clouds. Aeneas
stopped, struck by the sight. The snake slowly sweeping
along his length among the bowls and polished goblets   110
tasted the feast, then back he slid below the tomb,
harmless, slipping away from altars where he'd fed.

With fresh zeal Aeneas resumes his father's rites,
wondering, is the serpent the genius of the place?
Or his father's familiar spirit? Bound by custom
he slaughters a pair of yearling sheep, as many swine
and a brace of young steers with their sleek black backs,
then tipping wine from the bowls, he calls his father's ghost,
set free from Acheron now, the great Anchises' shade.

The comrades, too, bring on what gifts they can,   120
their spirits high, loading the altars, killing steers,
while others, setting the bronze cauldrons out in order,
stretch along the grass, holding spits over embers,
broiling cuts of meat.
                        The longed-for day arrived
as the horses of Phaëthon brought the ninth dawn on
through skies serene and bright. News of the day
and Acestes' famous name had roused the people
round about, and a happy crowd had thronged the shore,
some to behold Aeneas' men, some set to compete as well.
And first the trophies are placed on view amid the field: 130
sacred tripods, leafy crowns and palms, the victors' prizes,
armor, robes dyed purple, and gold and silver bars.
A trumpet blast rings out from a mound midfield—
let the games begin!
                     For the first event, enter,
four great ships, well matched with their heavy oars,
picked from the whole armada. Mnestheus commands the *Dragon*
swift with her eager crew, Mnestheus soon of Italy,
soon from him the Memmian clan would take its name.
Gyas commands the huge *Chimaera*, a hulk as huge
as a city—Trojans in three tiers drive her on,   140
churning as one man at three ranked sweeps of oars.
Sergestus, who gives his name to the Sergian house,
rides the tremendous vessel *Centaur.* Cloanthus
who bred your line, you Roman Cluentius, sails
the bright blue *Scylla.*
                         Far out in the offing,
fronting the foaming coastline, looms a rock. At times,
when the winter's Northwest winds blot out the stars,
it's all submerged, the breakers thunder it under.
In calm weather, up from the gentle swells it lifts
a quiet, level face, a favorite haunt of cormorants   150
basking in the sun. Here the good commander Aeneas
staked an ilex, leaves and all, as a turning-post
where crews would know to wheel their ships around
and begin the long pull home. They next draw lots

for starting places, captains stand on the sterns,
their purple-and-gold regalia gleaming far afield.
And the oarsmen don their wreaths of poplar leaves,
oil poured on their naked shoulders makes them glisten.
They crowd the thwarts, their arms tense at the oars,
ears tense for the signal; hearts pounding, racing   160
with nerves high-strung and a grasping lust for glory.
At last a piercing blare of the trumpet—suddenly all
the ships burst forth from the line, no stopping them now,
the shouts of the sailors hit the skies, the oarsmen's arms
pull back to their chests as they whip the swells to foam.
Still dead even, they plow their furrows, ripping the sea
wide open with thrashing oars and cleaving triple beaks.
Never so swift the teams in a two-horse chariot race
breaking headlong out of the gates to take the field,
not even when charioteers lay on the rippling reins,   170
leaning into the whip-stroke, giving the teams full head.
Resounding applause, cries of partisans fill the woods
and the curving bayshore rolls the sound around
and the pelted hillsides volley back the roar.

        Amid this din and confusion Gyas darts ahead,
leading the field at the start to race across the surf—
next Cloanthus, better oared but his pine hulk slows him down—
next, at an equal gap, the *Dragon* and *Centaur* fight it
out for third, and now the *Dragon* has it and now
the huge *Centaur* edges her out, now they're even,   180
prow to prow, cleaving the salt sea with long keels.
Soon they're nearing the rock, swerving into the turn
when Gyas, holding the lead, still victor at mid-course,
shouts out to his helmsman Menoetes: "Where are you heading?
Why so hard to starboard? Hold course! Hug the coast!
Your oars should barely shave that rock to port!
Leave the deep sea to the rest!"
                                Clear commands
but Menoetes, fearing some hidden reefs, veers
his prow to starboard, to open water, and Gyas
shouts again: "Where now? Still off course!   190

Head for the rocks, Menoetes!"
                    And glancing back,
watch, Cloanthus right in his wake—grazing past to port
on an inside track between Gyas' ship and the booming reefs—
races round into safe water, leaving the mark astern.
Young Gyas blazed in indignation deep to his bones,
tears streamed down his cheeks, he flings to the winds
all care for self-respect and the safety of his crew
and pitches the sluggish Menoetes off the stern,
headlong into the sea and takes the helm himself.
His own pilot now, he spurs his oarsmen, turning   200
the rudder hard to port and heads for home.
Old Menoetes, dead weight in his sodden clothes,
struggling up at last from the depths to break the surface,
clambered onto the rock and perched there high and dry.
The Trojan crews had laughed when he took the plunge,
then when he floundered round and now they laugh
as he retches spews of brine from his heaving chest.

A happy hope flared up in the last two captains now,
Sergestus and Mnestheus, to pass the flagging Gyas.
Sergestus gains the lead as they near the rock   210
but not by a whole keel's length—his prow's ahead
but the *Dragon*'s pressing prow overlaps his stern,
so Mnestheus, striding the gangplank, spurs his crew:
"Now put your backs in the oars, you comrades of Hector!
You are the ones I chose, my troops at Troy's last stand.
Now show the nerve, the heart you showed on Libya's reefs,
the Ionian Sea, the waves at Malea that attacked us!
It's not for first place now Mnestheus strives,
not for victory—
            Oh, if only—
                    No, let Neptune
pick the winner he wants but *we* must not come last,   220
what shame! Just win that victory—oh, my Trojans,
spare us that disgrace!"
                They bend hard to the oars
and pull for all they're worth, and the bronze hull shivers

under their massive strokes and the deep sweeps by beneath them—
gasping for breath, their chests wracked, mouths parched, sweat
rivering down their backs, but blind chance brings that crew
the prize they yearn for. Wild with striving, Sergestus—
wheeling his prow toward the rock, risking an inside track,
the dangerous straits—crashes into the jutting reefs,
unlucky man. The struck crag shudders, oars slamming   230
against its riptooth edges split, and the prow driven
onto the rock, hangs there, hoisted into the air.
The crew springs up, shouting, trying to backwater,
unshipping their iron pikes and sharp-tipped punting poles,
they scramble to rescue splintered oars from the surf.
Mnestheus riding high, the higher for his success—
oars at a racing stroke, wind at his beck and call—
shoots into open water, homing down the coast.
Swift as a dove, flushed in fear from a cave
where it nests its darling chicks in crannies,   240
a sudden burst of wings and out its home it flies,
terrified, off into open fields and next it skims
through the bright, quiet air and never beats a wing.
So Mnestheus, so his *Dragon* speeds ahead, cleaving
the swells on the homestretch, so she flies along
on her own forward drive.
                              First he leaves astern
Sergestus struggling still at his beetling rock,
splashing in shallows, crying for help—no use—
as he studies how to race with shattered oars.
Next Mnestheus goes for Gyas, the huge *Chimaera*   250
stripped of her helmsman, giving up the lead.
Now nearing the finish, that left one, Cloanthus—
Mnestheus goes for *him* all-out, urging his crews
to give it all they've got.
                              Roars of the crowd re-echo,
cheering on his challenge, the air resounds with cries.
One crew, stung by the shame of losing victory now
with glory won, would trade their lives for fame.
But Mnestheus and his crew, fired by their success,
can just about win the day because they think they can.

They were drawing abreast, perhaps they'd seize the prize   260
if Cloanthus had not flung his arms to the sea and poured
his prayers to the gods and begged them to hear his vows:
"You gods, you lords of the waves I'm racing over here,
I'll gladly steady a pure white bull at your altars,
there on shore, and pay my vows—scatter its innards
over the salt swell and tip out streams of wine!"

So he prayed, and far in the depths they heard him,
all the Nereids, Phorcus' chorus, virgin Panopea
and Father Portunus himself, with his own mighty hand,
drove the racing *Scylla* swifter than Southern winds   270
or a winging arrow, speeding toward the shore
to find her berth in the good deep-water harbor.
                                        Then
the son of Anchises summons all together, true to custom.
A herald's ringing voice declares Cloanthus the victor
and Aeneas crowns his brows with fresh green laurel.
He presents the prizes to each ship's crew, some wine,
three bulls of their choice and a heavy silver bar
and for each ship's captain lays on gifts of honor.
To the winner a cloak of braided gold that's fringed
with twin ripples of Meliboean crimson running round it,   280
and woven into its weft, Ganymede, prince of woody Ida
spins his javelins, wearing out the racing stags—
he's breathless, hot on the hunt, so true to life
as the eagle that bears Jove's lightning sweeps him
up from Ida into the heavens, pinned in its talons
while old guardsmen reach for the stars in vain
and the watchdogs' savage howling fills the air.

Then to the man whose prowess won him second place
he gives a coat of mail, glinting with burnished links
and triple-meshed in gold, a victor's trophy he himself   290
had dragged from Demoleos, killed near Simois' rapids
under Troy's high wall. This armor he gives Mnestheus,
a fighter's badge of honor to shield him well in war.
Two aides-de-camp, Phegeus and Sagaris, hefting it

on their shoulders now, could hardly bear it off
with all its heavy plies, yet Demoleos wore it once,
fully armed as he ran down Trojan stragglers. Aeneas
presents a pair of brazen cauldrons for third prize
and two cups of hammered silver, ridged in sharp relief.

Now with the gifts presented, all were moving off,   300
proud of their prizes, scarlet ribbons binding their brows
when here comes Sergestus, bringing in his ship. He'd barely
worked her free of the ruthless rock with craft and effort,
one bank of her oars gone, one in splinters. A laughingstock,
shorn of glory, she came crawling in . . . Like a snake caught,
as they often are, on a causeway, crushed by a bronze wheel
or heavy rock flung by a traveler—trampled, left half-dead,
trying to slip away, writhing in gnarled coils, no hope.
Part fighting mad, its eyes blazing, its hissing head
puffed high—part crippled, wounds cutting its pace,   310
struggling in knots, twitching, twisting round itself.
So the ship limped in, oars laboring, slowly, and still
she spreads her sails and enters the harbor, canvas taut.
Aeneas, glad that the ship is salvaged, crew restored,
gives Sergestus the prize that he had promised:
a slave girl, Pholoë, born of Cretan stock
and hardly inept at Minerva's works of hand,
nursing twins at her breast.
                              The ship-race over,
good Aeneas strides to the grassy level field
ringed by hills with woodland sloping down   320
to a vale that formed an enormous round arena.
There he went, the hero leading many thousands,
and took his own seat on a built-up platform
mid the growing crowd. And here, for those
who chanced to long for a breathless foot-race now,
Aeneas stirs their spirits, setting out the prizes.
Trojans mixed with Sicilians come from all directions,
with Nisus and Euryalus out in front. Euryalus radiant,
famed for the bloom of youth—Nisus, for the pure love
he devoted to the boy. Following them, Diores,   330

sprung from the stock of Priam's royal house.
Then Patron flanked by Salius, an Acarnanian,
one, and one an Arcadian born of Tegean blood.
Then two Sicilian youngsters, Helymus, Panopes,
hunters used to the woods, and friends of old Acestes,
and many others too, their names now lost
in the dark depths of time.
                              Among the crowds,
Aeneas addressed them all with: "Hear me now,
mark my words and fill your hearts with joy.
Not one of you leaves and lacks a gift from me.   340
I'll give two Cretan arrows with polished iron points
and a double axe embossed with knobs of silver.
The same honors await you, one and all.
But prize trophies go to the three front-runners,
brows crowned with the wreaths of braided golden olive.
First, the winner, shall have a horse with dazzling trappings.
The second, an Amazon's quiver bristling Thracian arrows,
slung from a sweeping sword-belt starred with gold
and clasped with a brilliant jewel.
The third can leave content with this Greek helmet."   350

    Soon as said they take their mark, ready, set—
a sudden signal—
                    go!—
                         and they break from the start,
pouring over the course like a stormcloud streaking on,
all eyes fixed on the goal, with Nisus far in the lead,
shooting out of the tight pack and faster than wind or
the winged lightning second, second at quite a gap,
comes Salius—next, and a good long way behind,
Euryalus coming third, and after Euryalus, Helymus,
then Diores flying hot on his heels and closer, closing,
watch, breathing over his shoulder and if there had been   360
more track to cover he would have caught and passed him
or run him a dead heat. Now down the stretch they come,
the exhausted runners closing on the goal when all at once
unlucky Nisus skids on a slick of blood they'd chanced to spill,

killing bullocks, soaking the turf and green grass surface,
here the racer, elated—victory won—pressing the pace
he stumbles, pitching face-first in the filthy dung
and blood of victims. But he won't forget Euryalus,
his great love, never, up from the slime he struggles,
flings himself in Salius' path to send him spinning,   370
reeling backward, splayed out on the beaten track
as Euryalus flashes past, thanks to his friend
he takes the lead—the victor flying along,
sped by the roaring crowd, with Helymus next
and Diores wins third prize.
                              But at this, Salius
bursts out with howls that ring through the huge arena,
round from the front-row elders to the crowd—a foul
had robbed him clean of the prize he wanted back.
True, but Euryalus has the people on his side,
plus modest tears and his own gallant ways,   380
favored all the more for his handsome build.
And Diores backs him up with loud appeals:
he finished third, but no third prize for him
if the victor's prize returned to Salius' hands.

    "Your prizes are yours," said captain Aeneas firmly,
"they all stand fast, young comrades. No one alters
our ranked list of winners now. Just let me
offer a consolation prize to a luckless man,
a friend without a fault."
                            And with that,
he handed Salius a giant African lion's hide,   390
a great weight with its shaggy mane and gilded claws.
"If losers win such prizes," Nisus erupted now,
"and the ones who trip, such pity—what gift
will you give to Nisus worth his salt? Why,
I clearly had earned the crown for first prize
if the same bad luck that leveled Salius had not
knocked me down!" And with each word he points
to the sopping muck that fouled his face and limbs.
The fatherly captain smiled down at his friend

and had them fetch a shield, Didymaon's work   400
the Greeks had torn from Neptune's sacred gate.
This gleaming trophy he gives the fine young runner.

Then with the racing over, the prizes handed out,
"Now," Aeneas announces, "let any man with heart,
with the fire in his chest, come forward—
put up your fists, strap on the rawhide gloves."
And he sets afield a pair of trophies for the boxing:
for the winner a bull with gilded horns and wreaths,
a sword and a burnished helm to console the loser.
No delay. Instantly there he stands, that immense man,   410
Dares, jaw thrust out, tremendous in all his power.
The crowd's abuzz as he hauls himself to his feet,
the one man who could trade blows with Paris,
Dares who, by the mound where great Hector lies,
crushed the champion Butes, that gigantic hulk,
a braggart who fought as Amycus' Bebrycian kin—
he laid him out on the yellow sand to gasp his last.
So strong, this Dares, first to cock his head for combat,
flaunting his broad shoulders, sparring, lefts and rights,
beating the air with blows.
                              Who will take him on?   420
Not one in the whole crowd would dare go up against him,
strap the gloves on. So, certain that all contenders
had withdrawn, the trophy his alone, he strode up
to Aeneas now and never pausing, full of swagger,
grasps the bull's horn with his left hand and boasts:
"Son of Venus, since no one dares to face me in the ring,
how long do I have to stand here? How long's right?
Just say the word—I'll lead my prize away."

With one accord the Trojans roared assent:
Give the man the prize that he'd been promised.   430

But now Acestes rebukes Entellus sharply,
sitting side by side on a grassy rise of ground:
"Entellus, once our bravest hero, where's it gone?

Look at this prize! How can you just sit back,
feckless, and let them cart it off without a fight?
Where's that god of ours, that Eryx, tell me—
our teacher once, renowned for nothing now?
Where's your fame that thrilled all Sicily once?
What of the trophies hanging from your rafters?"

    Entellus returns: "My love of glory, my pride   440
still holds strong, not beaten down by fear.
It's slow old age, that's what dogs me now.
My blood runs cold, my body's chill, played out.
But if I were now the man I was, full of the youth
that spurs that bantam there, cocksure and strutting so—
I'd need no bribe of a prize bull to bring me out.
I have no use for trophies."
                    Fighting words.
Down in the ring he threw his pair of gauntlets,
massive weights that violent Eryx used to sport,
binding his fists to fight with rawhide taut and tough.   450
The crowd was dazed—seven welted plies of enormous oxhide
stitched in ridges of lead and iron to make them stiff.
Dares, dazed the most, shrinks back from the bout.
But the hearty son of Anchises tests their heft,
turning over and over the heavy coiling straps.

    Now old Entellus' voice comes rising from his chest:
"What if you'd seen the gloves of Hercules himself
and the grim fight he fought on these very sands?
This is the gear your brother Eryx used to wield,
look, still crusted with blood and spattered brains—   460
with these he stood up against great Hercules,
and I used to wear them too,
when the blood ran warmer in me, made me strong
before old age, my rival, flecked my brows with gray.
But if this Trojan, Dares, cringes before my weapons,
if good Aeneas decides and Acestes my promoter nods,
we'll fight as equals here. These gloves of Eryx,

I'll give them up for your sake, Dares. Come,
nothing to fear, pull off your Trojan gauntlets!"

    With that challenge Entellus stripped his pleated cloak   470
from his shoulders, baring his great sinewy limbs,
his great bones and joints, and stood gigantic
in the center of the ring.
                      Officiating, Aeneas
produced two pairs of gauntlets matched in weight
and bound both fighters' hands with equal weapons.
At once each struck his stance, up on his toes,
fists raised high—not a twinge of fear now—
heads rearing back, out of range of the fists,
they mix punches, left, right, probe for openings,
Dares trusting to young blood and fancy footwork,   480
Entellus to brawn, to brute force, but his knees quake,
his huge, lumbering frame is racked with labored breathing.
Wasting blow after blow at each other, thrown but missed
then blow, blow upon hollow ribs, landing fast and furious,
pounding chestbones, flurry of blows to head and ears,
jaws cracking under the crush of hammering jabs—
massive Entellus, stock-still in his tracks, merely
rolls to avoid the salvos, eyes fixed on his rival.
Dares like some captain assaulting a steep city wall
or laying siege to a mountain stronghold under arms,   490
now this approach, now that, exploring the whole fort
with skill, with every kind of assault, and all no use.
Entellus towers up for a stunning roundhouse right
and Dares seeing it coming,
                ducks, quick,
                          he's gone—
but the giant's full force poured in the crashing blow
lands on empty air and his own weight brings him down,
a colossal man, a colossal fall, he slammed the earth,
toppled, as often a hollow pine, ripped up by the roots
on steep Mount Ida or Erymanthus, topples down to ground.
The crowd springs up, Sicilians, Trojans, rival outcries   500

hit the sky. Acestes, first to rush to his aged friend,
pities Entellus, hoists him off the ground.

                                    The champion,
never slowed by a fall, unshaken, goes back to fight
and all the fiercer, anger fueling his power now,
shame fires him up, and a sense of his own strength.
So in a blaze of fury he pummels Dares headlong over
the whole wide ring, lefts and rights, doubling blows,
no lull, no letup, thick and fast as the hailstones
pelting down from a stormcloud, rattling roofs,
so dense the champion's blows, both fists pounding   510
over and over, battering Dares reeling round—

                                    Enough.
Aeneas, the good captain, could not permit the fury,
the blind rage of Entellus to rampage any longer.
He stopped the fight, pulled the battle-weary Dares
out of the bout and consoled him with these words:
"Poor man, what insanity's got you in its grip?
You're up against superhuman power, can't you see?
The will of God's against you. Bow to God."

    With that command he parted both contenders.
Trusty friends conducted Dares back to the ships,   520
dragging his wobbly knees, his head lolling side to side,
spitting clots from his mouth, blood mixed with teeth.
His mates, called back, receive his sword and helmet,
leaving the bull and the victor's palm to Entellus.
Overflowing with pride, glorying over his bull
the old champion shouts: "Son of the goddess,
see, you Trojans too,
what power I had when I was in my prime,
and from what a death you rescue Dares now!"

                                    With that,
standing over against the bull's head steadied there,   530
the battle's prize, he drew the iron gauntlet back
and rearing up for the blow, swings it square between
both horns, crushing the skull and dashing out the brains,

and dying, quivering, down on the ground the great beast sprawls.
And rising over it now the champion's voice comes
pouring from his heart: "Here, Eryx,
I pay your spirit a better life than Dares'!
Here, in victory, I lay down my gloves, my skill."

    At once Aeneas invites all those who wish
to contend with winging shafts and names the prizes.   540
With powerful hands he steps the mast from Serestus' ship
and tethers atop it, looped by a cord, a fluttering dove,
a mark for steel-shod arrows. The archers gather now,
cast lots in a bronze helmet, and first to leap out,
to partisan shouts, is Hippocoön, son of Hyrtacus.
Next, Mnestheus, flushed with victory in the ships,
his brow still crowned with an olive wreath of green.
Third, Eurytion—your brother, famous Pandarus,
archer who once under orders broke that truce,
the first to whip an arrow into the Argive ranks.   550
The last lot, deep in the helm, was Acestes' own,
who dared to try his hand at young men's work.

                         Now
as they flex their bows to a curve with all their force,
all each man can muster, drawing shafts from quivers,
young Hippocoön shot first, his bowstring twanged,
his whizzing arrow ripped through the swift air
and struck home, fixed deep in the timber mast.
The mast shuddered, the dove fluttered in fright
and the whole arena round rang out with cheers.
And next, keen Mnestheus took his stand, bow drawn,   560
aiming higher, his eye and shaft both trained on the mark
but he had no luck, he missed the bird itself, his shaft
just slit a knot in the hempen cord that tied her foot
as the dove dangled high from the soaring mast and
off she flew to the South and the dark clouds.
Quick as a wink Eurytion, bow long bent and arrow
set for release, prayed to his archer brother,
aimed at the dove that reveled in open sky,

winging under a black cloud—
                    and struck—
                                and down
she dropped, dead weight, leaving her life in the stars   570
and bringing home the shaft that shot her through.

    Now Acestes alone remained, and his prize lost.
Still he whipped an arrow high in the lofting air
to display his seasoned art and make his bow ring out.
Suddenly, right before their eyes, look, a potent marvel
destined to shape the future! So the outcome proved
when the awestruck prophets sang the signs to later ages.
Flying up to the swirling clouds the arrow shot into flames,
blazing its way in fire, burning out into thin air,
lost like the shooting stars that often break loose,   580
trailing a mane of flames to sweep across the sky.
Transfixed, the men of Troy and Sicily froze and
prayed the gods on high. Nor did Prince Aeneas
hold back from the omen. He embraced Acestes
in all his glory, heaping splendid gifts
on the old king and urging: "Take them, father!
By this sign the great lord of Olympus has decreed
that you should bear off honors far from all the rest.
Here, you'll have a gift from old Anchises himself.
A mixing-bowl, richly engraved, the proud trophy   590
that Thracian Cisseus one day gave my father.
A memento of his host, a pledge of his affection."

    With that, he crowns his brows with laurel leaves
and declares Acestes first, the winner over all.
Good Eurytion never grudged him this distinction,
though he alone shot down the dove from the high sky.
Next in the prizes comes the one who slit the cord
and last the man whose shaft had drilled the mast.

    Even before the contest ended, great Aeneas calls
Epytides over, friend and bodyguard of the young Iulus,   600
and whispers in his trusted ear: "Go, and if Ascanius

has his troupe of boys prepared, their horses mustered
to ride through their maneuvers, have him parade
his squadrons now, to honor Anchises here
and display himself in arms."
                                        Aeneas commands
the flooding crowds to clear the whole broad arena,
leave the field wide open. Then in ride the boys,
trim in their ranks before their parents' eyes,
mounted on bridled steeds and glittering in the light
and as they pass, the men of Troy and Sicily   610
murmur a hum of admiration. All the riders,
following custom, wear their hair bound tight
with close-cut wreaths, each bearing a pair of lances,
cornel, tipped with steel. Some sling burnished quivers
over their shoulders, high on their necks the torques
of flexible, braided gold encircle each boy's neck.
Three squadrons with three captains weave their ways,
each leading a column of twelve, six boys in double file,
a trainer beside each troupe, all shining in the sun.

    The first young squadron parades along in triumph   620
led by little Priam, who bore his forebear's name—
your noble son, Polites, destined to sire Italians
riding a Thracian stallion dappled white, his pasterns
white and prancing, high brow flashing a blaze of white.
Next comes Atys, soon the source of the Latin Atians,
little Atys, a boy the boy Prince Iulus loved.
Last, handsomest captain of them all, comes Iulus
riding a mount from Sidon, radiant Dido's gift,
a memento of the queen, a pledge of her affection.
The rest of the youngsters ride Sicilian horses,   630
old Acestes' gifts, the riders awed by applause
the Dardans give their fine dressage, delighted
to see in their looks their own lost parents' faces.

    Now, once they'd paraded past the assembled crowd,
triumphant on horseback, bright in the eyes of kinsmen,
all riders took their places and Epytides from afar

called out
          "Get set"—
                       a crack of his whip, and watch,
the long column, split into three equal squads,
splits into rows of six, in bands dancing away,
then recalled at the next command they wheeled   640
and charged each other, lances tense for attack,
wheeling charge into countercharge, return and turn
through the whole arena, enemies circling, swerving back
in their armor, acting out a mock display of war,
now baring their backs in flight, now turning spears
for attack, now making peace and riding file by file.
So complex the labyrinth once in hilly Crete, they say,
where the passage wove between blind walls and wavered on
in numberless cunning paths that broke down every clue,
with nothing to trace and no way back—a baffling maze.   650
Complex as the course the sons of Troy now follow, weaving
their way through mock escapes and clashes all in sport
as swiftly as frisky dolphins skim the rolling surf,
cleaving the Libyan or Carpathian seas in play.
This tradition of drill and these mock battles:
Ascanius was the first to revive the Ride
when he girded Alba Longa round with ramparts,
teaching the early Latins to keep these rites,
just as he and his fellow Trojan boys had done,
and the Albans taught their sons, and in her turn   660
great Rome received the rites and preserved our fathers' fame.
The boys are now called *Troy,* their troupe the *Trojan Corps.*

    Here came to an end the games in honor of Aeneas'
hallowed father.
                  But here for the first time Fortune
veered in its course and turned against the Trojans.
While they consecrated the tomb with various games,
Saturnian Juno hurries Iris down from the sky
to the Trojan fleet, breathing gusts at her back
to wing her on her way. Juno brooding, scheming,

her old inveterate rancor never sated. Iris flies,   670
arcing down on her rainbow showering iridescence,
and no one sees the virgin glide along the shore,
past the huge assembly, catching sight of the harbor
all deserted now, and the fleet they left unguarded.
But there, far off on a lonely stretch of beach
the Trojan women wept for the lost Anchises.
Gazing out on the deep dark swells they wept
and wailed: "How many reefs, how many sea-miles
more that we must cross! Heart-weary as we are!"

They cried with one voice. A city is what they pray for.   680
All were sick of struggling with the sea.
                                        So down
in their midst speeds Iris—no stranger to mischief—
putting aside the looks and gown of a goddess,
turning into Beroë, aged wife of Doryclus
the Tmarian, a woman of fine, noble birth
who once had fame and sons. Like Beroë now,
Iris mingles in among all the Trojan mothers.
"How wretched we are," she cries, "that no Greek soldier
dragged us off to die in the war beneath our country's walls.
Oh, my poor doomed people! What is Fortune saving you for,   690
what death-blow? Seven summers gone since Troy went down
and still we're swept along, measuring out each land, each sea—
how many hostile rocks and stars?—scanning an endless ocean,
chasing an Italy fading still as the waves roll us on.
Here is our brother Eryx' land. Acestes is our host.
What prevents us from building walls right here,
presenting our citizens with a city? Oh, my country,
gods of the hearth we tore from enemies, all for nothing,
will *no* walls ever again be called the walls of Troy?
We're never again to see the rivers Hector loved,   700
the Simois and the Xanthus? No, come, action!
Help me burn these accursed ships to ashes.
The ghost of Cassandra came to me in dreams,
the prophetess gave me flaming brands and said:

'Look for Troy right here, your own home here!'
Act now. No delay in the face of signs like these.
You see? Four altars to Neptune. The god himself
is giving us torches, building our courage, too."

    Spurring them on and first to seize a deadly brand,
she held it high in her right hand, shook it to flame   710
and with all her power hurled the fire home.
Astounded, the hearts of the Trojan women froze,
stunned till one in the crowd, the eldest, Pyrgo,
once the royal nurse to Priam's several sons,
called out: "That's not Beroë, you women of Troy—
no Trojan wife of Doryclus!
Look at her beauty, her fiery eyes, immortal marks—
what pride, what features, and what a voice, what stride!
Why, I just left Beroë now, sick and bitter to be
the only one deprived of our lavish rites,   720
denied her part in the honors paid Anchises."
                                        Urging so,
but at first the women wavered, looking back
at the ships with hateful glances, torn between
their hapless love for the land they stood on now
and the fated kingdom, calling still—when all at once
the goddess towered into the sky on balanced wings,
cleaving a giant rainbow, flying beneath the clouds.
Now they are dumbstruck, driven mad by the sign
they scream, some seize fire from the inner hearths,
some plunder the altars—branches, brushwood, torches,   730
they hurl them all at once and the God of Fire unleashed
goes raging over the benches, oarlocks, piney blazoned sterns.

    The ships are ablaze. The herald Eumelus runs the news
to crowds wedged in the theater round Anchises' tomb—
even they can see the black cloud churn with sparks.
Out in the lead, Ascanius, still heading his horsemen,
still in triumph, swerves for the ships at full tilt,
his breathless handlers helpless to rein him back,

and finding the camp in chaos, shouts out: "Madness,
beyond belief! What now? What drives you on?   740
Wretched women of Troy, it's not the enemy camp,
the Greeks—you're burning your own best hopes!
Look, it's your own Ascanius!"
                              Down at his feet
he flung his useless helmet, the one he donned
when he played at war, acting out mock battles.
Just then Aeneas hurries in with his Trojan troops
but the women, terrified, scatter down the beaches,
fleeing, stealing away into woods and rocky caverns,
anywhere they can hide. They cringe from the daylight,
shrink from what they've done. They come to their senses,   750
know their people, and Juno is driven from their hearts.

     Despite all that, the flames, the implacable fire
never quits its fury. Under the sodden beams
the tow still smolders, reeking a slow, heavy smoke
that creeps along the keels, the ruin eating into the hulls,
and all their heroic efforts, showering water, get them nowhere.
At once devoted Aeneas ripped the robe on his shoulders,
called the gods for help and flung his hands in prayer:
"Almighty Jove, if you still don't hate all Trojans,
if you still look down with your old sense of devotion,   760
still respect men's labors, save our fleet from fire!
Now, Father, snatch the slim hopes of the Trojans
out of the jaws of death! Or if I deserve it,
come, hurl what's left of us down to death
with all your angry bolts—
overwhelm us here with your iron fist!"

     No sooner said than a wild black flood of rain
comes whipping down in fury, claps of thunder—highlands,
lowlands quake and a raging tempest bursts from the whole sky
dense and dark with the lashing Southwind's blast.   770
The decks are awash, the charred timbers drenched
till all the fires are slaked and all the ships,

except for the four hulls lost, are saved from ruin.

    But captain Aeneas, dazed by this swift sharp blow,
kept wrestling the overriding anguish in his heart,
now this way, that way. Should he forget his fate
and settle in Sicily now, or head for Italian shores?
Then old Nautes, the one man Tritonian Pallas taught,
making him famous for his knowledge of her arts,
giving him answers for what the gods' great rage   780
might mean or what the march of Fate cried out for—
Nautes speaks, consoling Aeneas with his counsel:
"Son of Venus, whether the Fates will draw us on
or draw us back, let's follow where they lead.
Whatever Fortune sends, we master it all
by bearing it all, we must!
You have Acestes, a Trojan born of the gods,
a ready adviser. Invite him into your councils.
Make your plans together. Hand them over to him,
the people left from the burnt ships and those worn out   790
by the vast endeavor you've begun, your destiny, your fate.
The old men bent with age, the women sick of the sea,
ones who are feeble, ones who shrink from danger:
set them apart, and exhausted as they are,
let them have their walls within this land.
If he lends his name, they'll call the town Acesta."

    Inspired now by the plans of his old friend,
Aeneas is torn by anguish all the more
as dark Night, looming up in her chariot,
took command of the heavens, and all at once,   800
down from the sky his father Anchises' phantom seemed
to glide and the words came rushing from him toward Aeneas:
"My son, dearer to me than life while I was still alive!
Oh my son, so pressed by the fate of Troy—I've come
by the will of Jove, who swept the fire from your ships
and now from the heights of heaven pities you at last.
So come, follow old Nautes' good sound advice:

choose your elite troops, your bravest hearts,
and sail them on to Italy. There in Latium you
must battle down a people of wild, rugged ways.   810
But first go down to the House of Death, the Underworld,
go through Avernus' depths, my son, to seek me, meet me there.
I am not condemned to wicked Tartarus, those bleak shades,
I live in Elysium, the luminous fields where the true
and faithful gather. A chaste Sibyl will guide you there,
once you have offered the blood of many pure black sheep.
And then you will learn your entire race to come
and the city walls that will be made your own.
Now farewell. Dank Night wheels around
in mid-career, cruel Dawn breaks in the East,   820
and I feel her panting stallions breathing near."

      With that, he fled into thin air like a wisp of smoke.
"Racing away, but where?" Aeneas cries, "So rushed!
Whom do you flee? Who keeps you from our embrace?"

      Calling so, he rakes the slumbering coals to worship
the household god of Troy and the sacred shrine
of white-haired Vesta, offering up a suppliant's
hallowed meal, and mist from an overflowing censer.

                                              At once
he summons his friends, Acestes first, to report
the will of Jove, his dear father's commands   830
and the firm resolve now settled in his mind.
No time for debate, and no dissent from Acestes.
Consigning the women to the town, they disembark
all those who elect to stay, who feel no need for glory.
The rest repair the thwarts, replace the charred beams
with new ship timbers, refit the oars and cables;
no large troop, but their spirits burn for war.
Meanwhile Aeneas is plowing out the city limits,
assigning homes by lot. One sector, as he decrees,
called Troy, another, Ilium. Trojan-born Acestes   840
relishes his new kingdom, holding court,

giving laws to the elders called in session.
Then on the peak of Eryx reaching for the stars,
he founds a temple to Venus of Mount Ida, round it
a spreading sacred grove, and appoints a priest
to tend Anchises' tomb.
                              Now the assembled people
have feasted nine days, the altars have their gifts,
a placid breeze has lulled the swells, and a pulsing
breath of the Southwind calls them back to sea.
A great wail rises up from the deep curved bay as   850
they linger out the night and day in each other's arms.
And the same women, the same men who once believed
the face of the sea, its mighty god, too cruel to bear,
now long to embark and brave the pains of exile to the end.
But good Aeneas, consoling them all with heartfelt words,
weeps as he commends them to Acestes, their blood kin.
Three calves to Eryx, then a ewe to the god of storms—
he orders killed, and the crewmen slip the cables,
one after another. Apart at the prow, Aeneas
takes his stand, crowned with a trim olive wreath,   860
and raises a wine bowl high and scatters innards
over the salt swell and tips out streams of wine.
Shipmates race each other, thrashing the waves
and a rising sternwind surges, drives the vessels on.

     But now Venus, her anguish mounting, goes to Neptune,
pouring out her heart in a flood of lamentation:
"Juno—her lethal rage, her insatiable spirit,
Neptune, makes me stoop to every kind of prayer.
No lapse of time, no reverence, nothing tames her,
no decree of Jove or the Fates can break her will,   870
she never rests. Not even devouring a city,
the heart of the Phrygian race, in all her hatred,
dragging the remnant down through pains of every sort:
it's not enough for her. Now she stalks the bones,
the ashes of murdered Troy! Such fury's beyond me—
no doubt she has her reasons. Neptune, you yourself,
you're my witness to what great instant chaos

she unleashed, just now, in Libya's heaving seas,
mixing the sea and wind and backed by Aeolus' blasts,
all for nothing, but all dared in your own realm.   880
What outrage! Why, she drove the Trojan women
down the path of crime, goading them on to gut
the ships with fire—so hateful—the fleet lost
and their friends abandoned here on alien soil.
The survivors? I beg you, give them all safe passage
across your waters, let them reach the Tiber—
if only my prayers are granted,
if Fate will grant the Trojans city walls."

Saturn's son, the king of the deep, complied:
"By all rights, Cytherea, you should trust my realm,   890
it gave you birth. I've earned your trust, what's more.
Time and again I tamed the wild rage of sky and sea,
the same on land—Xanthus and Simois be my witness—
I cared for your Aeneas.
                    "Once when Achilles harried
the breathless Trojans, pounding their ranks against their walls,
slaughtering thousands, rivers crammed with corpses groaned
and the Xanthus could find no channel rolling down to sea,
and then as Aeneas went up against the mighty Achilles—
hardly a match for the man's gods, the man's power—
then I saved him, wrapped him into a fold of clouds,   900
though I longed to crush their ramparts roots and all,
the walls I built with my own hands—those lying Trojans!
And now as then, my concern for him stands firm.
So cast your fear to the winds. Just as you wish,
he will arrive at Avernus' haven safe and sound.
Only one will be lost, one you'll seek at sea.
One life, for the lives of many men."
                            Welcome words,
and soon as Father Neptune had soothed the goddess' heart,
he harnesses up his team with their yoke of gold,
slips the frothing bits in their chafing jaws,   910
slacks the reins and the team goes running free,
the sea-blue chariot skimming lightly over the crests

and the waves fall calm, and under the axle's thunder
the sea swell levels off and the stormclouds flee
from the wild skies. And now his retinue rises
in all their forms, enormous beasts of the deep,
the veteran troupe of Glaucus, Ino's son Palaemon,
wind-swift Tritons, Phorcus' army in full force
with Thetis, Melite, virgin Panopea out on the left,
Fair-Isle, Sea-Cave, Spray, and the Waves' Embrace.   920

    No more wavering now, now buoyant spirits seize
Aeneas' heart. The good commander orders all masts
stepped at once and the yardarms hung with sail.
All as one they make sheets fast and let out canvas
bellying now to port and now to starboard, all as one
they swing the lofty spars around and swing them back
as a favoring sternwind sweeps the fleet straight on.
Far in front, Palinurus leads the tight formation,
a line commanded to set their course by him.
                                        By now
dank Night had nearly reached her turning-point in the sky,   930
and stretched on the hard thwarts beneath their oars
the crews gave way to a deep, quiet rest, when down
from the stars the God of Sleep came gliding gently,
cleaving the dark mists and scattering shadows,
hunting you, Palinurus, bringing you fatal sleep
in all your innocence. Like Phorbas to the life,
the god sat high astern, pouring his persuasions
into your ears: "Son of Iasius, Palinurus, the sea,
all on its own, is sweeping the squadrons on,
the wind is blowing steady. Time to sleep.   940
Come, put your head down, steal some rest
for your eyes worn out from labor.
For a moment I'll take on your work myself."

    Barely raising his eyes, Palinurus answers:
"You tell *me* to forget my sense of the sea?—
the placid face of the swells, the sleeping breakers?
You tell *me* to put my trust in that, that monster?

How could I leave Aeneas prey to the lying winds?
I, betrayed so often by calm, deceptive skies!"

     So the pilot countered, iron grip on the tiller,   950
never loosing his grasp, his eyes fixed on the stars.
But watch, the god with a bough drenched in Lethe's dew
and drowsy with all the river Styx's numbing power
shakes it over the pilot's temples left and right
and fight as he does, his swimming eyes fall shut.
Just as an instant sleep stole in and left him limp,
the god, rearing over him, hurled him into the churning surf
and down he went, headfirst, wrenching a piece of rudder off
and the tiller too, and crying out to his shipmates
time and again—no use—   960
as the god himself goes winging off into thin air.
And the squadrons forge ahead undaunted, swift as ever,
sailing safely along as Father Neptune promised,
true, but carried closer in to the Sirens' rocks—
hard straits once, white with the bones of many men—
now roaring out with the sounding boom of surf on reef
when captain Aeneas felt his ship adrift, her pilot lost,
and took command himself, at sea in the black night,
moaning deeply, stunned by his comrade's fate:
"You trusted—oh, Palinurus—   970
far too much to a calm sky and sea.
Your naked corpse will lie on an unknown shore."

BOOK SIX

The Kingdom of the Dead

So as he speaks in tears Aeneas gives the ships free rein
and at last they glide onto Euboean Cumae's beaches.
Swinging their prows around to face the sea,
they moor the fleet with the anchors' biting grip
and the curved sterns edge the bay. Bands of sailors,
primed for action, leap out onto land—Hesperian land.
Some strike seeds of fire buried in veins of flint,
some strip the dense thickets, lairs of wild beasts,
and lighting on streams, are quick to point them out.
But devout Aeneas makes his way to the stronghold   10
that Apollo rules, throned on high, and set apart
is a vast cave, the awesome Sybil's secret haunt
where the Seer of Delos breathes his mighty will,
his soul inspiring her to lay the future bare.
And now they approach Diana's sacred grove

and walk beneath the golden roofs of god.
                                            Daedalus,
so the story's told, fleeing the realm of Minos,
daring to trust himself to the sky on beating wings,
floated up to the icy North, the first man to fly,
and hovered lightly on Cumae's heights at last.   20
Here, on first returning to earth, he hallowed
to you, Apollo, the oars of his rowing wings
and here he built your grand, imposing temple.
High on a gate he carved Androgeos' death
and then the people of Athens, doomed—so cruel—
to pay with the lives of seven sons. Year in, year out,
the urn stands ready, the fateful lots are drawn.

    Balancing these on a facing gate, the land of Crete
comes rising from the sea. Here the cursed lust for the bull
and Pasiphaë spread beneath him, duping both her mates,   30
and here the mixed breed, part man, part beast, the Minotaur—
a warning against such monstrous passion. Here its lair,
that house of labor, the endless blinding maze,
but Daedalus, pitying royal Ariadne's love so deep,
unraveled his own baffling labyrinth's winding paths,
guiding Theseus' groping steps with a trail of thread.
And you too, Icarus, what part you might have played
in a work that great, had Daedalus' grief allowed it.
Twice he tried to engrave your fall in gold and
twice his hands, a father's hands, fell useless.
                                            Yes,   40
and they would have kept on scanning scene by scene
if Achates, sent ahead, had not returned, bringing
Deiphobe, Glaucus' daughter, priestess of Phoebus
and Diana too, and the Sibyl tells the king:
"This is no time for gazing at the sights.
Better to slaughter seven bulls from a herd
unbroken by the yoke, as the old rite requires,
and as many head of teething yearling sheep."
Directing Aeneas so—and his men are quick

with the sacrifice she demands—   50
the Sibyl calls them into her lofty shrine.

Now carved out of the rocky flanks of Cumae
lies an enormous cavern pierced by a hundred tunnels,
a hundred mouths with as many voices rushing out,
the Sibyl's rapt replies. They had just gained
the sacred sill when the virgin cries aloud:
"Now is the time to ask your fate to speak!
The god, look, the god!"
                              So she cries before
the entrance—suddenly all her features, all
her color changes, her braided hair flies loose   60
and her breast heaves, her heart bursts with frenzy,
she seems to rise in height, the ring of her voice no longer
human—the breath, the power of god comes closer, closer.
"Why so slow, Trojan Aeneas?" she shouts, "so slow
to pray, to swear your vows? Not until you do
will the great jaws of our spellbound house gape wide."
And with that command the prophetess fell silent.

An icy shiver runs through the Trojans' sturdy spines
and the king's prayers come pouring from his heart:
"Apollo, you always pitied the Trojans' heavy labors!   70
You guided the arrow of Paris, pierced Achilles' body.
You led me through many seas, bordering endless coasts,
far-off Massylian tribes, and fields washed by the Syrtes,
and now, at long last, Italy's shores, forever fading,
lie within our grasp. Let the doom of Troy pursue us
just this far, no more. You too, you gods and goddesses,
all who could never suffer Troy and Troy's high glory,
spare the people of Pergamum now, it's only right.
And you, you blessed Sibyl who knows the future,
grant my prayer. I ask no more than the realm   80
my fate decrees: let the Trojans rest in Latium,
they and their roaming gods, their rootless powers!
Then I will build you a solid marble temple,
Apollo and Diana, establish hallowed days,

Apollo, in your name. And Sibyl, for you too,
a magnificent sacred shrine awaits you in our kingdom.
There I will house your oracles, mystic revelations
made to our race, and ordain your chosen priests,
my gracious lady. Just don't commit your words
to the rustling, scattering leaves—   90
sport of the winds that whirl them all away.
Sing them yourself, I beg you!" There Aeneas stopped.

   But the Sibyl, still not broken in by Apollo, storms
with a wild fury through her cave. And the more she tries
to pitch the great god off her breast, the more his bridle
exhausts her raving lips, overwhelming her untamed heart,
bending her to his will. Now the hundred immense
mouths of the house swing open, all on their own,
and bear the Sibyl's answers through the air:
"You who have braved the terrors of the sea,   100
though worse remain on land—you Trojans will reach
Lavinium's realm—lift that care from your hearts—
but you will rue your arrival. Wars, horrendous wars,
and the Tiber foaming with tides of blood, I see it all!
Simois, Xanthus, a Greek camp—you'll never lack them here.
Already a new Achilles springs to life in Latium,
son of a goddess too! Nor will Juno ever fail
to harry the Trojan race, and all the while,
pleading, pressed by need—what tribes, what towns
of Italy won't you beg for help! And the cause of this,   110
this new Trojan grief? Again a stranger bride,
a marriage with a stranger once again.
But never bow to suffering, go and face it,
all the bolder, wherever Fortune clears the way.
Your path to safety will open first from where
you least expect it—a city built by Greeks!"
                                        Those words
re-echoing from her shrine, the Cumaean Sibyl chants
her riddling visions filled with dread, her cave resounds
as she shrouds the truth in darkness—Phoebus whips her on
in all her frenzy, twisting his spurs below her breast.   120

As soon as her fury dies and raving lips fall still,
the hero Aeneas launches in: "No trials, my lady,
can loom before me in any new, surprising form.
No, deep in my spirit I have known them all,
I've faced them all before. But grant one prayer.
Since here, they say, are the gates of Death's king
and the dark marsh where the Acheron comes flooding up,
please, allow me to go and see my beloved father,
meet him face-to-face.
Teach me the way, throw wide the sacred doors!   130
Through fires, a thousand menacing spears I swept him off
on these shoulders, saved him from our enemies' onslaught.
He shared all roads and he braved all seas with me,
all threats of the waves and skies—frail as he was
but graced with a strength beyond his years, his lot.
He was the one, in fact, who ordered, pressed me on
to reach your doors and seek you, beg you now.
Pity the son and father, I pray you, kindly lady!
All power is yours. Hecate held back nothing,
put you in charge of Avernus' groves. If Orpheus   140
could summon up the ghost of his wife, trusting so
to his Thracian lyre and echoing strings; if Pollux
could ransom his brother and share his death by turns,
time and again traversing the same road up and down;
if Theseus, mighty Hercules—must I mention them?
I too can trace my birth from Jove on high."
                                             So he prayed,
grasping the altar while the Sibyl gave her answer:
"Born of the blood of gods, Anchises' son,
man of Troy, the descent to the Underworld is easy.
Night and day the gates of shadowy Death stand open wide,   150
but to retrace your steps, to climb back to the upper air—
there the struggle, there the labor lies. Only a few,
loved by impartial Jove or borne aloft to the sky
by their own fiery virtue—some sons of the gods
have made their way. The entire heartland here
is thick with woods, Cocytus glides around it,

coiling dense and dark.
But if such a wild desire seizes on you—twice
to sail the Stygian marsh, to see black Tartarus twice—
if you're so eager to give yourself to this, this mad ordeal,   160
then hear what you must accomplish first.
                              "Hidden
deep in a shady tree there grows a golden bough,
its leaves and its hardy, sinewy stem all gold,
held sacred to Juno of the Dead, Proserpina.
The whole grove covers it over, dusky valleys
enfold it too, closing in around it. No one
may pass below the secret places of earth before
he plucks the fruit, the golden foliage of that tree.
As her beauty's due, Proserpina decreed this bough
shall be offered up to her as her own hallowed gift.   170
When the first spray's torn away, another takes its place,
gold too, the metal breaks into leaf again, all gold.
Lift up your eyes and search, and once you find it,
duly pluck it off with your hand. Freely, easily,
all by itself it comes away, if Fate calls you on.
If not, no strength within you can overpower it,
no iron blade, however hard, can tear it off.

     "One thing more I must tell you.
A friend lies dead—oh, you could not know—
his body pollutes your entire fleet with death   180
while you search on for oracles, linger at our doors.
Bear him first to his place of rest, bury him in his tomb.
Lead black cattle there, first offerings of atonement.
Only then can you set eyes on the Stygian groves
and the realms no living man has ever trod."
Abruptly she fell silent, lips sealed tight.

     His eyes fixed on the ground, his face in tears,
Aeneas moves on, leaving the cavern, turning over
within his mind these strange, dark events.
His trusty comrade Achates keeps his pace   190

and the same cares weigh down his plodding steps.
They traded many questions, wondering, back and forth,
what dead friend did the Sibyl mean, whose body must be buried?
Suddenly, Misenus—out on the dry beach they see him,
reach him now, cut off by a death all undeserved.
Misenus, Aeolus' son, a herald unsurpassed
at rallying troops with his trumpet's cry,
igniting the God of War with its shrill blare.
He had been mighty Hector's friend, by Hector's side
in the rush of battle, shining with spear and trumpet both.   200
But when triumphant Achilles stripped Hector's life,
the gallant hero joined forces with Dardan Aeneas,
followed a captain every bit as strong. But then,
chancing to make the ocean ring with his hollow shell,
the madman challenged the gods to match him blast for blast
and jealous Triton—if we can believe the story—
snatched him up and drowned the man in the surf
that seethed between the rocks.
                              So all his shipmates
gathered round his body and raised a loud lament,
devoted Aeneas in the lead. Then still in tears,   210
they rush to perform the Sibyl's orders, no delay,
they strive to pile up trees, to build an altar-pyre
rising to the skies. Then into an ancient wood
and the hidden dens of beasts they make their way,
and down crash the pines, the ilex rings to the axe,
the trunks of ash and oak are split by the driving wedge,
and they roll huge rowans down the hilly slopes.

    Aeneas spurs his men in the forefront of their labors,
geared with the same woodsmen's tools around his waist.
But the same anxiety keeps on churning in his heart   220
as he scans the endless woods and prays by chance:
"If only that golden bough would gleam before us now
on a tree in this dark grove! Since all the Sibyl
foretold of you was true, Misenus, all too true."

    No sooner said than before his eyes, twin doves

chanced to come flying down the sky and lit
on the green grass at his feet. His mother's birds—
the great captain knew them and raised a prayer of joy:
"Be my guides! If there's a path, fly through the air,
set me a course to the grove where that rich branch   230
shades the good green earth. And you, goddess,
mother, don't fail me in this, my hour of doubt!"

   With that he stopped in his tracks, watching keenly—
what sign would they offer? Where would they lead?
And on they flew, pausing to feed, then flying on
as far as a follower's eye could track their flight
and once they reached the foul-smelling gorge of Avernus,
up they veered, quickly, then slipped down through the clear air
to settle atop the longed-for goal, the twofold tree, its green
a foil for the breath of gold that glows along its branch.   240
As mistletoe in the dead of winter's icy forests
leafs with life on a tree that never gave it birth,
embracing the smooth trunk with its pale yellow bloom,
so glowed the golden foliage against the ilex evergreen,
so rustled the sheer gold leaf in the light breeze.
Aeneas grips it at once—the bough holds back—
he tears it off in his zeal
and bears it into the vatic Sibyl's shrine.
                                   All the while
the Trojans along the shore keep weeping for Misenus,
paying his thankless ashes final rites. And first   250
they build an immense pyre of resinous pitch-pine
and oaken logs, weaving into its flanks dark leaves
and setting before it rows of funereal cypress,
crowning it all with the herald's gleaming arms.
Some heat water in cauldrons fired to boiling,
bathe and anoint the body chill with death.
The dirge rises up. Then, their weeping over,
they lay his corpse on a litter, swathe him round
in purple robes that form the well-known shroud.
Some hoisted up the enormous bier—sad service—   260
their eyes averted, after their fathers' ways of old,

and thrust the torch below. The piled offerings blazed,
frankincense, hallowed foods and brimming bowls of oil.
And after the coals sank in and the fires died down,
they washed his embers, thirsty remains, with wine.
Corynaeus sealed the bones he culled in a bronze urn,
then circling his comrades three times with pure water,
sprinkling light drops from a blooming olive spray,
he cleansed the men and voiced the last farewell.
But devout Aeneas mounds the tomb—an immense barrow   270
crowned with the man's own gear, his oar and trumpet—
under a steep headland, called after the herald now
and for all time to come it bears Misenus' name.

                                   The rite
performed, Aeneas hurries to carry out the Sibyl's orders.
There was a vast cave deep in the gaping, jagged rock,
shielded well by a dusky lake and shadowed grove.
Over it no bird on earth could make its way unscathed,
such poisonous vapors steamed up from its dark throat
to cloud the arching sky. Here, as her first step,
the priestess steadies four black-backed calves,   280
she tips wine on their brows, then plucks some tufts
from the crown between their horns and casts them
over the altar fire, first offerings, crying out
to Hecate, mighty Queen of Heaven and Hell.
Attendants run knives under throats and catch
warm blood in bowls. Aeneas himself, sword drawn,
slaughters a black-fleeced lamb to the Furies' mother,
Night, and to her great sister, Earth, and to you,
Proserpina, kills a barren heifer. Then to the king
of the river Styx, he raises altars into the dark night   290
and over their fires lays whole carcasses of bulls
and pours fat oil over their entrails flaming up.
Then suddenly, look, at the break of day, first light,
the earth groans underfoot and the wooded heights quake
and across the gloom the hounds seem to howl
at the goddess coming closer.
                          "Away, away!"
the Sibyl shrieks, "all you unhallowed ones—away

from this whole grove! But you launch out on your journey,
tear your sword from its sheath, Aeneas. Now for courage,
now the steady heart!" And the Sibyl says no more but   300
into the yawning cave she flings herself, possessed—
he follows her boldly, matching stride for stride.
                                              You gods
who govern the realm of ghosts, you voiceless shades and Chaos—
you, the River of Fire, you far-flung regions hushed in night—
lend me the right to tell what I have heard, lend your power
to reveal the world immersed in the misty depths of earth.

    On they went, those dim travelers under the lonely night,
through gloom and the empty halls of Death's ghostly realm,
like those who walk through woods by a grudging moon's
deceptive light when Jove has plunged the sky in dark   310
and the black night drains all color from the world.
There in the entryway, the gorge of hell itself,
Grief and the pangs of Conscience make their beds,
and fatal pale Disease lives there, and bleak Old Age,
Dread and Hunger, seductress to crime, and grinding Poverty,
all, terrible shapes to see—and Death and deadly Struggle
and Sleep, twin brother of Death, and twisted, wicked Joys
and facing them at the threshold, War, rife with death,
and the Furies' iron chambers, and mad, raging Strife
whose blood-stained headbands knot her snaky locks.   320

    There in the midst, a giant shadowy elm tree spreads
her ancient branching arms, home, they say, to swarms
of false dreams, one clinging tight under each leaf.
And a throng of monsters too—what brutal forms
are stabled at the gates—Centaurs, mongrel Scyllas,
part women, part beasts, and hundred-handed Briareus
and the savage Hydra of Lerna, that hissing horror,
the Chimaera armed with torches—Gorgons, Harpies
and triple-bodied Geryon, his great ghost. And here,
instantly struck with terror, Aeneas grips his sword   330
and offers its naked edge against them as they come,
and if his experienced comrade had not warned him

they are mere disembodied creatures, flimsy
will-o'-the-wisps that flit like living forms,
he would have rushed them all,
slashed through empty phantoms with his blade.
                                            From there
the road leads down to the Acheron's Tartarean waves.
Here the enormous whirlpool gapes aswirl with filth,
seethes and spews out all its silt in the Wailing River.
And here the dreaded ferryman guards the flood,   340
grisly in his squalor—Charon . . .
his scraggly beard a tangled mat of white, his eyes
fixed in a fiery stare, and his grimy rags hang down
from his shoulders by a knot. But all on his own
he punts his craft with a pole and hoists sail
as he ferries the dead souls in his rust-red skiff.
He's on in years, but a god's old age is hale and green.

    A huge throng of the dead came streaming toward the banks:
mothers and grown men and ghosts of great-souled heroes,
their bodies stripped of life, and boys and unwed girls   350
and sons laid on the pyre before their parents' eyes.
As thick as leaves in autumn woods at the first frost
that slip and float to earth, or dense as flocks of birds
that wing from the heaving sea to shore when winter's chill
drives them over the waves to landfalls drenched in sunlight.
There they stood, pleading to be the first ones ferried over,
reaching out their hands in longing toward the farther shore.
But the grim ferryman ushers aboard now these, now those,
others he thrusts away, back from the water's edge.
                                            Aeneas,
astonished, stirred by the tumult, calls out: "Tell me,   360
Sibyl, what does it mean, this thronging toward the river?
What do the dead souls want? What divides them all?
Some are turned away from the banks and others
scull the murky waters with their oars!"

    The aged priestess answered Aeneas briefly:
"Son of Anchises—born of the gods, no doubt—

what you see are Cocytus' pools and Styx's marsh,
Powers by which the gods swear oaths they dare not break.
And the great rout you see is helpless, still not buried.
That ferryman there is Charon. Those borne by the stream   370
have found their graves. And no spirits may be conveyed
across the horrendous banks and hoarse, roaring flood
until their bones are buried, and they rest in peace . . .
A hundred years they wander, hovering round these shores
till at last they may return and see once more the pools
they long to cross."
              Anchises' son came to a halt
and stood there, pondering long, while pity filled his heart,
their lot so hard, unjust. And then he spots two men,
grief-stricken and robbed of death's last tribute:
Leucaspis and Orontes, the Lycian fleet's commander.   380
Together they sailed from Troy over windswept seas
and a Southern gale sprang up and
toppling breakers crushed their ships and crews.
                        Look,
the pilot Palinurus was drifting toward him now,
fresh from the Libyan run where, watching the stars,
he plunged from his stern, pitched out in heavy seas.
Aeneas, barely sighting him grieving in the shadows,
hailed him first: "What god, Palinurus, snatched you
from our midst and drowned you in open waters?
Tell me, please. Apollo has never lied before.   390
This is his one reply that's played me false:
he swore you would cross the ocean safe and sound
and reach Italian shores. Is *this* the end he promised?"

    But the pilot answered: "Captain, Anchises' son,
Apollo's prophetic cauldron has not failed you—
no god drowned me in open waters. No, the rudder
I clung to, holding us all on course—my charge—
some powerful force ripped it away by chance
and I dragged it down as I dropped headlong too.
By the cruel seas I swear I felt no fear for myself   400
to match my fear that your ship, stripped of her tiller,

steersman wrenched away, might founder in that great surge.
Three blustery winter nights the Southwind bore me wildly
over the endless waters, then at the fourth dawn, swept up
on a breaker's crest, I could almost sight it now—Italy!
Stroke by stroke I swam for land, safety was in my grasp,
weighed down by my sodden clothes, my fingers clawing
the jutting spurs of a cliff, when a band of brutes
came at me, ran me through with knives, the fools,
they took me for plunder worth the taking.   410
The tides hold me now
and the stormwinds roll my body down the shore.
By the sky's lovely light and the buoyant breeze I beg you,
by your father, your hopes for Iulus rising to his prime,
pluck me up from my pain, my undefeated captain!
Or throw some earth on my body—you know you can—
sail back to Velia's port. Or if there's a way and
your goddess mother makes it clear—for not without
the will of the gods, I'm certain, do you strive
to cross these awesome streams and Stygian marsh—   420
give me your pledge, your hand, in all my torment!
Take me with you over the waves. At least in death
I'll find a peaceful haven."
                              So the pilot begged
and so the Sibyl cut him short: "How, Palinurus,
how can you harbor this mad desire of yours?
You think that you, unburied, can lay your eyes
on the Styx's flood, the Furies' ruthless stream,
and approach the banks unsummoned? Hope no more
the gods' decrees can be brushed aside by prayer.
Hold fast to my words and keep them well in mind   430
to comfort your hard lot. For neighboring people
living in cities near and far, compelled by signs
from the great gods on high, will appease your bones,
will build you a tomb and pay your tomb due rites
and the site will bear the name of Palinurus
now and always."
                        That promise lifts his anguish,
drives, for a while, the grief from his sad heart.

He takes delight in the cape that bears his name.

So now they press on with their journey under way
and at last approach the river. But once the ferryman,   440
still out in the Styx's currents, spied them moving
across the silent grove and turning toward the bank,
he greets them first with a rough abrupt rebuke:
"Stop, whoever you are at our river's edge,
in full armor too! Why have you come? Speak up,
from right where you are, not one step more! This
is the realm of shadows, sleep and drowsy night.
The law forbids me to carry living bodies across
in my Stygian boat. I'd little joy, believe me,
when Hercules came and I sailed the hero over,   450
or Theseus, Pirithous, sons of gods as they were
with their high and mighty power. Hercules stole
our watchdog—chained him, the poor trembling creature,
dragged him away from our king's very throne! The others
tried to snatch our queen from the bridal bed of Death!"

But Apollo's seer broke in and countered Charon:
"There's no such treachery here—just calm down—
no threat of force in our weapons. The huge guard
at the gates can howl for eternity from his cave,
terrifying the bloodless shades, Persephone keep   460
her chastity safe at home behind her uncle's doors.
Aeneas of Troy, famous for his devotion, feats of arms,
goes down to the deepest shades of hell to see his father.
But if this image of devotion cannot move you, here,
this bough"—showing the bough enfolded in her robes—
"You know it well."
                        At this, the heaving rage
subsides in his chest. The Sibyl says no more.
The ferryman, marveling at the awesome gift,
the fateful branch unseen so many years,
swerves his dusky craft and approaches shore.   470
The souls already crouched at the long thwarts—
he brusquely thrusts them out, clearing the gangways,
quickly taking massive Aeneas aboard the little skiff.

Under his weight the boat groans and her stitched seams
gape as she ships great pools of water pouring in.
At last, the river crossed, the ferryman lands
the seer and hero all unharmed in the marsh,
the repellent oozing slime and livid sedge.
                                                These
are the realms that monstrous Cerberus rocks with howls
braying out of his three throats, his enormous bulk   480
squatting low in the cave that faced them there.
The Sibyl, seeing the serpents writhe around his neck,
tossed him a sop, slumbrous with honey and drugged seed,
and he, frothing with hunger, three jaws spread wide,
snapped it up where the Sibyl tossed it—gone.
His tremendous back relaxed, he sags to earth
and sprawls over all his cave, his giant hulk limp.
The watchdog buried now in sleep, Aeneas seizes
the way in, quickly clear of the river's edge,
the point of no return.
                              At that moment, cries—   490
they could hear them now, a crescendo of wailing,
ghosts of infants weeping, robbed of their share
of this sweet life, at its very threshold too:
all, snatched from the breast on that black day
that swept them off and drowned them in bitter death.
Beside them were those condemned to die on a false charge.
But not without jury picked by lot, not without judge
are their places handed down. Not at all.
Minos the grand inquisitor stirs the urn,
he summons the silent jury of the dead,   500
he scans the lives of those accused, their charges.
The region next to them is held by those sad ghosts,
innocents all, who brought on death by their own hands;
despising the light, they threw their lives away.
How they would yearn, now, in the world above
to endure grim want and long hard labor!
But Fate bars the way. The grisly swamp
and its loveless, lethal waters bind them fast,
Styx with its nine huge coils holds them captive.

Close to the spot, extending toward the horizon—   510
the Sibyl points them out—are the Fields of Mourning,
that is the name they bear. Here wait those souls
consumed by the harsh, wasting sickness, cruel love,
concealed on lonely paths, shrouded by myrtle bowers.
Not even in death do their torments leave them, ever.
Here he glimpses Phaedra, Procris, and Eriphyle grieving,
baring the wounds her heartless son had dealt her.
Evadne, Pasiphaë, and Laodamia walking side by side,
and another, a young man once, a woman now, Caeneus,
turned back by Fate to the form she bore at first.   520

And wandering there among them, wound still fresh,
Phoenician Dido drifted along the endless woods.
As the Trojan hero paused beside her, recognized her
through the shadows, a dim, misty figure—as one
when the month is young may see or seem to see
the new moon rising up through banks of clouds—
that moment Aeneas wept and approached the ghost
with tender words of love: "Tragic Dido,
so, was the story true that came my way?
I heard that you were dead . . .   530
you took the final measure with a sword.
Oh, dear god, was it I who caused your death?
I swear by the stars, by the Powers on high, whatever
faith one swears by here in the depths of earth,
I left your shores, my Queen, against my will. Yes,
the will of the gods, that drives me through the shadows now,
these moldering places so forlorn, this deep unfathomed night—
their decrees have forced me on. Nor did I ever dream
my leaving could have brought you so much grief.
Stay a moment. Don't withdraw from my sight.   540
Running away—from whom? This is the last word
that Fate allows me to say to you. The last."

Aeneas, with such appeals, with welling tears,
tried to soothe her rage, her wild fiery glance.
But she, her eyes fixed on the ground, turned away,

her features no more moved by his pleas as he talked on
than if she were set in stony flint or Parian marble rock.
And at last she tears herself away, his enemy forever,
fleeing back to the shadowed forests where Sychaeus,
her husband long ago, answers all her anguish,   550
meets her love with love. But Aeneas, no less
struck by her unjust fate, escorts her from afar
with streaming tears and pities her as she passes.

   From there they labor along the charted path
and at last they gain the utmost outer fields
where throngs of the great war heroes live apart.
Here Tydeus comes to meet him, Parthenopaeus
shining in arms, and Adrastus' pallid phantom. Here,
mourned in the world above and fallen dead in battle,
sons of Dardanus, chiefs arrayed in a long ranked line.   560
Seeing them all, he groaned—Glaucus, Medon, Thersilochus,
Antenor's three sons and the priest of Ceres, Polyboetes,
Idaeus too, still with chariot, still with gear in hand.
Their spirits crowding around Aeneas, left and right,
beg him to linger longer—a glimpse is not enough—
to walk beside him and learn the reasons why he's come.
But the Greek commanders and Agamemnon's troops in phalanx,
spotting the hero and his armor glinting through the shadows—
blinding panic grips them, some turn tail and run
as they once ran back to the ships, some strain   570
to raise a battle cry, a thin wisp of a cry
that mocks their gaping jaws.

   And here he sees Deiphobus too, Priam's son
mutilated, his whole body, his face hacked to pieces—
Ah, so cruel—his face and both his hands, and his ears
ripped from his ravaged head, his nostrils slashed,
disgraceful wound. He can hardly recognize him,
a cowering shadow hiding his punishments so raw.
Aeneas, never pausing, hails the ghost at once
in an old familiar voice: "Mighty captain,   580

Deiphobus, sprung of the noble blood of Teucer,
who was bent on making you pay a price so harsh?
Who could maim you so? I heard on that last night
that you, exhausted from killing hordes of Greeks,
had fallen dead on a mangled pile of carnage.
So I was the one who raised your empty tomb
on Rhoeteum Cape and called out to your shade
three times with a ringing voice. Your name and armor
mark the site, my friend, but I could not find you,
could not bury your bones in native soil   590
when I set out to sea."

    "Nothing, my friend," Priam's son replies,
"you have left nothing undone. All that's owed
Deiphobus and his shadow you have paid in full.
My own fate and the deadly crimes of that Spartan whore
have plunged me in this hell. Look at the souvenirs she left me!
And how we spent that last night, lost in deluded joys,
you know. Remember it we must, and all too well.
When the fatal horse mounted over our steep walls,
its weighted belly teeming with infantry in arms—   600
she led the Phrygian women round the city, feigning
the orgiastic rites of Bacchus, dancing, shrieking
but in their midst she shook her monstrous torch,
a flare from the city heights, a signal to the Greeks.
While I in our cursed bridal chamber, there I lay,
bone-weary with anguish, buried deep in sleep,
peaceful, sweet, like the peace of death itself.
And all the while that matchless wife of mine
is removing all my weapons from the house,
even slipping my trusty sword from under my pillow.   610
She calls Menelaus in and flings the doors wide open,
hoping no doubt by this grand gift to him, her lover,
to wipe the slate clean of her former wicked ways.
Why drag things out? They burst into the bedroom,
Ulysses, that rouser of outrage right beside them,
Aeolus' crafty heir. You gods, if my lips are pure,

I pray for vengeance now—
deal such blows to the Greeks as they dealt *me!*
But come, tell me in turn what twist of fate
has brought you here alive? Forced by wanderings,   620
storm-tossed at sea, or prompted by the gods?
What destiny hounds you on to visit these,
these sunless homes of sorrow, harrowed lands?"

    Trading words, as Dawn in her rose-red chariot
crossed in mid-career, high noon in the arching sky,
and they might have spent what time they had with tales
if the Sibyl next to Aeneas had not warned him tersely:
"Night comes on, Aeneas. We waste our time with tears.
This is the place where the road divides in two.
To the right it runs below the mighty walls of Death,   630
our path to Elysium, but the left-hand road torments
the wicked, leading down to Tartarus, path to doom."

    "No anger, please, great priestess," begged Deiphobus.
"Back I go to the shades to fill the tally out.
Now go, our glory of Troy, go forth and enjoy
a better fate than mine." With his last words
he turned in his tracks and went his way.
                                            Aeneas
suddenly glances back and beneath a cliff to the left
he sees an enormous fortress ringed with triple walls
and raging around it all, a blazing flood of lava,   640
Tartarus' River of Fire, whirling thunderous boulders.
Before it rears a giant gate, its columns solid adamant,
so no power of man, not even the gods themselves
can root it out in war. An iron tower looms on high
where Tisiphone, crouching with bloody shroud girt up,
never sleeping, keeps her watch at the entrance night and day.
Groans resound from the depths, the savage crack of the lash,
the grating creak of iron, the clank of dragging chains.
And Aeneas froze there, terrified, taking in the din:
"What are the crimes, what kinds? Tell me, Sibyl,   650

what are the punishments, why this scourging?
Why such wailing echoing in the air?"

The seer rose to the moment: "Famous captain of Troy,
no pure soul may set foot on that wicked threshold.
But when Hecate put me in charge of Avernus' groves
she taught me all the punishments of the gods,
she led me through them all.
Here Cretan Rhadamanthus rules with an iron hand,
censuring men, exposing fraud, forcing confessions
when anyone up above, reveling in his hidden crimes,   660
puts off his day of atonement till he dies, the fool,
too late. That very moment, vengeful Tisiphone, armed
with lashes, springs on the guilty, whips them till they quail,
with her left hand shaking all her twisting serpents,
summoning up her savage sisters, bands of Furies.
Then at last, screeching out on their grinding hinge
the infernal gates swing wide.
                            "Can you see that sentry
crouched at the entrance? What a specter guards the threshold!
Fiercer still, the monstrous Hydra, fifty black maws gaping,
holds its lair inside.
                    "Then the abyss, Tartarus itself   670
plunges headlong down through the darkness twice as far
as our gaze goes up to Olympus rising toward the skies.
Here the ancient line of the Earth, the Titans' spawn,
flung down by lightning, writhe in the deep pit.
There I saw the twin sons of Aloeus too, giant bodies
that clawed the soaring sky with their hands to tear it down
and thrust great Jove from his kingdom high above.

"I saw Salmoneus too, who paid a brutal price
for aping the flames of Jove and Olympus' thunder.
Sped by his four-horse chariot, flaunting torches,   680
right through the Greek tribes and Elis city's heart
he rode in triumph, claiming as *his* the honors of the gods.
The madman, trying to match the storm and matchless lightning

just by stamping on bronze with prancing horn-hoofed steeds!
The almighty Father hurled his bolt through the thunderheads—
no torches for him, no smoky flicker of pitch-pines, no,
he spun him headlong down in a raging whirlwind.

                                        "Tityus too:
you could see that son of Earth, the mother of us all,
his giant body splayed out over nine whole acres,
a hideous vulture with hooked beak gorging down   690
his immortal liver and innards ever ripe for torture.
Deep in his chest it nestles, ripping into its feast
and the fibers, grown afresh, get no relief from pain.

    "What need to tell of the Lapiths, Ixion, or Pirithous?
Above them a black rock—now, now slipping, teetering,
watch, forever about to fall. While the golden posts
of high festal couches gleam, and a banquet spreads
before their eyes with luxury fit for kings . . .
but reclining just beside them, the oldest Fury
holds back their hands from even touching the food,   700
surging up with her brandished torch and deafening screams.

    "Here those who hated their brothers, while alive,
or struck their fathers down
or embroiled clients in fraud, or brooded alone
over troves of gold they gained and never put aside
some share for their own kin—a great multitude, these—
then those killed for adultery, those who marched to the flag
of civil war and never shrank from breaking their pledge
to their lords and masters: all of them, walled up here,
wait to meet their doom.
                              "Don't hunger to know their doom,   710
what form of torture or twist of Fortune drags them down.
Some trundle enormous boulders, others dangle, racked
to the breaking point on the spokes of rolling wheels.
Doomed Theseus sits on his seat and there he will sit forever.
Phlegyas, most in agony, sounds out his warning to all,
his piercing cries bear witness through the darkness:
'Learn to bow to justice. Never scorn the gods.

You all stand forewarned!'

"Here's one who bartered his native land for gold,
he saddled her with a tyrant, set up laws for a bribe,   720
for a bribe he struck them down. This one forced himself
on his daughter's bed and sealed a forbidden marriage.
All dared an outrageous crime and what they dared, they did.

"No, not if I had a hundred tongues and a hundred mouths
and a voice of iron too—I could never capture
all the crimes or run through all the torments,
doom by doom."
                      So Apollo's aged priestess
ended her answer, then she added: "Come,
press on with your journey. See it through,
this duty you've undertaken. We must hurry now.   730
I can just make out the ramparts forged by the Cyclops.
There are the gates, facing us with their arch.
There our orders say to place our gifts."
                                        At that,
both of them march in step along the shadowed paths,
consuming the space between, and approach the doors.
Aeneas springs to the entryway and rinsing his limbs
with fresh pure water, there at the threshold,
just before them, stakes the golden bough.

       The rite complete at last,
their duty to the goddess performed in full,   740
they gained the land of joy, the fresh green fields,
the Fortunate Groves where the blessed make their homes.
Here a freer air, a dazzling radiance clothes the fields
and the spirits possess their own sun, their own stars.
Some flex their limbs in the grassy wrestling-rings,
contending in sport, they grapple on the golden sands.
Some beat out a dance with their feet and chant their songs.
And Orpheus himself, the Thracian priest with his long robes,
keeps their rhythm strong with his lyre's seven ringing strings,
plucking now with his fingers, now with his ivory plectrum.   750

Here is the ancient line of Teucer, noblest stock of all,
those great-hearted heroic sons born in better years,
Ilus, and Assaracus, and Dardanus, founder of Troy.
Far off, Aeneas gazes in awe—their arms, their chariots,
phantoms all, their lances fixed in the ground, their horses,
freed from harness, grazing the grasslands near and far.
The same joy they took in arms and chariots when alive,
in currying horses sleek and putting them to pasture,
follows them now they rest beneath the earth.

                                              Others, look,
he glimpses left and right in the meadows, feasting,   760
singing in joy a chorus raised to Healing Apollo,
deep in a redolent laurel grove where Eridanus River
rushes up, in full spate, and rolls through woods
in the high world above. And here are troops of men
who had suffered wounds, fighting to save their country,
and those who had been pure priests while still alive,
and the faithful poets whose songs were fit for Phoebus;
those who enriched our lives with the newfound arts they forged
and those we remember well for the good they did mankind.
And all, with snow-white headbands crowning their brows,   770
flow around the Sibyl as she addresses them there,
Musaeus first, who holds the center of that huge throng,
his shoulders rearing high as they gaze up toward him:
"Tell us, happy spirits, and you, the best of poets,
what part of your world, what region holds Anchises?
All for him we have come,
we've sailed across the mighty streams of hell."

      And at once the great soul made a brief reply:
"No one's home is fixed. We live in shady groves,
we settle on pillowed banks and meadows washed with brooks.   780
But you, if your heart compels you, climb this ridge
and I soon will set your steps on an easy path."

      So he said and walking on ahead, from high above
points out to them open country swept with light.
Down they come and leave the heights behind.

Now father Anchises, deep in a valley's green recess,
was passing among the souls secluded there, reviewing them,
eagerly, on their way to the world of light above. By chance
he was counting over his own people, all his cherished heirs,
their fame and their fates, their values, acts of valor.   790
When he saw Aeneas striding toward him over the fields,
he reached out both his hands as his spirit lifted,
tears ran down his cheeks, a cry broke from his lips:
"You've come at last? Has the love your father hoped for
mastered the hardship of the journey? Let me look at your face,
my son, exchange some words, and hear your familiar voice.
So I dreamed, I knew you'd come, I counted the moments—
my longing has not betrayed me.
Over what lands, what seas have you been driven,
buffeted by what perils into my open arms, my son?   800
How I feared the realm of Libya might well do you harm!"

      "Your ghost, my father," he replied, "your grieving ghost,
so often it came and urged me to your threshold!
My ships are lying moored in the Tuscan sea.
Let me clasp your hand, my father, let me—
I beg you, don't withdraw from my embrace!"

      So Aeneas pleaded, his face streaming tears.
Three times he tried to fling his arms around his neck,
three times he embraced—nothing . . . the phantom
sifting through his fingers,   810
light as wind, quick as a dream in flight.

      And now Aeneas sees in the valley's depths
a sheltered grove and rustling wooded brakes
and the Lethe flowing past the homes of peace.
Around it hovered numberless races, nations of souls
like bees in meadowlands on a cloudless summer day
that settle in flowers, riots of color, swarming round
the lilies' lustrous sheen, and the whole field comes alive
with a humming murmur. Struck by the sudden sight,
Aeneas, all unknowing, wonders aloud, and asks: 820

"What is the river over there? And who are they
who crowd the banks in such a growing throng?"

    His father Anchises answers: "They are the spirits
owed a second body by the Fates. They drink deep
of the river Lethe's currents there, long drafts
that will set them free of cares, oblivious forever.
How long I have yearned to tell you, show them to you,
face-to-face, yes, as I count the tally out
of all my children's children. So all the more
you can rejoice with me in Italy, found at last."   830

    "What, Father, can we suppose that any spirits
rise from here to the world above, return once more
to the shackles of the body? Why this mad desire,
poor souls, for the light of life?"
                          "I will tell you,
my son, not keep you in suspense," Anchises says,
and unfolds all things in order, one by one.
                                 "First,
the sky and the earth and the flowing fields of the sea,
the shining orb of the moon and the Titan sun, the stars:
an inner spirit feeds them, coursing through all their limbs,
mind stirs the mass and their fusion brings the world to birth.   840
From their union springs the human race and the wild beasts,
the winged lives of birds and the wondrous monsters bred
below the glistening surface of the sea. The seeds of life—
fiery is their force, divine their birth, but they
are weighed down by the bodies' ills or dulled
by earthly limbs and flesh that's born for death.
That is the source of all men's fears and longings,
joys and sorrows, nor can they see the heavens' light,
shut up in the body's tomb, a prison dark and deep.
                                     "True,
but even on that last day, when the light of life departs,   850
the wretches are not completely purged of all the taints,
nor are they wholly freed of all the body's plagues.
Down deep they harden fast—they must, so long engrained

in the flesh—in strange, uncanny ways. And so the souls
are drilled in punishments, they must pay for their old offenses.
Some are hung splayed out, exposed to the empty winds,
some are plunged in the rushing floods—their stains,
their crimes scoured off or scorched away by fire.
Each of us must suffer his own demanding ghost.
Then we are sent to Elysium's broad expanse,   860
a few of us even hold these fields of joy
till the long days, a cycle of time seen through,
cleanse our hard, inveterate stains and leave us clear
ethereal sense, the eternal breath of fire purged and pure.
But all the rest, once they have turned the wheel of time
for a thousand years: God calls them forth to the Lethe,
great armies of souls, their memories blank so that
they may revisit the overarching world once more
and begin to long to return to bodies yet again."

    Anchises, silent a moment, drawing his son and Sibyl   870
with him into the midst of the vast murmuring throng,
took his stand on a rise of ground where he could scan
the long column marching toward him, soul by soul,
and recognize their features as they neared.
                      "So come,
the glory that will follow the sons of Troy through time,
your children born of Italian stock who wait for life,
bright souls, future heirs of our name and our renown:
I will reveal them all and tell you of your fate.
                             "There,
you see that youth who leans on a tipless spear of honor?
Assigned the nearest place to the world of light,   880
the first to rise to the air above, his blood
mixed with Italian blood, he bears an Alban name.
Silvius, your son, your last-born, when late
in your old age your wife Lavinia brings him up,
deep in the woods—a king who fathers kings in turn,
he founds our race that rules in Alba Longa.
                          "Nearby,
there's Procas, pride of the Trojan people, then come

Capys, Numitor, and the one who revives your name,
Silvius Aeneas, your equal in arms and duty,
famed, if he ever comes to rule the Alban throne.   890
What brave young men! Look at the power they display
and the oakleaf civic crowns that shade their foreheads.
They will erect for you Nomentum, Gabii, Fidena town
and build Collatia's ramparts on the mountains,
Pometia too, and Inuis' fortress, Bola and Cora.
Famous names in the future, nameless places now.

                                        "Here,
a son of Mars, his grandsire Numitor's comrade—Romulus,
bred from Assaracus' blood by his mother, Ilia.
See how the twin plumes stand joined on his helmet?
And the Father of Gods himself already marks him out   900
with his own bolts of honor. Under his auspices, watch,
my son, our brilliant Rome will extend her empire far
and wide as the earth, her spirit high as Olympus.
Within her single wall she will gird her seven hills,
blest in her breed of men: like the Berecynthian Mother
crowned with her turrets, riding her victor's chariot
through the Phrygian cities, glad in her brood of gods,
embracing a hundred grandsons. All dwell in the heavens,
all command the heights.

                           "Now turn your eyes this way
and behold these people, your own Roman people.   910
Here is Caesar and all the line of Iulus
soon to venture under the sky's great arch.
Here is the man, he's here! Time and again
you've heard his coming promised—Caesar Augustus!
Son of a god, he will bring back the Age of Gold
to the Latian fields where Saturn once held sway,
expand his empire past the Garamants and the Indians
to a land beyond the stars, beyond the wheel of the year,
the course of the sun itself, where Atlas bears the skies
and turns on his shoulder the heavens studded with flaming stars.   920
Even now the Caspian and Maeotic kingdoms quake at his coming,
oracles sound the alarm and the seven mouths of the Nile

churn with fear. Not even Hercules himself could cross
such a vast expanse of earth, though it's true he shot
the stag with its brazen hoofs, and brought peace
to the ravaged woods of Erymanthus, terrorized
the Hydra of Lerna with his bow. Not even Bacchus
in all his glory, driving his team with vines for reins
and lashing his tigers down from Nysa's soaring ridge.
Do we still flinch from turning our valor into deeds?   930
Or fear to make our home on Western soil?

                               "But look,
who is that over there, crowned with an olive wreath
and bearing sacred emblems? I know his snowy hair,
his beard—the first king to found our Rome on laws,
Numa, sent from the poor town of Cures, paltry land,
to wield imperial power.

                        "And after him comes Tullus
disrupting his country's peace to rouse a stagnant people,
armies stale to the taste of triumph, back to war again.
And just behind him, Ancus, full of the old bravado,
even now too swayed by the breeze of public favor.

                                "Wait,   940
would you like to see the Tarquin kings, the overweening
spirit of Brutus the Avenger, the fasces he reclaims?
The first to hold a consul's power and ruthless axes,
then, when his sons foment rebellion against the city,
their father summons them to the executioner's block
in freedom's noble name, unfortunate man . . .
however the future years will exalt his actions:
a patriot's love wins out, and boundless lust for praise.

                                "Now,
the Decii and the Drusi—look over there—Torquatus too,
with his savage axe, Camillus bringing home the standards.   950
But you see that pair of spirits? Gleaming in equal armor,
equals now at peace, while darkness pins them down,
but if they should reach the light of life, what war
they'll rouse between them! Battles, massacres—Caesar,
the bride's father, marching down from his Alpine ramparts,

Fortress Monaco, Pompey her husband set to oppose him
with the armies of the East.

                                "No, my sons, never inure
yourselves to civil war, never turn your sturdy power
against your country's heart. You, Caesar, you
be first in mercy—you trace your line from Olympus—   960
born of my blood, throw down your weapons now!

                                            "Mummius here,
he will conquer Corinth and, famed for killing Achaeans,
drive his victor's chariot up the Capitol's heights.
And there is Paullus, and he will rout all Argos
and Agamemnon's own Mycenae and cut Perseus down—
the heir of Aeacus, born of Achilles' warrior blood—
and avenge his Trojan kin and Minerva's violated shrine.

                                                    "Who,
noble Cato, could pass you by in silence? Or you, Cossus?
Or the Gracchi and their kin? Or the two Scipios,
both thunderbolts of battle, Libya's scourge?   970
Or you, Fabricius, reared from poverty into power?
Or you, Serranus the Sower, seeding your furrow?
You Fabii, where do you rush me, all but spent?
And you, famous Maximus, you are the one man
whose delaying tactics save our Roman state.

      "Others, I have no doubt,
will forge the bronze to breathe with suppler lines,
draw from the block of marble features quick with life,
plead their cases better, chart with their rods the stars
that climb the sky and foretell the times they rise.   980
But you, Roman, remember, rule with all your power
the peoples of the earth—these will be your arts:
to put your stamp on the works and ways of peace,
to spare the defeated, break the proud in war."

      They were struck with awe as father Anchises paused,
then carried on: "Look there, Marcellus marching toward us,
decked in splendid plunder he tore from a chief he killed,
victorious, towering over all. This man on horseback,

he will steady the Roman state when rocked by chaos,
mow the Carthaginians down in droves, the rebel Gauls.   990
He is only the third to offer up to Father Quirinus
the enemy's captured arms."

                            Aeneas broke in now,
for he saw a young man walking at Marcellus' side,
handsome, striking, his armor burnished bright
but his face showed little joy, his eyes cast down.
"Who is that, Father, matching Marcellus stride for stride?
A son, or one of his son's descendants born of noble stock?
What acclaim from his comrades! What fine bearing,
the man himself! True, but around his head
a mournful shadow flutters black as night."

                                      "My son,"   1000
his tears brimming, father Anchises started in,
"don't press to know your people's awesome grief.
Only a glimpse of him the Fates will grant the world,
not let him linger longer. Too mighty, the Roman race,
it seemed to You above, if this grand gift should last.
Now what wails of men will the Field of Mars send up
to Mars' tremendous city! What a cortege you'll see,
old Tiber, flowing past the massive tomb just built!
No child of Troy will ever raise so high the hopes
of his Latin forebears, nor will the land of Romulus take   1010
such pride in a son she's borne. Mourn for his virtue!
Mourn for his honor forged of old, his sword arm
never conquered in battle. No enemy could ever
go against him in arms and leave unscathed,
whether he fought on foot or rode on horseback,
digging spurs in his charger's lathered flanks.
Oh, child of heartbreak! If only you could burst
the stern decrees of Fate! You will be Marcellus.
Fill my arms with lilies, let me scatter flowers,
lustrous roses—piling high these gifts, at least,   1020
on our descendant's shade—and perform a futile rite."

    So they wander over the endless fields of air,
gazing at every region, viewing realm by realm.

Once Anchises has led his son through each new scene
and fired his soul with a love of glory still to come,
he tells him next of the wars Aeneas still must wage,
he tells of Laurentine peoples, tells of Latinus' city,
and how he should shun or shoulder each ordeal
that he must meet.
                    There are twin Gates of Sleep.
One, they say, is called the Gate of Horn   1030
and it offers easy passage to all true shades.
The other glistens with ivory, radiant, flawless,
but through it the dead send false dreams up toward the sky.
And here Anchises, his vision told in full, escorts
his son and Sibyl both and shows them out now
through the Ivory Gate.
                    Aeneas cuts his way
to the waiting ships to see his crews again,
then sets a course straight on to Caieta's harbor.
Anchors run from prows, the sterns line the shore.

BOOK SEVEN

Beachhead in Latium, Armies Gather

In death, Caieta, Aeneas' nurse, you too
have granted our shores a fame that never dies.
And now your honor preserves your resting place,
and if such glory is any glory at all, your name
marks out your bones in the Great Land of the West.

But devout Aeneas now—the last rites performed
and the grave-mound piled high—once the seas lie calm,
sets sail on his journey, puts the port astern.
Freshening breezes blow as night comes on
and a full moon speeds their course,   10
its dancing light strikes sparkles off the waves.
And they closely skirt the coasts of Circe's land
where the Sun's rich daughter makes her deadly groves
resound with her endless song, and deep in her proud halls
she kindles fragrant cedar flaring through the night

as her whirring shuttle sweeps her fine-spun loom.
From there you could hear the furious growls of lions
bridling at their chains, roaring into the dead of night,
the raging of bristly boars and bears caged in their pens
and the looming forms of howling wolves: the men whose shapes   20
the brutal goddess Circe changed with her potent drugs,
tricked them out in the hides and look of wild beasts.
But to spare the loyal Trojans such a monstrous fate—
risking that harbor, touching those lethal shores—
Neptune swelled their sails with following winds
and gave them a swift escape,
speeding them past the churning shoals unharmed.

    Now the sea was going red with the rays of Dawn,
from the heavens gold Aurora shone in her rose-red car
when the wind died down, suddenly every breeze fell flat   30
and the oars struggle against a sluggish, leaden swell.
But now Aeneas, still at sea, scanning the offing,
spots an enormous wood and running through it,
the Tiber in all its glory, rapids, whirlpools
golden with sand and bursting out to sea. And over it,
round it, birds, all kinds, haunting the riverbed and banks,
entrance the air with their song and flutter through the trees.
"Change course!" he commands his men. "Turn prows to land!"
And he enters the great shaded river, overjoyed.

                              Now come,
Erato—who were the kings, the tides and times, how stood   40
the old Latin state when that army of intruders
first beached their fleet on Italian shores?
All that I will unfold, I will recall
how the battle first began . . .
And you, goddess, inspire your singer, come!
I will tell of horrendous wars, tell of battle lines
and princes fired with courage, driven to their deaths,
Etruscan battalions, all Hesperia called to arms.
A greater tide of events springs up before me now,
I launch a greater labor.

                King Latinus, already old,   50

had governed the fields and towns through long years of peace.
Faunus' son he was, and the Latian nymph's, Marica,
so we hear. Picus was Faunus' father, and Picus
boasted you as his sire, Great Saturn, you,
the founder of the bloodline. Latinus had no son,
his one male issue torn from him by the gods' decrees,
in the first bloom of youth. One daughter alone
was left to preserve the house and royal line—
ripe for marriage now, a full-grown woman now.
Many suitors sought her all through Latium,   60
all Ausonia too, and the handsomest of the lot
was Turnus, strong in his noble birth and breeding.
The queen mother burned with a will to wed him
to her daughter, true, but down from the gods
came sign on sign of alarm to block the way.

   Far in the palace depths there stood a laurel,
its foliage sacred, tended with awe for many years.
Father Latinus, they say, had found it once himself,
building his first stronghold, hallowed it to Phoebus
and named his settlers after the laurel's name, Laurentes.   70
Now sweeping toward this tree from a clear blue sky—
a marvel, listen, a squadron of bees came buzzing
to high heaven, swarmed in an instant, massed
on the tree's crown and hooking feet together,
bent the laurel's leafy branches down.
A prophet cries at once: "A stranger—I see him!
A whole army of men arriving out of the same quarter,
bent on the same goal, to rule our city's heights!"

   What's worse, as the young virgin Lavinia lit
the altar with pure torches, flanking her father,   80
look—what horror!—her flowing hair caught fire,
her lovely regalia crackled in the flames,
her regal tresses blazed, her crown blazing,
studded with flashing jewels—the next moment
the girl was engulfed in a smoky yellow glare,
strewing the God of Fire's power through the house.

That sight was bruited about as a sign of wonder, terror:
for Lavinia, prophets sang of a brilliant fame to come,
for the people they foretold a long, grueling war.

    Dismayed by the signs, the king seeks out the oracle   90
of Faunus, his vatic father. He consults the grove
below Albunea's heights, where the grand woods resound
with a holy spring and exhale their dark, deadly fumes.
Here all the Italian tribes and all Oenotria's land
seek out the oracle's response in hours of doubt.
Here the priest, when he brings the sacred gifts
and looks for sleep beneath the silent night—
stretched out on the hides of slaughtered sheep—
will see whole hosts of phantoms, miracles on the wing,
hear the voices swarm, engage with the gods in words   100
and speak with Acheron in Avernus' deepest pools.
Here too, Latinus himself, seeking out responses,
slaughtered a hundred yearling sheep in the old way
and there he lay ensconced, at rest on fleecy hides
when a sudden voice broke from the grove's depths:
"Never seek to marry your daughter to a Latin,
put no trust, my son, in a marriage ready-made.
Strangers will come, and come to be your sons
and their lifeblood will lift our name to the stars.
Their sons' sons will see, wherever the wheeling Sun   110
looks down on the Ocean, rising or setting, East or West,
the whole earth turn beneath their feet, their rule!"

    This response from father Faunus, a warning sent
in the silent night—Latinus did not seal his lips,
Rumor had spread it already, flying far and wide
through Ausonia's towns before the sons of Troy
tied up their fleet at the river's green embankments.

    Now Aeneas, his ranking chiefs and handsome Iulus
stretch out on the grass below the boughs of a tall tree,
then set about their meal, spreading a feast on wheaten cakes—   120
Jove himself impelled them—heaping the plates with Ceres' gifts,

her country fruits. And once they'd devoured all in sight,
still not sated, their hunger drove them on to attack
the fateful plates themselves, their hands and teeth
defiling, ripping into the thin dry crusts, never
sparing a crumb of the flat-bread scored in quarters.
Suddenly Iulus shouted:

       "What, we're even eating
our platters now?"

       Only a joke, and nothing more,
but his words, once heard, first spelled an end of troubles.
As they first fell from the boy's lips, his father   130
seized upon them, struck by the will of god,
and made him hold his peace, and Aeneas cries
at once: "Hail to the country owed to me by Fate!
Hail to you, you faithful household gods of Troy!
Here is our home, here is our native land!
For my own father—now I remember—Anchises
left to me these secret signs of Fate:
'When, my son, borne to an unknown shore,
reduced to iron rations, hunger drives you
to eat your own platters, then's the moment,   140
exhausted as you are, to hope for home.
There—never forget—your hands must labor
to build your first houses, ring them round with mounds.'
This is the hunger he meant, this the last trial,
the last limit set to our pains of exile. Come,
with the first light of day, our spirits high,
let's explore the land. What people hold it?
Where are their towns? Scatter out from port
on different routes. But now pour cups to Jove
and call on Father Anchises with our prayers,   150
set out the wine on tables once again!"

          With that,
he wreathes his brows with a leafy green spray
and prays to the spirit of the place, and Earth,
first of the gods, and nymphs and rivers still unknown,
and then to the Night and the rising stars of Night.
He calls on Jove of Ida, calls the Phrygian Mother,

both gods in turn, and then his two parents,
his mother high above and his father down below.
The Almighty Father answered, three times over,
rending the cloudless sky with claps of thunder,   160
flourishing high in his own hand from heaven's peak
a cloud on fire with rays of gold, with radiance.
The rumor spread at once through Trojan ranks
that the day had come to build their destined city.
Impelled by the great omen, hearts filled with joy,
they rush to refresh the banquet, set out bowls
and crown the wine with wreaths.
                                    The next day,
when the sun's first torch had flared across the earth,
taking different routes they explore the town,
the borderlands and coasts these people hold.   170
Here are the pools where Numicus' springs rise
and here is the Tiber River,
here the hardy Latins make their homes.
And then Aeneas orders a hundred envoys,
picked from all ranks, to approach the king's
imperial city—bearing an olive branch of Pallas
wound in wool, bearing gifts for the great man—
and sue for peace for all the Trojan people.
They waste no time, moving out on command,
setting a brisk pace.
                                    And Aeneas himself lines up   180
his walls with a shallow trench, he starts to work the site
and rings his first settlement on the coast with mounds,
redoubts and ramparts built like an armed camp.
Soon his envoys, having covered the distance,
sight the Latins' rising roofs and towers
and go up under the walls. There before the city,
boys and young men in their vibrant pride of strength
are training as riders, breaking teams in the whirling dust,
bending their tough, lithe bows, and hurling honed javelins,
full shoulder throws, challenging friends to race or box,   190
when a herald comes riding up ahead of the Trojans,
bringing news to the old king's ears: "Powerful men

in strangers' dress, they're on their way here now!"
King Latinus has them summoned into the palace
and takes his fathers' throne amidst them all.
                                              August,
immense, its hundred columns soaring, the house
commanded the city heights, Laurentine Picus' home
with its shuddering grove and ancestral, awesome aura.
Here ritual said that kings should receive the scepter,
first raise the rods of power. This shrine is their senate,   200
this the site of their sacred banquets. Here the elders
slaughtered rams, then sat to dine at an endless line of trestles.
Yes, and here, carved in seasoned cedar, rows of statues,
rows of the founding forebears: Italus, Father Sabinus,
the vintner's figure still wielding his hooked knife;
old Saturn and Janus' figure facing right and left.
All stand in the forecourt, and all the other kings
from the start of time, and those who had taken
wounds in war, fighting to save their country.
Many weapons, too, hang on the hallowed doors,   210
captured chariots, curved axes, crested helmets,
enormous bolts from gates, and lances, shields
and ramming beaks ripped from the prows of ships.
There with the augur's staff sat Picus to the life,
girt up in the short robe of state, his left hand
holding the sacred buckler. Picus, breaker of horses,
whom his bride, Circe—seized with a blinding passion—
struck with her golden wand and then with magic potions
turned him into a bird and splashed his wings with color.

So grand, the temple of the gods where King Latinus   220
assumed his fathers' throne and summoned the Trojans
to him in the halls. As they came marching in,
he hailed them first with peaceful words of welcome:
"Tell us, sons of Dardanus—for we know your city,
your stock, and we heard that you were sailing here—
what do you search for now? What cause, what craving
has sailed your ships to Italy, crossing many seas?
Whether you're lost or storms have swept you far off course,

dangers that sailors often suffer, facing open ocean—
shielded now by our riverbanks, you ride at anchor.   230
Don't resist our welcome. Never forget the Latins
are Saturn's people, fair and just, and not because
we are bound by curbs or laws, but kept in check
of our own accord: the way of our ancient god.
I can recall, though the years have blurred the tale,
that Auruncan elders liked to tell how Dardanus
sprang up in these fields, then wandered East
to the towns of Phrygian Ida, Thracian Samos,
called Samothrace these days. From here,
his old Tuscan home of Corythus, he set sail,   240
and now a golden palace high in the starry heavens
welcomes him to a throne, and his altars add
a name to the growing roster of the gods."

       As Latinus ended, Ilioneus followed:
"King, great son of Faunus, no black gales,
no stormy seas have swept us here to your country,
nor did the stars or landmarks throw us far off course.
With a firm resolve and willing hearts we've reached your city,
driven out of our own kingdom, once the grandest realm
the wheeling Sun could see from Olympus' heights.   250
Our race takes root from Jove, the sons of Dardanus
triumph in Father Jove—of the Father's highest stock,
our king himself, Aeneas of Troy, who sent us to your gates.
How savage the storm that broke from brute Mycenae,
scourging Ida's plains! How Fate compelled
the worlds of Europe and Asia to clash in war!
All people know the story, all at the earth's edge,
cut off where the rolling Ocean pounds them back,
and all whom the ruthless Sun in the torrid zone,
arching amidst the four cool zones of earth,   260
sunders far from us.
                      "Escaping that flood
and sailing here over many barren seas,
now all we ask is a modest resting place
for our fathers' gods, safe haven on your shores,

water, and fresh air that's free for all to breathe.
We will never shame your kingdom, nor will your fame
be treated lightly, no, our thanks for your kind work
will never die. Nor will Italy once regret
embracing Troy in her heart.
I swear by Aeneas' fate, by his right hand   270
proved staunch in loyalty, strong in feats of arms,
that many nations, many—and don't slight us now
because we come with an olive branch held out
and desperate pleas—that many people have
urged us, strongly, to join them as allies.
But the gods' will spurred us on to seek your land,
their power forced us here. Here Dardanus was born.
Here the clear commands of Apollo call him back
as the god impels us toward the Tuscan Tiber,
the Numicus' sacred springs.
                              "Aeneas, moreover,   280
offers you these gifts, remains of his former riches,
meager relics plucked from the fires of burning Troy.
From this gold goblet Father Anchises tipped the wine
at the high altars. This was Priam's regalia when,
in the way he liked to rule, he handed down the laws
to his gathered people—the scepter, the holy coronet
and the robes that Trojan women used to weave."

As Ilioneus ends his appeal, Latinus keeps on
looking down at the ground, stock-still,
only his eyes moving, rapt in concentration.   290
The brocaded purple stirs him, king that he is,
and Priam's scepter too, but he is stirred far more,
dwelling long on his daughter's marriage, her wedding bed,
and mulling deeply over the vision of old Faunus. "So this,"
he thinks, "is the man foretold by Fate. That son-in-law
from a foreign home, and he's called to share my throne
with equal power! His heirs will blaze in courage,
their might will sway the world."
And at last he speaks out, filled with joy:
"May the gods speed the plans that we launch here,   300

their own omens too! Your wish will be my command,
Trojan, I embrace your gifts. While Latinus rules,
you'll never lack rich plowland, bounty great as Troy's.
Just let Aeneas—if he needs us so, and presses so
to join in alliance and take the name of comrade—
come in person and never shy from the eyes of friends.
Let this be part of our peace, to grasp your leader's hand.
Take back to your king this answer I give you now.
I have a daughter. Signs from my father's shrine
and a host of omens from the skies forbid me   310
to wed her to a bridegroom chosen from our race.
Our sons-in-law will arrive from foreign shores:
that is the fate in store for Latium, so the prophets say,
a stranger's blood will raise our name to the stars.
This is the one the Fates demand. So I believe
and if I can read the future with any truth,
I welcome him as ours."
                              On that warm note
Latinus picks out horses from his entire stable:
three hundred strong, standing sleek in their lofty stalls.
At once he orders them led out to the Trojans, one for each,   320
swift with their winging hoofs, decked in embroidered
purple saddle-blankets, golden medallions dangling
from their chests, their trappings gold, pure gold
the bridle bits they champ between their teeth.
For absent Aeneas, a chariot, twin chargers too,
sprung from immortal stock, their nostrils flaring fire,
born of the mixed breed that crafty Circe bred,
making off with one of her father's stallions
to mate him with a mare.
Riding high with Latinus' gifts and words,   330
Aeneas' envoys bring back news of peace.
                                   But look,
the merciless wife of Jove was winging back from Argos,
Inachus' city, holding course through the heavens when,
from far in the air, as far as Sicily's Cape Pachynus,
she spied Aeneas exulting, Trojan ships at anchor.
Men building their homes already, trusting the land

already, their fleet abandoned now. Juno stopped,
transfixed with anguish, then, shaking her head,
this exclamation came pouring from her heart:
"That cursed race I loathe—their Phrygian fate   340
that clashes with my own! So, couldn't they die
on the plains of Troy? So, couldn't they stay
defeated in defeat? Couldn't the fires of Troy
cremate the Trojans? No, through the shocks of war,
through walls of fire, they've found a way! What,
am I to believe my powers broken down at last,
glutted with hatred, now I rest in peace? Oh no,
when they were flung loose from their native land
I dared to hunt those exiles through the breakers,
battle them down the ocean far and wide. I've spent   350
all power of sea and sky against those Trojans.
What good have the Syrtes been to me, or Scylla
or gaping Charybdis? The Trojans have settled down
secure in the Tiber channel they so craved,
safe from the waves—and me.
                              "Why, Mars had the force
to destroy the giant Lapith race! And Father Jove
in person gave old Calydon up to Diana's rage,
and for what foul crimes did Calydon and the Lapiths
merit so much pain? Oh but I, powerful Juno,
wife of Jove, wretched Juno, I endured it all,   360
left nothing undared, I stooped to any tactic,
still he defeats me—Aeneas! But if my forces
are not enough, I am hardly the one to relent,
I'll plead for the help I need, wherever it may be—
if I cannot sway the heavens, I'll wake the powers of hell!
It's not for me to deny him his Latin throne? So be it.
Let Lavinia be his bride. An iron fact of Fate.
But I can drag things out, delay the whole affair:
that I can do, and destroy them root and branch,
the people of either king. What a price they'll pay   370
for the father and son-in-law's alliance here! Yes,
Latin and Trojan blood will be your dowry, princess—
Bellona, Goddess of War, your maid-of-honor! So,

Hecuba's not the only one who spawned a firebrand,
who brought to birth a wedding torch of a son.
Venus' son will be the same—a Paris reborn,
a funeral torch to consume a second Troy!"

                                        That said,
the terrible goddess swooped down to the earth and
stirred Allecto, mother of sorrows, up from her den
where nightmare Furies lurk in hellish darkness.   380
Allecto—a joy to her heart, the griefs of war,
rage, and murderous plots, and grisly crimes.
Even her father, Pluto, loathes the monster,
even her own infernal sisters loathe her since
she shifts into so many forms, their shapes so fierce,
the black snakes of her hair that coil so thickly.
Juno whips her on with a challenge like a lash:
"Do me this service, virgin daughter of Night,
a labor just for me! Don't let my honor, my fame
be torn from its high place, or the sons of Aeneas   390
bring Latinus round with their lures of marriage,
besieging Italian soil. You can make brothers
bound by love gear up for mutual slaughter,
demolish a house with hatred, fill it to the roofs
with scourges, funeral torches. You have a thousand names,
a thousand deadly arts. Shake them out of your teeming heart,
sunder their pact of peace, sow crops of murderous war!
Now at a stroke make young men thirst for weapons,
demand them, grasp them—now!"

                                        In the next breath,
bloated with Gorgon venom, Allecto launches out,   400
first for Latium, King Latinus' lofty halls,
and squats down at the quiet threshold of Amata
seething with all a woman's anguish, fire and fury
over the Trojans just arrived and Turnus' marriage lost.
Allecto flings a snake from her black hair at the queen
and thrusts it down her breast, the very depths of her heart,
and the horror drives her mad to bring the whole house down.
It glides between her robes and her smooth breasts but she
feels nothing, no shudder of coils, senses nothing at all

as the viper breathes its fire through the frenzied queen.   410
The enormous snake becomes the gold choker around her throat,
the raveling end of a headband braiding through her hair,
writhing over her body.
                              At the fever's first attack
with its clammy poison still stealing over the queen,
trickling through her wits and twining her bones with fire—
before her mind was seized by the flames within her spirit
she could still speak softly, a mother's tender way,
sobbing over her daughter's marriage to a Phrygian:
"So, Lavinia goes in wedlock to these Trojans—exiles?
You, her father, have you no pity for your daughter,   420
none for yourself? No pity for me, her mother? Wait,
with the first Northwind that lying pirate will desert us,
setting sail on the high seas, our virgin as his loot!
Isn't that how the Phrygian shepherd breached Sparta
and carried Leda's Helen off to the towns of Troy?
What of your sacred word? Your old affection
for your people? Your right hand pledged,
time and again, to Turnus, *your* blood kin?
Now, if the Latin people must seek a son
of strangers' stock, if that is fixed in stone   430
and your father Faunus' orders press you hard,
well then I'd say all countries free of our rule
are total strangers. That's what the gods must mean.
And Turnus too: track down the roots of his house
and who are his forebears? Inachus and Acrisius,
Mycenae to the core!"
                          Desperate appeals—no use.
When she sees Latinus steeling himself against her,
when the serpent's crazing venom has sunk into her flesh,
the fever raging through her entire body, then indeed
the unlucky queen, whipped insane by ghastly horrors,   440
raves in her frenzy all throughout the city.
Wild as a top, spinning under a twisted whip
when boys, obsessed with their play, drive it round
an empty court, the whip spinning it round in bigger rings
and the boys hovering over it, spellbound, wonderstruck—

the boxwood whirling, whip-strokes lashing it into life—
swift as a top Amata whirls through the midst of cities,
people fierce in arms. She even darts into forests,
feigning she's in the grip of Bacchus' power,
daring a greater outrage, rising to greater fury,   450
hiding her daughter deep in the mountains' leafy woods
to rob the Trojans of marriage, delay the marriage torch.
"Bacchus, hail!" she shouts. "You alone," she cries,
"you deserve the virgin! For you, I say, she lifts
the thyrsus twined with ivy, dancing in your honor,
letting her hair grow long, your sacred locks!"

    Rumor flies, and the hearts of Latian mothers
flare up with the same fury, the same frenzy
spurs them to seek new homes. Old homes deserted,
baring their necks, they loose their hair to the winds;   460
some fill the air with their high-pitched, trilling wails,
decked in fawnskins, brandishing lances wound with vines.
And Amata mid them all, shaking a flaming brand of pine,
breaks into a marriage hymn for Turnus and her daughter—
rolling her bloodshot eyes she suddenly bursts out,
wildly: "Mothers of Latium, listen, wherever you are,
if any love for unlucky Amata still stirs your hearts,
your loyal hearts—if any care for a mother's rights
still cuts you to the quick, loose your headbands,
seize on the orgies with me!"   470
Mad—while through the woods and deserted lairs
of wild beasts Allecto whips Amata on
with the lash that whips her Maenads.

                                        Once Allecto
saw her first arrows of madness piercing home
and Latinus' plans and his whole house overwhelmed,
the grim goddess takes flight on her black wings and
heads straight for the walls of bold Rutulian Turnus.
Danaë once, they say, swept ashore by a Southern gale,
built that town for her father's settlers, King Acrisius.
Ardea, our forebears called the place in the old days,   480

and the mighty name of Ardea still stands firm
but its glory is gone forever.
Here, under steep roofs in the dark night,
Turnus, dead to the world, lay fast asleep . . .
and Allecto strips away her ghastly features,
her fury's writhing limbs—transforms herself,
her face like an old crone's, she furrows her brow
with hideous wrinkles now and takes on snowy hair,
binds it with ribbons, braids it with sprays of olive.

    Now she's Calybe, aged priestess of Juno's temple,   490
so she appears in the young king's eyes and urges:
"Turnus, how can you lie back and let your labors
come to nothing? Your own scepter's handed over
to settlers fresh from Troy! The king denies you
your bride, denies you your dowry earned in blood,
he seeks a stranger as heir to his royal throne.
Now go and offer yourself to thankless dangers,
you, you laughingstock! Go mow the Tuscans down,
armor your Latins well with pacts of peace!
This message mighty Juno in person ordered me   500
to give you here, asleep in the dead of night.
Action! In high spirits alert your men and arm them,
move them out through the gates to the field of battle!
Burn them to ash, those Phrygian chiefs encamped at ease
along our lovely river, and all their painted ships!
The great gods on high decree it so.
King Latinus—if he won't yield your bride
and keep his word, then he must learn his lesson,
taste, at last, the force of Turnus' sword!"
                                      Laughing,
ready with his reply, the prince mocks the prophet: 510
"So, a fleet's sailed into the Tiber. The tale's
not failed—as you imagine—to reach my ears.
Stop concocting this panic for me, please.
Queen Juno has hardly wiped me from her mind.
It's your dotage, mother—you, you doddering wreck

too spent to see the truth—that shakes you with anguish
all for nothing now. You and your warring kings,
your false alarms, you mockery of a prophet!
See to your own chores,
go tend the shrines and statues of the gods.   520
Men will make war and peace. War's their work."
                                          Enough—
Allecto ignited in rage. The challenge still on his lips,
a sudden shuddering seized him, eyes fixed in terror,
the Fury was looming up with so many serpents hissing,
so monstrous her features now revealed. Rolling
her eyes, fiery as he faltered, struggling
to say more, she hurled the man back and
reared twin snakes from her coiling hair and
cracked her whips and raved in her rabid words:
"So, I'm in my dotage, am I? A doddering wreck   530
too spent to see the truth? I and my warring kings—
a mockery of a prophet, am I? False alarms?
Well, look at these alarms!
I come to you from the nightmare Furies' den,
I brandish war and death in my right hand!"
                                          With that
she flung a torch at the prince and drove it home
in his chest to smoke with a hellish black glare.
A nightmare broke his sleep and the sweat poured
from all over his body, drenched him to the bone.
He shouts for armor, frenzied, cries for his armor,   540
rifling through his bed and the whole house to find it.
He burns with lust for the sword, the cursed madness of war
and rage to top it off. He roars like blazing brush
piled under the ribs of a billowing bronze cauldron—
the water seethes in the heat and a river boils inside it,
bubbling up in spume—the bowl can't hold it, it overflows
and a thick cloud of steam goes shooting into the air.
So, violating the peace, he tells his captains:
"March on King Latinus—gear up for war!
Defend Italy! Hurl the enemy from the borders!   550
Turnus comes, a match for Trojans and Latins both!"

Commands given, he called the gods to witness.
His keen Rutulians spur each other to arms,
some moved by his matchless build and youth,
some by his royal bloodline,
some by his sword-arm's shining work in war.

                              While Turnus
fills his Rutulian troops with headlong daring,
Allecto flies to the Trojan camp on Stygian wings—
a fresh plot in the air—to scout out the place
where handsome Iulus was hunting along the shore,   560
coursing, netting game. Here the infernal Fury throws
an instant frenzy into the hounds, she daubs their nostrils
wet with a well-known scent, and they burn to chase a stag.
This was the first cause of all the pain and struggle,
this first kindled the country people's lust for war.
There was a stag, a rare beauty, antlers branching,
torn from his mother's dugs. And the sons of Tyrrhus
nursed it with father Tyrrhus, who kept the royal herds,
charged with tending the broad, spreading pastures.
Their sister, Silvia, trained the stag to take   570
the commands she gave with love,
wreathed its horns with tender, fresh-cut garlands,
curried the wild creature, bathed it in running springs.
Tame to the touch, it liked to frequent its master's table.
Roving the forests, home to the well-known door it came,
all on its own, even at dead of night.

                         This fine beast,
straying from home, chanced to be floating down a stream,
cooling off on a grassy bank when the frenzied hounds
of the hunter Iulus started it—Iulus himself, fired
with a love of glory, aimed a shaft from his tensed bow   580
and Allecto steadied his trembling hand and the arrow shot
with a whirring rush and pierced through womb and loins.
Back to its well-known home the wounded creature fled,
struggled into its stall and groaning, bleeding,
filling the long halls with cries of pain,
it seemed to plead for help.

                    The sister,

Silvia, she is the first to call for rescue,
hands beating her arms, summoning hardy rustics.
Unexpectedly in they come, for savage Allecto stalks
the silent forests—some with torches charred to a point,   590
some with heavy knotted clubs, whatever they find to hand
their anger hones to weapons. Tyrrhus rallies his troops,
he's just been splitting an oak in four with wedges;
now, breathing fury, he seizes a woodsman's axe.

    Savage Allecto, high on a lookout, spots her chance
to wreak some havoc. Winging up to the stable's steep roof,
she lights on the highest peak and sounds the herdsman's
call to arms, a hellish blast from her twisted horn,
and straightway all the copses shiver, all the woods
resound to their darkest depths. Far in the distance   600
Trivia's lake could hear it, the glistening sulfur stream
of the Nar could hear it, so could the springs of Lake Velinus
and anxious mothers clutched their babies to their breasts.
Then, quick to the call that cursed trumpet gave,
the wild herdsmen gather from every quarter,
snatching arms in haste. Young Trojans too,
their camp gates spread wide, come pouring out
to help Ascanius now. The battle lines form up.
No rustic free-for-all with clubs and charred stakes—
they'll fight to the finish now with two-edged swords.   610
A black harvest of naked steel bristles far and wide,
and the bronze struck by the sun gleams bright
and hurls its light to the clouds
like a billow whitening under the wind's first gust as
crest on crest the ocean rises, its breakers rearing higher
until it surges up from its depths to hit the skies.
                                                        Here
a youngster breaks from the front—
                                and an arrow whizzes in
and down he goes, Almo, the eldest son of Tyrrhus—the point
lodges deep in his throat and chokes off the moist path
for his voice and his faint life breath with blood.   620
Around him, heaps of dead, and among them old Galaesus

killed as he set himself in their midst to beg for peace,
the most righteous man in all the Italian fields,
long ago, the richest too. Five flocks of cattle
he had in tow and five came home from pasture,
a hundred plowshares made his topsoil churn.

    As the battle draws dead even across the plain
the Fury's power has lived up to her promise.
She's fleshed the war in blood, inaugurated
the slaughter with a kill and now she leaves   630
Hesperia, wheeling round in the heavens to report
success to Juno—the Fury's voice triumphant:
"Look, I've done your bidding,
perfected a work of strife with ghastly war!
Go tell them to join in friendship, seal their pacts,
now I've spattered the Trojans red with Italian blood.
I'll add this too, if I can depend on your good will:
With rumors I will draw the border towns into war,
ignite their hearts with a maddening lust for battle.
They'll rush to the rescue now from every side—   640
I'll sow their fields with swords!"

    "Enough terror," Juno counters, "treachery too.
The causes of war stand firm. Man to man they fight
and the weapons luck first brought are dyed with fresh blood now.
Let them sing of such an alliance, such a wedding hymn,
the matchless son of Venus and that grand King Latinus!
You're roving far too freely, high on the heavens' winds,
and the Father, king of steep Olympus, won't allow it.
You must give way. Whatever struggle is still to come,
I'll manage it myself."

                      Quick to Juno's command,   650
she lifts her wings, hissing with snakes, and quitting
the airy heights of heaven, seeks her home in hell.
Deep in Italy's heart beneath high mountains
lies a famous place renowned in many lands:
the Valley of Amsanctus. A dark wooded hillside
thick with foliage closes around it right and left,

with a crashing torrent amidst it roaring over boulders,
rapids roiling white. And here they display a cavern,
an awesome breathing-vent for the savage God of Death,
and a vast swirling gorge spreads wide its lethal jaws   660
where the Acheron bursts through, and here the Fury
hid her hateful power, releasing earth and sky.

       But no letup yet. Saturn's queenly daughter
is just now putting the final touches to the war.
Out of the field of battle, streaming into town
whole troops of herdsmen are bringing home the dead—
Almo the young boy, Galaesus with his butchered face—
and they beg the gods for rescue, pleading with Latinus.
But there stands Turnus now, and amid their hot fury
and rising cries of murder, he fires up their fears: 670
"Trojans are called to share our realm! Phrygian blood
will corrupt our own, and I, I'm driven from the doors!"
And all whose mothers, maddened by Bacchus, dance in frenzy
through the trackless woods—Amata's name has no lightweight—
swarm in from all sides, wearying Mars with war cries.
Suddenly all are demanding this accursed war,
against all omens, against the divine power of Fate,
they're spurred by a wicked impulse. They rush to ring
the palace of King Latinus round, but he stands fast
like a rock at sea, a seabound rock that won't give way: 680
when a big surge hits and the howling breakers pound it hard,
its bulk stands fast though its foaming reefs and spurs roar on,
all for nothing, as seaweed dashing against its flanks
swirls away in the backwash.   But finding he lacks
the power to quash their blind fanatic will,
and the world rolls on at a nod from brutal Juno,
time and again he calls the gods and empty winds
to witness: "Crushed by Fate," the father cries,
"we're wrenched away by the tempest! My poor people,
you will pay for your outrage with your blood. You,   690
Turnus, the guilt is yours, and a dreadful end awaits you—
you will implore the gods with prayers that come too late!

Myself, now that I've reached my peaceful haven, here
at the harbor's mouth I'm robbed of a happy death."

He said no more. He sealed himself in his house
and dropped the reins of power.

There was a custom in Latium, Land of the West,
and ever after revered in Alban towns and now
great Rome that rules the world reveres it too,
when men first rouse the war-god into action,   700
whether bent on bringing the griefs of war
to the Getae, the Hyrcanians, or the Arabs
or marching on India, out to stalk the Dawn
and reclaim the standards taken by the Parthians.
There are twin Gates of War—so they are called—
consecrated by awe and the dread of savage Mars,
closed fast by a hundred brazen bolts and iron
strong forever, nor does Janus the watchman
ever leave the threshold. And here it is,
when the fathers' will is set on all-out war,   710
the consul himself, decked out in Romulus' garb,
his toga girt up in the ceremonial Gabine way,
will unbar the screeching gates and cry for war.
The entire army answers his call to arms and
brazen trumpets blast their harsh assent.
                                                    Then too
Latinus was pressed to declare war on Aeneas' sons
with the same custom, to unbar the deadly gates.
But the father of his people refused to touch them,
cringed at the horrid duty, locked himself from sight
in his shadowed palace. So the Queen of the Gods,   720
Saturn's daughter swooping down from the heavens,
struck the unyielding doors with her own hand,
swinging them on their hinges, bursting open
the iron Gates of War. All Italy blazed—
until that instant all unstirred, inert. Now
some gear up to cross the plains on foot, some,
riding high on their horses, wildly churn the dust

and all shout out "To arms!"—polishing shields smooth,
burnishing lances bright with thick rich grease,
honing their axes keen on grindstones.
                                    Ah what joy   730
to advance the banners, hear the trumpets blare!
Five great cities, in fact, plant their anvils,
forge new weapons: staunch Atina, lofty Tibur,
Ardea, Crustumerium, Antemnae proud with towers.
They beat the helmets hollow to guard the head,
they weave the wicker tight to rib their shields,
others are pounding breastplates out of bronze,
hammering lightweight greaves from pliant silver.
So it has given way to this, this: all their pride
in the scythe and harrow, all their love of the plow.   740
They reforge in the furnace all their fathers' swords.
Now the trumpets blare. The watchword's out for war.
One warrior wildly tears a helmet from his house,
one yokes his panting, stamping team to a chariot,
donning his shield and mail, triple-meshed in gold
and he straps a trusty sword around his waist.

    Now throw Helicon open, Muses, launch your song!
What kings were fired for war, what armies at their orders
thronged the plains? What heroes sprang into bloom,
what weapons blazed, even in those days long ago,   750
in Italy's life-giving land? You are goddesses,
you remember it all, and you can tell it all—
all we catch is the distant ring of fame.
                                    First
to march to war is brutal Mezentius, scorner of gods,
fresh from the Tuscan coasts to deploy his troops for battle.
Beside him, his son, Lausus, second in build and beauty
to Latian Turnus alone: Lausus, breaker of horses,
hunter of wild game. From Agylla town he led
a thousand men—who could not save his life—
a son who deserved more joy in a father's rule,   760
anyone but Mezentius for a father.
                                    Following them

comes Aventinus, handsome Hercules' handsome son,
parading his victor's team across the field, his chariot
crowned with the victor's palm, his shield emblazed
with his father's sign: the Hydra's hundred snakes,
the serpents twisting round. Deep in the woods
on Aventine hill the priestess Rhea bore him
all in secret, into the world of light.
A woman matched with a god, with Hercules,
hero of Tiryns come to the Latin land in glory,   770
fresh from cutting the monster Geryon down,
to wash the herds of Spain in the Tiber River.
The men bear spears and grim pikes into battle,
fight with sword-blades ground to a razor edge
and Sabellian hurling spears. The man himself
came out on foot, swirling a giant lion's hide,
its shaggy head hooding his head with its white teeth,
a terrible sight as he marched up to the palace,
the wild battle-dress of his father Hercules
wrapped around his shoulders.
                              Next in the march   780
come twin brothers, leaving Tibur's walls and
people named for their brother's name, Tiburtus—
Catillus and fearless Coras, boys from Argos.
Out of the front lines,
into the thick-and-fast of spears they'd charge
as two Centaurs born in the clouds come bolting
headlong down from a steep summit, speeding down from
Homole or from Othrys' snowy slopes, and the tall timber
cleaves wide at their onrush, thickets split
with a huge resounding crash.
                              Nor was Praeneste's   790
founder lacking from the ranks: King Caeculus born
to Vulcan among the flocks, all ages still believe,
and found on a burning hearth. His rustic bands
escort him now from near and far, the men who live
on Praeneste's heights, on the fields of Gabine Juno,
men from the Anio's icy stream, the Hernici's dripping rocks,
men you nourish, rich Anagnia—bathed in your river,

Father Amasenus. Not all of them march to war
with armor, shields and chariots rumbling on.
Mostly slingers spraying pellets of livid lead,   800
some brandish a pair of lances, all heads cowled
with tawny wolfskin caps, their left feet planted,
making a naked print, their right feet shod
with a rugged rawhide boot.
                              Next Messapus,
breaker of horses, Neptune's son, a king
whom neither fire nor iron could bring down:
he suddenly grasps his fighting sword again,
calls back to arms his people long at peace,
his rusty contingents long at rest from battle.
Men who hold Fescennia's ridge, Aequi Falisci too,   810
the steep slopes of Soracte and all Flavina's fields,
the lake of Ciminus rimmed with hills, and Capena's groves.
They marched in cadence and sang their ruler's praise
like snowy swans you'll see in the misting clouds,
winging back from their feeding grounds, their song
bursting out of their long throats with beat on beat,
resounding far from the river banks and Asian marsh
that their pulsing chorus pounds.
You'd never think such a throng of men in bronze
were massing for battle now, but high in the sky   820
a cloud of birds with their raucous song were surging
home from open sea to shore.
                              But look—Clausus,
born of the age-old Sabine blood, heading a mighty force,
a mighty force himself. From Clausus spreads through Latium
both the Claudian tribe and clan, once Rome had long
been shared with Sabine people. Under his command
came huge divisions from Amiternum, the first Quirites,
all the ranks from Eretum, Mutusca green with olives, all
who live in Nomentum city, the Rosean fields by Lake Velinus,
all on Tetrica's shaggy spurs and grim-set Mount Severus,   830
all in Casperia, Foruli, on the Himella River's banks,
men who drink the Tiber and Fabaris, men dispatched
from icy Nursia, musters from Orta, the Latin tribes,

men that the Allia—ominous name—divides as it flows on.
Men as many as breakers rolling in from the Libyan sea
when savage Orion sets low in the winter waves or
dense as the ears of corn baked by an early sun
on Hermus' plain or Lycia's burnished fields.
Shields clang and under the trampling feet
the earth quakes in fear.
                              Next Agamemnon's man   840
who hated the very name of Troy—Halaesus,
yoking his team to a chariot, speeds along
a thousand diehard clans in Turnus' cause.
Men whose mattocks till the Massic earth for wine,
Auruncans their fathers sent from the rising hills
and Sidicine flats close by, and men just come from Cales,
men who make their homes along the Volturnus' shoals
and beside them rough Saticulans, squads of Oscans.
Their weapons are long, pointed stakes they like
to fit with a supple thong for swifter hurling.   850
They have bucklers to shield their left side,
sickle-swords for combat, cut-and-thrust.
                                        Nor will you,
Oebalus, go unsung in our songs. You, they say,
the river-nymph Sebethis once bore Telon,
an old man now, when Telon ruled over Capreae,
the Teleboean isle. But the son unlike the father,
not content with his forebears' holdings, even now
held sway over broader realms: the Sarrastian clans,
their meadows washed by the Sarnus, men from Rufrae,
Batulum and Celemna's farms, and soldiers overseen   860
by the high walls of Abella rife with apples,
fighters who whirl the barbed lance, Teutonic style,
their heads wrapped with the bark they strip from cork-trees,
bronze shields gleaming—gleaming bronze, their swords.

    You too, Ufens, Nersae's foothills sent you to war
with your glowing fame, your brilliant luck in arms
and your Aequian clans, most rugged men alive,
seasoned to rough hunting in thicket groves

on their hardscrabble land. Armed to the hilt
they work the earth, their constant joy to haul   870
fresh booty home and live off all they seize.
                                        Next,
from the Marsian stock a priest came marching in,
his helmet crowned with a leafy olive spray:
sent by King Archippus, Umbro, no man braver,
an old hand, with his touch and spells, at shedding
sleep on the vipers' spawn and lake-snakes hissing death,
at soothing their anger, healing bites with his magic arts.
But he had no cure for the stab of a Trojan lance,
none of his drowsy incantations, no drugs culled
on the Marsian hills could heal him of his wounds.   880
For you the grove of Angitia wept, for you
the crystal swells of Fucinus Lake, for you
the clear quiet pools.
                        He rode to war as well,
Virbius, striking son of Hippolytus, sent to fight
by his mother Aricia: Virbius in his triumph, bred
in Egeria's grove that rings the marshy banks
where Diana's altar stands, rich with victims
fit to win her favor. For they say Hippolytus,
once his stepmother's craft had laid him low
and he'd paid the price his father set in blood   890
and his horses went berserk and tore the man apart,
back he came, under the world of stars and windy sky,
reborn by the Healer's potent herbs and Diana's love.
Then Father Almighty, enraged that any mortal rise
from the shades below, return to the light of life,
Jove with his lightning bolt struck down Apollo's son
who honed such healing skills, down to the Styx's flood.
But kind Diana hides the man away in a secret haunt,
sends him off to Egeria, deep in the nymph's grove
where, alone in Italian woods and all unsung—   900
Virbius, his new name—he might live out his time.
And so it is that horn-hoofed steeds are barred
from Diana Trivia's shrine and holy groves
since horses, panicked by monsters of the deep,

scattered the man and chariot out along the shore.
Nevertheless his son was lashing fiery chargers
down the level fields, his chariot hurtling
Virbius into battle.
                            And there the man himself,
Turnus, his build magnificent, sword brandished,
marches among his captains, topping all by a head.   910
Triple-plumed, his high helmet raises up a Chimaera
with all the fires of Etna blasting from its throat
and roaring all the more, its searing flames more deadly
the more blood flows and the battle grows more fierce.
There on the burnished shield, Io, blazoned in gold,
her horns raised, her skin already bristly with hair,
already changed to a cow—
an awesome emblem—as Argus guards the girl and
Father Inachus pours his stream from a chased urn.
And following Turnus comes a cloud of troops on foot,   920
shield-bearing battalions swarming the whole plain.
Men in their prime from Argos, ranks of Auruncans,
Rutulians, Sicanian veterans on in years, Sacranians
in columns, Labicians bearing their painted shields,
men who plow your glades, old Tiber, the Numicus'
holy banks, whose plowshare turns the Rutulian slopes
and Circe's high-ridged cape. Then men from fields
where Jove of Anxur reigns and Goddess Feronia
takes joy in her fine green grove, and troops
from Satura's black marsh where the frigid Ufens   930
weaves his way through a valley's bottom land
and plunges down to sea.
                            Topping off the armies
rides Camilla, sprung from the Volscian people,
heading her horsemen, squadrons gleaming bronze.
This warrior girl, with her young hands untrained
for Minerva's spools and baskets filled with wool,
a virgin seasoned to bear the rough work of battle,
swift to outrace the winds with her lightning pace.
Camilla could skim the tips of the unreaped crops,
never bruising the tender ears in her swift rush   940

or wing her way, hovering over the mid-sea swell
and never dip her racing feet in the waves.
Young men all come pouring from homes and fields
and crowding mothers marvel, stare at her as she strides—
awestruck, breathless, how the beauty of royal purple
cloaks her glossy shoulders! How her golden brooch
binds up her hair—how she cradles a Lycian quiver,
her shepherd's staff of myrtle spiked with steel.

BOOK EIGHT

The Shield
of Aeneas

Soon as Turnus hoisted the banner of war from Laurentum's heights
and the piercing trumpets blared, soon as he whipped his horses
rearing for action, clashed his spear against his shield—
passions rose at once, all Latium stirred in frenzy
to swear the oath, and young troops blazed for war.
The chiefs in the lead, Messapus, Ufens, Mezentius,
scorner of gods, call up forces from all quarters
and strip the fields of men who worked the soil.
They send Venulus out to great Diomedes' city
to seek reserves and announce that Trojan ranks   10
encamp in Latium: "Aeneas arrives with his armada,
bringing the conquered household gods of Troy,
claiming himself a king demanded now by Fate.
And the many tribes report to join the Dardan chief
and his name rings far and wide through Latian country.
But where does the build-up end? What does he long to gain,
if luck is on his side, from open warfare? Clearly,

Diomedes would know—better than King Turnus,
better than King Latinus."

So things went in Latium. Watching it all,   20
the Trojan hero heaved in a churning sea of anguish,
his thoughts racing, here, there, probing his options,
shifting to this plan, that—as quick as flickering light
thrown off by water in bronze bowls reflects the sun
or radiant moon, now flittering near and far, now
rising to strike a ceiling's gilded fretwork.

                                        The dead of night.
Over the earth all weary living things, all birds and flocks
were fast asleep when captain Aeneas, his heart racked
by the threat of war, lay down on a bank beneath
the chilly arc of the sky and at long last   30
indulged his limbs in sleep. Before his eyes
the god of the lovely river, old Tiber himself,
seemed to rise from among the poplar leaves,
gowned in his blue-grey linen fine as mist
with a shady crown of reeds to wreathe his hair,
and greeted Aeneas to ease him of his anguish:

    "Born of the stock of gods, you who bring back Troy
to us from enemy hands and save her heights forever!
How long we waited for you, here on Laurentine soil
and Latian fields. Here your home is assured, yes,   40
assured for your household gods. Don't retreat.
Don't fear the threats of war.
The swelling rage of the gods has died away.
I tell you now—so you won't think me an empty dream—
that under an oak along the banks you'll find a great sow
stretched on her side with thirty pigs just farrowed,
a snow-white mother with snow-white young at her dugs.
By this sign, after thirty years have made their rounds
Ascanius will establish Alba, bright as the city's name.
All that I foresee has been decreed.

                                        "But how to begin   50
this current struggle here and see it through,

victorious all the way?
I'll explain in a word or so. Listen closely.
On these shores Arcadians sprung from Pallas—
King Evander's comrades marching under his banner—
picked their site and placed a city on these hills,
Pallanteum, named for their famous forebear, Pallas.
They wage a relentless war against the Latin people.
Welcome them to your camp as allies, seal your pacts.
I myself will lead you between my banks, upstream,   60
making your way against the current under oars—
I'll speed you on your journey. Up with you,
son of Venus! Now, as the first stars set,
offer the proper prayers to Juno, overcome
her anger and threats with vows and plead for help.
You will pay me with honors once you have won your way.
I am the flowing river that you see, sweeping the banks
and cutting across the tilled fields rich and green.
I am the river Tiber. Clear blue as the heavens,
stream most loved by the gods who rule the sky.   70
My great home is here,
my fountainhead gives rise to noble cities."

                                                        With that,
the river sank low in his deep pool, heading down
to the depths as Aeneas, night and slumber over,
gazing toward the sunlight climbing up the sky,
rises, duly draws up water in cupped hands
and pours forth this prayer to heaven's heights:
"You nymphs, Laurentine nymphs, you springs of rivers,
and you, Father Tiber, you and your holy stream,
embrace Aeneas, shield him from dangers, now at last.   80
You who pity our hardships—wherever the ground lies
where you come surging forth in all your glory—always
with offerings, always with gifts I'll do you honor,
you great horned king of the rivers of the West.
Just be with me. Prove your will with works."

    So he prays and choosing a pair of galleys
from the fleet, he mans them both with rowers

while fitting out his troops with battle gear.
                                        But look,
suddenly, right before his awestruck eyes, a marvel,
shining white through the woods with a brood as white,   90
lying stretched out on a grassy bank for all to see—
a great sow. Devout Aeneas offers her up to you,
Queen Juno on high, a blood sacrifice to you,
standing her at your altar with her young.
And all night long the Tiber lulled his swell,
checking his current so his waves would lie serene,
silent, still as a clear lagoon or peaceful marsh,
soothing its surface smooth, no labor there for oars.
So they embark with cheers to speed them on their way
and the dark tarred hulls go gliding through the river,   100
amazing the tides, amazing the groves unused to the sight
of warriors' shields, flashing far, and blazoned galleys
moving on upstream. And on and on they row, wearying
night and day as they round the long, winding bends,
floating under the mottled shade of many trees and
cleave the quiet stream reflecting leafy woods.
The fiery Sun had climbed to mid-career when,
off in the distance, they catch sight of walls,
a citadel, scattered roofs of houses: all that now
the imperial power of Rome has lifted to the skies,   110
but then what Evander held, his humble kingdom.
Quickly they swerve their prows and row for town.

     As luck would have it, that day Arcadia's king
was holding solemn annual rites in honor of Hercules,
Amphitryon's powerful son, and paying vows to the gods
in a grove before the city. Flanked by his son,
Pallas, the ranking men and the lowly senate,
all were offering incense now, and warm blood
was steaming on the altars. As soon as they saw
the tall ships gliding through the shadowed woods   120
and the rowers bending to pull the oars in silence—
alarmed by the unexpected sight, all rise as one
to desert the sacred feast. But Pallas forbids them

to cut short the rites, and fearless, seizes a spear
and runs to confront the new arrivals by himself.
"Soldiers," he shouts from a barrow some way off,
"what drives you to try these unfamiliar paths?
Where are you going? Who are your people?
Where's your home? Do you bring peace or war?"

Then captain Aeneas calls from his high stern,   130
his hands extending the olive branch of peace:
"We're Trojans born. The weapons you see are honed
for our foes, the Latins. They drive us here—as exiles—
with all the arrogance of war. We look for Evander.
Tell him this: Leading chiefs of Dardania come,
pressing to be his friends-in-arms."
                              Dardania . . .
Pallas, awestruck by the famous name, cries out:
"Come down onto dry land, whoever you are,
speak with my father face-to-face.
Come under our roofs—our welcome guest."   140
Clasping Aeneas' right hand, he held it long
and heading up to the grove they leave the river.

There Aeneas hails Evander with winning words:
"Best of the sons of Greece, Fortune has decreed
that I pray to you for help, extend this branch
of olive wound in wool. I had no fear of you
as a captain of the Greeks, Arcadia-born
and bound by blood to Atreus' twin sons.
For I am bound to you by my own strength,
by oracles of the gods and by our fathers—   150
blood-kin—and your own fame that echoes
through the world. All this binds me to you,
and Fate drives me here, and glad I am to follow.
Dardanus, first and founding father of Ilium,
came to the land of Troy. A son, as Greeks will tell,
of Electra, that Electra, daughter of Atlas, mighty Atlas
who bears the grand orb of the heavens on his shoulders.
Your father is Mercury, conceived by radiant Maia

and born on a snow-capped peak of Mount Cyllene.
But Maia's father—to trust what we have heard—   160
is Atlas, the same Atlas who lifts the starry skies.
So our two lines are branches sprung from the same blood.

"Counting on this, I planned my approach to you.
Not with envoys or artful diplomatic probes,
I come in person, put my life on the line,
a suppliant at your doors to plead for help.
The same people attack us both in savage war,
Rutulians under Turnus, and if they drive us out,
nothing, they do believe, can stop their forcing all
of Italy, all lands of the West beneath their yoke,   170
the masters of every seaboard north and south.
Take and return our trust. Brave hearts in war,
our tempers steeled, our armies proved in action."

Aeneas closed. While he spoke, Evander had marked
his eyes, his features, his whole frame, and now
he replies, pointedly: "Bravest of the Trojans,
how I welcome you, recognize you, with all my heart!
How well I recall the face, the words, the voice
of your father, King Anchises.
                                    "Once, I remember . . .
Priam, son of Laomedon, bound for Salamis,   180
out to visit his sister Hesione's kingdom,
continued on to see Arcadia's cold frontiers.
Then my cheeks still sported the bloom of youth
and I was full of wonder to see the chiefs of Troy,
wonder to see Laomedon's son, Priam himself, no doubt,
but one walked taller than all the rest—Anchises.
I yearned, in a boy's way, to approach the king
and take him by the hand. So up I went to him,
eagerly showed him round the walls of Pheneus.
At his departure he gave me a splendid quiver   190
bristling Lycian arrows, a battle-cape shot through
with golden mesh, and a pair of gilded reins my son,
Pallas, now makes his. So the right hand you want

is clasping yours. We are allies bound as one.
Soon as tomorrow's sun returns to light the earth
I'll see you off, cheered with an escort and support
I'll send your way. But now for the rites,
since you have come as friends,
our annual rites it would be wrong to interrupt.
So, with a warm heart celebrate them with us now.   200
High time you felt at ease with comrades' fare."

     That said, he orders back the food and cups already
cleared away, and the king himself conducts his guests
to places on the grass. Aeneas, the guest of honor,
he invites to a throne of maple, cushioned soft
with a shaggy lion's hide. Then picked young men
and the altar priest, outdoing themselves, bring on
the roasted flesh of bulls and heap the baskets high
with the gifts of Ceres, wheaten loaves just baked,
and in Bacchus' name they keep the winecups flowing.   210
And now Aeneas and all his Trojan soldiers feast
on the oxen's long back cut and sacred vitals.

                                             Once
their hunger was put aside, their appetites content,
King Evander began: "These annual rites, this feast,
a custom ages old, this shrine to a great spirit—
no hollow superstition, and no blind ignorance
of the early gods has forced them on us. No,
my Trojan guest, we have been saved from dangers,
brutal perils, and so we observe these rites,
we renew them year by year, and justly so.

                                        "Now then,   220
first look up at this crag with its overhanging rocks,
the boulders strewn afar. An abandoned mountain lair
still stands, where the massive rocks came rumbling down
in an avalanche, a ruin. There once was a cavern here,
a vast unplumbed recess untouched by the sun's rays,
where a hideous, part-human monster made his home—
Cacus. The ground was always steaming with fresh blood
and nailed to his high and mighty doors, men's faces

dangled, sickening, rotting, and bled white . . .
The monster's father was Vulcan, whose smoky flames   230
he vomited from his maw as he hauled his lumbering hulk.
But even to us, at last, time brought the answer
to our prayers: the help, the arrival of a god.
That greatest avenger, Hercules! On he came,
triumphant in his slaughter and all the spoils
of triple-bodied Geryon. The great victor,
driving those huge bulls down to pasture,
herds crowding these riverbanks and glens.
But Cacus, desperate bandit, wild to leave
no crime, no treachery undared, untested,   240
stole from their steadings four champion bulls
and as many head of first-rate, well-built heifers.
Ah, but to leave no hoofmarks pointing forward,
into his cave he dragged them by the tail,
turning their tracks backward—
the pirate hid his plunder deep in his dark rocks.
No hunter could spot a trace that led toward that cave.

        "Meanwhile, Hercules was about to move his herds out,
full fed from their grazing, ready to go himself when
the cows began to low at parting, filling the woods   250
with protest, bellowing to the hills they had to leave.
But one heifer, deep in the vast cavern, lowed back
and Cacus' prisoner foiled its jailer's hopes.
Suddenly Hercules ignited in rage, in black fury
and seizing his weapons and weighted knotted club,
he made for the hill's steep heights at top speed.
And that was the first we'd seen of Cacus afraid,
his eyes aswirl with terror—off to his cave he flees,
swifter than any Eastwind, yes, his feet were winged with fear.
He shut himself in its depths, shattered the chains and   260
down the great rock dropped, suspended by steel and
his father's skill, to wedge between the doorposts,
block the entrance fast.
Watch Hercules on the attack. Scanning every opening,
tossing his head, this way, that way, grinding his teeth,

blazing in rage, three times he circles the whole Aventine hill,
three times he tries to storm the rocky gates—no use—
three times he sinks down in the lowlands, power spent.

"Looming over the cavern's ridge a spur reared up,
all jagged flint, its steep sides sheering away,   270
a beetling, towering sight, a favorite haunt
of nestling vultures. This crag jutting over
the ridge, leaning left of the river down below—
he charged from the right and rocked it, prised it
up from its bedrock, tore it free of its roots,
then abruptly hurled it down and the hurl's force
made mighty heaven roar as the banks split far apart
and the river's tide went flooding back in terror.
But the cave and giant palace of Cacus lay exposed
and his shadowy cavern cleaved wide to its depths—   280
as if earth's depths had yawned under some upheaval,
bursting open the locks of the Underworld's abodes,
revealing the livid kingdom loathed by the gods,
and from high above you could see the plunging abyss
and the ghosts terror-struck as the light comes streaming in.

"So Cacus, caught in that stunning flood of light,
shut off in his hollow rock, howling as never before—
Hercules overwhelms him from high above, raining down
all weapons he finds at hand, torn-off branches, rocks
like millstones. A deathtrap, no way out for the monster now!   290
Cacus retches up from his throat dense fumes—unearthly,
I tell you—endless waves billowing through his lair,
wiping all from sight, and deep into his cave
he spews out tides of rolling, smoking darkness,
night and fire fused. Undaunted Hercules had enough—
furious, headlong down he leapt through the flames
where the thickest smoke was massing, black clouds
of it seething up and down the enormous cavern.
Here, as Cacus spouts his flames in the darkness,
all for nothing—Hercules grapples him, knots him   300
fast in a death-lock, throttling him, gouging out

the eyes in his head, choking the blood in his gullet dry.
He tears out the doors in a flash, opens the pitch-black den
and the stolen herds—a crime that Cacus had denied—
are laid bare to the skies, and out by the heels
he drags the ghastly carcass into the light.
No one can get his fill of gazing at those eyes,
terrible eyes, that face, the matted, bristling chest
of the brute beast, its fiery maw burnt out.

    "From then on, we have solemnized this service   310
and all our heirs have kept the day with joy.
Potitius first, the founder of the rites,
the Pinarian house too, that guards the worship
of Hercules. Potitius set this altar in the grove.
The Greatest Altar we shall always call it,
always the Greatest it will be.
                    "So come,
my boys, in honor of his heroic exploits
crown your hair with leaves, hold high your cups,
invoke the god we share with our new allies,
offer him wine with all your eager hearts."   320

    With that welcome, a wreath of poplar, hung
with a poplar garland's green and silver sheen
that shaded Hercules once,
shaded Evander's hair and crowned his head
and the sacred wooden winecup filled his hand.
In no time, all were tipping wine on the board
with happy hearts and praying to the gods.
                         Meanwhile
evening is coming closer, wheeling down the sky and
now the priests advance, Potitius in the lead,
robed in animal skins the old accustomed way   330
and bearing torches. They refresh the banquet,
bringing on the second course, a welcome savor,
weighing the altars down with groaning platters.
Then the Salii, dancing priests of Mars, come
clustering, leaping round the flaming altars,

raising the chorus, brows wreathed with poplar:
here a troupe of boys and a troupe of old men there,
singing Hercules' praises, all his heroic feats.
How he strangled the first monsters, twin serpents
sent by his stepmother, Juno—crushed them in his hands.   340
And the same in warfare: how he razed to the roots
those brilliant cities, Troy and Oechalia both.
How under Eurystheus he endured the countless
grueling labors, Juno's brutal doom.
                                   "Hercules,
you the unvanquished one! You have slaughtered
Centaurs born of the clouds, half man, half horse,
Hylaeus and Pholus—the bull, the monster of Crete,
the tremendous Nemean lion holed in his rocky den.
The Stygian tide-pools trembled at your arrival,
Death's watchdog cringed, sprawling over the heaps   350
of half-devoured bones in his gory cave. But nothing,
no specter on earth has touched your heart with fear,
not even Typhoeus himself, towering up with weapons.
Nor did Lerna's Hydra, heads swarming around you,
strip you of your wits. Hail, true son of Jove,
you glory added to all the gods! Come to us,
come to your sacred rites and speed us on
with your own righteous stride!"
                                   So they sing
his praise, and to crown it sing of Cacus' cave,
the monster breathing fire, and all the woods resound   360
with the ringing hymns, and the hillsides echo back.

And then, with the holy rites performed in full,
they turned back to the city. The king, bent with years,
kept his comrades, Aeneas and his son, beside him,
moving on as he eased the way with many stories.
Aeneas marveled, his keen eyes gazing round,
entranced by the site, gladly asking, learning,
one by one, the legendary tales of the men of old.

King Evander, founder of Rome's great citadel, begins:

"These woods the native fauns and the nymphs once held   370
and a breed of mortals sprung from the rugged trunks of oaks.
They had no notion of custom, no cultured way of life,
knew nothing of yoking oxen, laying away provisions,
garnering up their stores. They lived off branches,
berries and acorns, hunters' rough-cut fare. First
came Saturn, down from the heights of heaven, fleeing
Jove in arms: Saturn robbed of his kingdom, exiled.
He united these wild people scattered over the hilltops,
gave them laws and pitched on the name of Latium for the land,
since he'd lain hidden within its limits, safe and sound.   380
Saturn's reign was the Age of Gold, men like to say,
so peacefully, calm and kind, he ruled his subjects.
Ah, but little by little a lesser, tarnished age
came stealing in, filled with the madness of war,
the passion for possessions.
                                        "Then on they came,
the Ausonian ranks in arms, Sicanian tribes and
time and again the land of Saturn changed its name.
Then kings reared up and the savage giant Thybris,
and since his time we Italians call our river Tiber.
The true name of the old river Albula's lost and gone.   390
And I, cast from my country, bound for the ocean's ends—
irresistible Fortune and inescapable Fate have planted me
in this place, spurred on by my mother's dire warnings,
the nymph Carmentis, and God Apollo's power."

    No sooner said than, moving on, he points out
the Altar of Carmentis, then the Carmental Gate
as the Romans call it: an ancient tribute paid
to the nymph Carmentis, seer who told the truth,
the first to foresee the greatness of Aeneas' sons
and Pallanteum's fame to come. Next he displays   400
the grand grove that heroic Romulus restored
as a refuge—the Asylum—then shows him, under
its chilly rock, the grotto called the Lupercal,
in the old Arcadian way, Pan of Mount Lycaeus.
And he shows him the grove of hallowed Argiletum too,

he swears by the spot, retells the Death of Argus,
once his guest.
                    From there he leads Aeneas on
to Tarpeia's house and the Capitol, all gold now
but once in the old days, thorny, dense with thickets.
Even then the awesome dread of the place struck fear   410
in the hearts of rustics, even then they trembled
before the woodland and the rock.
                              "This grove," he says,
"this hill with its crown of leaves is a god's home,
whatever god he is. My Arcadians think they've seen
almighty Jove in person, often brandishing high
his black storm-shield in his strong right hand
as he drives the tempest on. Here, what's more,
in these two towns, their walls razed to the roots,
you can see the relics, monuments of the men of old.
This fortress built by Father Janus, that by Saturn: 420
this was called the Janiculum, that, Saturnia."
                                        So,
conversing and drawing near Evander's humble home,
they saw herds of cattle, everywhere, lowing loud
in the Roman Forum and Carinae's elegant district.
"These gates," Evander says, as he reaches his lodge,
"Hercules in his triumph stooped to enter here.
This mansion of mine was grand enough for him.
Courage, my friend! Dare to scoff at riches.
Make yourself—you too—worthy to be a god.
Come into my meager house, and don't be harsh."   430

   So he said, and under his narrow sloped roof
he led the great Aeneas, laid him down on a bed
of fallen leaves and the hide of a Libyan bear.
Night comes rushing down, embracing the earth
in its deep dark wings.
                    But his mother, Venus,
stirred by fear—no wonder—by all the threats
and the Latins' violent uproar, goes to Vulcan now
and there in their golden bridal chamber whispers,

breathing immortal love through every word:
"When Greek kings were ravishing Troy in war,   440
her fated towers, her ramparts doomed to enemy fires,
I asked no help for the victims then, I never begged
for the weapons right within your skill and power.
No, my dearest husband, I'd never put you to work
in a lost cause, much as I owed to Priam's sons,
however often I wept for Aeneas' grueling labors.
Now, by Jove's command he lands on Rutulian soil,
so now I do come, kneeling before the godhead I adore,
begging weapons for my Aeneas, a mother for her son!
Remember Aurora, Tithonus' wife, and Nereus' daughter?   450
Both wept and you gave way. Look at the armies massing,
cities bolting their gates, honing swords against me
to cut my loved ones down."
                    No more words.
The goddess threw her snow-white arms around him
as he held back, caressing him here and there,
and suddenly he caught fire—the same old story,
the flame he knew by heart went running through him,
melting him to the marrow of his bones. As thunder
at times will split the sky and a trail of fire goes
rippling through the clouds, flashing, blinding light—   460
and his wife sensed it all, delighting in her bewitching ways,
she knew her beauty's power.
                    And father Vulcan,
enthralled by Venus, his everlasting love, replied:
"Why plumb the past for appeals? Where has it gone,
goddess, the trust you lodged in me? If only
you'd been so passionate for him, then as now,
we would have been in our rights to arm the Trojans,
even then. Neither Father Almighty nor the Fates
were dead against Troy's standing any longer or
Priam's living on for ten more years. But now,   470
if you are gearing up for war, your mind set,
whatever my pains and all my skills can promise,
whatever molten electrum and iron can bring to life,
whatever the bellows' fiery blasts can do—enough!

Don't pray to me now. Never doubt your powers."

    With those words on his lips, he gave his wife
the embraces both desired, then sinking limp
on her breast he courted peaceful sleep
that stole throughout his body.
                   And then,
when the first deep rest had driven sleep away   480
and the chariot of Night had wheeled past mid-career,
that hour a housewife rises, faced with scratching out
a living with loom and Minerva's homespun crafts,
and rakes the ashes first to awake the sleeping fires,
adding night to her working hours, and sets her women
toiling on at the long day's chores by torchlight—
and all to keep the bed of her husband chaste
and rear her little boys—so early, briskly,
in such good time the fire-god rises up
from his downy bed to labor at his forge.
                    Not far   490
from Aeolian Lipare flanked by Sicily's coast,
an island of smoking boulders surges from the sea.
Deep below it a vast cavern thunders, hollowed out
like vaults under Etna, forming the Cyclops' forges.
You can hear the groaning anvils boom with mighty strokes,
the hot steel ingots screeching steam in the cavern's troughs
and fires panting hard in the furnace—Vulcan's home,
it bears the name Vulcania.
Here the firegod dove from heaven's heights.

    The Cyclops were forging iron now in the huge cave: 500
Thunder and Lightning and Fire-Anvil stripped bare.
They had in hand a bolt they had just hammered out,
one of the countless bolts the Father rains on earth
from the arching sky—part buffed already, part still rough.
Three shafts of jagged hail they'd riveted on that weapon,
three of bursting stormclouds, three of blood-red flame
and the Southwind winging fast. They welded into the work
the bloodcurdling flashes, crackling Thunder, Terror

and Rage in hot pursuit. Others were pressing on,
forging a chariot's whirling wheels for Mars   510
to harrow men and panic towns in war.
Others were finishing off the dreaded aegis
donned by Pallas Athena blazing up in arms—
outdoing themselves with burnished gilded scales,
with serpents coiling, writhing around each other,
the Gorgon herself, the severed head, the rolling eyes,
the breastplate forged to guard the goddess' chest.

"Pack it away!" he shouts. "Whatever you've started,
set it aside, my Cyclops of Etna, bend to this!
Armor must be forged for a man of courage!   520
Now for strength, you need it! Now for flying hands!
Now for mastery, all your skill! Cast delay to the winds!"

Enough said. At a stroke they all pitched into the work,
dividing the labors, share and share alike, and bronze
is running in rivers and flesh-tearing steel and
gold ore melting down in the giant furnace.
They are forging one tremendous shield, one
against all the Latin spears—welding seven plates,
circular rim to rim. And some are working the bellows
sucking the air in, blasting it out, while others   530
are plunging hissing bronze in the brimming troughs,
the ground of the cavern groaning under the anvils' weight,
and the Cyclops raising their arms with all their power,
arms up, arms down to the drumming, pounding beat
as they twist the molten mass in gripping tongs.

While Vulcan, the Lord of Lemnos, spurs the work
below that Aeolian coast, the life-giving light
and birdsong under the eaves at crack of dawn
awake Evander from sleep in his humble lodge.
The old man rises, pulls a tunic over his chest   540
and binds his Etruscan sandals round his feet.
Over his right shoulder, down his flank he straps
an Arcadian sword, swirling back the skin of a panther

to drape his left side. For company, two watchdogs
go loping on before him over the high doorsill,
friends to their master's steps. He makes his way
to the private quarters of his guest, Aeneas,
the old veteran bearing in mind their recent talk
and the help that he had promised. Just as early,
Aeneas is stirring too. One comes with his son, Pallas,   550
the other brings Achates. They meet and grasp right hands
and sitting there in the open court, are free at last
to indulge in frank discussion.
                                  The old king starts in:
"Greatest chief of the Trojans—for while you are alive
I'll never consider Troy and its kingdom conquered—
our power to reinforce you in war is slight,
though I know our name is great. Here the Tiber
cuts us off and there the Rutulians close the vise,
the clang of their armor echoes round our walls.
But I mean to ally you now with mighty armies,   560
vast encampments filled with royal forces—
your way to safety revealed by unexpected luck.
It's Fate that called you on to reach our shores."

"Now, not far from here Agylla city stands,
founded on age-old rock by Lydian people once,
brilliant in war, who built on Etruscan hilltops.
The city flowered for many years till King Mezentius
came to power—his brutal rule, barbaric force of arms.
Why recount his unspeakable murders, savage crimes? The tyrant!
God store up such pains for his own head and all his sons!   570
Why, he'd even bind together dead bodies and living men,
couple them tightly, hand to hand and mouth to mouth—
what torture—so in that poison, oozing putrid slime
they'd die by inches, locked in their brute embrace.
Then, at last, at the end of their rope, his people
revolt against that raving madman, they besiege
Mezentius and his palace, hack his henchmen down
and fling fire on his roof. In all this slaughter
he slips away, taking flight to Rutulian soil,

shielded by Turnus' armies, his old friend.   580
So all Etruria rises up in righteous fury,
demanding the king, threatening swift attack.
Thousands, Aeneas, and I will put you in command.
Their fleet is massed on the shore and a low roar grows,
men crying for battle-standards now, but an aged prophet
holds them back, singing out his song of destiny:
'You elite Lydian troops, fine flower of courage
born of an ancient race, oh, what just resentment
whips you into battle! Mezentius makes you burn
with well-earned rage. But still the gods forbid   590
an Italian commander to lead a race so great—
choose leaders from overseas!'

    "At that, the Etruscan fighting ranks subsided,
checked on the field of battle, struck with awe
by the warnings of the gods. Tarchon himself
has sent me envoys, bearing the crown and scepter,
offering me the ensigns, urging: 'Join our camp,
take the Etruscan throne.' Ah, but old age,
sluggish, cold, played out with the years,
has me in its grip, denies me the command.   600
My strength is too far gone for feats of arms.
I'd urge my son to accept, but his blood is mixed,
half Sabine, thanks to his mother, and so, Italian.
You are the one whose age and breed the Fates approve,
the one the Powers call. March out on your mission,
bravest chief of the Trojans, now the Italians too.
What's more, I will pair you with Pallas, my hope,
my comfort. Under your lead, let him grow hard
to a soldier's life and the rough work of war.
Let him get used to watching you in action,   610
admire you as his model from his youth.
To him I will give two hundred horsemen now,
fighting hearts of oak—our best—and Pallas
will give you two hundred more, in Pallas' name."

    He had barely closed and Anchises' son, Aeneas,

and trusty Achates, their eyes fixed on the ground,
would long have worried deep in their anxious hearts
if Venus had not given a sign from the cloudless sky.
A bolt of lightning suddenly splits the heavens,
drumming thunder—the world seems to fall in a flash,   620
the blare of Etruscan trumpets blasting through the sky.
They look up—the terrific peals come crashing over and over—
and see blood-red in a brilliant sky, rifting a cloudbank,
armor clashing out. All the troops were dumbstruck,
all but the Trojan hero—well he knew that sound,
his goddess mother's promise—and he calls out:
"Don't ask, my friend, don't ask me, I beg you,
what these portents bring. The heavens call for me.
My goddess mother promised to send this sign
if war were breaking out, and bring me armor   630
down through the air, forged by Vulcan himself
to speed me on in battle. But, oh dear gods,
what slaughter threatens the poor Laurentine people!
What a price in bloodshed, Turnus, you will pay me soon!
How many shields and helmets and corpses of the brave
you'll churn beneath your tides, old Father Tiber!
All right then, you Rutulians,
beg for war! Break your pacts of peace!"

Fighting words. Aeneas rises from his high seat
and first he rakes the fires asleep on Hercules' altar,   640
then gladly goes to the lowly gods of hearth and home
he worshipped just the day before. Evander himself
and his new Trojan allies, share and share alike,
slaughter yearling sheep as the old rite demands.
And next Aeneas returns to his ships and shipmates,
picks the best and bravest to take his lead in war
while the rest glide on at ease, no oars required
as the river's current bears them on downstream
to bring Ascanius news of his father and his affairs.
Horses go to the Trojans bound for Tuscan fields,   650
and marked for Aeneas, a special mount decked out
in a tawny lion's skin that gleams with gilded claws.

A sudden rumor flies through the little town:
"Horsemen are rushing toward the Tuscan monarch's gates!"
Mothers struck with terror pray and re-echo prayers,
the fear builds as the deadly peril comes closer,
the specter of War looms larger, ever larger . . .
Evander, seizing the hand of his departing son,
clinging, weeping inconsolably, cries out:
"If only Jove would give me back the years,   660
all gone, and make me the man I was, killing
the front ranks just below Praeneste's ramparts,
heaping up their shields, torching them in my triumph—
my right hand sent great King Erulus down to hell!
Three lives his mother Feronia gave him at his birth—
I shudder to say it now—three suits of armor for action.
Three times I had to lay him low but my right hand,
my right hand then, stripped him of all his lives
and all his armor too!
                       "Oh, if only! Then no force
could ever tear me *now* from your dear embrace,   670
my boy, nor could Mezentius ever have trod
his neighbor Evander down, butchered so many,
bereaved our city . . . so many widows left.
But you, you Powers above, and you, Jupiter,
highest lord of the gods: pity, I implore you,
a king of Arcadia, hear a father's prayers!
If your commands will keep my Pallas safe
and if the Fates intend to preserve my son,
and if I live to see him, join him again,
why then I pray for life—   680
I can suffer any pain on earth. But if
you are threatening some disaster, Fortune,
let me break this brutal life off now, now
while anxieties waver and hopes for the future fade,
while you, my beloved boy, my lone delight come lately,
I still hold you in my embrace. Oh, let no graver news
arrive and pierce my ears!"
                              So at their last parting
the words came pouring deep from Evander's heart.

He collapsed, and his servants bore him quickly
into the house.
           And even now the cavalry   690
had come riding forth through the open gates,
Aeneas out in the lead, flanked by trusty Achates,
then other Trojan captains, with Pallas in command
of the column's center, Pallas brilliant in battle cape
and glittering inlaid armor. Bright as the morning star
whom Venus loves above all the burning stars on high,
when up from his ocean bath he lifts his holy face
to the lofty skies and dissolves away the darkness.
Mothers stand on the ramparts, trembling, eyes trailing
the cloud of dust and the troops in gleaming bronze.   700
Over the brush, the quickest route, cross-country,
armored fighters ride. Cries go up, squadrons form,
galloping hoofbeats drum the rutted plain with thunder.

    Next to Caere's icy river a huge grove stands,
held in ancestral awe by people far and wide,
on all sides cupped around by sheltering hills
and ringed by pitch-dark pines. The story goes
that ancient Pelasgians, first in time long past
to settle the Latian borders, solemnized the grove
and a festal day to Silvanus, god of fields and flocks.   710
Not far from here, Tarchon and his Etruscans mustered,
all secure, and now from the hills his entire army
could be seen encamped on the spreading plain.
Down come captain Aeneas and all his fighters
picked for battle, water their horses well
and weary troops take rest.
            But the goddess Venus,
lustrous among the cloudbanks, bearing her gifts,
approached and when she spotted her son alone,
off in a glade's recess by the frigid stream,
she hailed him, suddenly there before him: "Look,   720
just forged to perfection by all my husband's skill:
the gifts I promised! There's no need now, my son,
to flinch from fighting swaggering Latin ranks

or challenging savage Turnus to a duel!"

    With that, Venus reached to embrace her son
and set the brilliant armor down before him
under a nearby oak.
                Aeneas takes delight
in the goddess' gifts and the honor of it all
as he runs his eyes across them piece by piece.
He cannot get enough of them, filled with wonder,   730
turning them over, now with his hands, now his arms,
the terrible crested helmet plumed and shooting fire,
the sword-blade honed to kill, the breastplate, solid bronze,
blood-red and immense, like a dark blue cloud enflamed
by the sun's rays and gleaming through the heavens.
Then the burnished greaves of electrum, smelted gold,
the spear and the shield, the workmanship of the shield,
no words can tell its power . . .
                There is the story of Italy,
Rome in all her triumphs. There the fire-god forged them,
well aware of the seers and schooled in times to come,   730
all in order the generations born of Ascanius' stock
and all the wars they waged.
             And Vulcan forged them too,
the mother wolf stretched out in the green grotto of Mars,
twin boys at her dugs, who hung there, frisky, suckling
without a fear as she with her lithe neck bent back,
stroking each in turn, licked her wolf pups
into shape with a mother's tongue.
             Not far from there
he had forged Rome as well and the Sabine women brutally
dragged from the crowded bowl when the Circus games were played
and abruptly war broke out afresh, the sons of Romulus   750
battling old King Tatius' hardened troops from Cures.
Then when the same chiefs had set aside their strife,
they stood in full armor before Jove's holy altar,
lifting cups, and slaughtered a sow to bind their pacts.
                    Nearby,
two four-horse chariots, driven to left and right, had torn

Mettus apart—man of Alba, you should have kept your word—
and Tullus hauled the liar's viscera through the brush
as blood-drops dripped like dew from brakes of thorns.

                                     Porsenna,
there, commanding Romans to welcome banished Tarquin back,
mounted a massive siege to choke the city—Aeneas' heirs   760
rushing headlong against the steel in freedom's name.
See Porsenna to the life, his likeness menacing, raging,
and why? Cocles dared to rip the bridge down, Cloelia
burst her chains and swam the flood.

                                Crowning the shield,
guarding the fort atop the Tarpeian Rock, Manlius
stood before the temple, held the Capitol's heights.
The new thatch bristled thick on Romulus' palace roof and
here the silver goose went ruffling through the gold arcades,
squawking its warning—Gauls attack the gates! Gauls
swarming the thickets, about to seize the fortress,   770
shielded by shadows, gift of the pitch-dark night.
Gold their flowing hair, their war dress gold,
striped capes glinting, their milky necks ringed
with golden chokers, pairs of Alpine pikes in their hands,
flashing like fire, and long shields wrap their bodies.

Here Vulcan pounded out the Salii, dancing priests of Mars,
the Luperci, stripped, their peaked caps wound with wool,
bearing their body-shields that dropped from heaven,
and chaste matrons, riding in pillowed coaches,
led the sacred marches through the city.

                              Far apart   780
on the shield, what's more, he forged the homes of hell,
the high Gates of Death and the torments of the doomed,
with you, Catiline, dangling from a beetling crag,
cringing before the Furies' open mouths.

                              And set apart,
the virtuous souls, with Cato giving laws.

                           And amidst it all
the heaving sea ran far and wide, its likeness forged
in gold but the blue deep foamed in a sheen of white

and rounding it out in a huge ring swam the dolphins,
brilliant in silver, tails sweeping the crests
to cut the waves in two.
                              And here in the heart   790
of the shield: the bronze ships, the battle of Actium,
you could see it all, the world drawn up for war,
Leucata Headland seething, the breakers molten gold.
On one flank, Caesar Augustus leading Italy into battle,
the Senate and People too, the gods of hearth and home
and the great gods themselves. High astern he stands,
the twin flames shoot forth from his lustrous brows and
rising from the peak of his head, his father's star.
On the other flank, Agrippa stands tall as he steers
his ships in line, impelled by favoring winds and gods   800
and from his forehead glitter the beaks of ships
on the Naval Crown, proud ensign earned in war.

    And opposing them comes Antony leading on
the riches of the Orient, troops of every stripe—
victor over the nations of the Dawn and blood-red shores
and in his retinue, Egypt, all the might of the East
and Bactra, the end of the earth, and trailing
in his wake, that outrage, that Egyptian wife!
All launch in as one, whipping the whole sea to foam
with tugging, thrashing oars and cleaving triple beaks   810
as they make a run for open sea. You'd think the Cyclades
ripped up by the roots, afloat on the swells, or mountains
ramming against mountains, so immense the turrets astern
as sailors attack them, showering flaming tow and
hot bolts of flying steel, and the fresh blood running
red on Neptune's fields. And there in the thick of it all
the queen is mustering her armada, clacking her native rattles,
still not glimpsing the twin vipers hovering at her back,
as Anubis barks and the queen's chaos of monster gods
train their spears on Neptune, Venus, and great Minerva.   820
And there in the heart of battle Mars rampages on,
cast in iron, with grim Furies plunging down the sky
and Strife in triumph rushing in with her slashed robes

and Bellona cracking her bloody lash in hot pursuit.
And scanning the melee, high on Actium's heights
Apollo bent his bow and terror struck them all,
Egypt and India, all the Arabians, all the Sabaeans
wheeled in their tracks and fled, and the queen herself—
you could see her calling, tempting the winds, her sails
spreading and now, now about to let her sheets run free.   830
Here in all this carnage the God of Fire forged her pale
with imminent death, sped on by the tides and Northwest Wind.
And rising up before her, the Nile immersed in mourning opens
every fold of his mighty body, all his rippling robes,
inviting into his deep blue lap and secret eddies
all his conquered people.
                              But Caesar in triple triumph,
borne home through the walls of Rome, was paying
eternal vows of thanks to the gods of Italy:
three hundred imposing shrines throughout the city.
The roads resounded with joy, revelry, clapping hands,   840
with bands of matrons in every temple, altars in each
and the ground before them strewn with slaughtered steers.
Caesar himself, throned at brilliant Apollo's snow-white gates,
reviews the gifts brought on by the nations of the earth
and he mounts them high on the lofty temple doors
as the vanquished people move in a long slow file,
their dress, their arms as motley as their tongues.
Here Vulcan had forged the Nomad race, the Africans
with their trailing robes, here the Leleges, Carians,
Gelonian archers bearing quivers, Euphrates flowing now   850
with a humbler tide, the Morini brought from the world's end,
the two-horned Rhine and the Dahae never conquered,
Araxes River bridling at his bridge.
                              Such vistas
the God of Fire forged across the shield
that Venus gives her son. He fills with wonder—
he knows nothing of these events but takes delight
in their likeness, lifting onto his shoulders now
the fame and fates of all his children's children.

BOOK NINE

Enemy at the Gates

Now, while off in the distance much was under way,
Saturnian Juno hurried Iris down from the sky
to Turnus brash in arms, seated then by chance
in a hallowed glen, his forebear Pilumnus' grove.
The messenger with her rosy lips bestirred the king:
"Turnus, what no god would dare to promise you—
the answer to your prayers—
time in its rounds has brought you all unasked.
Yes, Aeneas has quit his camp, his comrades and
his fleet, he's lighted out for the Palatine hill,   10
Evander's royal home. But still not satisfied,
he's made his way to the farthest towns of Corythus,
arming a band of Tuscans, countryfolk he's mustered.
Why hold back? Now's the time for horse and chariot.
Away with delay! Attack their shattered camp!"

She towered into the sky on balanced wings,
cleaving a giant rainbow, flying beneath the clouds.
And Turnus knew her and raised both hands to the stars,
calling after the goddess, trailing her flight with cries:
"Iris, pride of the sky! Who has sped you here to me,   20
swooping down from the clouds to reach the earth?
Why this sudden radiance lighting the heavens?
I can see the clouds parting, the stars riding
the arching skies. I follow a sign so clear,
whoever you are who calls me into action."

In that spirit he went to the river's edge,
drew pure water up from the brimming banks
and prayed to the gods, over and over,
weighing down the heavens with his vows.

                                        And next
his entire army was moving out across the plain,   30
rich in cavalry, rich in braided cloaks, bright gold.
Messapus heads the column, the rear's brought up
by the sons of Tyrrhus, Turnus commands the center:
a force like the Ganges rising, fed by seven quiet streams
or the life-giving Nile ebbing back from the plains
to settle down at last in its own banks and bed.
Suddenly, far off, a massive dust-cloud rises
black as night, darkness sweeping across the plain.
The Trojans spot it, and first from the landward wall
Caicus calls out: "What's that mass, my countrymen,   40
blackness rolling toward us? Quick, take arms,
pass out weapons, mount the walls,
the enemy's all but on us! Battle stations!"

With a deafening roar the Trojans all come pouring in
through the gates for shelter, mount the ramparts now.
So ran his parting orders, Aeneas, best of captains:
"If any crisis comes while I am away, don't risk
a pitched battle, no, don't trust to the open field,
just guard the camp and ramparts, safe behind the walls."

So, though shame and anger spur them to all-out war,   50
still they bar the gates, they follow their orders,
armed to the hilt, protected inside the turrets,
bracing for the foe.
                              But Turnus flying on ahead
of his slower column, flanked by a picked troop
of twenty horsemen, gains the town in no time,
borne by a Thracian charger blazed with white,
and helmed in his golden casque with crimson crest.
"Who's with me, men, who's first to attack the enemy?
Just watch!" he cries and hurls his javelin into the sky—
the opening shot of war—and high in his saddle races   60
down the plain as his shouting comrades speed him on,
riding in his wake with their war cries striking terror,
amazed at the Trojans' bloodless hearts, and calling:
"No trusting themselves to a level field of battle!
No braving our infantry, grappling hand to hand,
the cowards cling to camp!"
                              Wildly, back and forth,
Turnus gallops along the walls—a way in?—no way in.
As a wolf prowling in wait around some crowded sheepfold,
bearing the wind and rain in the dead of night, howls
at chinks in the fence, and the lambs keep bleating on,   70
snug beneath their dams. The wolf rages, desperate,
how can he maul a quarry out of reach? Exhausted,
frenzied with building hunger, starved so long,
his jaws parched for blood.
                              So wildly Turnus,
scanning the camp and rampart, flares in anger,
brute resentment sears him to the bone.
What tactic to try, to make a breakthrough, how
to shake those penned-up Trojans clear of their walls
and strew them down the plain? The armada, there.
Hard by the camp it lay tied up, riding at anchor,   80
shielded round by the high redoubts and river currents—
here he attacks, shouting out to his cheering comrades:
"Bring up fire!" A man on fire, he seizes a blazing
pine-tar torch in his fist and now, watch, his men

pitch into the work as Turnus urges them on in person
and whole battalions equip themselves with smoking brands.
They've plundered the hearthfires, sooty torches ignite
a murky glare, and the God of Fire hurls at the skies
a swirl of sparks and ash.
                              What god, you Muses,
warded off such savage flames from the Trojans?   90
Who drove from the ships such raging fire? Tell me.
Trust in the tale is old, yet its fame will never die . . .
In the early days on Phrygian Ida's slopes when Aeneas
first built his fleet, gearing up for the high seas,
they say the Berecynthian Mother of Gods herself
appealed to powerful Jove with pleading words:
"Grant this prayer, my son, that your loving mother
makes to you, since now you rule on Olympus' heights.
I had a grove on the mountain's crest where men
would bring me gifts, a pinewood loved for long,   100
dark with pitch-pine, shady with maple timber.
These woods I gladly gave the Dardan prince
when the prince lacked a fleet—
now dread and anguish have me in their grip.
Dissolve my fears, let a mother's prayers prevail!
May these galleys never be wrecked on any passage out
or overpowered by whirling storms at sea,
let their birth on our mountains be a blessing!"

    Her son who makes the starry world go round
replied: "Mother, what are you asking Fate to grant?   110
What privilege are you begging for your ships? Think,
should keels laid by a mortal hand enjoy an immortal's rights?
Should Aeneas go through scathing dangers all unscathed—
Aeneas? What god commands such power? Nevertheless,
one day, when their tour of duty is done at last
and they moor in a Western haven, all the ships
that survived the waves and bore the Trojan prince
to Latium's fields—I will strip them of mortal shape
and command them all to be goddesses of the deep
like Doto, Nereus' daughter, and Galatea too,   120

breasting high, cleaving the frothing waves."
                                        Jove had spoken.
Sealing his pledge by the Styx, his brother's stream,
by the banks that churn with pitch-black rapids,
whirlpools swirling dark, he nodded his assent
and his nod made all of Mount Olympus quake.

                                        And so
the promised day had arrived and the Fates filled out
the assigned time, when Turnus' rampage warned the Mother
to drive his brands from her consecrated ships. And first
a strange radiance flashed in all eyes and a great cloud
appearing out of the dawn came sweeping down the sky,   130
trailed by the Goddess' dancing troupes from Ida.
Then an awesome voice descended through the air,
surrounding the Trojan and Rutulian ranks alike:
"No frantic rush to defend my ships, you Trojans,
no rising up in arms! Turnus can sooner burn
the Ocean dry than burn these sacred pines of mine.
Run free, my ships—run, you nymphs of the sea!
Your Mother commands you now!"
                                        And all at once,
each vessel snapping her cables free of the bank,
they dive like dolphins, plunging headlong beaks   140
to the bottom's depths, then up they surface,
turned into lovely virgins—wondrous omen—
each a sea-nymph sweeping out to sea.

    The Rutulians shrank in panic. Messapus himself
was stunned with terror, his stallions reared, and the river,
roaring, checked its currents, Tiber summoned his outflow
back from open sea. But dauntless Turnus never loses
faith in his daring, he flares up more at his men,
inflaming their spirits more: "All these omens
threaten the Trojans! Jove himself has whisked away   150
their trusted line of defense. No waiting for us,
for Rutulian sword and torch to strike their ships!
So now the open sea is blocked to the Trojans,
no escape, no hope. They're robbed of half the world

and the other half, dry land, is in our grasp,
so many thousand Italians take up arms.
All their fateful oracles—words from the gods
these Phrygians bandy about—alarm me not at all.
Let it be quite enough for Fate and Venus both
that Trojans reach the rich green land of Italy—   160
Trojans!
                    "I have my own fate too, counter to theirs,
to stamp out these accursed people with my sword—
they've stolen away my bride! Atreus' sons,
they're not alone in suffering such a wound,
not only Mycenae has a right to go to war.
'To die once is enough'?
The crime they committed once should be enough!
If only they hated most all womankind so deeply!
These Trojans who borrow courage, build their trust
on the walls they raise, the ditch they dig between us—   170
what a flimsy buffer to shield them all from slaughter!
Haven't they seen Troy's ramparts, built by Neptune's hands,
collapse in flames?
                    "But you, my elite ones, who is ready
to hack their ramparts down with the sword, to join me now
and storm their panicked camp? I have no use for all
the armor Vulcan forged, nor for a thousand ships
to go against these Trojans. Let all the Etruscans
join them at once as allies! They need not fear our
stealing up on them in the dark like skulking cowards
to rob them of their Palladium, butcher their sentries   180
posted on the heights. No hiding ourselves away
in a horse's blind dark flanks. In naked daylight
I am determined now to ring their walls with fire!
I'll make certain they never think they're fighting
Greek and Pelasgian boys, the recruits that Hector
warded off ten years.
                    "But now, my comrades,
seeing the best part of the day is done,
for the rest, refresh yourselves, hearts high.
You've done good work. And trust to it now,

we're heading for a battle."
                      All the while   190
Messapus is ordered to cordon off the gates
with a sentry-line and gird the walls with fire.
Fourteen Rutulians are picked to guard the ramparts,
each commanding a hundred troops, their helmets crested
with purple plumes, their war-gear glinting gold.
They scatter to posts and man the watch by turns
or stretching out on the grass, enjoy their wine,
tilting the bronze bowls while the fires burn on
and the watchmen dice away a sleepless night . . .

    Scanning all of this from the walls aloft,   200
the Trojans hold the heights with men-at-arms
while edgy, anxious, they reinforce the gates,
building bulwarks, joining ramps to the outworks,
bringing weapons up. Mnestheus, fierce Serestus
are spurring on the work, the men whom captain Aeneas
charged, should crisis call, to marshal troops in ranks
and take command of the outpost. The whole army's on guard,
tense along the walls. With perilous posts assigned
they stand watch by turns, each fighter defending
what he must defend.
               Now Nisus guarded a gate—   210
matchless in battle, Hyrtacus' son, Aeneas' comrade.
Ida the Huntress sent him, quick as the wind with spears
and winging arrows, and right beside him came his friend,
Euryalus. None more winning among Aeneas' soldiers,
none who strapped on Trojan armor, a young boy
sporting the first down of manhood, cheeks unshaved.
One love bound them, side by side they'd rush to attack,
so now, standing the same watch, they held one gate.
                     "Euryalus,"
Nisus asks, "do the gods light this fire in our hearts
or does each man's mad desire become his god?   220
For a while now a craving's urged me on
to swing into action, some great exploit—
no peace and quiet for me. See those Rutulians?

What trust they put in their own blind luck!
Watchfires flickering far apart. Men sprawling,
sunk in their wine and sleep. Dead silence all around.
Now listen to what I'm mulling over, what new plan
is shaping in my mind. The people, the elders
all demand that Aeneas be recalled and
men dispatched to tell him how the land lies.   230
If they promise you my reward—the fame of the work's
enough for me—I think I can just make out a path,
under that hill, to Pallanteum's city walls."

Euryalus froze, his heart pounding with love of praise
and he checks his fiery friend at once: "So, Nisus,
grudging your friend a share in your fine exploit?
I'm to send you out alone into so much danger?
That's not how father, the old soldier, Opheltes,
brought me up in the thick of the Greek terror,
the death-throes at Troy. Nor has it been my way,   240
soldiering on beside you, following out the fate
of great-hearted Aeneas, right to the bitter end.
Here is a heart that spurns the light, that counts
the honor you're after cheap at the price of life!"

"No," Nisus insisted, "I had no such qualm about you—
how wrong I'd be. Just let great Jove or whatever
god looks down with friendly eyes on what we do,
carry me back to you in triumph! Ah, but if—
and you often see such things in risky straits—
if anything sends me down to death, some god,   250
some twist of Fate, you must live on, I say,
you're young, your life's worth more than mine.
Let someone commit my body to the earth,
snatched from battle or ransomed back for gold.
Or if Fortune, up to her old tricks, denies me rites,
pay them when I am gone and honor me with a hollow tomb.
Nor would I cause your mother so much grief, dear boy.
She alone, out of so many Trojan mothers, dared
to follow you all the way. She had no love

for great Acestes' city."
                              Euryalus countered: 260
"You're spinning empty arguments, they won't work.
No, my mind won't change, won't budge an inch.
Let's be gone!"
                  With that, he stirs the sentries
and up they march to take their turn on watch.
Leaving his post, he and his comrade, Nisus,
stride off to find the prince.
                              Across the earth
all other creatures were stretched out in sleep,
easing their cares, their spirits blank to hardship.
But the leading Trojan chiefs, the chosen men of rank
were holding a council now on grave affairs of state—   270
what should they do? Who'll take word to Aeneas?
There they stand, out on the open campgrounds,
leaning on spears, hands at rest on shields
when in rush Nisus and Euryalus side by side,
clamoring for admittance, being heard at once:
"We've something urgent, well worth your while!"
So intense, that Iulus was first to welcome both,
inviting Hyrtacus' son to speak, and so he did:
"Men of Aeneas, hear us out with open minds,
don't judge what we say by our young years.   280
The enemy's sunken deep in sleep and wine,
dead to the world. There's a place for mischief—
we've seen it ourselves—an open fork in the road,
at the gate that fronts the coast. It's dark there,
gaps in their watchfires, smoke blackens the sky.
Give us this chance to make our way to Aeneas,
Pallanteum too, and you'll soon see us back,
loaded with spoils, some bloody killing done.
The road won't play us false. Hunting the dark glens,
day after day, we've scouted the city's outposts,   290
reconnoitered every bend in the river."
                              Aletes,
bowed with the years, a seasoned adviser, cried out:
"Gods of our fathers, Troy's eternal shield! So,

you're not about to destroy us root and branch,
not if you plant such courage, such resolve
in our young soldiers' hearts."

                        He grasped them
both by the hands and hugged their shoulders,
tears rivering down his cheeks: "For you,
good men, what reward can I find to equal
the noble work you're set on? First and best   300
the gods will give, and your own sense of worth.
The rest a thankful Aeneas will repay at once,
and young Ascanius too. As long as he lives
he'll never forget such meritorious service."

   "Never!" Ascanius steps in, "my life depends
on father's safe return. By our great household gods,
by Assaracus' hearth-god and white-haired Vesta's shrine,
I swear to you both, Nisus, all my hope, my fortune
lies in your laps alone. Just call father back,
bring him back to my eyes. If he returns,   310
all griefs are gone! Two cups I'll give you,
struck in silver, ridged with engraving—father
took them both when Arisba fell—and a pair of tripods,
two large bars of gold, and a winebowl full of years,
Dido of Sidon's gift.

                        "But if, in fact, we capture
Italy, seize the scepter in triumph, allot the plunder . . .
You've seen the stallion Turnus rides, the armor he sports,
all gold—that mount, the shield, the blood-red plumes,
I exempt from the lot. Your trophies, Nisus, now.
Also, father will give twelve women, beauties all,   320
and a dozen captive soldiers, each in armor—more,
whatever lands their King Latinus claims for himself.
But you, Euryalus, you who outstrip me by a year,
I admire you, I receive you with all my heart,
through thick and thin embrace you as my comrade.
Never without you, when I am bent on glory,
whether in word or action, peace or war,
you have my trust forever."

Euryalus replied:
"No day will show me unequal to such brave work,
if only the dice of Fortune fall out well, not badly.   330
But topping all your gifts, I beg you, just one more.
My mother, of Priam's ancient stock—poor woman!
Neither the land of Troy could hold her back,
setting sail with me, nor King Acestes' city.
Now I leave her, unaware of the risk I run,
whatever it is, with no parting words because—
I swear by the night and your right hand—I cannot
bear the sight of my mother's tears. But you,
I beg you, comfort her in her frailty, brace her
in desolation. Let me carry this hope of you   340
and all the bolder I go to face the worst."

     The Trojans were moved to tears, handsome Iulus
the most of all. Touched by love for his own father,
this image stirred his heart. "Trust me," he said,
"all I do will be worthy of your great exploit:
your mother will be mine in all but the name, Creusa.
No small thanks awaits the one who bore such a son.
Whatever comes of your exploit—I swear by my life,
the oath my father used to take—all I promise you
on your return in glory, the same rewards await   350
your mother and your kin."

                    He weeps as he speaks
and draws from his shoulder-strap a sword of gold,
forged by one Lycaon of Crete: marvelous work,
fitted with ivory sheath and set for action.
Mnestheus hands Nisus a fine shaggy hide
stripped from a lion, and trusty old Aletes
exchanges helmets with him. Now, both armed,
they move out at once, and as they go an escort
of ranking Trojans, warriors young and old,
sees them off at the gates with many prayers.   360
Yet first the handsome Iulus—beyond his years,
filled with a man's courage, a man's concerns as well—
gives them many messages to carry to his father.

But the winds scatter them all, all useless,
fling them into the clouds.
                                      Now out they go,
crossing the trench and threading through the dark,
heading toward the enemy camp, destined to die
but make a bloodbath first. Bodies everywhere—
they can see them stretched in the grasses, sunk
in a drunken stupor, chariot poles tipped up on shore,   370
bodies of fighters trapped in the wheels and harness,
weapons and winecups too are strewn about . . .
and Nisus speaks up first: "Euryalus, now
for the daring sword-hand. Now the moment calls.
Here's the way. You keep guard at our back,
so no patrol can attack us from the rear—
you be on the alert,
a hawk's eye all around. I'll make a slaughter,
cut you a good clean swath."
                                      Nisus breaks off
as he plants his sword in lofty Rhamnes,   380
propped up by chance on a pile of rugs,
his chest puffed out, and heaving, dead asleep,
a king himself, King Turnus' favorite prophet,
but no prophecy now could save him from his death.
Three aides at his side the Trojan killed—off guard,
sprawled in a snarl of arms, then Remus' armor-bearer,
then his charioteer, he caught him under his horses' hoofs.
He hacks their lolling necks and lops the head of their master,
leaves the trunk of him spouting blood, the earth and bedding
warmed with the wet black gore. He cuts down Lamyrus too,   390
Lamus and Serranus—well-built soldier, he'd gamed away
till late at night and now lay numb in a drunken haze.
Lucky man, if only he'd stretched his gambling through the night
and played it out till dawn! Nisus, wild as a starved lion
raging through crowded pens as the hunger drives him mad,
and he mangles sheep, dumb with terror, rips to shreds
their tender flesh and roars from bloody jaws.
                                      No less
bloody Euryalus' work—the man's on fire, storming

down on the common ruck before him, Fadus, Herbesus,
Rhoetus, Abaris, quite unconscious now. But Rhoetus,   400
waking, witnessed it all and cowered, crouching
behind an enormous mixing-bowl, but Euryalus pounced
as Rhoetus rose—he rushed him, drove a sword in his heart,
up to the hilt then wrenched it back, dripping death.
Rhoetus vomits his red lifeblood, spewing out
gore and wine mixed with the man's last gasp.
But still Euryalus glowed with a killer's stealth,
he was stalking nearer Messapus' henchmen now,
he could spot the outer campfires flickering low
and horses tethered securely, grazing grass—the cavalry—   410
when Nisus, sensing his comrade run amok with bloodlust,
cuts him short: "Call it quits, the dawn's at hand,
our old foe. Enough revenge. We've hacked a path
through enemy lines—enough!"
                                    And they leave behind
a haul of soldiers' armor struck in solid silver,
mixing-bowls in the bargain, gorgeous rugs.
But Euryalus tears off Rhamnes' battle-emblems
and gold-studded belt: gifts that lavish Caedicus
once sent Remulus of Tibur, hoping to seal a pact
with a friend then far away, and Remulus, dying,   420
passed them on to his grandson and, once he died,
the Latins commandeered them in battle, spoils of war.
Euryalus seizes them, fits them onto his gallant shoulders
all for nothing. He dons Messapus' helmet crested
with tossing plumes. The raiders quit the camp
and race for safety.
                          But just then a troop
of cavalry sent on ahead from the Latin city—
the rest of the army waits, poised on the plain—
comes riding in with messages for King Turnus.
Three hundred strong, all men bearing shields   430
with Volcens in command. Just nearing the camp,
just coming up to the earthworks when they spot
at a distance two men swerving off to the left.
The helmet—Euryalus forgot—it glints in the dark,

it gives him away, it's caught in a shaft of moonlight.
A sight not lost on Volcens, shouting out from the vanguard:
"Soldiers, halt!
        Why on the road?—in armor!
                    Who are you?
Where are you headed?" No answer given. Off they scurry
into the woods and trust to night. But the troopers
fan out left and right, blocking the well-known paths,   440
the sentries ringing all ways out. The dense woods
spread far, the thickets and black ilex bristle,
briars crowd the entire place, with a rare track
showing a faint trace through the thick blind glades.
The dark branches, the heft of the plunder, all weigh down
Euryalus—fear leads him astray in the tangled paths.
But Nisus gets away, unthinkingly flees the foe
to a place called Alban later, named for Alba then,
a spot where Latinus kept his sturdy sheepfolds.
Here Nisus halts, looking back for his lost friend,   450
no use—
       "My poor Euryalus! Where did I lose you?
Where can I find you now?"
                 Nisus already picks his way,
wheeling, groping back through the whole deceptive wood,
retracing, scouring his tracks through the silent brush . . .
he hears hoofbeats, hears a commotion, orders, hot pursuit.
The next moment a cry hits his ears, and look, Euryalus!
Caught by the full band, undone by the dark, the place,
the treachery, sudden crashing attack—he's overwhelmed,
they're dragging him off, struggling, desperate, doomed.
What can Nisus do? How can he save his young friend—   460
what force, weapons, what bold stroke?
Pitch himself at the swords and die at once?
Race through wounds to a swift and noble death?
Quickly cocking his arm, his lance brandished high,
he cranes up at the moon and prays his heart out:
"You, goddess, Latona's daughter! Stand by me now!
Help me now in the thick of danger—glory of stars,
guard of the groves! If father Hyrtacus ever

gave you gifts in my name to grace your altars,
if I have ever adorned them with hunting trophies,   470
hanging them from your dome, fixing them to your roofs—
help me rout my enemies! Wing my spears through the air!"

    With that he hurled his spear, his whole body behind it—
whirring on through the dark night, it flies at Sulmo
and striking his turned back it splits—crack!—
and a splinter stabs his midriff through.
He twists over, vomiting hot blood from his chest,
chill with death, his flanks racked with his last gasps.
The Rutulians reel, looking about, but now Nisus,
all the bolder, watch, cocking another spear   480
beside his ear as the enemy panics—hurls and
the shaft goes hissing right through Tagus' brow,
splitting it, sticking deep in the man's warm brains.
Volcens burns with fury, stymied—where can he find
the one who threw it? Where can he aim his rage?
"No matter!" he cries. "Now you'll pay me
in full with your hot blood for both my men!"
With that he rushes Euryalus, sword drawn as
Nisus terrified, frenzied—no more hiding in shadows,
no enduring such anguish any longer—he breaks out: 490
"Me—here I am, I did it! Turn your blades on me,
Rutulians! The crime's all mine, he never dared,
could never do it! I swear by the skies up there,
the stars, they know it all! All he did was love
his unlucky friend too well!"
                                But while he begged
the sword goes plunging clean through Euryalus' ribs,
cleaving open his white chest. He writhes in death
as blood flows over his shapely limbs, his neck droops,
sinking over a shoulder, limp as a crimson flower
cut off by a passing plow, that droops as it dies   500
or frail as poppies, their necks weary, bending
their heads when a sudden shower weighs them down.
But Nisus storms the thick of them, out for Volcens,
one among all, Volcens his lone concern. His enemies

massing round him, trying to drive him back, left, right
but he keeps charging, harder, swirling his lightning sword
till facing Volcens, he sinks his blade in his screaming mouth—
Nisus dying just as he stripped his enemy of his life.
Then, riddled with wound on wound, he threw himself
on his lifeless friend and there in the still of death   510
found peace at last.
                How fortunate, both at once!
If my songs have any power, the day will never dawn
that wipes you from the memory of the ages, not while
the house of Aeneas stands by the Capitol's rock unshaken,
not while the Roman Father rules the world.
                         Triumphant,
the Rutulians gathered their battle-plunder, weeping now
as they bore the lifeless body of Volcens back to camp.
There they wept no less, finding Rhamnes bled white
and so many captains killed in one great slaughter.
Serranus, Numa too, and a growing crowd cluster   520
around the dead and dying men, and the ground lies warm
with the recent massacre, rivulets foam with blood.
Together they recognize the trophies of war—
Messapus' burnished helmet
and many emblems retrieved with so much sweat.
                        By now,
early Dawn had risen up from the saffron bed
of Tithonus, scattering fresh light on the world.
Sunlight flooded in and the rays laid bare the earth
as Turnus, fully armed himself, calls his men to arms.
And each commander marshals his own troops for battle,   530
squadrons sheathed in bronze, and whets their fury
with mixed accounts of the last night's slaughter.
They even impale the heads on brandished pikes,
the heads—a grisly sight—and strut behind them,
baiting them with outcries . . . Euryalus and Nisus.
On the rampart's left wing—the river flanks the right—
the hardened troops of Aeneas group in battle order,
facing enemy lines and manning the broad trench
or stationed up on the towers—wrung with sorrow,

men stunned by the sight of men they know too well,   540
their heads stuck on pikestaffs dripping gore.

   That moment, Rumor, flown through the shaken camp,
wings the news to the ears of Euryalus' mother.
Suddenly warmth drains from her grief-stricken body,
the shuttle's flung from her hand, the yarn unravels
and off she flies, poor thing. Shrilling a woman's cries
and tearing her hair, insane, she rushes onto the high walls,
seeking the front ranks posted there—without a thought
for the fighters, none for the perils, the spears, no,
she fills the air with wails of mourning: "You—   550
is this *you* I see, Euryalus? You, the only balm
of my old age! How could you leave me all alone?—
so cruel! When you set out on that deadly mission,
couldn't your mother have said some last farewell?
What heartbreak, now you lie in an unknown land,
fresh game for the dogs and birds of Latium!
Nor did your own mother lead her son's cortege
or seal your eyes in death or bathe your wounds
or shroud you round in the festive robe I wove,
speeding the work for you, laboring day and night,   560
lightening with the loom the pains of my old age.
Where can I go? What patch of ground now holds
your body cut to pieces, your mutilated corpse?
This head—it's all you bring me back, my son?—
it's all that I followed, crossing land and sea?
Stab me through, if *you* have any decency left,
whip all your lances into me, you Rutulians,
kill me first with steel! Or pity me, You,
Great Father of Gods, and whirl this hated body
down to hell with a bolt, the only way I know   570
to burst the chains of this, this brutal life!"

   Her wails dashed their spirits, a spasm of sorrow
went throbbing through them all. They were broken men,
their lust for battle numbed. As she inflames their grief,
Idaeus and Actor, ordered by Ilioneus and Iulus

weeping freely, cradle her in their arms and
bear her back inside.
                          A terrific brazen blast
went blaring out from the trumpets far and wide
and war cries echo the horns and the high sky resounds.
And now the Volscians charge, ranks of them packing under   580
a tortoise-shell of shields, bent on filling the trenches,
tearing down stockades. Some press hard for an entry,
scaling the walls with ladders, wherever a gap shows
in the thin defensive ring and light breaks through.
The opposing Trojans fling down missiles, any and all,
thrusting off the assault with rugged pikes—expert
from their years of war at defending city ramparts.
Great boulders they trundle down on the raiders,
huge weights, trying to break their shielded troops
but under the tortoise-shell they gladly take their blows.   590
Yet they can't hold out. Wherever Rutulians mass for attack,
the Trojans roll up immense rocks and heave them hurtling down,
cracking their armored carapace, crush them, send them reeling
and now the bold Rutulians lose all zest for battle under
a blind defensive shell, they struggle out in the open,
flinging spears to clear the enemy ramparts. Here
in another sector, Mezentius—grim sight—is shaking
a Tuscan pine beam, hurling fire and smoky pitch at the foe
as Messapus, breaker of horses, Neptune's son, is ripping
open a rampart, shouting: "Ladders—scale the walls!"   600

    I pray you, Calliope—Muses—inspire me as I sing
what carnage and death the sword of Turnus spread that day,
what men each fighter speeded down to darkness. Come,
help me unroll the massive scroll of war!
                                     Now a tower
reared high, a commanding, salient point with rampways
climbing up to it. All the Italians fought to storm it,
full strength, straining to drag it down, full force
while Trojans, jammed inside, fought to defend it,
barricade it with stones, hurling salvos of spears
through gaping loopholes. Turnus, first to attack,   610

whirled a flaming torch that stuck in the tower's flanks
and whipped by the wind it quickly seized on planking,
clinging fast to the doorway's posts it ate away.
Inside, panic, chaos, soldiers fighting to find
some way out of the flames—no hope. Men went cramming
back to the safe side, back from the killing heat but under
the sudden lurch of weight the tower came toppling down,
making the whole wide heaven thunder back its crash.
Fighters writhe in death, crushed on the ground,
the enormous wreckage right on top of them, yes,   620
impaling them on their own weapons, stabbing
splintered timbers through their chests.
                                             Only
Helenor and Lycus slip to safety, just—Helenor
still in the flush of youth. A slave, Licymnia,
bore him once to Maeonia's king in secret,
sent him to Troy, light-armed in forbidden gear,
a naked sword and a shield still blank, unblazoned.
Now he found himself in the thick of Turnus' thousands,
Latin battalions crowding, pressing at all points—
as a wild beast snared in a closing ring of hunters,   630
raging against their weapons flings itself at death,
staring doom in the face, leaping straight at the spears—
just so wild the young soldier leaps at the enemy's center,
rushing at death where he sees the spearheads densest.
But Lycus, far faster, escapes through enemy lines
and spears to reach the wall, clawing up to the coping,
trying to grasp his comrades' hands when Turnus, chasing
him down with a lance, shouts out in triumph:
                                             "Fool,
you hoped to escape my clutches?"—
                                      seizing him as he dangles,
tearing the man down along with a hefty piece of wall.   640
As the eagle that bears Jove's lightning snatches up
in his hooking talons a hare or snow-white swan
and towers into the sky, or the wolf of Mars that rips
a lamb from the pens and its mother desperate to find it

fills the air with bleating.

                     War cries rising, everywhere,
on and on they charge, packing the trench with earth,
some men hurling fiery torches onto the rooftops.
Ilioneus heaving a rock, a huge crag of a rock,
brings down Lucetius just assaulting the gates
with a flaming torch in hand as Liger kills Emathion,   650
Asilas lays out Corynaeus, one adept with javelin,
one with arrows blindsiding in from a distance—
Caeneus kills Ortygius—Turnus, triumphant Caeneus—
Turnus cuts down Itys, Clonius, Dioxippus and Promolus,
Sagaris, Idas, posted out in front of the steepest towers,
and Capys kills Privernus. Themillas' spear grazed him first,
he dropped his shield, the idiot, raised his hand to the gash
as the arrow flew and digging deep in his left side, deeper,
burst the ducts of his life breath with a deadly wound.
There stood Arcens' son, decked out in brilliant gear   660
and a war-shirt stitched blood-red with Spanish dye,
a fine, striking boy. His father reared him once
in the grove of Mars where Symaethus' waters swirl
and a shrine to the gods of Sicily stands, the Palaci,
quick to forgive, their altar rich with gifts—
and he sent his son to war . . .

                    Mezentius' hissing sling—
keeping its strap taut and dropping his spears, three times
he whipped it around his head, let fly and the lead shot,
sizzling hot in flight, split his enemy's skull and
splayed him out headfirst on a bank of sand.

                           Then,   670
they say, Ascanius shot for the first time in war
the flying arrow he'd saved till now for wild game,
routing, terrorizing them, now his bow-hand cut down
strong Numanus—Remulus by family name, just lately
bound in marriage to Turnus' younger sister. Numanus,
out of the front lines he swaggered, chest puffed up
with his newfound royal rank and he let loose
an indiscriminate string of ugly insults,

flaunting his own power to high heaven: "What,
have you no shame? You Phrygians twice enslaved,   680
penned up twice over inside blockaded ramparts,
skulking away from death behind your walls! Look
at the heroes who'd seize our brides in battle!
What god drove you to Italy? What insanity?
No sons of Atreus here, no spinner of tales, Ulysses.
We're rugged stock, from the start we take our young ones
down to the river, toughen them in the bitter icy streams.
Our boys—they're up all night, hunting, scouring the woods,
their sport is breaking horses, whipping shafts from bows.
Our young men, calloused by labor, used to iron rations,   690
tame the earth with mattocks or shatter towns with war.
All our lives are honed to the hard edge of steel,
reversing our spears we spur our oxen's flanks.
No lame old age can cripple our high spirits,
sap our vigor, no, we tamp our helmets down
on our gray heads, and our great joy is always
to haul fresh booty home and live off all we seize.
But you, with your saffron braided dress, your flashy purple,
you live for lazing, lost in your dancing, your delight,
blowzy sleeves on your war-shirts, ribbons on bonnets.   700
Phrygian women—that's what you are—not Phrygian men!
Go traipsing over the ridge of Dindyma, catch the songs
on the double pipe you dote on so! The tambourines,
they're calling for you now, and the boxwood flutes
of your Berecynthian Mother perched on Ida!
Leave the fighting to men. Lay down your swords!"

    Flinging his slander, ranting taunts—Ascanius
had enough. Facing him down and aiming a shaft
from his bowstring, horse-gut, tense, he stood there,
stretching both arms wide, praying first to Jove   710
with a fervent heartfelt vow: "Jove almighty,
nod assent to the daring work I have in hand!
All on my own I'll bring your temple yearly gifts!
I'll steady before your altar a bull with gilded brows,

bright white with its head held high as its mother's,
butting its horns already, young hoofs kicking sand!"

And the Father heard and thundered on the left
from a cloudless sky—the instant the lethal bow sings out
and the taut shaft flies through Remulus' head with a vicious hiss
and rends his empty temples with its steel. "Go on,   720
now mock our courage with high and mighty talk!
Here's the reply the Phrygians, twice enslaved,
return to you Rutulians!"
                    That's all he says.
The Trojans echo back with a roar of joy,
their spirits sky-high.
               By chance Apollo,
god of the flowing hair enthroned on a cloud
in the broad sweeping sky, was glancing down
at Ausonia's troops and camp and calls to Iulus
flushed with triumph now: "Bravo, my boy, bravo,
your newborn courage! That's the path to the stars—   730
son of the gods, you'll father gods to come!
All fated wars to come will end in peace,
justly, under Assaracus' future sons—
Troy can never hold you!"
               In the same breath
the god Apollo dives from the vaulting skies and
cleaving the gusty winds searches for Ascanius.
He assumes the form and features of old Butes,
armor-bearer, once, to Dardan Anchises,
trusty guard of his gates until Aeneas
made him Ascanius' aide. So Apollo approached   740
like Butes head to foot—the man's age, his voice,
the shade of his skin, white hair, weapons clanging grimly,
and counsels Iulus now in his full glow of triumph:
"Son of Aeneas, stop! Enough that Numanus fell
to your flying shafts and you've not paid a price.
Apollo has granted this, your first flush of glory,
he never envied your arrows, a match for the Archer's own.

For the battles to come, hold back for now, dear boy!"

    This order still on his lips, Apollo vanished
from sight into empty air.
                            But the Trojan captains   750
recognized the god, his immortal arms, and heard
his arrows rustling in his quiver as he flew.
So they restrain Ascanius blazing for battle,
pressing on him Apollo's will and last commands
but they themselves go rushing back to fight
and expose their lives to peril.
Cries rock the ramparts, up and down the walls—
they're tensing murderous bows, whipping spear-straps,
weapons strewing the ground, shields and hollow helmets
ringing out under impact—fighting surges, raging strong   760
as a tempest out of the West when the Kids are rising great
with rain that lashes the earth, and thick and fast as the hail
that stormclouds shower, pelting headlong down on the waves
when Jupiter fierce with Southwinds spins a whirlwind,
thunderheads exploding down the sky.
                            Pandarus and Bitias—
Alcanor of Ida's offspring born by the nymph Iaera
once in Jupiter's grove—men like pines and peaks
of their native land, who trusted so to their swords
they fling wide the gate their captain entrusted to them,
all on their own inviting enemy ranks to breach the walls.   770
There they loom in the gateway, left and right like towers,
armored in iron, crests on their high heads flaring—
tall as a pair of oaks along a stream in spate,
by the Po's banks or the Adige's lovely waters,
rearing their uncropped heads to the high sky,
their twin crowns waving tall.
                            But in they charge,
the Rutulian forces seeing the way wide open now.
In an instant Quercens, Aquiculus striking in armor,
Tmarus—daredevil heart—and Haemon, son of Mars,
with all their squadrons routed, turn tail and run   780
or throw their lives down right at the gateway's mouth.

And the more they fight, the hotter their battle fury grows
and now the Trojans mass, regrouping to storm the site,
clashing man to man, daring to foray farther out.
                                                    Turnus,
the great captain, is blazing on in another zone,
stampeding the Trojan ranks when the news arrives:
The enemy flushed with the latest carnage offers up
their gates flung open now. And Turnus wheels,
dropping the task at hand and full of fury, speeds
to the Trojan gate to face the headstrong brothers.   790
But first Antiphates, he was the first to charge,
Sarpedon's bastard son by a mother born in Thebes—
but Turnus cuts him down, his Italian cornel spearshaft
wings through the melting air and piercing the man's stomach
thrusts up into his chest, and froth from the wound's black pit
comes bubbling up as the steel heats in the lung it struck.
Then Merops and Erymas die at his hands, then Aphidnus,
even Bitias, eyes ablaze, all rage at heart, and not
by a spear—he'd never give up his life to a spear—
a massive pike with a giant blade comes hurtling, roaring   800
into him, driven home like a lightning bolt and neither
the two bull's-hides of his shield nor trusty breastplate,
double-mailed with its scales of gold, can block its force.
His immense limbs collapse, and earth groans as his giant shield
thunders down on his body.
                                Huge as a masoned pier that
falls at times on the shore of Euboean Baiae—first
they build it of massive blocks, then send it crashing over,
dragging all in its wake and it crushes down on the ocean floor
as the waves roil and black sand goes heaving into the air
and Prochyta Island quakes to its depths and the craggy bed   810
of Inarime weighting Typhoeus down by Jove's command.
                                                            Here,
Mars, power of war, injects new heart and force in the Latins,
twisting his sharp spurs in their chests and loosing Flight
and dark Fear at the Trojan ranks, and the Latins swarm in
from all directions, seize the moment for all-out assault
as the war-god strikes their spirits. Pandarus, seeing his brother's

body spread on the ground and sensing how Fortune falls—
disaster rules the day—with all his might he rams
his massive shoulder into the gate and wheels it
shut on its hinges, shuts out many comrades now   820
outside the ramparts, facing an uphill battle,
and shuts in many others, ushering fighters home
as in they rush, along with himself, the crazy fool—
not to have spotted Turnus charging in with the crowds
and all unwittingly shut him up inside the walls
like a claw-mad tiger among some helpless flock.
Suddenly strange light flares from Turnus' eyes
and his armor clangs, horrific, the blood-red plumes
shake on his head and his shield shoots bolts of lightning.
They know him at once, his hated face, his immense frame,   830
and Aeneas' troops are stunned.
                                    But enormous Pandarus
breaks ranks, afire with rage at his brother's death,
and shouts: "No palace here, your dowry from Amata!
Look, no Fortress Ardea hugging her native Turnus!
What you see is your enemy's camp—you can't escape!"

    And Turnus replied with a cool, collected smile:
"On with it now, if you have the backbone in you,
let's trade blows. You'll tell the ghost of Priam
you found an Achilles—even here!"
                                    No more talk.
Putting all his strength behind it, Pandarus hurls   840
his spear, unpolished, knotted, bark still rough
but the breezes whisk it away, Saturnian Juno flicks
aside the approaching wound and the weapon stabs the gate.
"But you won't escape my blade, whirling in my right hand,"
cries Turnus. "No, this sword and the man who wields it,
the wounds they deal are fatal!" Rearing to full height,
sword high, the steel hacks the brows, splitting the temples—
gruesome wound—and it cleaves the soft unshaven cheeks.
A great crash! Under his huge weight the earth quakes,
his limbs fall limp, his armor splattered with brains,   850
he sprawls on the ground in death—in perfect halves

over both his shoulders, right and left, his head
goes lolling free.
                    The Trojans swerve and scatter
in panic and if the conquering hero had thought at once
of smashing the gate-bolts, letting his cohorts in,
this day would have been the last day of the war,
the last of the Trojans too. But Turnus' hot fury,
his mad lust for carnage drives him against his foes.
First he seizes Phaleris, cuts the knees from under Gyges—
snatching their spears he whips them into the backs of men   860
who break and run as Juno builds his courage, his war-lust.
Halys next, he sends him packing along with comrades,
Phegeus too, as a spear impales him through his shield,
then men on the ramparts keen for combat, blind to Turnus
who picks them off, Alcander and Halius, Prytanis and Noëmon.
Lynceus swings to attack, shouting his comrades on—but first
from the right-hand rampart Turnus spins with one stroke
of his dazzling sword, close-up, that brings down Lynceus,
slashes his head off, head and helmet tumbling far away.
Next he brings down Amycus, gifted killer of wild game—   870
no hand more skilled at dipping an arrow's point or
capping a lance with poison—then Clytius, Aeolus' son,
then Cretheus, friend of the Muses, the Muses' comrade,
Cretheus, always dear to his heart the song and lyre,
tuning a verse to the taut string, always singing
of cavalry, weapons, wars and the men who fight them.
                                                At last
the Trojan captains hear of the massacre of their troops.
Mnestheus, fierce Serestus, both come rushing in and
seeing their ranks in panic, ranks of enemies
lodged inside the gates, Mnestheus shouts out: 880
"Where are you heading? Where are you flying now—
what other walls, what other ramparts have you got?
My countrymen, can one man, penned up in your fortress
on all sides, spread such slaughter through the city?
Send such a rout of first-rate fighters down to death
and never pay the price?
You feckless, craven—have you no pity? No shame

for your wretched land, your gods of old? For great Aeneas?"

That ignites them, stiffens their spines and closing ranks
they halt . . . as Turnus pulls back from the melee, heading   890
step by step for the banks where the river rings the camp.
All the more fiercely Trojans swarm him, war cries breaking,
ranks packed tight as a band of huntsmen bristling spears,
attacking a savage lion. Terrified, true, but glaring still,
ferocious still as he backs away, but his heart, his fury
keep him from turning tail, yet for all his wild desire
he still can't claw his way through spears and huntsmen.
Just so torn, so slowly but surely Turnus backs away,
his spirit churning with anger. Twice he charged
the thick of his foes, twice he broke their lines,   900
stampeding the Trojans down their walls at speed.
But a whole battalion marching out of the camp
comes massing hard against him—not even Juno
dares reinforce his power to counterattack.
No, Jove sped Iris down from the high heavens,
winging strict commands for his sister, Juno,
if Turnus did not quit the Trojans' looming walls.

So now no shield, no sword-arm helps the fighter
stand up under the onslaught, overpowering salvos
battering down on him left and right. Over and over   910
the helmet casing his hollow temples rings out shrill,
the solid bronze of it splits wide open under the rocks,
the plumes are ripped from his head, the boss of his shield
caves in to the hammering blows. And the Trojan ranks,
with lightning-bolt Mnestheus out in the lead, unleash
an immense barrage of spears, and sweat goes rippling over
Turnus' entire body, rivering down, black with filth—
can't catch his breath, gasping, weak knees quaking,
bone-tired until at last he dives headfirst,
plunging into the river, armor and all, and Tiber   920
swept him into its yellow tide, catching him as he came,
then bore him up in its soothing waves and bathing away
the carnage, gave the elated fighter back to friends.

BOOK TEN

Captains Fight and Die

Now the gates of mighty Olympus' house are flung wide open.
The Father of Gods and King of Men convenes a council
high in his starry home, as throned aloft he gazes
down on the earth, the Trojan camp and Latian ranks.
The gods take seats in the mansion, entering there
through doors to East and West, and Jove starts in:
"You great gods of the sky,
why have you turned against your own resolve?
Why do you battle so? Such warring hearts!
I ordered Italy not to fight with Troy.   10
What's this conflict flouting my command?
What terror has driven one or the other side
to rush to arms and rouse their enemies' swords?
The right time for war will come—don't rush it now—
one day when savage Carthage will loose enormous ruin
down on the Roman strongholds, breach and unleash
the Alps against her walls. Then is the time

to clash in hatred, then to ravage each other.
Be at peace for now. Spirits high, consent
to the pact I have decreed."   20

    Jove is just that brief, but golden Venus
is far from brief as she replies: "Oh Father,
everlasting king over men and all the world,
what other force could we implore to save us now?
You see the Rutulians on the rampage? Turnus amidst them,
proud in his chariot, puffed up with his new success,
spurring the war-lust on! Their thick armored walls
no longer can shield the Trojans. Now they are even
fighting inside their gates, it's combat cut-and-thrust,
right on their own ramparts, trenches bathed in blood!   30
And Aeneas knows nothing, the man is miles away . . .
When will you ever let them lift the siege?
Once more a new force, a new army threatens the walls
of newborn Troy. Once more he springs from Arpi,
that Aetolian, Diomedes. So once again, I see,
some wounds are in store for me, your daughter,
and I must block the mortals hurling spears!

    "If without your assent, against your will
the Trojans have reached Italy, let them pay
for their latest outrage, never grant them rescue.   40
But if they have followed the oracles laid down
by the gods on high and the great shades below,
how can anyone overturn your edicts now
and plant the Fates anew? Why recall it all,
the armada burned to ash on the shores of Eryx?
The storm-king lashing gales from Aeolia into fury?
Iris swooping down from the clouds? Now she even
stirs the dead, the one realm in the world still left
untested, yes, and Allecto, suddenly loosed on earth,
tears like a Maenad through the heart of Italian cities.   50
Empire stirs me no longer now. That was our hope
while Fortune still smiled. Now let those win out . . .
the ones you *want* to win. If there is no patch of earth

that your ruthless queen could grant the Trojans now,
I beg you, Father, by the smoking wreck of Troy,
let Ascanius have safe passage out of battle,
spare my grandson's life!
                         "As for Aeneas,
let the man be tossed on strange new seas,
follow the course where Fortune leads the way.
Just give me the strength to shield my grandson,   60
bear him quite unscathed from the raw clash of arms.
Why, I have Amathus, Paphus' heights, and Cythera too,
an Idalian mansion—there with his weapons laid away,
let him live his life out, all unsung. And so,
give the command for Carthage to crush Italy,
overwhelm her with force. From Italy comes
no barrier posed against the towns of Tyre.
What good has it been to flee the plague of war,
to slip through the thick of fires set by the Greeks?
Drain to the lees the perils at sea and the whole wide earth   70
while the Trojans hunt for Latium, hunt for Troy reborn!
Better, no, to settle down on their country's dying ashes,
the ground where Troy once stood? I beg you, Father,
give them back their Xanthus and their Simois
if these luckless Trojans must, once more,
relive the fall of Troy!"
                         At that, Queen Juno
looses her fury, bursting out: "Why drive me
to break my deep silence, to open up my wounds,
long scarred over, and bruit them to the world?
How could anyone—man or god—force your Aeneas   80
to pitch on war, to harry King Latinus as his foe?
So, he sought out Italy under the Fates' command?
The Fates? Cassandra's raving spurred him on! Did I
press him to leave his camp or cast his life to the winds?
To trust his walls, the whole command of the battle to a boy?
To disrupt the Tuscans' faith, inflame a peaceful people?
What god, what ruthless power of mine drove him to ruin?
Where's Juno in this? Or Iris sped from the clouds? So,
it's wrong for Italians to ring your newborn Troy with fire?

For Turnus to plant his feet on his own native soil?   90
His forebear is Pilumnus, his mother a goddess, Venilia!
What of the Trojans putting the Latins to the torch?
Yoking the fields of others, hauling off the plunder?
Taking their pick of daughters, tearing the sworn bride
from her husband's arms? Their hands pleading for peace
while they arm their sterns with spears! Oh, you can
whisk Aeneas clear of the clutches of the Greeks,
in place of a man puff up some vapid fume of air!
You can change an armada into sea-nymphs, yes,
but if we in our turn offer the Latin side   100
a helping hand, is that such a horrid crime?
'Aeneas knows nothing, the man is miles away'?
Unknowing let him stay there!
Why, you have Paphus, Idalia, steep Cythera too—
why tamper with brute Italians, a city rife with war?
Is it I who try to overwhelm from the roots up
your sinking Phrygian state? Not I! Wasn't it
he who exposed your wretched Trojans to the Greeks?
What inspired Europe and Asia to surge up in arms,
underhandedly break the bonds of friendship?   110
Was it I who lured the Trojan adulterer on
to lay Sparta low? Or I who equipped the man
with weapons, fanned the flames of war with lust?
You should have feared for your chosen people then.
It's too late now for rising up with your groundless
accusations—flinging empty slander in my face!"

    While Juno harangued the gods with her appeals,
all were murmuring low, assenting, dissenting . . .
low as the first stir of stormwind caught in the trees
when the rustling unseen murmur keeps on rolling,   120
warning sailors that gales are coming on. Then
the almighty Father, power that rules the world,
begins, and as he speaks the lofty house of the gods
falls silent, earth rocks to its roots, the heights
of the sky are hushed and the Western breezes drop
and the Ocean calms its waters into peace: "So then,

take what I say to heart and stamp it in your minds.
Since it is not allowed that Latins and Trojans
join in pacts of peace, and there is no end
to your eternal clashes—now, whatever the luck   130
of each man today, and whatever hope he follows,
Trojan or Italian, I make no choice between them.
Whether Italy's happy fate lays siege to the camp
or the Trojans' folly, the deadly prophecies they follow.
Nor do I exempt the Italians. How each man weaves
his web will bring him to glory or to grief.
King Jupiter is the king to all alike.
The Fates will find the way."
                                        And now, sealing
his pledge by the river Styx, his brother's stream,
by the banks that churn with pitch-black rapids,   140
whirlpools swirling dark, he nodded his assent
and his nod made all of Mount Olympus quake.
The great debate had closed.
Jupiter rises up from his golden throne
as the gods of heaven flock around him there
and escort him to the gateway of his mansion.
                                        All day
the Rutulians encircle every entry, battling on to bring
their enemies down in blood and ring their walls with fire.
But Aeneas' force is locked fast in its own ramparts now,
no hope of a breakout. Shattered, helpless, posted high   150
on the turrets, girding walls with a thin defensive ring
are Asius, son of Imbrasus, Thymoetes, Hicetaon's son,
the Assaraci twins and Castor with aged Thymbris
up in front: behind them, both Sarpedon's brothers,
Clarus and Thaemon, new allies from Lycia's highlands.
One man puts his weight into heaving up a boulder,
no mean piece of a crag—Acmon born in Lyrnesus,
strong as his father Clytius, his brother Menestheus.
All of them struggle there to defend their walls,
some with javelins, some with rocks or flinging   160
blazing torches, nocking arrows to bowstrings.
There amidst them, look, the Dardan boy himself,

Venus' favorite, rightly—handsome head laid bare,
he shines like a brilliant gemstone set in tawny gold,
adorning a head or neck, or aglow as ivory deftly
inlaid in box or black Orician terebinth wood
and over his milk-white neck his long locks fall,
clasped tight by a torque of hammered gold.
Ismarus, you too, your fine hardy fighters
watched you dipping your arrowheads in poison,   170
winging wounds at the enemy. You, the noble son
of a proud Maeonian house, where the farmhands work
the loamy soil and Pactolus floods the fields with gold.
And there was Mnestheus too, his glory riding high
with yesterday's triumph—driving Turnus off the walls—
and Capys too, whose name comes down to us in Capua,
the famed Campanian town.
                          And so both sides
had clashed in the cruel thick-and-fast of war
while Aeneas plowed the sea in the dead of night.
Once he left Evander and entered the Tuscan camp,   180
he seeks King Tarchon, tells him his name and stock
and the help he needs and the help he brings himself.
He tells him Mezentius musters fighters to his side,
tells him the heart of Turnus flares for battle,
warns him of what to trust in men's affairs,
concluding all with his own strong appeals.
Then no delay, Tarchon joins forces at once
and seals a pact. And so, free of Fate's demand,
since they are sworn to a foreign leader now,
under the will of god the Etruscans set sail.   190
Aeneas' ship's in the lead, with Phrygian lions
fixed on her beak, Mount Ida looming aloft,
a god-sent sign of home to Trojan exiles.
There sits great Aeneas . . .
musing over the shifting tides of war
as Pallas flanks him closely on his left, asking
now of the stars that guide them through the night
and now of the hardships he had braved on land and sea.

Now throw Helicon open, Muses, launch your song!
What forces sail with Aeneas fresh from the Tuscan shores,   200
manning their ships for battle, sweeping through the waves?

Massicus first. He plows the sea in the bronze-sided *Tiger*.
Under him sail battalions, a thousand men who put astern
the walls of Clusium, Cosae too; their weapons, arrows,
shouldering lightweight quivers, bows bristling death.
Fierce Abas joins him, all his fighters shining in arms
with a brilliant gilded Apollo stationed at the stern.
Six hundred men his motherland Populonia gave him,
soldiers drilled for war, three hundred more from Ilva,
the Blacksmiths' inexhaustible island rife with iron ore.   210
Asilas third, the famous seer who bridges the worlds
of gods and men, a reader of animals' entrails,
stars that sweep the sky and the cries of birds
and the lightning charged with Fate. A thousand men
he rushes aboard, tight ranks spiked with spears.
Pisa placed them at his command, a Greek city
born by the river Alpheus, bred by Tuscan soil.
And following in his wake sails irresistible Astyr,
Astyr who trusts to his horse and armor rainbow-hued.
And swelling his ranks, three hundred, all as one   220
alert to obey his orders, men whose home is Caere,
men from Minio's fields, from ancient Pyrgi
and fever-racked Graviscae.
                              Nor could I pass you by,
Cunarus, staunchest in war of all Liguria's chiefs,
or you with your modest band of men, Cupavo.
Topping your crest the swan plumes toss,
a fabulous mark of your father's altered form,
and all for offending you, Love, you and Venus.
They tell how Cycnus, wrung by grief for his lover,
lifting a song to soothe his broken heart for Phaëthon—   230
shadowed by leafy poplars, Phaëthon's sisters once—
Cycnus donned the downy white plumage of old age,
left the earth behind and soared up to the stars

on wings of song. And now his son, Cupavo,
flanked by fighters his own age on deck,
drives along under oars the giant *Centaur*—
the monster high on the figurehead makes threats
to heave from aloft a massive boulder down on the waves
while the long keel cuts its furrow through the deep.

        Ocnus too, heading an army come from native coasts,   240
a son of Manto the seer and the Tuscan river Tiber.
He gave you, Mantua, walls and his mother's name,
Mantua, rich in the rosters of her forebears.
Not all of a single tribe but three in one,
four clans under each, and Mantua leads them all
and the city draws her force from Tuscan blood.
Mantua, source of the five hundred men Mezentius
goaded on to fight against himself: men the Mincius,
son of Father Benacus gowned in gray-green reeds,
steers down to the sea in warships built of pine.   250

        Aulestes bears down too, surging on with the beat
of a hundred oaken oars that thrash the swells,
churning the sea's clean surface into spume.
He sails the massive *Triton*, her sea-horn making
the blue deep quake, and as she runs on her prow displays
a shaggy man to the waist, all dragon to the tail and
under the monster's breast, part man, part beast,
the foaming swells resound.
                                So many chosen captains
heading thirty warships, speeding to rescue Troy,
cleft the fields of salt with beaks of bronze.
                                By now   260
the day had slipped from the sky and the gentle moon
was riding high through the heavens at mid-career,
her horses pounding through the night. As pressures
gave no rest to his limbs, Aeneas sat astern,
guiding the tiller, trimming sail, when suddenly,
look—a troop of his comrades comes to meet him,
halfway home, the nymphs that kindly Cybebe told

to rule the sea in power, changing the ships
to sea-nymphs swimming abreast, cutting the waves,
as many as all the bronze prows berthed at anchor once.   270
They know their king far off, circling, dancing round him
and one, most eloquent of them all, Cymodocea swims in
on his wake and grips his stern with her right hand,
arching her back above the swells as her left hand
rows the silent waves, and she calls out to Aeneas,
lost to it all: "Awake, Aeneas, son of the gods?
Wake up! Fling your sheets to the winds, sail free!
Here we are, the pines from the sacred ridge of Ida,
now we're nymphs of the sea—we are your fleet!
When traitorous Turnus forced us headlong on   280
with sword and torch, we burst your mooring lines,
we had no choice, and now we scour the seas
to find our captain. The Great Mother pitied us,
changed our shape, she made us goddesses, yes,
and so we pass our lives beneath the waves.
                                        "But not
your son, Ascanius, trapped now by the wall and trench,
in the thick of the spears, the Latins spiked for war.
Already Arcadian horsemen flanked by strong Etruscans
hold assigned positions. But Turnus is dead against
their joining up with the Trojan camp. He's setting   290
his own squadrons between their closing forces now.
Up with you! Call your men to arms with the dawn.
That first, then seize the indestructible shield
the God of Fire gave you, ringed with gold.
Daybreak, if you find my urgings on the mark,
will see vast heaps of Rutulians cut down in blood!"

She closed with a dive and drove the tall ship on
with her right hand—how well she knew the ropes!
and on it flies, faster than spear or wind-swift shaft
while the rest race on in her wake.   300
The Trojan son of Anchises, stunned with awe,
his spirits lift with the sign and scanning the skies
above his head Aeneas prays a few strong words:

"Ida's generous queen and Mother of the Gods,
by Dindyma dear to your heart, by towered cities,
the double team of lions yoked to your reins,
lead me in war, bring on the omen, goddess,
speed the Trojans home with your victor's stride!"

No more words. As the wheeling sun swung round
to the full light of day and put the dark to flight,   310
first he commands his troops to follow orders,
brace their hearts for battle, gear for war.
                                        Now Aeneas,
standing high astern, no sooner catches a glimpse
of his own Trojan camp than he quickly hoists
his burnished, brazen shield in his left hand.
The Trojans up on the ramparts shout to the skies—
fresh hope ignites their rage—and wing their spears
like cranes from the river Strymon calling out commands
as they swoop through the air below the black clouds,
flying before the Southwinds, cries raised in joy.   320
The Rutulian king and the Latin captains marvel
till, glancing back, they see an armada heading
toward the shore and the whole sea rolling down
on them now in a tide of ships. From the peak
of Aeneas' helmet flames are leaping forth
and a deadly blaze comes pouring from its crest.
The golden boss of his shield spews streams of fire,
strong as the lethal, blood-red light of comets streaming
on in a clear night, or bright as the Dog Star, Sirius,
bearing plague and thirst to afflicted mortals,   330
rises up to shroud the sky with gloom.
                                        But dauntless Turnus
never lost his faith in his daring, certain to seize
the beaches first and hurl the invader off the land:
"Now then, here is the answer to your prayers—
we'll break them all by force!
The god of battle is in your hands, my men.
Let each fighter think of his own wife, his home,
remember the great works, the triumphs of our fathers.

Down to the shore we go to take them on. They're dazed,
they've just debarked, they've got no land-legs yet!   340
Fortune speeds the bold!"
                              Urging them on but torn:
whom to lead to the shore assault? Whom to trust
to besiege the embattled walls?
                              And all the while
Aeneas lands his men by planks from the high sterns.
Many, who watch for the ebbing waves to slip away,
go vaulting into the shallows, others row for shore.
Tarchon, on the watch for a welcome stretch of beach
where the shoals don't churn, no breakers booming low
but a smooth unbroken groundswell glides toward the sand,
abruptly swerves his prow around and spurs his shipmates: 350
"Now, my chosen hands, you bend to your sturdy oars!
Lift up your prows, thrust them on, beaks plowing
this enemy coast, keels cutting their own furrows!
I don't flinch from a wreck in such a mooring
once I've seized the land!"
                              At Tarchon's command
his shipmates rise to their oars and drive their vessels
foaming onto the Latian shore until their beaks have
gripped dry land, all keels beached safe and sound,
all but your own ship, Tarchon. Aground on the shoals,
long impaled on a jagged reef it teeters back and forth,   360
tiring the waves—and suddenly breaks up, flinging
crews in the surf, ensnared in the shattered oars
and bobbing thwarts as the heavy backwash drags
their feet from shore.
                              But Turnus wastes no time,
he deploys his full force quickly against the Trojan force
to fight them at the beaches. Trumpets blare. Aeneas
is the first to attack the beleaguered farmers and—
sign of the battle's outcome—brings the Latins down,
killing mighty Theron who dared to attack Aeneas.
His sword pierces the bronze mesh of Theron's tunic,   370
stiff with its golden scales, and drains his gaping flank.
Lichas next—cut live from his dead mother's womb

and hallowed to you, the Healer—
but what good now to elude the knife at birth?
Next Aeneas, as rugged Cisseus, giant Gyas clubbed
their way through his ranks: he flung both down to death.
No help to them now, the weapons of Hercules, no,
nor their own strong arms or their father Melampus,
Hercules' mainstay, long as the earth afforded
the man his grueling labors.

                              Here's Pharus, watch,   380
hurling his hollow threats as Aeneas hurls his javelin,
stakes it square in the man's howling mouth. You too,
unlucky Cydon, pursuing Clytius, your new love,
his cheeks soft with the first gold down of youth—
you would have gone down under the Trojan's hand
and died a pitiful death,
with all recall of your young boy lovers lost,
if a pack of your brothers had not blocked Aeneas,
seven of Phorcus' offspring rifling seven spears,
some glancing off his shield and his helmet, harmless,   390
others, that loving Venus flicked away, just scratched his body.
Aeneas cries to Achates: "Give me a sheaf of weapons!
I won't miss a single Rutulian with my spear,
just as my spears impaled the Greeks at Troy!"

    With that he seizes a heavy lance and wings it hard
and straight through the bronze of Maeon's shield it pounds,
ripping open his breast and breastplate both at once.
His brother Alcanor runs to brace his falling brother,
quick, but the spear's already flown its bloody way,
stabbing his dying arm that hangs from his shoulder,   400
dangling loose by the tendons. Another, Numitor,
wrenching out the shaft from his brother's body,
went at Aeneas, praying to hit him, pay him back
but not a chance of that—he could only graze
the stalwart Achates in the thigh.

                             Now up steps
Clausus from Cures, flushed with his young strength
and flings his burly spear from a distance, hitting Dryops

under the chin full force to choke the Trojan's throat
as he shouted, cutting off both his voice and life
in the same breath, and his brow slams the ground   410
as he vomits clots of blood.
Three Thracians too, of the Northwind's lofty stock,
and three whom their father, Idas, and fatherland Ismarus
sent away to the wars, but Clausus kills them all
with a novel twist of death for each. Halaesus
rushes in with Auruncan troops and Messapus,
Neptune's son, as well, the brilliant horseman.
Trojans and Latins, struggling to rout each other,
seesawing back and forth as they fight it out
on Italy's very doorstep. Like clashing winds   420
in the vast heavens, bursting forth into battle,
matched in spirit, in power—no gust surrendering,
one to another, neither the winds nor clouds nor seas:
all hangs in the balance, the world gripped in a deadlock.
So they clash, the Trojan armies, armies of Latins,
foot dug in against foot, man packed against man.

                                          Another zone
where a torrent had hurled down boulders, heaving them
far and wide and torn out trees from its banks . . .
When Pallas saw his Arcadians, untrained to attack
on foot and turning tail before the Latins' pursuit—   430
the lay of the rock-choked land convinced them all
to desert their horses—so, seizing on one last way
to stem disaster, now with prayers, now stinging taunts,
he fires up their war-lust: "Where are you flying, friends?
I beg you now by your self-respect, your own brave work,
by your chief Evander's name, your victories won,
by my own rising hopes to match my father's fame,
don't trust to your feet—hack the foe with swords,
that's the way! Over there, where the massed infantry
pushes forward, that's where your famous land   440
demands you back with Pallas in the lead.
No gods force us on—
we're mortals, harried by mortal enemies.
They have as many hands and lives as we. Look,

the ocean shuts us in with immense blockades of waves,
no land to fly to! What, shall we head for the sea—
or Troy?"

        Fighting words, and he hurls himself
at the enemy's massed ranks.

                    First to confront him?
Lagus, lured on by a harsh fate. As he tries to lift
an enormous rock, Pallas rifles a spear that strikes his spine   450
midway where it parts the ribs, and wrenches back the shaft
that's wedged in the bone as Hisbo pounces down on him,
filled with the hope to take his man off guard.
But Pallas takes him first—Hisbo rushing in fury,
off *his* guard, berserk with his comrade's death
as Pallas welcomes him in with the naked sword
he plunges into his lungs puffed up with rage.
Next he goes for Sthenius, then Anchemolus
sprung from Rhoeteus' age-old line, a man
who dared befoul his own stepmother's bed.   460

    You too, you twins, went down on Latian fields,
Thymber, Larides, Daucus' sons: identical twins,
an endearing puzzlement to your parents till
Pallas made a strict distinction between you.
Thymber—he lops off your head with one sweep
of Evander's sword and, Larides, chops your hand
and the fighter's dying hand gropes for its body,
quivering fingers claw for the sword once more.
Enflamed by his taunts and watching his brilliant work,
the Arcadians, armed with grief and shame, stand braced   470
to meet the enemy.

                Suddenly Pallas runs Rhoeteus through
as he races past in his two-horse chariot. That much
respite and breathing room had Ilus won—at Ilus
Pallas had flung a rugged spear at long range,
but Rhoeteus pausing between them
takes the point head-on as he flees from you,
distinguished Teuthras, you and your brother Tyres—
Rhoeteus spilling out of his car in death-throes,

drumming the fields of Italy with his heels. So
as in summer, just when the winds he prayed for rise   480
and a shepherd kindles fires scattered through the forest,
suddenly all in the midst ignite into one long jagged
battle line of fire rampaging through the fields and high
on his perch he gazes down in triumph, seeing the blaze
exulting on—just as your comrades' courage speeds
to your rescue, all at a single point, Pallas,
and joy fills your heart.
                                        But Halaesus hot for combat
charges against them now, compressing all his force
behind his weapons. Ladon he butchers, Pheres, Demodocus—
a flash of his sword and he slices off Strymonius' hand   490
just as it clutched his throat. He smashes Thoas full
in the face with a rock and crushes out his skull
in a spray of brains and blood. Halaesus' father,
foreseeing his son's doom, hid him deep in the woods,
but when the old man's eyes went glazing blind in death,
the Fates, taking the son in hand, devoted him here
to Evander's lance. Pallas attacks him, praying first:
"Now, Father Tiber, grant the spear I'm about to hurl
a lucky path through rugged Halaesus' chest—
I'll strip him of weapons, hang them on your oak!"   500
The Tiber heard his prayer. As Halaesus guarded Imaon,
the hapless fighter left his chest defenseless,
bared to the Arcadian lance.
                                        But Lausus, who plays
a front-line role in war, won't let his soldiers flinch
at Pallas' carnage. First he finishes Abas, quick
to face him there: that burly knot, that bulwark of battle.
Arcadia's prime he hacks down, hacks down the Tuscans
and you whose bodies went unscarred by the Greeks,
you Trojans too. And the lines of fighters clash,
matched in chiefs, in power, the rearguard packs tight,   510
no room for maneuver, no spear hurled in the press.
Here Pallas drives and lunges, Lausus opposes him,
all but equal in age, remarkably handsome, both,
but Fortune grudged them both safe passage home.

Yet Jove would not allow those fighters to clash;
he saved each man for his own fate, soon now, under
a stronger foe.
                      Now his loving sister, Juturna,
spurs her brother Turnus quickly to Lausus' side.
Turnus races his chariot straight through the ranks
and shouts as he sees his comrades: "Now's the time   520
to halt your fighting! *I* will go after Pallas,
Pallas is mine now, my prize alone. If only
his father were here to watch it all in person!"

    At that, his comrades cleared off from the field
and as they withdrew, young Pallas, struck dumb
by that arrogant command, runs his eyes over Turnus'
enormous frame, scanning every feature from where he stood
and glancing grimly, Pallas volleys back these words
to counter the words his high and mighty enemy used:
"Now's my time to win some glory, either for stripping   530
off a wealth of spoils or dying a noble death—
my father can stand up under either fate.
Enough of your threats!"
                            Enough said.
Pallas marches out to the center of the field
and the blood runs cold in each Arcadian heart.
Down from his chariot Turnus vaulted, nerved
to attack the enemy face-to-face on foot.
Like some lion that spots from his high lookout,
far off on the plain and flexing for combat there,
an immense bull, and the lion plunges toward his kill—   540
and that is the image of Turnus coming on for battle.
When Pallas judged him just in range of his spear
he moved up first—if only Fortune would speed
his daring, pitting himself against unequal odds,
and he cries out to the arching heavens: "Hercules,
by my father's board, the welcome you met as a stranger,
I beg you, stand by the great task I'm tackling now.
May Turnus see me stripping the bloody armor off his body,
bear the sight of his conqueror—eyes dulled in death!"

Hercules heard the young man's prayer, suppressed a groan   550
that rose up from his heart, and wept helpless tears
as the Father said these tender words to his son:
"Each man has his day, and the time of life
is brief for all, and never comes again.
But to lengthen out one's fame with action,
that's the work of courage. How many sons of gods
went down under Troy's high wall! Why, I lost
a son of my own with all the rest—Sarpedon.
For Turnus too, his own fate calls, and the man
has reached the end of all his days on earth."   560

So Jove declares, and turns his glance away
from the Latian fields below . . .

Where Pallas rifles his spear full force
and sweeps his flashing sword from its casing sheath.
The spear goes flying on and it hits the armor high up
where the bronze rims the shoulder's ridge, and glancing off,
it rams its way through the shield's plies and finally
scrapes the skin of Turnus' massive body. But Turnus,
balancing long his oakwood spear with its iron tip,
flings it at Pallas with winging words: "Now we'll see   570
if *my* spear pierces deeper!" And Pallas' shield, for all
its layers of iron and bronze, its countless layers of oxhide
rounding it out for strength—still Turnus' vibrant spear
goes shattering through the shield with stabbing impact,
piercing the breastplate's guard and Pallas' broad chest.
Pallas wrenches the spearhead warm from his wound—no use—
his blood and his life breath follow hard on the same track out.
Collapsing onto his wound, his armor clanging over him,
Pallas dies, pounding enemy earth with his bloody mouth
as Turnus trumpets over him: "You Arcadians, listen!   580
Take a message home to Evander, tell him this:
The Pallas I send him back will serve him right!
Whatever tribute a tomb can give, whatever
balm a burial, I am only too glad to give.
But the welcome he gave Aeneas costs him dear."

  With that, he stamped his left foot on the corpse
and stripped away the sword-belt's massive weight
engraved with its monstrous crime: how one night,
their wedding night, that troop of grooms was butchered,
fouling their wedding chambers with pools of blood—   590
all carved by Clonus, Eurytus' son, in priceless gold.
Now Turnus glories in that spoil, exults to make it his.
How blind men's minds to their fate and what the future holds,
how blind to limits when fortune lifts men high. Yes,
the time will come when Turnus would give his all
to have Pallas whole, intact,
when all this spoil, this very day he'll loathe.
But a huge throng of friends is attending Pallas,
moaning, weeping, and bears him back upon his shield.
Oh you return to your father, his great grief and glory!   600
This day first gave you to war and this day takes you off
and still you leave behind great heaps of Latian dead.

  Such a heavy blow. Now a trusted herald,
no empty rumor, wings the news to Aeneas:
His men stand on the razor edge of death—
now is the time to rescue his routed Trojans.
The closest enemy ranks he mows down with iron,
reaping a good wide swath through the Latian front,
blazing with rage as his sword-blade hacks that path,
hunting for you, Turnus, so proud of your latest kill.   610
As Pallas, Evander, all of them rise before Aeneas' eyes,
the welcoming board that met him that first day,
the right hands clasped in trust—
                              And four sons of Sulmo,
fighters all, and the same number reared by Ufens:
Aeneas takes them alive to offer Pallas' shade
and soak his flaming pyre with captive blood.
And next he wings from afar a deadly spear at Magus
ducking under it, quick, as the quivering shaft flies past
and Magus, hugging Aeneas' knees, implores: "I beg you now
by your father's ghost, by your hopes for rising Iulus,   620
spare this life of mine for my father and my son!

Ours is a stately mansion, deep inside lie buried
bars of ridged silver and heavy weights of gold,
some of it tooled, some untooled—mine alone!
Now how can a Trojan victory hinge on me?
How can a single life make such a difference?"

    Magus begged no more as Aeneas lashed back:
"All those bars of silver and gold you brag of,
save them for your sons! Such bargaining in battle,
Turnus already cut it short when he cut Pallas down!   630
So the ghost of my father, so my son declares."
And seizing Magus' helmet tight in his left hand
and wrenching back his neck as the man prays on,
he digs his sword-blade deep down to the hilt.
                          Hard by,
the son of Haemon and priest of Phoebus and Diana,
his temples wreathed in the consecrated bands,
all white in his robes, brilliant in his array—
Aeneas confronts him, coursing him down the field
and rearing over him as he stumbles, slaughters him,
shrouding his brilliant robes with a mighty shade.   640
Serestus gathers the armor, shoulders it home
to you, King Mars, your trophy now.
                           Now Caeculus,
Vulcan's stock, and Umbro fresh from the Marsian highlands
rally their troops as Aeneas rages on against them.
His slashing sword had already hacked off Anxur's
left arm and his round buckler slammed the ground.
He'd shouted some great boast, trusting his strength
would match his words, probably lifting his spirits
sky-high and promising gray hairs for himself
and a ripe old age—
                    as Aeneas faced down Tarquitus   650
gloating in burnished gear and born to Faunus,
god of the woods, by the wood-nymph Dryope.
Tarquitus blocked his path as Aeneas blazed on
and cocking back his spear he flings it and stakes
the breastplate fast to the shield's groaning weight.

Then as Tarquitus begs him, struggling to keep on begging,
all for nothing, Aeneas dashes his head to the ground
and rolling the man's warm trunk along and looming
over him vaunts with all the hatred in his heart:
"Now lie there, you great horrific sight!   660
No loving mother will bury you in the ground
or weight your body down with your fathers' tomb.
You'll be abandoned now to carrion birds or plunged
in the deep sea and swept away by the waves and
ravening fish will dart and lick your wounds!"

      Plunging on he goes, overtaking their finest,
Turnus' front-line troops: Antaeus, Lucas
and stalwart Numa and Camers with tawny locks,
magnanimous Volcens' son, the richest landholder
in all Italy once, the lord of Amyclae, quiet town.   670
Aeneas like Aegaeon who, they say, had a hundred arms
and a hundred hands, and flames blazed from his fifty maws
and chests when he fought down Jupiter's bolts of lightning,
clashing as many matching shields, unsheathing as many swords—
so Aeneas now, rampaging in triumph all across the plain,
once his sword had warmed to the slaughter. Look there,
he heads for Niphaeus' car and his four horses raising
their chests against him, but as they see him ramping
on in his loping strides and hear him groan in fury,
round they wheel in terror, rearing backward, spilling   680
their driver out the chariot, whirling it down to shore.

      While into the melee hurry Lucagus and his brother Liger,
chariot-borne by two white steeds, the brother reinsman
guiding the team as Lucagus flaunts his naked steel.
But Aeneas could not suffer their fiery charge—
he charged *them*, looming, huge, his spear poised
as Liger shouted out: "What you see here are not
Diomedes' team, Achilles' car, or the plains of Troy—
now on our own land you see the end of your wars,
of your own life too!"
                        Such maddened words   690

he hurls but no words come from Aeneas now—
he hurls his spear in reply against his foe and
then as Lucagus, bending into the stroke, slaps
the team with his flat sword, his left foot thrust out,
braced for attack, Aeneas' weapon pierces the bottom plies
of his gleaming buckler, ripping into his left groin.
Flung from the car he writhes on the field in death
as righteous Aeneas sends some bitter words his way:
"Lucagus, no panicked pair has let your chariot down,
no horses shying away from an enemy's empty shade—   700
it's you, tumbling off your chariot, you desert your team!"
He seized the yoke as the luckless brother, slipping
off the war-car, flinging his helpless arms toward
Aeneas, prayed: "I beg you, beg by the ones who bore
a son like you, great man of Troy, now spare my life,
pity my prayers!" Praying on as Aeneas broke in:
"A far cry from the words you mouthed before—
die! No brother deserts a brother here!" Then
with his blade he carved wide open Liger's chest,
his hidden cache of life.
       So much slaughter   710
the Trojan commander spreads throughout the plain
like a stream in spate or black tornado storming on
till at last the young Ascanius and his troops break free
and put the camp behind. The great blockade is over.

At the same moment Jove adeptly spurs on Juno:
"My own sister, my sweet wife as well, it's Venus,
just as you thought, your judgment never fails.
She is the one who supports the Trojan forces,
not their own strong hands that clutch for combat,
not their unflinching spirits seasoned hard to peril."   720

And Juno replies, her head bent low: "My dearest husband,
why rake my anxious heart? I dread your grim commands.
Your love for me, if it held the force it once held
and should hold still, you'd never deny me this,
All-powerful One: the power to spirit Turnus

clear of battle, save him all unscathed
for his father, Daunus. But now, as it is,
let him die and pay his debt to the Trojans,
pay with his own loyal blood. Still, Turnus
takes his birth from our own breed, his name too—   730
Pilumnus was his forebear, four generations back—
and his lavish hand has heaped your threshold high
with treasure troves of gifts!"

The king of lofty Olympus countered briefly:
"If what you want is reprieve from instant death,
some breathing space for the doomed young man,
and you acknowledge the limits I lay down,
then whisk your Turnus away,
pluck him out of the closing grip of Fate.
That much room for indulgence I will give you.   740
But if some deeper longing for mercy stirs beneath
your prayers, some notion the whole thrust of the war
can shift and change, you're feeding empty hopes."

Juno replies in tears: "What if your heart should grant
what you begrudge in words, and the life of Turnus
were firmly set for years to come? For now,
a crushing end awaits an innocent man,
unless I'm lost to the truth and swept away.
Oh, if only my fears were false and I deceived!
If only you—you have the power—would bend   750
your will to a better goal!"
                                    With that appeal,
headlong down from the heights of heaven she dove,
girt up in clouds, unfurling a whirlwind through the air
and winging straight at the Trojan ranks and Latian camp.
Then, out of thin mist the goddess creates a phantom:
Aeneas' double, but a strange, unearthly sight,
a shadow stripped of power,
and decking it out in Trojan armor, matching
the shield and crest on Aeneas' godlike head,
she fills it with hollow words, gives it a voice,   760

sound without sense, and it apes his marching stride.
Like ghosts that after our death, they say, will flutter on
or dreams that deceive our senses lost in sleep . . .
But the buoyant shade parades before the front,
shaking a spear in his enemy's face and taunting—
Turnus attacks it, rifling a vibrant lance, a long cast
but the phantom swerves away and Turnus in turmoil,
thinking *Aeneas* had really turned tail and fled,
and drinking deep of the vapid cup of hope,
cries out: "Where are you racing, Aeneas?   770
Don't abandon your sworn bride! My right hand
will give you the earth you crossed the seas to find."

       He shouts in hot pursuit, flashing his naked sword,
blind to the winds that scatter all his triumph.

       A ship chanced to be moored to a spur of cliff,
her ladders and gangways set for action. King Osinius
sailed her here, straight from the shores of Clusium.
Here Aeneas' frightened shadow throws itself into hiding,
Turnus hard on its heels, nothing can keep him back,
bounding over the gangways, leaping the high decks.   780
He had barely touched the prow when Juno bursts the cables,
rips the ship from her moorings, blows her out to sea
on the tide ebbing fast. And now the misty phantom,
no longer hunting for cover, flutters up on high,
dissolving into a dark cloud. And all the while
Aeneas calls on Turnus to fight but the man is gone,
so the many men who block his way he sends to death
as Juno's winds are spinning Turnus around in mid-sea
and glancing backward, knowing nothing, no thanks for escape,
he lifts his hands in prayer, his voice to the stars: 790
"Almighty Father, so, you find my guilt so great?
You're dead set on my paying such a price?
Where have I come from? Where am I racing now?
What is this flight that takes me home?—a coward!—
Will I ever see my Laurentine walls and camp again?
What of those gallant men who backed my sword and me?
All of them—what disgrace—I deserted them all to die

an unspeakable death. Now I see them straggling, lost,
I hear them groaning as they go under. What shall I do?
If only the earth gaped deep enough to take me down.   800
Better, pity me, winds! Turnus begs you with all his heart,
dash this ship on a reef or cliff or run her aground
on the Syrtes' savage shoals where no Rutulian,
no rumor that knows my shame can dog my heels!"

    Praying, his mind at sea, wavering here, there,
crazed by his own disgrace—should he fling himself
on his sword and thrust the ruthless blade through his ribs?
Or plunge in the heavy swells and swim back to the bay
and pitch himself at the Trojan spears once more?
Three times he probed each way, three times Juno   810
with all her power held the prince's fury down,
pitying him in her heart, and kept him hard on course,
cutting the deep as favoring tide and current sweep him
home to his father Daunus' ancient city.
                                            But now
Mezentius' turn. That moment at Jove's command
he carries on the fight, attacks the victorious Trojans,
true, but his own Etruscan troops with all their hate
and showering weapons rush to attack *him* quite alone,
their one and only target. He, like a headland jutting
into the ocean wastes and bared to the winds' rage,   820
braving the breakers, weathering out all force
and fury of sea and sky, stands firm himself.
He hacks to ground Dolichaon's son, Hebrus,
Latagus with him and Palmus who spins and runs—
he smashes Latagus square in the face and mouth
with a rock, a crag of a rock, and cuts the knees
from under the racing Palmus, leaves him slowly
writhing in pain and gives his armor to Lausus,
bronze for his shoulders, plumes to crown his crest.

    The next to die? Euanthes the Phrygian, Mimas too,   830
a comrade of Paris just his age. On the same night
Theano brought into light the son of Amycus,

Hecuba, great with the torch, bore Paris.
Paris lies dead in the city of his fathers,
Mimas lies unsung on the Latian shores.
                                        Mezentius . . .
Picture the wild boar that's harried down from a ridge
by snapping packs of hounds, some beast Mount Vesulus
shielded for long or long the Latian forests fed
on the reeds that crowd their marshes:
once stampeded into the nets he jolts to a halt,   840
snorts, at bay, the hackles rising up on his neck,
no hunter bold enough to approach him, take him on,
at a safe remove they attack with spears and shouts.
But the boar stands fast, unflinching—where to charge?—
anywhere—grinding his tusks and shaking spears from his back.
So Mezentius now, for all his attackers' rightful fury,
none of them has the spine to fight him, swords drawn,
they just bait him with missiles, far-flung cries,
all at a safe remove.
                        Now Acron, a Greek,
had just arrived from Corythus' old frontier,   850
an exile, leaving his marriage in the lurch.
As Mezentius spied him routing the lines far off,
crested in purple plumes, the blue of his bride-to-be—
like a famished lion stalking the cattle pens for prey,
for the hunger will often drive him mad, just let him spot
some goat on the run or a stag's antlers branching high:
his big jaws gape at the sport, his mane bristles, then
a pouncing assault! and he clenches his quarry's flesh
as the sopping gore soaks his ruthless maw—just so
Mezentius pounces hotly onto the enemy masses.   860
He lays unlucky Acron low, his heels pounding
the dark earth as he gasps his life away and dyes
the weapon splintered off in his body blood-red.

Orodes darts away but Mezentius would not stoop
to killing him on the run with a spearcast from behind,
stabbing him, unseen, no, he dueled him man to man,
proving himself the better man by force of arms,

not stealth, and next, stamping his foot on the corpse
and leaning hard on the spear, Mezentius shouts out:
"Here, men, lies no mean part of their battle strength,   870
Orodes, once so tall!" And his comrades shout back,
redoubling the victor's cry as Orodes pants his last:
"You don't have long to crow, whoever you are, my victor!
Vengeance waits, the same fate watches over you too,
you'll lie here in the same field—very soon."
"Die now!" Mezentius cries,
grinning through his rage: "As for my own death,
the Father of Gods and King of Men will see to that."
Mezentius, vaunting, pries the spear from Orodes' body.
Grim repose and an iron sleep press down his eyes   880
and seal their light in a night that never ends.

    Caedicus chops Alcathous down—Sacrator, Hydaspes—
Rapo kills Parthenius, then the indestructible Orses.
Messapus levels Clonius, then Lycaon's son, Erichaetes,
one thrown from a reinless horse and sprawled aground,
the other fighting on foot. On foot a Lycian too,
one Agis strode up now but Valerus, no poor heir
to his fathers' battle prowess, hurled him down
as Thronius fell to Salius, Salius to Nealces,
crack marksman with spears and arrows both,   890
blindsiding in front afar.
                          Ruthless Mars
was drawing the battle out, dead even now,
equaling out the grief, the mutual slaughter.
Victors and victims killing, killed in turn:
both sides locked, not a thought of flight, not here.
The gods in the halls of Jove are filled with pity,
feeling the futile rage of both great armies,
mourning the labors borne by mortal men . . .
Here Venus, over against her, Juno gazing down,
as Tisiphone seethes amid the milling thousands,   900
that livid, lethal Fury.
                       But here Mezentius comes,
brandishing high his massive spear and storming on

like a whirlwind down the plain, and enormous as Orion
marching in mid-sea, plowing a path through the deep swells,
his shoulders rearing over the waves, or hauling down
from a ridge the trunk of an age-old mountain ash,
as he treads the ground he hides his head in clouds—
so vast, Mezentius marching on in gigantic armor.
Aeneas, spotting him out in the long front ranks,
comes up to cross his path. But he holds firm,   910
unafraid, awaiting his great-hearted foe,
stands firm in all his mass. His eyes narrow,
gauging the length his spear will need, he cries:
"Let this right arm—my only god—and the spear I hurl
be with me now! I dedicate you, Lausus, decked
in the spoils I strip from that pirate's corpse—
my son, my living trophy over Aeneas!"
                         Enough.
He hurled his spear and whizzing in from a distance,
winging on, it ricocheted off Aeneas' shield to hit
that hardy fighter Antores, yards away, between   920
the flank and groin: Antores sent from Argos,
Hercules' aide who bound himself to Evander,
settling down in the king's Italian city.
Laid low by a wound aimed for another,
luckless man, he looks up at the heavens,
longing for his dear Argos as he dies.
                     Next
the grave Aeneas flings a spear at Mezentius—
right through the buckler's three round plates of bronze,
through the linen plies and bull's-hide triply stitched
the spear pierced, plunging deep in the man's groin   930
but its force stopped short of home. In a flash Aeneas,
overjoyed now at the sight of the Tuscan's blood,
sweeps his sword from its sheath and closes fast
on his staggered foe. But Lausus, seeing it all,
groaned low with the love he bore his father,
tears poured down his face and now, Lausus,
your fated, brutal death and your brave deeds—
if glorious work long ages old can win belief—

neither your record nor yourself will I ever fail
to sing, young soldier, you deserve our praise.
                                    Now   940
his father was backing off, defenseless, weighed down,
dragging his enemy's spearshaft trailing from his shield,
so the son sprang forward, darting into the moil and
just as Aeneas rose up, his arm reared for attack,
Lausus, ducking under the stroke, parried the sword,
holding the Trojan off while shouting comrades
harried Aeneas with missiles pelting in from afar
till under his son's shield the father could escape.
Aeneas keeps down, huddling under his own shield, enraged . . .
Think of a cloudburst bearing down with gusts of hail   950
and every plowman, every farmhand quits the fields
and the traveler keeps safe in a welcome refuge
under some river's banks or cavern's rocky arch
while rain pelts the earth, so when the sun returns
they can all get on with the day's work. So Aeneas,
overpowered by missiles left and right, braves out
the cloudburst of war till its thunder dies away
and then he taunts Lausus, threatens Lausus:
"Why hurry your death? Daring beyond your powers!
Your love for your father lures you into folly."   960

    But Lausus rages on, berserk as the savage fury
surges higher now in the Trojan captain's heart.
The Fates bind up the last threads of Lausus' life
as Aeneas drives his tempered sword through the youth,
plunging it home hilt-deep. The point impaled his shield,
a flimsy defense for the youngster's brash threats,
and the shirt his mother wove him of soft gold mesh
and his lap filled up with blood, and then his life
slipped through the air, sorrowing down to the shades
and left his corpse behind.
                        Ah but then,   970
when the son of Anchises saw his dying look,
his face—that face so ashen, awesome in death—
he groaned from his depths in pity, reached out his hand

as this picture of love for a father pierced his heart,
and said: "Forlorn young soldier, what can Aeneas,
in all honor, give you to match your glory now?
What gifts are worthy of such a noble spirit?
Keep your armor that gave you so much joy.
I give you back to your fathers' ash and shades
if it offers any solace. And this, at least,   980
may comfort you for a death so cruel, unlucky boy:
you went down under the hand of great Aeneas."

    With that, he rounded hard on Lausus' comrades,
slow to move, and lifted their captain's body
off the ground where Lausus was defiling
his braided hair with blood.
                            But Lausus' father
was just stanching his wounds in the Tiber's waters,
leaning his body against a tree trunk, resting now.
Nearby, his brazen helmet swings from a branch
and his heavy armor lies on the grass, in peace.   990
Picked young soldiers stand in a ring around him.
His combed, flowing beard spreading across his chest,
he tries to limber his neck, panting, heaving in torment.
Time and again he asks for news of Lausus, again
he dispatches runners to recall him, bearing
a stricken father's orders. Yes, but Lausus—
weeping comrades are bearing his lifeless body
home on his shield, a great soldier taken down
by a great wound. But his father hears their wails
far off and stirred by a grim foreboding, knows it all.   1000
Soiling his gray hair with dust, flinging both hands
to the skies, he clings to his son's body, crying:
"Was I so seized by the lust for life, my son,
I let you take my place before the enemy's sword?
My own flesh and blood! What, your father saved
by your own wounds? Kept alive by your death?
Oh, now at last I know the griefs of exile—
I, in all my pain—at last a wound strikes home . . .
I've stained your name, my son, with my own crimes,

detested, drummed from my fathers' scepter and their throne!   1010
I owed a price to my land and people who despise me.
If only I'd paid in full with my own guilty life,
by any death on earth! But I live on, not yet
have I left the land of men and light of day
but I will leave it all!"
                              In the same breath
he struggles to stand erect on his damaged thigh
and though his strength is sapped by his deep wound,
his spirit is unbroken. He calls for his horse,
his pride, his mainstay, always the mount he rode
triumphant from every battle. Seeing it grieving,   1020
he begins: "Long have we lived together, Rhaebus,
if anything in this mortal world lives long. Today,
either you'll carry back those bloody arms we strip
in triumph, parade Aeneas' head and avenge together
Lausus' pains. Or if no force can clear our path,
you will go down with me.
For I can't believe, my brave one, you could bend
to a stranger's orders, bear a Trojan master."

Mezentius mounted up, his weight settling
onto the horse's back in the old familiar way,   1030
both hands holding the heft of well-honed spears,
his helmet aflash with bronze and bristling horsehair crest,
and into the surge of battle so he plunged, churning
with mighty shame, with grief and madness all aswirl
in that one fighting heart. Three times he shouted
out to Aeneas, a great resounding shout, and Aeneas
knew that voice and his prayer rose up in joy:
"So grant it, Father of Gods and high Apollo,
bring the battle on!"
                      That challenge made,
he closes on his enemy, spear poised for the kill   1040
as Mezentius answers back: "Why, you king of cruelty,
now that you've killed my son, why try to make me cringe?
That was the only way you could destroy me. I never
flinch at death or bow to a single god. No more words.

I'm here to die, but I bring you these gifts first!"
And with that he flung a javelin at his enemy,
planting one shaft after another, racing round
in a sweeping ring but the golden boss of Aeneas' shield
stands fast. Three times Mezentius rides around him,
hurling his weapons, keeping the Trojan on his left;   1050
three times Aeneas wheels round with him, bearing
a grisly thicket of lances bristling on his shield.
Then, tired of all delays, of ripping out the shafts—
outmatched, on the defensive—Aeneas now at last,
at his wit's end, bursts forth and hurls his spear
and it splits the temples of Mezentius' warhorse.
Back it rears, flailing the air with flying hoofs
and throwing its rider, pitching headlong down
in a tangled mass, it's shoulder-joint torn out,
it crushes Mezentius' body to the ground.   1060
Trojan and Latin war cries set the sky on fire as
Aeneas dashes up and wrenching his sword from its sheath,
he triumphs over him: "Where's the fierce Mezentius now?
Where's his murderous fury?"
                              And the Tuscan fighter,
gazing up at the sky and drinking in the air as he
returned to his senses, said: "My mortal enemy,
why do you ridicule me, threaten me with death?
Killing is no crime. I never engaged in combat
on such terms. No such pact did Lausus seal
between you and me that you would spare my life.   1070
One thing is all I ask, if the vanquished
may ask a favor of the victor: let my body
be covered by the earth. Too well I know
how my people's savage hatred swirls around me.
Shield me, I implore you, from their fury!
Let me rest in the grave beside my son,
in the comradeship of death."
                              With those words,
fully aware, he offers up his throat to the sword
and across his armor pours his life in waves of blood.

BOOK ELEVEN

Camilla's Finest Hour

Now as Dawn rose up and left her Ocean bed,
Aeneas, moved as he is by grief to pause and
bury comrades, desolate with their deaths, still
the victor pays his vows to the gods as first light breaks.
An enormous oak, its branches lopped and trunk laid bare,
he stakes on a mound and decks with the burnished arms
he stripped from Mezentius, that strong captain:
a trophy to you, Mars, the great god of war.
Aeneas fixes the crests still dripping blood,
the enemy's splintered spears and breastplate   10
battered hard and pierced in a dozen places.
Fast to the left hand he straps the brazen shield
and down from the neck he hangs the ivory-hilted sword.
Then he turns to his comrades, bands of officers
pressing round him there, and Aeneas starts in
to stir their spirits flushed with recent triumph:

"What magnificent things we've done, my friends!
Dismiss all fears for what's still left to do.
These are the spoils stripped from a proud king,
our first fruits of battle, this is Mezentius,   20
the work of my right hand!
Now on we go to the Latian king, his city walls.
Sharpen your swords with heart and pin your hopes on war!
No taking us off guard, no hanging back, no dread
must cripple our steps with anxious second thoughts
when the gods allow us to pull our standards up,
strike camp, and move the army out. But now
commit our friends' unburied bodies to the earth,
their only tribute down in the depths of hell. Go!"
he cries, "deck with funeral gifts those heroes' souls.   30
They won this land for us with their own blood.
But first send Pallas home to Evander's grieving city,
a soldier who never lost heart when the black day
swept him off and drowned him in bitter death."

                                                      So

Aeneas says, in tears, turning back to his gates
where Pallas' lifeless body lay outspread,
guarded by old Acoetes. He bore Evander's arms
in Arcadia once, but the omens were less bright
when he marched out with Pallas, beloved foster-son.
Around them flocked a retinue, crowds of Trojans and   40
Trojan women, their hair unbound in the mourners' way.
But then, as soon as Aeneas entered the high-built gates,
they beat their breasts and raised their cries to the sky
and the royal lodging groaned with wails of grief.
Aeneas, gazing at Pallas resting there, his head,
his face bled white, and his smooth chest splayed
apart by a Latin spear, the tears came welling up
with words of sorrow: "Child of heartbreak, was it you
whom Fortune denied me, coming to me all smiles?
Now you will never live to see our kingdom born,   50
never ride in triumph home to your father's house.
A far cry from the pledge I made Evander for his son!
Embracing me as I left that day, he sent me out

to win ourselves an empire—fearful, warning that
we would face brave men, a battle-hardened people.
So even now, gripped by his own empty hopes,
he may be paying his vows,
perhaps, and loading the altars down with gifts
while we, with shows of grief and hollow tributes,
bring him a lifeless son who owes no more, now,   60
to any god on high.
                    "Unlucky man, you must
behold the agonizing burial of your son . . .
Is this how we return? Our longed-for triumph?
Is this my binding pledge? Ah, but Evander, you
will never see him retreat, hit by a shameful wound,
never pray for a father's wretched death, disgraced
by a son who still lives safely on. Oh, Italy,
oh, what a rugged bastion you have lost,
how great your loss, my Iulus!"
                    Mourning done,
he commands his troops to lift the stricken body high   70
and sends a thousand men, picked from the whole corps
to escort the rites and join in the father's tears.
A small comfort offered a grief so great but owed
to a father's heartache. Others lost no time,
braiding with wickerwork a soft, pliant bier,
weaving shoots of arbutus, sprigs of oak,
shrouding the piled couch with shady leaves.
Here on his raised rustic bed they place the boy
and there he lies like a flower cut by a young girl's hand,
some tender violet bloom or drooping hyacinth spray,   80
its glow and its lovely glory still not gone,
though Mother Earth no longer nurses it now
or gives it life. Then Aeneas carried out
twin robes, stiff with purple and gold braid,
that Dido of Sidon made with her own hands once,
just for Aeneas, loving every stitch of the work
and weaving into the weft a glinting mesh of gold.
Heartsick, he cloaks the boy with one as a final tribute,

covering locks that soon will face the fire.

                        Then,
heaping a mass of plunder seized in the Latin rout,   90
Aeneas orders it borne home in a long cortege,
adding the steeds and arms he stripped from foes.
Behind their backs he strapped their hands, the captives
he planned to send below as gifts to appease the shades,
sprinkling Latin blood on the pyre that burned their corpses.
He orders his own captains to carry tree-trunks clad
in enemy arms, with the hated names engraved.
Unlucky old Acoetes, weighed down with the years,
they help along as he beats his chest with fists,
claws his cheeks with his nails and stumbling on,   100
flings his full length to the ground. Chariots too
are rolled along, splashed to the rails with Latin blood.
And here comes Pallas' warhorse, Blaze, regalia set aside,
weeping, ambling on, big tears rivering down his face.
And others bear the spear and helmet of Pallas.
Turnus, the victor, commandeered the rest.

                            There follows
an army of mourners, Trojans all, and all the Tuscans,
all the Arcadians march with arms reversed.
After the long cortege of Pallas' friends
had moved on well ahead, Aeneas drew to a halt,   110
groaned from his depths and spoke these last words:
"The same dark fate of battle commands me back
to other tears. Hail forever, our great Pallas!
Hail forever and farewell!"

                        Aeneas said no more.
Back he strode to his ramparts, back to camp.

    Now in came envoys sent from the Latin city,
bearing olive branches and pleading for a truce . . .
"Those bodies felled by the sword and strewn about the field:
return them, let them lie with mounds of earth for cover.
There is no fighting defeated men, robbed of the light.   120
Spare them now. You called them your hosts, once,

and the fathers of your brides!"

    Good Aeneas grants the appeal he'd never shun.
He treats them kindly and adds these gracious words:
"What unmerited stroke of fortune, men of Latium,
traps you so in war that you flee from us, your friends?
Peace for the dead, cut down by the lots of battle,
that's your plea? I'd grant that to the living too.
I'd never have come if Fate had not ordained me here
a house and home. Nor do I make war with your people.   130
It's your king, who renounced our pact of friendship,
choosing to trust to Turnus' force of arms. Why,
it would have been fairer for Turnus to meet this death!
If the soldier means to finish off our war by force,
to rout the Trojans now, he should have clashed
with me and my weapon then, in combat man to man.
One of us would have lived, the one whom Mars—
or his own right arm—had granted life. Go now.
Ignite the pyre beneath your luckless dead."

    Aeneas closed. They all stood silent, trading   140
startled glances fixed on each other, hushed.

    Then aged Drances—always quick to attack
the young captain, Turnus—full of hatred
and accusations, breaks forth to have his say:
"Man of Troy, great in fame, greater in battle,
how can I sing your praises to the skies?
What to commend first? Your sense of justice,
your awesome works of war? Surely we'll carry back
to our walls these words of yours with grateful hearts,
and if Fortune points the way, ally you with our king,   150
Latinus. Turnus can find his allies for himself.
We'll even be glad to raise your mighty walls
ordained by Fate, glad to shoulder up
the foundation stones of Troy!"
                All as one,

his comrades murmured Yes to Drances' offer.
Now for a dozen days they made their truce and,
peace intervening, Trojans and Latins mingled safely,
ranging the woods and mountain ridges side by side.
And soaring ash trees ring to the two-edged iron axe
and they bring down pines that towered toward the skies.   160
There is no pause in the work as the wedges split
the oak and fragrant cedar, the groaning wagons
haul down from the slopes huge rowan trunks.

                              Rumor,
already in flight with the first alarms of sorrow,
fills Evander's ears, Evander's walls and palace,
Rumor that just had trumpeted Pallas' Latian triumph.
Arcadians throng to gateways, grasping funeral brands
in the old archaic way. And the torches light the road,
searing a long line through flatlands far and wide.
Joining forces with them, the Trojan escorts mass   170
to form a growing column of mourners on the march.
Once Arcadia's mothers saw them nearing their homes,
their wailing set the walls on fire with grief.

    And no force in the world can stop Evander now.
Into the crowds he goes and as the bier is lowered,
throws himself on Pallas, clinging for dear life,
sobbing, groaning, his sorrow all but choking
his voice that thrusts a passage through at last:
"A far cry from the pledge you made your father, Pallas,
that you would do nothing rash the day you trusted   180
yourself to the savage God of War! How well
I knew the thrill of a boy's first glory in arms,
the heady sweetness of one's first fame in battle.
But how bitter the first fruits of a man's youth,
the hard lessons learned in a war so near at hand,
and none of the gods would hear my vows, my prayers.
And you, my wife, most blessed woman in all the world,
how lucky you were to die, spared this wrenching grief!
But I defeated Fate, a father doomed to outlive his son.

If only I'd joined ranks with our Trojan comrades here   190
and Latin spears had hurled me down! And I had given
my own life, and the long last march brought me,
not Pallas, home! Not that I blame you, Trojans,
nor our pacts, our friendship sealed by a handclasp.
No, this fate was assigned to me in my old age.
But if my son was doomed to an early death,
to know he died after killing Volscian hordes
and died as he led the Trojans into Latium:
that will be my joy.
                    "Nor do I think you merit
any other burial rites than good Aeneas grants,   200
and the Trojan heroes, Tuscan chiefs as well
and Tuscan armies, bearing your great trophies
stripped from the men your right arm killed in war.
And you too, Turnus, would now be standing here,
a tremendous trunk of oak decked out in armor
if Pallas had had your years and strength to match.
But why in my torment hold the Trojans back from battle?
Go. Take this word to your king. Remember it well.
The reason I linger out this life I loathe, Aeneas,
now Pallas is dead and gone, is your right arm   210
that owes, as you well know, the life of Turnus
to son and father both. That is the only field
left free to you now, to prove your worth and fortune.
I look for no joy in life—the gods have ruled that out—
just to bear the news to my son among the dead."
                                        Soon
the Dawn had raised her light that gives men life,
wretched men, calling them back to labor
and mortal struggle. Now captain Aeneas, now
Tarchon erected pyres along the sweeping shore.
And here they carried the bodies of their dead   220
in the old ancestral way, as the dark funeral fires
blazed up from below to shroud the high skies
in pitch-dark smoke. Three times they ran
their ritual rounds about the burning pyres,

armed in gleaming bronze, three times they rode
on horseback, circling the fires lit in mourning,
lifting their wails of sorrow. Tears wet the earth,
tears wetting their armor. The shouting of fighters soars,
the clashing blare of trumpets.
      Some heave on the flames
the plunder stripped from the Latin ranks they killed—   230
their helmets, burnished swords, bridles, chariot wheels
still glowing hot, while others burn the offerings
well-known to the dead, their shields, their spears
that had no luck. And round about they slaughter
droves of cattle, carcasses offered up to Death,
and bristling swine and beasts led in from the fields
are butchered over the flames. Then down the entire shore
they watch their comrades burn as men stand guard at the pyres
now dying out . . . Nor can they tear themselves away
till the dank night comes wheeling round the heavens   240
studded with fiery stars.
     No less in another zone
the grieving Latins raise up countless pyres too.
For they had many dead, and some they bury in earth,
some they lift and bear off to the nearby fields
and the other dead they carry back to town.
All the rest they burn, unnumbered and unsung,
an enormous tangled mass of bloody carnage waits
and the wasteland far and wide lights up with fires,
with pyre on pyre striving to outblaze the last.
The third day rose, driving the night's chill from the sky   250
as the mourners raked the embers, leveling off the ashes
mixed with bones, and piled the gravesite high
with mounds of earth still warm.
      Now in the homes,
in King Latinus' city that overflowed with wealth,
the breaking wails and the long dirges reach their climax.
Here the mothers and grief-stricken brides of the dead
and their loving sisters, hearts torn with sorrow,
and young boys robbed of their fathers—

curse this horrendous war and Turnus' marriage.
"He himself," they cry, "he should decide it all   260
with his own sword and shield, since he lays claim
to the realm of Italy, claims the lion's share
of honor for himself!" And caustic Drances
lends weight to their side. He swears that Turnus
alone is summoned, he alone called forth to battle.
But opposing them at once, a mix of views and voices
rises up for Turnus. The famous name of the queen
holds out its shield, and the hero wins support
for his many feats, his trophies won in war.
                                                    Now
amid the din, as the fiery controversy flared,   270
look, to top it off, the grim-set envoys enter,
bearing the news from Diomedes' noble city:
"Nothing has been won, for all our attempts.
Nothing achieved by all our gifts, our gold,
our fervent appeals. We Latins must look elsewhere,
hunt for other allies or press for peace at once
at the hands of the Trojan king."
                                            Crushing news.
Even King Latinus is overwhelmed. It's clear,
Aeneas comes by the will of Fate, the word on high.
So the wrath of the gods declares, the fresh-dug graves   280
before Latinus' eyes. And so he convenes a council,
all the leading captains mustered at his command,
inside the lofty gates. They all collected now,
crowding into the royal halls through milling streets.
Throned in their midst, greatest in years and first in power,
sits Latinus, the king's brow hardly marked by joy.
He orders the envoys, home from Aetolia's city,
to tell all, all the reports they carry back,
demanding the truth from each man in turn.

    A hush fell as Venulus, following orders,   290
tells his story: "My countrymen, we have seen
Diomedes, seen the Argive camp. We've made
the long march and survived its many dangers—

we have grasped the hand that toppled Troy.
The victor king was still building his city,
Argyripa, named for his father's Argive stock—
in Iapyx' realm, the fields round Mount Garganus.
Once we entered, allowed to appeal before the king,
we offered our gifts, told him our names, our native land,
and who had attacked us, what had drawn us to Arpi.   300

     "He heard our pleas and replied with calming words:
'You happy, happy people, men of old Ausonia,
land where Saturn ruled, what drives you now
to shatter your blessed peace? What spurs you
to rouse the hells of war you've never known?
We who defiled the fields of Troy with swords—
why mention all the pain we drank to the dregs,
fighting beneath those walls, or the men we lost,
drowned in Simois River? Strewn across the world,
we all have borne unspeakable punishments, yes,   310
we've paid the price in full for all our crimes.
Even Priam might pity our embattled troops.
The grim star of Minerva, she bears witness,
so do Euboea's crags and Caphereus' vengeful cliffs.
Caught in that war's wake, we have been driven
to many shores. Atreus' son, Menelaus, right up
to the Pillars of Proteus—long an exile now.
Ulysses has seen the Cyclops on Mount Etna.
Shall I tell you of Neoptolemus' brief reign?
The house of Idomeneus tumbled to the ground?   320
The Locrians stranded out on Libya's coast?
Even he, the Mycenaean commander of all Greece:
the moment he crossed his threshold, down he went
at the hands of his wicked queen. The conqueror of Asia . . .
an adulterer crouched in wait to lay him low.

     "'Just think. The envious gods denied me my return
to my fathers' altars, or one glimpse of the wife
I yearned for so, or the lovely hills of Calydon.
I'm still stalked by the sight of terrifying omens.

My comrades gone! Flown off to the sky on wings   330
or they roam the streams, as birds—how brutal,
the punishments all my people have endured—
and they make the cliffs re-echo with their cries.
Such disasters were in the stars, from that day on
that I like a maniac attacked an immortal's body,
my sword defiled the hand of Venus with a wound!

    "'No, don't press me to face such battles now.
I've had no strife with Trojans since Troy fell,
nor do I think of those old griefs with any joy.
And as for the gifts you bring me from your homeland,   340
give them to Aeneas. I've stood up against his weapons,
we've gone man to man. Trust me, I know just how
fiercely the fighter rises up behind his shield,
what a whirlwind rides on that man's spear!
If Troy had borne two others to match Aeneas,
Trojan troops would have marched on Greece's cities,
Greece would now be grieving, Fate turned upside down.
Whatever the stand-off round the sturdy walls of Troy,
with Greek victory hanging fire until the tenth year came,
was all thanks to Aeneas' and Hector's strong right arms.   350
Both men shone in courage, both men blazed in combat,
Aeneas the more devout. Join hands in pacts of peace
while you still have the chance. Don't join battle,
sword to sword. Be on your guard.'
                         "Now then,
you have heard, great king, the king's response,
the view he takes of this mighty war of ours."

    The envoys had barely closed when a troubled groan
came murmuring from the Italians' anxious lips and
mounted as when the rocks resist a stream in spate
and the dammed-up tide goes churning, sounding out   360
as it beats from bank to bank with water roaring white.
Once their spirits calmed and the anxious din died down,
first the king salutes the gods from his high throne
and then begins: "If only before now, men of Latium,

we had resolved this dire crisis! How I wish
we had called a council then. Far better then,
not now, with the enemy camped before our walls.
What an ominous war we wage, my countrymen!
Fighting people descended from the gods,
unbeaten heroes, never wearied in battle,   370
even in defeat they can't put down the sword.
If you had any hope of winning Aetolian allies,
give it up now. Each man to his own best hope,
but now you can see how slim your hopes have been.
The rest of your prospects? All lie in shambles—
look with your own eyes, feel with your own hands.
I blame no one. The most that valor could do,
valor has done. We have fought the good fight
with all our kingdom's power.
                              "Now, at this point,
torn as I am with doubts, here is what I propose,   380
I will tell it in brief. Come, listen closely . . .
I have an age-old tract along the Tiber River,
stretching West, beyond the Sicanian border.
Here the Auruncans and Rutulians sow their crops,
plow the rugged hills and graze the wildest banks.
Let this entire spread, plus highlands ringed with pines,
be given the Trojans now to win their friendship.
And let us draft a treaty, just in every term,
and invite the Trojans in to share our kingdom.
Let them settle here, if so their hearts desire,   390
and build their city walls. But if they are bent
on seizing other countries, other people now,
and it's in their power to put our land astern,
then we'll build them twenty ships of Italian oak.
More, if they have the crews. The timber's stacked ashore.
Let them set out the number, the class of ship they need.
We can supply the bronze, the shipwrights, docks and tackle.
I also propose—to bear the news, confirm the pact—
that a hundred envoys be dispatched, elite Latin stock,
their arms laden with boughs of peace and bearing gifts,   400
hundred-weights of gold and ivory, throne and robe,

our royal emblems. Confer among yourselves.
Shore up our shattered fortunes."
                                        Drances rises,
aggressive as always, stung by Turnus' glory,
spurred by smarting, barely hidden envy—
a lavish spender, his rhetoric even looser,
but a frozen hand in battle. No small voice
in the public councils, always a shrewd adviser,
a power in party strife. On his mother's side,
well born, but his father's side remains a blank.   410
Drances rises now. His urgings fuel their fire:
"Our situation is clear for all to see,
and it needs no voice of ours in council now,
my noble king. The people know, they admit they know
what destiny has in store, but they flinch from speaking out.
Let *him* allow us to speak and quit his puffed-up pride,
that man whose unholy leadership and twisted ways—
Oh, I'll let loose, he can threaten me with death!—
so many leading lights among us he's snuffed out
that we see our entire city plunged in grief while he,   420
trusting that he can break and run, attacks the Trojans,
terrorizing the heavens with his spears!
                                        "Just add
one gift to the hoards you tell us now to give and
pledge the Dardans. Just one more, my generous king!
Let no one's violence overwhelm your power here
as a father to give his daughter to a man,
an outstanding man, a marriage earned in full
and sealed by pacts of peace that last forever.
But if such terror grips our hearts and minds,
let us beg a favor of our fine prince.
                                        "Turnus,   430
surrender to king and country their due rights!
Why keep flinging your wretched people into naked peril?
You are the root and spring of all the Latins' griefs!
There's no salvation in war. Peace—we all beg you,
Turnus—bound with the one inviolate pledge of peace!

"I've come first, the man you think your enemy—
and what if I am? I'm here to implore you now:
pity your own people. Surrender your pride.
You're beaten, now retreat! Routed so,
we have seen our fill of death. Vast tracts   440
we have left a wasteland. Or if glory spurs you on,
if your strength is still like oak, if the dowry
of a palace seems so very dear to your heart,
courage! Chest out, meet your enemy head-on!
But of course—so Turnus can fetch his royal bride—
our lives are cheap, scattered in piles across the field,
unburied and unwept. Come, prince, if you have the spine,
if you have any spark of your fathers' warring spirit,
look, your challenger calls you out to fight!"
                                              Turnus
groans under that barrage, his fury breaks into fire   450
and the outrage bursts from the soldier's deep heart:
"Always a mighty flood of words from you, Drances,
when battle demands our fighting hands! Whenever
the senate's called, you're first to show your face.
But there is no earthly need to fill these halls
with the talk that flies so bravely from your mouth,
safe as you are while the ramparts keep the enemy out
and the trenches still don't overflow with blood. So,
bluster away with your bombast—that's your style!
Brand *me* for cowardice, Drances, once your arm   460
has left as many piles of slaughtered Trojans,
decked as many fields with brilliant trophies. Now
we're free to see what courage and quickness can achieve.
No long hunt for the foe. As you may have noticed,
they camp around our walls on every side. Come,
shall we march against them? You hang back—why?
Will your warlust always lie in your windy words
and your craven, racing feet? Beaten, am I?
Who could rightly call me beaten—you, you swine—
who bothers to see the Tiber crest with Trojan blood   470
and Evander's house uprooted, razed to the earth

and all his Arcadian fighters stripped of arms?
That's hardly the man that Pandarus and Bitias
met when those two giants confronted me—
and the thousand men whom I, in a single day,
sent down to hell in all my triumph, trapped
as I was inside the enemy's rugged walls.
                                                    "So,
'there's no salvation in war,' you say? Go sing that song,
you fool, for the Trojan chief—your own prospects too.
Keep on striking your huge panic in all our hearts,   480
praising to high heaven the strength of a people
beaten twice. Disdaining the forces of Latinus!
Now, I suppose, the Myrmidon captains cringe before
the Phrygian armies, now Diomedes, now Larisaean Achilles,
and Aufidus' rapids rush back from the Adriatic's waves!
But here's Drances, feigning terror at my rebukes,
a scoundrel's shabby dodge,
just to hone his charges hurled against me!
You, you'll never lose your life, such as it is,
not by my right hand—fear not—just let it rest,   490
beating inside that coward's chest of yours!
                                        "But now,
Father, I come back to you and your resolves . . .
If you no longer harbor any hope for our armies,
if we are so alone, and at one repulse our forces
are totally overwhelmed, good fortunes lost forever,
let us reach out our helpless arms and plead for peace.
Oh, if only we had a shred of our old courage left!
I rate that man the luckiest one among us, first
in the work of war, first in strength of heart,
who spurning the sight of our surrender, falls,   500
dying, and bites the dust for one last time.
But if we have troops and provisions still intact
and the towns and men of Italy still support our side,
if the Trojans have also paid a bloody price for glory—
they have their burials too, the same storm's struck us both—
then why this shameful collapse before it all begins?

Why tremble so before the trumpet blares?
                                        "Many things
the run of the days and shifting works of fickle time
have turned from bad to good. Many men has two-faced
Fortune cheated, only to come back and set them up   510
on solid ground once more. Diomedes, true,
and his city, Arpi, will offer us no relief.
But Messapus will, I trust, Tolumnius will,
that soldier of fortune, and all the captains
sent by so many lands, and no small glory waits
for the men picked out from Latian and Laurentine fields.
And Camilla too, our ally sprung from Volscian stock,
heading her horsemen, squadrons gleaming bronze.

        "But if the Trojans call me to single combat,
if that's your will as well, and I am such a bar   520
to the public good, then Victory has not spurned
or so hated these hands of mine that I would
shrink from any risk when hopes are riding high.
I will take him on with a will. Let him outfight
the great Achilles, strap on armor the match for his,
forged by Vulcan's hands. Bring him on, I say!
To all, to Latinus, the father of my bride,
I, Turnus, second in fighting strength to none
of the men who came before me—I devote my life.
Aeneas challenges me alone? Challenge away,   530
I beg you. And if the gods are raging now,
don't let Drances appease them with his death
instead of mine. If courage and glory are at stake,
don't let Drances carry off the prize!"
                                        But now,
while they debated their heated, divisive issues,
sparring back and forth, Aeneas struck camp
and deployed his lines for battle.
Then in the thick of the din, suddenly, look,
a messenger rushes in through the royal palace,
spreading panic across the city: "Armies marching!   540

Trojan and Tuscan allies pouring down from the Tiber,
sweeping the whole plain!"
                              Confusion reigns at once,
the people's spirits distraught, raked by the spur of rage.
Shaking fists, they shout "To arms!" "Arms!" the ranks shout out
while their fathers weep and groan. And now from all sides
an enormous uproar, cries in conflict lift on the winds—
like cries of bird-flocks landing in some tall grove by chance
or swans with their hoarse calls clamoring out across
the sounding pools of Padusa River stocked with fish.
"All right then, citizens!" seizing his moment Turnus   550
calls: "Summon your councils, sit there praising peace!
Our enemies swoop down on our country, full force!"
No more for them. Up he leapt and raced from the halls,
shouting: "You, Volusus, call your Volscian units to arms,
move your Rutulians out. Messapus, array the cavalry—
you and your brother Coras, range them down the plains.
Another contingent guard the gates and man the towers.
The rest attack with me where I command!"
                                        At once
they rush to the walls from all parts of the city.
King Latinus himself, shocked by the sudden crisis,   560
leaves the council, delays his own noble plans
till a better hour, over and over faults himself
for not embracing Trojan Aeneas with open arms,
adopting him as his son to shield the city.
Others are digging trenches before the gates,
hauling up on their shoulders stones and pikes.
And the raucous trumpet sounds the signal—bloody war!
Then a mixed cordon of boys and mothers rings the walls
as the long last struggle calls them all to gather.
Here is the queen, with a grand cortege of ladies   570
bearing gifts and riding up to Minerva's temple,
set on the heights, and beside her rides the girl,
the princess Lavinia, cause of all their grief,
her lovely eyes bent low . . .
Taking their lead, the ladies fill the shrine

with the smoke of incense, pouring out their wails
from the steep threshold: "You, power of armies,
queen of the battle, Pallas, virgin goddess,
shatter that Phrygian pirate's spear! Himself?
Hurl him headlong down, sprawled at our high gates!"   580

    And Turnus in matchless fury gears himself for war.
Now he's buckled his breastplate, gleaming, ruddy bronze
with its bristling metal scales—encased his legs in gold,
his temples still bare, but his sword was strapped to his side
as down from the city heights he speeds in a flash of gold
in all his glory, in all his hopes already locked fast
with the enemy—wild as a stallion bolting the paddock,
burst free of the reins at last
he commands the open plain, making for pasture,
out for the herds of mares or keen for a plunge   590
in the river runs he knows so well, he charges off,
his proud head flung back, neighing, racing on,
reveling in himself, his mane sporting over
his neck and shoulders.
                              Rushing to meet him came
Camilla, riding up with her armed Volscian ranks
and under the gates the princess sprang from her horse,
and following suit her entire troop dismounted
in one gliding flow as their captain speaks out:
"Turnus, if the brave deserve to trust themselves,
I'm steeled, I swear, to engage the cavalry of Aeneas,   600
foray out alone to confront the Tuscan squadrons.
Permit me to risk the first shock of battle.
You stay here on foot and guard the walls."
                                        Turnus,
his eyes trained on the awesome young girl, responded:
"Pride of Italy, Princess, what can I do or say
to show my thanks? But since that courage of yours
would leap all bounds, come share the struggle with me.
Aeneas, as rumor has it and posted scouts report,
has recklessly sent his light horse on ahead

to harass the plains, while he himself, crossing   610
the mountain heights by a lonely, desolate ridge,
he's moving on the city. I am setting an ambush
deep in a hollowed woody path and posting troops
to block the passage through at both ends of the gorge.
You take on the Etruscan cavalry—frontal assault,
flanked by brave Messapus, the Latin horsemen
and squadrons of Tiburtus. You too assume
a captain's joint command." With equal zeal
he rallies Messapus, rallies allied chiefs and
spurring them into battle, marches on the foe.   620

  There is a valley full of twists and turns,
a perfect spot for the lures and subterfuge of battle,
both of its sides closed off and dark with thick brush.
A cramped path leads the way, a tightening pass,
a difficult entry takes you in—a ready trap.
And over it all, amid the hilltop lookout points
there's high ground, hidden, good safe shelter.
Whether you'd like to attack from left or right
or stand on the ridge and roll huge boulders down.
Now here Turnus heads, by a track he knows by heart   630
and staking his ground, he lurks in the woods, in ambush.

  While high on Olympus, Diana called swift Opis,
one of her virgin comrades, one of her sacred troop,
and the goddess spoke in tears: "Camilla's moving out
to a brutal war, dear girl, strapping on our armor
all for nothing. I love her like no one else!
And it's no new love, you know, that stirs Diana,
no sweet lightning bolt of passion . . .
                                       "Once,
when that tyrant, Metabus, loathed by people
for his abuse of power, was drummed from his kingdom,   640
leaving Privernum's ancient town, he took his daughter,
a baby, with him, fleeing the thick-and-fast of battle,
a friend to share his exile. Camilla, he called her,
changing her mother's name, Casmilla, just a bit.

Holding her in his arms, he made for the ridges,
wild, dense with woods, with enemy weapons raining
down around them, Volscian forces closing for the kill.
And suddenly as they flew, the Amasenus overflowed, look,
foaming over its banks, such violent cloudbursts broke.
About to swim for it, Metabus stops short, stayed   650
by love for his child, fear for that dear burden.
As he racked his brains, desperate, deeply torn,
he lit on a quick decision. His own huge spear—
the fighter luckily bore it in his grip—
rugged with knots, the oakwood charred hard.
Rolling her up in cork-bark stripped from trees,
he lashed her fast to the weapon, just mid-haft and
balancing both in his right hand, he prays to the skies:
'Bountiful one, to you, lover of groves, Latona's daughter,
a father devotes his baby girl. Yours is the first spear   660
she grasps as she flees the enemy through the air,
pleading for your mercy!
Receive her, goddess—your very own—I pray you,
now I commit my child to the fickle winds!'
                         "With that,
cocking back his arm he sends the javelin whirring on
and the river roars out as over the churning rapids
poor Camilla flies along on the whizzing shaft.
But now as enemy fighters harry Messapus even more,
he flings himself in the stream and, flushed with triumph,
pries from the turf his spear and baby girl as one,   670
his gift to you, Diana, Goddess of the Crossroads.
No homes, no city walls would give them shelter,
nor would he have consented, fierce man that he was,
no, a shepherd's life on the lonely mountains,
that's the life he led. There in the brush
and the rough lairs of beasts he nursed his child
on raw milk from the dugs of a wild brood-mare,
milking its udders into her tender lips. And then,
when the toddler had taken her first hesitant steps,
Metabus armed her hand with a well-honed lance   680
and slung from her tiny shoulder bow and arrows.

No gold band for her hair, no long flaring cape,
a tiger-skin that covered her head hung down her back.
With a hand uncallused still she flung her baby spears,
swirled a sling-shot round her head with its supple strap
and bagged a crane or snowy swan by the Strymon's banks.
Many a mother in Tuscan cities yearned for her
as a daughter. Futile. Diana's her only passion.
She nurses a lifelong love of chastity and the hunt
while she remains untouched. If only she'd never   690
been carried away to serve in such a war—
bent on challenging Trojans. She'd still be
one of my loyal comrades, still my own dear girl.

"Action! Watch, a terrible destiny drives her on!
Down you dive from the high skies, Opis my nymph,
light out for the Latin lands where battle flares
and the omens all are bad. These weapons, take them,
pluck from the quiver an arrow fletched for vengeance!
Use it. Whoever defiles her sacred body with a wound—
Trojan, Italian: make him pay me an equal price in blood!   700
Then I will fold her in cloud, poor girl, with all her gear
and bear Camilla's unsullied body home to a tomb
and lay her to rest in her own native land."
                                        At that,
Opis dove down from the sky through a light breeze,
her body wrapped in a whirlwind dark as night
and whirring on her way.
                        But all the while
the Trojan forces are closing on the walls,
Etruscan chiefs and a massed army of cavalry
squaring off in squadrons rank by rank. Across
the entire field the snorting chargers stamping,   710
fighting their tight reins and veering left and right
and the plains are bristling a jagged crop of iron spears,
everywhere, fields ablaze with weapons brandished high.
At the same time, grouping against the Trojan lines,
Messapus, the swift Latins, Coras, his brother too
and young Camilla's wing—all march into sight,

right arms cocked back, thrusting javelins forward,
shaking vibrant lances, infantry tramping into position,
battle stallions panting, plains mounting to fever pitch.
And once both armies had closed to a spearcast away   720
they reined back to a halt—
then abruptly surge forward, shouting, whipping
their teams into combat frenzy, weapons pelting
thick as a snowstorm shrouds the skies in darkness.
At once Tyrrhenus and fierce Aconteus charge each other
full tilt with their spears, and both are first to crash,
shattering down with tremendous impact, splintering ribs
of their battle stallions ramming chest to chest.
Aconteus, hurled off, drops like a lightning bolt
or a dead weight shot forth from a siege engine,   730
heaving headlong far away from his charger,
gasping out his life breath on the winds.
                                        That moment
the lines of fighters buckle, Latins, routed, sling
their shields on their backs and wheel their horses
round to the walls as the Trojans drive them on
with Asilas in the lead, his squadrons charging.
Now they are nearing the gates when again the Latins
raise a war cry, wrenching the horses' supple necks around
while the Trojans, all reins slack, beat a deep retreat . . .
Picture an ocean rolling, waves ebbing and flowing,   740
now flooding onto the shore, smashing over the cliffs
in a burst of foam and drenching the bay's sandy edge—
now rushing in fast retreat, swallowing down the scree
lost in the backwash, leaving the shallows high and dry:
so twice the Etruscans hurled the Latins toward their walls,
twice routed, glancing round they cover their backs with shields.
But when at the third assault the whole front locked fast,
fighting hand-to-hand, and each man picked out his man,
then, truly, the groans of the dying men break loose,
weapons, bodies, a sea of blood, massacred riders,   750
half-dead horses writhing together now in death
and the pitched battle peaks.
                            Orsilochus fearing

to face the horseman Remulus, whirls a lance
at his horse instead, planting the point below its ear
and furious, wild with the wound, it cannot bear the agony,
rearing back, chest high, its hoofs thrashing the air
as Remulus, thrown free, rolls around in the dust.
And Catillus brings down Iollas, then Herminius,
massive in courage, immense in brawn and armor,
his blond locks flowing bare and his shoulders bare,   760
no fear of wounds, so huge his body exposed to spears.
But Catillus' shaft goes hammering through him, quivering out
his broad back and it doubles up the man impaled with pain.
Everywhere, black tides of blood, iron clashing, slaughter,
fighters striving for death with glory through their wounds.

    Watch, exulting here in the thick of carnage, an Amazon,
one breast bared for combat, quiver at hand—Camilla—now
she rifles hardened spears from her hand in salvos, now
she seizes a rugged double axe in her tireless grasp,
Diana's golden archery clashing on her shoulder.   770
Even forced to withdraw she swerves her bow
and showers arrows, wheeling in full flight.
And round Camilla ride her elite companions, Tulla,
young Larina, Tarpeia brandishing high her brazen axe—
daughters of Italy, all, she chose to be her glory,
godlike Camilla's aides in peace and war and wild
as Thracian Amazons galloping, pounding along
the Thermodon's banks, fighting in burnished gear
around Hippolyte, or when Penthesilea born of Mars
comes sweeping home in her car, an army of women   780
lifts their rolling, shrilling cries in welcome,
exulting with half-moon shields.
                              Fierce young girl,
who is the first and who the last your spear cuts down?
How many dying bodies do you spread out on the earth?
Eunaeus, son of Clytius, first. His chest, unshielded,
charging Camilla now, who runs her enemy through
with her long pine lance and he vomits spurts of blood,

gnawing the gory earth, twisting himself around his wound
as the Trojan breathes his last. Then Liris, Pagasus over him:
Liris struggling to clutch his reins, thrown from his horse   790
as it goes sprawling under him—Pagasus rushes to help
his falling comrade, reaches out with an unarmed hand
and both of them side by side pitch headlong down.
And adding kills, she takes Amastrus, Hippotas' son,
then attacking at long range, with spearcasts pierces
Tereus and Harpalycus, then Demophoön, Chromis too
and for every shaft the girl let fly from her hand
another Phrygian fighter bit the dust.
                               Here's Ornytus
riding his Apulian charger in from a distance,
all decked out in exotic armor, the huntsman   800
setting up for a soldier. A bull's-hide covers
his broad shoulders, the big yawning maw of a wolf
with glistening fangs in its jaws protects his head
and a hunter's hook-tipped javelin arms his hand
as into the press he goes, topping all by a head
but Camilla runs him down—easy work with the ranks
in full retreat—and spears him through, exulting
over his body with all the hatred in her heart:
"Still in the woods, you thought, and flushing game,
my fine Etruscan hunter? Well, the day has come   810
when a woman's weapons prove your daydreams wrong!
Still, you carry no mean fame to your fathers' shades—
just tell them this: You died by Camilla's spear!"
                                    Lunging
she kills a pair of massive Trojans, Butes and Orsilochus.
Butes, his back turned, she stabs between the helmet and
breastplate, just where the horseman's neck shines bare
and the shield on his left arm dangles down, off guard.
And fleeing Orsilochus now
as the Trojan drives her round in a huge ring,
Camilla tricks him, wheeling inside him, quick,   820
the pursuer now the pursued as she rears above him—
praying, begging for mercy—her battle-axe smashes down,

blow after blow through armor, bone, splitting his skull,
warm brains from the wound go splashing down his face.

                                        Suddenly

right before Camilla, stunned with terror to see her here,
stands Aunus' fighting son, an Apennine man and not
the least of Liguria's liars while the Fates allow.
Once he sees there is no running away from battle,
no turning aside Camilla's attack, he tries
to devise a ruse with all his craft and cunning,   830
letting loose: "Now where's the glory, tell me,
a woman putting her trust in a powerful horse?
No more running away. Meet me on level ground,
in combat, hand-to-hand, gear up to fight on foot.
You'll soon see whose windy boasts of glory
cheat him blind!"
                        Raked by the scathing taunt
Camilla blazes up in rage, hands off her horse
to an aide and takes her stand against the Ligurian:
fearless on foot and armed like him with a naked sword
and still unbattered shield. But quick as a flash   840
the soldier, certain his guile had won the day,
runs away himself, yanking his reins around and
digging iron spurs in his racing stallion's flanks.
"Ligurian fool! So bloated with all your empty pride,
pulling your slippery inbred tricks for nothing!
Fraud will never carry you home, safe and sound,
to your lying father Aunus!"
                              So young Camilla cries
and lightning-fast on her feet outruns the charger,
snatches the reins and facing her enemy dead-on,
makes him pay with his own detested blood—   850
quick as Apollo's falcon wheeling down from a crag
outraces a dove in flight to a high cloud, seizes it,
clutches it, hooked talons ripping its insides out,
its blood and plucked feathers drifting down the sky.

    But the Father of Men and Gods, far from blind,
throned on his steep Olympian peak observes it all

and stirs Etruscan Tarchon into the savage fighting,
lashing the trooper on with the rough spur of rage.
So into the bloody, buckling lines rides Tarchon,
goading his horsemen on with a burst of mixed cries,   860
rallying each by name, spurring the routed back to battle:
"What's your fear, you Tuscans forever deaf to shame?
Always slacking off! What cowardice saps your courage?
What, is a woman routing squadrons strong as ours?
Why have swords or useless lances gripped in our fists?
But you're not slow when it comes to nightly bouts of love,
when the curved flute strikes up some frantic Bacchic dance!
Linger on for the feasts and cups at the groaning board—
that's your love, your lust—
till the seer will bless and proclaim the sacrifice   870
and the rich victim lures you into the deep groves!"

    With that, he whips his warhorse into the press,
braced to die himself, he rushes Venulus headlong,
sweeps him off his mount and hugging his enemy
tight to his chest with his clenched right arm,
gallops away with him, racing off full tilt.

                                        A cry
hits the skies, all the Latins turning to watch
as Tarchon flies like wildfire down the field,
bearing the man and weapons both, then wrenches off
the iron point of Venulus' spear and delves around   880
for a spot laid bare where a lethal blow might land,
the other fighting off the enemy's hand from his throat,
pitting force against fury. Swift as a golden eagle seizes
a snake and towers into the sky, talons knotted round it,
claws clutching fast but the wounded serpent writhes
in its rippling coils, stiffens, scales bristling,
hissing through its fangs as it rears its head,
but all the more the eagle keeps on digging into
its struggling victim, its hooked beak ripping away,
its wings thrashing the air—so Tarchon sweeps his kill   890
right from the Tiber's columns, Tarchon flushed with triumph.
Following hard on their captain's feat and clear success

the Etruscans swing to attack . . . as Arruns starts
to circle swift Camilla, a match for her spear yet
more adept at cunning. His life is doomed by the Fates
but now he tests his luck for the quickest way in.
Wherever Camilla rages, plunging into the front,
there Arruns stalks her, quietly tracks her steps;
whenever she downs a foe and turns around for home,
round he tugs at his fast reins and ducks from sight.   900
Now this approach, now that, exploring the circuit
round from every side, he shakes his fatal spear
in his ruthless fist.
                    By chance, one Chloreus,
sacred to goddess Cybebe, once her priest—Camilla
spied him at long range, gleaming in Phrygian gear,
spurring a lathered warhorse decked with coat of mail,
its brazen scales meshing with gold like feathers stitched.
He himself, aflame in outlandish reds and purples,
shot Gortynian shafts from a Lycian bow, a bow
of gold slung from the priest's shoulders, gold   910
his helmet too, and he'd knotted his saffron cape
and flaring linen pleats with a tawny golden brooch,
his shirt and barbarous leggings stiff with needled braid.
Camilla, keen to fix some Trojan arms on a temple wall
or sport some golden plunder out on the hunt,
she tracked him now, one man in the moil of war,
she stalked him wildly, reckless through the ranks,
afire with a woman's lust for loot and plunder when,
grasping his chance at last, rising up from ambush
Arruns flings his spear with a winged prayer aloft: 920
"Apollo, highest of gods, lord of holy Soracte!
We worship you first and foremost, honor your fires
stoked by cords of pine! And we your celebrants firm
in our faith, we plant our feet in your embers glowing hot!
Grant, Father, our shame be blotted out by our spears,
almighty God Apollo! I am not bent on plunder
stripped from a girl, no trophy over her corpse.
My other feats of arms will win me glory. If only
this murderous scourge drops dead beneath my strokes,

back I'll go to my fathers' towns—unsung!"

                                        Apollo heard   930
and willed that part of the prayer would win the day
but part he scattered abroad on the ruffling winds.
That Arruns should cut Camilla down in sudden death:
that he granted, true, but not that his noble land
should see him home again
and the gusting Southwinds swept that prayer away.

    So when he sent his javelin hissing through the air
and all the Volscians, wheeling, trained their eyes
and alert minds on the princess, she was numb to it all,
the draft, the hiss, the weapon sent from the blue—until   940
the spear went ripping through her, under her naked breast
and it struck deep, it hammered home and drank her virgin blood.
Her frightened comrades hurry to brace their falling queen
but Arruns races off, more frantic than all the rest—
his triumph mixed with terror—no longer trusting his spear
or daring to meet the young girl's weapons point-blank.
Like the wolf that's killed some shepherd or hulking ox
and before attacking spears can catch him, races off
at once, darting into the pathless hills for cover—
he knows he's done some outrage—frantic now,   950
he tucks his trembling tail between his legs
and heads for the woods. So Arruns, shaken,
slinking from sight, content with a bare escape,
loses himself in the milling lines of fighters.

                                        Camilla,
dying, tugs at the spear but the iron point stands
fixed in the deep wound, wedged between her ribs.
She's faint from loss of blood, her eyes failing,
chill with death, and the glowing color she had,
once, fades away. Then as she breathes her last,
she calls to Acca, alone of her young comrades,   960
more than all the others true to Camilla,
the only one with whom she shares her cares,
and here is what she says: "This far, Acca,
my sister, and I can go no further. Now

the raw wound saps my strength . . .
darkness, everywhere, closing in around me.
Go, quickly, carry my last commands to Turnus:
Take over the fighting, free the town from Trojans!
Now farewell."
                         With Camilla's last words she lost
her grip on the reins and, all against her will,   970
slipped down to the ground. Little by little
she grew cold, and wholly freed of her body,
laid down her head as her neck drooped limp
in the clutch of death, and she let her weapons fall.
Camilla's life breath fled with a groan of outrage
down to the shades below.
                         And then, at that,
an immense cry rose up and hit the golden stars.
With Camilla down, the melee peaks to a new pitch,
the masses surging forward, the whole Trojan army,
Etruscan captains, Evander's Arcadian wings.   980

    But all the while Diana's sentry, Opis,
posted high on a ridge, has scanned the fighting
unperturbed. And when at a distance she could see—
clear in the thick of battle, war cries, warriors' fury—
Camilla beaten down by the brutal stroke of death,
she moaned, crying out from the bottom of her heart:
"Too cruel, dear girl, too cruel the price you pay
for trying, begging to challenge the men of Troy in combat!
What gain for you, your lonely life in the forest,
serving Diana, our quiver round your shoulder?   990
But your queen has not deserted you, shorn of honor,
not in your hour of death, nor will your death lack glory
among the race of man, nor will you bear the shame
of dying unavenged. Whoever defiled your body with
that wound will pay with the death that he deserves!"
                                                 Under
the mountain ridges stood an immense mound of earth,
hedged with shady ilex, the tomb of Dercennus,
an old Laurentine king. Here with a swoop

the lovely goddess first took up her post,
from the high ground looking round for Arruns . . .   1000
and seeing him gleam in armor, puffed with pride,
"Why running away?" she shouted. "Step right up,
just come this way—to die! Collect the reward
you've earned for Camilla's death. Just think,
you are to die by the arrows of Diana!"
                    That said,
the Thracian goddess, plucking a wind-swift shaft
from her golden quiver, drew her bow with a vengeance,
back to a full draw till the curved horns all but touched,
her balanced hands tense—left hand at the iron point,
right hand at the bowstring stretched to her breast—   1010
then, the instant that Arruns heard the whizzing shaft
and whirring air the iron struck home in his flesh.
As he gasps out his last, his oblivious comrades
leave him sprawled in the nameless dust and
Opis flies away to Mount Olympus.
                    Their captain gone,
Camilla's light horse squadrons are first to flee,
the harried Rutulians flee and brave Atinas too,
leaders routed, and front-line men, their leaders lost,
make for safety, swerving their horses, racing for the walls.
But nothing can halt the Trojans' fierce offensive now,   1020
no weapons can stop them, nothing stand against them.
Home the Latins go, slack bows on sagging shoulders,
galloping hoofbeats pound the rutted plain with thunder.
As a dust storm dark as night goes whirling toward the walls,
the mothers stand at the lookouts, beating their breasts,
raising the women's shrilling wails to the starry sky.

    And the first Latins to rush through the open gates?
Enemies mixing in with their own ranks crowd them hard,
nor can they find escape from a wretched death, no,
right at the entrance, just in their native walls,   1030
in the safe retreat of home they're pierced by spears
and pant their lives away. Some shut the gates,
not daring to clear a safe way in for comrades,

beg as they will, and a ghastly bloodbath follows,
defenders killed at the entries, enemies flung on swords.
Shut out in front of their parents' faces, eyes streaming tears,
some pitch headlong into the trenches, pressed by the rout,
some charge wildly, reins flying, ramming the gateways
blocked by the rugged posts.
And even mothers up on the ramparts strive—   1040
their genuine love of country marks the way,
they'd seen Camilla fight—they hurl their weapons
with trembling hands, daring to do the work of iron
with pikes of rugged oak and poles charred hard.
Defending their city walls, they all burn
to be the first to die.
                    At the same time
the wrenching news hits Turnus still in the woods.
It arrives in force as Acca brings her commander
word of stark disaster: Volscian units routed,
Camilla fallen, enemy armies surging on, attacking   1050
on all fronts, and Mars in his triumph, panic already
shakes the city walls. Turnus in all his fury—
that's what the ruthless will of Jove demands—
abandons his hilltop ambush, quits the shaggy grove.
He was barely out of sight and about to range the plain
when captain Aeneas, moving through the exposed pass,
climbs the ridge and comes forth from the shady woods.
So now both men are speeding toward the walls—not many
strides between their armies marching in total strength.
Then, the moment Aeneas spied the dust storm swirling   1060
down the plain and the long lines of Latian fighters,
Turnus spied Aeneas, savage in full armor, and caught
the tramp of marching infantry, battle stallions panting.
They would have clashed at once and tried their luck in war
but the ruddy Sun has plunged his weary team in the Western sea
and as daylight slips away he brings the nightfall on.
Now both armies come to a halt before the city,
building dikes to fortify their camps.

BOOK TWELVE

The Sword
Decides All

Once Turnus sees his ranks of Latins broken in battle,
their spirits dashed and the war-god turned against them,
now is the time, he knows, for him to keep his pledge.
All eyes are fixed on him—his blood is up
and nothing can quench the fighter's ardor now.
Think of the lion ranging the fields near Carthage . . .
the beast won't move into battle till he takes
a deep wound in his chest from the hunters, then
he revels in combat, tossing the rippling mane on his neck
he snaps the spear some stalker drove in his flesh and   10
roars from bloody jaws, without a fear in the world.
So Turnus blazes up into full explosive fury,
bursting out at the king with reckless words:
"Turnus spurns all delay! Now there's no excuse
for those craven sons of Aeneas to break their word,
to forsake the pact we swore. I'll take him on, I will!

Bring on the sacred rites, Father, draft our binding terms.
Either my right arm will send that Dardan down to hell,
that rank deserter of Asia—my armies can sit back
and watch, and Turnus' sword alone will rebut   20
the charge of cowardice trained against them all.
Or let him reign over those he's beaten down.
Let Lavinia go to him—his bride!"

    Latinus replied in a calming, peaceful way:
"Brave of the brave, my boy, the more you excel
in feats of daring, the more it falls to me to weigh
the perils, with all my fears, the lethal risks we run.
The realms of your father, Daunus, are yours to manage,
so are the many towns your right arm took by force.
Latinus, too, has wealth and the will to share it.   30
We've other unwed girls in Latian and Laurentine fields,
and no mean stock at that. So let me offer this,
hard as it is, yet free and clear of deception.
Take it to heart, I urge you. For me to unite
my daughter with any one of her former suitors
would have been wrong, forbidden:
all the gods and prophets made that plain.
But I bowed to my love of you, bowed to our kindred blood
and my wife's heartrending tears. I broke all bonds,
I tore the promised bride from her waiting groom,   40
I brandished a wicked sword.
                  "Since then, Turnus,
you see what assaults, what crises dog my steps,
what labors you have shouldered, you, first of all.
Beaten twice in major battles, our city walls
can scarcely harbor Italy's future hopes.
The rushing Tiber still steams with our blood,
the endless fields still glisten with our bones.
Why do I shrink from my decision? What insanity
shifts my fixed resolve? If, with Turnus dead,
I am ready to take the Trojans on as allies,   50
why not stop the war while he is still alive?
What will your Rutulians, all the rest of Italy

say if I betray you to death—may Fortune forbid!—
while you appeal for my daughter's hand in marriage?
Oh, think back on the twists and turns of war.
Pity your father, bent with years and grief,
cut off from you in your native city Ardea
far away."
                    Latinus' urgings deflect the fury
of Turnus not one bit—it only surges higher.
The attempts to heal enflame the fever more.   60
Soon as he finds his breath the prince breaks out:
"The anguish you bear for my sake, generous king,
for my sake, I beg you, wipe it from your mind.
Let me barter death as the price of fame.
I have weapons too, old father, and no weak,
untempered spears go flying from my right hand—
from the wounds we deal the blood comes flowing too.
His mother, the goddess, she'll be far from his side
with her woman's wiles, lurking in stealthy shadows,
hiding him in clouds when her hero cuts and runs!"   70

    But the queen, afraid of the new rules of engagement,
wept, and bent on her own death embraced her ardent
son-in-law to be: "Turnus, by these tears of mine,
by any concern for Amata that moves your heart,
you are my only hope, now, you the one relief
to my wretched old age. In your hands alone
the glory and power of King Latinus rest,
you alone can shore our sinking house.
One favor now, I pray you.
Refrain from going hand to hand with the Trojans!   80
Whatever dangers await you in that one skirmish,
Turnus, await me too. With you I will forsake
the light of this life I hate—never in shackles
live to see Aeneas as my son!"
                              As Lavinia heard
her mother's pleas, her warm cheeks bathed in tears,
a blush flamed up and infused her glowing features.
As crimson as Indian ivory stained with ruddy dye

or white lilies aglow in a host of scarlet roses,
so mixed the hues that lit the young girl's face.
Turnus, struck with love, fixing his eyes upon her,   90
fired the more for combat, tells Amata, briefly:
"Don't, I beg you, mother, send me off with tears,
with evil omens as I go into the jolting shocks of war,
since Turnus is far from free to defer his death.
Be my messenger, Idmon. Take my words to Aeneas,
hardly words to please that craven Phrygian king!
Soon as the sky goes red with tomorrow's dawn,
riding Aurora's blood-red chariot wheels,
he's not to hurl his Trojans against our Latins,
he must let Trojan and Latian armies stand at ease.   100
Our blood will put an end to this war at last—
that's the field where Lavinia must be won!"

                                        No more words.
Rushing back to the palace Turnus calls for his team
and thrills to see them neighing right before him,
gifts from Orithyia herself to glorify Pilumnus,
horses whiter than snow, swifter than racing winds.
Restless charioteers flank them, patting their chests,
slapping with cupped hands, and groom their rippling manes.
Next Turnus buckles round his shoulders the breastplate,
dense with its golden mesh and livid mountain bronze,   110
and straps on sword, shield, and helmet with horns
for its bloody crest—that sword the fire-god forged
for Father Daunus, plunged red-hot in the river Styx.
And next with his powerful grip he snatches up
a burly spear aslant an enormous central column—
plunder seized from an enemy, Actor—shakes it hard
till the haft quivers and "Now, my spear," he cries,
"you've never failed my call, and now our time has come!
Great Actor wielded you once. Now you're in Turnus' hands.
Let me spill his corpse on the ground and strip his breastplate,   120
rip it to bits with my bare hands—that Phrygian eunuch—
defile his hair in the dust, his tresses crimped
with a white-hot curling-iron dripping myrrh!"

Frenzy drives him, Turnus' whole face is ablaze,
showering sparks, his dazzling glances glinting fire—
terrible, bellowing like some bull before the fight begins,
trying to pour his fury into his horns, he rams a tree-trunk,
charges the winds full force, stamping sprays of sand
as he warms up for battle.

                  At the same time, Aeneas,
just as fierce in the arms his mother gave him,   130
hones his fighting spirit too and incites his anger,
glad the war will end with the pact that Turnus offers.
Then he eases his friends' and anxious Iulus' fears,
explaining the ways of Fate, commanding envoys now
to return his firm reply to King Latinus,
state the terms of peace.

              A new day was just
about to dawn, scattering light on the mountaintops,
the horses of the Sun just rearing up from the Ocean's depths,
breathing forth the light from their flaring nostrils when
the Latins and Trojans were pacing off the dueling-ground   140
below the great city's walls, spacing the braziers out
between both armies, mounding the grassy altars high
to the gods they shared in common. Others, cloaked
in their sacred aprons, brows wreathed in verbena,
brought out spring water and sacramental fire.
The Italian troops march forth, pouring out
of the packed gates in tight, massed ranks
and fronting them, the entire Trojan and Tuscan
force comes rushing up, decked out in a range of arms,
no less equipped with iron than if the brutal war-god   150
called them forth to battle. And there in the midst
of milling thousands, chiefs paraded left and right,
resplendent in all their purple-and-gold regalia:
Mnestheus, blood kin of Assaracus, hardy Asilas,
then Messapus, breaker of horses, Neptune's son.
The signal sounds. All withdraw to their stations,
plant spears in the ground and cant their shields against them.
Then in an avid stream the mothers and unarmed crowds

and frail old men find seats on towers and rooftops,
others take their stand on the high gates.
                                    But Juno,   160
looking out from a ridge now called the Alban Mount—
then it had neither name, renown nor glory—gazed
down on the plain, on Italian and Trojan armies
face-to-face, and Latinus' city walls.
At once she called to Turnus' sister, goddess
to goddess, the lady of lakes and rilling brooks,
an honor the high and mighty king of heaven bestowed
on Juturna once he had ravished the virgin girl:
"Nymph, beauty of streams, our heart's desire,
well you know how I have favored you, you   170
above all the Italian women who have mounted
that ungrateful bed of our warm-hearted Jove—
I gladly assigned you a special place in heaven.
So learn, Juturna, the grief that comes your way
and don't blame me. While Fortune seemed to allow
and Fate to suffer the Latian state to thrive,
I guarded Turnus, guarded your city walls.
But now I see the soldier facing unequal odds,
his day of doom, his enemy's blows approaching . . .
That duel, that deadly pact—I cannot bear to watch.   180
But if *you* dare help your brother at closer range,
go and do so, it becomes you. Who knows?
Better times may come to those in pain."
                                    Juno
had barely closed when tears brimmed in Juturna's eyes
and three, four times over she beat her lovely breast.
"No time for tears, not now," warned Saturn's daughter.
"Hurry! Pluck your brother from death, if there's a way,
or drum up war and abort that treaty they conceived.
The design is mine. The daring, yours."
                                    Spurring her on,
Juno left Juturna torn, distraught with the wound   190
that broke her heart.
                       As the kings come riding in,
a massive four-horse chariot draws Latinus forth,

his glistening temples ringed by a dozen gilded rays,
proof he owes his birth to the sun-god's line,
and a snow-white pair brings Turnus' chariot on,
two steel-tipped javelins balanced in his grip.
And coming to meet them, marching from the camp,
the great founder, Aeneas, source of the Roman race,
with his blazoned starry shield and armor made in heaven.
And at his side, his son, Ascanius, second hope of Rome's   200
imposing power, while a priest in pure white robes leads on
the young of a bristly boar and an unshorn yearling sheep
toward the flaming altars. Turning their eyes to face
the rising sun, the captains reach out their hands,
pouring the salted meal, and mark off the brows
of the victims, cutting tufts with iron blades,
and tip their cups on the sacred altar fires.

 Then devoted Aeneas, sword drawn, prays:
"Now let the Sun bear witness here
and this, this land of Italy that I call.   210
For your sake I am able to bear such hardships.
And Jove almighty, and you, his queen, Saturnia—
goddess, be kinder now, I pray you, now at last!
And you, Father, glorious Mars, you who command
the revolving world of war beneath your sway!
I call on the springs and streams, the gods enthroned
in the arching sky and gods of the deep blue sea!
If by chance the victory goes to the Latin, Turnus,
we agree the defeated will depart to Evander's city,
Iulus will leave this land. Nor will Aeneas' Trojans   220
ever revert in times to come, take up arms again
and threaten to put this kingdom to the sword.
But if Victory grants our force-in-arms the day,
as I think she may—may the gods decree it so—
I shall not command Italians to bow to Trojans,
nor do I seek the scepter for myself.
May both nations, undefeated, under equal laws,
march together toward an eternal pact of peace.
I shall bestow the gods and their sacred rites.

My father-in-law Latinus will retain his armies,   230
my father-in-law, his power, his rightful rule.
The men of Troy will erect a city for me—
Lavinia will give its walls her name."

    So Aeneas begins, and so Latinus follows,
eyes lifted aloft, his right hand raised to the sky:
"I swear by the same, Aeneas, earth and sea and stars,
by Latona's brood of twins, by Janus facing left and right,
by the gods who rule below and the shrine of ruthless Death,
may the Father hear my oath, his lightning seals all pacts!
My hand on his altar now, I swear by the gods and fires   240
that rise between us here, the day will never dawn
when Italian men will break this pact, this peace,
however fortune falls. No power can bend awry
my will, not if that power sends the country
avalanching into the waves, roiling all in floods
and plunging the heavens into the dark pit of hell.
Just as surely as this scepter"—raising the scepter
he chanced to be grasping in his hand—"will never
sprout new green or scatter shade from its tender leaves,
now that it's been cut from its trunk's base in the woods,   250
cleft from its mother, its limbs and crowning foliage lost
to the iron axe. A tree, once, that a craftsman's hands
have sheathed in hammered bronze and given the chiefs
of Latium's state to wield."
                              So, on such terms
they sealed a pact of peace between both sides,
witnessed by all the officers of the armies.
Then they slash the throats of the hallowed victims
over the flames, and tear their pulsing entrails out
and heap the altars high with groaning platters.

    But in fact the duel had long seemed uneven   260
to all the Rutulians, long their hearts were torn,
wavering back and forth, and they only wavered more
as they viewed the two contenders at closer range,
poorly matched in power . . .

Turnus adds to their anguish, quietly moving toward
the altar, eyes downcast, to pray. A suppliant now,
his fresh cheeks and his strong young body pallid.
Soon as his sister Juturna saw such murmurs rise
and the hearts of people slipping into doubt,
into the lines she goes like Camers to the life,   270
a soldier sprung from a grand ancestral clan:
his father a name for valor, brilliant deeds,
and he himself renowned for feats of arms.
Into the center lines Juturna strides,
alert to the work at hand,
and she sows a variety of rumors, urging:
"Aren't you ashamed, Rutulians, putting at risk
the life of one to save us all? Don't we match them
in numbers, power? Look, these are all they've got—
Trojans, Arcadians, and all the Etruscan forces,   280
slaves to Fate—to battle Turnus in arms! Why,
if only half of us went to war, each soldier
could hardly find a foe. But Turnus, think,
he'll rise on the wings of fame to meet the gods,
gods on whose altars he has offered up his life:
he will live forever, sung on the lips of men!
But we, if we lose our land, will bow to the yoke,
enslaved by our new high lords and masters—
we who idle on amid our fields!"
                                        Stinging taunts
inflame the will of the fighters all the more   290
till a low growing murmur steals along the lines.
Even Laurentines, even Latins change their tune,
men who had just now longed for peace and safety
long for weapons, pray the pact be dashed
and pity the unjust fate that Turnus faces.
Then, crowning all, Juturna adds a greater power.
She displays in the sky the strongest sign that ever
dazed Italian minds and deceived them with its wonders.
The golden eagle of Jove, in flight through the blood-red sky,
was harrying shorebirds, routing their squadron's shrieking ranks   300
when suddenly down he swoops to the stream and grasps a swan,

out in the lead, in his ruthless talons. This the Italians
watch, enthralled as the birds all scream and swerving
round in flight—a marvel, look—they overshadow
the sky with wings, and forming a dense cloudbank,
force their enemy high up through the air until,
beaten down by their strikes and his victim's weight,
his talons dropped the kill in the river's run
and into the clouds the eagle winged away.
                                                      Struck,
the Italians shout out, saluting that great omen,   310
all hands eager to take up arms, and the augur
Tolumnius urges first: "This, this," he cries,
"is the answer to all my prayers! I embrace it,
I recognize the gods! I, I will lead you—
reach for your swords now, my poor people!
Like helpless birds, terrorized by the war
that ruthless invader brings you,
devastating your shores by force of arms.
He too will race in flight and wing away,
setting his sails to cross the farthest seas.   320
Close ranks. Every man of you mass with one resolve!
Fight to save your king the marauder seized!"
                                                      Enough.
Lunging out he whips a spear at the foes he faced
and the whizzing javelin hisses, rips the air dead-on—
and at that instant a huge outcry, ranks in a wedge
in disarray, lines buckling, hearts at a fever pitch
as the shaft wings on where a band of nine brothers
with fine bodies chanced to block its course. One
mother bore them all, a Tuscan, loyal Tyrrhena wed
to Gylippus, her Arcadian husband. And one of these,   330
in the waist where the braided belt chafes the flesh
and the buckle clasps the strap from end to end—
a striking, well-built soldier in burnished bronze—
the spear splits his ribs and splays him out on the sand.
But his brothers, a phalanx up in arms, enflamed by grief,
some tear swords from sheaths and some snatch up their spears
and all press blindly on. As the Latian columns charge them,

charging *them* come Agyllines and Trojans streaming up
with Arcadian ranks decked out in blazoned gear and
one lust drives them all: to let the sword decide.   340
Altars plundered for torches, down from menacing clouds
a torrent of spears, and the iron rain pelts thick-and-fast
as they carry off the holy bowls and sacred braziers.
Even Latinus flees, cradling his defeated gods and
shattered pact of peace. Others harness teams
to chariots, others vault up onto their horses,
swords brandished, tense for attack.
                                   Messapus,
keen to disrupt the truce, whips his charger straight
at Tuscan Aulestes, king adorned with his kingly emblems,
forcing him back in terror. And back he trips, poor man,   350
stumbling, crashing head over shoulders into the altar
rearing behind him there, and Messapus, fired up now.
flies at him, looming over him, high in the saddle
to strike him dead with his rugged beamy lance,
the king begging for mercy, Messapus shouting:
"This one's finished! Here,
a choicer victim offered up to the great gods!"—
and the Latins rush to strip the corpse still warm.
Rushing to block them, Corynaeus grabs a flaming torch
from the altar—just so Ebysus can't strike first—and hurls   360
fire in the Latin's face and his huge beard flares up,
reeking with burnt singe. And following on that blow
he seizes his dazed foe's locks in his left hand and
pins him fast to the ground with a knee full force
and digs his rigid blade in Ebysus' flank.
                                   Podalirius,
tracking the shepherd Alsus, hurtles through the front
where the spears shower down, he's rearing over him now
with his naked sword but Alsus, swirling his axehead back,
strikes him square in the skull, cleaving brow to chin
and convulsive sprays of blood imbrue his armor.   370
Grim repose and an iron sleep press down his eyes
and shut their light in a night that never ends.
                                   But Aeneas,

bound to his oath, his head exposed and the hand unarmed
he was stretching toward his comrades, shouted out:
"Where are you running? Why this sudden outbreak,
why these clashes? Rein your anger in!
The pact's already struck, its terms are set.
Now I alone have the right to enter combat.
Don't hold me back. Cast your fears to the wind!
This strong right arm will put our truce to the proof.   380
Our rites have already made the life of Turnus mine."

        Just in the midst of these, these outcries, look,
a winging arrow whizzes in and it hits Aeneas.
Nobody knows who shot it, whirled it on to bring
the Rutulians such renown—what luck, what god—
the shining fame of the feat is shrouded over now.
Nobody boasted he had struck Aeneas. No one.
                                             Turnus,
soon as he saw Aeneas falling back from the lines,
his chiefs in disarray, ignites with a blaze of hope.
He demands his team and arms at once, in a flash of pride   390
he leaps up onto his chariot, tugging hard on the reins
and races on and droves of the brave he hands to death
and tumbles droves of the half-dead down to earth
or crushes whole detachments under his wheels or
seizing their lances, cuts down all who cut and run.
Amok as Mars by the banks of the Hebrus frozen over—
splattered with blood, fired to fury, drumming his shield
as he whips up war and gives his frenzied team free rein and
over the open fields they outstrip the winds from South and West
till the far frontiers of Thrace groan to their pounding hoofs   400
and round him the shapes of black Fear, Rage and Ambush,
aides of the war-god gallop on and on. Just so madly
Turnus whips his horses into the heart of battle,
chargers steaming sweat, trampling enemy fighters
killed in agony—kicking gusts of bloody spray,
their hoofs stamping into the sand the clotted gore.
Now he's dealing death to Sthenelus, Thamyris, Pholus:
Sthenelus speared at long-range, the next two hand-to-hand,

at a distance too both sons of Imbrasus, Glaucus and Lades.
Imbrasus had reared them himself in Lycia once and   410
equipped them both with matching weapons either
to fight close-up or outrace the winds on horseback.

    Another sector. Eumedes charges into the melee,
grandson of old Eumedes, bearing that veteran's name
but famed for his father Dolon's heart and hand in war.
Dolon, who once dared to ask for Achilles' chariot,
his reward for spying out the Achaean camp
but Diomedes paid his daring a different reward—
now he no longer dreams of the horses of Achilles.
Eumedes . . . spotting him far out on the open meadow,   420
Turnus hits him first with a light spear winged across
that empty space then races up to him, halts his team, and
rearing over the dying Trojan, plants a foot on his neck
and tears the sword from his grip—a flash of the blade—
he stains it red in the man's throat, and to top it off
cries out: "Look here, Trojan, here are the fields,
the great Land of the West you fought to win in war.
Lie there, take their measure. That's the reward
they all will carry off who risk my blade,
that's how they build their walls!"
                                  A whirl of his spear   430
and Turnus sends Asbytes to join him, Chloreus too
and Sybaris, Dares, Thersilochus, then Thymoetes,
pitched down over the neck of his bucking horse.
Like a blast of the Thracian Northwind howling over
the deep Aegean, whipping the waves toward shore, wherever
the winds burst down the clouds take flight through the sky,
so Turnus, wherever he hacks his path, the lines buckle in
and the ranks turn tail and run as his own drive sweeps him on,
his rushing chariot charging the gusts that toss his crest.
Phegeus could not face his assault, his deafening cries;   440
he flung himself before the chariot, right hand wrestling
the horses' jaws around as they came charging into him,
frothing at their bits, then dragged him dangling down
from the yoke as Turnus' spearhead hit his exposed flank

and ripping the double links of his breastplate, there it stuck,
just grazing the fighter's skin. But raising his shield,
swerving to brave his foe, he strained to save himself
with his naked sword—when the wheel and whirling axle
knocked him headlong, ground him into the dust. Turnus,
finishing up with a stroke between the helmet's base   450
and the breastplate's upper rim, hacked off his head
and left his trunk in the sand.
                                   And now, while Turnus
is spreading death across the plains in all his triumph,
Mnestheus and trusty Achates, Ascanius at their side,
are setting Aeneas down in camp—bleeding, propping
himself on his lengthy spear at every other step . . .
Furious, struggling to tear the broken arrowhead out,
he insists they take the quickest way to heal him:
"Cut the wound with a broadsword, open it wide,
dig out the point where it's bedded deep   460
and put me back into action!"

    Now up comes Iapyx, Iasius' son, and dear
to Apollo, more than all other men, and once,
in the anguished grip of love, the god himself
gladly offered him all his own arts, his gifts,
his prophetic skills, his lyre, his flying shafts.
But he, desperate to slow the death of his dying father,
preferred to master the power of herbs, the skills that cure,
and pursue a healer's practice, silent and unsung. But Aeneas,
pressed by a crowd of friends and Iulus grieving sorely—   470
the fighter stood there bridling, fuming, hunched
on his rugged spear, unmoved by all their tears.
The old surgeon, his robe tucked back and cinched
in the healer's way, with his expert, healing hands
and Apollo's potent herbs he works for all he's worth.
No use, no use as his right hand tugs at the shaft
and his clamping forceps grip the iron point.
No good luck guides his probes,
Apollo the Master lends no help, and all the while
the ruthless horror of war grows greater, grimmer   480

throughout the field, a disaster ever closer . . .
Now they see a pillar of dust upholding the sky
and the horsemen riding on and dense salvos of weapons
raining down in the camp's heart, and the cries of torment
reach the heavens as young men fight and die beneath
the iron fist of Mars.
                    At this point, Venus,
shocked by the unfair pain her son endures,
culls with a mother's care some dittany fresh
from Cretan Ida, spear erect with its tender leaves
and crown of purple flowers. No stranger to wild goats   490
who graze it when flying arrows are planted in their backs.
This she bears away, her features veiled in a heavy mist,
this she distils in secret into the river water poured
in burnished bowls, and fills them with healing power
and sprinkles ambrosial juices bringing health,
and redolent cure-all too. With this potion,
aged Iapyx laved the wound, quite unaware, and
suddenly all the pain dissolved from Aeneas' body, all
the blood that pooled in his wound stanched, and the shaft,
with no force required, slipped out in the healer's hand   500
and the old strength came back, fresh as it was at first.
"Quick, fetch him his weapons! Don't just stand there!"—
Iapyx cries, the first to inflame their hearts against the foe.
"This strong cure, it's none of the work of human skills,
no expert's arts in action. My right hand, Aeneas,
never saved your life. Something greater—
a god—is speeding you back to greater exploits."

     Starved for war, Aeneas had cased his calves in gold,
left and right, and spurning delay, he shakes his glinting spear.
Once he has fitted shield to hip and harness to his back,   510
he clasps Ascanius fast in an iron-clad embrace
and kissing him lightly through his visor, says:
"Learn courage from me, my son, true hardship too.
Learn good luck from others. My hand will shield you
in war today and guide you toward the great rewards.
But mark my words. Soon as you ripen into manhood,

reaching back for the models of your kin, remember—
father Aeneas and uncle Hector fire your heart!"

    Urgings over, out of the gates he strode,
immense in strength, waving his massive spear.   520
Antheus and Mnestheus flank him closely, dashing on
and from the deserted camp roll all their swarming ranks.
The field is a swirl of blinding dust, the earth quaking
under their thundering tread. From the opposing rampart
Turnus saw them coming on, his Italians saw them too
and an icy chill of dread ran through their bones.
First in the Latin ranks, Juturna caught the sound,
she knew what it meant and, seized with trembling, fled.
But Aeneas flies ahead, spurring his dark ranks on and storming
over the open fields like a cloudburst wiping out the sun,   530
sweeping over the seas toward land, and well in advance
the poor unlucky farmers, hearts shuddering, know
what it will bring—trees uprooted, crops destroyed,
their labor in ruins far and wide—and the winds come first,
churning in uproar toward the shore. So the Trojans storm in,
their commander heading them toward the foe, their tight ranks
packed in a wedge, comrade linked with comrade massing hard.
A slash of a sword—Thymbraeus finished giant Osiris,
Mnestheus kills Arcetius, Achates hacks Epulo down
and Gyas, Ufens. Even the seer Tolumnius falls,   540
the first to wing a lance against the foe.
Cries hit the heavens—now it's the Latins' time
to turn tail and flee across the fields in a cloud of dust.
Aeneas never stoops to leveling men who show their backs
or makes for the ones who fight him fairly, toe-to-toe,
or the ones who fling their spears at longer range.
No, it's Turnus alone he's tracking, eyes alert
through the murky haze of battle, Turnus alone
Aeneas demands to fight.
                              Juturna, terror-struck
at the thought, the woman warrior knocks Metiscus,   550
Turnus' charioteer, from between the reins he grasps
and leaves him sprawling far from the chariot pole

as she herself takes over, shaking the rippling reins
like Metiscus to the life, his voice, his build, his gear.
Quick as a black swift darts along through the great halls
of a wealthy lord, and scavenging morsels, banquet scraps
for her chirping nestlings, all her twitterings echo now
in the empty colonnades, now round the brimming ponds.
So swiftly Juturna drives her team at the Trojan center,
darts along in her chariot whirling through the field,   560
now here, there, displaying her brother in his glory, true,
but she never lets him come to grips, she swerves far away.
But Aeneas, no less bent on meeting up with the enemy,
stalks his victim, circling round him, turn by turn
and his shrill cries call him through the broken ranks.
As often as he caught sight of his prey and strained
to outstrip the speed of that team that raced the wind,
so often Juturna wheeled the chariot round and swooped away.
What should he do? No hope. He seethes on a heaving sea
as warring anxieties call him back and forth.
                              Then Messapus,   570
just sprinting along with a pair of steel-tipped spears
in his left hand, training one on the Trojan, lets it fly—
right on target. Aeneas stopped in his tracks and huddled
under his shield, crouching down on a knee but the spear
in its onrush swiped the peak of his helmet off and
swept away the plumes that crowned his crest.
Aeneas erupts in anger, stung by treachery now
and seeing Turnus' horses swing his chariot round
and speed away, over and over he calls out to Jove,
to the altars built for the treaty now a shambles.   580
Then, at last, he hurtles into the thick of battle
as Mars drives him on, and terrible, savage, inciting
slaughter, sparing none, he gives his rage free rein.

Now what god can unfold for me so many terrors?
Who can make a song of slaughter in all its forms—
the deaths of captains down the entire field,
dealt now by Turnus, now by Aeneas, kill for kill?
Did it please you so, great Jove, to see the world at war,

the peoples clash that would later live in everlasting peace?

    Aeneas takes on Rutulian Sucro—here was the first duel   590
that ground the Trojan charge to a halt—and meets the man
with no long visit, just a quick stab in his flank and
the ruthless sword-blade splits the ribcage, thrusting
into the heart where death comes lightning fast.
                                  Turnus,
hurling the brothers Amycus and Diores off their mounts,
attacks them on foot and one he strikes with a long spear,
rushing at Turnus, one he runs through with a sword and
severing both their heads, he dangles them from his car
as he carts them off in triumph dripping blood.
                                 Aeneas
packs them off to death, Talos, Tanais, staunch Cethegus,   600
all three at a single charge, then grim Onites too,
named for his Theban line, his mother called Peridia.
                                 Turnus
kills the brothers fresh from Apollo's Lycian fields
and next Menoetes who, in his youth, detested war
but war would be his fate. An Arcadian angler
skilled at working the rivers of Lerna stocked with fish,
his lodgings poor, a stranger to all the gifts of the great,
and his father farmed his crops on rented land.
                               Like fires
loosed from adverse sides into woodlands dry as tinder,
thickets of rustling laurel, or foaming rivers hurling   610
down from a mountain ridge and roaring out to sea,
each leaves a path of destruction in its wake.
Just as furious now those two, Aeneas, Turnus
rampaging through the battle, now their fury
boils over inside them, now their warring hearts
at the breaking point—they don't concede defeat—
and now they hack their wounding ways with all their force.

    Here's Murranus sounding off the names of his forebears,
all his fathers' fathers' line from the start of time,
his entire race come down from the Latin kings . . .   620

Headlong down Aeneas smashes the braggart with a rock,
a whirling boulder's power that splays him on the ground,
snarled in the reins and yoke as the wheels roll him on
and under their thundering hoofbeats both his galloping horses—
all thought of their master vanished—trample him to death.
Here's Hyllus rushing in with his bloodcurdling rage
but Turnus rushing to block him whips a spear at his brow
that splits his gilded helmet, sticks erect in his brain.
And your sword-arm, Cretheus, bravest Greek afield—
it could not snatch you from Turnus,   630
nor did the gods he worshipped save Cupencus' life
when Aeneas came his way: he thrust his chest at the blade
but his brazen shield, poor priest, could not put off his death.
And Aeolus, you too, the Laurentine fields saw you go down
and your body spread across the earth. Down you went,
whom neither the Greek battalions could demolish,
nor could Achilles, who razed the realms of Priam.
Here was your finish line, the end of life.
Your halls lie under Ida, high halls at Lyrnesus
but here in Laurentine soil lies your tomb.

                                  All on attack—   640
the armies wheeling around for combat, all the Latins,
all the Trojans—Mnestheus, fierce Serestus,
Messapus breaker of horses, brawny Asilas—
the Etruscan squadron, Evander's Arcadian wings,
each fighter at peak strength, all force put to the test
as they soldier on, no rest, no letup—total war.

                                     And now
his lovely mother impelled Aeneas to storm the ramparts,
hurl his troops at the city—fast, frontal assault—
and panic the Latins faced with swift collapse.
And he, stalking Turnus through the moil of battle,   650
Aeneas' glances roving left and right, sights the town
untouched by this ruthless war, immune, at peace and
an instant vision of fiercer combat fires his soul.
He summons Mnestheus, Sergestus, staunch Serestus,
chosen captains, takes his stand on a high rise
where the rest of the Trojan fighters cluster round,

tight ranks that don't throw down their shields and spears
as Aeneas, rising amidst them, urges from the earthwork:
"No delay in obeying my orders—Jove backs us now!
No slowing down, I tell you, we must strike at once!   660
That city, the cause of the war, the heart of Latinus' realm—
unless they bow to the yoke, brought low this very day,
I'll topple their smoking rooftops to the ground.
What, wait till Turnus deigns to take me on?
Consents to fight me again, defeated as he is?
That city, my people, there's the core and crux
of this accursed war. Quick, bring torches!
Restore our truce with fire!"
                              A call to arms
and they pack in wedge formation bent on battle,
advancing toward the walls in a dense fighting mass—   670
in a moment you see ladders slanted, brands aflame.
Some charge at the gates and cut the sentries down
and others whirl their steel, blot out the sky with spears.
Aeneas himself, up in the lead beneath the ramparts,
raises his arm and thunders out, upbraiding Latinus,
calling the gods: "Bear witness, I've been dragged
into battle once again! The Latins are our enemies
twice over—this is the second pact they've shattered!"
And Discord surges up in the panic-stricken citizens,
some insisting the gates be flung wide to the Dardans,   680
yes, and they hale the king himself toward the walls.
Others seize on weapons, rush to defend the ramparts . . .
Picture a shepherd tracking bees to their rocky den,
closed up in the clefts he fills with scorching smoke
and all inside, alarmed by the danger, swarming round
through their stronghold walled with wax, hone sharp
their rage to a piercing buzz and the black reek
goes churning through their house and the rocks hum
with a blind din and the smoke spews out into thin air.

    Now a new misfortune assailed the battle-weary Latins,   690
rocking their city to its roots with grief. The queen—
when from her house she sees the enemy coming strong,

walls assaulted, flames surging up to the roofs and no
Rutulian force in sight to block their way, no troops of Turnus,
then, poor woman, she thinks him killed in the press of war
and suddenly lost in the frenzied grip of sorrow, claims
that she's the cause, the criminal, source of disaster—
shrilling wild words in her crazed, grieving fit and
bent on death, ripping her purple gown for a noose,
she knots it high to a rafter, dies a gruesome death.   700
As soon as the wretched Latin women hear the worst,
the queen's daughter Lavinia is the first to tear
her golden hair and score her lustrous cheeks,
the rest of the women round her mad with grief and
the long halls resound with trilling wails of sorrow.
From here the terrible news goes racing through the city,
spirits plunge—Latinus, rending his robes to tatters,
stunned by his wife's death and his city's fall,
fouls his white hair with showers of dust.
                                        Turnus
at this point, fighting off on the outskirts of the field,   710
is hunting a few stragglers. Yet he's less avid now,
exulting less and less when his horses win the day.
But the winds bring him a hint of hidden terrors,
mingled cries drifting out of the town in chaos.
A muffled din. He cocks his ears, listening . . .
hardly the sound of joy. "What am I hearing,
why this enormous grief that rocks the walls,
this clamor echoing from the city far away?"

    So he wonders, madly tugging the reins back
and makes the chariot stop.
                            But his sister, changed   720
to look like his charioteer, Metiscus, handling the car
and team and reins, she faced him with this challenge:
"This way, Turnus! We'll hunt these Trojans down
where victory opens up the first way in.
Other hands can defend our city walls. Aeneas
hurtles down on the Latins—all-out assault—
but we can deal out savage death to his Trojans.

You'll return from the front no less than Aeneas
in numbers killed and battle honors won!"

                                        "My sister,"
Turnus replies, "I recognized you long ago, yes,   730
when you first broke up our treaty with your wiles
and threw yourself into combat. No hiding your godhood,
you can't fool me now. But what Olympian wished it so,
who sent you down to bear such heavy labor? Why,
to witness your luckless brother's painful death?
What do I do now? What new twist of Fortune
can save me now? I've seen with my own eyes,
calling out to me 'Turnus!' as he fell . . .
Murranus—no one dearer to me survived,
a great soldier taken down by a great wound.   740
Unlucky Ufens died before he could see my shame
and the Trojans commandeered his corpse and weapons.
Must I bear the sight of Latinus' houses razed—
the last thing I needed—and not rebut
the ugly slander of Drances with my sword?
Shall I cut and run? Shall the country look
on Turnus in full retreat? To die, tell me,
is that the worst we face? Be good to me now,
you shades of the dead below, for the gods above
have turned away their favors. Down to you I go,   750
a spirit cleansed, utterly innocent as charged,
forever worthy of my great fathers' fame!"

        The words were still on his lips when, look,
Saces, riding his lathered horse through enemy lines
and slashed where an arrow raked his face, comes racing up,
calling for help, crying the name of Turnus: "Turnus,
you are our last best hope! Pity your own people.
Aeneas strikes like lightning! Up in arms he threatens
to topple Italy's towers, bring them down in ruins,
already the flaming brands go winging toward the roofs.   760
The Latins, their eyes, their looks are trained on you.
Latinus, the king himself, moans and groans with doubt—
whom to call his sons? Which pact can he embrace?

And now the queen, whose trust lay all in you,
she's dead by her own hand,
terrified, she's fled the light of life.
Alone before the gates Messapus and brave Atinas
hold our front lines steady, ringed by enemy squadrons
packed tight, bristling a jagged crop of naked blades!
While look at you, wheeling your chariot round   770
the abandoned grassy fields!"

                              Stunned by pictures
of these disasters blurring through his mind,
Turnus stood there, staring, speechless, churning
with mighty shame, with grief and madness all aswirl
in that one fighting heart: with love spurred by rage
and a sense of his own worth too. As soon as the shadows
were dispersed and the light restored to his mind,
he turned his fiery glance toward the ramparts,
glaring back from his chariot to the town.

                              But now,
look, a whirlwind of fire goes rolling story to story,   780
billowing up the sky, and clings fast to a mobile tower,
a defense he built himself of wedged, rough-hewn beams,
fitting the wheels below it, gangways reared above.
"Now, now, my sister, the Fates are in command.
Don't hold me back. Where God and relentless
Fortune call us on, that's the way we go!
I'm set on fighting Aeneas hand-to-hand,
set, however bitter it is, to meet my death.
You'll never see me disgraced again—no more.
Insane as it is, I beg you, let me rage before I die!"   790

      He leapt from his chariot, hit the ground at a run
through enemies, Trojan spears, and left his sister
grieving as he went bursting through the lines.
Wild as a boulder plowing headlong down from a summit,
torn out by the tempests—whether the stormwinds washed it free
or the creeping years stole under it, worked it loose,
down the cliff it crashes, ruthless crag of rock
bounding over the ground with enormous impact,

churning up in its onrush woods and herds and men.
So Turnus bursts through the fractured ranks, charging   800
toward the walls where the earth runs red with blood
and the winds hiss with spears and, hand flung up,
he cries with a ringing voice: "Hold back now,
you Rutulians! Latins, keep your arms in check!
Whatever Fortune sends, it's mine. Better
for me alone to redeem the pact for you
and let my sword decide!"
                                        All ranks scattered,
leaving a no-man's-land between them both.
                                        But Aeneas,
the great commander, hearing the name of Turnus,
deserts the walls, deserts the citadel's heights   810
and breaks off all operations, jettisons all delay—
he springs in joy, drums his shield and it thunders terror.
As massive as Athos, massive as Eryx or even Father
Apennine himself, roaring out with his glistening oaks,
elated to raise his snow-capped brow to the winds. And then,
for a fact, the Rutulians, Trojans, all the Italians,
those defending the high ramparts, those on attack
who batter the walls' foundations with their rams:
all armies strained to turn their glances round
and lifted their battle-armor off their shoulders.   820
Latinus himself is struck that these two giant men,
sprung from opposing ends of the earth, have met,
face-to-face, to let their swords decide.
                                        But they,
as soon as the battlefield lay clear and level,
charge at speed, rifling their spears at long range,
then rush to battle with shields and clanging bronze.
The earth groans as stroke after stroke they land
with naked swords: fortune and fortitude mix
in one assault. Charging like two hostile bulls
fighting up on Sila's woods or Taburnus' ridges,   830
ramping in mortal combat, both brows bent for attack
and the herdsmen back away in fear and the whole herd
stands by, hushed, afraid, and the heifers wait and wonder,

who will lord it over the forest? who will lead the herd?—
while the bulls battle it out, horns butting, locking,
goring each other, necks and shoulders roped in blood
and the woods resound as they grunt and bellow out.
So they charge, Trojan Aeneas and Turnus, son of Daunus,
shields clang and the huge din makes the heavens ring.
Jove himself lifts up his scales, balanced, trued,   840
and in them he sets the opposing fates of both . . .
Whom would the labor of battle doom? Whose life
would weigh him down to death?

              Suddenly Turnus
flashes forward, certain he's in the clear and
raising his sword high, rearing to full stretch
strikes—as Trojans and anxious Latins shout out,
with the gaze of both armies riveted on the fighters.
But his treacherous blade breaks off, it fails Turnus
in mid stroke—enraged, his one recourse, retreat,
and swifter than Eastwinds, Turnus flies as soon   850
as he sees that unfamiliar hilt in his hand,
no defense at all. They say the captain, rushing
headlong on to harness his team and board his car
to begin the duel, left his father's sword behind
and hastily grabbed his charioteer Metiscus' blade.
Long as the Trojan stragglers took to their heels and ran,
the weapon did its work, but once it came up against
the immortal armor forged by the God of Fire, Vulcan,
the mortal sword burst at a stroke, brittle as ice,
and glinting splinters gleamed on the tawny sand.   860
So raging Turnus runs for it, scours the field,
now here, now there, weaving in tangled circles
as Trojans crowd him hard, a dense ring of them
shutting him in, with a wild swamp to the left
and steep walls to the right.

              Nor does Aeneas flag,
though slowed down by his wound, his knees unsteady,
cutting his pace at times but he's still in full fury,
hot on his frantic quarry's tracks, stride for stride.
Alert as a hunting hound that lights on a trapped stag,

hemmed in by a river's bend or frightened back by the ropes   870
with blood-red feathers—the hound barking, closing, fast
as the quarry, panicked by traps and the steep riverbanks,
runs off and back in a thousand ways but the Umbrian hound,
keen for the kill, hangs on the trail, his jaws agape—
and now, now he's got him, thinks he's got him, yes
and his jaws clap shut, stymied, champing the empty air.
Then the shouts break loose, and the banks and rapids round
resound with the din, and the high sky thunders back. Turnus—
even in flight he rebukes his men as he races, calling
each by name, demanding his old familiar sword.   880
Aeneas, opposite, threatens death and doom at once
to anyone in his way, he threatens his harried foes
that he'll root their city out and, wounded as he is,
keeps closing for the kill. And five full circles
they run and reel as many back, around and back,
for it's no mean trophy they're sporting after now,
they race for the life and the lifeblood of Turnus.

      By chance a wild olive, green with its bitter leaves,
stood right here, sacred to Faunus, revered by men
in the old days, sailors saved from shipwreck.   890
On it they always fixed their gifts to the local god
and they hung their votive clothes in thanks for rescue.
But the Trojans—no exceptions, hallowed tree that it was—
chopped down its trunk to clear the spot for combat.
Now here the spear of Aeneas had stuck, borne home
by its hurling force, and the tough roots held it fast.
He bent down over it, trying to wrench the iron loose and
track with a spear the kill he could not catch on foot.
Turnus, truly beside himself with terror—"Faunus!"
he cried, "I beg you, pity me! You, dear Earth,   900
hold fast to that spear! If I have always kept
your rites—a far cry from Aeneas' men
who stain your rites with war."
                                    So he appealed,
calling out for the god's help, and not for nothing.
Aeneas struggled long, wasting time on the tough stump,

no power of *his* could loose the timber's stubborn bite.
As he bravely heaves and hauls, the goddess Juturna,
changing back again to the charioteer Metiscus,
rushes in and returns her brother's sword to Turnus.
But Venus, incensed that the nymph has had her brazen way,   910
steps up and plucks Aeneas' spear from the clinging root.
So standing tall, with their arms and fighting hearts refreshed—
one who trusted all to his sword, the other looming fiercely
with his spear—confronting each other, both men breathless,
brace for the war-god's fray.
                                        Now at the same moment
Jove, the king of mighty Olympus, turns to Juno,
gazing down on the war from her golden cloud, and says:
"Where will it end, my queen? What is left at the last?
Aeneas the hero, god of the land: you know yourself,
you confess you know that he is heaven bound,   920
his fate will raise Aeneas to the stars.
What are you plotting? What hope can make you
cling to the chilly clouds? So, was it right
for a mortal hand to wound, to mortify a god?
Right to restore that mislaid sword to Turnus—
for without your power what could Juturna do?—
and lend the defeated strength? Have done at last.
Bow to my appeals. Don't let your corrosive grief
devour you in silence, or let your dire concerns come
pouring from your sweet lips and plaguing me forever.   930
We have reached the limit. To harass the Trojans
over land and sea, to ignite an unspeakable war,
degrade a royal house and blend the wedding hymn
with the dirge of grief: all that lay in your power.
But go no further. I forbid you now."
                                        Jove said no more.
And so, with head bent low, Saturn's daughter replied:
"Because I have known your will so well, great Jove,
against my *own* I deserted Turnus and the earth.
Or else you would never see me now, alone
on a windswept throne enduring right and wrong.   940
No, wrapped in flames I would be up on the front lines,

dragging the Trojan into mortal combat. Juturna?
I was the one, I admit, who spurred her on
to help her embattled brother, true, and blessed
whatever greater daring it took to save his life,
but never to shower arrows, never tense the bow.
I swear by the unappeasable fountainhead of the Styx,
the one dread oath decreed for the gods on high.

                            "So,
now I yield, Juno yields, and I leave this war I loathe.
But this—and there is no law of Fate to stop it now—   950
this I beg for Latium, for the glory of your people.
When, soon, they join in their happy wedding-bonds—
and wedded let them be—in pacts of peace at last,
never command the Latins, here on native soil,
to exchange their age-old name,
to become Trojans, called the kin of Teucer,
alter their language, change their style of dress.
Let Latium endure. Let Alban kings hold sway for all time.
Let Roman stock grow strong with Italian strength.
Troy has fallen—and fallen let her stay—   960
with the very name of Troy!"

                           Smiling down,
the creator of man and the wide world returned:
"Now there's my sister. Saturn's second child—
such tides of rage go churning through your heart.
Come, relax your anger. It started all for nothing.
I grant your wish. I surrender. Freely, gladly too.
Latium's sons will retain their fathers' words and ways.
Their name till now is the name that shall endure.
Mingling in stock alone, the Trojans will subside.
And I will add the rites and the forms of worship,   970
and make them Latins all, who speak one Latin tongue.
Mixed with Ausonian blood, one race will spring from them,
and you will see them outstrip all men, outstrip all gods
in reverence. No nation on earth will match the honors
they shower down on you."

                       Juno nodded assent to this,

her spirit reversed to joy. She departs the sky
and leaves her cloud behind.
                        His task accomplished,
the Father turned his mind to another matter, set
to dismiss Juturna from her brother's battles.
They say there are twin Curses called the Furies . . .   980
Night had born them once in the dead of darkness,
one and the same spawn, and birthed infernal Megaera,
wreathing all their heads with coiled serpents,
fitting them out with wings that race the wind.
They hover at Jove's throne, crouch at his gates
to serve that savage king
and whet the fears of afflicted men whenever
the king of gods lets loose horrific deaths and plagues
or panics towns that deserve the scourge of war.
Jove sped one of them down the sky, commanding: 990
"Cross Juturna's path as a wicked omen!"

    Down she swoops, hurled to earth by a whirlwind,
swift as a darting arrow whipped from a bowstring
through the clouds, a shaft armed by a Parthian,
tipped with deadly poison, shot by a Parthian
or a Cretan archer—well past any cure—
hissing on unseen through the rushing dark.
So raced this daughter of Night and sped to earth.
Soon as she spots the Trojan ranks and Turnus' lines
she quickly shrinks into that small bird that often,   1000
hunched at dusk on deserted tombs and rooftops, sings
its ominous song in shadows late at night. Shrunken so,
the demon flutters over and over again in Turnus' face,
screeching, drumming his shield with its whirring wings.
An eerie numbness unnerved him head to toe with dread,
his hackles bristled in horror, voice choked in his throat.

    Recognizing the Fury's ruffling wings at a distance,
wretched Juturna tears her hair, nails clawing her face,
fists beating her breast, and cries to her brother:

"How, Turnus, how can your sister help you now?   1010
What's left for me now, after all I have endured?
What skill do I have to lengthen out your life?
How can I fight against this dreadful omen?
At last, at last I leave the field of battle.
Afraid as I am, now frighten me no more,
you obscene birds of night! Too well I know
the beat of your wings, the drumbeat of doom.
Nor do the proud commands of Jove escape me now,
our great, warm-hearted Jove. Are these his wages
for taking my virginity? Why did he grant me life   1020
eternal—rob me of our one privilege, death?
Then, for a fact, I now could end this agony,
keep my brother company down among the shades.
Doomed to live forever? Without you, my brother,
what do I have still mine that's sweet to taste?
If only the earth gaped deep enough to take me down,
to plunge this goddess into the depths of hell!"
                                                With that,
shrouding her head with a gray-green veil and moaning low,
down to her own stream's bed the goddess sank away.

All hot pursuit, Aeneas brandishes high his spear,   1030
that tree of a spear, and shouts from a savage heart:
"More delay! Why now? Still in retreat, Turnus, why?
This is no foot-race. It's savagery, swordplay cut-and-thrust!
Change yourself into any shape you please, call up
whatever courage or skill you still have left.
Pray to wing your way to the starry sky
or bury yourself in the earth's deep pits!"

Turnus shakes his head: "I don't fear you,
you and your blazing threats, my fierce friend.
It's the gods that frighten me—Jove, my mortal foe."   1040

No more words. Glancing around he spots a huge rock,
huge, ages old, and lying out in the field by chance,

placed as a boundary stone to settle border wars.
A dozen picked men could barely shoulder it up, men
of such physique as the earth brings forth these days,
but he wrenched it up, hands trembling, tried to heave it
right at Aeneas, Turnus stretching to full height, the hero
at speed, at peak strength. Yet he's losing touch with himself,
racing, hoisting that massive rock in his hands and hurling,
true, but his knees buckle, blood's like ice in his veins   1050
and the rock he flings through the air, plummeting under
its own weight, cannot cover the space between them,
cannot strike full force . . .
                    Just as in dreams
when the nightly spell of sleep falls heavy on our eyes
and we seem entranced by longing to keep on racing on,
no use, in the midst of one last burst of speed
we sink down, consumed, our tongue won't work,
and tried and true, the power that filled our body
fails—we strain but the voice and words won't follow.
So with Turnus. Wherever he fought to force his way,   1060
no luck, the merciless Fury blocks his efforts.
A swirl of thoughts goes racing through his mind,
he glances toward his own Rutulians and their town,
he hangs back in dread, he quakes at death—it's here.
Where can he run? How can he strike out at the enemy?
Where's his chariot? His charioteer, his sister? Vanished.

    As he hangs back, the fatal spear of Aeneas streaks on—
spotting a lucky opening he had flung from a distance,
all his might and main. Rocks heaved by a catapult
pounding city ramparts never storm so loudly, never   1070
such a shattering bolt of thunder crashing forth.
Like a black whirlwind churning on, that spear
flies on with its weight of iron death to pierce
the breastplate's lower edge and the outmost rim
of the round shield with its seven plies and right
at the thick of Turnus' thigh it whizzes through,
it strikes home and the blow drops great Turnus

down to the ground, battered down on his bent knees.
The Rutulians spring up with a groan and the hillsides
round groan back and the tall groves far and wide   1080
resound with the long-drawn moan.
                                        Turnus lowered
his eyes and reached with his right hand and begged,
a suppliant: "I deserve it all. No mercy, please,"
Turnus pleaded. "Seize your moment now. Or if
some care for a parent's grief can touch you still,
I pray you—you had such a father, in old Anchises—
pity Daunus in his old age and send me back
to my own people, or if you would prefer,
send them my dead body stripped of life. Here,
the victor and vanquished, I stretch my hands to you,   1090
so the men of Latium have seen me in defeat.
Lavinia is your bride.
Go no further down the road of hatred."

    Aeneas, ferocious in armor, stood there, still,
shifting his gaze, and held his sword-arm back,
holding himself back too as Turnus' words began
to sway him more and more . . . when all at once
he caught sight of the fateful sword-belt of Pallas,
swept over Turnus' shoulder, gleaming with shining studs
Aeneas knew by heart. Young Pallas, whom Turnus had overpowered,   1100
taken down with a wound, and now his shoulder flaunted
his enemy's battle-emblem like a trophy. Aeneas,
soon as his eyes drank in that plunder—keepsake
of his own savage grief—flaring up in fury,
terrible in his rage, he cries: "Decked in the spoils
you stripped from one I loved—escape my clutches? Never—
Pallas strikes this blow, Pallas sacrifices you now,
makes you pay the price with your own guilty blood!"
In the same breath, blazing with wrath he plants
his iron sword hilt-deep in his enemy's heart.   1110
Turnus' limbs went limp in the chill of death.
His life breath fled with a groan of outrage
down to the shades below.

1

"*Homer* makes us Hearers, and *Virgil* leaves us Readers." So writes Alexander Pope in his preface to the *Iliad,* and so the great translator of Homer, no doubt unwittingly, sets at odds the claims of an oral tradition and those of a literary one, as we would call them now, or as C. S. Lewis calls their two protagonists, the Primary and the Secondary Epics. Much in their opposition rings true, especially with regard to Homer. Surely his work should impress us, audibly and irresistibly, as a performance and even in part a public, musical event. Homer makes us hearers indeed, and that may be a major source of his speed, directness, and simplicity, and his nobility too, elusive yet undeniable, that Matthew Arnold praised in recommending Homer, well more than a century after Pope, to the Victorian era and beyond. And yet Pope's contrast may be too extreme, and his characterization of Virgil, beyond the fact that Virgil was a writer, may be open to question. For according to Suetonius' "Life" of the poet, as the Introduction makes abundantly clear, Virgil was hardly a stranger to recitation. He was a remarkably effective reciter at that, especially when he read his work aloud in the presence of Augustus Caesar and Octavia, his sister.

And so, to turn to the translator, who writes at a far remove from Virgil in every way, I have tried to lend my work a performative cast as well. My approach to the *Aeneid,* in other words, resembles the one I took in rendering the *Iliad* and the *Odyssey*. With the *Aeneid,* however, I have aimed for certain more literary effects—occasional pauses for second thoughts, phrases that resonate a few ways at once—that writing, more than singing, will allow. And I have tried to modulate my voice a little further than I did with Homer, making it somewhat more intimate for Virgil, particularly for his introspective, often heartrending moments, and yet at the same time more formal too, for his famous, lapidary lines. In other words, at every step I have seen how impossible it is to translate Virgil, especially his unequaled blend of grandeur and accessibility (as Brooke Holmes suggests), of eloquence and action, heroics and humanity, and countless other features too. To cite only one, my voice is willing, if less than able, to sound "a thin wisp of a cry" (6.571), like that of the Greek dead in hell, for Virgil's great crescendos of battle that dominate the last four books.

Yet my versions of all three poems, different as those versions may be, share a common impulse. Again I have tried to find a middle ground (and not a no-man's-land, if I can help it) between the features of an ancient author and the expectations of a contemporary reader. Not a line-by-line translation, my version of the *Aeneid* is, I hope, neither so literal in rendering Virgil's language as to cramp and distort my own—though I want to convey as much of what he writes as possible—nor so "literary," in the stilted, bookish sense, as to brake his forward motion once too often. For the more literal approach would seem to be too little English, and the more "literary," too little Latin. I have tried to find a cross between the two: a modern English Virgil.

Of course it is a risky business, stating what one has tried to do, or worse, the principles one has used (petards that will probably hoist the writer later). Yet a few words of explanation seem in order, some further thoughts about "the Virgilian performance," at least as I understand it, and how it may condition my translation. I return to what many would observe, that, short of reciting in public, even our private acts of reading, and especially the Romans' private acts of reading, have by nature a dramatic side as well. As W. A. Camps reminds us, drawing from Quintilian, the Roman rhetorician, Latin education in the first century A.D. "laid a particular emphasis on the element of sound in style," and "sensitivity to this was general in a world in which the normal way of reading to oneself was to read aloud" (note p. 67). Virgil, to put it in Pope's terms, may write in order to "leave us readers," yet his writing "makes us hearers" too, reading alone and yet aloud, and listening for the writer's own distinctive voice.

And Virgil invites us to play a still more active role, as his preference for verbs in the historical present, rather than in the past tenses, may imply. The predominance of the historical present throughout the poem ("nearly two-thirds of all indicative verbs in the *Aeneid*," as Sara Mack reports, p. 48) has a range of effects upon the reader. They go from generating the broad, irrepressible sweep of the poem, which K. W. Gransden (1984, p. 76) and others note, to all that the Greek word *enargeia* can convey: the vividness, the immediacy, the dramatic impact of every action and every speech, as clear as Venus in Aeneas' eyes, "her pure radiance shining down upon [him] through the night" (2.731). Similarly, the reader is surrounded by a luminous, recurrent Now that not only captures his or her attention but also makes the reader a witness and even, within one's private study, a participant in a series of events. It is as if— Gransden again, to whom many of these remarks are much indebted— the "when" of an action is less important than the fact and "how" of its occurrence. And as Andreola Rossi pursues the point, most occurrences in the poem are presented "here and now" instead of "then and there," as Virgil creates "a forged continuum, even an identity, between the past retold and the present perceived" (p. 130).

Consequently the scenes on the Libyan temple that recall the late Trojan War unite with the unfolding, tragic events in Carthage that will take the life of Dido and, evoked by her dying curses, ultimately lead to the Punic Wars. The legendary Cyclops beat their metal into Aeneas' shield, emblazoning it with the triumphs of Rome that lie a thousand years ahead, yet the weld between the mythic and the historical, the miraculous work of Vulcan and the battle of Actium, is seamless. As T. S. Eliot muses in his Heraclitean way:

Time present and time past
are both perhaps present in time future,
and time future contained in time past.   (*Burnt Norton*, 1)

So frequent is Virgil's use of the historical present that he can intersperse the imperfect among his verbs, producing a confident shuttling back and forth in time, even within the same verse paragraph. The translation suggests the effect in a more cautious, discretionary way, to spare the English reader some confusion. Yet the historical present prevails, to register one of Virgil's leading ways of bringing home the *Aeneid* to his audience.

Other features of his performance do the same, each reinforcing the *enargeia* of his epic, and each has a bearing, however distant, on the translation at hand. One is Virgil's reputation, during his lifetime and cited by others now, for directness of speech, his preference for the plain instead of the "poetic" word, a preference I have often tried to follow. Another is Virgil's way of echoing himself. As John Swallow analyzes the matter, some echoes may be temporary props or *tibicines*, which Virgil used to keep his narrative flowing, rather than stop and search for the *mots justes* he hoped to find when he revised his work, like "a she-bear," as he described the process in Suetonius' "Life" (p. 473), and "gradually licked it into shape." But other echoes express the moral symmetry we call "poetic justice"—as when the lines describing Camilla's death by treachery (11.973–74) echo in the last lines of the poem, where Turnus dies at Aeneas' hands, not by treachery but as retribution outright for the death of Pallas. A contrast, yet also an echo reminding us, as R. D. Williams (1973, note 12.948) and W. S. Macguinness (1953, p. 13) remark, that far from stressing Aeneas' conquest rather than his cruelty, Virgil binds his final act to the other acts of cruelty that pervade the closing books. This and other echoes—when Latin context and English sense and syntax will permit—the translation often sounds within itself.

Even more important in bringing the *Aeneid* home are Virgil's numberless forms of expression that alert and delight the reader, galvanizing one's imagination, winning one's belief. I refer to the magnificent panoply of the epic poem, whose forms extend, to mention only a few, from the dramatic, when Aeneas recounts the fall of Troy for Dido—until, like Desdemona, she may wish "that heaven had made her such a man"—to the operatic, in Dido's arias and agonies of passion, to the pastoral interludes, formal elegies, martial catalogues, duels to the death, vehement debates between the gods on high, and urgent invocations of the Muse. And perhaps the most epic feature of all is one already mentioned: the pulsing sweep of the narrative itself, borne along by Virgil's voice, its rise and fall throughout the *Aeneid*'s length and breadth, "the enormous onward pressure" that C. S. Lewis felt as strongly in Virgil as he did in Milton, "of the great stream on which you are embarked" (1961, p. 46). No wonder Tennyson praises Virgil not only for his ennoblements, for wielding "the stateliest measure / ever moulded by the lips of man," but also for his sheer kinetic power, his "ocean-roll of rhythm" ("To Virgil"). And nothing makes it stronger than the rhythmic variety that Virgil offers, as Knox observes in his review of Fitzgerald's *Aeneid* (*The New Republic*, November 28, 1983, p. 36), "the infinite variations on the play of the Latin stress accent against the quantitative Greek meter [that] all combine to produce a music that works like an incantation."

So if, as Knox remarks in his Introductions to our *Iliad* and *Odyssey*, "the strongest weapon in [Homer's] poetic arsenal" is variety within a metrical norm, Virgil creates an analog in Latin, and the English translation tries, in a far-off way, to follow suit. However remotely, I have sought a compromise between Virgil's spacious hexameter, his "ocean-roll of rhythm," and a tighter line more native to English verse. Yet I have opted for a freer give-and-take, for more variety than uniformity with Virgil than with Homer. This may be unavoidable in trying to "unpack" Virgil's more compressed effects, his virtuoso displays of highly inflected, and deeply suggestive, word order, which can take one's breath away. In any event, working from a five- or six-beat line while leaning more to six, I expand at times to seven, to convey the reach of an "Homeric" simile in the *Aeneid,* or the vehemence of a storm at sea or a battle waged on land. Or I contract at times to three or four beats, not when Virgil does (perhaps implying with his half lines that revision is on its way), but to give a speech or action sharper stress in English. Free as it is, such variety in unity results, I suppose, from a kind of tug-of-war peculiar to translation: in this case, from trying to convey the meaning of the Latin on the one hand, and trying to find a cadence for one's English on the other, while joining hands, if possible, to make a line of verse. All told, I hope not only to give my own language a slight stretching now and then, but also to lend Virgil the sort of range in rhythm, pace and tone that may make a version of the *Aeneid,* like a version of the two Homeric poems, engaging to a modern reader.

For Virgil's performance in Latin is a reperformance of the *Iliad* and the *Odyssey* in Greek, a "Homerization" of the legendary past of Rome. This, of course, is a subject that has engaged generations of scholars and brought forth many a brilliant study over time. I can only touch on the broadest outlines of the matter here, and I do so from the viewpoint of a translator. At any rate, what announces the bond between Virgil's work and Homer's, as readers from Suetonius onward have remarked, are the first three words of the *Aeneid, arma virumque cano,* that sing the themes of war and humankind—the *Iliad* and the *Odyssey,* in effect—in one and the same phrase, and eventually in the same epic poem. As many observe, like Knox in his Introduction, Virgil presents an *Odyssey* of wandering in the first half of the *Aeneid* and an *Iliad* of warfare in the second. And as others have continued the analogy (usefully, for this translator), the Odyssean half of Virgil's epic has many Iliadic elements: Aeneas' narrative of the fall of Troy, and the funeral games for Anchises, and the return of many Trojan figures, some still alive, like Andromache and Helenus, and several more as ghosts. Similarly, the second, Iliadic half of the *Aeneid* has many Odyssean elements, chief among them perhaps the objective of the warfare waged: not to destroy an enemy capital but to found one's own, or as a later idiom would have it, to "win home" to the promised city, Rome.

Home, for since, as Gransden and Knox's Introduction remind us, the legendary founder of Troy and an ancestor of Aeneas was Dardanus, who migrated from Italy to Troy, Aeneas' arrival in Latium is a kind of *nostos* too, a return to the homeland of his forebears. His linear journey to a point is circular in result, like the motion of Achilles' rage and the homing of Odysseus, yet Virgil conceives his hero's journey on a larger, more historical—but in no way more compelling—scale. As Gransden sums up the matter, "Rome became in due time the new Troy, risen like the phoenix from the ashes of the destroyed city of Priam; indeed in the perspective of history the fall of Troy could be seen as the necessary precursor of the rise of Rome, and the whole mighty sequence as part of a divine plan, the working out of fate" (1990, p. 27). Or as Knox puts it, pungently, "The death agonies of Troy are the birthpangs of Rome" (Commager, p. 125), and the entire chain reaction binds together the *Iliad*, the *Odyssey*, and the *Aeneid*.

Virgil is the great translator of Homer, from phrase to simile to episode to epic scope and goal. And Virgil's every act of translation honors his source, not only by imitation but by emulation, a strenuous, competitive struggle in which Virgil may have found it "easier," as Virgil himself would say, "to filch his club from Hercules than a line from Homer" (Suetonius' "Life," p. 483). But in the *Aeneid* one may sense the exhilaration of influence as much as the anxiety, and watch the two at work in all their force, as when Aeneas narrates the fall of Troy, completing—and competing with?—Homer, who leaves the catastrophe, more dramatically for many, foreshadowed yet forever still to strike. Emulatively too, Virgil's leading characters often undertake a sequence or a composite of Homeric roles. Dido portrays the temptresses in the *Odyssey*, Circe and Calypso, who impede the hero's progress. But Dido is potentially still more vivid as Arete, who rules her ideal kingdom well, and as Nausicaa, who lends it a fresh young beauty, and ultimately as Penelope, loyal to Aeneas, if only he will embrace her as his queen.

Yet it is the hero himself who plays, at times inverting, at times asserting, the most consequential range of Homeric roles throughout the poem, until in his climactic action—killing Turnus—Aeneas resembles, at one and the same moment, an Achilles avenging the death of a cherished comrade, a Hector defending his homeland successfully, and an Odysseus winning his rightful bride by killing her suitor, reclaiming his kingdom, and laying the groundwork for its future. And Aeneas' range of Homeric roles within the *Aeneid* reflects his possible roles in later history as well. For he prefigures, in his tenuous way, Romulus the founder and Augustus the first emperor of Rome, and as some may see the ancient hero, a modern hero in the making.

2

Seeing is believing that all three epic poems coexist, but giving voice to that belief is another matter—enough to leave one standing "silent, upon a peak in Darien." So let me extend these questions of style to others that also affect a translator, his mood and mind, and his appreciation of his author. Whether or not such things find full expression, they may inform his approach, and perhaps a part of his work as well. Yves Bonnefoy, the celebrated French poet and translator of Yeats and Shakespeare, says that "if a work does not compel us, it is untranslatable" (Schulte and Biguenet, p. 192). Yet the obverse may be just as true. If a work does compel us, we will try to find a way, some way, to translate it or, as they say, die trying. What follows, then, are some of the features of Virgil that I have found especially compelling.

First, mindful of Virgil's relationship with Homer, their kinship and their contrasts, I have drawn on my translations of the *Iliad* and the *Odyssey* to suggest an Homeric echo here, an adaptation there, in the *Aeneid*. This, for example, is the simile that describes Achilles' pursuit of Hector as he races to escape his mortal enemy. One pursuing, the other pursued, and both caught in a blur of perpetual motion—

> endless as in a dream . . .
> when a man can't catch another fleeing on ahead
> and he can never escape nor his rival overtake him—
> so the one could never run the other down in his speed
> nor the other spring away. . . .   (*Iliad* 22.237–41)

—until Zeus with his golden scales decrees Hector's death, and Apollo deserts the hero, and Achilles, aided by Athena, takes his life. However vivid the moment and the simile that keeps its pace, the situation is strangely removed from us at first. It occurs in the third person, and the action itself in the past tense, as if to stress how far beyond our reach is Hector's fate, how remote and impersonal his doom.

But Virgil "translates" Homer's simile to tell another story as Aeneas pursues his enemy Turnus to his death:

> Just as in dreams
> when the nightly spell of sleep falls heavy on our eyes
> and we seem entranced by longing to keep on racing on,
> no use, in the midst of one last burst of speed
> we sink down, consumed, our tongue won't work,
> and tried and true, the power that filled our body
> fails—we strain but the voice and words won't follow.
> So with Turnus.   (12.1053–60)

As Michael Putnam remarks, "Vergil humanizes this description in an extraordinary way. He turns third-person narrative—one man chases, one flees—into first-person. It is now we, the readers, who suffer the dream, we who follow" (Spence, p. 91). We are drawn into a sympathy for, and even an identification with, Turnus, until the Fury in Aeneas could kill us all in the same moment that it chokes off Turnus' life. The more personal our involvement in his fate, the more inhuman it becomes. The two perspectives, Homeric and Virgilian, could hardly be more opposed, and their difference is underscored by Rossi, describing the recurrent immediacy of Virgil (pp. 148–49), and Andrew Ford, the far-off time and place of Homer's actions (pp. 52–55). Yet the final impression that each poet presents is equally intense. The terror that Homer creates by turning us into spectators—struck by a life-or-death event that sweeps us back to an era older and yet more vivid than our own—Virgil creates through direct engagement: we are racers too, and like Turnus we are transfixed by Aeneas' sword.

Central to the give-and-take between the two great poets, as this translator sees it (his vision largely shaped by Putnam and others), is Virgil's cumulative, Homeric presentation of Aeneas. As with an Homeric hero—unlike some later heroes whose qualities are winnowed down to a few strong traits—by gradually enlarging Aeneas' qualities, which multiply as his situations multiply about him, Virgil displays his hero in the round, not as the distillation but the sum of all his parts.

"What hero?" asked "the plain sailor man" whom Yeats befriended once, according to a famous anecdote mentioned in the Introduction and recorded in Ezra Pound's *ABC of Reading* (p. 44):

> [the sailor] took a notion to study Latin, and his teacher [Yeats] tried him with Virgil; after many lessons he asked him something about the hero.
> Said the sailor: "What hero?"
> Said the teacher: "What hero, why, Aeneas, the hero."
> Said the sailor: "Ach, a hero, him a hero? Bigob, I t'ought he waz a priest."

So have others, impressed, perhaps, by Aeneas' many acts of service to a higher power, which often seem performed at the price of his own self-assertion. But however faceless Aeneas may appear in the first half of the *Aeneid*—although that half includes his narrative of the fall of Troy, where he strives at first to be a headlong Iliadic hero, and his desperate grief at the loss of his wife, Creusa—throughout the second half of the poem he begins to be himself. The crux of his career, it seems, is his visit to the Underworld—"the dream center of the sixth book" as Arthur Hanson sees it (Luce, vol. 1, p. 697)—where Aeneas witnesses his father's visionary pageant of the Roman chiefs to come. From that experience, no matter how frail Aeneas' understanding or flawed his memory of it may be—and the Introduction clearly demonstrates his limits—he emerges from the Underworld as nothing more and nothing less than human. Moreover, bearing the mantle of his mission on his shoulders, which once had borne his father, he is "fired . . . with a love of glory still to come" (6.1025).

So Aeneas prepares for the second half of the *Aeneid*, Virgil's "greater labor" (7.50), which tells how the Trojans fight to found an Italian settlement where Rome will one day rise. That task requires of the hero, in addition to his growing prowess, a growing resolve to endure the hardships he must face, as his father's ghost describes them (6.1024–29), and the dual fate that he must undertake. For if the gradual, cumulative growth of Aeneas is Homeric, his ultimate identity within the *Aeneid* is not. He is at last as far from Achilles—who will blaze out on the crest of battle, his tomb to be a beacon on a headland—as he is from Odysseus, "the man of twists and turns" (*Odyssey* 1.1), the wily paterfamilias who wins home to reclaim his wife and son, his father and his kingdom here and now. But Aeneas, for all his potential, ends in a paradoxical position.

He is both deprived and empowered, a lost and a latent hero, too late to impersonate Achilles or Odysseus fully, too early to live within Augustus' promised reign. Aeneas will live, in fact, only three years after his marriage to Lavinia, and so he will die 330 years before the founding of Rome. Cut short as he is, however, it seems a hopeful sign that his arrival at the site should fall one calendar day before Augustus' triumph a thousand years thereafter.

For Aeneas may well be, particularly after Jupiter's abdication from the workings of human history in Book 10, "the loneliest man in literature" (Gransden, 1996, p. xix), yet he is still the founder of his people. As C. S. Lewis sees him, he is "a ghost of Troy until he becomes the father of Rome" (1961, p. 37). That consummation is incomplete. Even at the end of the poem, the hero remains a work in progress, and for Virgil to pretend otherwise would be too comforting, too pat and absolute. But Aeneas has made an impressive start. He has begun to unify his sense of duty and his sense of desire, and the two together will comprise his sense of destiny. In word and action both, he has begun to meet that destiny, for all its demands, with stoic endurance, a warrior's readiness, and even Homeric ferocity when required: a range of strengths that marks his enlargement throughout the *Aeneid* and most visibly in its second half. His *aristeia*—his heroic demonstration of excellence—is proof not only of his martial prowess but also, especially in his compassion for a world at war, of his emerging moral awareness, his humanity and its powers.

Yet for all his progress, Aeneas has some way to go. His destiny, like his character, remains double-edged, a "yoking by violence together" of opposing tugs, of profit and loss, of gain and bitter grief. Indeed as Aeneas wrestles with his destiny, so his creator wrestles with the epic tradition, its gods and its heroes, its rigors and rewards. For Virgil, as we have known for long, thanks to Adam Parry, Putnam, and others, was a poet *agonistes,* one whose hardest struggle may have been to find his voice, or rather his two voices, as Parry heard them (1989, pp. 78–96), and to forge a bond between them. One voice is devoted to the emperor Augustus, who, to borrow from Wendell Clausen's formulation (Introduction, Conington-Symonds trans., 1965, p. xv), may have urged, though he did not order the *Aeneid.* This voice is the public, "official" voice of imperial triumph, that sounds out the blare of the battle trumpets, the drumbeat of bronze squadrons marching in formation. The other voice is the muted, intimate voice of loss and suffering, the personal voice that bravely confronts, and unforgettably laments, "the burdens of mortality

[that] touch the heart" (1.559) and the anguish that appears throughout the *Aeneid* in many haunting forms, the "Italian fields forever / receding on the horizon" (3.582–83), and the beloved ghosts that vanish, "sifting through [the] fingers, / light as wind, quick as a dream in flight" (2.985–86).

Time and again one hears the two Virgilian voices at odds, echoing an opposition between action and reflection, patriotism and personal assertion, public exultation and wrenching private sorrow. Rather than hear the two voices clashing, in fact, it may be the modern preference, in response to dubious, often shattered national hopes, to hear in Virgil's lines the private voice to the exclusion of the public. His version of "the price of empire," as it is often called, is very high indeed, and it extends from the deaths that end the majority of books in the *Aeneid*, to the poem's grim, unforgiving perspective at the end, to the legacy of suffering it bequeaths to all of us. For it seems to be a price we keep on paying, in the loss of blood and treasure, time-worn faith and hard-won hope, down to the present day.

Yet both of Virgil's voices ask to be heard, even though their relationship may remain ambiguous. That is one of the reasons the poem seems to stop but never end. Another is that much of the hero's work, especially that of adjusting to a postwar era, is still to be performed, and there are prophecies—Creusa's about her husband's second wife (2.972), and Jupiter's about the nationhood of Aeneas' people (1.304–55)—still to be fulfilled. And yet another reason, as the Introduction recounts, is that Virgil left instructions at his death that the *Aeneid*, still unfinished, be destroyed. For he thought it needed three more years of licking into shape, time spent, perhaps, in harmonizing the voices he had sounded out. Or was he simply driven by his perfectionism as a poet? It is impossible to say, but fortunately, as we know, Augustus countermanded Virgil's "final orders" and preserved the *Aeneid* as we have it now. And so, despite the conclusiveness of Turnus' death, the poem still feels open-ended, its eventual outcome "'something evermore about to be'" (Wordsworth, quoted by Gransden, 1984, p. 209)—an effect that owes a good deal to Virgil's choice of the historical present as his favored tense. For it may enable his two voices, one devoted to Roman prowess, the other to its human costs, to be held in suspension, side by side, as opposites that share the Virgilian experience of power and pathos both. The saddest poem one may know may be among the strongest.

So whether Aeneas is "the loneliest man in literature" or "the founder of his people," or something of both, is a matter of prophecy, for it concerns a future still unfolding, even now. To recall the opening lines of W. H. Auden's "Secondary Epic"—

No, Virgil, no:
Not even the first of the Romans can learn
His Roman history in the future tense,
Not even to serve your political turn;
Hindsight as foresight makes no sense.

—in the light of the historical present, hindsight may make a bit more sense as foresight than we thought. "Prophecy is really hard," an American sage once said, "especially about the future." But a few things may be ventured even so. One is Sara Mack's conclusion: "The *Aeneid*, rooted in time, becomes itself timeless, for all time. It involves all its readers in Rome's destiny; it makes us all Romans" (p. 87). That is the paradox of the historical present: it makes the eternal timely, the timely eternal. So since we are Romans all, their story still resounds within us, reading in private, and at times aloud, of Roman greatness or Roman grief, or both at once.

What shall we hear when we read the *Aeneid* today? The story of Aeneas' bleak reward as Eliot describes it? "Hardly more than a narrow beachhead and a political marriage in a weary middle age: his youth interred, its shadow moving with the shades the other side of Cumae" (1957, p. 70)? Or worse, as Hanson hears the *Aeneid*, a story that stops "suicidally where it began, without resolving the conflicts it so forcefully portrays" (Luce, vol. 1, p. 700). Or as Clausen hears it, more complexly still, a story of affirmation as well as of regret, "a perception of Roman history as a long Pyrrhic victory of the human spirit that makes Virgil his country's truest historian" (Commager, p. 86). And so he may speak, from a distance that seems to narrow every year, to our own history as well, particularly to the tug of war between "private life, public destiny," as Garry Wills would phrase it, that Aeneas begins to reconcile within himself, but that tears apart the lives of many modern readers. As Auden says of Virgil, "Behind your verse so masterfully made / We hear the weeping of a Muse betrayed" ("Secondary Epic"). Yet we can also hear Augustus' triumph over Antony at Actium, and the ghost of Anchises who foretells the power of Rome to place the world beneath the rule of law.

So, if the two voices are concurrent in Virgil's time and ours, might they be dissonant yet moving, with proper encouragement, toward a state of harmony? Or might they work together even more effectively? Might one voice reinforce the other, conspiring to make the modern reader, like Aeneas, more complete, more accepting of uncertainties, and so perhaps more seasoned and humane, as Virgil calls us toward a future far beyond our ken and our control? His "ocean-roll of rhythm" may well serve, as another has suggested, quoting Arnold, to "bring / the eternal note of sadness in." A note we cannot, should not avoid. For Virgil's world of tears, like that of Keats, may become a "vale of Soul-making" after all, a place to restore ourselves and our societies to wholeness, health, and peace.

ACKNOWLEDGMENTS

These, at least, are some of the things that have occurred to the translator, and in trying to express them I have had many kinds of help. The strongest has come from Bernard Knox, my teacher once and my collaborator now, whom I prefer to call a comrade. Much as we worked together on Sophocles' Theban plays and the two Homeric poems, so we have worked on the *Aeneid*. Not only has he written the Introduction to the translation, but he has commented on my drafts for many years. And when I leaf through the pages now, his reactions ring my manuscript so completely that I might be looking at a worse-for-wear, dog-eared copy encircled by a scholiast's remarks. Yet Knox's gifts are more magnanimous than that. All told, he has offered me what I have needed most: "Doric discipline," in Yeats's words, and "Platonic tolerance" too. It has been my great good luck to work with such a man.

Michael Putnam has stood by the undertaking from the start, offering me his help in conversation, in encouragement, and even more essentially in his masterful writings about Virgil, which extend from matters of diction to the resonance of a simile or a symbol, to the dramatic construction of a scene, to the vision of the *Aeneid*. Still more immediately, with Putnam serving as classical authority, he and I have worked together closely to produce the Suggestions for Further Reading, the Notes on the Translation, and the Pronouncing Glossary that conclude the book. He has been swift in his pace, unstinting in his erudition, and the soul of generosity—I owe him "more than word can wield the matter."

Several other scholars and critics, cited among the Suggestions for Further Reading, have instructed me as well. Of the commentaries I would underscore those of R. G. Austin on Books 1, 2, 4 and 6; of R. D. Williams on Books 1 through 12; C. J. Fordyce on 7 and 8; K. W. Gransden on 8 and 11; Philip Hardie on 9; W. S. Macguinness on 12; and, often relayed by Knox as the occasion required, the commentaries of Conington et al., Mackail, and Servius. All their writings have been resources to me, assisting in matters that include the proper English phrase and syntax for the Latin, the background of Virgil's place-names, their geographical locations, folk tales and founding myths, and the broad historical reaches of the Roman world.

Several modern translators of the *Aeneid* have helped as well. Each has introduced me to a new aspect of the poem, another potential for the present. "For if it is true," as Maynard Mack proposes, "that what we translate from a given work is what, wearing the spectacles of our time, we see in it, it is also true that we see in it what we have the power to translate" (*The Norton Anthology of World Literature*, 5th ed., p. 2045). So the help I have derived from others is considerable, and dividing them for convenience into groups, I say my thanks to each in turn. First, to those who have translated the *Aeneid* into prose: John Conington, edited by J. A. Symonds; H. R. Fairclough as revised by G. P. Goold; W. F. Jackson Knight (for his translation, and for the genealogical table of the royal houses of Troy and Greece drawn by Bernard Vasquez appearing within it); and David West (for his translation and also his comprehensive introduction to the poem). Each presents an example of accuracy as well as grace, and the stronger that example, the more instructive each has been in bringing me a little closer to the Latin. Next, my thanks to the translators who have turned the *Aeneid* into verse: F. O. Copley, Patrick Dickinson, Robert Fitzgerald, Rolfe Humphries, C. Day Lewis, Stanley Lombardo, Allen Mandelbaum (for his translation and also his extremely helpful glossary), Edward McCrorie, and C. H. Sisson. Each presents a kind of aspiration, a striving to find the strongest English line for Virgil's Latin line; and I have learned from each in turn, probably most from Fitzgerald, for the Latinity of his stamina and his style.

And finally, there are the unapproachables, all impossible to reach, who have caught the Virgilian spirit on the wing and turned it into words. I will mention only a few. John Dryden, who produced his *Aeneid* at the end of the seventeenth century, is far and away the first among them, and its greatness is anticipated, in brief, by his elegy "To the Memory of

Mr. Oldham," perhaps the most Virgilian poem that I know in English. Dryden's work is preceded by certain Virgilian adaptations in the English Renaissance, particularly Marlowe's *Dido, Queen of Carthage,* and followed by many selections, new as well as old, in Gransden's generous edition of *Virgil in English.* Closest to me in time are Auden's "Secondary Epic" and "Memorial for the City," Allen Tate's "Aeneas at Washington" and "The Mediterranean," Robert Lowell's "Falling Asleep over the *Aeneid,*" and several other works discussed in Theodore Ziolkowski's *Virgil and the Moderns,* with its superb analysis of Hermann Broch's *Death of Virgil.*

Of the more recent translators, I have known only a few in person, yet we all may know each other in a way, having trekked across the same territory, perhaps having had the same nightmare that haunted Pope throughout his Homeric efforts. "He was engaged in a long journey," as Joseph Spence reports Pope's dream, "puzzled which way to take, and full of fears" that it would never end. And if you reach the end, the fears may start in earnest. Your best hope, I suppose, a distant one at that (and for some not all that hopeful), is the one held out by Walter Benjamin in his famous essay "The Task of the Translator." "Even the greatest translation," he writes, "is destined to become part of the growth of its own language and eventually to be absorbed by its renewal" (p. 73).

Many classicists have helped as well, with prompting and advice, some viva voce and some in their writings: Paul Alpers, Charles Beye, Ward Briggs Jr., Edward Champlin, Andrew Feldherr, Andrew Ford, Eric Grey, Arthur Hanson, Georgia Nugent, David Quint, Sarah Spence, and James Zetzel. And many other friends, most of them writers, have helped with caution or encouragement or a healthy blend of both. Most heartening of all, none has asked me, "Why another *Aeneid*?" Each understands, it seems, that if Virgil was a performer, even in his writerly way, his translator might aim to be one as well. And no two performances of the same work—surely not of a musical composition, so probably not of a work of language either—will ever be the same. The tempo and timbre of each will be distinct, let alone its deeper resonance, build, and thrust. So there may always be room for one translation more, especially as idioms and eras change, and I thank the following friends for suggesting that I try my hand at Virgil: André Aciman, Christopher Davis, James Dickey, Charles Gillispie, Shirley Hazzard, Christopher Hedges, Robert Hollander, John McPhee, Jeffrey Perl, Theodore Weiss, and Theodore Ziolkowski.

I have been especially fortunate in finding readers for the work in progress. First the classicists. Robert Kaster went through books 1, 4, 6, 10, and 11 in considerable detail; Denis Feeney generously did the same—amid a demanding chairmanship—throughout the entire poem; and the late Douglas Knight, having worked through the first four books with me, no sooner saw Dido out of this world than he followed her himself. And then there were the writers, Edmund Keeley, Chang-rae Lee, J. D. McClatchy, Paul Muldoon, and C. K. Williams with Catherine Mauger. Each has read my drafts with sharp eyes and open minds and a tireless fellow feeling. They have looked a gift horse in the mouth, as Robert Graves once said to a would-be writer, and prescribed the dentistry it needed.

I would also thank the friends who asked me to read the work in public and perhaps improve it in the bargain. First my hosts at Princeton University, who invited me to their classes, their colloquia and other convenings—Sandra Bermann, Andrew Feldherr, Brooke Holmes, Nancy Malkiel, Susan Taylor, and Michael Wood. Then Robert Goheen at the Wistar Association, Karl Kirchwey at Bryn Mawr College, and Rosanna Warren and Steven Shankman at the Association of Literary Scholars and Critics.

The roofs of some great houses have extended welcome shelter to the translator and his work. My thanks to Mary and Theodore Cross for turning Nantucket into Rome West with their Virgilian hospitality. And my thanks to the house of Viking Penguin that has produced the book at hand. My editor, Kathryn Court, assisted by Alexis Washam, once again has treated the writer and the writing too with insight, affection, and address. My senior development editor has been Beena Kamlani, and once again her efforts to tame and train a fairly unruly piece of work have been heroic. And all the good people at Viking Penguin—Susan Petersen Kennedy, Clare Ferraro, Paul Slovak, Paul Buckley, Leigh Butler, Maureen Donnelly, Francesca Belanger, Florence Eichin, John Fagan, Matt Giarratano, Dan Lundy, Patti Pirooz, John McElroy, Nancy Sheppard—all have been loyal allies in New York, joined by Adam Freudenheim and Simon Winder in London. And through it all, without the unfailing strategies and support of my friend and agent Georges Borchardt, assisted by DeAnna Heindel and Jonathan Zev Berman in turn, this translation might not have seen the light.

In closing, I thank the familiar spirits of Anne and Adam Parry, dear ghosts who pour the wine and lead the way. And first and last, my abiding thanks to Lynne, the Muse, and to our daughters, Katya and Nina, their husbands and their children. They have borne me through the work with the power of their love.

R. F.

Princeton, N. J.
Thanksgiving 2005

A NOTE ON THIS PAPERBACK EDITION:
THIS PRINTING CONTAINS MINOR REVISIONS OF THE TEXT.

R. F.

Princeton, N. J.
September 11, 2007

House of Atreus

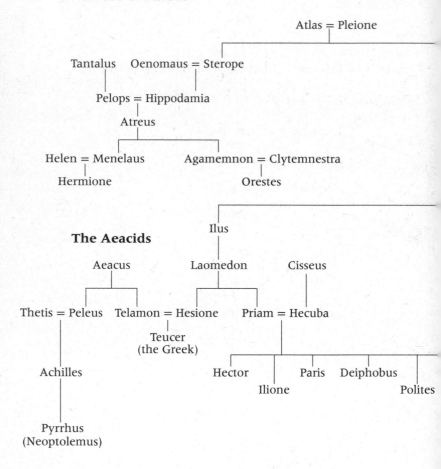

Atlas = Pleione

Tantalus   Oenomaus = Sterope

Pelops = Hippodamia

Atreus

Helen = Menelaus   Agamemnon = Clytemnestra

Hermione   Orestes

The Aeacids

Ilus

Aeacus   Laomedon   Cisseus

Thetis = Peleus   Telamon = Hesione   Priam = Hecuba

Teucer
(the Greek)

Achilles   Hector   Paris   Deiphobus

Ilione   Polites

Pyrrhus
(Neoptolemus)

THE ROYAL HOUSES OF GREECE AND TROY

Ancestors of the Trojans

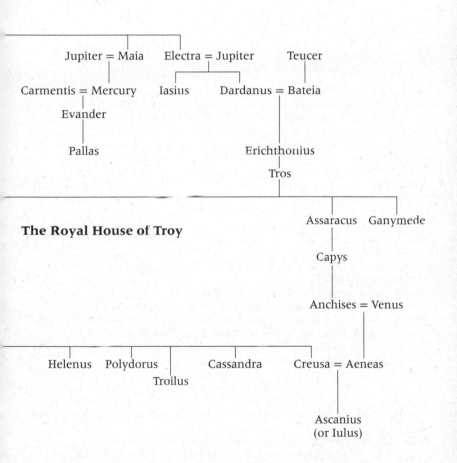

The Royal House of Troy

SUGGESTIONS FOR FURTHER READING

I. Texts and Commentaries

Austin, R. G., ed., *P. Vergili Maronis Aeneidos Liber Quartus* (Oxford, 1955).

———, ed., *P. Vergili Maronis Aeneidos Liber Secundus* (Oxford, 1964).

———, ed., *P. Vergili Maronis Aeneidos Liber Primus* (Oxford, 1971).

———, ed., *P. Vergili Maronis Aeneidos Liber Sextus* (Oxford, 1977).

Conington, J., H. Nettleship, and F. Haverfield, eds. with commentary, *The Works of Virgil*, 3 vols. (Oxford, 1858–83; repr. Hildesheim, 1963).

Eden, P. T., ed., *A Commentary on Virgil Aeneid VIII* (Leiden, 1975).

Fairclough, H. R., ed. and trans., 2 vols. *Virgil*: vol. 1: *Eclogues, Georgics, Aeneid I–VI* (Cambridge, 1916); vol. 2: *Aeneid VII–XII. Appendix Vergiliana* (Cambridge, 1918); rev. by G. P. Goold (Cambridge, 1999, 2000).

Fordyce, C. J., ed., *P. Vergili Maronis Aeneidos Libri VII–VIII* (Oxford, 1977).

Gransden, K. W., ed., *Virgil Aeneid Book VIII* (Cambridge, 1976).

———, ed., *Virgil Aeneid Book XI* (Cambridge, 1991).

Greenough, J. B., G. L. Kittredge, and Thornton Jenkins, eds. *Virgil and Other Latin Poets* (Boston, 1930).

Hardie, P., ed., *Virgil Aeneid Book IX* (Cambridge, 1994).

Harrison, S. J., ed., *Virgil Aeneid 10* (Oxford, 1991).

Henry, J., *Aeneidea, or Critical, Exegetical, and Aesthetical Remarks on the Aeneid* (London, Dublin, Edinburgh, Meissen, 1873–92; repr. New York, 1972).

Horsfall, N., ed., *Virgil Aeneid 7: A Commentary* (Leiden, 2000).

———, ed., *Virgil Aeneid 11: A Commentary* (Leiden, 2004).

Mackail, J. W., ed., *The Aeneid of Virgil* (Oxford, 1930).

Maguinness, W. S., ed., *Virgil: Aeneid Book XII* (London, 1953; repr. London, 1992).

Mynors, R. A. B., ed., *P. Vergili Maronis Opera* (Oxford Classical Text: Oxford, 1969).

Norden, E., ed., *P. Vergilius Maro: Aeneid Buch VI* (Leipzig, 1916; 4th ed.: Darmstadt, 1957).

Page, T. E., ed., *The Aeneid of Virgil*, 2 vols. (London, 1894, 1900).

Pease, A. S., ed., *P. Vergili Maronis Aeneidos Liber Quartus* (Cambridge, 1935).

Rolfe, J. C., ed. and trans., *Suetonius*, 2 vols. (Cambridge, 1913,1914). See vol. 2, 464–83, for "The Life of Vergil" contained in *The Lives of Illustrious Men*.

Servius, *Commentarii*, eds. G. Thilo and H. Hagen, 3 vols. (Leipzig, 1878–87; repr. Hildesheim, 1961).

Williams, R. D., ed., *P. Vergil Maronis Aeneidos Liber Quintus* (Oxford, 1960).

———, ed., *P. Vergili Maronis Aeneidos Liber Tertius* (Oxford, 1962).

———, ed., *The Aeneid of Virgil,* 2 vols. (London, 1972, 1973).

II. Critical Works

Anderson, W. S., *The Art of the Aeneid* (Englewood Cliffs, 1969; repr. Wauconda, 1989).

——— and L. N. Quartarone, eds., *Approaches to Teaching Vergil's Aeneid* (Publications of the Modern Language Association of America: New York, 2002).

Barchiesi, A., *La Traccia del Modello: Effetti Omerici nella Narrazione Virgiliana* (Pisa, 1984).

Bernard, J., ed., *Vergil at 2000: Commemorative Essays on the Poet and His Influence* (New York, l986).

Benjamin, W., *Illuminations,* trans. W. Zohn; ed. and intro. H. Arendt (New York, 1969). See "The Task of the Translator," 69–82.

Beye, C. R., *The Iliad, the Odyssey, and the Epic Tradition* (New York, 1966); rev. and repr. as *Ancient Epic Poetry: Homer, Apollonius, Virgil* (Ithaca, 1993); expanded 2nd ed., with a chapter on the Gilgamesh poems (Wauconda, 2006).

Bloom, H., ed., *Virgil: Modern Critical Views* (New York, 1986).

———, ed., *Modern Critical Interpretations: Virgil's Aeneid* (New York, 1987).

Bowra, C. M., *From Virgil to Milton* (London, 1945).

Boyle, A. J., *The Chaonian Dove: Studies in the Eclogues, Georgics, and Aeneid of Virgil* (Leiden, 1986).

Broch, H., *Der Tod des Vergil* (New York, 1945); trans. by J. S. Untermeyer as *The Death of Virgil* (New York, 1945).

Cairns, F., *Virgil's Augustan Epic* (Cambridge, 1989).

Camps, W., *Introduction to Virgil's Aeneid* (Oxford, 1969).

Clausen, W. V., *Virgil's Aeneid and the Tradition of Hellenistic Poetry* (Berkeley, 1987.)

Commager, S., ed., *Virgil: A Collection of Critical Essays* (Englewood Cliffs, 1966). See B. M. W. Knox "The Serpent and the Flame: The Imagery of the Second Book of the *Aeneid,*" 124–42 (from *American Journal of Philology* 71 [1950], 379–400); R. A. Brooks "*Discolor Aura*: Reflections on the Golden Bough," 143–63 (from *American Journal of Philology* 74 [1953], 160–80); W. V. Clausen "An Interpretation of the *Aeneid,*" 75–88 (from *Harvard Studies in Classical Philology* 68 [1964], 139–47).

Conte, G. B., *The Rhetoric of Imitation: Genre and Poetic Memory in Virgil and Other Latin Poets* (*Cornell Studies in Classical Philology* #44: Ithaca, 1986).

Di Cesare, M., *The Altar and the City: A Reading of Vergil's Aeneid* (New York, 1974).

Duckworth, G., *Structural Patterns and Proportions in Vergil's Aeneid* (Ann Arbor, 1962).

Eliot, T. S., *What Is a Classic?* (London, 1945); repr. in *On Poetry and Poets* (London, 1957).

Farron, S., *Vergil's Aeneid: A Poem of Grief and Love* (Leiden, 1993).

Feeney, D., *The Gods in Epic: Poets and Critics of the Classical Tradition* (Oxford, 1991).

Ford, A., *Homer: The Poetry of the Past* (Ithaca, 1992).

Frank, T., *Vergil: A Biography* (New York, 1922).

408   SUGGESTIONS FOR FURTHER READING

Galinsky, G. K., *Aeneas, Sicily and Rome* (Princeton, 1969).

Gillis, D., *Eros and Death in the Aeneid* (Rome, 1983).

Gransden, K. W., *Virgil's Iliad: An Essay on Epic Narrative* (London, 1984).

———, *Virgil: The Aeneid* (New York, 1990).

———, *Virgil in English* (*Penguin Poets in Translation*: London, 1996).

Greene, T., *The Descent from Heaven: A Study in Epic Continuity* (New Haven, 1963).

Griffin, J., *Virgil* (Oxford, 1986).

Hardie, P., *Virgil's Aeneid: Cosmos and Imperium* (Oxford, 1986).

———, *The Epic Successors of Virgil: A Study in the Dynamics of a Tradition* (Cambridge, 1993).

———, *Virgil* (*New Surveys in the Classics* #28: Oxford, 1998).

———, ed., *Virgil: Critical Assessments of Classical Authors*, 4 vols., (London, 1999).

Harrison, S. J., ed., *Oxford Readings in Vergil's Aeneid* (Oxford, 1990).

Heinze, R., *Vergils epische Technik* (Leipzig, 1915); trans. as *Virgil's Epic Technique*, by H. Harvey, D. Harvey, and F. Robertson (Berkeley, 1993).

Highet, G., *The Speeches in Vergil's Aeneid* (Princeton, 1972).

Hollander, R., *Il Virgilio dantesco: tragedia nella "Commedia"* (Firenze, 1983).

Horsfall, N., *A Companion to the Study of Virgil* (Leiden, 1995).

Hunt, J., *Forms of Glory: Structure and Sense in Virgil's Aeneid* (Carbondale, 1973).

Jenkyns, R., *Classical Epic: Homer and Virgil* (London, 1992).

———, *Virgil's Experience: Nature and History: Times, Names, Places* (Oxford, 1998).

Johnson, W. R., *Darkness Visible: A Study of Vergil's Aeneid* (Berkeley, 1976).

Klingner, F., *Virgil: Bucolica, Georgica, Aeneis* (Zurich, 1967).

Knauer, G. N., *Die Aeneis und Homer: Studien zur poetischen Technik Vergils mit der Homerzitate in der Aeneis* (*Hypomnemata* #7: Göttingen, 1964; repr. 1979).

Knight, W. F. J. Jackson, *Roman Vergil* (Harmondsworth, 1966).

Levi, P., *Virgil: His Life and Times* (London, 1998).

Lewis, C. S., *A Preface to Paradise Lost* (London, 1942, repr. 1961).

Luce, T. J., ed., *Ancient Writers: Greece and Rome* (2 vols., New York, 1982). See J. A. Hanson "Vergil" (vol. 2, 669–701).

Lyne, R. O. A. M., *Further Voices in Vergil's Aeneid* (Oxford, 1987).

———, *Words and the Poet: Characteristic Techniques of Style in Vergil's Aeneid* (Oxford, 1989).

Mack, S., *Patterns of Time in Vergil* (Hamden, 1978).

Martindale, C., ed., *Virgil and His Influence* (London, 1984).

———, ed., *The Cambridge Companion to Virgil* (Cambridge, 1997).

McAuslan, I., and P. Walcot, eds., *Virgil* (*Greece and Rome Studies* #1: Oxford, 1990).

Moskalew, W., *Formular Language and Poetic Design in the Aeneid* (*Mnemosyne Supplement* #73: Leiden, 1982).

Most, G., and S. Spence, eds., *Re-Presenting Virgil* (*Materiali e discussioni per l'analisi dei testi classici* #52: Pisa, 2004).

O'Hara, J. J., *Death and the Optimistic Prophecy in Vergil's Aeneid* (Princeton, 1990).

Otis, B., *Virgil: A Study in Civilized Poetry* (Oxford, 1964).

Parry, A., *The Language of Achilles and Other Papers* (Oxford, 1989). See "The Two Voices of Virgil's *Aeneid*," 78–96 (from *Arion* 2.4 [1963], 66–80).

Perkell, C., ed., *Reading Vergil's Aeneid: An Interpretive Guide* (Norman, 1999).

Pöschl, V., *Die Dichtkunst Vergils: Bild und Symbol in der Aeneis* (Wiesbaden, 1950); trans. as *The Art of Vergil: Image and Symbol in the Aeneid*, by G. Seligson (Ann Arbor, 1962).

Pound, E., *ABC of Reading* (New York, 1960).

Putnam, M. C. J., *The Poetry of the Aeneid* (Cambridge, 1965; repr. Ithaca, 1988).

———, *Virgil's Aeneid: Interpretation and Influence* (Chapel Hill, 1995).

———, *Virgil's Epic Designs: Ekphrasis in the Aeneid* (New Haven, 1998).

——— (with J. Hankins), ed. and trans., *Maffeo Vegio: Short Epics* (Cambridge, 2004).

———, "Virgil's *Aeneid*," in J. M. Foley, ed., *A Companion to Ancient Epic* (Malden/ Oxford, 2005), 452–75.

——— and J. Ziolkowski, *The Virgilian Tradition: The First Fifteen Hundred Years* (New Haven, 2006).

Quinn, K., *Virgil's Aeneid: A Critical Description* (London, 1968).

Quinn, S., ed., *Why Vergil? A Collection of Interpretations* (Wauconda, 2000).

Quint, D., *Epic and Empire: Politics and Generic Form from Virgil to Milton* (Princeton, 1993).

Reed, J. D., *Virgil's Gaze: Nation and Poetry in the Aeneid* (Princeton, 2007).

Rossi, A., *Contexts of War: Manipulation of Genre in Virgilian Battle Narrative* (Ann Arbor, 2004).

Schulte, R., and J. Biguenet, eds., *Theories of Translation. An Anthology of Essays from Dryden to Derrida* (Chicago, 1992). See Yves Bonnefoy "Translating Poetry," 186–92.

Smith, A. R., *The Primacy of Vision in Virgil's Aeneid* (Austin, 2005).

Sparrow, J., *Half-lines and Repetitions in Virgil* (Oxford, 1931; repr. New York, 1977).

Spence, S., ed., *Poets and Critics Read Vergil* (New Haven, 2001). See M. C. J. Putnam "Vergil's Aeneid: The Final Lines," 86–104.

Stahl, H.-P, ed., *Vergil's Aeneid: Augustan Epic and Political Context* (London, 1998).

Thibodeau, P., and H. Haskell, eds., *Being There Together: Essays in Honor of Michael C. J. Putnam* (Afton, 2003). See S. Scully "Eros and Warfare in Virgil's 'Aeneid' and Homer's 'Iliad,'" 181–97.

Thomas, R., *Virgil and the Augustan Reception* (Cambridge, 2001).

Van Nortwick, T., *Somewhere I Have Never Travelled* (Oxford, 1992).

West, D., and T. Woodman, eds., *Creative Imitation and Latin Literature* (Cambridge, 1979).

Williams, G., *Technique and Ideas in the Aeneid* (New Haven, 1983).

Williams, R. D., *The Aeneid* (London, 1987).

Wiltshire, S., *Public and Private in Vergil's Aeneid* (Amherst, 1989).

Woodman, T., and J. Powell, eds., *Author and Audience in Latin Literature* (Cambridge, 1992). See G. P. Goold "The Voice of Virgil: The Pageant of Rome in *Aeneid* 6," 110–23.

Zetzel, J., "*Romane Memento*: Justice and Judgment in *Aeneid* 6," *TAPA* 119 (1989), 263–84.

Ziolkowski, T., *Virgil and the Moderns* (Princeton, 1993).

VARIANTS FROM THE
OXFORD CLASSICAL TEXT

The Oxford Classical Text of Virgil's *Opera*, edited by R. A. B. Mynors and published in 1969, has been followed throughout the translation, except for the textual variants cited below:

1.427	*theatri*	6.383	*terrae*
2.587	*flammae*	8.588	*in*
2.691	*augurium*	10.280	*viri*
4.54	*incensum*	10.754	*insignis*
4.641	*celerabat*	10.850	*exilium*
5.29	*demittere*	11.149	*Pallanta*
5.520	*contorsit*	11.173	*armis*
5.595	add. *luduntque per undas*	12.218	*aequis*
6.255	*lumina*		

Bracketed as questionable by Mynors, lines 6.242, 8.46, and 10.278 are omitted from the translation; 3.230 and 4.273 are included. For a discussion of the inclusion of 2.567–88, see Introduction, pp. 11–12.

NOTES ON
THE TRANSLATION

Names in small capitals refer to entries in the Pronouncing Glossary, pp. 426–486.

1.49–55 *Minerva could burn the fleet to ash:* Minerva (Athena in the Greek pantheon), though she favored the Greeks, was angry over the Greek chieftain Little Ajax, son of Oileus. He had violated Cassandra, King Priam's daughter, in the Trojan temple of Minerva, where she had taken refuge (see AJAX). Little Ajax, son of Oileus, is to be distinguished from Great Ajax, son of Telamon, the hero of Sophocles' play who committed suicide before Troy fell and, questioned by Ulysses (Odysseus) in the Underworld, refused to speak (*Odyssey* 11.617–49). Oilean Ajax is mentioned by Virgil as fighting against Aeneas (2.516).

1.236–237 *Scylla's howling rabid dogs, / . . . the Cyclops' boulders:* The stories of the Trojans' encounter with (or their avoidance of) Scylla and Charybdis and their contact with the Cyclops are told through Aeneas in 3.496–508 and 3.711–86.

1.287–97 *Antenor could slip out . . . :* Antenor was a Trojan elder who at one point advised the Trojans to give Helen back to the Greeks. He somehow escaped from Troy with his people, sailed west through the Aegean, north up the Adriatic, passed the Timavus River (adjacent to Aquileia), and founded the city of Padua, some seventy miles farther west.

1.320–21 For *Ascanius . . . Iulus . . . Ilus,* see Glossary, especially ILUS (1), and Introduction, pp. 11–17.

1.322–25 *thirty sovereign years . . . :* As Austin says (1971, Note 1.269), "a grand periphrasis."

1.351 *Gates of War:* This reference would recall to readers of the *Aeneid* the temple of the god Janus at Rome. He was the god of doors and gates and his temple was closed, twice in the Republic's history but on three occasions under Augustus, in times of peace. See 7.705–15.

1.352–55 *The Frenzy / of civil strife . . . :* for the historical background of recent Italian civil war, see Introduction, pp. 1–3.

1.379–80 *Suddenly . . . his mother / crossed his path:* Though the reader now knows that the huntress is Venus (Aphrodite) in disguise, Aeneas is not allowed to make the identification until she begins to disappear, and then it comes as a surprise to him, 1.488–97.

1.446 *Byrsa, the Hide:* The legend was that the Africans sold the Tyrians as much land as they could cover with a bull's-hide, but the Tyrians cut it into thin strips and so encircled a much larger area than intended. See BYRSA.

1.534–37 *the Tyrians . . . first unearthed that sign . . . :* Digging after their first landfall, they unearthed the head of a fiery stallion, which was afterward to be seen on Carthaginian coinage.

1.561–95 The "empty, lifeless pictures" that Aeneas sees on the walls of Juno's temple in Carthage all portray people and events from the Trojan War. The mention of RHESUS (567–73) alludes to the events narrated in *Iliad* 10. Diomedes and Ulysses raid the Trojan camp at night and kill the recently arrived Rhesus, a Thracian ally of Troy. They then drive his magnificent horses back to the Greek camp, because an oracle had said that if the horses could crop the grass of Troy or drink from the river Xanthus, the city would not fall. TROILUS (573–79), a very young warrior, is killed by Achilles (not in the *Iliad*; his story comes from later epic work). The Trojan women (579–83) are seen as unsuccessful suppliants of Athena, who refuses, as in the *Iliad* (6.338–66), to divert the battle fury of Diomedes from the Trojans. In the *Iliad* (Books 22–25), Achilles drags the body of Hector (*Aeneid* 1.583–89) not around the walls of Troy but around the tomb of Patroclus, and gives his body back to Priam, his father. The Trojan ally MEMNON (591), from the East, and the Amazon PENTHESILEA (592–95) are all from post-Iliadic epics that exist now only in fragments.

1.571–73 *high-strung teams . . . :* for the prophecy attached to these fine horses, see Note 1.561–95.

1.699 *Just one is lost:* Orontes. See LEUCASPIS, LYCUS, and ORONTES.

1.746–47 *Teucer, your enemy . . . / claiming his own descent from Teucer's ancient stock:* See TEUCER (2) and (1).

2.56 *Ulysses:* According to a later epic poem, when Ulysses tried to escape service in the war at Troy by pretending madness, Palamedes proved him sane by placing Ulysses' infant son Telemachus in the path of the oncoming plow. Later, at Troy, Ulysses avenged himself by forging a letter from Priam that exposed Palamedes as a Trojan agent. Palamedes was stoned to death by the Greeks.

2.149–52 *With blood you appeased the winds . . . :* The oracle refers to the prewar sacrifice of Iphigenia, the daughter of Agamemnon, and the future sacrifice (i.e., of Sinon) which the oracle foresees.

2.211 *the fateful image of Pallas:* The Palladium; a small, sacred statue of Pallas Athena in full armor, and a talisman that safeguarded Troy, but was carried away from its shrine on the city heights by Diomedes and Ulysses, leaving the city vulnerable and the goddess outraged, 9.180.

2.259 *Laocoön, the priest of Neptune picked by lot:* Laocoön and his sons are the subject of a famous statue, probably copied from a Hellenistic original, discovered in Rome in 1506, now housed in the Vatican Museum.

2.551 *under a tortoise-shell of shields:* The "tortoise" formation was a screen formed when soldiers held their interlocked shields over their heads as they advanced.

2.686–92 *Such was the fate of Priam . . . :* For the historical resonance of these lines, see Introduction, pp. 24–25.

2.702–28 For a discussion of the Helen passage, the debate it has prompted, and its authenticity and effectivness in context, see Introduction, pp. 11–12.

2.795–96 *I have seen / one sack of my city:* Anchises refers to an earlier sack of Troy at the hands of Hercules, in payment for Laomedon's reneging on his offer of famous horses as a gift to Hercules. See 3.558–59 and Note ad loc.

2.804–5 *the Father . . . scorched me with its fire:* As Williams relates it (1972, note 2.649), "the story was that Anchises boasted of Venus' love for him, for which Jupiter resolved to punish him with a thunderbolt; Venus however diverted it so that he was scorched but not killed." See Austin, 1964, Note 2.649.

2.862 *thunder crashes on the left:* In Roman augury, signs appearing on the left were generally regarded as favorable. The opposite is true for Greek divination. See 9.717–20.

2.888 *an old shrine of forsaken Ceres stands:* "Forsaken" here probably means solitary. In other words the temple would be a safe spot for the refugees to meet.

2.983–86 *Three times I tried to fling my arms around her neck . . . :* These lines echo the lines that, beginning with Homer, describe the grief of the living who try but cannot seize a cherished ghost, of Achilles to seize Patroclus (*Iliad* 23.111–19), then of Ulysses to seize his mother (*Odyssey* 11.233–39), here of Aeneas to seize his wife, Creusa, and later (6.808–11) his father's spirit in the Underworld. Each encounter demonstrates that, between the living and the dead, "there yawns a gulf," as Auden might express it, "embraces cannot bridge."

3.20–21 *here I sail / and begin to build our first walls:* Aeneas has been told by Creusa (2.967–72) that he would travel very far and found a city in Hesperia, through which the Tiber runs, so his building of a city in Thrace at this point is one of the details that Virgil might have corrected if he had had the opportunity to revise the poem later.

3.102 *Grant us our own home, god of Thymbra:* THYMBRA was the site of a famous shrine to APOLLO. It was there, according to some ancient sources, that Achilles killed Troilus. See Note 1.561–95.

3.123 *the land of our return:* For Aeneas' arrival in Italy as a kind of *nostos* or return, see DARDANUS.

3.126 *Crete, great Jove's own land:* Jupiter was born on the island of Crete, where, according to legend, he was watched over by the nymphs of Mount Dicte and fed by bees, as described by Virgil in Book 4 of his *Georgics* (4.152).

3.159 *the old Curetes' harbor:* See CURETES. The noise made by the clashing cymbals of the Curetes hid the wailing of the baby Jupiter from his father, who would otherwise have devoured him.

3.205 *There Dardanus was born:* See DARDANUS.

3.219 *He recalls at once the two lines of our race, two parents:* Anchises had previously forgotten the double Trojan ancestry, from Teucer (1) and Dardanus, a native of Italy.

3.258 *after Phineus' doors were locked against them all:* Phineus was blinded by the gods for having blinded his own sons. He was harried by HARPIES sent by Jupiter, and the demons snatched away his food and contaminated what was left. He was rescued by two sons of the Northwind, Boreas, the Argonauts Zetes and Calais.

3.262 *Styx's waters:* Milton has made the names of the infernal rivers and their Greek etymologies resonate in *Paradise Lost:*

> . . . four infernal rivers that disgorge
> Into the burning lake their baleful streams:
> Abhorred Styx the flood of deadly hate,
> Sad Acheron of sorrow, black and deep;
> Cocytus, named of lamentation loud
> Heard on the rueful stream; fierce Phlegethon
> Whose waves of torrent fire inflame with rage.
> Far off from these a slow and silent stream,
> Lethe the river of oblivion rolls
> Her watery labyrinth, whereof who drinks,
> Forthwith his former state and being forgets,
> Forgets both joy and grief, pleasure and pain.   2.575–86

(See ACHERON, COCYTUS, LETHE, RIVER OF FIRE, and WAILING RIVER.)

3.374 *where's my Hector now?:* As Williams reasons (1960, note 3.310–12): "Andromache can hardly believe that Aeneas is really present in person . . . She half believes he is a phantom, come in response to her invocations at Hector's tomb (303)—why then has he come and not Hector?"

3.384–85 *She was the one, /* . . . *Priam's virgin daughter:* Polyxena, daughter of Priam and Hecuba, was sacrificed on the tomb of Achilles.

3.389–400 *But I, our home in flames . . . :* See ANDROMACHE. After Hector's death and the fall of Troy, she became the slave and concubine of Achilles' son, Pyrrhus (Neoptolemus). He deserted her in favor of Hermione, a daughter of Helen and one to whom he had been affianced. Hermione was also pursued by Orestes, however, who killed Pyrrhus, his bitter rival for her affections. Andromache, abandoned by Pyrrhus, married Helenus, her fellow captive and a son of Priam with prophetic powers, and together they founded at Buthrotum a miniature town modeled after Troy. See HELENUS and HERMIONE.

3.405 *whom in the old days at Troy:* As Williams observes (1960, note 3.340), "This is the only half-line in the *Aeneid* where the sense is incomplete, for it is impossible to regard it as an aposiopesis like Neptune's *quos ego—!" (Aen.* 1.135).

3.558–59 *Twice they plucked you safe / from the ruins of Troy:* Once when Hercules sacked the city, and then again when the Greeks did the same. See Note 2.795–96.

3.644 *Hercules' town:* Hercules is the greatest of the Greek heroes; he eventually, after his death, became an immortal god. He was the son of Jupiter and a mortal woman, Alcmena. Jupiter intended that he should lord it over all who dwell around him, but Jupiter's jealous wife, Juno, contrived to have that destiny conferred on Eurystheus, king of Argos, to whom Hercules was to be subject. At Eurystheus' command, Hercules performed the famous Twelve Labors: among them was the capture of the three-headed dog, Cerberus, the guardian of the entrance to the Underworld (6.452–54). For Hercules' adventures on the site of Rome, where he kills the villain Cacus, see CACUS, 8.220–320, and Note 7.770.

3.713 *My father Adamastus was poor, and so I sailed to Troy:* He would have received money in payment for services as a mercenary.

4.21–22 *my first love deceived me . . . / by his death:* Sychaeus' murder deceived Dido in the sense that it unexpectedly disappointed her future hopes.

4.179 *Apollo leaving his Lycian haunts:* See LYCIA. Apollo presumably leaves his winter residence at Patara in Lycia, when travel becomes feasible, to hold a festival at his birthplace, Delos.

4.219–36 *Rumor . . . :* The associations surrounding Rumor as sister of Coeus, a Titan, and Enceladus, one of the Giants, are deliberately unpleasant, smacking of anger and vengeance. For Jupiter had destroyed the Giant and the Titan, and Mother Earth "bore one last child, Fama [Rumor]," as Williams explains (1972, Note 4.179) "to be their sister and take vengeance on gods and men with her evil tongue."

4.285 *not for* this *did she save him twice from Greek attacks:* As Williams explains (1972, Note 4.228), "once from Diomedes . . . and once from burning Troy." See *Iliad* 5.347–56 and *Aeneid* 2.729–52.

4.305–6 *[Mercury's] wand . . . that unseals our eyes in death:* He seals the eyes of the dead, then opens them when the body is placed on the pyre, perhaps to grant them vision after the dead have been cremated. There is a passage in Pliny's *Historia Naturalis* (11.150) that refers to the custom.

4.376–77 *the cyclic orgy . . . / and Cithaeron echoes round . . . :* The festival was "triennial," which is to say held every other year, in the ancient system of counting. Mount Cithaeron was the setting for the *Bacchae* of Euripides.

4.431–32 *Grynean Apollo's oracle . . . / his Lycian lots . . . :* Lots here stand for some written version of the oracle's utterances that would have stated simply "Italy."

4.641–48 *She'd sprinkled water . . . :* Dido's many ritual acts and implements, the water sprinkled, the potent herbs, the bronze sickles, the love-charm ripped from a foal's brow, the moonlight, the sacred grain, the one foot freed from its sandal, the robes unbound—all are concerned with traditional aspects of magic.

4.710–11 *Woman's a thing / that's always changing, shifting like the wind: Varium et mutabile semper / femina* [4.569–70] is, according to Dryden, "the sharpest satire, in the fewest words, that ever was made on womankind; for both the adjectives are neuter, and *animal* must be understood, to make them grammar. Virgil does well to put the words into the mouth of Mercury. *If a god had not spoken them, neither durst he have written them, nor I translated them* [Dryden's italics]" (*Dedication of the Aeneis*, 1697). Referred to by Williams, 1972, note 4.569–70.

4.779 *Come rising up from my bones, you avenger still unknown:* For Hannibal as the avenger whom Dido cannot know and so must leave nameless, see Introduction, pp. 24ff.

4.818–19 *So— / so—:* The tradition that the repetition of "so" (Latin *sic*) represents Dido's suicidal sword-strokes is as early as Virgil's fourth-century A.D. commentator, Servius (on line 4.660).

4.868 *Proserpina had yet to pluck a golden lock from her head:* Proserpina would ordinarily have snipped a lock of hair from the dead as an offering. Her role here is taken by Iris because, as a suicide, Dido's death was seen as premature.

5.134–318 *For the first event, enter / four great ships . . . :* A ship-race in which Cloanthus pilots the *Scylla* to victory, MNESTHEUS pilots the *Dragon* to second place, GYAS the *Chimaera* to third, and SERGESTUS the *Centaur* to fourth and last. See Williams, 1960, Note 5.114–50.

5.325–402 *a breathless foot-race now . . . :* In which Euryalus finishes first, Helymus second, Diores third, Salius fourth, and Nisus fifth, followed by Patron and Panopes and "many others too, their names now lost / in the dark depths of time" (336–37). See Williams, 1960, Note 5.315–39.

5.400–1 *Didymaon's work / the Greeks had torn from Neptune's sacred gate:* Didymaon is otherwise unknown. The reference may be to an event in the Trojan War.

5.539–98 *those who wish / to contend with winging shafts . . . :* In the archery contest Acestes places first, Eurytion second, Mnestheus third, and Hippocoön fourth. See Williams, 1960, note 5.485–518.

5.548–50 *famous Pandarus, / archer who once . . . :* For the Iliadic background of this passage, see PANDARUS (1), Trojan archer who at Troy, under Athena's orders, "broke that truce [between the Trojans and the Argives], / the first to whip an arrow into the Argive ranks," and wounded Menelaus. For the event and its consequences, see *Iliad* 4.99–167.

5.575–76 *a potent marvel / destined to shape the future:* Though there has been debate about the meaning of the sign, its positive nature and association with Acestes probably is meant to anticipate the latter's founding of ACESTA.

5.612 *hair bound tight:* Since at lines 743–45 Ascanius doffs his helmet, we must assume that there was a change of headgear after the initial moments of the ceremony.

5.655–62 *This tradition . . . :* The earliest reference we have to the equestrian maneuvers known as "the Game of Troy," or simply "Troy," dates from the time of Sulla, which is to say the late second or early first century B.C. As with so many other details in Book 5, the anachronism is deliberate on Virgil's part. See TROY (3).

5.757 *devoted Aeneas ripped the robe:* To tear one's garments is a customary sign of grief in many cultures.

5.894–903 *I cared for your Aeneas . . . :* To support his point, Neptune refers to two incidents, one at the start of the *Aeneid*, in the storm off Carthage, which only the king of the sea can calm, and another in *Iliad* 20.314–86, where Neptune removes Aeneas from mortal combat with Achilles.

5.906 *Only one will be lost:* Palinurus; see 5.929–72.

5.920 *Fair-Isle, Sea-Cave, Spray, and the Waves' Embrace:* Throughout the *Aeneid*, the translation attempts to render many, but far from all, "significant names" in terms of their Greek or Latin roots. Following the lead of such translators as Arrowsmith, Rouse, and Fitzgerald, this has been the translator's practice with certain Homeric names—the marine names of the Nereids, for example, in the *Iliad* (18.43–56, and Note ad loc), and the nautical names of the Phaeacian sea-men in the *Odyssey* (8.129–39, and Note ad loc). Here in *Aeneid* 5.920, where Virgil has borrowed a few Homeric names for the Nereids (*Iliad* 18.45–46), the translator borrows and adapts a few of his own English names in turn. Elsewhere, the names "Fire-Anvil,""Lightning," and "Thunder" (8.501) for the Cyclops who forge Aeneas' shield, and the name "Blaze" for Pallas' charger (11.103), reflect the same approach. (The translator has refrained, however, from rendering the name of Mezentius' mount—*Rhaebus* [10.1021], "Bandy-Legs" in Greek—lest it recall the awkward American champion, Seabiscuit.)

5.964–65 *the Sirens' rocks— / hard straits once . . . . :* See SIRENS. Servius connected the Sirens with Capreae, modern Capri, off the southern coast of the Bay of Naples. It is with one of the Sirens, Parthenope standing for Naples itself, that Virgil connects the writing of the *Georgics* (see *Georgics* 4.564).

6.53 *an enormous cavern pierced by a hundred tunnels:* See the detailed discussion, with illustrations, by Austin (1977, Note 6.42–76).

6.89–90 *don't commit your words / to the . . . leaves:* A reference to the Sibyl's typically helter-skelter way of delivering her oracles, which prompts Aeneas' prayer that she sing those oracles herself, presumably in the interests of clarity and permanence.

6.106 *a new Achilles:* For the significance of the Sibyl's expression, see Note 7.434–36, and TURNUS.

6.111 *Again a stranger bride:* As Williams explains (1972, note 6.93–94), "the first foreign bride was Helen, this one will be Lavinia." The first was the cause of the Trojan War; the second, the cause of the war in Latium.

6.116 *a city built by Greeks:* The Sibyl refers, in her riddling way, both to Evander and his Greek roots, and to Pallanteum, his Italian capital (later Rome), and the assistance it can offer Aeneas and his armies. See 8.50–59, and Williams, 1972, Note 6.97.

6.158–59 *twice / to sail the Stygian marsh, to see black Tartarus twice:* As Williams notes, "instead of the normal once" (1972, note 6.134); or as Circe praises Ulysses for his courage in descending to the Underworld while still alive, "doomed to die twice over—others die just once" (*Odyssey* 12.24).

6.239–45 *the twofold tree, its green / a foil for the breath of gold . . . :* See R. A. Brooks under Commager in Suggestions for Further Reading.

6.384–423 *Palinurus . . . / fresh from the Libyan run . . . :* The discrepancies between Virgil's accounts of Palinurus' death, here and at 5.921–72, are discussed by Williams, 1960, Note 5.827f., and in his Introduction to Book 5, pp. xxv–xxviii.

6.395 *Apollo's prophetic cauldron:* The *cortina* was actually the cauldron that stood on top of the tripod, hence a metonymy for Delphi and for Apollo.

6.557–58 *Here Tydeus . . . Parthenopaeus . . . / Adrastus' pallid phantom:* The first three ghost-heroes mentioned here, Tydeus, Parthenopaeus, and Adrastus, formed part of the so-called Seven against Thebes. This failed expedition, which was organized by Polynices, son of Oedipus and Jocasta, to retake the throne of Thebes from his brother, Eteocles, was led by Adrastus, who alone survived. Parthenopaeus receives a succinct but moving lament at the conclusion of Statius' epic *Thebaid*, which takes the ill-fated adventure as its subject.

6.588 *three times with a ringing voice:* The triple cry raised as a funeral rite, presumably a farewell to the dead; three times presumably to make sure the dead hear the cry.

6.615–16 *Ulysses . . . / Aeolus' crafty heir:* Ulysses is here called *Aeolides*, which is to say grandson of AEOLUS (1), a caustic reference to the story that Ulysses had been fathered by Sisyphus, son of Aeolus, on Anticleia before her marriage to Laertes.

6.877 *bright souls, future heirs of our name and our renown:* For the figures in Anchises' pageant, see Introduction, pp. 25–33.

6.879 *that youth who leans on a tipless spear of honor:* i.e. Silvius; see Introduction, p. 29.

6.900–1 *[Jupiter] marks him out / with his own bolts of honor:* The most likely sign that would associate Romulus with Jupiter is the lightning bolt, which he presumably carried in his hand. The *spolia opima*, weapons taken from an enemy chieftain and dedicated to Jupiter—a tradition begun by Romulus, have also been suggested.

6.942 *the fasces he reclaims:* For "fasces," see Introduction, p. 30.

6.925 *the stag with its brazen hoofs:* i.e., the Hind of Ceryneia, which Hercules stalked through Arcadia and hunted down as the fourth of his labors.

6.1035–36 *shows them out now / through the Ivory Gate:* For the distinction between the Gate of Ivory and the Gate of Horn as passageways for our dreams, see 6.1029–33, and Introduction, p. 32.

7.127–28 *eating / our platters now:* The reference goes back to 3.295–310, where, however, the prophecy is uttered by the Harpy Celaeno, not Anchises.

7.176–77 *an olive branch of Pallas / wound in wool:* The olive branch, traditional symbol of peace, is here wreathed with woolen bands, as Aeneas makes his supplication.

7.260 *the four cool zones of earth:* Ilioneus considers the earth as divided into five zones. The central torrid zone is flanked by the remaining four, two temperate, adjacent to it, and two cold, at the extremes.

7.327 *the mixed breed that crafty Circe bred:* Circe was able to mate the immortal horses of her father, the Sun, with mortal stock to create a mixed breed.

7.358–59 *for what foul crimes did Calydon and the Lapiths / merit so much pain?* Calydon was ravaged by a boar sent by Diana to destroy the countryside, because its king, Oeneus, had slighted her. It was finally killed by Meleager. The Lapiths, among whom Ixion and Pirithous are to be numbered, were at the latter's wedding set to fighting the Centaurs by Mars, because he was not invited to the feast. At *Aeneid* 6.694 they are among the sinners perpetually punished in Tartarus.

7.375–77 *wedding torch . . . funeral torch . . . :* Hecuba dreamed, before giving birth to Paris, that she was pregnant with a burning torch. Juno sees Aeneas as a second Paris, snatching Lavinia as the latter did Helen, to become himself a bane to Troy as the city is reborn.

7.434–36 *Turnus too: track down the roots . . . :* His Greek roots, delineated here, together with his Iliadic ferocity, support the Sibyl's designation of him, at 6.106, as "a new Achilles."

7.770 *hero of Tiryns:* Hercules was born in Tiryns, in the Argolid, and his mother, Alcmena, was the daughter of the king of Tiryns.

7.850 *a supple thong for swifter hurling:* Horsfall on 7.731 says that the throwing-strap was "to impart rotatory motion."

7.884–908 *Virbius, striking son of Hippolytus . . . :* Hippolytus, son of Theseus and Hippolyte, was torn apart by his horses at his father's command, for his supposed involvement with his stepmother, Phaedra. He was restored to life by Aesculapius, with the help of Diana. He settled in Aricia, a town in Latium east of Rome where there was a grove and temple sacred to Diana, on the edge of modern Lago di Nemi.

8.54–57 *On these shores Arcadians sprung from Pallas* . . . : Evander, descendant of PALLAS (2), king of Arcadia in the western Peloponnese, was driven into exile for killing his father. With his Arcadian followers he settled in the Tiber valley, founding Pallanteum on the future site of Rome.

8.84 *you great horned king of the rivers of the West:* Rivers are often depicted with the face and horns of a bull, emblematic of its roar and, more generally, power. See 8.852.

8.315 *The Greatest Altar:* The *Ara Maxima* was dedicated to Hercules Invictus, the Unconquered, to whom an annual sacrifice was offered on August 12. It was located in the Forum Boarium on the banks of the Tiber. Its remains may lie beneath the present Church of Santa Maria in Cosmedin.

8.346 *Centaurs born of the clouds:* Ixion attempted to rape Hera, but Zeus substituted for her a cloud, resulting in the first Centaur; see CENTAURS and IXION.

8.426–30 *Hercules in his triumph stooped to enter here* . . . : As Gransden remarks (note 8.364–65), "On this celebrated sentiment Dryden observed 'I am lost in the admiration of it. I contemn the world when I think of it, and myself when I translate it.'"

8.450 *Remember Aurora . . . and Nereus' daughter:* Thetis, sea-nymph and mother of Achilles, had asked Hephaestus (Vulcan) to make armor for her son, the same request as that of Aurora, wife of Tithonus, for her son Memnon. The shield of Achilles is described in *Iliad* 18.558–709.

8.738–853 *There is the story of Italy* . . . : For the historical events emblazoned on the shield of Aeneas, see Introduction, pp. 33–36.

9.166–71 *'To die once is enough'? / The crime they committed once should be enough* . . . : See Fairclough's reading, reproduced by Goold, of this difficult passage: "The argument is this: one would have expected them to be haters of women, rather than commit a second offence like that of abducting Helen, especially as they are cowards who refuse to face a fight" (rev. Fairclough, 2000, note 9.6). See Hardie, 1994, note 9.140–42.

9.466–68 *You, goddess, Latona's daughter:* That is, the MOON.

9.604 *help me unroll the massive scroll of war:* The metaphor is based on the unfolding of a large book-scroll dealing with the martial events to follow.

9.681 *penned up twice over inside blockaded ramparts:* First at Troy, and now in Italy.

10.96–97 *you can / whisk Aeneas clear of the clutches of the Greeks:* As Williams explains (1973, note 10.81f.), "The reference here is to the story told in Homer

[*Iliad* 5.347–55] of how Aphrodite saved Aeneas from Diomedes and Apollo concealed him in a cloud."

10.132 *Trojan or Italian, I make no choice between them:* Is this an expression of Jupiter's impartiality, or is it in fact a momentary act of abdication from human affairs? See Introduction, p. 21.

10.242 *Mantua:* Mantua (modern Mantova) lies in the Po valley, south of Verona and some ten miles north of the river itself. Virgil was born just to the south of Mantua, in the village of Andes. Archeology has confirmed its Etrurian origin, which Virgil details at 10.242–46. See Introduction, pp. 2, 3, 11.

10.587–90 *the sword-belt's massive weight / engraved with its monstrous crime . . . :* The baldric contains depictions of the forty-nine of the fifty daughters of Danaus, the Danaids, who murdered their cousin-husbands, sons of Aegyptus, on their wedding night.

10.917 *my son, my living trophy over Aeneas:* A trophy (*tropaeum* in Latin) consisted of a tree trimmed to human shape and decked with the armor of a slain warrior so as to resemble the dead. Lausus according to Mezentius will be a living trophy of Aeneas once he dons the Trojan's weaponry. Further, see Aeneas' construction of a trophy in the image of Mezentius, his victim, 11.5–13.

11.315–36 *we have been driven / to many shores:* For the fateful homeward journeys of many Greek leaders, see AGAMEMNON ("the Mycenaean commander," 11.322), ULYSSES (see CYCLOPS), DIOMEDES (see PALLADIUM and Notes 2.211, 11.335–6), IDOMENEUS, LOCRI, and MENELAUS (see PROTEUS).

11.335–36 *I like a maniac attacked . . . Venus . . . :* As one of the highpoints of his *aristeia* in *Iliad* 5.370–494, Diomedes assaulted Venus, an outrageous action for which, as he maintains in this passage, the gods have punished him and his people ever since.

11.483–85 *the Myrmidon captains cringe . . . :* We have here two examples of *adunata* (impossibilities), the one historical—the Greeks will be afraid of the Trojans—the other natural—the Aufidus will reverse its current.

12.488–96 *some dittany fresh / from Cretan Ida . . . and redolent cure-all too:* In addition to the dittany in her potion, Venus distills ambrosia which, as food or unguent, is always associated with the immortal gods and their powers. Panacea ("cure-all") was an herb noted for its medicinal properties.

12.573–77 *Aeneas . . . stung by treachery now:* This seems to refer to the Latins' treachery in violating the truce, "attacking [Aeneas] when he was not fighting them [12.544–46] but only seeking Turnus" (Williams, 1973, note 12.494).

12.870–71 *frightened back by the ropes / with blood-red feathers:* Virgil describes a cord, with crimson feathers attached, which hunters would use to surround game and pen them in.

12.980–88 *They say there are twin Curses called the Furies . . . :* The twin Furies are Allecto and Tisiphone, sisters of Megaera. The Curses (*Dirae*) and the Furies are regularly synonymous.

The main purpose of this Glossary is to indicate pronunciation. Identifications are typically brief, and are amplified by reference to the Translation, and often to the Introduction, the Notes on the Translation, and other Glossary entries as well. Usually only the first appearance of a name is listed.

The Latin vowels vary in pronunciation, sometimes but not always according to the length of the Latin syllable, and the reader will have to find guidance in the rhythm of the English line or consult this Glossary, where, for example, long 'i' is conveyed either through 'eye' (Anchises: *an-keye'-seez*) or 'ee' (Aequi Falisci: *ee'-kwee fa-lees'-kee*). Stress is indicated by an apostrophe *after* the stressed syllable (*af'-ter*). When a name is Anglicized, or has a standard English equivalent, we follow English pronunciation as a guide.

Phonetic Equivalents:

a as in *cat*   *o* as in *pot*
ay as in *day*   *oh* as in *bone*
aw as in *raw*   *oo* as in *boot*
ai as in *air*   *or* as in *bore*
ah as in *father*   *oy* as in *boy*

e as in *pet*   *s* as in *hiss*
ee as in *feet*   *th* as in *thin*

i as in *bit*   *u* as *us*
eye as in *bite*   *ur* as in *burst*

ABARIS (*a'-ba-ris*): Rutulian in Turnus' forces, killed by Euryalus, 9.400.

ABAS (*a'-bas*): (1) one of Aeneas' captains, his ship caught in the storm off Carthage, 1.142. (2) Ancient king of Argos, 3.342. (3) Etruscan from Populonia, an ally of Aeneas, 10.206.

ABELLA (*a-bee'-la*): Campanian town noted for its profusion of apples, 7.861.

ACAMAS (*a'-ka-mas*): Greek, son of Theseus, raider hidden in the Trojan horse, 2.333.

ACARNANIAN (*a-kar-nay'-ni-an*): Greek from Acarnania, an area in west-central Greece, 5.332.

ACCA (*ay'-ka*): ally and confidante of Camilla, 11.960.

ACESTA (*a-kees'-ta*): western Sicilian city, named after King Acestes, now Segesta, 5.796.

ACESTES (*a-kees'-teez*): king of Sicily, born of Trojan stock, son of Crinisus, and an ally of Anchises and Aeneas, whom he hosts in his island home; he places first in the archery contest at Anchises' funeral games, since his arrow shoots into a flaming omen, 1.230. See Note 5.539–98.

ACHAEMENIDES (*a-kee-men'-i-deez*): comrade of Ulysses, who abandons him on the Cyclops' island; saved from the one-eyed monsters by Aeneas and his Trojans, 3.712.

ACHAEANS (*a-kee'-anz*): Greeks and their allies ranged against the Trojans in the ten year siege of the city; 6.962, more generally, a collective name for all Greek people, and ACHAEAN (*a-kee'-an*) for their effects, 12.417.

ACHATES (*a-kah'-teez*): loyal confidante and steadfast comrade of Aeneas, 1.142.

ACHERON (*a'-ke-ron*): "Sad Acheron of sorrow, black and deep," in Milton's phrase, one of the major rivers in the Underworld, 5.119. See Note 3.262.

ACHILLES (*a-kil'-eez*): son of Peleus and Thetis, grandson of Aeacus, father of Pyrrhus (also called Neoptolemus); commander of the Myrmidons, killer of Hector and many other Trojans, killed by Paris empowered by Apollo; the hero of the *Iliad*, 1.38.

ACMON (*ayk'-mon*): comrade of Aeneas, born in Lyrnesus; his father, Clytius (2); his brother, Menestheus, 10.158.

ACOETES (*a-kee'-teez*): Arcadian, armor-bearer of King Evander, comrade-in-arms of Pallas (3), whom he treats as a foster son, 11.37.

ACONTEUS (*a-kohn'-tyoos*): Latin, pitched off his horse by Tyrrhenus, who takes his life, 11.725.

ACRAGAS (*a'-kra-gas*): Greek name (meaning "steep") for a city on the southern coast of Sicily, one of Aeneas' seamarks when he sails around the island; famous for breeding horses; now called Agrigento, 3.812.

ACRISIUS (*ay-kree'-si-us*): king of Argos, father of Danaë; legendary builder of a capital city, Ardea, to the south of Rome, for his Rutulian people, 7.435.

ACRON (*ay'-kron*): Greek killed by Mezentius, 10.849.

ACTIUM (*ak'-ti-um*): a town and promontory off the northwestern coast of Greece, site of a decisive naval battle between the armada of Octavian and that of Antony and Cleopatra in 31 B.C., 3.329; ACTIAN (*ak'-ti-an*), belonging to that locale, 3.334. See 8.791–836 and Introduction, p. 35.

ACTOR (*ayk'-tor*): Trojan under Aeneas' command, 9.575.

ADAMASTUS (*a-da-mays'-tus*): Ithacan, father of Achaemenides, 3.713.

ADIGE (*a'-di-jay*): ancient Athesis, a river in the Veneto, in northern Italy, 9.774.

ADRASTUS (*a-dras'-tus*): king of Argos, father-in-law of Tydeus and Polynices, 6.558. See Note 6.557–58.

ADRIATIC (*ay-dree-at'-ik*): the modern Adriatic Sea, ancient Hadria, between the Balkan peninsula and the Eastern coast of Italy, 11.485.

AEAEA (*ee-ee'-a*): island home of Circe, 3.458, placed by Virgil off the Latian coast, southeast of Rome. It later became a headland called by the Romans Circeii (modern Monte Circeo).

AEACUS (*ee'-a-kus*): father of Peleus, grandfather of Achilles, 6.966. See PAULLUS, PERSEUS, and Introduction, p. 30.

AEGAEON (*ee-jee'-on*): name used by mortals for the hundred-handed giant called Briareus by the gods, 10.671. See *Iliad* 1.479–80.

AEGEAN (*ee-jee'-an*): the modern Aegean sea, between the Balkan peninsula and Asia Minor, 12.435.

AENEAS (*ee-nee'-as*): son of Anchises and Venus, commander of the Dardanians and, after the death of Anchises, king of the Trojans and the central figure in the *Aeneid*, 1.111. See Introduction, Notes, and Glossary, passim, and *Iliad* 20.95–402.

AENUS (*ee'-nus*): Thracian colony putatively named after Aeneas, who was its founder, 3.23. See Williams, 1962, note 3.18.

AEOLIAN (*ee-oh'-li-an*): belonging to islands of the winds, located to the north of Sicily, ruled by Aeolus (1) and named for their king, 1.62. Identified with Lipare, 8.491.

AEOLUS (*ee'-o-lus*): (1) lord of the winds, 1.64, father of Salmoneus and, in all likelihood, Misenus, 6.196; and so-called grandfather of Ulysses, 6.615–16; see Note ad loc. (2) Father of Clytius (1) a Trojan killed by Turnus, 9.872. (3) Trojan comrade of Aeneas, killed by Turnus, 12.634.

AEQUI FALISCI (*ee'-kwee fa-lees'-kee*): a town in southern Etruria, on the western edge of the Tiber valley some twenty-five miles north of Rome. More commonly called Falerii (near modern Civita Castellana), 7.810.

AEQUIAN (*ee'-kwee-an*): of a rugged Italian tribe living in the foothills of the Apennines, largely east of Rome, 7.867.

AETOLIAN (*ee-toh'-li-an*): 10.35, like Diomedes, a native of AETOLIA (*ee-toh'-li-a*), a region in northwestern Greece, 11.287.

AFRICA: referring mainly, in the *Aeneid*, to Libya, a northern region of the continent, 4.47.

AGAMEMNON (*a-ga-mem'-non*): Greek, king of Mycenae, son of Atreus, husband of Clytemnestra, murdered by her and her paramour, Aegisthus; brother of Menelaus, supreme commander of all Achaea's armies, leader of the largest Greek contingent at Troy, and the conqueror of the city, 3.63. See Note 11.315–36, *Iliad*, passim, and for Homer's version of the death of the king, see *Odyssey* 4.573–604.

AGATHYRSIANS (*a-ga-theer'-shanz*): people of Scythia who tattooed their bodies, 4.183.

AGENOR (*a-jee'-nor*): legendary ruler and founder of Phoenicia, forebear of Dido, 1.412.

AGIS (*ay'-jis*): Lycian killed by Valerus, 10.887.

AGRIPPA (*a-gri'-pa*): Marcus Vipsanius Agrippa, son-in-law of Augustus and his potential successor; admiral, second in command of the Roman armada at the battle of Actium, 8.799. He was awarded the Naval Crown for his decisive role in the victory over Sextus Pompeius in the sea-battle off Naulochus in 36 B.C. See Introduction, p. 2.

AGYLLA (*a-gee'-la*): 7.758, Greek name for CAERE, Etrurian city whose contingent of AGYLLINES (*a-gee'-leyenz*), Tuscan allies of Turnus, is led by Lausus, 12.338.

AJAX (*ay'-jaks*): Greek, son of Oileus, Oilean or Little Ajax, at Troy the commander of the Locrian contingent. For ravishing Cassandra in the Trojan temple of Minerva, the goddess destroyed him and his fleet on the homeward run from Troy, 1.51. See Note 1.49–55 and *Odyssey* 4.560–73.

ALBAN (*al'-ban*): 1.8, person or place belonging to ALBA LONGA (*al'-ba long'-a*), the foundational city of Rome, some fifteen miles to its southeast, 1.325.

ALBULA (*ayl'-bu-la*): legendary name of the Tiber, 8.390.

ALBUNEA (*ayl-bun'-e-a*): a woodland and fountain or sulfur spring near Lavinium, 7.92.

ALCANDER (*ayl-kayn'-der*): Trojan killed by Turnus, 9.865.

ALCANOR (*al-kay'-nor*): (1) Trojan, father by the nymph Iaera of Pandarus (2) and Bitias, 9.766. (2) Latin ally of Turnus, brother of Maeon, killed by Aeneas, 10.398.

ALCATHOUS *(ayl-ka'-tho-us)*: Trojan killed by Caedicus (2), 10.882.

ALETES *(a-lee'-teez)*: Trojan, survivor of shipwreck off the Libyan coast, a seasoned adviser of Aeneas, 1.143.

ALLECTO *(a-lek'-toh)*: one of the three Furies, 7.379. See Introduction, p. 20.

ALLIA *(ay'-li-a)*: small tributary of the Tiber, six miles upriver from Rome, where, in 390 B.C., the Romans suffered a harsh defeat by the Gauls, and so an "ominous name" from that time on, 7.834.

ALMO *(ayl'-moh)*: Latin, Tyrrhus' eldest son, and first to fall in the open warfare between Latins and Trojans, 7.618.

ALOEUS *(a-lee'-us)*: father of the giants, Otus and Ephialtes, who were confined in Tartarus for attempting to overthrow Jupiter, 6.675.

ALPS: the great mountain range of central Europe, 10.17. See Introduction, p. 26.

ALPHEUS *(al-fee'-us)*: river and its legendary god in the western Peloponnese; driven underground by his unsatisfied desire for the nymph ARETHUSA, he surges up to mingle with her spring in Syracuse on Sicily, 3.802.

ALSUS *(ayl'-sus)*: Rutulian shepherd who kills Podalirius, 12.366.

ALTARS: a great reef between Africa and Sicily, and a constant danger to mariners, 1.130. Cf. Longfellow's "reef of Norman's Woe" in "The Wreck of the Hesperus," about a wreck off Gloucester, Massachusetts.

AMASENUS *(a-ma-see'-nus)*: Latian river associated with the contingent from Praeneste, allies of Turnus, 7.798.

AMASTRUS *(a-mays'-trus)*: Trojan killed by Camilla, 11.794.

AMATA *(a-mah'-ta)*: wife of King Latinus and mother of Lavinia; victim of the Fury Allecto, she takes her own life upon thinking that Turnus has been killed, 7.402.

AMATHUS *(a'-ma-thus)*: town in southern Cyprus, a favored, sacred haunt of Venus, 10.62.

AMAZONS *(a'-ma-zonz)*: a mythical nation of women warriors, vaguely located in the north, who are supposed to have invaded Phrygia in Asia Minor, 1.592.

AMITERNUM *(a-mi-teer'-num)*: a town in the Sabine territory, its contingent led by Clausus, allies of Turnus, 7.827.

AMPHITRYON *(am-fi'-tri-on)*: Alcmena's husband and supposed father of her son, Hercules, who was actually sired by Jupiter, 8.115.

AMSANCTUS (*aym-saynk'-tus*): sulphurous lake in the territory of the Samnites, inland from Naples, a breathing vent for the God of Death, and "the navel of Italy," according to Servius, 7.655.

AMYCLAE (*a-mee'-klee*): a town in Latium, ruled by Camers. Its "silence" has been explained in various ways, none of them convincing, 10.670.

AMYCUS (*a'-mi-kus*): (1) Trojan, comrade of Aeneas, shipwrecked off the coast of Libya, 1.261. (2) Harsh king of the Thracian Bebrycians, and a champion boxer ultimately taken down by Pollux, 5.416. (3) Trojan, comrade of Aeneas and an expert hunter, killed by Turnus, 9.870. (4) Father of Mimas by Theano, killed by Mezentius, 10.832. (5) Trojan, brother of Diores, killed by Turnus, 12.595.

ANAGNIA (*a-nayg'-ni-a*): Latian town east of Rome (modern Anagni), source of a contingent allied with Turnus, 7.797.

ANCHEMOLUS (*an-ke'-mo-lus*): son of Rhoeteus, king of the Marsi; killed by Pallas (3), 10.458.

ANCHISES (*an-keye'-seez*): Trojan of royal descent, grandson of Assaracus, son of Capys (2), second cousin of Priam, father by Venus of Aeneas, his son who accompanies him from Troy to Sicily, where Anchises dies, 1.739. See Introduction, Notes, and Glossary, passim.

ANCUS (*an' kus*): Ancus Martius, the fourth king of Rome, 6.939. See Introduction, p. 30.

ANDROGEOS (*ayn-dro'-je-os*): (1) Greek captain killed at the fall of Troy, 2.463. (2) Son of Minos the king of Crete; when the Athenians murdered Androgeos, his father demanded in restitution the yearly sacrifice to the Minotaur of seven Athenian girls and seven boys, 6.24.

ANDROMACHE (*an-dro'-ma-kee*): daughter of Eetion, wife of Hector, then of Pyrrhus, and finally of the prophet Helenus; mother of Astyanax, and one of the leading heroines of the *Iliad*. See *Aeneid* 2.569, 3.389–400, and Note ad loc.

ANGITIA (*ayn-gi'-ti-a*): a sorceress, sister of, or perhaps epithet of Medea herself; Lake Fucinus, modern Piano del Fucino east of Avezzano, was sacred to her for its healing powers, 7.881.

ANIO (*a'-ni-o*): a tributary of the Tiber, rising in the Apennines and passing through the territory of the Sabines, source of a contingent allied with Turnus, 7.796.

ANIUS (*a'-ni-us*): priest of Apollo and king of Delos, who welcomes Aeneas' party to the island, 3.97.

ANNA (*an'-a*): sister of Dido, who attempts to intercede between Dido and Aeneas, 4.11.

ANTAEUS (*an-tee'-us*): Latin under Turnus' command, killed by Aeneas, 10.667.

ANTANDROS (*an-tan'-dros*): town under the heights of Phrygian Mount Ida (1), where Aeneas builds his fleet, 3.6.

ANTEMNAE (*ayn-teem'-nee*): Sabine town at the juncture of the Anio and the Tiber; a source of armaments for Turnus' forces, 7.734.

ANTENOR (*an-tee'-nor*): Trojan escapee from the fall of Troy, who precedes Aeneas to Italy, founder of Patavium, now Padua, 1.287. See Note 1.287–97.

ANTHEUS (*ayn'-theus*): Trojan, companion of Aeneas, fathered by Sarpedon, and pilot of a shipwrecked vessel in his fleet, 1.215.

ANTIPHATES (*an-ti'-fa-teez*): an ally of Aeneas, killed by Turnus, 9.791.

ANTONY (*an'-toh-nee*): triumvir, Marcus Antonius, 8.803. See Introduction, pp. 2–6.

ANTORES (*ayn-toh'-reez*): Hercules' aide who affiliated himself with Evander, comrade of Aeneas, killed by Mezentius, 10.920.

ANUBIS (*a-noo'-bis*): Egyptian deity in Cleopatra's train at the battle of Actium; protector of tombs, typically portrayed with the head of a dog or jackal and the body of a man, 8.819.

ANXUR (*aynks'-oor*): (1) Volscian town in Latium, sacred to Jupiter, also known as Tarracina or Terracina (modern Terracina) and renowned for its grove where Jupiter presided, 7.928. (2) Rutulian killed by Aeneas, 10.645.

APENNINE (*a'-pe-neyen*): belonging to the central mountain ridge of the Italian peninsula 11.826; its divinity is "Father / Apennine himself," 12.813–14.

APHIDNUS (*a-feed'-nus*): Trojan killed by Turnus, 9.797.

APOLLO (*a-pol'-oh*): god, son of Jupiter and Latona (Leto), twin brother of Diana, a patron of the arts, especially music and poetry. Also an archer, a healer, and a prophet with a famous oracular shrine at Delphi, in central Greece. The principal divine champion of the Greeks, 1.400. As Augustus' patron divinity, he presides appropriately over the battle of Actium, in Virgil's description, 8.826. See Note 4.179 and PHOEBUS.

AQUICULUS (*a-kwee'-cu-lus*): Rutulian stopped at the gates of Aeneas' encampment, 9.778.

ARABIANS: inhabitants of Arabia Felix, modern Yemen, against which the Romans sent an ill-fated expedition in 24 B.C., 8.827.

ARAXES (*a-rak'-seez*): river in Armenia, bridged by Alexander, but the span was ripped from its moorings by the stream's powerful current, 8.853.

ARCADIANS (*ar-kay'-di-anz*): 8.54, inhabitants of ARCADIA (*ar-kay'-di-a*), a region in the rugged central Peloponnese where Evander was born, 8.113. It is treated by Virgil in his *Eclogues* as the place of origin of pastoral poetry.

ARCENS (*ayr'-kens*): Sicilian, father of a nameless ally of Aeneas, killed by Mezentius, 9.660.

ARCETIUS (*ayr-ket'-i-us*): Rutulian killed by Mnestheus, 12.539.

ARCHIPPUS (*ayr-kee'-pus*): Marsian king who sent Umbro to fight on Turnus' side, only to be killed by Trojans, 7.874.

ARCTURUS (*ark-too'-rus*): the Bear-Watcher, most brilliant star in the constellation called the Wagon; its rising coincides with heavy spring rains, 1.894. See GREAT AND LITTLE BEARS.

ARDEA (*ayr'-de-a*): the Rutulians' capital city, south of Rome; the home of Turnus and place where he was born, 7.480.

ARETHUSA (*a-re-thoo'-sa*): fountain at the seaward edge of Syracuse, that, according to legend, draws its waters underground from the ALPHEUS River in Greece, 3.804.

ARGILETUM (*ar-gi-lee'-tum*): a main artery leading from the Roman Forum northeast toward the Esquiline and Viminal hills. Virgil derives its name from "the death of Argus" (2), but it more likely stems from *argilla* (clay), 8.405.

ARGOS (*ar'-gos*): 1.30, city or district in the northeastern Peloponnese, or the general region of the Achaeans, mainland Greece, inhabited by the ARGIVE (*ar'-geyev*) people, 1.50.

ARGUS (*ar'-gus*): (1) hundred-eyed monster, guardian assigned to Io by Juno and killed by Mercury, 7.918. (2) Legendary guest of Evander, who was killed for plotting against his host, 8.406.

ARGYRIPA (*ayr-gi'-ri-pa*): city in Apulia, established by Diomedes and called thereafter Arpi, 11.296.

ARICIA (*a-ree'-si-a*): Latian city named for its resident nymph, the mother of Virbius, 7.885. See Note 7.884–908.

ARISBA (*a-reez'-bah*): city in the Troad conquered by Aeneas, 9.313. Beyond Virgil's mention, the connection with Aeneas is obscure.

ARPI (*ayr'-pi*): alternative name for Argyripa, 10.34.

ARRUNS (*ay'-runz*): an Etruscan ally of Aeneas, and the killer of Camilla, 11.893.

ASBYTES (*ays-bee'-teez*): Trojan killed by Turnus, 12.431.

ASCANIUS (*as-kay'-ni-us*): grandson of Anchises, son of Aeneas and Creusa, also called Iulus, 1.320–21; see ILUS (1). For his relationship to the later Julian family, see Introduction, pp. 12–17.

ASIA: actually Asia Minor in the context of the *Aeneid*; a region originally named for a Lydian city there, 1.467.

ASILAS (*a-see'-las*): (1) Rutulian, who kills the Trojan Corynaeus (1), 9.651. (2) Etruscan seer and a fighting ally of Aeneas, 10.211.

ASIUS (*a'-si-us*): Trojan, defender of Aeneas' camp, 10.152.

ASSARACI (*ay-sa'-ra-kee*): two Trojans, both defenders of Aeneas' camp, 10.153.

ASSARACUS (*ay-sa'-ra-kus*): son of Tros, brother of Ilus (2) and Ganymede, father of Capys (2), grandfather of Anchises, great-grandfather of Aeneas, 1.339.

ASTYANAX (*as-teye'-a-naks*): "Lord of the City" in Greek, infant son of Hector and Andromache, flung to his death from the walls of Troy by the victorious Greeks, 2.571. See *Iliad* 6.471–577, 22.566–96.

ASTYR (*ay'-stir*): Etruscan comrade of Aeneas, 10.218.

ASYLUM: the Asylum, a grove between the two summits of the Capitoline hill, was established by Romulus as a place of refuge, 8.402.

ATHENA (*a-thee'-na*): 2.208; see MINERVA, PALLAS (1), and TRITONIAN; Notes 1.49–55, 2.211; and Introduction p. 17.

ATHOS (*a'-thos*): mountain on a promontory in the northern Aegean Sea, 12.813.

ATINA (*a-tee'-na*): Italian town, still bearing the same name, that housed a Volscian clan, 7.733.

ATINAS (*a-tee'-nas*): Rutulian captain, routed along with other allies of Turnus at Aeneas' gates, 11.1017.

ATLAS (*at'-las*): father of Electra and Maia, tutor of Iopas, the Carthaginian bard, a Titan who upheld the pillars separating the earth and sky (for Atlas' powers, see *Odyssey* 1.62–64), and was transformed into Mount Atlas, a peak in northern Africa, 1.889.

ATREUS (*ay'-tryoos*): grandson of Tantalus, son of Pelops, brother of Thyestes, king of Mycenae, and father of Agamemnon and Menelaus, the Atridae, 1.553.

ATYS (*a'-tis*): Trojan youth in the equestrian display at Anchises' funeral games, soon to be the source of the Latin ATIANS (*ay'-shanz*) (5.625). By the name Atys, Virgil is suggesting the origin of the *gens* Atia and hence of Augustus, whose mother Atia, married to Caius Octavius, was the niece of Julius Caesar. See Introduction, pp. 1–2.

AUFIDUS (*aw'-fi-dus*): river in Apulia, now the Ofanto, whose strong currents empty into the Adriatic, and so the river cannot possibly flow backward from the Adriatic, 11.485. See Note 11.483–85.

AUGUSTUS (*aw-gus'-tus*): imperial title, awarded in 27 B.C. to the first Roman emperor, Octavius Caesar: the grand-nephew of Julius Caesar and adopted as his son, 6.914. See ATYS; CAESAR, JULIUS; ILUS (1); JULIUS; and Introduction passim.

AULESTES (*aw-lees'-teez*): allied to Aeneas, an Etruscan captain who sails the *Triton,* 10.251.

AULIS (*aw'-lis*): district in the narrow strait between Euboea and the Greek mainland, where the Greek fleet gathered before sailing for Troy and Agamemnon sacrificed his daughter, Iphigenia, 4.534.

AUNUS (*aw'-nus*): Ligurian, his son killed by Camilla, 11.826.

AURORA (*aw-roh'-ra*): interchangeable with Dawn, 3.684.

AURUNCAN (*aw-run'-kan*): of the original Italian people, named after Aurunca, an ancient Campanian town northwest of Naples, 7.236.

AUSONIA (*aw-soh'-ni-a*): 7.61, land of the AUSONIANS (*aw-soh'-ni-anz*), people of southern Italy, and a collective name for all of Italy too, 9.728.

AUTOMEDON (*aw-to'-me-don*): Achilles' henchman, charioteer, and armor-bearer, 2.594.

AVENTINUS (*a-ven-teye'-nus*): son of Hercules (mentioned nowhere else, see Williams, 1973, note 7.655f.) by a priestess, Rhea, 7.762; eponym for the AVENTINE (*a'-ven-teyen*) hill, one of the seven hills of Rome, 7.767.

AVERNUS (*a-ver'-nus*): modern Lago di Averno, lake in a volcanic crater just east of Cumae and west of Naples; "birdless" or "over which no birds will fly," as the name implies, since the caldera emitted noxious fumes; located near a legendary entrance to the Underworld, and so the name is often used of the Underworld in general, 3.519.

BACCHUS (*bah'-kus*): son of Jupiter and Semele, the god of wine, the vine, and ecstasy, 1.877; also called *Lyaeus* ("the Liberator," see 4.73).

BACTRA (*bak'-tra*): remote Eastern region bounded by the Oxus to the north and the Hindu Kush to the south, whose forces fought on the side of Antony and Cleopatra at the battle of Actium, 8.807.

BAIAE (*bah'-yee*): bayside town of Campania, just south of Cumae; one of the Romans' favorite spas and resorts, known by the Augustan era for the luxury of its villas built on piers out into the water, 9.806.

BARCE (*bayr'-see*): Sychaeus' old nurse, Dido's attendant, 4.788.

BARCAN (*bar'-kan*): of a Libyan people inhabiting the city of Barce, and known for their marauding ways, 4.55.

BATULUM (*ba'-tu-lum*): town in Campania, allied to Turnus, 7.860.

BEBRYCIAN (*be-bri'-shan*): of Bebrycia, a region in Asia Minor, forming the southern border of the Black Sea, 5.416.

BELLONA (*be-loh'-na*): Roman goddess of battle, cult-partner of Mars, 7.373.

BELUS (*bee'-lus*): (1) Father of Dido, 1.742. (2) First founder of Dido's Phoenician royal line of descent, 1.872. (3) Father of Palamedes and, according to Virgil, of Danaus and Aegyptus, 2.103.

BENACUS (*bee-nay'-kus*): "Father Benacus," personification of northern Italian lake, now Lago di Garda, and source of the Mincius River, 10.249.

BERECYNTHIAN (*be-re-sin'-thi-an*): of Berecynthia, a mountainous area in Phrygia, sacred to the Great Mother, Cybebe (Cybele), 6.905.

BEROË (*be'-roh-ee*): aged wife of Doryclus, impersonated by Iris in her machinations to destroy Aeneas' fleet, 5.684.

BITIAS (*bi'-ti-as*): (1) Tyrian nobleman in Dido's retinue, 1.884. (2) Brother of Pandarus (2), both born of Alcanor (1) and Iaera, Trojan comrade of Aeneas, killed by Turnus, 9.765.

BLACKSMITHS: i.e., Chalybes, people from Pontus, a region along the southern coast of the Black Sea, who were reputed to be master iron-workers and the originators of steel, 10.210.

BOLA (*boh'-la*): town in Latium, promised to the heirs of Aeneas, 6.895.

BRIAREUS (*bri-a'-ryoos*): name used by the gods for the hundred-handed giant called Aegaeon by mortals, 6.326. See *Iliad* 1.477–83.

BRUTUS (*broo'-tus*): Lucius Junius Brutus, the founder and first consul of the Roman Republic, known as Brutus the Avenger, because he avenged the allegiance of his sons to Tarquin, after he had been expelled, by executing them, 6.942. See Introduction, p. 30.

BUTES (*boo'-teez*): (1) braggart kin of Amycus (2), king of the Bebrycians, who was once overpowered by Dares in a boxing-match, 5.415. (2) Armor-bearer of Anchises, who, at Aeneas' bidding, protects Ascanius, 9.737. (3) Trojan killed by Camilla, 11.814.

BUTHROTUM (*boo-throh'-tum*): coastal city in Epirus, inhabited after the fall of Troy by the Trojans Helenus and Andromache and their people, who founded a miniature version of Troy, 3.350. See Note 3.389–400.

BYRSA (*beer'-sa*): the citadel of Carthage, from the Greek word for bull's-hide, 1.446. See Note ad loc.

CACUS (*ka'-kus*): son of Vulcan, fire-breathing monster who once lived on the Aventine hill in Pallanteum, savaging Evander's people until Hercules destroyed him, the occasion for yearly rites of celebration among the town's inhabitants, 8.227.

CAECULUS (*kee'-ku-lus*): Vulcan's son, found on a burning hearth, who established Praeneste; comrade-in-arms of Turnus, 7.791.

CAEDICUS (*kee'-di-kus*): (1) Latin companion and guest of Remulus (1), to whom he presented many gifts, 9.418. (2) Etruscan, comrade of Mezentius, 10.882.

CAENEUS (*kee'-nyoos*): (1) Thessalian girl changed by Neptune into a young man and then turned back by Fate to her original form, 6.519. (2) Trojan, killer of Ortygius; killed by Turnus, 9.653.

CAERE (*kee'-ree*): Etrurian city, called Agylla once, and now Cervetri, its banks a center of worship of Silvanus, god of forests, and the source of a contingent led by Lausus, 8.704.

CAESAR, JULIUS (*see'-zar, jool'-yus*): Caius Julius Caesar, known to history as Caesar. His family, the Julian *gens*, is "a name passed down from Iulus, his great forebear," 1.342–44. See ATYS, AUGUSTUS, ILUS (1), and Introduction, pp. 1–2.

CAICUS (*ka-ee'-kus*): Trojan, companion of Aeneas, his ship temporarily lost in the storm off Libya, 1.217.

CAIETA (*kay-ee'-ta*): (1) port and promontory on the western coast of Latium, now Gaeta, 6.1038, that derives its name from the name of Gaeta (2), Aeneas' nurse, since she is buried there, 7.1.

CALCHAS (*kal'-kas*): son of Thestor, prophet of the Achaeans in the service of Apollo and the armies of the Greeks, 2.126.

CALES (*kay'-leez*): town in central Campania, now Calvi, north of Capua, that sent a contingent to fight on Turnus' side, 7.846.

CALLIOPE (*ka-leye'-o-pee*): leader of the nine Muses; her province is epic poetry, and she is invoked by Virgil to help unfold the wars in Italy, 9.601.

CALYBE (*ka'-li-bee*): Rutulian priestess of Juno, impersonated by Allecto when she incites Turnus to battle, 7.490.

CALYDON (*ka'-li-don*): city in Aetolia, where Diomedes was born, the site of a legendary struggle between Aetolians and Curetes, 7.357; see Note 7.358–59.

CAMERINA (*ka-me-ree'-na*): town on the southern coast of Sicily; the settlement and its surrounding marshland are held in place by the Fates, 3.809.

CAMERS (*ka'-meers*): Rutulian, Volcens' son and an ally of Turnus, killed by Aeneas, 10.668.

CAMILLA *(ka-mil'-a)*: Volscian commander, comrade of Turnus, comparable to an Amazon like Penthesilea, "a warrior queen who dares to battle men" (1.595), 7.933.

CAMILLUS *(ka-meel'-us)*: Marcus Furius Camillus liberated Rome from the Gauls, 6.950. See Introduction, p. 30.

CAMPANIAN *(kam-pan'-yan)*: of Campania, a region of western central Italy, the name of whose major city, Capua, Virgil derives from the Trojan Capys (1), 10.176–77.

CAPENA *(ka-peen'-a)*: town in Etruria on the west bank of the Tiber, due north of Rome, its contingent allied with Turnus' forces, 7.812.

CAPHEREUS *(ka-fee'-ryoos)*: eastern headland of Euboea, where Greeks on the homeward run from Troy were stormed and sunk as part of Minerva's vengeance against Oilean Ajax for violating Cassandra, 11.314.

CAPITOL: the Capitoline hill in Rome, its southern height crowned by the temple of Jupiter Optimus Maximus, where Roman triumphal processions came to a conclusion, 6.963. See Introduction, pp. 20, 34.

CAPREAE *(ca'-pre-ee)*: modern Capri, an island off the peninsula that forms the southern edge of the Bay of Naples, and the source of a contingent allied to Turnus, 7.855.

CAPYS *(ka'-pis)*: (1) Trojan companion of Aeneas, restored to him after the storm off Libya; supposed founder of Capua (see CAMPANIAN), whose name the city bears; killer of Privernus, 1.217. (2) A king of Alba Longa, 6.888.

CARIANS *(kay'-ri-anz)*: Trojan allies, inhabitants of Caria, a region in southern Asia Minor facing the Aegean, 8.849.

CARINAE *(ka-reen'-ee)*: "the Keels," elegant district of future Rome, just north of the Roman Forum, at the base of the Esquiline, home to the fashionable and the powerful, 8.424.

CARMENTAL GATE *(kar-men'-tal)*: ancient entrance to the city of Rome, located at the western base of the Capitoline hill and named after Carmentis, 8.396.

CARMENTIS *(kar-men'-tis)*: nymph, prophetess, and mother of Evander, 8.394.

CARPATHIAN *(kar-pay'-thi-an)*: of Carpathus, an island in the Aegean, lying between Crete and Rhodes, 5.654.

CARTHAGE *(kar'-thage)*: capital city of Phoenician exiles, led by Dido, who settled them in northern Libya, a nation greatly favored by Juno, and later to become the mortal enemies of Rome in the Punic Wars, 1.15. See Introduction, passim.

CASMILLA *(kas-mee'-la)*: mother of Camilla by Metabus, 11.644.

CASPERIA (*kay-sper'-i-a*): Sabine town, whose contingent was allied with Turnus, 7.831.

CASPIAN (*kas'-pi-an*): inland sea, the largest in the world, between Europe and Asia, 6.921.

CASSANDRA (*ka-san'-dra*): daughter of Priam, sister of Hector, lover of Agamemnon, murdered with him by Aegisthus and Clytemnestra. She was a prophetess who foresaw the doom of Troy, her visions inspired by Apollo who, his love rebuffed, denied her the power ever to be believed, 2.311. See *Iliad* 24.819–30.

CASTOR (*kas'-tor*): Trojan comrade of Aeneas, 10.153.

CATILINE (*ka'-ti-leyen*): Lucius Sergius Catilina who, in 63 B.C., organized a conspiracy, which bears his name, to overthrow the Roman government, 8.783. See Introduction, pp. 1, 34.

CATILLUS (*ka-teel'-us*): twin brother of Coras, brother of Tiburtus, and with his brothers, one who established Tibur and was allied with Turnus' forces, 7.783.

CATO (*kay' toh*): (1) Marcus Porcius Cato, the Censor, harsh giver of laws, 6.968. (2) Marcus Porcius Cato, called Uticensis because he committed suicide at Utica in Africa rather than endure the victory of Caesar; great-grandson of Cato the Censor, 8.785. See Introduction, p. 34.

CAUCASUS (*kaw'-ka-sus*): a mountain range between the Black and Caspian seas, where an eagle perpetually devoured the liver of Prometheus, shackled to a rocky ledge, 4.458.

CAULON (*kaw'-lon*): a town near the tip of the southwestern coast of Italy, 3.646.

CELAENO (*se-lee'-noh*): leader of the Harpies, possessed of prophetic power, 3.257.

CELEMNA (*se-leem'-na*): inland town in northern Campania, source of a contingent allied with Turnus, 7.860.

CENTAUR (*sen'-tawr*): name of ship, captained by Sergestus, that founders in the ship-race at the funeral games of Anchises, placing fourth and last, 5.143. See Note 5.134–318.

CENTAURS (*sen'-tawrz*): wild creatures, part man and part horse, who live in the vicinity of Mount Pelion, 6.325. See Notes 7.358–59, 8.346.

CERAUNIA (*se-raw'-ni-a*): mountains and promontory on the northern coast of Epirus, a menace to mariners, 3.593, that tapers into Acroceraunia, a point of land extending into the narrow straits—the shortest route to Italy, 3.594. See MINERVA.

CERBERUS (*ser'-be-rus*): watchdog with three heads that guards the entrance to the Underworld, whom Hercules took to the upper world and then brought back to hell as his twelfth and final labor, 6.452–55.

CERES (*see'-reez*): (Demeter), mother of Proserpina, and goddess of grainlands and, by extension, of their products, flour and bread, 1.210.

CETHEGUS (*se-thee'-gus*): Rutulian killed by Aeneas, 12.600.

CHAONIA (*kay-ohn'-ni-a*): a sector of Epirus where Dodona, the site of an oracle sacred to Jupiter, is located, 3.349; CHAONIAN (*kay-ohn'-i-an*), belonging to that locale, 3.398, which was named by Helenus after his brother, CHAON (*kay'-on*), a Trojan, son of Priam, 3.399.

CHAOS: the Underworld, and god of the Underworld, father of Erebus, or darkness, and Night, 4.639.

CHARON (*ka'-ron*): a god of the Underworld, and son of Erebus and Night, who chooses the dead souls that he will ferry across the river Styx, 6.341. Regarding those who are eligible for transport, see Introduction, pp. 28, 37.

CHARYBDIS (*ka-rib'-dis*): monster in the form of a giant whirlpool, supposedly located across from Scylla in the Straits of Messina, 3.497.

CHIMAERA (*keye-mee'-ra*): name of ship, captained by Gyas (1), that finishes third in the ship-race at the funeral games of Anchises, 5.139. See Note 5.134–318.

CHIMAERA: monster breathing fire, "all lion in front, all snake behind, all goat between" (*Iliad* 6.214), that stands watch in the Underworld, 6.328, and forms an ornament on Turnus' helmet, 7.911.

CHLOREUS (*kloh'-ryoos*): Trojan, sacred to the goddess Cybebe (Cybele), once her priest, stalked by Camilla first, then killed by Turnus, 11.903.

CHROMIS (*kroh'-mis*): Trojan killed at long range by Camilla with her spears, 11.796.

CIMINUS (*si'-mi-nus*): lake in Etruria surrounded by hills, its contingent allied with Turnus, 7.812.

CIRCE (*sir'-see*): goddess and enchantress of Aeaea, who changes men to animals and beasts, 3.458. See Note 7.327 and *Odyssey* 10.146–631.

CISSEUS (*see'-syoos*): (1) king of Thrace, father of Hecuba, who is consequently named Cisseis, 5.591. (2) Latin fighter, son of Melampus, killed by Aeneas, 10.375.

CITHAERON (*si-thee'-ron*): mountain in central Greece, renowned for its wild Dionysiac rites, 4.377.

CLARIAN (*kla'-ryan*): of Clarus, a town near Colophon in Ionia, site of a temple and oracle sacred to Apollo, 3.427.

CLARUS (*kla'-rus*): Lycian; he and Thaemon are two of Sarpedon's brothers, and both are allies of Aeneas, 10.155.

CLAUDIAN (*klaw'-di-an*): belonging to a Roman *gens,* or tribe, according to Virgil descended from Clausus, 7.825.

CLAUSUS (*klaw'-sus*): Sabine warrior allied to Turnus, 7.822.

CLOANTHUS (*kloh-ayn'-thus*): Trojan, comrade of Aeneas, lost in the storm off Carthage but restored to pilot the *Scylla* and win the ship-race at the funeral games for Anchises, 1.263. See Note 5.134–318.

CLOELIA (*klee'-li-a*): Roman girl who, eluding her captor, Porsenna, broke free of her chains and swam across the Tiber, 8.763. See Introduction, p. 34.

CLONIUS (*klo'-ni-us*): (1) Trojan killed by Turnus, 9.654. (2) A second Trojan, killed by Messapus, 10.884.

CLONUS (*klo'-nus*): son of Eurytus, goldsmith who engraved the sword-belt stripped by Turnus from the body of Pallas (3), 10.591.

CLUENTIUS (*klu-een'-ti-us*): name of Roman family descended from Cloanthus, 5.144.

CLUSIUM (*kloo'-si-um*): modern Chiusi, prominent Etrurian city near Lake Trasimene, and source of a contingent allied with Aeneas, 10.204.

CLYTIUS (*kli'-ti-us*): (1) Trojan, son of Aeolus (2), killed by Turnus, 9.872. (2) Father of Acmon and Menestheus, allies of Aeneas who hail from Lyrnesus, 10.158. (3) Rutulian ally of Turnus, lover of Cydon and a warrior protected from Aeneas by his brothers, 10.383. (4) Trojan, father of Eunaeus, killed by Camilla, 11.785.

CNOSSUS (*kno'-sus*): principal city of Crete, lying on its north coast, 3.139.

COCLES (*koh'-kleez*): Publius Horatius Cocles, who famously held the bridge over the Tiber against the attack of Lars Porsenna until it could be cut down, 8.763. See Introduction, p. 34.

COCYTUS (*koh-see'-tus*): "named of lamentation loud / Heard on the rueful stream," in Milton's phrase; one of the major rivers in the Underworld, 6.156, "the Wailing River," 6.339. See Note 3.262.

COEUS (*see'-us*): Titan, father of Latona, brother of Enceladus and Rumor, born to Mother Earth, 4.226.

COLLATIA (*koh-lay'-ti-a*): Sabine town in Latium, built by descendants of Silvius Aeneas, 6.894. See Introduction, p. 29.

CORA (*koh'-ra*): town in Latium, on the northwest edge of the Volscian mountains, built by descendants of Silvius Aeneas, 6.895.

CORAS (*koh'-ras*): Argive, brother of Tiburtus, twin brother of Catillus, he fights on Turnus' side, 7.783.

CORINTH (*ko-'rinth*): city that gives its name to the gulf north of the Peloponnese, in the kingdom of Agamemnon, conquered by Lucius Mummius in 146 B.C., 6.962. See Introduction, p. 30.

COROEBUS (*ko-ree'-bus*): Phrygian, fiancé of Cassandra, comrade of Aeneas, killed by the Greek Peneleus at the fall of Troy, 2.430.

CORYBANTES (*ko-ri-ban'-teez*): priests of the Great Mother of Mount Cybelus, who worshipped her with ecstatic dances and clashing cymbals, 3.135.

CORYNAEUS (*ko-ri-nee'-us*): (1) Trojan priest who gathered the bones from Misenus' funeral pyre; killed by Asilas (1), a Rutulian, 6.266. (2) A second Trojan, who overpowers Ebysus, 12.359.

CORYTHUS (*ko'-ri-thus*): (1) town in Etruria, a potential ally of Aeneas, 3.209. (2) Founder of the Etrurian town, 9.12.

COSAE (*koh'-see*): legendary Etrurian coastal city, northwest of Graviscae, its contingent allied to Aeneas, 10.204.

COSSUS (*koh'-sus*): Aulus Cornelius Cossus, Roman general, 6.968. See Introduction, p. 31.

CRETE (*kreet*): 3.126, the large island south of the Peloponnese in the Aegean, the kingdom of Idomeneus; CRETANS (*kree'-tanz*), its inhabitants, 3.128; CRETAN (*kree'-tan*), 3.146, their effects.

CRETHEUS (*kree'-thyoos*): (1) Trojan singer and soldier killed by Turnus, 9.873. (2) Greek soldier in the Trojan ranks, killed by Turnus, 12.629.

CREUSA (*kre-oo'-sa*): daughter of Priam by Hecuba, wife of Aeneas, mother of Ascanius, lost in the fall of Troy, 2.697.

CRINISUS (*kri-nee'-sus*): river in Sicily and its god; father of Acestes, king of Sicily, 5.47.

CRUSTUMERIUM (*kroos-too-mer'-i-um*): town of the Sabines, north of Rome, provider of armaments for the Latin forces, 7.734.

CUMAE (*koo'-mee*): Campanian town, founded by Greeks who migrated from Chalcis on the island of Euboea; northwest of Naples, a legendary entrance to the Underworld, its cavern a favorite haunt of the Sibyl, who is Aeneas' guide, 3.518; CUMAEAN (*koo-mee'-an*), belonging to it and its inhabitants, 6.117.

CUNARUS (*ku'-na-rus*): strongest of the Ligurian chiefs, an ally of Aeneas, his emblem a swan, in honor of his alleged father, Cycnus, 10.224.

CUPAVO (*ku-pay'-vo*): son of Cycnus, Ligurian chief in league with Aeneas, captain of the *Centaur* on her missions, 10.225.

CUPENCUS (*ku-peen'-kus*): Rutulian, warrior-priest killed by Aeneas, 12.631.

CUPID (*kyoo'-pid*): personification of love, son of Venus, 1.783.

CURES (*koo'-reez*): Sabine town, where Numa lived before becoming Rome's second king, 6.935.

CURETES (*koo-ree'-teez*): legendary people of Crete, priests of Jupiter in later time, 3.159.

CYBEBE (*si-bee'-bee*): (Cybele) goddess of the Phrygians, and the Great Mother of the Romans, 10.267. For the origin, customs, and extent of her cult, see 3.134–7, and William, 1962, note 3.111f.

CYBELUS (*si-bee'-lus*): Phrygian mountain sacred to Cybebe (Cybele), 3.134.

CYCLADES (*si'-cla-deez*): ring of islands surrounding Delos in the Aegean Sea, 3.153.

CYCLOPS (*seye'-klops*): 3.664, a cannibal clan of one-eyed giants who dwelled in Sicily, in the neighborhood of Mt. Etna; also a name for Polyphemus in particular, blinded by Ulysses and his crewmen (see *Odyssey* 9.118–630). They labor in the forge of Vulcan as well, in a great cavern called Vulcania off the coast of Sicily, where they forge Aeneas' shield. For the Cyclops at their labors, see 8.500–35. For the Cyclops' names, see 8.501 and Note 5.920. For the shield they forge, see 8.737–858 and Introduction, pp. 33–36. See LIPARE and VULCANIA.

CYCNUS (*keek'-nus*): Ligurian, father of Cupavo, transformed into a swan while mourning for his lover, Phaëthon, who mourned in turn for his dead sisters, who had been transformed into poplars, 10.229. See CUNARUS.

CYDON (*see'-don*): Latin soldier in Turnus' ranks, 10.383.

CYLLENE (*see-lee'-nee*): mountain in Northern Arcadia, the site of Mercury's birth and sacred to the god, 8.159.

CYMODOCEA (*see-mo-do-see'-a*): sea-nymph in Neptune's retinue, and known for her powers of speech, 10.272. See Note 5.920.

CYMOTHOË (*see-mo'-tho-ee*): sea-nymph who with Triton hauls the shipwrecked Trojan vessels off the rocks, 1.169.

CYNTHUS (*sin'-thus*): mountain on Delos, place of Apollo and Diana's birth, and a favorite haunt of both immortals, 1.601.

CYPRUS (*seye'-prus*): the large island in the eastern Mediterranean and sacrosanct to Venus, who regards it as her home, 1.742.

CYTHERA (*si-the'-ra*): 1.307, island off the southeastern coast of the Peloponnese and sacred to Venus, CYTHEREA (*si-the-ree'-a*) or the Cytherean, who often bears its name; see 5.890.

DAEDALUS (*dee'-da-lus*): "the fabulous artificer," in Joyce's phrase, in the service of Minos, king of Crete, for whom he built the famous labyrinth, 6.16.

DAHAE (*da'-hee*): wandering Scythian tribe that ranges east of the Caspian Sea; among the conquered people who march at Augustus' triumph after the battle of Actium, 8.852.

DANAË (*da'-na-ee*): daughter of Acrisius, king of Argos; mother, by Zeus, of Perseus, she established Ardea, 7.478. Servius tells the story of how her father shut her in a chest that he threw into the sea; it washed to shore off the coast of Italy, southwest of Rome.

DARDANIA (*dar-day'-ni-a*): the kingdom of Dardanus, originally founded as a colony on the foothills of Mount Ida (1), and the predecessor of Troy, 8.135.

DARDANUS (*dar'-da-nus*): son of Jupiter and Atlas' daughter, Electra, forebear of Priam and the kings of Troy, ancestor of Aeneas; reputed to have been born in Italy, 2.977. (For possible associations of Dardanus with Etruria, see Horsfall on 7.206–11, 207, and 219–20.) Dardanus' birth in Italy makes the arrival there of Aeneas, his descendant, a kind of *nostos,* or return; see 3.114–23, 3.200–6. The Trojans are occasionally referred to as DARDANS (*dar'-danz*), 2.305, and their effects as DARDAN (*dar'-dan*), 1.719. See Introduction, pp. 12, 17, and *Iliad* 20.251–82.

DARES (*day'-reez*): veteran Trojan boxer defeated by Entellus at the funeral games for Anchises and later killed by Turnus, 5.411.

DAUCUS (*daw'-kus*): Rutulian, father of the identical twins, Thymber and Larides, both killed by Pallas (3), 10.462.

DAUNUS (*daw'-nus*): according to myth, a king of Daunia, a sector of Apulia, and the father of Turnus, 10.727.

DAWN: goddess of the morning, Hyperion's daugther, wife of Tithonus, and mother by Tithonus of Memnon, 1.591.

DEATH: God of the Underworld, twin brother of Sleep, 6.126.

DECII (*de'-ki-ee*): father and son with the same name, Publius Decius Mus, heroes of the Roman Republic, 6.949. See Introduction, p. 30.

DEIOPEA (*dee-i-o-pee'-a*): sea-nymph offered by Juno to Aeolus (1) as an inducement to destroy Aeneas' fleet with a tempest off the coast of Carthage, 1.85.

DEIPHOBE (*dee-i'-fo-bee*): the Sibyl of Cumae, daughter of Glaucus (2), and Aeneas' guide to the Underworld, 6.43.

DEIPHOBUS (*dee-i'-fo-bus*): son of Priam, commander-in-chief of the Trojans after Hector's death; consort of Helen after Paris dies; Aeneas sees his comrade's ghost in the Underworld, his body mangled by Menelaus during Troy's final night, 2.390.

DELOS (*dee'-los*): Aegean island, "chief isle of the embowered Cyclades," according to Keats, the birthplace of Diana and Apollo and sacred to both gods, 3.88. It drifted until the moment when Latona gave birth to her twin progeny. See GYAROS, MYCONOS, and ORTYGIA (1).

DEMODOCUS (*dee-mo'-do-kus*): comrade of Aeneas, killed by Halaesus, 10.489.

DEMOLEOS (*dee-mo'-le-os*): Greek, whose armor, stripped from his dead body by Aeneas, forms second prize in the ship-race at Anchises' funeral games, 5.291. See Note 5.134–318.

DEMOPHOÖN (*dee-mo'-fo-on*): Trojan killed by Camilla at close range, 11.796.

DERCENNUS (*der-see'-nus*): ancient Laurentine king, whose tomb forms a lookout point for Opis, messenger of Diana, 11.997.

DIANA (*deye-an'-a*): (Artemis), daughter of Latona and Jupiter, twin sister of Apollo, goddess of childbirth, the hunt, and the moon, 1.600. In her tri-form aspect, she is the goddess of the moon in the sky, of wild nature on earth, and, under the name of Hecate, of the Underworld: "Trivia" (7.601), also referred to, in the translation, as "triple Hecate, Diana the three-faced virgin" (4.640), "Diana Trivia" (7.903), or "Diana, Goddess of the Crossroads" (11.671), where she is worshipped for her mystic, magic powers. See HECATE and TRIVIA, and Note 7.884–908.

DICTE (*dik'-tee*): mountain in eastern Crete, synonymous with that island; the birthplace of Jupiter and the site of a cavern where he was concealed from his father, Saturn, who would have devoured the infant god, 3.210.

DIDO (*deye'-doh*): Phoenician exile, queen and founder of Carthage, wife of Sychaeus first, then consort of Aeneas, who commits suicide upon his departure for Italy, 1.358.

DIDYMAON (*di-di-may'-on*): artisan who practised his craft as a metal-smith, 5.400.

DINDYMA (*din'-di-ma*): mountain in Phrygia, consecrated to the Great Mother, Cybebe (Cybele), and site of her female followers' rites, 9.702.

DIOMEDES (*deye-o-mee'-deez*): Greek, son of Tydeus, king of Argos, founder of Argyripa, later called Arpi, in Apulia (see RHESUS for Diomedes' capture of Rhesus' Thracian horses), 1.116. For Diomedes' capture, with Ulysses, of the horses, see *Iliad* 10.528–670. For Diomedes' outraging of Pallas Athena during the Trojan War, see PALLADIUM and Note 2.211; for his wounding of Venus in combat and his subsequent punishment, see Notes 11.315–36, 11.335–36.

DIONE (*di-oh'-nee*): goddess, mother of Venus, 3.24.

DIORES (*di-oh'-reez*): Trojan, competitor who places third in the foot-race at Anchises' funeral games; brother of Amycus (5), and beheaded by Turnus, 5.330. See Note 5.325–402.

DIOXIPPUS (*di-ohks-ip'-us*): Trojan killed by Turnus, 9.654.

DISCORD: strife personified, with particular reference to civil war, 12.679.

DODONA (*doh-doh'-na*): site in Epirus, in northwestern Greece; the sanctuary of an oracle of Zeus, whose prophecies were communicated through the rustling leaves of a great oak, 3.548.

DOG STAR: Orion's Dog, or Sirius, whose rising is a "fatal sign" (*Iliad* 22.36) since it carries plague to humankind and blights their crops, 3.174.

DOLICHAON (*doh-li-kay'-on*): Trojan, father of Hebrus (2); killed by Mezentius, 10.823.

DOLON (*doh'-lon*): Trojan scout, son of the old herald Eumedes, lured by the reward of Achilles' team and chariot to spy on the Greek camp at night, but killed by Diomedes, 12.415. See *Iliad* 10.351–527.

DOLOPIAN (*do-loh'-pi-an*): person from Phthia, a sector of southern Thessaly, kingdom of Peleus and home of Achilles, 2.9.

DONUSA (*do-noo'-sa*): Aegean island among the Cyclades, to the southeast of Delos located at their center, 3.152.

DORYCLUS (*do-ree'-klus*): Rutulian, specifically a Tmarian from Epirus, husband of Beroë, 5.684.

DOTO (*doh'-toh*): sea-nymph, daughter of Nereus, 9.120.

DRAGON: name of a ship, captained by Mnestheus, that finishes second in the ship-race at the funeral games of Anchises, 5.136. See Note 5.134–318.

DRANCES (*dran'-seez*): fellow-Rutulian of Turnus, and his outspoken critic, 11.142.

DREPANUM (*dre'-pa-num*): town on the northwest coast of Sicily, now Trapani, the site of Anchises' death, 3.817.

DRUSI (*droo'-zee*): great patrician family of Rome, 6.949. See Introduction, p. 30.

DRYOPE (*dri'-o-pee*): wood-nymph, mother by Faunus, god of the woods, of Tarquitus, a Rutulian killed by Aeneas, 10.652.

DRYOPIANS (*dri-oh'-pi-anz*): ancient people said to live near Mount Parnassus in northern Greece, 4.183.

DRYOPS (*dri'-ops*): Trojan killed by Clausus from Cures, 10.407.

DULICHIUM (*doo-li'-ki-um*): Ionian island near Ithaca, off the western coast of Greece, 3.324.

DYMAS (*di'-mas*): Trojan, aide of Aeneas, accidentally killed by his own comrades in the chaos of Troy's fall, 2.429.

EARTH: the earth personified, 4.209.

EBYSUS (*e'-bi-sus*): Rutulian killed by Corynaeus (2), 12.360.

EGERIA (*e-jee'-ri-a*): Latian water-nymph, whose healing grove safeguarded Hippolytus, and where, after being tormented to death by his father and stepmother, he returned to life as Virbius, 7.886. See Note 7.884–908.

EGYPT: the country in northern Africa, synonymous with Cleopatra, the Egyptian queen, 8.806.

ELEAN (*ee-lee'-an*): 3.803, belonging to ELIS (*ee'-lis*), realm of the Epeans in the northwestern Peloponnese to the north of Nestor's Pylos; its principal city, Olympia, became the site of the Olympic games, 6.681.

ELECTRA (*e-lek'-tra*): one of the seven daughters of Atlas, who compose the Pleiades; sister of Maia, the mother by Jupiter of Dardanus, the founder of Troy. 8.156.

ELYSIUM (*ee-li'-zi-um*): home in the Underworld of the fortunate after death, the site of Aeneas' reunion with the spirit of his father, 5.814. For Homer's description of the Elysian Fields, see *Odyssey* 4.634–39.

EMATHION (*ee-ma'-thi-on*): Trojan killed by Liger, 9.650.

ENCELADUS (*en-sel'-a-dus*): giant rebel against the rule of Jupiter, who struck him dead with a lightning-bolt and buried him under Mount Etna as his eternal doom, 3.673.

ENTELLUS (*en-tee'-lus*): veteran Sicilian boxer who overpowers Dares at the funeral games for Anchises, 5.431.

EPEUS (*e-pee'-us*): Greek, builder of the Trojan horse, and one of the raiders hidden in its hollows, 2.334.

EPIRUS (*ee-peye'-rus*): mountainous area in northwestern Greece on the Adriatic coast, 3.348.

EPULO (*e'-pu-lo*): Rutulian killed by Achates, 12.539.

EPYTIDES (*e-pi-teye'-deez*): Trojan friend and bodyguard of Ascanius, 5.600.

EPYTUS (*ee'-pi-tus*): Trojan, comrade-in-arms of Aeneas in Troy's last hours, 2.427.

ERATO (*e'-ra-toh*): the Muse of love, one of the nine Muses, she is invoked at the start of Book 7, because the second half of the *Aeneid* involves, in part, Turnus' efforts to wrest his expected bride, Lavinia, from the claims of Aeneas, 7.40. See Introduction, p. 19.

EREBUS (*e'-re-bus*): child of Chaos, god of the Underworld and darkness, 4.639.

ERETUM (*e-ree'-tum*): city on the east bank of the Tiber north of Rome; settled by Sabines, its contingent led by Clausus, 7.828.

ERICHAETES (*e-ri-kee'-teez*): Trojan, Lycaon's (2) son, killed by Messapus, 10.884.

ERIDANUS (*ee-ri'-da-nus*): river that, according to legend, rises in Elysium in the Underworld, and runs through the living world above; commonly thought to be the Po, 6.762.

ERIPHYLE (*e-ri-fee'-lee*): wife of the prophet Amphiaraus, who accepted from Polynices, leader of the Seven against Thebes, a necklace as a bribe for persuading her husband to join the expedition, in which he met his death; she met her death, in turn, at the hands of her son, Alcmaeon, 6.516.

ERULUS (*e'-ru-lus*): king of Praeneste, son of Feronia who gave her son three lives, requiring the young Evander to kill him three times over, 8.664.

ERYMANTHUS (*e-ri-man'-thus*): mountain range in Arcadia, in the northwest Peloponnese, and the home of a great boar that Hercules killed as the third of his Twelve Labors, 5.499.

ERYMAS (*e'-ri-mas*): Trojan comrade of Aeneas, killed by Turnus, 9.797.

ERYX (*e'-riks*): (1) mountain and town in the northwestern corner of Sicily, 1.684. (2) Son of Venus and Butes (2), half-brother of Aeneas; king of Sicily, champion boxer killed by Hercules in a legendary bout, 5.29.

ETHIOPIAN (*ee-thee-oh'-pi-an*): of a region in the northeast of Africa and a favorite haunt of Neptune. 4.602.

ETNA (*et'-na*): volcanic peak in eastern Sicily, home of the Cyclops, 3.648.

ETRURIA (*ee-troo'-ri-a*): region in Italy north of Rome, settled by the Etruscans, 8.581.

ETRUSCAN (*ee-trus'-kan*): belonging to people of Tuscany in central Italy, who may have originated in Lydia in Asia Minor 7.48; alternatively called TUSCAN (*tus'-kan*), 1.80, as belonging to the TUSCANS (*tus'-kanz*), 7.498. See Introduction, pp. 20–23, 35–36.

EUANTHES (*yoo-ayn'-theez*): Phrygian fighter in the Trojan ranks, 10.830.

EUBOEAN (*yoo-bee'-an*): belonging to the large island lying off the coast of eastern Greece, 6.2, EUBOEA (*yoo-bee'-a*), 11.314. See CUMAE.

EUMEDES (*yoo-mee'-deez*): Trojan, offspring of Dolon, 12.413.

EUMELUS (*yoo-mee'-lus*): Trojan herald who alerts the Trojans to the burning of their fleet, 5.733.

EUNAEUS (*yoo-nee'-us*): Trojan, son of Clytius (4), killed by Camilla with a long pine lance, 11.785.

EUPHRATES (*yoo-fray'-teez*): river in Asia Minor, enclosing together with the Tigris the Fertile Crescent, 8.850.

EUROPE: the continent named for Europa, daughter of Agenor (or Phoenix, according to Homer). She was abducted by Jupiter, in the form of a bull, and became by him the mother of Minos and Rhadamanthus and perhaps Sarpedon too, 1.467.

EUROTAS (*yoo-roh'-tas*): river running alongside Sparta in Lacedaemon, 1.601.

EURYALUS (*yoo-reye'-a-lus*): Trojan, comrade-in-arms of Nisus, victor in the foot-race at Anchises' funeral games, later killed by Volscians, 5.328. See Note 5.325–402.

EURYPYLUS (*yoo-ri'-pi-lus*): Greek, emissary to Apollo's oracle during the siege of Troy, 2.146.

EURYSTHEUS (*yoo-ris'-thyoos*): king of Mycenae, grandson of Perseus and taskmaster of Hercules who, at Eurystheus' command, carried out the legendary Twelve Labors, 8.343.

EURYTUS (*yoo'-ri-tus*): father of the goldsmith Clonus, 10.591.

EURYTION (*yoo-ri'-ti-on*): Trojan, son of the famous archer Pandarus (1) and, at the funeral games for Anchises, a contestant in the archery contest who hits the target dove yet places second to Acestes, whose arrow shoots into a flaming omen, 5.548. See Note 5.539–98.

EVADNE (*ee-vayd'-nee*): among the lovelorn ghosts in hell; the wife of Capaneus, one of the Seven against Thebes, she burned herself alive on her husband's pyre, 6.518.

EVANDER (*ee-van'-der*): son of Mercury and Carmentis, king who migrated from Arcadia with his people to found the city of Pallanteum on the site of Rome; host to Aeneas and his Trojans, and father of Pallas (3), who becomes Aeneas' comrade, 8.55. See Note 8.54–57 and Introduction, p. 16.

FABARIS (*fa'-ba-ris*): branch of the Tiber, 7.832.

FABII (*fa'-bi-ee*): famous Roman family that produced several leaders of the Roman state, 6.973. See MAXIMUS and Introduction, p. 31.

FABRICIUS (*fay-bri'-shus*): Caius Fabricius Luscinus, the conqueror of Pyrrhus, whom he treated nobly, in the third century B.C., renowned for his rise from poverty into power; his austere integrity, the epitome of old Roman virtues, 6.971. See Introduction, p. 31.

FADUS (*fay'-dus*): Rutulian killed by Euryalus, 9.399.

FALISCI (*fa-lees'-kee*): inhabitants of southern Etruria, their contingent allied with Turnus (see AEQUI FALISCI), 7.810.

FATE(S): the three Parcae were visualized as three women spinning thread, a normal household occupation for women in antiquity, and the thread was a human life. Shortly after Homer they were given names: Clotho ("Spinner"), Lachesis ("Allotter"—she decides how long the thread should be), and Atropos ("one who cannot be turned back"), who cuts the thread. In general, these shadowy but potent figures ultimately control the destiny of mortals, 1.2, 1.21.

FAUNS (*fawnz*): half-human Roman spirits of the field and countryside, 8.370.

FAUNUS (*faw'-nus*): Roman deity often identified with Pan. He was son of Picus and the Latian nymph Marica; father of King Latinus, 7.52.

FERONIA (*fee-roh'-ni-a*): Italian nature divinity, worshipped chiefly in groves, mother of Erulus, 7.928.

FESCENNIA (*fee-skee'-ni-a*): town in southern Etruria, its contingent allied with Turnus, 7.810.

FIDENA (*fi-dee'-na*): Latian town just north of Rome, and founded by kings of Alba Longa, 6.893. See Introduction, p. 29.

FIELD OF MARS: The Campus Martius, originally an open space of level ground at Rome, north of the city's center and outside its walls. It was bounded on the west by the Tiber and on the east by the Capitoline, Quirinal, and Princian hills; and it contained the Mausoleum of Augustus, in which the younger Marcellus was the first to be buried (in 23 B.C.), 6.1006.

FLAVINA (*flay-veye'-na*): a city in southern Etruria, 7.811.

FORTUNE: chance or luck personified and deified, she had famous places of worship in Rome and especially Praeneste, 2.99.

FORULI (*fo'-ru-li*): town inhabited by Sabines, south of Amiternum, its contingent allied with Turnus, 7.831.

FUCINUS (*foo-see'-nus*): Latian lake in the Apennine range, in Marsian country, with the grove of Angitia on its western shore, the city of Marruvium on its eastern shore; the home of Umbro, 7.882.

FURIES: Allecto, Megaera, and Tisiphone, avenging spirits whose task it is to exact blood for blood when no human avenger is left alive. They are particularly concerned with injuries done by one member of a family to another, and they have regulatory powers as well, 3.303. See Note 12.980–88 and ALLECTO, MEGAERA, and TISIPHONE.

GABII (*ga'-bi-ee*): Latian town, due east of Rome, 6.893; GABINE (*ga'-beyen*) descriptive of its inhabitants' customs, 7.712. See Introduction, p. 29.

GAETULIAN (*gee-tool'-yan*): of a northern African tribe that settled in Morocco, 4.52.

GALAESUS (*gay-lee'-sus*): aged Latin, killed at the outbreak of hostilities between the Italians and the Trojans, 7.621.

GALATEA (*ga-la-tee'-a*): sea-nymph in Nereus' retinue, 9.120.

GANGES (*gan'-jeez*): river in India, flowing down from the Himalayas and emptying into the Bay of Bengal, 9.34.

GANYMEDE (*ga'-ni-meed*): one of three sons of Tros, the first king of Troy; "the handsomest mortal man on earth" (*Iliad* 20.269), snatched away for his beauty by the eagle of Jupiter and made immortal as the cup-bearer of Jupiter and the other gods, 1.35. See Introduction, p. 17.

GARAMANTS (*ga'-ra-mants*): African tribe, living in the eastern Sahara, conquered by Rome in 19 B.C., 6.917. See Introduction, p. 29.

GARGANUS (*gayr-gay'-nus*): mountainous headland of Apulia, 11.297.

GATES OF SLEEP: 6.1029; see Note 6.1035–36 and Introduction, p. 32.

GATES OF WAR: 1.351, see Note ad loc; 7.705–15.

GAULS (*gawlz*): people of Northern Europe, besiegers of the gates of Rome in 390 B.C., 6.990. See Introduction, pp. 30–33.

GELA (*jay'-la*): Sicilian city alongside a southern coastal river named Gela too, 3.810.

GELONIAN (*je-loh'-ni-an*): of a Scythian tribe renowned for its archery, 8.850.

GERYON (*je'-ri-on*): legendary monster with three bodies, killed three times over by Hercules, who rustled Geryon's herds of oxen out of Spain and drove them to the Tiber, the tenth of Hercules' Labors, 7.771.

GETAE (*je'-tee*): Thracian tribe that settled on the banks of the lower Danube, 7.702.

GLAUCUS (*glaw'-kus*): (1) sea-god in Neptune's retinue, and father of Deiphobe, the Cumaean Sibyl, 5.917. (2) Trojan, one of Antenor's three sons whom Aeneas sees among the war heroes in the Underworld, 6.561. (3) Son of Imbrasus, killed by Turnus, 12.409.

GOD OF FIRE: 5.731, see VULCAN.

GORGON (*gor'-gon*): daughter of Phorcus (1), sister of Medusa; fabulous female monster, whose glance could turn a person into stone; the centerpiece of Minerva's shield, 2.762.

GORTYNIAN (*gohr-tee'-ni-an*): of Gortyna, a city in Crete, renowned for archery, 11.909.

GRACCHI (*gra'-kee*): famous Roman family that produced two tribunes, 6.969. See Introduction, p. 31.

GRAVISCAE (*gra-vees'-kee*): coastal Etrurian city, "weighed down," as the name suggests, by varieties of illness, 10.223.

GREAT AND LITTLE BEARS: the constellations Ursa Major and Ursa Minor, the Big and Little Dippers, 1.894. See ARCTURUS.

GREAT MOTHER OF GODS: 2.978; see CYBEBE and CYBELUS, also BERECYNTHIAN, CORYBANTES, and DINDYMA.

GREATEST ALTAR: 8.315, see Note ad loc.

GREEKS: 1.38, and GREEK, their effects, 1.116. See ACHAEANS.

GRYNEAN (*gree-nee'-an*): of Grynia, an Aeolian city sacred to Apollo, who had an oracle there, 4.431.

GYAROS (*gee'-a-ros*): Aegean island, one of the mooring-points to which Apollo fastened his birthplace, the island of Delos, once adrift, to make it stable, 3.92.

GYAS (*gi'-as*): (1) Trojan, shipwrecked comrade of Aeneas, restored to captain the Chimaera to third place in the ship-race at Anchises' funeral games, 1.263. See Note 5.134–318. (2) Latin, son of Melampus, killed by Aeneas, 10.375.

GYGES (*geye'-jeez*): Trojan comrade of Aeneas, killed by Turnus, 9.859.

GYLIPPUS (*gi-lee'-pus*): Arcadian, father by Tyrrhena of nine sons who block an assault by the Latian Tolumnius, 12.330.

HAEMON (*hee'-mon*): (1) Rutulian, priest of Mars, who storms Aeneas' camp, 9.779. (2) Latin, father of one of Turnus' comrades, Haemonides, a priest of Apollo and Diana, killed by Aeneas, 10.635.

HALAESUS (*ha-lee'-sus*): once companion of Agamemnon, then an Italian chieftain and comrade of Turnus, killed while defending Imaon, 7.841.

HALIUS (*ha'-li-us*): Trojan, comrade of Aeneas, killed by Turnus, 9.865.

HALYS (*ha'-lis*): Trojan, comrade of Aeneas, killed by Turnus, 9.862.

HARPALYCE (*hayr-pa'-li-see*): huntress and expert rider, a woman warrior of Thrace, 1.382.

HARPALYCUS (*hayr-pa'-li-kus*): Trojan, comrade of Aeneas, killed by Camilla, 11.796.

HARPIES (*har'-peez*): "Snatchers" in Greek, winged female demons, birds with the faces of girls, 3.257. See Note 3.258.

HEBRUS (*hee'-brus*): (1) river in Thrace that flows into the Macedonian Sea, 1.383. (2) Trojan, son of Dolichaon, comrade of Aeneas, killed by Mezentius, 10.823.

HECATE (*he'-ka-tee*): goddess of the Underworld, yet a three-headed, tri-form divinity, who appears as Hecate in hell, Diana on earth (daughter of Latona), and Luna, the moon, in heaven, 4.640. See DIANA and TRIVIA.

HECTOR (*hek'-tor*): Trojan, supreme commander of Trojan forces, eldest son of Priam and Hecuba, husband of Andromache, father of Astyanax; killed by Achilles to avenge the death of Patroclus at Hector's hands, 1.118.

HECUBA (*he'-kyoo-ba*): daughter of Dymas, wife of Priam and his queen, mother of Hector, 2.622.

HELEN (*he'-len*): daughter of Jupiter and Leda, wife of Menelaus, consort of Paris; her abduction by him from Sparta was the cause of the Trojan War, 1.774. See Introduction, pp. 12, 17.

HELENOR (*he-lee'-nor*): Trojan, son of a slave, Licymnia, and a Maeonian king; killed by the Latin forces, 9.623.

HELENUS (*he'-le-nus*): Trojan, son of Priam, prophet and warrior, later married to Andromache, 3.351. See Note 3.389–400.

HELICON (*he'-li-kon*): Boeotian mountain, traditional home of the Muses, sacred place of Apollo, 7.747.

HELORUS (*he-loh'-rus*): a town and river in southeastern Sicily, surrounded by fertile fields, 3.807.

HELYMUS (*he'-li-mus*): Sicilian who places second in the foot-race at Anchises' funeral games, 5.89. See Note 5.325–402.

HERBESUS (*heer-bee'-sus*): Rutulian killed by Euryalus, 9.399.

HERCULES (*her'-kyoo-leez*): the hero of the Twelve Labors, 3.644. See Note ad loc, Note 7.770; AMPHITRYON, and passim.

HERMINIUS (*heer-mi'-ni-us*): Trojan killed by Catillus, 11.758.

HERMIONE (*her-meye'-o-nee*): Spartan, daughter of Menelaus and Helen, granddaughter of Leda; wife of Pyrrhus, she deserted him to marry Orestes, 3.392.

HERMUS (*heer'-mus*): Lydian river, 7.838.

HERNICI (*heer'-ni-kee*): people who settled a rock-strewn region in Latium, southeast of Rome, and sent a contingent to fight on Turnus' side, 7.796.

HESIONE (*he-seye'-o-nee*): sister of Priam, daughter of Laomedon, wife of Telamon, who was the father of Ajax and Teucer (2); she ruled over Salamis with her husband, 8.181.

HESPERIA (*he-sper'-i-a*): "Land of the West," Italy, 1.639. HESPERIAN (*he-sper'-i-an*): Western or Italian in general; belonging to the daughters of Hesperus in particular, who preside over a garden bountiful with golden apples, 4.606.

HICETAON (*hi-ke-tay'-on*): Trojan, father of Thymoetes (2), who is killed by Turnus, 10.152.

HIMELLA (*hi-meel'-a*): river in Sabine country, flowing into the Tiber; source of contingent allied with Turnus, 7.831.

HIPPOCOÖN (*hi-po'-ko-on*): Trojan, comrade of Aeneas, contender who places last in the archery contest at Anchises' funeral games, 5.545. See Note 5.539–98.

HIPPOLYTE (*hi-po'-li-tee*): legendary Amazon queen from Thrace, married to Theseus, 11.779.

HIPPOLYTUS (*hi-po'-li-tus*): son of Theseus and Hippolyte, father of Virbius, 7.884. See Note 7.884–908.

HIPPOTAS (*hi'-po-tas*): Trojan, father of Amastrus, who is killed by Camilla, 11.794.

HISBO (*hiz'-boh*): Rutulian killed by Pallas (3), 10.452.

HOMOLE (*ho'-mo-lee*): Thessalian mountain where the Centaurs (2) dwell, 7.788.

HYADES (*heye'-a-deez*): constellation, "the rainy Hyades," whose rising coincides with the onset of spring rains, 1.894.

HYDASPES (*hi-das'-peez*): Trojan killed by Sacrator, 10.882.

HYDRA (*heye'-dra*): (1) serpent with seven heads, that had its lair near Lerna in the Argolid and was killed by Hercules as his Second Labor. It appears as a monster at the entranceway to the Underworld, 6.327, and as a device on the shield of Hercules' son, Aventinus, 7.765. (2) Monster with fifty heads, guarding the realm of the damned in the Underworld, 6.669.

HYLAEUS (*hee-lee'-us*): Centaur killed by Hercules, 8.347.

HYLLUS (*hee'-lus*): Trojan killed by Turnus, 12.626.

HYPANIS (*hee'-pa-nis*): comrade of Aeneas at the fall of Troy, 2.429.

HYRCANIA (*heer-kay'-ni-a*): region south of the Caspian Sea, 4.459, inhabited by HYRCANIANS (*heer-kay'-ni-anz*), an Asian tribe, 7.702.

HYRTACUS (*heer'-ta-kus*): (1) Trojan, father of Hippocoön, who competes in the archery at Anchises' funeral games, 5.545. See Note 5.539–98. (2) Trojan, father of Nisus, 9.211.

IAERA (*i-ee'-ra*): wood-nymph, mother by Alcanor (1) of Pandarus (2) and Bitias, whom she bore in Jupiter's grove on Phrygian Mount Ida, 9.766.

IAPYX (*i-ah'-piks*): (1) Apulian who lives in the fields round Mount Garganus, 11.297. (2) Trojan, descendant of Iasius and loved by Apollo, who teaches him the healing skills he uses to treat Aeneas' wound; his name, Iapyx, suggests the Greek word for healing, 12.462.

IARBAS (*i-ayr'-bas*): African warlord, son of Jupiter Hammon, rebuffed by Dido in his advances toward her, 4.47.

IASIUS (*eye-a'-si-us*): Trojan, brother of Dardanus, son-in-law of Teucer (1), Aeneas' forebear who had settled in Italy. He is the father or ancestor of PALINURUS, Aeneas' helmsman, and of Iapyx (2), 3.206.

ICARUS (*i'-ka-rus*): son of Daedalus who, attempting to flee from the Cretan labyrinth by flying on artificial wings, soared too near the sun; it melted the wax that fastened the feathers and—as Auden saw him, "amazing, a boy falling out of the sky"—he dropped into the Aegean Sea and drowned, 6.37.

IDA (*eye'-da*): (1) central mountain range in Phrygia, south of Troy, and favored seat of Jupiter, 2.867. (2) Huntress, possibly mother of Nisus, 9.212. (3) Mountain in Crete, Venus' source of dittany, which heals Aeneas' wound, 12.489.

IDAEUS (*eye-dee'-us*): (1) charioteer of Priam, with his chariot still in tow, even when he is a ghost in the Underworld, 6.563. (2) Trojan comrade of Aeneas, 9.575.

IDALIUM (*eye-da'-li-um*): town and mountain grove on Cyprus; a favorite haunt of Venus, where her rites are performed, 1.812. IDALIAN (*eye-da'-li-an*), 1.826, belonging to Idalium or IDALIA (*eye-da'-li-a*), a variant of the place-name, 10.104.

IDAS (*eye'-das*): (1) Trojan killed by Turnus, 9.655. (2) Father of three Thracian fighters, comrades of Aeneas, all killed by Clausus, 10.413.

IDMON (*eyed'-mon*): Rutulian, messenger of Turnus, 12.95.

IDOMENEUS (*eye-doh'-men-yoos*): son of Deucalion, commander of the Cretan contingent at Troy, he was banished from Crete for killing his son and settled in Calabria where he founded a state among the Sallentini, 3.145. See Note 11.315–36.

ILIA (*eye'-li-a*): priestess of Mars, who produced for the god his twin sons, Romulus and Remus (1), 1.327. See Introduction, p. 18.

ILIONE (*eye-li'-o-nee*): Trojan, the eldest of Priam's daughters born of Hecuba, 1.777.

ILIONEUS (*eye-li'-o-nyoos*): Trojan, representative of Aeneas before Dido and Latinus, and killer of Lucetius, 1.141.

ILIUM (*i'-li-um*): Troy, the city of ILUS (2), 1.321; ILIAN (*i'-li-an*), belonging to Ilium, 3.400.

ILLYRIA (*i-lee'-ri-a*): region in northwestern Greece, fronting the Adriatic and forming a difficult passage for mariners, 1.288.

ILUS (*eye'-lus*): (1) the original name of Aeneas' son while Ilium (Troy) still stood. Afterward he has two names, Ascanius and Iulus, a modification of Ilus, to suggest his role as ancestor of the Julian *gens* and therefore of the emperor Augustus, 1.321. See Note 1.320–21. (2) Eldest son of Tros, father of Laomedon, grandfather of Priam, and founder of Troy, named Ilium after Ilus, 6.753. (3) Rutulian soldier in Pallas' (3) line of fire, 10.473.

ILVA (*eel'-va*): modern Elba, island off the Etrurian coast between Italy and Corsica, 10.209.

IMAON (*i-may'-on*): Rutulian comrade of Turnus, protected by Halaesus, 10.501.

IMBRASUS (*eem'-bra-sus*): (1) father of Asius, a defender of Aeneas' encampment, 10.152. (2) Lycian, father of Glaucus (3) and Lades, both sons killed by Turnus, 12.409.

INACHUS (*i'-na-kus*): founding king of Argos and father of Io (7.333), who is also treated by Virgil as the god of the Argolid's principal river, 7.919.

INARIME (*ee-nar'-i-mee*): island in the Tyrrhenian Sea, present-day Ischia, under which Jupiter buried Typhoeus, if he did not bury him under Etna (see TYPHOEUS), 9.811.

INDIANS: people from India, the territory bounded by the Indus River on the west and the Ganges on the east, as delimiting the easternmost boundary of the known world under Rome, 6.917.

INO (*eye'-noh*): daughter of Cadmus, once a mortal, now a sea-nymph in Neptune's retinue, 5.917.

INUIS (*i'-nu-is*): heavily defended Latian town near Rome, 6.895.

IO (*eye'-oh*): daughter of the river-god Inachus, guarded by Argus (1), a monster with a hundred eyes; Io was loved by Jupiter and turned by vengeful Juno into a cow, 7.915.

IOLLAS (*i-oh'-las*): Trojan killed by Catillus, 11.758.

IONIAN (*eye-ohn'-i-an*): of Ionia, a sea-reach below the Adriatic, stretching between southern Italy and Greece, 3.256.

IOPAS (*i-oh'-pas*): bard of Carthage, taught his art by Atlas, 1.887.

IPHITUS (*eye'-fi-tus*): Trojan, Aeneas' comrade-in-arms at Troy's demise, 2.542.

IRIS (*eye'-ris*): goddess, messenger of the gods, who typically comes arcing down to earth in a rainbow, 4.864.

ISMARUS (*iz'-ma-rus*): (1) Lydian who fights at the side of Iulus, 10.169. (2) Mountain in Thrace, and city bearing its name, which, like the mountain, is also called Ismarus or Ismara, 10.413.

ITALIAN: 1.3, of Italy, 1.15; Italians, people of the region, 1.130. See HESPERIA, and Introduction, passim.

ITALUS (*eye'-ta-lus*): one of the legendary, founding fathers of Italy, 1.642.

ITHACA (*i'-tha-ka*): Ionian island off the western coast of Greece, 2.131, and traditional home of Ulysses—who is sometimes called "the Ithacan" (2.156)—together with his forebears and his family.

ITYS (*i'-tis*): Trojan killed by Turnus, 9.654.

IULUS (*i-u'-lus*): see ILUS (1), 1.321, and Note 1.320–21.

IXION (*eek-see'-on*): lord of the Lapiths, reputed father of Pirithous, who was actually sired by Jove with Ixion's wife; for attempting to rape Juno, Ixion was spread-eagled on a wheel that revolved forever in the Underworld, 6.694.

JANICULUM (*ja-ni'-cu-lum*): a hilly ridge on the western side of the Tiber, on which Janus was said to have built a fortress, 8.421.

JANUS (*jay'-nus*): ancient two-headed Italian god of crossings, entrances and beginnings, facing left and right, equally toward the past and toward the future, 7.206.

JOVE (*johv*): (Zeus) alternative name for Jupiter, 1.52.

JUDGMENT OF PARIS: see 1.34 and Introduction, p. 17; *Iliad* 24.35–36; and Note ad loc.

JULIUS (*jool'-yus*): "a name passed down from Iulus, his great forebear," a member of the Julian *gens* and forerunner of Caius Julius Caesar Octavianus, the first Roman emperor, who bore the title Augustus, 1.344. See ATYS, AUGUSTUS, and ILUS (1).

JUNO (*joo'-noh*): (Hera), queen of the gods, daughter of Saturn, wife and sister of Jupiter, her special province, marriage; among the Olympians, the principal antagonist of Aeneas, because of his Trojan origins, 1.5. See Introduction, passim.

JUPITER (*joo'-pi-ter*): (Zeus), son of Saturn, king of the gods, alternatively called JOVE, husband and brother of Juno, father of the Olympians and many mortals too. His spheres include the sky and the weather, hospitality and the rights of guests and suppliants, the punishment of injustice, the sending of omens, and the governance of the universe, controlled to some extent by Fate as well, 1.94. See Introduction, passim.

JUTURNA (*joo-tur'-na*): Italian water-nymph, sister of Turnus and servant of Juno; her name, like her allegiance, belongs equally to Juno and to Turnus, 12.168.

KIDS: constellation that "marks stormy weather at both its rising in spring and its setting in late September" (Hardie, 1994, note 9.668), 9.761.

LABICIANS (*la-bi'-shanz*): people of Labicum, a town in Latium southeast of Rome, their contingent allied to Turnus, 7.924.

LABYRINTH: a baffling maze devised for King Minos by Daedalus to house the Minotaur in the royal palace at Cnossus on Crete, 5.647.

LACINIAN (*la-see'-ni-an*): of Lacinium, a headland on the toe of southern Italy, sacred to Juno and the site of a temple devoted to her, 3.646.

LADES (*la'-deez*): Lycian, son of Imbrasus, brother of Glaucus, both brothers killed by Turnus, 12.409.

LADON (*la'-don*): Arcadian, an ally of Aeneas, killed by Halaesus, 10.489.

LAERTES (*lay-er'-teez*): son of Arcesius, husband of Anticleia, father of Ulysses, 3.325.

LAGUS (*la'-gus*): Rutulian killed by Pallas (3), 10.449.

LAMUS (*la'-mus*): Rutulian killed by Nisus, 9.391.

LAMYRUS (*la'-mi-rus*): Rutulian killed by Nisus, 9.390.

LAOCOÖN (*lay-o'-ko-on*): Trojan, priest of Neptune, who opposed the admittance of the Trojan horse into the city and was strangled by sea-serpents, 2.51. See Note 2.259.

LAODAMIA (*lay-o-da-mee'-a*): wife of Protesilaus, she committed suicide when her husband died at Troy, 6.518.

LAOMEDON (*lay-o'-me-don*): king of Troy, son of Ilus (2), father of Priam; he reneged on the payment set by Apollo and Neptune to construct the walls of Troy, and so acquired a reputation for treachery, 3.298.

LAPITHS (*la'-piths*): a Thessalian tribe among the condemned in hell; their legendary battle with the Centaurs, at the wedding of their king, Pirithous, and Hippodamia, was a favorite theme for temple sculpture, 6.694. See Note 7.358–59.

LARIDES (*la-ree'-deez*): Rutulian comrade of Turnus; son of Daucus, twin brother of Thymber, both brothers killed by Pallas (3), 10.462.

LARISAEAN (*la-ri-see'-an*): belonging to Larisa, a town in Thessaly, and used as an epithet of Achilles, who hails from that large region of northeastern Greece, 11.484.

LATAGUS (*la'-ta-gus*): comrade of Aeneas, killed by Mezentius, 10.824.

LATINUS (*la-teye'-nus*): king of Latium, son of Faunus, father by his wife Amata of Lavinia, his only child, who was fated to become the wife of Aeneas, 6.1027.

LATIUM (*lay'-shum*): 1.7, source of the LATIN (noun or adj.) or LATIAN (adj., *lay'-shan*) people and their effects, 3.449; a region between the Tiber and Campania, settled by Saturn, according to legend, when in exile from Jupiter; the land where Saturn had "lain hidden" (8.380) and established the Age of Gold. For Latin, see Introduction, passim.

LATONA (*lay-toh'-na*): (Leto), goddess, mother of Apollo and Diana by Jupiter, 1.605.

LAURENTES (*law-reen'-teez*): 7.70, and LAURENTINE (*law-reen'-teyen*), 7.197, the inhabitants of, and belonging to, LAURENTUM (*law-reen'-tum*), a coastal city in Latium, south of Rome, 8.1.

LAUSUS (*law'-sus*): comrade of Turnus, son of Mezentius, who lays down his life to save his father and is killed by Aeneas, 7.756.

LAVINIA (*la-veen'-i-a*): daughter of Latinus and Amata; Turnus considers her his betrothed, but her father Latinus recognizes that she is fated to marry Aeneas, 6.884. LAVINIAN (*la-veen'-i-an*): 1.3, of the capital city of Latium, LAVINIUM (*la-veen'-i-um*), destined to be established by Aeneas and named after his queen, Lavinia, 1.309.

LEDA (*lee'-da*): wife of Tyndareus and mother of Clytemnestra; mother by Jupiter, transformed into a swan, of Helen and the twins Castor and Pollux, 1.776.

LELEGES (*le'-le-jeez*): early people of northwestern Asia Minor, conquered by Caesar Augustus; in Homer, allies of the Trojans, 8.849.

LEMNOS (*lem'-nos*): island in the northeastern Aegean, noted for its volcanic gasses, where Vulcan landed when he was flung from Olympus by Jupiter; thereafter a center of the cult of Vulcan, 8.536.

LERNA (*ler'-na*): marshland near the Greek city of Argos, where Hercules, for his Second Labor, killed the Hydra (1), 6.327.

LETHE (*lee'-thee*): "the river of oblivion," in Milton's phrase; one of the major rivers in the Underworld, 5.952. See Note 3.262.

LEUCASPIS (*loo-kays'-pis*): Trojan, lost at sea, presumably during the storm that opens Book 1, considered by Servius to be the helmsman of the ship of Orontes, 6.380.

LEUCATA (*loo-kay'-ta*): headland at the southern end of Leucas, an island off the shores of Acarnania in the Ionian Sea, and sacred to Apollo, 3.327. See 8.793.

LIBURNIANS (*li-bur'-ni-anz*): coastal people of Illyria, close to the northern waters of the Adriatic, 1.289.

LIBYA (*li'-bi-ya*): region of northern Africa that faces the Mediterranean Sea; Carthage was its capital, 1.26. LIBYAN (*li'-bi-yan*): belonging to the region, 1.457.

LICHAS (*li'-kas*): Latin, born by Caesarian section from his dead mother's womb, and consequently hallowed to Apollo the Healer, but killed by Aeneas, 10.372.

LICYMNIA (*li-keem'-ni-a*): a slave, mother of Helenor, 9.624.

LIGER (*li'-jer*): Etruscan, comrade of Turnus, killer of Emathion; brother of Lucagus, both killed by Aeneas, 9.650.

LIGURIA (*li-goor'-i-a*): 10.224, a region north of Etruria, in Cisalpine Gaul, inhabited by the LIGURIAN (*li-goor'-i-an*) people, 11.838.

LILYBAEUM (*li-li-bee'-um*): headland on the extreme western coast of Sicily and a dangerous reach for mariners, 3.816.

LIPARE (*li'-pa-ree*): island among the cluster of Aeolian islands off the northern coast of Sicily; it lies not far from Vulcan's home, called Vulcania, and is also associated with Aeolus (1), the king of the winds, 8.491. See VULCANIA.

LIRIS (*leye'-ris*): Trojan killed by Camilla, 11.789.

LOCRI (*loh'-kree*): people of Locris, a region in central Greece, or Locri, a specific settlement; LOCRIANS (*loh'-kri-ans*): belonging to the Locri, 11.321. Their contingent at Troy was shipwrecked on their return from Asia Minor; some survivors founded a Greek colony, Naryx (Narycium), also known as Locri Epizephyrii, on the toe of Italy, 3.472. See Note 11.315–36.

LOVE: see CUPID.

LUCAGUS (*loo'-ka-gus*): Etruscan, comrade of Turnus, brother of Liger, both killed by Aeneas, 10.682.

LUCETIUS (*loo-se'-ti-us*): Latin killed by Ilioneus, 9.649.

LUPERCAL (*loo'-per-kal*): a grotto on the Palatine hill, where Romulus and Remus were alleged to have been suckled by a wolf, and a site held sacred for its powers of fertility, 8.403.

LUPERCI (*loo-per'-kee*): priests of Lupercus or Lycaean Pan, 8.777.

LYCAEUS (*li-kee'-us*): mountain in western Arcadia, sacred haunt of Pan, 8.404.

LYCAON (*li-kay'-un*): (1) Cretan metal-worker, 9.353. (2) Father of the Trojan warrior Erichaetes, 10.884.

LYCIAN (*li'-shan*): 1.134, of LYCIA (*li'-sha*), a region in southern Asia Minor allied to Troy, the kingdom of Sarpedon and Glaucus, and a winter haunt of Apollo, where he offered oracles to his devotees, 4.179. See Note ad loc.

LYCTOS (*leek'-tos*): city in Crete, its contingent led to Troy by Idomeneus, 3.473.

LYCURGUS (*li-kur'-gus*): son of Dryas, king of Thrace, he attacked Dionysus and was blinded by Jupiter in turn, 3.18.

LYCUS (*li'-kus*): Trojan, for a moment considered lost in the epic's initial storm, 1.262. (Since all the others named at 1.261–63, except Orontes, survive, it is a reasonable assumption that the Lycus of Books 1 and 9.623 are one and the same.)

LYDIAN (*li' di-an*): 2.969, from Lydia in Asia Minor, an area settled by Lydians, supposedly the ancestors of the Etruscans, and so, along with Tuscans and Etrurians, an alternative name for the Etruscan people, 8.565. See Introduction, p. 35.

LYNCEUS (*leen'-syoos*): Trojan killed by Turnus, 9.866.

LYRNESUS (*leer-ne'-sus*): a city in the Troad below Trojan Mount Ida, 10.157.

MACHAON (*ma-kay'-on*): Greek healer, son of Asculapius, co-commander of the Thessalians at Troy, and one of the raiding party hidden inside the Trojan horse, 2.334.

MAENADS (*mee'-nadz*): literally "madwomen." They are the female devotees of the god Bacchus, who range the hills in ecstasy, carrying the thyrsus (the "sacred stave"), a staff wreathed with ivy and topped by a pine cone, 3.151.

MAEON (*mee'-on*): Rutulian, comrade of Turnus, killed by Aeneas, 10.396.

MAEONIA (*mee-oh'-ni-a*): equivalent to Lydia in Asia Minor, and to Etruria in Italy too, since the region was the supposed source of the Maeonidae, the Etruscans, 9.625.

MAEOTIC (*mee-o'-tik*): of Lake Maeotis, an area settled by Scythian warriors, which formed the northeastern boundary of the Roman Empire; today the Sea of Azov, 6.921.

MAGUS (*ma'-gus*): Rutulian killed by Aeneas, 10.617.

MAIA (*meye'-a*): daughter of Atlas, mother by Jupiter of Mercury, constellated among the seven Pleiades, 1.356.

MALEA (*ma'-le-a*): stormy southeastern cape of the Peloponnese, a perilous reach for sailors, 5.217.

MANLIUS (*man'-li-us*): Marcus Manlius Capitolinus, Roman who saved the Capitol from being overpowered by the Gauls, 8.765. See Introduction, p. 34.

MANTO (*man'-to*): daughter of Tiresias, prophetess married to the Tiber; together they bore a comrade of Aeneas, Ocnus, who called his place of origin Mantua, after his mother's name, 10.241.

MANTUA (*man'-tu-a*): city in the Po River valley and capital of the Etruscan alliance, 10.242. See Note ad loc and Introduction, pp. 2, 3, 11, 36.

MARCELLUS (*mar-sel'-us*): (1) Marcus Claudius Marcellus, Roman general, 6.986. See Introduction, pp. 31–32. (2) Augustus' nephew and adopted son who died in 23 B.C., 6.1018. See FIELD OF MARS and Introduction, pp. 3, 31–32.

MARICA (*ma-ree'-ka*): Latian water-nymph, mother by Faunus of King Latinus, 7.52.

MARS (*marz*): (Ares), Roman god of war, son of Jove and Juno, and father of Romulus and Remus, 1.328.

MARSIAN (*mar'-si-an*): of the Marsi or Marsians, a Sabellian tribe opposed to Aeneas, who lived in the vicinity of Lake Fucinus, 7.872.

MASSIC (*ma'-sik*): of the vine-rich mountain slope on the borders of Latium and Campania, source of a contingent allied with Turnus, 7.844.

MASSICUS (*ma'-si-kus*): leader of an Etruscan contingent in support of Aeneas, and captain of the TIGER, 10.202.

MASSYLIAN (*ma-si'-li-an*): of a North African tribe, the Massylians, to the west of Carthage, 6.73.

MAXIMUS (*mak'-si-mus*): Quintus Fabius Maximus, general who saved the Republic after the disastrous defeat of the Roman army by Hannibal at Cannae in 216 B.C., 6.974. See Introduction, p. 31.

MEDON (*mee'-don*): Trojan, one of Antenor's three sons whom Aeneas sees among the war heroes in the Underworld, 6.561.

MEGAERA (*me-gee'-ra*): one of the Furies, sister of Allecto and Tisiphone, 12.982. See Note 12.980–88.

MEGARA (*me'-ga-ra*): town on the Eastern coast of Sicily, named for the Greek city between Corinth and Athens on the Saronic Gulf, 3.796.

MELAMPUS (*me-laym'-pus*): Latin, comrade of Hercules, father of Cisseus (2) and Gyas (2), two brothers killed by Aeneas, 10.378.

MELIBOEAN (*me-li-bee'-an*): of Meliboea, a city in Thessaly, in the kingdom of Philoctetes, 3.476.

MELITE (*me'-li-tee*): sea-nymph in Neptune's retinue, 5.919.

MEMMIAN (*me'-mi-an*): of a Roman clan called the Memmii. Virgil draws a connection between the Greek and Latin verbs *memnêsthai* and *meminisse*—"to remember"—so as to connect Mnestheus and the name Memmius, 5.138.

MEMNON (*mem'-non*): king of the Ethiopians, son of Tithonus and Dawn; his armor forged by Vulcan, he fought for the Trojans at Troy and was killed by Achilles, 1.591.

MENELAUS (*me-ne-lay'-us*): son of Atreus, king of Lacedaemon, brother of Agamemnon, rightful husband of Helen, 2.334. See PROTEUS and Note 11.315–36.

MENESTHEUS (*me-nees'-thyoos*): Trojan, grandson of Laomedon, son of Clytius (2), brother of Acmon, 10.158.

MENOETES (*me-nee'-teez*): (1) Trojan, helmsman of Gyas who captains the *Chimaera* to finish third in the ship-race at Anchises' funeral games, 5.184. See Note 5.134–318. (2) Arcadian soldier and gifted angler killed by Turnus, 12.604.

MERCURY: (Hermes), messenger of the gods, son of Jupiter and Maia, giant-killer, and guide of dead souls to the Underworld, 1.360.

MEROPS (*me'-rops*): Trojan killed by Turnus, 9.797.

MESSAPUS (*mee-say'-pus*): son of Neptune, comrade of Turnus, commander of a contingent from southern Etruria, 7.804.

METABUS (*me'-ta-bus*): Volscian commander, father of Camilla, 11.639.

METISCUS (*me-tees'-kus*): Rutulian, Turnus' charioteer impersonated by Juturna once she has put the driver out of action, 12.550.

METTUS (*mee'-tus*): Mettus Fufetius, leader of Alba Longa, 8.756. See Introduction, p. 34.

MEZENTIUS (*me-zen'-ti-us*): Etruscan king, father of Lausus, 7.754. See Introduction, pp. 20–22.

MIMAS (*mi'-mas*): Trojan comrade of Aeneas, killed by Mezentius, 10.830.

MINCIUS (*min'-si-us*): river of Cisalpine Gaul, now known as the Mincio, "fathered" by Lake Benacus (Lago di Garda) and source of a contingent supporting Aeneas, 10.248.

MINERVA (*mi-ner'-va*): (Athena), goddess, daughter of Jupiter, defender of the Greeks. A patron of human ingenuity and resourcefulness, whether exemplified by handicrafts, such as spinning and weaving, or by skill in human relations, or in battle. She joins Neptune and Venus to represent Roman divinity at the battle of Actium, 1.49. Minerva's "temple on the heights" (3.620) refers to Castrum Minervae, a site at the heel of Italy sacred to the goddess, where Aeneas, taking the shortest route by sea from Greece, makes his first Italian landfall. See CERAUNIA.

MINIO (*mi'-ni-oh*): river in Etruria, whose people are Trojan allies, 10.222.

MINOS (*meye'-nos*): son of Jupiter and Europa, king of Crete, father of Deucalion, a formidable judge in the Underworld, 6.17.

MINOTAUR (*min'-o-tawr*): half man, half bull, issue of Pasiphaë, wife of Minos, and a bull; and killed by Theseus, 6.31. See LABYRINTH.

MISENUS (*meye-see'-nus*): Trojan, son of Aeolus (2), trumpeter and herald of Aeneas, who, having challenged the gods, was punished by them, 3.288. Misenum, the cape that forms the northern headland of the Bay of Naples, was named after the herald in compensation for his death (see 6.270–73).

MNESTHEUS (*mnees'-thyoos*): Trojan, one of Aeneas' captains, who pilots the *Dragon* to second place in the ship-race and finishes third in the archery contest at Anchises' funeral games, 4.356. See Note 5.134–318, Note 5.539–98, and MEMMIAN.

MONACO (*mo'-na-koh*): (Latin *Monoecus*), headland of Liguria, sacred to Hercules, whose temple was erected there, 6.956.

MOON: the moon personified, one of the aspects of Diana, the tri-form goddess, 1.891. See 10.260–63, DIANA, HECATE.

MORINI (*mo-ri'-nee*): a people of northern Gaul, conquered by Caesar Augustus, 8.851.

MUMMIUS (*moo'-mi-us*): Lucius Mummius, the conqueror of Corinth in 146 B.C., 6.961; see CORINTH, and Introduction, p. 30.

MURRANUS (*moo-ray'-nus*): Rutulian killed by Aeneas, 12.618.

MUSAEUS (*moo-see'-us*): according to legend, a Greek singer reputed to have come from Thrace and been instructed by Orpheus, 6.772.

MUSE: goddess, daughter of Jupiter, one of a group of nine, who preside over literature and the arts and are the sources of memory and artistic inspiration, 1.9.

MUTUSCA (*mu-toos'-ka*): Sabine town, its contingent allied with Turnus, 7.828.

MYCENAE (*meye-see'-nee*): city in the Argolid, Agamemnon's capital, just north of the city of Argos in the Peloponnese, 1.340. MYCENAEAN (*meye-se-nee'-an*), belonging to the city, 11.322. For "the Mycenaean commander" (ibid.), see AGAMEMNON.

MYCONOS (*mee'-ko-nos*): island in the Cyclades, to which Apollo chained the island of Delos, his birthplace, to keep it stationary, 3.92.

MYGDON (*mig'-don*): father of Coroebus; an ally of Aeneas, affianced to Cassandra, killed by Peneleus, 2.430.

MYRMIDON (*mur'-mi-don*): a resident of Phthia, in southern Thessaly; one of the savage fighters ruled by King Peleus and commanded at Troy by his son, Achilles, 2.8.

NAR (*nar*): Sabine river, a sulphurous stream that flows from the foothills of the Apennines into the Tiber, 7.602.

NARYCIAN (*na-ri'-shan*): of Naryx, see LOCRI, 3.472.

NAUTES (*naw'-teez*): Trojan, elder seer and counselor of Aeneas, 5.778.

NAXOS (*nak'-sos*): Aegean island in the Cyclades, south of Delos, a favorite haunt of the Maenads, 3.150.

NEALCES (*ne-ayl'-seez*): Trojan who kills Salius (2), 10.889.

NEMEAN (*ne-mee'-an*): of Nemea, a sector of the Argolid and home of an enormous lion; killing it was the first of Hercules' Twelve Labors imposed on him by King Eurystheus, 8.348.

NEOPTOLEMUS (*ne-ohp-to'-le-mus*): "New Soldier" in Greek, son of Achilles, who came to Troy after his father's death and, together with Philoctetes, led the fight against the Trojans; also known as Pyrrhus, married to Hermione, the daughter of Helen and Menelaus, 2.333. For the brevity of Neoptolemus' life, see Note 3.389–400.

NEPTUNE (*nep'-tyoon*): (Poseidon), Roman god of the sea, son of Cronus and Rhea, younger brother of Jupiter, father of Polyphemus the Cyclops; partisan of Aeneas, 1.145. See Note 5.894–903.

NEREUS (*nee'-ryoos*): sea-god, father of Thetis, the mother of Achilles, and of all the Nereids, 2.521.

NEREIDS (*nee'-re-idz*): sea-nymphs, daughters by Doris of Nereus, who form the sea-lord's retinue, 3.89. See Note 5.920.

NERITOS (*nee'-ri-tos*): Ionian island close to Ithaca, which Virgil may conflate with Mount Neriton, which dominates Ithaca itself, 3.324.

NERSAE (*neer'-see*): city of the Aequi, east of Rome, who are Latian allies of Turnus, 7.865.

NIGHT: personified, mother of the Furies, sister of Earth, she drives her chariot through the sky, a goddess who wields power over gods and men, and even Jupiter responds to her with fear, 3.600.

NILE: the famous river of Egypt, known for its delta with seven mouths that empty into the Mediterranean, pictured by Virgil as receiving back Antony and Cleopatra after their defeat by Octavian (Augustus) at the battle of Actium, 6.922.

NIPHAEUS (*ni-fee'-us*): Rutulian spilled from his horses by Aeneas, 10.677.

NISUS (*neye'-sus*): Trojan, comrade of Euryalus, competitor in the foot-race who places fifth, later killed by Volscians, when he tries to save his younger friend during their exploit in behalf of Aeneas, 5.328. See Note 5.325–402.

NOËMON (*no-ee'-mon*): Trojan killed by Turnus, 9.865.

NOMENTUM (*noh-men'-tum*): Sabine town northeast of Rome, 6.893.

NUMA (*noo'-ma*): (1) Numa Pompilius, legendary king of Rome, 6.935; see Introduction, p. 29. (2) Rutulian, one among many, killed in the melee led by Nisus and Euryalus, 9.520. (3) Rutulian comrade of Turnus, routed by Aeneas, 10.668.

NUMANUS (*noo-may'-nus*): Rutulian, also called Remulus (2), married to Turnus' younger sister and a braggart killed by Ascanius, 9.674.

NUMICUS (*noo-mee'-kus*): small stream in Latium near the Tiber, where Aeneas was said to have died, 7.171.

NUMIDIANS (*noo-mi'-di-anz*): nomadic North African tribe of daring bareback riders, 4.53.

NUMITOR (*nu'-mi-tor*): (1) king of Alba Longa, grandfather of Romulus, 6.888. (2) Rutulian, comrade of Turnus who fails in his attempt on Aeneas' life, 10.401.

NURSIA (*noor'-si-a*): mountain town inhabited by Sabines, near Umbria in the Apennines, 7.833.

NYMPHS: Semi-divine female beings who inspirit many features of the natural world, woodlands and mountain slopes, waters, springs and streams, 1.198.

NYSA (*nee'-sa*): mountain and city in India, legendary birthplace of Bacchus, center of his cult where the Bacchic rites were allegedly begun, and one of the god's favorite haunts, 6.929.

OCEAN: the great river that surrounds the world and the god who rules its waters, 1.343.

OCNUS (*ohk'-nus*): founding father of Mantua, son of Manto the seer and the Tuscan river Tiber, leader of a contingent allied with Aeneas, 10.240.

OEBALUS (*ee'-ba-lus*): son of Telon, the king of Capreae, and the water-nymph Sebethis; he extended his father's holdings to the mainland; leader of a contingent allied with Turnus, 7.853.

OECHALIA (*ee-ka'-li-a*): town on the island of Euboea, razed by Hercules when its king, Eurytus, denied the hero his daughter's hand in marriage, 8.342.

OENOTRIANS (*ee-noh'-tri-anz*): 1.641, people of OENOTRIA (*ee-noh'-tri-a*), region of southern Italy, 7.94.

OILEUS (*oh-eye'-lyoos*): Locrian king, father of Little Ajax, 1.51.

OLEAROS (*oh le' a ros*): island among the Cyclades, named for its profusion of olives, 3.152.

OLYMPUS (*o-lim'-pus*): mountain in northeastern Thessaly, home of the gods, and a general term for the sky and the heavens above it, 1.453.

ONITES (*o-neye'-teez*): Rutulian killed by Aeneas, 12.601.

OPHELTES (*o-feel'-teez*): Trojan, father of Euryalus, who taught his son the skills of soldiery at Troy, 9.238.

OPIS (*oh'-pis*): nymph who serves as an aide of Diana and messenger of the goddess, 11.632.

ORESTES (*o-res'-teez*): grandson of Atreus, son of Agamemnon and Clytemnestra, he avenged his father's murder by murdering his mother and her lover, Aegisthus, and was driven mad by her Furies, 3.394. See ANDROMACHE and HELENUS.

ORICIAN (*o-ri'-shan*): of Oricia, a town in Epirus known for its black terebinth wood, 10.166.

ORION (*o-reye'-on*): mythical hunter loved by the Dawn and murdered by Diana; and the constellation called the Hunter in his name, 1.644.

ORITHYIA (*oh-ree-theei'-a*): daughter of Erectheus, ancient king of Athens, and wife of the North Wind, Boreas. Her gifts are horses, 12.105.

ORNYTUS (*ohr'-ni-tus*): Etruscan killed by Camilla, 11.798.

ORODES (*o-roh'-deez*): Trojan killed by Mezentius, 10.864.

ORONTES (*o-rohn'-teez*): Trojan allied to Aeneas, leader of the Lycian contingent, who meets his death in a storm at sea, 1.134.

ORPHEUS (*orf'-yoos*): legendary bard who could sing the world into order and even attempt to lead his beloved Eurydice up from the Underworld, 6.140. See Introduction, pp. 9–10.

ORSES (*ohr'-seez*): Trojan killed by Rapo, 10.883.

ORSILOCHUS (*ohr-si'-lo-kus*): Trojan killed by Camilla, 11.752.

ORTA (*ohr'-ta*): Etrurian town near the juncture of the Tiber and the Nar, source of a contingent allied to Turnus, 7.833.

ORTYGIA (*ohr-ti'-ji-a*): (1) legendary "Quail Island" where Diana killed Orion, amd usually identified with Delos, 3.149. (2) Island in the harbor of Syracuse on Sicily, 3.801.

ORTYGIUS (*ohr-ti'-ji-us*): Rutulian killed by Caeneus (2), 9.653.

OSCANS (*os'-kanz*): tribe of Campania, allied with Turnus, 7.848.

OSINIUS (*o-seye'-ni-us*): king of Clusium, his Etrurian contingent allied with Aeneas, 10.776.

OSIRIS (*oh-seye'-rus*): Rutulian killed by Thymbraeus, 12.538.

OTHRYS (*oh'-thris*): (1) father of Panthus, 2.401. (2) Snow-capped peak in Thessaly, home of Centaurs, 7.788.

PACHYNUS (*pa-kee'-nus*): headland at the southeastern-most point of Sicily, 3.506.

PACTOLUS (*payk-toh'-lus*): river in Lydia, whose waters run with silt and reflect a golden cast, 10.173.

PADUA (*pa'-dyoo-a*): ancient Patavium, Antenor's city in Cisalpine Gaul, 1.295. See Note 1.287–97.

PADUSA (*pa-doo'-sa*): one of the mouths of the river Po, 11.549.

PAGASUS (*pa'-ga-sus*): ally of Aeneas, killed by Camilla, 11.789.

PALAEMON (*pa-lee'-mon*): son of Ino and Athamas, transformed into a sea-god, and so a member of Neptune's retinue, 5.917.

PALAMEDES (*pa-la-mee'-deez*): legendary Greek hero, son of Belus (3); falsely accused of treason by Ulysses—whom he had exposed as a draft-dodger at the outbreak of the Trojan War—and consequently put to death, as narrated by Sinon, 2.102.

PALATINE (*pa'-la-teyen*): one of Rome's seven hills, the site of Augustus' home in the city, 9.10.

PALICI (*pa-leye'-kee*): twin sons of Jupiter, born to him by Thalia, 9.664.

PALINURUS (*pa-li-noo'-rus*): Trojan helmsman of Aeneas' ship; washed overboard, his burial site becomes a cape (Palinuro) on the western coast of Lucania that bears his name, 3.243. See Note 6.384–423 and Introduction, p. 27.

PALLADIUM (*pa-lay'-di-um*): a miniature statue of Athena in full armor, with which the destiny of Troy, and then Rome, was closely linked, 9.180. See Note 2.211.

PALLANTEUM (*pay-layn'-tee-um*): Evander's first, Arcadian city, named for Pallas (2), son of Lycaon and forebear of Evander; next, the name of Evander's Etruscan city built on the Palatine hill, a prefiguration of Rome itself, 8.57.

PALLAS (*pa'-las*): (1) an epithet of the Greek goddess Athena, who is equivalent to Minerva in the Roman pantheon, 1.580. (2) A legendary king of Arcadia, grandfather of Evander, 8.54. (3) Son of Evander, comrade of Aeneas, killed by Turnus, who strips the sword-belt from his body, 8.117.

PALMUS (*payl'-mus*): comrade of Aeneas, killed by Mezentius, 10.824.

PAN (*pan*): Lycaean Pan in particular, guardian god of woods and shepherds, half man, half goat, who takes his title from Mount Lycaeus in Arcadia, 8.404.

PANDARUS (*pan'-da-rus*): (1) Trojan, son of Lycaon, and a famous archer, 5.548. See Note 5.548–50. (2) Trojan, son of Alcanor (1) by Iaera; brother of Bitias, both brothers killed by Turnus, 9.765.

PANOPEA (*pa-no-pee'-a*): a sea-nymph in Father Portunus' retinue, 5.268.

PANOPES (*pa'-no-peez*): Sicilian also-ran who enters the foot-race at Anchises' funeral games, 5.334. See Note 5.325–402.

PANTAGIAS (*payn-ta'-gi-as*): river in eastern Sicily, 3.795.

PANTHUS (*payn'-thus*): son of Othrys, priest of Apollo at Troy, 2.401.

PAPHOS (*pa'-fos*): city on the island of Cyprus, its temple a favorite haunt of Venus and sacred to the goddess, 1.504.

PARIAN (*pa'-ri-an*): 1.709, belonging to PAROS (*pa'-ros*): island among the Cyclades, renowned for its marble, 3.152.

PARIS (*pa'-ris*): Trojan, son of Priam and Hecuba, who abducted Helen from Menelaus in Lacedaemon, and started the Trojan War, 1.34. See Note 7.375–77 and Introduction, p. 17.

PARTHENIUS (*payr-then'-i-us*): Trojan killed by Rapo, 10.883.

PARTHENOPAEUS (*payr-then-o-pee'-us*): son of Meleager and Atalanta, ruler of Argos, one of the Seven against Thebes, whose ghost Aeneas meets in the Underworld, 6.557. See Note 6.557–58.

PARTHIANS (*par'-thi-anz*): a people living southwest of the Caspian Sea in a part of modern Iraq; renowned for their feats in archery, 7.704. See Introduction, pp. 1, 30.

PASIPHAË (*pa-si'-fa-ee*): wife of Minos, the king of Crete, 6.30. See MINOTAUR.

PATRON (*pay'-tron*): Arcadian comrade of Aeneas, who enters the foot-race at Anchises' funeral games, 5.332. See Note 5.325–402.

PAULLUS (*paw'-lus*): Lucius Aemilius Paullus, Roman military leader, victor over Perseus of Macedon, 6.964. See Introduction, p. 30.

PELASGIANS (*pe-laz'-ji-anz*): early inhabitants of Greece who are considered by Virgil to be pre-Etruscan settlers of the area north of Rome, 8.708.

PELIAS (*pe'-li-as*): Trojan, comrade of Aeneas in Troy's last hours, 2.542.

PELOPS (*pee'-lops*): ancient king of Argos, son of Tantalus, father of Atreus, grandfather of Agamemnon and Menelaus, 2.250.

PELORUS (*pe-loh'-rus*): headland of northeastern Sicily, fronting the Straits of Messina that separate the island from the mainland, 3.486.

PENELEUS (*pee-ne'-le-us*): Greek who kills Coroebus at the fall of Troy, 2.530.

PENTHESILEA (*pen-the-si-lee'-a*): queen of the Amazons, killed by Achilles at Troy, 1.592.

PENTHEUS (*pen'-thyoos*): king of Thebes who, for spurning the rites of Dionysus, is maddened by the god and dismembered by his mother, Agave, with her troop of raving Bacchantes. In Virgil's context, the king's double vision is produced, one may suppose, by his manic state of mind, 4.588.

PERGAMUM (*per'-ga-mum*): (1) 3.161, the name Aeneas gives the city he founds in Crete, after (2) Pergamum (or Pergama), the citadel of Troy as well as a collective name for the city itself, 6.78.

PERIDIA (*pe-ri-deye'-a*): mother of Onites, a Rutulian killed by Aeneas, 12.602.

PERIPHAS (*pe'-ri-fas*): Greek, comrade of Pyrrhus in Troy's last hours, 2.593.

PERSEUS (*per'-syoos*): Macedonian king who claimed descent from Achilles and his line, 6.965. See PAULLUS, and Introduction, p. 30.

PETELIA (*pe-tee'-li-a*): small, inland town in the toe of Italy, built by Philoctetes, according to legend, when he fled his home in Thessaly, 3.475.

PHAEACIA (*fee-ay'-sha*): (Corcyra, modern Corfu), an island kingdom in the Ionian Sea, ruled by Alcinous and Arete; its inhabitants, the Phaeacians, renowned for the hospitality they offered Ulysses and other travelers, 3.347.

PHAEDRA (*fee'-dra*): daughter of Minos, wife of Theseus, seductress of his son, Hippolytus, and a suicide whose ghost Aeneas sees among the lovelorn ladies in the Underworld, 6.516. See Note 7.884–908.

PHAËTHON (*fay'-e-thon*): (1) equivalent to Helios, god of the sun, 5.125. (2) More particularly, the son of Helios by Clymene; lover of Cycnus, killed by Jupiter's thunderbolt as he attempted to guide his father's chariot, 10.230. See CYCNUS.

PHARUS (*fa'-rus*): Rutulian killed by Aeneas, 10.380.

PHEGEUS (*fee'-gyoos*): (1) Trojan, aide-de-camp of Aeneas, 5.294. (2) Trojan killed by Turnus, perhaps identical with (1), 9.863. (3) Trojan beheaded by Turnus, 12.440.

PHENEUS (*fe'-ne-us*): town in Arcadia displayed to Anchises by the young Evander, 8.189.

PHERES (*fee'-reez*): Trojan killed by Halaesus, 10.489.

PHILOCTETES (*fi-lok-tee'-teez*): son of Poias, the great archer of the Trojan War, original commander of the Thessalians from Methone, marooned on Lemnos suffering from an infected snake bite, 3.475. See MELIBOEAN and PETELIA.

PHINEUS (*fee'-nyoos*): son of Agenor and king of Thrace, blinded by the gods for having blinded his own sons, and harried by the Harpies sent by Jupiter; they either snatched his food away from him or contaminated what was left, 3.258. See Note ad loc.

PHLEGYAS (*fle'-gi-as*): father of Ixion, tormented for having torched Apollo's temple at Delphi, and one of the most agonized figures in the Underworld, doomed to warn mankind to submit to the will of the gods, 6.715.

PHOEBUS (*fee'-bus*): title of Apollo, derived from a Greek word meaning "luminous," "brilliant," with a sense of purity implied as well, 3.120.

PHOENICIAN (*fee-ni'-shan*): of Phoenicia, a narrow coastal strip of land between Syria and the Mediterranean, known for its navigators, traders, and artisans, and the cities of Sidon and Tyre; the original homeland of Dido, 1.413. See Introduction, p. 25.

PHOENIX (*fee'-niks*): son of Amyntor, aged tutor and comrade of Achilles, 2.946.

PHOLOË (*foh'-lo-ee*): Cretan slave girl, Sergestus' prize for entering the ship-race at Anchises' funeral games, 5.316.

PHOLUS (*foh'-lus*): (1) a Centaur killed by Hercules, 8.347. (2) Trojan killed by Turnus, 12.407.

PHORBAS (*fohr'-bas*): Trojan shipmate of Palinurus, impersonated by the god of sleep to tempt Aeneas' helmsman to his doom, 5.936.

PHORCUS (*fohr'-kus*): (1) an old god of the sea, leader of the Nereids, 5.268. (2) Latin, father of Cydon and his brothers, seven warriors hurling as many spears against Aeneas, 10.389.

PHRYGIAN (*fri'-jan*): 1.461, of the PHRYGIANS (*fri'-janz*), Trojan allies, inhabitants of Phrygia, a land mass in Asia Minor including Troy and stretching eastward from the city into Anatolia, 9.158. In Latin poetry, Phrygian often stands derogatorily for oriental, and thence effeminate.

PICUS (*pee'-kus*): son of Saturn, father of Faunus, transformed into a woodpecker (*picus* in Latin) by Circe who, stung by his rebuff of her advances, covered his wings with color, 7.53.

PILLARS OF PROTEUS: 11.317; see PROTEUS.

PILUMNUS (*pee-loom'-nus*): son of Daunus, forebear of Turnus, a patron deity of house and household, 9.4.

PINARIAN (*pee-nay'-ri-an*): of a Roman family, the Pinarii, that, together with the family of the Potitii, founded the rites for Hercules and performed them in antiquity, 8.313.

PIRITHOUS (*pee-ri'-tho-us*): son of Zeus, king of the Lapiths, who, with his comrade Theseus, attempted to abduct Persephone, the Queen of the Underworld, from the bridal bed of Death; in punishment Pirithous was clapped in chains for all time, 6.451.

PISA (*pee'-za*): city in Etruria, supposedly established by colonists from Pisa in Elis in the northwestern Peloponnese, 10.216.

PLEMYRIUM (*plee-mi'-ri-um*): Sicilian headland to the south of the Bay of Syracuse, 3.800.

PLUTO (*ploo'-toh*): king of the Underworld, 7.383.

PO: river in northern Italy, Latin *Padus*, 9.774.

PODALIRIUS (*po-da-leye'-ri-us*): Trojan killed by Alsus, 12.365.

POLITES (*po-leye'-teez*): Trojan, son of Priam, killed by Pyrrhus, 2.652.

POLLUX (*po'-luks*): brother of Helen and twin of Castor, sons of Leda. The extraordinary privilege granted them—that they should come back to life on alternate days—was attributed to the fact that one (Pollux) was the son of immortal Jupiter and the other (Castor) of Tyndareus, Leda's human husband, 6.142.

POLYBOETES (*po-li-bee'-teez*): Trojan priest whose ghost Aeneas encounters among the war heroes in the Underworld, 6.562.

POLYDORUS (*po-li-doh'-rus*): Trojan, son of Priam, who placed him under the guardianship of king Polymestor of Thrace; when Priam's fortunes failed, Polymestor took Polydorus' treasure together with his life, 3.53.

POLYPHEMUS (*po-li-fee'-mus*): Cyclops, son of Neptune, blinded by Ulysses and his crew in revenge for the monster's devouring of their shipmates, 3.742.

POMETIA (*po-mee'-ti-a*) or Pometii: town of the Volscians, southeast of Rome near the Pomptine Marshes, 6.895.

POMPEY (*pom' pee*) the Great: renowned Roman leader, Gnaeus Pompeius Magnus, 6.956. See Introduction, pp. 1, 30.

POPULONIA (*po-pu-loh'-ni-a*): coastal city of Etruria, source of Turnus' allies led by Abas (3). 10.208.

PORSENNA (*por-seen'-a*): king of Etruria, 8.758. See Introduction, p. 34.

PORTUNUS (*pohr-too'-nus*): god of harbors, who impels the *Scylla*, the victor in the ship-race at Anchises' funeral games, 5.269.

POTITIUS (*po-tee'-ti-us*): founder of the Potitian clan that, together with the Pinarian, established the rites of Hercules in Evander's kingdom, and so eventually in Rome as well, 8.312.

PRAENESTE (*pree-nees'-tee*): renowned city in Latium, now Palestrina, in the foothills of the Apennines east of Rome, 7.790.

PRIAM (*preye'-am*): (1) king of Troy, son of Laomedon of the line of Dardanus, father of Hector, Paris, and many others, 1.553. (2) Grandson of Priam (1), and son of Polites, 5.621.

PRIVERNUM (*pree-veer'-num*): Latian city southeast of Rome and inhabited by Volscians; the place where Camilla was born, 11.641.

PRIVERNUS (*pree-veer'-nus*): Rutulian killed by Capys (1), 9.656.

PROCAS (*pro'-kas*): Alban king, whose prefiguration is presented by Anchises to Aeneas in the Underworld, 6.887.

PROCHYTA (*pro'-ki-ta*): small, seismic island off the coast of Campania, southwest of Cape Misenum, at the northern tip of the Bay of Naples, 9.810.

PROCRIS (*proh'-krees*): daughter of Erectheus, wife of Cephalus, who inadvertently killed her while hunting, 6.516.

PROMOLUS (*pro'-mo-lus*): Trojan killed by Turnus, 9.654.

PROSERPINA (*pro-ser'-pi-na*): (Persephone), daughter of Ceres and wife of Pluto, who abducted her from earth to the Underworld where she rules among the dead, 4.868. See Note ad loc.

PROTEUS (*proh'-tyoos*): the Old Man of the Sea, servant of Neptune, and a prophet known for changing himself into any shape he chooses, 11.317. The Pillars of Proteus (ibid.), presumably the island of Pharus, off Alexandria in the Nile Delta—where Menelaus was marooned when homeward bound from Troy—gain their name by analogy with the Pillars of Hercules at the western end of the Mediterranean Sea.

PRYTANIS (*pri'-ta-nis*): Trojan killed by Turnus, 9.865.

PUNIC (*pyoo'-nik*): equivalent of Carthaginian, 1.411. For the Punic Wars between Rome and Carthage, see Introduction, pp. 25–27.

PYGMALION (*pig-may'-li-on*): brother of Dido, who murdered her husband, Sychaeus, and effectively drove her into exile from Tyre, 1.421.

PYRGI (*peer'-gee*): Etrurian coastal town, its contingent allied with Aeneas, 10.222.

PYRRHUS (*peer'-us*): son of Achilles, also known as Neoptolemus, and the killer of Priam, 2.585. See Introduction, p. 15.

QUERCENS (*kweer'-kens*): one of many Rutulians who storm the Trojans' fort by the Tiber, 9.778.

QUIRINUS (*kwi-ree'-nus*): "Father Quirinus," the name given the deified Romulus, 6.991.

QUIRITES (*kwi-ree'-teez*): the citizenry of Rome, 7.827. The Romans themselves considered the name to derive from the Sabine town of Cures, north of Rome, off the Via Salaria.

RAPO (*ra'-po*): Rutulian who kills the Trojan Parthenius and Orses, 10.883.

REMULUS (*rem'-yoo-lus*): (1) native of Tibur, guest of Caedicus (1), who presents him with lavish gifts, 9.419. (2) Family name of Numanus, Rutulian killed by Ascanius, his first kill in battle, 9.674. (3) Rutulian killed by Orsilochus, 11.753.

REMUS (*ree'-mus*): (1) brother of Romulus, whom he killed for leaping over the walls of Rome in a gesture of rivalry, 1.350. See Introduction, p. 21. (2) Rutulian whose armor-bearer is killed by Nisus, 9.386.

RHADAMANTHUS (*ra-da-man'-thus*): son of Jupiter and Europa, brother of Minos, and the lawgiver who, after dispensing justice in Crete, presides, sternly, in the Underworld, 6.658.

RHAEBUS (*ree'-bus*): Mezentius' charger, "Bandy-Legs" in Greek, 10.1021. See Note 5.920.

RHAMNES (*rahm'-neez*): Rutulian and prophet, in the service of Turnus, killed by Nisus, 9.380.

RHEA (*ree'-a*): priestess and mother by Hercules of Aventinus, who bore the boy in secret, 7.767.

RHINE: the Rhine, European river rising in the Swiss Alps and flowing into the North Sea, 8.852.

RHESUS (*ree'-sus*): Thracian king whose horses were seized by Diomedes and Ulysses, 1.568. See Note 1.561–95.

RHIPEUS (*reye'-pyoos*): Trojan, comrade-in-arms of Aeneas at the fall of Troy, 2.427.

RHOETEUM (*ree'-tee-um*): headland of the Troad, just north of Troy, 3.130.

RHOETEUS (*ree'-tyoos*): according to Servius, king of the Marsi, father of Anchemolus, and killed by Pallas (3), 10.459.

RHOETUS (*ree'-tus*): Rutulian killed by Euryalus, 9.400.

RIVER OF FIRE: Phlegethon, "whose waves of torrent fire inflame with rage," in Milton's phrase; one of the major rivers in the Underworld, 6.304. See Note 3.262.

ROMAN FORUM: the Forum Romanum, the main square of Rome and its civic center. Evidence of its use goes back at least to the 8th century B.C., 8.424.

ROME: 1.8, capital city of the ROMAN Empire, its people and their effects, 1.41. See Introduction, passim.

ROMULUS (*rom'-yu-lus*): legendary founder of Rome, son of Mars and Ilia, Remus's twin brother, after whom the ROMANS were named, 1.329. See Introduction, pp. 18 and 29.

ROSEAN (*roh'-see-an*): of the central Italian fields by Lake Velinus known for their fertility, a region whose contingent is allied with Turnus, 7.829.

RUFRAE (*roo'-free*): town in northern Campania, its contingent allied with Turnus, 7.859.

RUMOR: (Latin *Fama*), allegorical representation of public talk and the common tongue, 4.219. The associations surrounding Rumor as sister of Coeus, a Titan, and Enceladus, one of the Giants, are deliberately unpleasant, smacking of anger and vengeance. For Jupiter had destroyed the Giant and the Titan, and Mother Earth "bore one last child, Fama [Rumor]," as Williams explains (1972, Note 4.179) "to be their sister and take vengeance on gods and men with her evil tongue."

RUTULIAN (*ru-tul'-yan*): of a leading tribe within Latium; its capital city, Ardea; its commander-in-chief, Turnus, 7.477.

SABAEANS (*sa-bee'-anz*): people of an Arabian region, Saba or Sheba, allied with the forces of Cleopatra and Mark Antony at the battle of Actium, 8.827.

SABINUS (*sa-bee'-nus*): 7.204, portrayed as a vintner with his hooked knife, the founder of the SABINE (*say'-beyn*) people of ancient central Italy, 7.823. For the abduction of their women from the Roman Circus by Romulus' men, see 8.748–49, and Introduction, p. 34.

SACES (*sa'-keez*): Rutulian comrade of Turnus, 12.754.

SACRANIANS (*sa-kray'-ni-anz*): a people of ancient Latium, their contingent allied with Turnus, 7.923.

SACRATOR (*sa-kray'-tor*): Rutulian comrade of Turnus, killer of Hydaspes, 10.882.

SAGARIS (*sa'-gar-is*): Trojan, aide-de-camp of Aeneas, killed by Turnus, 5.294.

SALAMIS (*sa'-la-mis*): island off the coast of Athens in the Saronic Gulf, the home of Telamon and his son, Great Ajax, 8.180.

SALII (*sa'-li-ee*): dancing priests of Mars, whom Virgil has taking part in the rites of Hercules as well, 8.334.

SALIUS (*sa'-li-us*): (1) Acarnanian, who enters the foot-race at Anchises' funeral games and places fourth, 5.332. See Note 5.325–402. (2) Rutulian killed by Nealces, 10.889.

SALLENTINE (*say-leen'-teyen*): of the Sallentini, an Italian people of Calabria, taken over by Idomeneus on his return from Troy, 3.474.

SALMONEUS (*sal-mohn'-yoos*): son of Aeolus (1), a king of Elis, struck by a bolt from Jove for simulating the Father's lightning with torches, Jove's thunder with his horses' stamping hooves, and so the man was confined in hell forever, 6.678. See Introduction, p. 28.

SAME (*sam'-ee*): island in the Ionian Sea, off the western coast of Greece (modern Cephalonia), near Ithaca in the kingdom of Ulysses, 3.324.

SAMOS (*sam'-os*): island off the central coast of Asia Minor, opposite Ephesus and famous for its temple to Juno, 1.18.

SAMOTHRACE (*sam'-o-thrays*): (Samothracia), island off the coast of Thrace, once called Samos, according to Virgil, and later, Samothrace, 7.238–39.

SARNUS (*sayr'-nus*): river in Campania, just east of Pompeii, its locale the source of a contingent allied with Turnus, 7.859.

SARPEDON (*sahr-pee'-don*): Trojan ally, son of Jupiter and Laodamia, co-commander of the Lycians, killed by Patroclus at Troy, 1.119.

SARRASTIAN (*say-rays'-ti-an*): of the Sarastes, a people in Campania, living in the vicinity of the river Sarnus between Naples and Salerno; their contingent allied with Turnus, 7.858.

SATICULANS (*sa-tee'-kew-lanz*): inhabitants of Saticula, a town in Campania, east of Capua, north of Mount Vesuvius; their contingent allied with Turnus, 7.848.

SATURA (*sa'-too-ra*): marshy area in Latium, location unknown, its inhabitants allies of Turnus, 7.930.

SATURN (*sa'-turn*): (Cronos), the Sower, legendary, apotheosized king of Latium, god of agriculture and of civilization in general, who established and presided over the Age of Gold, 1.37. SATURNIAN (*sa-tur'-ni-an*), belonging to Saturn, 3.451.

SATURNIA (*sa-tur'-ni-a*): (1) legendary settlement founded by Saturn on the Capitoline Hill, 8.421. (2) One of Juno's titles, since Saturn was her father, 12.212.

SCAEAN GATES (*see'-an*): the main gates of Troy, facing the Greek beachhead and beyond that, the sea, 2.758.

SCIPIOS (*ski'-pi-ohs*): powerful Roman family that produced two superb generals, Africanus the Elder (Publius Cornelius Scipio Africanus Major) and Africanus the Younger (Publius Cornelius Scipio Africanus Minor), who both wreaked destruction on Carthage in the Punic Wars, 6.969. See Introduction, pp. 25–27.

SCYLACEUM (*si-la'-see-um*): town on the south coast of the toe of Italy, its litoral a wrecker of ships, 3.647.

SCYLLA (*sil'-a*): (1) man-eating monster that lives in a cliffside cavern opposite the whirlpool of Charybdis, supposedly in the Straits of Messina, 3.496. See Note 1.236–37. (2) Vessel, captained by Cloanthus, that wins the ship-race at Anchises' funeral games, 5.145. See Note 5.134–318.

SCYROS (*skee'-ros*): island in the central Aegean off the coast of Euboea, 2.596.

SEBETHIS (*se-bee'-this*): water-nymph, mother by Telon of Oebalus, an ally of Turnus, 7.854.

SELINUS (*se-leye'-nus*): "city of palms" on the southwestern coast of Sicily, 3.814. As Williams observes (1972, note 3.705), however, the name "is more likely to mean 'conferring the victor's palm,' because the plant *sélinon* (selinon), a kind of parsley . . . was one of the plants used for the victor's crown, especially at the Isthmian games."

SERESTUS (*se-rees'-tus*): Trojan, shipwrecked companion restored to Aeneas, 1.732.

SERGESTUS (*seer-jees'-tus*): Trojan, shipwrecked companion restored to Aeneas, and captain who pilots the *Centaur* to finish fourth and last in the ship-race at Anchises' funeral games, 1.614. See Note 5.134–318.

SERGIAN (*seer'-jan*): Roman family named for Sergestus, 5.142.

SERRANUS (*see-ray'-nus*): (1) agnomen for the consul and hero of the First Punic War, Marcus Atilius Regulus, the Sower, 6.972. See Introduction, p. 31. (2) Rutulian killed by Nisus, 9.391.

SEVERUS (*se-veer'-us*): Sabine mountain among the Apennines; its people form a contingent allied with Turnus, 7.830.

SIBYL (*si'-bil*): Deiphobe, prophetess in Cumae, Aeneas' guide to the Underworld, 3.531.

SICANIAN (*si-kay'-ni-an*): one of an ancient people of Sicania or Sicily, their contingent allied with Turnus, 7.923.

SICILY (*si'-si-lee*): the large triangular island just off the southern tip of Italy in the Mediterranean, 1.42. SICILIAN (*si-si'-li-an*): belonging to the island, 1.231.

SIDICINE (*si'-di-seyen*): of the Sidicines, a tribe in Campania, their contingent allied with Turnus, 7.846.

SIDON (*seye'-don*): the major city of Phoenicia and its citizens, the Sidonians, 1.740.

SIGEAN (*si-jee'-an*): of Sigeum, headland facing the Aegean to the north of Troy, 2.392.

SILA (*see'-la*): a woody mountain range in Bruttium, in southern Italy, 12.830.

SILVANUS (*seel-vay'-nus*): a Roman god of forests, 8.710.

SILVIA (*seel'-vi-a*): Latin woman, daughter of Tyrrhus; her appeals for her tamed deer, fortuitously killed by Ascanius, set off the warfare between the Latins and the Trojans, 7.570.

SILVIUS (*seel'-vi-us*): last born of Aeneas and Lavinia, as prophesied by Anchises in the Underworld, 6.878–86; see Introduction, p. 29.

SILVIUS AENEAS (*seel'-vi-us*): Aeneas' namesake, his equal in military prowess and sense of duty, and a future Alban king, 6.888–90.

SIMOIS (*sim'-oh-is*): river of Troy, brother and tributary of the Xanthus (Scamander), 1.119.

SINON (*seye'-non*): Greek, master of fraud, whose cunning induces the Trojans to lead the wooden horse into their city, 2.101.

SIRENS: enchantresses of the sea, half woman, half bird, whose song can tempt a sailor to his ruin, 5.964. See Note 5.964–65.

SIRIUS (*see'-ri-us*): see DOG STAR, 10.329.

SLEEP: god of sleep, twin brother of Death, son of the Underworld and Night, 5.933. For the GATES OF SLEEP, 6.1029, see Note 6.1035–36 and Introduction, p. 32.

SORACTE (*soh-rak'-tee*): Etrurian mountain west of the Tiber to the north of Rome, and sacred to Apollo, 7.811.

SPARTAN (*spar'-tan*): 1.381, belonging to SPARTA (*spar'-ta*), the capital city of Laconia or Lacedaemon in the southern Peloponnese, ruled by Menelaus, and home to him and Helen, 2.716.

STHENELUS (*sthe'-ne-lus*): (1) Greek, Diomedes' charioteer, 2.331. (2) Trojan killed by Turnus, 12.407.

STHENIUS (*sthe'-ni-us*): Rutulian attacked by Pallas (3), 10.458.

STROPHADES (*stroh'-fa-deez*): islands in the Ionian Sea, their name is derived from the Greek word for "turn," *stréphesthai*, as Williams observes (1972, note 3.210–11), because the two sons of Boreas, "in one version of the story . . . were here turned back from their pursuit of the Harpies by the goddess Iris," after a promise that no more harm would come to Phineus, 3.254. See Note 3.258 and PHINEUS.

STRYMON (*stree'-mon*): Thracian river, favorite haunt of water-birds, especially cranes, 10.318.

STRYMONIUS (*stree-mon'-i-us*): Trojan whose hand is severed by Halaesus, 10.490.

STYX (*stiks*): "abhorred Styx the flood of deadly hate," in Milton's phrase; the main river in the Underworld, by which the gods swear their binding oaths, 3.262 (see Note ad loc); STYGIAN (*sti'-jan*), belonging to the river, 6.159.

SUCRO (*soo'-kroh*): Rutulian killed by Aeneas, 12.590.

SULMO (*sool'-moh*): (1) Rutulian under Volscian command; killed by Nisus, 9.474. (2) Another Rutulian, father of four sons, comrades of Turnus, captured by Aeneas to be slaughtered at Pallas' (3) funeral, 10.613.

SUN: the sun personified, 1.682. See PHAËTHON (1) and (2), 5.125, and TITAN.

SYBARIS (*si'-bar-is*): Trojan killed by Turnus, 12.432.

SYCHAEUS (*si-kee'-us*): Dido's Phoenician husband, to whom the ghost of the queen returns in the Underworld, 1.417. See PYGMALION.

SYMAETHUS (*see-mee'-thus*): Sicilian river southwest of Catania, in the foothills of Mount Etna, 9.663.

SYRACUSE (*si'-ra-kyooz*): the major city of Sicily in classical antiquity, founded by colonists from Corinth on the southeastern coast of the island and the putative birthplace of Theocritus. See ORTYGIA (2), PLEMYRIUM, and 3.800.

SYRTES (*seer'-teez*): the Sandbanks, two great shoals near the southern coast of the Mediterranean off Libya and Carthage, and a menace to mariners, 1.132.

TABURNUS (*ta-boor'-nus*): Monte Taburno, a mountain range in the Samnite region of southern Italy, 12.830.

TAGUS (*ta'-gus*): Rutulian under Volcens' command, killed by Nisus, 9.482.

TALOS (*ta'-los*): Rutulian killed by Aeneas, 12.600.

TANAIS (*ta'-na-is*): Rutulian killed by Aeneas, 12.600.

TARCHON (*tar'-kon*): Etruscan chieftain of forces allied with those of Aeneas, 8.595. See Introduction, p. 35.

TARENTUM (*ta-ren'-tum*): now Taranto, a Calabrian coastal city and harbor on the Gulf of Tarentum in southern Italy, 3.644.

TARPEIA (*tar-pay'-a*): woman warrior, comrade-in-arms of Camilla, 11.774.

TARPEIAN (*tar-pay'-an*): of a cliff on the Capitoline hill, with which it is often synonymous, named after Tarpeia, daughter of one of Romulus' generals, who treacherously opened Rome to the Sabines, 8.765.

TARQUIN (*tar'-kwin*): the name of two kings of Rome, Tarquinius Priscus and Tarquinius Superbus, "the Proud," 6.941. The latter, Rome's last king, was expelled by Brutus, 8.759. See BRUTUS and Introduction, pp. 30, 34.

TARQUITUS (*tayr'-kwi-tus*): born to Faunus by the wood-nymph Dryope and a Latin champion, comrade of Turnus, killed by Aeneas, 10.650.

TARTARUS (*tar'-ta-rus*): the lowest, darkest depths of the house of Hades, the kingdom of the dead, where Jupiter incarcerates his defeated enemies, the Titans in particular, 5.813. TARTAREAN (*tar-tar-ee'-an*), belonging to the region, 6.337.

TATIUS (*ta'-ti-us*): king of the Sabines, who, after the abduction of the Sabine women and his incursion against the Romans in revenge, shared with Romulus the joint rule of both their peoples, 8.751.

TEGEAN (*te-jee'-an*): resident of Tegea, a town in central Arcadia and synonymous with the region, 5.333.

TELEBOEAN (*te-le-bee'-an*): of an Acarnanian people who settled on Capreae, 7.856.

TELON (*te'-lon*): king of the Teleboeans, ruler of Capreae, father by Sebethis of Oebalus, who enlarged his father's holdings, 7.854.

TENEDOS (*ten'-e-dos*): island in the northeastern Aegean off the coast of Troy, where the Greek fleet regroups for the final assault on the city, 2.28.

TEREUS (*tee'-ryoos*): Trojan killed by Camilla, 11.796.

TETRICA (*te'-tri-ka*): an Apennine mountain ridge in the Sabines' realm, source of a contingent allied with Turnus, 7.830.

TEUCER (*too'-sur*): (1) first king of the Trojans or Teucrians, father of Bateia, the wife of Dardanus, forebear of Aeneas, 1.279. (2) Achaean, bastard son of Telamon, half-brother of Great Ajax and a master archer, 1.740.

TEUTHRAS (*too'-thras*): Arcadian comrade of Pallas (3) and under Aeneas' command, 10.477.

TEUTONIC (*too-ton'-ik*): describing a people of Germany. To Roman historians, the epitome of a savage northern tribe, 7.862.

THAEMON (*thee'-mon*): Lycian, brother of Clarus and Sarpedon, and an ally of Aeneas, 10.155.

THAMYRUS (*tham'-i-rus*): Trojan killed by Turnus, 12.407.

THAPSUS (*thap'-sus*): a town and a point of land on Sicily's eastern coast, 3.796.

THEANO (*the-ayn'-oh*): Trojan woman who bore Mimas to Amycus (4), 10.832.

THEBES (*theebz*): seven-gated city of the Thebans in Boeotia, attacked by Polynices and the Seven; the scene of Euripides' *Bacchae*, 4.590. See PENTHEUS.

THEMILLAS (*the-meel'-as*): Trojan, whose spear grazes Privernus, a Rutulian killed by the Trojan Capys (1), 9.656.

THERMODON (*theer'-moh-don*): river in Pontus which empties into the southern coast of the Black Sea, and a favorite haunt of the Amazons, 11.778.

THERON (*thee'-rohn*): Latin killed by Aeneas, 10.369.

THERSILOCHUS (*theer-si'-lo-kus*): (1) Trojan, one of Antenor's three sons whom Aeneas sees among the war heroes in the Underworld, 6.561. (2) Trojan killed by Turnus, 12.432.

THESEUS (*thees'-yoos*): son of Aegeus, king of Athens, who abducted Ariadne from Crete to Naxos and, with his comrade, Pirithous, descended to the Underworld and tried, unsuccessfully, to kidnap Persephone; in punishment, Theseus was condemned to sit on a seat for eternity, 6.36.

THESSANDRUS (*thee-sayn'-drus*): Greek raider hidden in the Trojan horse, 2.331.

THETIS (*the'-tis*): sea-goddess, daughter of Nereus, married to Peleus and by him the mother of Achilles, 5.919.

THOAS (*thoh'-as*): (1) Greek raider concealed in the Trojan horse, 2.333. (2) Trojan killed by Halaesus, 10.491.

THRACIAN (*thray'-shan*): 1.382, belonging to THRACE (*thrays*), a country north of the Aegean and the Hellespont, and west of the Black Sea, 3.41.

THRONIUS (*thro'-ni-us*): Trojan killed by Salius (2), 10.889.

THYBRIS (*thee'-bris*): legendary Etruscan king, eponymous hero of the river Tiber, where Thybris met his death, 8.388.

THYMBER (*theem'-ber*): Rutulian, twin brother of Larides, sons of Daunus, both killed by Pallas (3), 10.462.

THYMBRA (*theem'-bra*): town in the Troad, south of Troy, on the Xanthus (Scamander) River, and sacred to Apollo, 3.102.

THYMBRAEUS (*theem-bree'-us*): Trojan, killer of the Latin Osiris, 12.538.

THYMBRIS (*theem'-bris*): Trojan veteran, comrade of Aeneas, 10.153.

THYMOETES (*thi-mee'-teez*): (1) Trojan who urges the admittance of the Trojan horse into the city. 2.41. (2) Trojan, son of Hicetaon and defender of Aeneas' garrison, killed by Turnus, 10.152.

TIBER (*teye'-ber*): the river Tiber, the main river of central Italy, that rises in the Apennines and runs south; the city of Rome was established along its left bank; a name for the god of the river as well, 1.15.

TIBUR (*tee'-bur*): venerable town of Latium, now called Tivoli, built along the Anio, northeast of Rome, 7.733.

TIBURTUS (*tee-boor'-tus*): Greek, brother of Catillus and Coras, one of the three legendary founders of Tibur, the town that bears Tiburtus' name; all are allied with Turnus, 7.782.

TIGER: name of ship captained by MASSICUS, an Etruscan ally of Aeneas, 10.202.

TIMAVUS (*ti-may'-vus*): northern Italian river that empties into the Adriatic near its headwaters, 1.290. See Note 1.287–97.

TIRYNS (*tir'-inz*): ancient city in the Argolid, in the kingdom of Diomedes, and known for its rugged Cyclopean walls, 7.770. See Note ad loc.

TISIPHONE (*ti-si'-foh-nee*): one of the three Furies, she metes out punishments in the Underworld; guardian of the gates that enclose the damned, 6.645.

TITAN (*teye'-tan*): one of the elder gods, children of Uranus confined by Jupiter in Tartarus for their rebellion against the Olympians, 6.673–74. For the Sun as "child of the Titan Hyperion" (Austin, 1955, note 4.118 f.) see 4.147, 6.838.

TITHONUS (*ti-thoh'-nus*): consort of the Dawn, son of Laomedon and brother of Priam, father of Memnon, 4.731.

TITYUS (*ti'-ti-us*): legendary figure doomed to eternal torture in the Underworld for having assaulted Latona, mother of Diana and Apollo, who joined forces to kill the giant in revenge, 6.687.

TMARIAN (*tma'-ri-an*): inhabitant of mountainous region in Epirus, 5.685.

TMARUS (*tma'-rus*): Rutulian routed or killed by Aeneas' forces, 9.779.

TOLUMNIUS (*to-loom'-ni-us*): Rutulian prophet, comrade of Turnus, 11.513.

TORQUATUS (*tohr-kwah'-tus*): Titus Manlius, early Roman consul, named for the torque he wore, having seized it from a Gaul he killed in battle, 6.949. For his execution of his son for insubordination, see Introduction, p. 30.

TRITON (*treye'-ton*): (1) sea god, son of Neptune, who, as Wordsworth heard him, "blow[s] his wreathéd horn," 1.169. (2) Name of ship under Aulestes' command, that carries a contingent of Etruscans allied to Aeneas, 10.254.

TRITONIAN (*treye-tohn'-yan*): epithet of Athena or Minerva, the goddess also called Tritonia, either because she is "the Third-born of the Gods" and daughter of Jupiter, or because she was reared in the vicinity of Lake Tritonis in Northern Africa, or was associated with the river Triton in Boeotia, 5.778.

TRIVIA (*tri'-vi-a*): 7.601; "she of the three ways," as Goold in his Index (2000), following Fairclough, renders "an epithet of Diana or Hecate, whose images were placed at the intersection of roads." For "Trivia's lake" (7.601), the modern Lago di Nemi, see Note 7.884–908, and see DIANA and HECATE.

TROILUS (*troy'-lus*): Trojan, son of Priam, killed by Achilles, 1.574. See Note 1.561–95.

TROY (*troy*): (1) 1.2, capital city of the Troad, city of Tros, the TROJAN (*tro'-jan*) people and their effects, 1.23; alternatively called ILIUM, after ILUS (2), eldest son of Tros. (2) Miniature of original Troy, founded by Helenus and Andromache in Buthrotum, a coastal city in Epirus, 3.414. (3) An equestrian ritual, named "the Game of Troy," or simply "Troy," performed by Roman boys, and thought to have originated in the funeral games for Anchises, 5.662; see Note 5.655–62. (4) Sector of the Sicilian city of Acesta, 5.840.

TULLA (*too'-la*): aide-in-arms of Camilla, 11.773.

TULLUS (*too'-lus*): Tullus Hostilius, the third king of Rome, 6.936. See Introduction, pp. 29, 34.

TURNUS (*tur'-nus*): son of Daunus by the water-nymph Venilia, king of the Rutulians, suitor of Lavinia, and so the major opponent of Aeneas, who ultimately takes his life in battle, 7.62. For Turnus' role as a "new Achilles," see Note 7.434–36.

TUSCAN SEA (*tus'-kan*): also called the Tyrrhenian Sea, an extension of the Mediterranean, bounded to the east by the Italian peninsula and, as Williams remarks (1972, note 1.67), "the sea nearest to Rome," 1.80.

TUSCANS (*tus'-kanz*): 7.498; see ETRUSCAN.

TYDEUS (*tee'-dyoos*): son of Oeneus, father of Diomedes and one of the Seven against Thebes, killed in the unsuccessful assault on the city, 6.557. See Note 6.557–58.

TYPHOEUS (*ti-fee'-us*): hundred-headed, fire-breathing, rebellious monster struck dead by a lightning-bolt of Jupiter, who interred him beneath either Mount Etna or the island Inarime, modern Ischia, 1.794.

TYRES (*ti'-reez*): one of Aeneas' Arcadian comrades who, with his brother Teuthras, pursues Rhoetus until Pallas (3) takes his life, 10.477.

TYRIAN (*ti'-ri-an*): 1.14, a general term for the Phoenicians, especially those in exile from the principal city of Phoenicia, TYRE (*teyer*), renowned for its deep blue dye, who have settled in Carthage, 1.411.

TYRRHENA (*tee-ree'-na*): Tuscan woman wed to an Arcadian, Gylippus, to whom she bore several sons, 12.329.

TYRRHENUS (*tee-ree'-nus*): Etruscan who kills Aconteus, 11.725.

TYRRHUS (*tee'-rus*): Latin who, together with his sons, maintained the herds of King Latinus, 7.567.

UCALEGON (*oo-ka'-le-gon*): Trojan elder, whose house is torched by the Greeks in Troy's last hours, 2.391.

UFENS (*oo'-fens*): (1) Rutulian leader of a contingent composed of hunters and hard-scrabble farmers, 7.865. (2) River in Latium, whose natives are allies of Turnus, 7.930.

ULYSSES (*yoo-lis'-eez*): (Odysseus), grandson of Arcesius and Autolycus, son of Laertes, husband of Penelope, father of Telemachus, king of Ithaca and the surrounding islands, who helped to plot the deceit of the Trojan horse, 2.9. See CYCLOPS and Note 11.315–36; Notes and Glossary, passim. He is the hero of Homer's *Odyssey*.

UMBRIAN (*oom'-bri-an*): of an area in north-central Italy, inhabited by the Umbri or Umbrians and renowned for its keen-scented hunting hounds, 12.873.

UMBRO (*oom'-bro*): Marsian comrade of Turnus, and a healer killed by a Trojan lance, 7.874.

VALERUS (*val'-er-us*): Etruscan who overpowers Agis, 10.887.

VELIA (*ve'-li-a*): coastal town of western Lucania, 6.417.

VELINUS (*ve-lee'-nus*): lake in the region of the Sabines, source of a contingent allied with Turnus, 7.602.

VENILIA (*ve-nee'-li-a*): sea-nymph, mother of Turnus by Daunus, ruler of Ardea, 10.91.

VENULUS (*ven'-u-lus*): Latin, Turnus' envoy to Diomedes, to appeal for his support, 8.9.

VENUS (*vee'-nus*): (Aphrodite), goddess of love, daughter of Jupiter and Dione, wife of Vulcan, and mother of Aeneas by Anchises, and of Cupid, 1.270. For her role in the Judgment of Paris and the narrative action of the *Aeneid*, see Introduction, passim.

VESTA (*ves'-ta*): Roman goddess of the hearth, the home and family, and like her celebrants' devotion to her, her hearthfire was kept continuously burning, 1.349. Her temple was prominent among the monuments of the Roman Forum.

VESULUS (*ves'-u-lus*): Ligurian mountain, where the Po River rises, 10.837.

VIRBIUS (*veer'-bi-us*): (1) Son of Hippolytus and Aricia, his mother, who sent him into battle as a comrade-in-arms of Turnus, 7.884. (2) The name attached to Hippolytus when he had been restored to life, 7.901. See Note 7.884–908.

VOLCENS (*vohl'-kens*): Latin commander allied with Turnus; father of Camers and leader of a cavalry unit that kills Euryalus before Nisus cuts down Volcens in return, 9.431.

VOLSCIAN (*vohl'-shan*): 7.933, of a Latin tribe, the VOLSCIANS (*vohl'-shanz*), that migrated from the Apennines to southern Italy; despite later hostilities with the Romans, they are considered allies of Turnus in the *Aeneid,* 9.580.

VOLTURNUS (*vohl-toorn'-us*): the main river in Campania, that empties into the Tyrrhenian Sea, 7.847.

VOLUSUS (*voh-loo'-sus*): Rutulian, commander of the Volscians and comrade of Turnus, 11.554.

VULCAN (*vul'-kan*): (Hephaestus), god of fire, the great metallurgist, son of Juno, husband of Venus, who at the behest of Venus and assisted by his Cyclopean smiths, forges the shield of Aeneas, 7.792. See Introduction, passim.

VULCANIA (*vul-kay'-ni-a*): a volcanic island off the northern coast of Sicily, beneath which is a great cavern where Vulcan makes his home and the Cyclops labor at their forges, 8.498. See CYCLOPS and LIPARE.

WAILING RIVER: 6.339; see COCYTUS and Note 3.262.

XANTHUS (*ksan'-thus*): (1) river of the Troad, so called by the gods but called Scamander by mortals; brother or tributary of the river Simois, 1.573. (2) Brook in Epirus, called after (1) in the miniature Troy at Buthrotum, 3.416; see Note 3.389–400. (3) River in Lycia, a favorite haunt of Apollo, until the winter cold impels the god to Delos, 4.180.

ZACYNTHOS (*za-kin'-thus*): island off the western coast of Greece, south of Ithaca, in the kingdom of Ulysses, 3.324.

ZEPHYRS (*ze'-firz*): collective name for the West Winds, whether unruly or, more typically, favorable to mariners, 3.145.

AVAILABLE FROM
PENGUIN CLASSICS

The Odyssey

Homer

Translated by Robert Fagles

The Odyssey is literature's grandest evocation of everyman's journey through life. In the myths and legends that are retold here, renowned translator Robert Fagles has captured the energy and poetry of Homer's original in a bold, contemporary idiom and given us an *Odyssey* to read aloud, to savor, and to treasure for its sheer lyrical mastery. This is an *Odyssey* to delight both the classicist and the general reader, and to captivate a new generation of Homer's students.

ISBN 978-0-14-303995-2

PENGUIN
CLASSICS

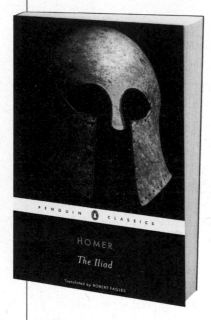